BLACKBEARD'S SHIP

THE VOYAGES OF
QUEEN ANNE'S REVENGE
COLLECTION ONE

JEREMY MCLEAN

POINTS OF SAIL
PUBLISHING

Points of Sail Publishing
P.O. Box 30083 Prospect Plaza
FREDERICTON, New Brunswick
E3B 0H8, Canada

Edited by Ethan James Clarke
http://silverjay-editing.com/

This is a work of fiction. Any similarity to persons, living or dead, is purely coincidental... Or is it?

ACKNOWLEDGEMENTS

This compilation of my first four novels represents, to me, a great accomplishment in my career. It also shows a transformative work, of my journey as a writer to become better at my craft. I couldn't have done it without all my friends and family who've read the books over the years, as well as the many editors I've employed to help me find, understand, and fix the common mistakes that plague my drafts. Without their help I would not have grown to the level I am at now, and without their support I may not have published these books in the first place.

Thank you all.

PREFACE

(OR, WHAT TO KNOW
BEFORE DIVING IN.)

Hello, and thank you for taking an interest in this collection of stories. If you're not familiar with them, they're the first two books in my two ongoing series'. One is called The Voyages of Queen Anne's Revenge and is action adventure with a dash of fantasy, and the other is called The Pirate Priest and is more straight historical fiction.

I've always had a love of pirates, and Blackbeard, like many, was my favourite. The scourge of the seas who lit his hair aflame and carried six pistols strapped to his chest during battle. Many myths and legends surround the historical Blackbeard. To this day, it's debated where he came from before becoming the dreaded pirate we all know. Even Edward Teach's name (or the classical spelling this book uses, Thatch) may have been a pseudonym because many pirates changed their names to protect their families.

When I started writing Blackbeard's Freedom, the first book I've ever written, I wanted to create an origin story for Blackbeard. I also wanted to make a book that would be fun without being bogged down in historical accuracy or language. When hearing about Blackbeard's exploits as a child, he sounded almost too surreal, larger than life, and in this book, I hoped to capture some of that magic. As such, while it carries the veneer of a book set in the 1700s, it's best to treat it as an alternate history. Or better yet, think of it as historical fantasy, given many of the things that happen in these books.

If you enjoy pirate movies from the big screen (I hope you know the ones I'm referring to), then I think you'll enjoy this series. If you're a young adult like me (I was in my early twenties when I first started writing this) and you, like me, enjoy video games, superheroes, and all things nerdy, then I think you'll like this series. If you want to read about a fisherman's gradual descent into darkness to become the most ruthless pirate on the seven seas across several books, then I think you'll love this series.

I only hope that you enjoy it as much as I enjoyed writing it.

TABLE OF CONTENTS

BOOK ONE OF
THE VOYAGES OF QUEEN
ANNE'S REVENGE

BLACKBEARD'S
FREEDOM

1. EDWARD THATCH

Salt water and sweat mixed as it fell from Edward's hair and fore-head. The drops went down his cheek, falling onto his lips and leaving a sickening taste in his mouth. But it was not the hot sun which caused him to perspire so. No, it was the twenty marines, in their stark blue uniforms, with their rifles pointed at him. He steadied his shaking hand on the flintlock pistol he had pointed at the back of their captain's head.

Oh Father, what am I doing?

"Think about what you're doing, boy. The way you're going, there's no ending with you free. We can negotiate here. You have a choice to make: one can lead to a happy life… and the other never ends well."

No… no, I will be free. And I won't let you stand in my way. It's too late for choices.

Edward cocked the gun against the captain's head, his mind clear on what he needed to do. "Listen carefully," Edward said aloud for all to hear, "for I'm only going to say this once."

Five Hours Ago

Edward Thatch breathed deep, taking in the full scent of that salty sweet air he so loved. He held that breath far longer than normal, like a jealous lover who thinks he could lose his love at any moment. He had to let go, but with another breath it was back again.

"Still don't feel real, does it?" A man came up beside Edward and placed his arm around Edward's shoulder. He glanced sideways to see Henry Morgan, a third generation Welshman and his best friend.

Henry was not as tall as Edward, but he made up for the height with might. His straight brown hair was in a ponytail, and his rolled sleeves displayed his farmer's tan.

"Well, it has only been a few days since we started whaling," Edward replied. "Any man would be hard pressed to come back to earth after too much heaven."

Henry laughed with vigor. "We need you here on the ship, Cap-tain."

Edward smiled. "You know me, Henry. You couldn't keep me from this beauty with a loaded pistol."

Blackbeard's Ship

Edward and Henry watched the crew of the ship called *Freedom* from the raised aft deck. The men milled about, performing various duties aboard the three-masted ship.

On the aft deck there were some fixing the sails and rigging. On the quarterdeck the helmsman concentrated on changes in the skies and sea with help from a cabin boy. On the main deck some were checking on the main mast while others cleaned. Far ahead on the raised foredeck there were men loafing about as far from their captain's eye as possible.

"Despite the oddness of how Benjamin Hornigold sold us the vessel," Henry said, his eyes wandering the floorboards of the sole, "… it is a fine ship."

Edward cringed. "Let us never speak of the incident again. My stomach churns with the mention of his name."

"Come now, it's not every day that one buys a warship while tanked off whiskey." He slapped Edward on the back as he laughed.

"Yes… but as we are trying to be whalers, we've no need—" Yelling from the waist of the ship stopped Edward's voice and called their attention.

"Ye lilly-white kencracker. You stole me money, I know ye did!" Sam was yelling to another crewman on deck.

Samuel Bellamy, the apparent aggressor, was a young man of around five feet eleven inches, but like a true cockney Londoner he acted as if he were ten feet tall. Despite his prettiness, which no doubt made women ogle, there was darkness in his jet-black eyes.

"I stole nuthin' of yers," the other crewman yelled back. "Why don't ye check it again? All that black hair gettin' in yer way."

"Stop yer lyin' and give back me money!" Sam rushed up to the man and pushed him hard, sending him sprawling against the starboard railing.

This can't be good, Edward thought, before bolting down to the waist of the ship. Henry followed a few steps behind him.

The other crewmembers gathered around in anticipation of a fight. The crewman accused of stealing pushed Sam back, and then they circled each other as the rest chanted. Edward pushed through the throng. Sam threw the first punch straight in the face of the other man, who countered with a right upper to his chin.

Sam's head snapped back, but he seemed unfazed by the blow. His lips drew back in a cruel smile, and his eyes glistened as if he were enjoying himself. He burst like a cannon with a punch to the crewman's gut, and followed it with a downward right against his jaw. The crewman fell to the floor, unconscious, but Sam kept beating on him. Edward still had not reached them.

William, the crew's boatswain, jumped from the main mast and slid down a rope to the deck. He grabbed Sam by the arm, flipped

2

him over on his back, and pinned him to the deck.

William was mature in demeanor despite his young age. His eyes and face were devoid of expression, and he seemed incapable of smiling. He could blend in with anyone else among the ship, but, upon closer inspection, revealed a man sharper in mind and stronger in body than most.

Sam struggled and writhed but was unable to escape William's grip. Edward, finally at the centre of the throng, shouted, "Let him go, William." William rose to his feet just as Henry forced his way to the front of the crowd.

Henry glared angrily at the beaten and bloodied crewman and at Sam, who had just gotten to his knees. "You bastard!" He leveled Sam again with a thunderous punch.

Edward stepped between Sam and Henry. "Henry, stop! I will have no more fighting aboard my ship!" He pointed to the unconscious crewman. "Someone help that poor sod." Two crewmen carried the injured man below deck.

Edward walked to Sam, still stretched out on the deck, and looked daggers down at him. His dark eyes pierced Sam, carrying a force greater than Henry's punch.

"Another incident like this… and you're off my ship, and maybe I won't wait for us to make port," he said.

"That rat bastard stole me money, I knows it!"

Edward knelt and leaned close to Sam's face. Henry and William stood on either side of him. "We'll question the man when he's well again, but my warning stands. You are not to get into another fight. Understood?"

Sam tried to stare down Edward, but the intensity of Edward's gaze made him turn away. "You got it, Chief."

"What was that?"

"Captain," Sam replied with emphasis.

Edward offered his hand, but Sam ignored it and picked himself up off the floor before stalking off.

Edward watched Sam go. Then he looked at his officers and the crowd of seamen. "Back to work," he ordered.

The crew resumed their duties with a fresh reminder of who their captain was. They also knew now to stay away from Sam.

Edward turned to Henry and William. "William, keep an eye on Sam. I don't want him causing problems again. You stop him at the first sign of trouble."

William saluted in his no-nonsense way. "Yes, Captain." He was about to turn and walk away with his orders, but something caught his keen eye. "Captain, there's a storm approaching. We must warn the helmsman," he stated in his perfect English, so unlike Sam's cockney twang.

Blackbeard's Ship

Edward searched the sky. In the east, the clouds were practically roiling, already black and heavy with a promise of rain. "Hard to starboard!" he called out. "Keep this ship beating to the wind. We don't want to be here when that menace hits!"

Henry stopped Edward before he went to help the crew prepare. "We'll never escape that storm without releasing the foresail."

Edward glanced to the front mast and the sail Henry mentioned. It had been stuck in place since he'd bought the ship, and whenever they tried to find the reason it was an exercise in futility.

I've never seen a storm come in so quickly without warning... Henry's right, this ship is too slow with only two sails.

"I need five strong arms with me now!" No sooner did Edward yell the command than Sam, Henry, and William joined him on his way to the bow of the ship. "We're unfurling the topsail one way or the other. Our lives depend on it. We need to find the reason it's stuck and make it unstuck. Go, go, go! No time to waste!"

Darkness was descending upon them as the smell of the sea air faded and clean rain flooded in.

The group of sailors inspected the rigging and climbed up to the sail by the ropes. They checked the knots, pulling and tugging on whatever they thought might be holding the sail down. Before they made any progress, the rain began. Everyone knew what this meant, and they worked all the harder to accomplish their task. Many of the rest of the crew broke out the oars and started rowing to make the ship move faster.

Sam was in the middle of the mast checking the rigging when he suddenly yelled, "I found it!" He pointed excitedly to a spot on the mast where a metal notch held a rope down. "I need a knife!" Someone on the foredeck heard his cry and tossed him a small knife. He placed the knife in the notch and pried at it. He went this way and that as the rain worsened and the wind picked up. Slowly the notch inched its way out of the wood. Minutes passed like hours as the storm grew worse. Edward and the crew watched, their lives in the hands of the one who had almost killed a mate not minutes ago.

With one final snap, the metal hook flew out and hit the deck with a clang. Several men released the restraining ropes and the topsail unfurled.

The crew of the *Freedom* started to cheer, but those cries of victory died very quickly in every throat. Painted on the topsail was a black skull with two crossed bones beneath it. Lightning flashed a brilliance of white light and a crash of thunder followed soon after. Sounds of astonishment rippled through the crew. The Jolly Roger, the sign of a pirate, was painted on their sail.

Edward couldn't believe what he saw. He felt sick. Sweat broke out on his brow, mixed with the rain and ran down his face. He stood still as a statue. *What is that doing on my ship?*

"There's no time to worry about that right now, Ed!" Henry shouted. "Hold it together!"

Edward blinked his eyes back into focus. "You… you're right. We must hurry." Edward ran to the edge of the foredeck. "Pull those oars in before they get taken away. Soon we'll be moving too fast for them to do any good." A mate nodded and yelled back something in the affirmative before issuing commands to the other men. "This storm will not beat us, gentlemen! We're sailors, not craven landlubbers."

Edward joined in hoisting the heavy oars onto the deck and securing them. "Do not yield, men. This storm cannot topple us!"

The crew ran this way and that, keeping the sails and the ship together in the strong winds. Edward stayed in the thick of it with the other crewmates, and soon his arms legs burned with the strain.

After what seemed like hours, the wind and rain had abated somewhat, and Edward knew from his father's teaching that this was a crucial time. If the sails were left up now the ship could be blown in the wrong direction.

"Secure those sails before the wind changes!" Edward shouted while he ran to the aft sail. He and the other free crewmembers rushed to pull up the sails. The rain had made the ropes slick and harder to work with.

Edward pulled on the rigging with all his might. His arms burned with the struggle. The rough grain of the rope dug into his calloused hand, but he gritted his teeth to push away the pain.

Edward finished raising the aft sail, but noticed the crew still furling the foresail. "Hand that foresail!" Then he looked beyond the sails, beyond the bow, and saw a thing more shocking to him than the sight of the Jolly Roger.

A ship was heading straight for the *Freedom.*

He removed a spyglass from his coat pocket and peered through it. Judging from the new ship's size, it was a frigate much like the *Freedom*. It was a marine vessel and, unlike the *Freedom*, was equipped with cannons. The name emblazoned on the side was H.M.S. *Pearl.*

He spun on his heels and shouted, "Everyone! Finish what you're doing, and raise your hands in the air. A marine vessel is approaching off our bow! Someone bring me something white tied to a plank!"

In a flurry of frantic activity, the crew rigged the sails and a cabin boy brought Edward a white shirt fastened to a pole. He ran to the front of the deck and waved it in the direction of the oncoming vessel. Everyone else did as ordered and raised their hands in the air in submission. Henry had come onto the main deck, ready for the inevitable. Sam was trying to hide behind others, but still had his hands raised. William was also trying to hide, but was doing a better job of it than Sam. Edward kept waving the pole as the marine ship pulled up beside them. He then dropped the pole and went down to the main deck to join Henry. He opened up a hinge on the railing of the ship to allow a gangplank to be placed down and the marine officers to board. He then backed away and raised his hands in the air.

We'll talk our way out of this. They have to believe us...

Marines tied the ships together with grappling hooks, and extended gangplanks over the water. The officers and guards boarded with muskets raised. Their leader was a man of no more than average height who nonetheless carried himself with the deadly grace of a lion on the prowl. He had the clean-shaven face of a youth, but his uniform revealed him to be an accomplished military captain.

"Who is your captain?" He glanced around at the ragged crew, who stood frozen in poses of surrender. "And would you put your hands down? You've already lost any credibility as a threat." Everyone obeyed. "Now, which one of you is the captain of this ship? Speak up!"

"I am... sir." Edward stepped forward.

The marine commander looked Edward up and down. Edward was much taller and imposing than the captain, being six foot four inches, but the battle-hardened marine didn't appear fazed. An amused smile flitted across his face and then disappeared. "A fine ship you have for a pirate."

"We're not pirates!" Henry yelled from behind Edward.

"I did not ask you, powder-monkey."

Edward turned to Henry. "Henry, I can handle this." Henry pursed his mouth and did his best to be quiet.

"Your man says you aren't pirates, yet you bear the mark of them on your sail. You own a high-class warship, and clearly are not marines or any merchants I've ever seen. If you aren't pirates, and this ship isn't stolen, then I must be the son of Davy Jones himself." The captain's men laughed.

"I told you we're not pirates!" cried Henry. "We're whalers. This is a misunderstanding. Edward paid for this ship fair and square!"

The commander signaled to one of his men. The marine walked over and smashed the butt of his musket into Henry's face, sending him crumpling to the deck.

Henry! Edward struggled to resist the impulse to rush over and help his friend, and fought hard to control his anger and panic. *God damn him! How will we get out of this?*

"Order your men to tend to him," the captain commanded.

Edward turned to some of his crew. "You heard him, take him

below deck." Then he met the captain's eyes. "Despite my friend's... outburst, his word is true. We are no pirates and I purchased this vessel fairly."

"Can you produce papers of sale or title of ownership to prove your man's claim?"

Edward felt his stomach turn. "N-no. The previous owner forgot to entrust the papers to me."

"Of course he did." The captain glanced over his shoulder at his men and smiled.

"I-it has only been a few weeks since the sale, if you just return with us to Badobos I'm sure we can find him to corroborate my story. His name is Benjamin Hornigold."

At the mention of Hornigold's name, the marine captain's eyes widened and he missed a step. "Do you take me for a fool?"

Edward was taken aback and tried to stammer out a response, but couldn't think of any.

"I am Captain Isaac Smith of the Royal Navy, and I am hereby taking control of this vessel. You will all be brought to Clarendon Parish where you will be jailed until your trial."

"Trial! W-we haven't done anything! We're simple whalers. Look at our equipment, look at us, we're not pirates. My name is Edward Thatch. I... I was raised in Badobos by the Hughes family. You can ask them about it." Edward hated to flash his adopted family's name around, but he was overcome with desperation.

"Save it, pirate. We're onto your deception. It's obvious you were damaged during the storm and wanted to try talking your way out of a fight."

"Are you even listening? We live on Badobos a few days southwest of here. I just bought this ship and I didn't even know about the sail."

"Enough excuses. Your story is as vaporous as the deed you seem to have misplaced. I'm claiming your ship as my own. You will be tried and executed in a court of law, which is more than you deserve."

Edward's mind raced. *Executed? ... I can't die, not now, not like this!*

Captain Smith turned and motioned for two of his men, who walked over to Edward, sheathing their weapons and pulling out shackles. He noticed a pistol on the captain's belt. *We're not pirates. We don't deserve to be treated like this! I won't let him have his way!*

Edward put Smith in a choke hold, grabbed his gun from its holster, and pointed it at his temple. "Nobody move or I shoot!"

The marines all aimed their firearms at Edward as his crew watched on in horror. "Drop your weapons, you fools!" commanded Smith. "Do as he says."

He walked backwards with Smith in tow, his elbow tight around the captain's neck. He felt like he should be breathing rapidly, but his breaths were steady, calm almost.

"Now you have my attention, boy, but you're not doing yourself any favours," Smith said, his hands held up to calm his men. "If you didn't want us thinking you were pirates you're doing a piss-poor job of it."

"Shut it!" Edward glanced swiftly back and forth to the marines in front of him. He thought out his options, and came to only one conclusion. "Sam?" Edward called.

"Yea?" Sam was only a few feet away.

Edward pushed Smith forward, but kept the pistol trained on him. "Bind the captain's arms and feet," Edward commanded.

Sam followed the order without question. He grabbed spare rope from the foot of one of the masts, then tied Smith's arms behind his back in a handcuff knot. He wore a wicked smile as he made the captain kneel down, then used the slack from the handcuff knot to tie Smith's feet to his hands. The more Smith pulled against the knots, the more they tightened.

"Think about what you're doing, boy. The way you're going, there's no ending with you free," Smith whispered with a pause for Edward to consider his words. Edward cocked the gun in response. "We can negotiate here. You have a choice to make: one can lead to a happy life... and the other never ends well."

It's too late for choices, Edward thought before echoing the words into Smith's ear.

"Listen carefully," Edward said loudly for all to hear. "for I'm only going to say this once. Drop your muskets, pistols, and other equipment near the mast and then back away to the starboard railing with your hands behind your backs."

The marines seemed unsure of what to do, but they were quick to action. They followed his order immediately, eyeing their captain nervously.

Edward's crew stared in rapt attention as the soldiers delivered their weapons and gear without a murmur. They were in awe of him, he could feel it; him, the man who, not two weeks ago, had not even met the lot of them.

"Take their weapons, men." The crew's eyes went from Edward to the guns as if they didn't know what they were. "Do it!" he shouted. They obeyed. Then, to Smith, "Now order your crew to gather up all the food, supplies, and weapons aboard your ship and bring them over here."

Edward knew he was pushing his luck—the marine crew looked uncertain, offended even—but fortunately Smith applied his own pressure. "Do it," he ordered.

"Leave enough food so you can make it back to port."

Some of Edward's crew pointed the muskets at the marines and some held them like foreign objects, filthy and wrong in their hands.

"This will never work," Smith whispered. "My men will have your portrait posted at every port from here to the Bahamas by next month. Think this through! I'll cut you a break if you stop this madness right now."

"Just like you were going to cut us a break earlier? Ha!"

A few minutes later the marines walked back with bags and barrels filled with supplies: swords, muskets, pistols, a few rifles, and barrels of gunpowder. They also had more spices and food than necessary for a short voyage on a small ship. They dropped them in the centre of the *Freedom* and returned to the starboard rails, awaiting the next commands from Edward.

"Now tell your men to head south until they've lost sight of us. Their lives depend on it. I'm a deadly pirate, remember? You don't know what I'm capable of." *How is my voice so calm? My heart's about to explode!*

Smith examined the man in front of him once again, as if he was re-assessing his first impression of Edward. "Men, I want you to sail away from here," Smith commanded. "Sail until you cannot see this ship any longer…"

"But, Captain—"

"Don't worry, I'll be fine. These men are whalers, remember?" As his men were leaving, he muttered to Edward, "I'll make you pay for this humiliation, Thatch."

"We'll see about that, now won't we?" *I'm a dead man.*

The marine crew pulled the gangplanks back into their own ship, cut the grappling hooks, and released their sails. The enemy ship headed south, slowed by the wind against them.

Edward cried out, "Men, I want those sails unfurled and this ship underway!" No one moved. "That's an order!" Those who had guns dropped them where they stood and went to work unfurling the sails again. The ship moved fast with the wind, and in no time at all the marines were out of sight.

Edward now took hold of Smith's arm and dragged him to the side of the ship. He pulled a knife from his pocket and cut the ropes binding Smith, then backed away a short distance. After Smith rose, Edward pointed the pistol at him. "Now jump."

Smith's face froze in astonishment. "You cannot be serious!" He looked at the water, then at Edward, then at some crewmembers who stood watching.

Edward didn't lower the pistol an inch. "Get off my ship."

Smith slowly climbed up the port side of the ship. "You can't hide from me, Thatch. The stench of a pirate is all over you. We will meet again, and then the tables will turn." Smith spat on Edward's ship as one last act of contempt before he jumped off the side.

Edward and the crew watched as the marine did his best to stay afloat. "Throw him a plank!" Edward commanded. A cabin boy obliged. Smith grabbed onto it and floated there, the waves pushing him up and down.

Edward and his crew kept staring at the marine captain until his tiny, bobbing form could be seen no longer.

What have I done?

2. MUTINY

Henry sat with two men on a pier, their legs dangling into the water, looking out to the ocean. They sat watching the sun set in silence; it would be the last sunset they would all see together.

"Let's make a promise," Robert Maynard said.

Robert was sitting in the middle, with Henry on the left and Edward on the right. He was younger than the other two and of smaller stature. He had wispy blond curls and a smile that made women swoon and men envious.

"Let's promise that we shall meet again when we fulfill our dreams and have something to show for it. We will reunite either right here, in Badobos, or out on the open seas." He looked up to his taller friends and placed one hand on each of their shoulders.

Henry looked to Robert and Edward, smiling to them both. "It's a promise," Henry and Edward both replied in unison.

⚓ ⚓ ⚓

Henry woke with a start. He took deep breaths through his mouth; his nose hurt something fierce. The crew cabin's wooden plank ceiling and swaying hammocks were spinning, but he could see Edward and two other crewmembers. They were arguing over something.

"Can you all shut it? The devil's knocking on my brain."

Edward's face turned to Henry, and he flashed a small smile. Then he turned his attention back to the other crewmembers. "We'll discuss this later." The men shook their heads and left the crew's quarters.

Henry leaned up on his elbows so he could see everything. "What happened? Did you convince the captain we were whalers?"

"Yes, about that…"

Edward described what had happened. As he listened, Henry's expression changed from interest, to shock, to disgust, and finally to anger.

"What in the devil's name were you thinking, Edward? You… you pulled a gun on a marine officer? You fool!"

"I am no fool! Any man would have done the same thing!" he argued. "He wasn't listening to reason; I did what I had to do to secure the lives of the crew... Your life," he said while pointing at his friend.

Henry sighed as he ran his fingers through his hair. "What are we to do now? Where are we to go? Where *can* we go? From what the marine captain told us, he'll make sure you're infamous before we next reach port."

"Yes, and judging by his character he'll embellish the story and make us out to be the truest of villains to cover his blunder."

"He'll probably say we were the devil's own children and we used our deadly powers to compel him and his men to do our bidding." Edward and Henry shared a grim chuckle.

Edward looked over his shoulder and noticed their quarter-master, John, trembling as he paced. He was a somewhat plump man, the type who had seen action in their glory years and then rested on their laurels for too long.

"John," Edward said, and the older man jumped in fright. "You're just the man who we need to talk to. Come," Edward commanded. John dragged himself over to Edward and Henry, adjusting his rounded glasses nervously. "Do you have any idea where we could escape to after this nasty business?"

Edward and Henry awaited their quartermaster's response, though he seemed to be on the point of breaking at the light questioning. John glanced back and forth from one of them to the other, as if he were at gunpoint. "I... I... don't know of anywhere, Edward." He was almost cowering with fear as he replied. He ran a shaking hand through his salt-and-pepper hair.

Edward glanced at Henry, then back to John. "John, what's wrong? You won't look me in the eyes."

"It's nothing," John said, still not looking up.

"No, please, John. You're from Badobos; you know us. You know that you can tell us anything," Henry reassured the man.

John gained confidence at Henry's reassuring words, then focused on Edward. "Wh-when you had the marine hostage, there was something a-about your eyes. They were dark like the devil's, and you had a smile on your face, like it was all a joke. The men are saying you seemed like you were having fun."

"What? I think I would remember if I was smiling. I don't remember doing that. Why would I smile? I didn't smile!"

"Ed, calm down. We know you wouldn't do that. They're probably mistaken. Right, John?"

John looked at Edward and then back at Henry. "Y-yes... They must have been s-seeing things, Edward."

"Yes... they must have."

"Well," said Henry, trying to cut the tension, "this still leaves open the question of where we can safely land."

"We'll have to discuss it with the crew. John, call everyone to the deck. We'll see if anyone has a good suggestion."

"Right away, Captain." John left and went straight up the ladder, telling everyone he saw along the way to meet on the deck.

Edward wanted to make sure Henry was all right before heading up. He could walk fine; his nose was the problem, and they weren't able to do much about it.

The two walked up to the top deck where the crew was waiting, then moved to the quarterdeck. John followed them up soon after.

The sun was high in the sky after the harsh storm. It was almost as if the storm had never happened, but the remnants of the wind and rain remained as a reminder. The smell of the gunpowder and spices on the deck gave the crew a memento to the second storm that happened.

Edward stood there for a minute, staring at his men. He didn't know what to say, and the number of people confronting him was already working on his nerves. Speaking to crowds was always a problem, but Henry had been trying to help him get better. He slowed his breathing and did what Henry had taught him to do: focus on one person in the audience at a time.

"You all know of what has happened, and, unfortunately, there's not much we can do. That is why I ask you, men, what should our next course of action be?"

The crew murmured to each other. Some had raised brows in a questioning manner, and others tightened their fists as they talked in hushed voices. No one knew what to say until an angry-looking crewman spoke up. His name was Frederick. A fisherman by trade, he had worked in Badobos all his life. Edward knew him well and wasn't surprised to be hearing from him.

"You got us into this mess and now you're asking us for help? Because of you, the marines think we're pirates! Why should we help you at all?"

Henry's technique wasn't working any more. Edward started to panic. His breathing became more rapid, and his eyes flitted to all the other men looking at him for an answer.

Henry came to the rescue. "We're all in this mess. Fighting over who to blame won't solve anything."

"Why can't we just sail home?" another crewman asked. Several more agreed with him.

"The marines know where we're from. That will be the first place they inspect. We can't return home, at least not now. We might be able to revisit when we figure out how to clear our names, but for now we need something else."

Frederick spoke up again. "I think we should seek out the marines and explain the situation to them. Maybe if they hear the words of a few sane people then they'll understand." Many in the crew agreed loudly.

Henry sighed. "Oh, you think they'll understand? Like the last marines did? You think when they hear the account from Captain Smith they'll let the charges drop? Don't be a fool. They'll never believe our word against his. We can't go to the marines." Henry was trying his best to protect Edward, but Frederick was having none of it.

"I think you're afraid of what they'll do to your friend the 'Captain.' *He's* the one pulled the gun on Smith; *he's* the one who ordered him around. He's the one they want, not us." Frederick turned to face the men. "If we take him to the marines, then they'll absolve us of his wrongdoing! I say we tie him up and put our lot in with the authorities! Who's with me?"

Half the crew yelled in agreement and started making their way up to the quarterdeck.

"This is insane!" shouted Edward. "You think they'll treat you differently because you bring me in? They'll think you're trying to save your own skin."

"Don't listen to him, men! The captain is the one who's labelled a pirate, and he'll be the one put on trial if we turn him in."

At least fifty men crowded onto the quarterdeck, and thirty more waited on the ladder, ready to beat the tar out of Edward, Henry, and John. "Any suggestions?" Henry asked Ed as they put their backs against each other.

"Not unless you count fighting off eighty sailors as a suggestion."

William ran up the railing leading to the quarterdeck. He had four swords in hand, taken from the marine ship. He leapt over to Edward, Henry, and John and handed them each a sword. Then he pointed his own at the ringleader, Frederick.

"You dare direct your anger at the man who saved your lives? He is your captain. You owe him your allegiance!" William yelled above the rising din.

"He didn't save our lives. He put us into this situation, and he's going to get us out of it, one way... or the other. You can't take on all of us! Surrender so we can return home."

Edward gritted his teeth. "I had already tried to explain to him how we were whalers and he didn't care. You think he'll change his mind because a different person tells him?"

"Well... I'd rather take my chances with a marine who believes in justice than live the rest of my life as a pirate! We'll be able to cut a deal with him over your life."

The standoff held for a whole minute, with neither side willing to budge. The mutinous crewmembers didn't want to risk injury, and the four armed men didn't want to hurt them.

Then a loud bang sounded from the main deck, causing everyone to duck for cover. They turned their attention there, where Sam stood, brandishing a pistol.

"You should all stop what yer doin'. Captain's right. Whatever you do it won't do a lick o' good in your situation. You'd be right old fools to take 'im to the marines, and even bigger fools if ye kill 'im."

"Oh yes? And how would you know?"

"I know 'ow the marines think. If you off the captain, they jus' find the ship and execute you all at sea. If you take 'im in, they really will think you're jus' tryin' to cut a deal and you'll be chained before the piss stains yer pants. If the lot of us'd been put on trial, you'd have been found guilty regardless of what you said and then executed. We all be alive 'cause he was bold. The best thing you can do now is take the ship to a good port, and go our separate ways. The marines only have 'is name and this ship to go by. Edward Thatch is the one they're after."

Frederick considered Sam's words as he peered at the crew and Edward. After a moment of thought, he lowered his sword. "Let's stop, everyone. Sam's right."

Despite the attempt at placating the situation, the crew was reluctant to stand down. They talked to each other in loud whispers, debating whether they could take Sam's words at face value. When they convinced themselves, or at least calmed themselves, they lowered their weapons.

Edward, Henry, John, and William all let out a collective sigh of relief as the crew lowered their weapons. The clang of swords falling on the deck meant their throats were safe for another day.

The threat over, the crew who had started the mutiny returned to the main deck, and Edward turned to Sam.

"So what are you suggesting we do?"

"We're close to a port soft on pirates. Dole out a little coin to the harbourmaster and he won't say a word."

Edward thought it over for a minute. "We need to be in agreement on this. All those in favor of following Bellamy's plans, raise your hands and say 'aye.'" The whole crew did so. "All opposed?" No one spoke up. "Right. Then move those weapons into barrels and into the corners of the steps. Move any excess to the crew's quarters. Put all the gunpowder in the crew's quarters for the time being. Lay aloft and loose all sails! Sam, what's the name of the place we're sailing to?"

"Port Royal."

3. PORT ROYAL

"This is my decision, and that is all that matters," Edward said, arms folded.

"Why stay with the ship, Ed?" Henry objected, his melodic Welsh accent undercutting his obstinate tone. "We can leave it and never be seen again. If we stay with the ship, it'll be like a target on our backs."

"I bought this ship, Henry. It took me a week just to say I'd keep it, and now... I'm attached to it. I can't explain it, but I feel bound to this ship. Besides, as I told you, Smith knows my name and my face. No matter where I run I'll be hunted like a pirate."

Henry folded his massive arms in front of him. "And should they find you? You'll fight them?"

"If I must, yes."

"And what if it's Robert chasing after you? What then? He plans on becoming a marine to stop pirates. Would you fight him too?"

The words hit Edward like a shot to the chest. Edward, Henry, and Robert had been best friends since childhood. "I guess... I never thought about it."

"No, you didn't. I can tell from the look in your eyes that no matter what I say you'll keep the ship. But it's not worth dying over, or killing."

"Maybe to you the *Freedom* isn't worth dying over, but to me it is. I don't want to kill anyone... but if someone tries to take my *Freedom*, I will fight them. I don't care how long I'm chased. I will not relinquish this ship."

"Even to Robert?"

"Robert would understand. He would believe our side. He's still our friend. Besides, we're not killing and stealing from anyone."

Henry sighed. "Well I can't leave you on your own. I'll stay with you... to whatever end," he said with a melancholic smile. "Besides, you know you're lost without me."

"Ha! I bet you just can't stand the thought of being apart from me," Edward said with a playful push.

Henry rolled his eyes. "Yea, I sure do love gettin' my face bashed in and being bossed about by a tosspot like you." They laughed together a moment, but then grew silent as the swaying hammocks caught their attention. They could hear the splash of waves and the shouts of orders above them. "You know, it's a bit like one of them books your Dad had. The tattered ones with the heroes who get into a spot of trouble, enemies chasing them down, but they outsmart them at every turn. You think that could be us some day? And with pirates there's supposed to be treasure, right? What do you think?"

Edward scratched his face. "I guess."

The two sat thinking of the past, and what they left behind.

"Have you thought about Lucy?"

The mention of that name brought Edward back to the small Caribbean island of Badobos. Aside from his friend Robert, Lucy was the only person he missed from home.

Edward fondly remembered Lucy as fair and gentle, demure in bearing and dainty in appearance, but with a fire inside her. Edward had not found that spirit in any other woman, nor did he think he would. Her sky blue eyes filled him with joy more so than the sea air.

"You know I have," he replied.

Henry gave him an exasperated look. "And? You're just going to leave her behind, no so much as a letter explaining what's happened?"

"She's better off not knowing. It will make letting me go easier."

"Ed, she will find out one way or another. At least if you send her a letter explaining that you aren't a pirate it will be better than the alternative. You owe her that."

"I will be the one to decide what I owe her or not, thank you." Edward knew Lucy. If she thought there was any way she might be able to help, she would not hesitate to find him. Better she thought he left her than to hold out hope to find him again. That way they could both move on.

Henry rubbed his eyes in frustration. "At least tell me that you will think it over. The poor girl will be worried sick when you do not return."

"I will think it over," Edward lied. "I'm going to check on things above deck."

Edward left to head above, and Henry went to have something to eat. It was turning into a nice day with a full sun, and the wind in their sails was bringing them to Port Royal at a quick pace.

The salt air was back and Edward could smell it stronger than ever. He thought he should feel bad with all that had happened, but there was no weight on his shoulders.

Edward noticed William brooding on the main deck next to the weapons they had procured from the marines. He surveyed the arms, running his fingers down the length of a rifle in a familiar way.

"Best be careful. The sparks from your gaze may ignite the gunpowder," Edward joked.

Blackbeard's Ship

"Gunpowder is added prior to firing, not while in storage," William pointed out.

Edward's face flushed and he coughed. "Right." He stood there for a few more seconds with nothing to say as the wind swayed the ship and the crew walked about on the deck. "William, I was curious of your decision to stay with me at the risk of being labelled a pirate. You seem like one who would brook no such thing."

"I know the truth of the situation. You were in the right. You are my captain now, so I follow you. If you wish for me to leave, I will. If not, I will help you however I can."

"Good to know." Edward nodded, and William returned the gesture.

"I have a query," William said a few moments later, when another uncomfortable silence threatened to settle between them. "I notice that some of the doors on the ship are locked and we are unable to access certain sections."

Edward's mouth made a line. "Yes, that. Well, after purchasing this vessel, the previous owner, Benjamin Hornigold, only left a few keys for us. Thus our locked door predicament."

At the mention of the name Benjamin Hornigold, William, for the first time, showed a hint of shock on his face. He turned speechless for a moment.

"What's wrong, William?" Edward asked, looking over his own shoulder.

William recovered quickly. "Nothing. Did you meet with this Hornigold personally?"

Edward grinned. "I believe so. It's an amusing tale, actually. After a particularly... eventful celebration with Henry, I awoke the next morning with my life savings gone and a note explaining the sale of this ship in my pocket." Edward laughed, until he noticed William staring at him with a straight face and his arms crossed.

"Perhaps a list of the doors locked would be prudent. We can have some of the crew attempt forcing the locks later."

"Right, I'll get on that right now. Good idea, William."

Edward turned around, but glanced back at the other man. He seemed lost in thought once again, but this time he wasn't looking at the marines' guns. Edward decided not to pry and returned to his task.

He made a mental note of the two cabins aft and fore of the main deck, as they were among the sections locked off.

Edward moved on to the bow to descend to the lower decks. The gun deck was first, but was currently only used to access the crew cabin as the doors in the hallway were locked as well.

Edward gazed at the doors on either side of the hallway. *How are we to ever open you? I suppose a locksmith could give picking it a try.*

Sam walked up the ladder from the crew cabin and noticed Edward. "Isn't that just the rub, mate? A full set of cannons and no way ta fire 'em. Jus' like when you're about ta get with a girl and she leaves before ye can clank yer rocks, eh?" He laughed at his own crude humour.

Edward ignored the comment. "Sam, I wish to thank you for the other day. You saved my skin."

"Just returning the favor, mate."

"I'm curious why you're choosing to remain aboard. Why aren't you leaving?"

"Well… I guess it would have come outta the woodwork sooner or later. I used ta work on a pirate ship a few years back. Got away and managed ta stay away from the gallows. I wasn't no one special, s'no one cared about me. From then on, it's been port to port fer me. And here ye come, yer labelled as a pirate, and I'm back in the same spot. Figure I'm destined for this life. It be a sign if there ever was one."

Edward thought it over. "I guess that makes sense." *To a madman.*

"I knew you'd understand. Ya do what you've gotta do, right, mate? And boy, when I saw you take that marine's gun, then force 'im to give you all his stuff? I said to meself: this guy's one to watch. Figure I'll set eyes on a great show if I tag along fer a while. Y'understand. Right, mate?"

Edward nodded as he walked away. "Glad to have you aboard, Sam," he said over his shoulder. *He is mad.*

Edward moved on to the crew cabin, just below the gun deck. The crew cabin was empty now, and he couldn't see Henry anywhere.

Perhaps Henry is still eating.

Hammocks lined the crew cabin bow to stern—two hundred forty-eight altogether. A few beds were also built into the side of the hull at intervals. At the stern was a door leading to a dining hall unlike any ship Edward was familiar with, and at the bow was another door locked from use.

Five in total. I have half a ship thanks to that Benjamin Hornigold. Edward gazed at the dim wooden estate he now owned, taking in the smells and sounds of his ship. The vessel creaked and groaned as it swayed over the waves. The smell of pine and salt air mixed in his nostrils; it was distinct, and familiar, as if he had smelled the same thing before somewhere.

Well, he did provide me half a beautiful ship at least. Edward leaned against the wall of the crew cabin deck, gazing at the *Freedom*.

His ship. His *Freedom*. His home.

"You look so much like your father, Edward," a voice said behind Edward.

He turned to see John, feeling a stab of melancholy at hearing John's compliment and thinking of his father. He managed a small smile. "Was there something you needed, John?"

"Uhh… yes, Captain. There is something that we should discuss in p-private, if you please."

"Certainly." Edward followed John a short distance to the only spot on the ship they could have a private conversation—the galley.

The galley had a swiveling door for easy entrance to the dining area. Various pots and pans hung on hooks overhead, and plates were stacked on closed shelves. On the port side was a pantry filled with plenty of food; lemons, limes, salted meats, and exotic spices were some of the treasures left by Hornigold or taken from the marines.

"So what is this about, John?"

John reached into his pocket. "This," he said as he pulled out a piece of paper folded in quarters. "This slipped my mind until it fell from my pocket. I found it nailed to the front of the quarterdeck after our mysterious friend Benjamin left me the keys to the *Freedom* for you."

Edward took the paper, unfolded it, and read: "To whomever owns this ship—Salutations. I am the previous owner of this fine ship and to you I present a game to prove yourself worthy. On the back of this paper is a clue to finding the first missing key to one part of the *Freedom* along with a bit of 'incentive' to sweeten the teeth."

Edward turned over the paper, and sure enough, there was more writing. It was in the form of a cryptic puzzle.

From two ports of two crescent moons, two and two islands north and north northwest. Two by two islands, two by two tests. Two by two crews, one of wit, one of grit. Each test gains one key for the chest. Bring the keys and find the chest in the belly of the fifth.

Edward lowered the paper and frowned. "John, I don't want you to tell anyone about this, all right?"

"I promise I won't tell a soul, Captain. But… what does it mean?"

"I don't know…" *A riddle to some treasure, probably.* With misgivings, Edward pocketed the paper. "Let us forget about that for now, as a question came to me that I've been meaning to ask. Why are you deciding to stay with me, after what has happened?"

"It was because of you I joined this crew, Edward, and it is that same reason why I am still here."

"Me! Why me, John?"

"Because you're your father's son. He was my captain years ago, and now you are my captain. Besides, now that we're in this mess you'll need me even more. I promised your father I would protect and help you in any way I could."

"John, are you sure you'll be able to handle being on this ship? There will be battles if we have to escape from marines."

"Edward, I know sometimes I can be a bit… timid. But it's different when I'm in an actual battle. I was in the Nine Years' War, you know?" He seemed lost in thought for a moment. "I know how to load and shoot a gun, and you can count on me outside battle as your quartermaster as well."

Edward paused a moment, seeing John with different eyes. *It is true. When the crew was in their mutinous phase, he held his sword even steadier than I did.* "All right then, John. You can stay. Don't let me regret my decision."

"Yes, Captain."

"So what was my father like as a whaling captain?"

"That's right, you were too young to join us back then. He was a true man of the sea. No matter what storm came, your father held everything together. He was an inspiration to the crew, and some say he was the best captain they ever had."

"So what happened?"

John's nervousness set in again. "N-no one knows. He had been acting odd, and then one day he left his regular crew and went on a journey with another group of sailors. They say a storm caught them and killed the whole crew." Edward's face fell at the words. John pulled the younger man's chin back up. "If you ask me or anyone who was on his crew, they'll tell you there's no way your father would have died. He was too stubborn. He's p-probably out there somewhere, trying to find his way home."

Edward scrubbed at his nose and clapped the quartermaster on the back. "Thank you, John." *I'll find you, Father. I'll bring you home, wherever you are.*

John looked for a moment like he wanted to say something else, but instead he gave a grin and a sloppy salute, and then left to let him have a moment alone.

⚓ ⚓ ⚓

Henry was on the main deck and Sam was passing by with a piece of cheese in his hand. "Sam?"

"What is it, mate?" Sam asked before taking a bite of his cheese.

"When we reach Port Royal, I want you off this ship. Permanently."

Sam snorted, a bit startled but unfazed. "No," he answered in a flat tone, starting to walk away, but Henry grabbed his arm.

"Why don't you drop your hand from me arm before I remove

it meself?"

"I want you gone," Henry seethed. "You're more trouble than you're worth, so find another ship. I don't care what you do afterward, but I don't want to see you again."

Sam leaned in. "Well, mate, you ain't the captain, now, is ya?" he said with a grin. "You got a problem with me, take it up with him. Otherwise, piss off. I don't got time for nancies like you."

Sam pulled his arm away and sauntered off to the foredeck.

"You'd better watch it, Sam," Henry called after him. "The next time you decide to take your frustration out on someone, I'll be there. You won't like it when that happens."

Sam looked back over his shoulder. "Oh. I'm sure I will, mate. I'd like to see what you think you can do." Sam tore another piece off his cheese and shot Henry a cocky smile.

Henry watched the younger man walk away. Moments later Edward walked up to him from the crew cabin.

"What were you talking with Sam about?"

"Oh, nothing... You wanted to talk with the crew about the spoils today, didn't you?"

"Yes, but there's something else."

Edward pulled out a piece of paper he had folded up in his pocket. It was the paper John had found on the ship when he first tried to sell it. He handed it to Henry.

"What's this?"

"Open it up and take a look. John just showed it to me. He found it on the ship before we set sail."

Henry unfolded the sheet with care and examined it, back and front, all the while muttering to himself. "Sweeten the teeth... Two by two islands, two by two tests... One key for the chest... Belly of the fifth?" He cocked his brow. "You know what this is?"

Edward whispered, "It's the location of one of the keys to the ship. Seeing as how this is a pirate ship, it might be a safe bet there's treasure too." He smiled at Henry's widened eyes.

"This is..." Henry started to say, but stopped himself. "This is unbelievable, Edward! Do you know where it's talking about?"

"No idea."

Henry read the cryptic message over once more. "Well, since our current helmsman plans to leave, we won't bother showing him. Our new one will have to make sense of it."

Edward smiled widely. "Go gather the crew together, would you?"

Henry nodded and, with William's assistance, gathered the crew on the main deck. They and John then joined Edward on the quarterdeck.

Henry did the talking.

"It will take John a little more than a week to sell everything we acquired, and then we can divide the spoils. You will all receive a share regardless of your decision to leave or to stay, but you have to be here if you want the money. You can wander around town, but if you're not here when we hand it out, you're given nothing."

The crew of the *Freedom* shouted gleefully their understanding.

"Also, for those who do not want the shares, we would appreciate it if you keep your mouths shut. You know Edward did what he had to; he's not a pirate. For the sake of those who wish to have their fair share, some of whom you no doubt know from Badobos, please leave the authorities out of this."

Edward spoke up at that. "I hope it's clear to you all that I… I didn't mean to bring any of this upon you. You've been a fine crew and… I mean to say, you've earned your reward. All I ask is your understanding."

Many in the crew nodded to Edward, with a fair number of sympathetic looks. Henry dismissed them, and they returned to their duties in a buoyant mood, the thought of money no doubt speeding their hands and feet.

Edward turned to Henry after the crew went back to work. "Let's talk in the galley. We have a few things to discuss in private."

Edward took Henry, John, William, and Sam below deck to the crew cabin. They walked past the swaying hammocks, past the pine benches and dining tables, and into the stone and metal kitchen. Sam guarded the door as Edward opened the conference.

Edward leaned against the stove. "We'll leave right after we divide the shares. No later." Edward fixed them all with a grim frown to emphasise his seriousness.

"Do you think someone will still try to turn us in?" asked Henry.

Edward stroked his chin in contemplation. There was one plain-looking sailor in particular he had in mind.

"Frederick. He seems to want retribution."

"It makes sense. He was like that in Badobos too," Henry agreed. "I remember one time he and James had an argument. James' house burned down later in the week. Everyone suspected it was Frederick, but no one could prove it."

"William, would you be able to keep an eye on him? All you'd have to do is stay out of sight, and if he talks with anyone, let us know."

"Yes, Captain."

Edward turned to Henry. "What about the crew? Who will we need?"

"We'll need new able-bodied seamen all around. We should purchase cannons as we could run into a fight on the sea, and we'll need gunners to support them," Henry said. "A new sailing master too, as our current one is leaving us." He scratched his chin, and then ran his fingers though his hair. "A surgeon is a must if we will be getting into battles."

With care, John wrote down everything Henry proposed; he was becoming famous for keeping lists and not neglecting any detail.

"That's a good point, we'll want to keep the guns and gunpowder, but only sell the spices and our bounty from our brief time as whalers." Edward chuckled. "And we can't forget the... disposition... of these crewmembers. They need to know this has been labelled a pirate ship and be so branded when they come aboard." Edward glanced at the door. "Sam mentioned he knew some people who might join."

"I don't trust him," Henry stated, folding his arms. He didn't care that Sam might be listening right outside the door. "He's a troublemaker, and the same goes for anyone he would have join us."

"He scuffled with another crewmember. It's not as if you've never had a temper problem before."

"I don't care. I don't think we should keep him aboard."

"We don't have the luxury of choice. He stays," Edward declared with finality. "Now, anyone else have suggestions?" No one came forward. "Well, Henry and I can first ask around for surgeons when we have his nose examined."

"What? My nose is fine! Never been better. See?" Henry took in several large breaths through his nose, but Edward could tell he was suppressing a wince. He moved from the stove, walked over to Henry, and then flicked his nose. "Ow! Damn you, Edward! That hurts!"

"See? You need to see a surgeon. Everyone else clear on what they are doing?" They nodded in agreement. "On to Port Royal!"

With their plan of action in place, it was a straight sail to Port Royal. After the marine incident had passed they were not far away from port, and soon after they docked the *Freedom* at the farthest end of the harbour of Port Royal. Long before landing they had furled the foresail so none would see the Jolly Roger, and they planned to replace it later when they had new canvas and no prying eyes. Rowers brought the ship in, then retracted their oars at the command of the sailing master to let the *Freedom* slip the rest of the way into port.

They were quite a sight to behold. To begin with, it was most unusual for a frigate to be in the Port Royal harbour. If Edward was a captain of a wealthy merchant ship, he certainly didn't look the part, clothed as he was almost in rags. The crew, if anything, looked even worse.

From the pier, Edward could see much of Port Royal itself. It was midday, and the bazaar was bustling with activity. The smell of meat and vegetables cooking wafted in all the way to their ship. Edward heard vendors hawking their wares, buyers trying to haggle, and locals catching up while shopping. The island was green and lush, and had an abundance of swaying palms contrasting against the stone streets of colonisation.

As the crew was preparing supplies to sell, the harbourmaster met them at the west end of the pier where they had docked. The crew placed gangplanks out on the pier and the harbourmaster boarded without an invitation. Edward went to greet him.

"Hello, and welcome to Port Royal, sirs. No doubt you are in a hurry, so may I have your name, please?" the harbourmaster asked.

Bollocks! What do I tell him my name is? "Edward Hughes. Pleasure to be in your town." Edward shook the harbourmaster's hand.

The harbourmaster returned the handshake while glancing at the ship, the haggard crew, the muskets, and the whaling equipment. Edward could tell that at each glance the harbourmaster became more wary of the newcomers. "There is a docking fee of a piece of eight."

Edward called John and took from him two pieces of eight. He gave both to the harbourmaster with a smile. "Here you are, one piece of eight," he said with much emphasis on the word 'one'.

The harbourmaster looked at the two coins with delight, pocketing one. "Welcome to Port Royal," he said with a smile and a bow.

"Thank you," Edward replied. The man left without another word, writing something in his ledger regarding their ship.

"Captain, are you sure it was wise to b-bribe the man? We don't even know him." John shifted his gaze from the harbourmaster and then back to Edward in quick succession while wringing his hands.

"We ensured his silence."

"How c-can you be sure?"

"Did you see the way he pocketed the money? He won't say anything." Edward turned around to speak to the whole crew. He took a few deep breaths and focused on a few people in the crowd. "Everyone, listen please. I know because of all that has happened some of you want to leave, but I want you to know I appreciate your help in everything you've done here. I'd have any one of you as a drinking mate across the Caribbean and back again."

The crew was silent until Sam yelled, "Hear, hear!" and everyone joined in with a shout. Then they were back at the task of unloading the cargo and piling it up on the pier in preparation for sale.

"Captain, may I make a suggestion?" William asked in his usual formal tone.

"Yes, William, what is it?"

"If we are purchasing cannons, you should buy smaller ones."

Edward folded his arms. "Why would we do that?"

Blackbeard's Ship

"It makes more sense to have smaller ones on deck. They can be operated by one person rather than the two or more required to operate the larger ones. You can have more cannons in total, and still have money left over. I estimate we can fit ten cannons on each side of the ship. Given market pricing of the whaling equipment, blubber, and spices, you should have money to spare."

Edward thought it over a minute. "John!" John came running. "When you buy our cannons, make them small so one crewman can operate it, ten for each side of the ship. And the necessary ammunition, of course."

"I'll put it on the list, Captain."

"Now, come, Henry. We need to find you a surgeon."

Edward and Henry walked into town and headed to a surgeon who, Sam claimed, didn't ask questions. They wanted to make sure they recruited a person they could trust, as well as one who might be willing to join the crew.

As they moved through town, they could smell the sweet salt air of the sea, grass, perfumed women, and the aroma of roasting meat wafting from various establishments. The closer they got to the surgeon's shop, the less sweet the smell became. They passed shabby houses, dank bars, and ruddy-faced roughs loitering about drunk at midday. Some structures were falling apart and seemed like a strong breeze might push them over. By the time they reached the farthest side of the town, no longer could they smell the salt air, the grass, or the meat, and instead they smelled some foul concoction of mud and rotten food.

"Do you see it anywhere?" Edward asked.

Henry was still rubbing his nose with care. "No... Wait, I think I see it. Over there." He pointed to a doorway in the middle of a stone alley with a sign hanging in front. The dirty, rusted sign read *'barbier chirurgien'* and as it swung in the breeze it made a horrible screeching noise. The door was also in a dilapidated condition with what appeared to be bullet holes strewn about on its surface, and it hung crooked on its rusty hinges. "Are you sure about this, Edward? Sam's information was second-hand. I don't know if we can trust it."

"Only one way to find out." Edward grabbed the handle and pushed at the door. Before he had opened the door a quarter of the way, someone pulled the door inward with his hand still latched to the handle. It dragged him forward and soon he was looking straight down the barrel of a pistol.

"Who sent you, knaves? Speak or be shot. *Tu comprends?*"

Edward spoke as quickly as he could, his hands in the air. "We are here of our own accord, sir."

The eyes of the man holding the pistol darted back and forth between Edward and Henry, and then, popping his head past the doorway, outside to the alley. He pulled the gun away and stepped back.

"Come in, gentlemen."

Edward and Henry shook their heads to each other, and then entered the establishment. "My friend has a—"

"Broken nose," the man said dismissively. "I know this already. Sit down. I need to *expérimenter* something first."

"How did you know his nose was broken?"

"I am observant where others are not," the surgeon said as he worked with something at the back of the room.

Edward and Henry got a good look at the room. It was small and almost barren, and not well kept in the slightest. The wood on the walls was rotting, the floorboards were broken beyond repair, and the only chair in the room was old, dirty, and falling apart.

There was a peculiar smell, like vinegar and pure alcohol, and something else that Edward couldn't put his finger on. He had to cover his nose for the first minute to stifle the smell.

Henry sat down in a tall chair with wool spilling from holes in the upholstery. "I noticed the more than casual rubbing your friend was doing to *son nez*. The redness and swelling around the bridge and left eye suggest he was struck with a rather large blunt object that hit the right side of the face."

Edward's jaw dropped. "That's… impressive."

The surgeon turned around with a flourish and a bow. "Alexandre Exquemelin, at your service." After Alexandre rose from his bow, he lifted his pistol and shot it at the front of the room.

Edward jumped to the left and ducked down. Henry fell off the side of the chair and took cover behind it. "Ed, are you all right?" Henry yelled.

"Yes, I am fine. Were you shot?"

A moment passed. "No."

Edward rose back to his full height of six feet four inches, flexing his muscles in an attempt to intimidate the Frenchman in front of them. "What are you bloody doing, man? You could have hit us!"

"Relax, *mon ami*. I added rifling in the barrel, it's perfectly safe." Alexandre loaded another bullet into the pistol.

Edward looked to the front of the room and noticed a dead pig hanging from the ceiling. The pig was riddled with bullet holes and cuts that appeared to be from a fencing sword.

Alexandre aimed once more at the pig and fired. The noise of the gun was deafening in the small room. Edward was already having trouble hearing after the first shot, and the second compounded the problem. "To answer your question, I am trying to make a *balle* that is piercing and more accurate. So far, the *expérimenter* is going well."

Edward took a better look at the Frenchman. His thin jawline was clean-shaven and he had a prominent nose, but his eyes were what Edward noticed most: Baggy, dark, sullen eyes, set deep in his bony face. They gave the impression he would as soon slice your neck open as shave your beard. Those eyes were wild and unpredictable, and it made Edward's skin crawl almost as much as the place in which he now found himself.

I suppose that attribute is perfect on a pirate ship.

Henry sat back in the chair at Alexandre's beckoning, but eyed Edward with worry. Before he could voice his concerns, Alexandre was on him.

Alexandre grabbed Henry's nose and yanked it hard to the left. There was a distinct cracking noise, followed by a range of colourful expletives from Henry. "Ow! Ahh that hurt, you bloody git! I thought you were a surgeon! Bugger! That *smarts*!" Henry kept rubbing his nose as he muttered some Welsh curses for good measure.

"There, that should heal properly now. Is that all, *messieurs*?"

Henry gave Edward the evil eye, saying without words that he didn't want this man on the ship, but Edward shrugged his shoulders. "There is another matter which we would like to discuss with you."

Before Edward could continue, Alexandre held up his hand to silence him. "Let me guess. The salty, sweaty smell on you means you were recently at sea. You want me to join your *rassemblement*?"

Edward's and Henry's jaws slowly dropped as they listened. "That's… exactly right. How did you…?"

"How did you do that?" Henry finished, dumbfounded.

"*Je viens se dire cela.* I'm observant." Alexandre's strange face softened into a smile of satisfaction. "Now: to answer the question you have no need to ask… You have to tell me what type of vessel you're on and what I'll be treating onboard. That will determine my answer."

"Why?"

"Because I want excitement. I want *défi*. I want to see things you cannot see in normal everyday work. Can you provide, *messieurs*? The smell of gunpowder on you tells me you can."

Edward and Henry looked at each other. "You want to tell him?" Edward asked.

"Me? Why don't you tell him?"

"I don't want to tell him, you tell him."

"You're the captain, you tell him."

"Tell me what, *messieurs*?" Alexandre jumped in.

Edward sighed. "Fine. I'll tell him," he said. "We are the right people for you, Alexandre." Edward whispered as if someone might hear him and place him under arrest. "We've been labelled pirates.

More than enough excitement, I'd say."

"*Vous plaisantez*! I've been dying for a chance like this! I knew moving here was the right idea. So much excitement! It will be *un grand plaisir* to join you."

Alexandre took a large bag from under his desk and loaded his surgical and barbering equipment into it. He also grabbed a sack to hold an extra set of clothes and his experiment with bullets, excluding the pig.

"You'll be labelled as a pirate after this, you know."

"Oui. I know that, *monsieur…*?"

"Henry."

"*Monsieur* Henry. Labels mean nothing to me. I merely wish to enhance my skills and keep things interesting. Caring for the elderly or *les enfants*, it is boring. The life of a pirate is full of excitement and danger. I have no incertitude caring for you while in the midst of battle will also be exciting. Now if that is all, we should be leaving quickly. What is the name of your ship in case we are separated?"

In case we get separated? "It's called the *Freedom*. Why would we be separated?"

No sooner had the words left Edward's mouth than Alexandre's door burst open with a crash and fell off its hinges. Two burly men, thugs who seemed to be used to heavy drinking, busted through.

"That's why," Alexandre answered.

"Alexandre, you filthy French pisspot! You stole all our money!" The man on the right, closest to Edward, pointed to Alexandre as he spoke.

Edward turned to Alexandre, his brow raised. "What's he talking about?"

"I'll tell you what I'm talking about. That arsehole put something in our drinks that made us fall asleep, and then he stole our money. Now he'll pay. *You'll* need a surgeon after this, Alexandre!"

"It is a simple *malentendu* really. It was an experiment, and *messieurs*, you were excellent subjects." The man walked to Alexandre, not swayed by his words. Edward and Henry were ready to fight, but didn't know what to do, as they weren't the ones being targeted. Alexandre kicked the man's groin hard, sending him to the floor. Then he punched the other, knocking him back. "*Courons!* Run, *messieurs!* The experiment has gone awry!" Alexandre yelled as he rushed out the door.

Edward and Henry ran out the door as well. "Let's split up. I'll go to the right. Meet at the ship!"

"Right!" Henry yelled, and then he and Alexandre headed back to the main street and on to the *Freedom*.

The men who were after Alexandre ran out soon after, but they didn't see Henry and the surgeon leaving on the main street. They saw only Edward, stepping off onto a side street. They chased after him, hot on his heels.

Damn! Why are both of them chasing me? I thought they would split up!

Edward ran as fast as he could. He bobbed and weaved in and out of the streets, darting around people and wagons and vendors' stalls. He was making good speed, but the two large men kept pace with him. They were light on their feet for their size, and smashed and shoved anything in their way. Edward tried to pass between buildings to lose them, but they didn't slow down. He didn't dare look back, but the grunts and shouts from bystanders told him they were still at his heels.

And then he tripped over a rainwater barrel in an alley.

They were on him at once, picking him up off the ground and throwing him against the nearest wall. There was no one around to help him.

"Where's Alexandre? You obviously know each other. Where do you hide out?"

"We arrived in Port Royal not a few hours before and just met him. We needed the work of a cheap surgeon and then you busted in."

"Yea, and I'm the Queen of England," one of the men said with sarcasm dripping from every word. "We'll just have to make you talk." He punched Edward in the stomach, and Edward doubled over and fell to the ground. Then the two of them cracked their knuckles and smiled.

"Welcome to Port Royal."

4. PUSH VS. SHOVE

Edward was staring into the faces of men he didn't know, for a theft he didn't commit, involving a man he had met not ten minutes before.

When I get my hands on Alexandre, he will pay.

"You'd better start talking or we start breaking bones."

Edward said nothing as he struggled to find a way to escape. It was then that he noticed Henry sneaking up behind the men. Henry grabbed an empty glass bottle from the ground in his hands and nodded to him.

The thugs were about to pounce on him when Henry smashed the bottle down on the head of the one on the right. The other man turned to the noise, and Edward took his chance and punched the second man straight in the jaw. The man's head was flung to the side, and down he went.

Before it had even started, the fight was over.

Edward clasped hands with Henry and thanked him for the help. "I thought you and Alexandre were headed to the ship."

"We were, until I noticed that we weren't being followed. Alexandre said he could find the ship on his own, so I came back to save you. Just like I always do," Henry added, folding his arms.

"Yea, yea, rub it in." Edward pushed his friend, then thanked him again. "Let's head back to the ship. I want to have some words with this surgeon."

When they returned to the ship, they found Alexandre there, sitting pretty on the port railing. When Alexandre noticed them he rose to his feet.

"Ah, *mon Capitaine*, I trust you are well?"

Edward glared at Alexandre. "No thanks to your friends. I was trapped in an alley but Henry saved me. Do you mind explaining why those men wanted your head?"

"*Toutes mes excuses.* As I mentioned to them, it was merely a misunderstanding. I made a... *préparation* causing the men to fall asleep. It worked and my experiment was *complète*. However, when I left, someone must have stolen their money. It was not I, but the men assume. *Incorrectement*, I might add."

Edward shook his head, exasperated. "It matters not. Find a place for your things in the crew cabin."

"*Votre souhait est mon commandement*," Alexandre said with a flourish, and then descended into the lower decks.

"So now what?" Henry asked.

"We'll rent a room at an inn and stay there for the time being. Tomorrow we can search for a sailing master."

"Pray to God everything else goes smoothly, friend." Henry patted Edward on the back. "I know I have."

"Pray he fixes your nose. I would like to have a first mate that at least looks intimidating. Right now a slight breeze could break you."

"Oh? And who saved you from a couple of drunkards? At least I took my punishment."

Edward slowly brought his hand up in a manner suggesting he was going to flick Henry's nose again.

"Don't you dare."

Edward and Henry had a good chuckle before leaving the ship to find an inn. They found many just above the harbour, and Edward decided to look at one alone first and left Henry standing outside. He emerged not ten minutes later and motioned Henry on without a word.

"What was that about?" Henry asked.

"I secured us a room at this inn for the week, but we'll find another to stay at."

Henry cocked his brow. "Why?"

"This way, with William on the prowl and ready to notify us when Frederick makes his move, we can slip into this inn. Frederick will think we're at the next inn, which we'll stay at for the next few days, but he won't find us there."

Henry dwelled on it. "I have to admit, that is clever." Edward smiled at the praise. "For you," he added, for which his captain punched him in the arm.

They both went into the next inn and Edward rented them a room for the next ten days.

The room was what they might have expected for the price: small, well-worn beds, no furniture, rats and bugs everywhere. The smell of sweat and even less savoury fluids emanated from the floors and sheets.

"This is a fine choice a lodgings you've found us," Henry remarked as he scanned the room.

"No one claimed the life of a pirate was glamorous."

"You would do well not to utter the P-word. We aren't pirates, remember? The marines only think we are. Besides, someone might hear you."

"And what of it?" Edward took off his boots and lay down on his bed. Henry did the same and flashed Edward a nasty look.

"So you're fine with it? You're fine with having people think we are pirates?"

"There are some advantages to it."

"This is what I was talking about before," Henry said, his melodic Welsh accent appearing with his anger. "What would Robert think of this? You stole from those marines. You can try and gussy it up however you want, but taking something that isn't yours is theft. Before, I could understand your stance, but now you should stop saying you've been labelled a pirate as though it was unjust."

"I'm not a pirate. We needed to make sure they wouldn't attack us afterwards. Taking their weapons was the only way. If we could have taken their cannons, I would have."

"If you say so, Captain."

Edward ignored the jab and laid his head down. *I shouldn't have to justify my actions. He's a part of this too.*

The two laid in silence as the noises outside the inn died down, and all they could hear were the occasional drunkard and night-birds singing a song. They drifted off to sleep and it washed away the tension between Edward and Henry. After they voiced good mornings, Edward got down to business.

"We only need to find ourselves a sailing master and our job will be done." He touched his hand to the pocket that held Benjamin Hornigold's mysterious gift. *Then we can start on this.*

"We need one who's not only willing to take the position, but has the necessary fortitude for it. Where will we find a man of such disposition?"

The salty air blew at Edward's face, and the sun hit his eyes as it inched up on the horizon. "Well, we are near the pier. What say we start our journey here and work our way up?"

First they returned to the ship and told some trustworthy crewmembers where they were staying. They were to keep it secret from all except William, should he need Edward or Henry. Then the two traversed the entire pier, asking if anyone knew of any sailing masters craving work. Finding no success, they took their search to town, but after three days they still hadn't found anyone for the position.

Everything else seemed to be proceeding according to plan. John was nowhere to be seen until the fourth day, but the results of his efforts were apparent. New crewmembers were showing up by the dozens. From riggers to gunners, more showed up with each day's passing, and each one was more capable than the last. Some appeared shady, but hardy and eager to leave shore nonetheless.

Also new to the ship were the cannons. Just as planned, they were able to buy twenty small ones and still had a good chunk of money left over.

When Edward and Henry weren't searching for a sailing master, they familiarised themselves with the new crewmembers. They wanted to know who the newcomers were and what skills they had. Edward thought certain men might be trouble later on, but he couldn't be picky about the crew at this time.

Close to night on the fourth day, John and William both returned to the ship with urgent concerns. Edward, Henry, John, William, and Sam all met in the galley once again for a private meeting.

John and William said simultaneously: "We have a problem." They looked at each other, but William nodded to John to go first.

"I heard in t-town that Port Royal has anti-piracy laws that are s-strictly enforced," he said, wiping sweat from his bushy brows.

"Anti-piracy laws?" Edward frowned.

John nodded. "Port Royal isn't the p-pirate safe haven Sam made it out to be. The new governor appointed in Jamaica set up anti-piracy laws. If we're found out, we'll all be h-hung, Captain." The man was shaking.

Edward turned to Sam, his arms folded.

"Don' look at me! I 'aven't been 'ere in years. Not since the war ended."

"That's exactly when it happened. Queen Anne appointed him specifically to rid Jamaica of pirates after the war ended."

"How soon can we leave?"

"This very minute should it please you, Captain. We've sold everything and bought all we need; all that remains is to divide the spoils among the crew."

"Very good. We'll divide the spoils as soon as we find a sailing master, and then leave immediately. No one knows about us except the harbourmaster, and as long as he continues to cover for us we'll be all right."

John moved to speak, but William cut him off. "That is where my problem comes in. Frederick made his move. He knows of where you're staying in Port Royal, and the marines plan to arrest you tonight. He's hoping to avoid having to send them to the ship, but I think they plan to make either him or you talk."

"Bollocks! How long would you say we have?"

"Provided you and Henry aren't captured tonight… a day or two at most."

"We have need of a sailing master before we leave. There's no other way. None of us are skilled enough to read the seas." Edward stood and paced the room.

"C-Captain?" John said meekly.

"We need options. Plans to abscond."

"Captain?" John repeated a little louder.

"How are we to make it to the next port without someone to guide us? I need suggestions, mates. If you have any ideas now would be a good time."

"Captain!" John yelled.

"Yes, John, what is it?"

"I may have a solution. I happened upon a sailing master who may be willing to leave these shores, but…"

"Great! John, you've proven yourself time and time again! William, Sam, prepare everything for departure in the morning! Tomorrow at the break of dawn we set sail!"

Edward, full of purpose, left the ship to find John's sailing master. He had John guide him to the man's house, and dragged Henry along. He didn't want to waste any time in this place which was suddenly so dangerous to men like them.

They approached a rather secluded home at the peak of the hill on Port Royal. With bare walls and a flat roof and only one level, it looked more like a warehouse than lodging. The lawn was unkempt, grass growing everywhere, and the windows were caked with dirt.

"This is the place?" Edward asked, unimpressed.

"Yes, Captain, this should be the one, if my information is correct."

"How can we be sure he'll join us? Aside from the upkeep of his home, he seems like a normal everyday citizen, from what John mentioned." Henry peered at the fading sun. Night was creeping up on them. William would be dividing the spoils at that moment, and Sam letting everyone know when they'd be leaving. Most would stay the night on the ship, Edward hoped.

"We'll have to do our best to convince him, won't we, Henry?" Edward knocked on the door to the house. He waited a minute, and then knocked again.

"Who is it?" a voice asked from behind the door.

"My name is Edward. I have heard there is a sailing master living here. I'd like to speak to him."

There was a pause on the other side. "What about?"

"I'm a captain. I'm here to discuss a position on my ship. May we enter?"

Another pause, and then: "Please wait a moment." Edward could hear someone shuffling and picking something up, then a clicking noise. "Come in."

Edward shrugged to John and Henry and then opened the door, only to walk right into the barrel of a musket. *Oh shit!* He dropped to the floor and covered his head. The noise of a gun firing filled his ears. Then he heard a struggle and the same voice he had heard from behind the door saying, "No! Let go!"

"It's all right, Ed, you can get up now."

Edward pulled his arms down from atop his head, hoisted himself up from the floor, and looked the shooter over. It was a young man, about the same age as Edward and Henry, sitting slumped in a wheelchair. Ragged, tatty clothes covered his small frame. His legs were thin, but his arms appeared strong. He had dark circles under his eyes, and Edward thought that the man had long ago lost his hope in this life, and over time it had given him a perpetual slouch in his chair.

"Why did you shoot at me?"

"Humph." The young man folded his arms and pursed his lips.

"Fine. John, Henry, clearly we won't meet a decent sailing master here. Let's leave. If we're quick we can find someone else. Good day, sir." Edward left, with Henry and John following right behind.

"What? That's it?"

Edward turned back to the man. "You shot me! You expect me to stay and have tea with you?"

"No, no, that's not... I'm sorry. This is a misunderstanding. Please, sir, let me explain," he said. The young man looked genuinely contrite, and upset with himself over his anger.

Edward was dubious and furrowed his brow. "Fine, but this better be a damned good explanation, mate." He walked over to a low table in the house, and the others followed. The man motioned for them to sit down in the—to put it nicely—*modest* couch and chairs available.

"So you truly are a captain?"

"Yes."

"And you're really looking for a sailing master to guide your ship?"

"Yes. Now can you please explain yourself?"

"I'm sorry. I... I'm in debt, and I thought you were collectors. I don't have many visitors. As you can tell, I've had my share of hardships. But my biggest problem is no one will hire me. So if you are here to offer me a job, I would be more than willing to take it."

Edward waited a moment before speaking. "How long have you been in debt to these... collectors?"

"Not long. But for these types 'not long' is too long."

"So why should I hire you to sail my ship?"

"I've studied the science of sailing in great detail, I pride myself on my ability to read clouds, and I know everything needed to run a ship." The man's eyes lit up with a hope long suppressed. "If you take me on, you'll never find a better sailing master. No one has more knowledge and intuition than I have. And no one could be more loyal or more dedicated."

Edward thought for a moment. "Any specific conditions for joining?"

The man thought on the question a moment. "Yes, there is one... My fourteen-year-old sister has to come with me. I can't leave her here."

"Done," Edward announced before Henry and John could object. "But I have two conditions of my own."

The man was smiling and almost on the verge of tears. It was clear he hadn't had a job in some time, and sailing was his passion.

"Name them," he said.

"First, I know not how my men will react to having a woman aboard. It's a common superstition that it's bad luck to bring one out to sea. Not mine, but I'm not the only person aboard. Dress her in boy's clothes, cut her hair, whatever is necessary. Second, you'd best not have any objections to you and your sister being in battle, as we've been labelled pirates."

"Edward!" Henry yelled.

"A pirate ship? You're pirates?"

Edward threw his hands up at Henry. "It's easier just to say it!" Then, to the young man: "Not exactly. We were *accused* of piracy, and we may end up in danger because of it. If you've no desire for the life, then you're free to stay here and await the collectors. The choice is yours: the freedom of the seas, or slavery to money."

The man thought about it for a while. His struggle was evident. "I have one more condition."

"Oh?" Edward asked with raised brow.

"If we meet the pirate Calico Jack, or any of his subordinates, we will kill them." He spoke of killing as if it were a business transaction.

"And why are we to kill this Calico Jack and his men?"

"My reasons are my own. I need for you to promise me if we meet him or any of his men, we will kill them."

Edward thought about it for a moment. "Done." They shook hands, sealing their deal of death.

"Pack your things, only essentials, and be ready to leave in the early morning. We're setting sail at dawn."

"Understood… Captain." The man smiled.

"Oh, and it would be good to have your name."

"Ah. My name is Herbert Blackwood. My sister's name is Christina Blackwood."

"All right then, Herbert, I'll be back here early in the morning and we'll escort you to our ship. Be ready."

"Understood, Captain."

Edward stood and left the house without saying another word. As he left the house, the last rays of light shining upon him, he felt elated that they now had a sailing master.

"What the hell are you doing?" Henry said on their way back to town.

"What are you talking about?" Edward kept walking as the others followed.

Blackbeard's Ship

"What am I talking about?" Henry counted off the offences on his fingers. "I'm talking about hiring a cripple, bringing a girl aboard our ship, and agreeing to kill a ruthless band of pirates? Are you out of your bleedin' mind?"

Edward stopped and turned to Henry. "I'm helping this man and his sister. My father never had a problem with women aboard as long as they pulled their weight, and neither do I. Besides, we need him. We need to leave right away, and this man appears to be an expert sailing master. Shall I remind you that I make the decisions here, Henry, not you?"

"You think they'll be safer? On a pirate ship? The man's a cripple, Edward. What do you expect will happen during a battle? What if he falls over? Who will pick him up? What if we're in a storm and he can't stick to the wheel?"

"Enough, Henry." Edward resumed walking.

"And what about the girl? I don't care if your father was fine with it, you know it's bad luck to have a woman aboard. If the crew finds out, she'll be thrown overboard at the first sign of trouble. Either that or they'll rape her. You think the crew we've gathered is as noble as you? Don't be a fool, Edward!"

Edward turned to Henry once more. He pointed his finger in his face. "I said enough, Henry! Both of them are joining the crew and that's final. If you don't like it, then maybe you're on the wrong ship!"

Henry's expression changed from anger to surprise to hurt. After a few moments, he walked away. Not in the direction of the inn, and not to the pier either. Edward stood and watched him leave. John stood with his mouth agape as if he wanted to say something, until Edward motioned to resume their walk to the inn.

"W-what do you want me to do, Captain?"

"Leave him. If he wants to have a fit right before we set sail, then fine. He knows when we weigh anchor. Prepare some men to escort Herbert and Christina to the ship in the morning. Make sure they're armed."

"Yes, Captain. B-but what about you? Do you need someone to watch over you tonight? You know, with Frederick and all?"

"No, I'll be fine. I want to be alone anyway." *Henry just needs to cool off ... And maybe I need to cool off as well.*

⚓ ⚓ ⚓

Edward watched from his room on the second floor as the marines went into the other inn. He could tell they wanted to be silent and catch him by surprise. But Edward was ready. He wouldn't be found in that inn. He was down the road, at the inn he had set aside at the beginning of the week.

After Edward watched them enter the decoy inn, he went back to sleep, satisfied that they were not onto him. In his slumber he did not hear the screams from the other man they *had* found there.

⚓ ⚓ ⚓

Early the next morning, William, John, and four other crewmates went to Herbert's house and helped him back to the ship. Edward met them on the pier by the *Freedom*. He could see Herbert in his wheelchair and a young one at his side. *That must be Christina.*

Edward waved to them and turned to William as they approached. "You didn't see anyone suspicious on your way here, did you?"

"Nothing worth noting, Captain. None are up at this hour. We chose a longer route back, but it kept us away from prying eyes."

Edward nodded in satisfaction. *I expected nothing less, William, but these skills make me wonder who you were before joining our crew.* Edward walked over to Herbert. "How are you feeling? Must have been a while since you were last on a ship."

Herbert smiled. "And a fine ship it is…" he said as he gazed at his new home. "You are right, it has been a while. My brother Christopher and I are a little nervous."

Edward stroked his chin. *Christopher… Nice touch.* "Don't worry, everything will go smoothly. Excited, Christopher?" Edward asked to the young one beside Herbert. The girl nodded, but didn't say anything. Edward could see blue eyes and short blond hair sticking out from beneath a cap. *She is young. I hope I haven't made a mistake.* Edward felt a pang of regret at the fight he'd had with Henry over this, but suppressed it. "Come, let's get you on board."

Edward, Herbert, and Christina went up the gangplank onto the main deck. They were greeted by various men of the *Freedom*'s crew loading supplies, packing things away, and arranging the rigging. Some were reeling in the anchor, while a few stragglers were just arriving.

"Well, Herbert, what do you think?"

"It's beautiful. Thank you, Captain." Herbert's gaze travelled the length of the ship, but then went back to shore. He scanned the pier and docks with a noticeable look of concern.

"As long as you're aboard this ship, you'll be free. They won't find you here," Edward reassured him quietly.

"I know. You live one way for so long, it's tough to change."

"Well, you're part of our family now. We'll take care of you."

"You're different, you know."

Edward laughed. "What do you mean?"

"A regular captain wouldn't want someone like me aboard his ship, especially after I shot at him. I know I wouldn't."

Edward knelt down next to Herbert and smiled. "Well, I'm not a regular captain then, am I?"

"No, I guess not." Herbert smiled back. As he boarded, he wheeled his chair straight to the aft ladder and stopped.

Edward saw the problem. "Need someone to help you?"

"No, I have someone." Herbert hopped off his wheelchair, and his sister grabbed it and carried it to the top of the cabin.

Several crewmembers watched as Herbert climbed the steep steps, one by one, accompanied by what they took to be an adolescent boy. They shook their heads as they carried on with their work, some making rude comments to each other. Herbert pressed on, ignoring them. After a few moments of hard labour, he made it to the top, sat back in his wheelchair, and took his position at the ship's wheel. He showed Edward his thumb, saying he was ready to work.

We need to find a better system for Herbert to move across the ship. Edward became lost in thought trying to think of something that would help Herbert manoeuvre around.

John grabbed Edward's attention. "Captain, I have something to show you."

"What is it, John?" Edward followed John's prompts into the crew's quarters.

"This."

John pointed to a set of clothes hanging against the wall. They were garments meant for a man of the sea, and a man of rank: a pair of long boots, black breeches, a white tunic with half-length sleeves, a black leather vest, a knee-length black coat and, to top it off, a black tricorn hat befitting a captain. The smell of new leather accentuated the quality.

"John! These are incredible! Wherever did you find them?" Edward examined the clothing, amazed at the workmanship.

"I bought them at one of the local shops. I thought it would be appropriate for you to have something good to wear as captain. You have to be a figure of authority and an inspiration to the crew. I hope they fit you well."

"These are... for me?"

"Why yes, Captain. No one should wear that hat but you."

Edward picked up the hat and examined it, smiling. "I'll put it on right away!"

"Hurry, your crew awaits." John left Edward to change into his fine new clothes.

Edward soon emerged from the lower decks wearing the clothes, feeling that he would be able, for the first time, to present to his crew the visible image of authority.

"It suits you," John said.

"Thank you, John." Edward inspected the assembled crew for someone he had not seen since the day before.

"Looking for Henry, Captain?" John asked.

"I guess he's made his decision…" he said.

His eyes were cast to the sole of the ship, and he felt a wrench in his heart. The two of them had been inseparable for many years, and in a few short moments it was over. They might not see each other ever again, and over a foolish argument. Edward thought to run out looking for Henry, but his pride steadied his feet.

Edward let out a shaky sigh. "Ready the sails before anyone else makes the same decision. Or before we're discovered."

"Right, Captain."

Edward heard a couple of crewmembers boarding at the last minute, talking about something that drew his attention.

"You there!" Edward shouted.

"Yes, Captain?"

Misplaced anger welled within Edward. "What is so important that you were almost late for departure?"

The two men explained hastily. "Well, beggin' yer pardon, Captain. It was about a hangin' they suddenly announced. It's set for noon today. They say some unlucky sod of a pirate was caught. At least the ones like us know not to be flauntin' our nature about."

Edward felt a pang in his stomach. "Who is it being hanged?"

"Uhh, I think it was two actually. Fred something, and… who was the other? Henry, I believe."

The words pierced like a knife. Edward spun around and looked at John, who had heard every word. They both knew beyond doubt the Henry the men were talking about was their Henry.

Edward's best friend, Henry Morgan, was about to be hanged.

5. A TRIP TO THE GALLOWS

The sun was nearing noon over Port Royal Point. The point was a finger of land projecting out into the sea, ending in a high bluff. It was much like the one Henry, Edward, and Robert had climbed as boys in Badobos. Today a crowd of more than three hundred gathered inside the stone enclosure at the peak, with still more spilling out of the arches and onto the grassy hill. Henry and Frederick stood on a wooden platform at the back of the square, nooses around their necks, waiting for the inevitable. The hot sun beat down on them and the salt air blew in their faces. Adults and children alike were jeering and throwing vegetables and fruit at them.

Ironic it would end at a place like this, Henry thought, remembering the bluff and his friends back home. He scanned the crowd, and he could see the disgust and rage in their faces. *I didn't even do anything, and yet they hate me. I wonder how many innocent people have stood here like this. There wasn't even a trial.* Someone threw a cabbage and it hit him square in the jaw, missing his nose by an inch.

Frederick was right beside him, stone-faced but shaking. "I'll haunt you after I die," he threatened.

"This was your doing," Henry spat. "William followed you and saw you talking with the authorities. What I don't understand is how you ended up here if you sold us out."

"I refused to tell them the name of the ship you were on because some of my friends were still on it. So they accused me of conspiring with pirates. But if it wasn't for your friend Edward, we wouldn't be in this situation."

Henry clenched his teeth, hot fury on his cheeks. "If you had kept your mouth shut then we wouldn't be here either, now would we?"

A marine rammed the butt of his rifle into Henry's stomach. Frederick smiled, but the officer did the same to him. "Stow it, you two!"

Damn! Why did Edward and I have to argue over something so stupid? If I hadn't of been so angry I would have remembered to leave the decoy inn.

Someone in the mob caught Henry's eye—a man dressed in black garb like a captain of a ship was strolling through the crowd. He bore several weapons, but no one seemed to notice or care. The man stopped just shy of the podium and then lifted his face.

Edward? Is that Ed? What the hell is he doing here? He's going to get himself killed! Henry stared at Edward, and the man smiled and winked at him. Then he disappeared into the crowd again, weaving ever closer to the stairs of the podium. *No, you stupid sod! Leave me! I'm not worth it!* Henry searched the crowd and could make out a few other familiar faces. John, William, and Sam were all there. *There's probably more of them too, the bleedin' idiots! They'll die trying to save me.* Henry forgot about his own plight and could think only of the danger to his friends. *What are they planning to do?*

The militia prodded the crowd to part so the magistrate of Port Royal could walk to the podium in front of the gallows. The militia kept the crowd at bay while he climbed the steps. The magistrate was a large man accustomed to a life of ease. He carried himself with an air of superiority to the rabble gathered for the show, and especially to Henry and Frederick.

At a gesture of his hands, the crowd grew quiet and he began his speech. The man droned on about the supposed villainy that Henry and Frederick had participated in—none of it true, but it riled the crowd up regardless. It culminated in the magistrate sweeping his arm through the air in a grand flourish as a sign to the executioners. They stepped up to pull the levers that would spell Henry's and Frederick's doom.

Before they could reach the levers, someone in the crowd yelled "Now!" Henry saw Edward and William strike the two guards standing at the foot of the stairs unconscious. There was a loud bang and Henry felt the noose around his neck loosen. Then Edward jumped up to the railing, sprang to where the astonished magistrate stood, and placed his sword at the magistrate's throat.

"Nobody move or this man dies!" he yelled.

The authorities on the wooden podium made a move towards Edward, but William appeared brandishing a pistol, and backed them into a corner

"Tell all your men to move away from the podium!" Edward hissed into the magistrate's ear.

"I'd rather die than help you escape!" the magistrate hissed back.

"I had a feeling you might have that attitude… so I took some precautions to ensure your cooperation. Look toward the eastern entrance to the square."

The magistrate turned his head to the right and noticed his family there. A middle-aged woman in a nice dress of green held two children, a boy and girl of the same age, close to her. Sam was standing behind the three.

"You see that man? He's with me, and he has a gun pointed at your wife right now. If you don't cooperate, she'll die first. Don't push me." Edward pressed the sword harder against the magistrate's throat, drawing blood.

Blackbeard's Ship

Sweat poured down the magistrate's face and neck. "Men, move away from the podium now!" The guards hesitated in confusion, but then slowly drew back, providing a wide berth around the platform.

"W-what is it you want here?"

"I'm here to save my friend. The one whom you were about to hang."

"Y-you're pirates in league with him? I should have known."

"We aren't pirates, and had there been a trial, that would have become apparent. Instead, you would condemn an innocent man on the word of one you were also going to hang? A fool if I ever saw one."

William went over to Henry and Frederick and released them from their bonds. Then they all walked down the podium with the magistrate in tow. Sam herded the magistrate's family forward, and they all went to the edge of the bluff with the officers following every step of the way.

"What do you plan to do? You're surrounded. Give up," the magistrate said.

"Ha! You think I'd yield now you prat? Don't worry, Magistrate. If I can help it, no one will die today. Not even you."

When everyone reached the edge of the bluff, William nodded to Edward, and he moved right up to the edge, until the magistrate whispered: "Who are you?"

Edward laughed an almost maniacal laugh. "My name is Edward Thatch." Then he shoved the magistrate back into the crowd of shocked soldiers—and he, followed by his companions, jumped off the edge of Port Royal Point.

"Are they insane? Those fools will never survive the drop!" the magistrate yelled as he and the guards ran to the edge to see the pirates plummeting—but not to their deaths. For right there, beneath the bluff, the *Freedom* drifted in the water—and on the aft deck the ship's crew had a sail stretched out for Edward and the others to fall into. Everyone on the bluff was in awe and disbelief.

The crew let Edward and his companions gently down onto the deck. Edward stood up, stretched his muscles and shook his head; he raised his eyes to the people gathered far above on the bluff, and laughed as he waved to them.

The sails of the *Freedom* were dropped soon after, with the foremost sail still showing the Jolly Roger. The pirate ship sailed away, their stolen crewmates in hand.

6. BATTLE-PROVEN

"Captain, they're sending ships out to pursue us." John pointed towards the port.

Edward turned around, a smile still on his face. "I have the notion it's best if we leave, wouldn't you agree John?" Without waiting for an answer, he walked to the edge of the deck overlooking the rest of the ship. "Gentlemen, we've overstayed our welcome in Port Royal. Put those sails in a broad reach and get us out of here!"

The new crew—Edward's new crew—rushed to work in a frenzy. The ship pitched and rolled with the waves, and the men without sea legs were having a hard time navigating the deck. That, coupled with the men not knowing what their duties were, was like too many cooks spoiling the broth. Men were bumping, tripping, and falling on top of each other as they ran to adjust the sails. Soon everyone was yelling and fights were breaking out.

Edward, Henry, and William went straight into the thick of it in an attempt to bring order to the chaos. The three were frantic in issuing orders, breaking up fights, and focusing the crew on the task at hand to save their lives.

A three-masted ship with at least twenty-six cannons was gaining on them from the rear. It didn't have any affiliated markings that denoted it being part of the British Navy and was most likely part of Port Royal's militia. The ship was smaller than the *Freedom* and thus faster and likely more maneuverable.

Edward was fighting to stop two crewmates arguing and to focus them on rigging the sails when he noticed the pursuing ship approaching broadside.

"Cannons!" Edward bellowed, jumping to the floor of the ship and dragging the crewmen he was arguing with down.

A thunder like none he had ever heard before erupted. It sounded very much like the real thing, only quicker, more uniform, and almost hollow. A second volley followed soon after.

A hail of cannonballs hit the *Freedom*. The large, speeding iron ripped and crushed the wood in its path. One hit the starboard railing right next to Edward, breaking the wood to splinters and showering the pieces over his head.

Edward rose on unsteady hands and feet amid the new sounds, moving at a snail's pace. Once on his feet, he glanced about at the other crewmates. Some were still in shock, but others who had been through battles before were quick to man the cannons themselves. Edward couldn't see any injured.

John came over to Edward and shook him by the shoulders. "Captain, we need you on earth! We need to counter."

"Yes," Edward replied. "Yes," he repeated, coming to his senses again. He turned to his crew. The men were still running around with no idea what to do, and Edward's anger was rising. "Men!" he yelled at the top of his lungs. His voice seemed louder than the cannons and the crew stopped what they were doing to look at him. Only then did he notice all the eyes on him, but his anger fought off his nervousness. "Prepare for battle."

With their captain's simple decree, the crew was brought to heel. The gunners gathered powder and cannonballs and manned the cannons. Others grabbed muskets and loaded them with balls, and the rest worked on moving the sails to fill them with wind and regain lost speed.

"Herbert!" Edward called. The new sailing master was sitting at the helm in his wheelchair, and from the look on his face he was well aware of what trial by fire awaited him now. "Keep those cannons from harming us," Edward commanded.

"Aye, Captain," Herbert replied with a grin.

Herbert swung the wheel hard turned the *Freedom* starboard to the south until its stern faced the other ship, presenting less of a target. He shouted to the crew to adjust the sails so they were running with the south wind, and then ordered some other crewmates to lower the jib sails to ease the fore mast.

Edward went up to the stern and pulled out a spyglass. He examined the other ship and could see that its name was *Gentry*, and it was turning forward to renew the chase against the *Freedom*. It would not be long before it caught up. Beyond the enemy ship, Edward could see other ships at the dock of Port Royal preparing to leave.

Damn! If those other ships catch up to us, we're done for. If only our gun deck wasn't locked. Curse you, Benjamin!

Edward ran back down to the main deck and grabbed a musket. *Wait a minute. I don't even know how to load this.* He glanced at the other crewmates, who loaded their muskets as if they were experts, and he could not help but feel like he'd have very little to contribute were it to come to a battle.

John, noticing his captain's plight, came to his rescue. "Here, Captain," he said, gracious enough to offer his own musket. Edward traded his empty weapon for the loaded one. "Keep your wits about you Captain; the other ship is approaching."

Edward turned to see the other ship gaining on them. Herbert had managed to coax enough speed from the sails to slow the *Gentry*'s progress, but soon the smaller ship would overtake the *Freedom*.

Edward went for cover behind the stern ladder. John went behind some barrels lined up against the starboard railing. Henry, musket in hand, crouched near the bow, ducking behind a cannon and peering at the approaching ship.

"Full and by the sails. Prepare to fire starboard!" Herbert yelled.

Fire starboard? Why are we firing? We aren't even close.

As if in answer to Edward's thoughts, Herbert gritted his teeth and flung the wheel hard to port. The ship lurched to the right as the crew gave the sails some slack, easing the turn. With the wind full in the sails, the *Freedom* passed in front of the *Gentry* before they could fire another broadside volley.

"Fire starboard!" Herbert commanded.

The gunners complied; the thunder was more distinct this time, louder, and it hurt Edward's ears.

Most of the iron balls met their mark, hitting the *Gentry* on the bow and starboard side. Some of the cannonballs hit the sea and splashed water into the air around the other ship.

Herbert pulled the wheel back to starboard, turning the ship to port. The *Freedom* evened back out, heading south from Port Royal again. The *Gentry* was still following on their heels, on the port side this time. Soon it would be in line to deliver a volley, despite Herbert's gambit.

The hot, metallic smell of burnt gunpowder tickled Edward's nose and mixed with the salty, sweet sea air and the *Freedom*'s pine planks. The smell of war overpowered the smells of nature, and the combination was unlike anything Edward had smelled before. His heart was pumping as fast as a storm wind turns a weather vane and it invigorated him. He wouldn't easily admit it, but he was enjoying it; the smells, the situation—all of it filled him with the excitement of battle, a thrill he had never known until now.

The two ships were closer now, close enough for bullets. The sound of small pops filtered into Edward's ears, and he noticed the crew on the port side ducking behind cover. He crawled over to the port side and peered out from behind cover. A bullet nicked the railing right next to his head and he dropped back down behind the ladder in an instant. When there was a lull in the pops of bullets hitting the ship, he ventured out of cover once more. This time, no stray bullets came at him. He lifted the musket, a far cry from the whaler's harpoon he was used to, and copied his neighbours in peering down the barrel. He moved the musket around until he was staring at someone down the sights.

Blackbeard's Ship

As he watched the man down his sights, Edward couldn't pull the trigger. *I have to.* He gritted his teeth. *I will not let them take Henry. I will not let them take my* Freedom. *If I want to keep my* Freedom *and save my crew, this is something I have to do.* He stared down the barrel another moment. *Sorry.* He pulled the trigger and closed his eyes from the sudden burst of light and smoke in his face. The muzzle flared as the bullet left the chamber. When he opened his eyes, they stung and watered from the smoke. He was still staring down the barrel, but he'd lost sight of the man he was aiming at. *Did I hit him?* He would never know for certain.

A rain of cannonballs crashed into the *Freedom*, decimating part of the port-side railing. Edward fell back from the blast of wood splinters in his face, and a cannonball skimmed across the deck five feet from him. It churned up the wooden planks of his home before falling off the other side.

Edward landed on his back and dropped the musket. His face and chest and eyes hurt. He thought he tasted blood in his mouth. The coppery warmth slid on his tongue, and he spat red onto the deck.

Henry ran up next to him. "Are you all right, Ed?" he asked as he grabbed Edward's hand and lifted him up to his feet.

"I am well. Just a scratch. What of the crew?"

"No serious injuries, but we can't keep going like this," Henry said.

Edward nodded in agreement. "We need to escape, and we can't do that unless we take the wind out of the *Gentry*'s sails."

Henry looked like he had been hit in the face. "That's it! We need to take the wind out of their sails."

"What?" Edward asked, dumbfounded. "How?"

"Focus our fire on the sails. No ship can be quick with holes in the canvas."

Edward smiled. "Brilliant." He turned to the crew. "Men! Focus cannon-fire on the sails. We're getting out of here."

The gunners responded with a yell and began raising the mouths of their cannons. The small cannons were easy to use, just as William had predicted, but with an extra hand they were able to fire that much quicker.

The *Gentry* was returning fire at will, and the shots were more erratic now. Where before they took the time to line up the shot and fire as one, now the enemy gunners seemed to be hastier in their aim. Cannonballs fell into the water in front of the *Freedom*, splashing waves onto the deck, or overshot and went between the masts and into the water.

Edward noticed the same thing happening with his crew. They weren't taking time to aim, and their shots were wild. A few grazed the masts of the *Gentry* here and there, but nothing did too much in the way of damage.

Edward thought he recognised the issue. "Herbert," he called, "why is the *Gentry* not circling around us if they're faster?"

Herbert glanced at the enemy ship, then at Edward again. "They've chosen to match our speed, Captain. They must feel they have superior firepower."

Damn! Edward thought. *They must have noticed how we haven't fired anything from the gun deck. We'll never hit the sails with this angle.* Edward used his spyglass to peer at Port Royal once more. He could see ships almost ready for departure. *We need to end this now.* "Crew, listen up!" he yelled. "Move all the cannons to the starboard side and ready for a broadside volley on the enemy sails."

The crew stared at Edward as if he were mad. They had a right to, given that the enemy ship was on the port side, and this was their first time with him in battle. He hadn't earned their trust yet.

We don't have time for this. His anger again pushed through the nervousness he felt at everyone staring at him. "Move it, men!" he bellowed. Despite his youth, his height made Edward an imposing figure and he had a deep voice, and the crew reacted accordingly.

They hopped to their task, helping the gunners move the cannons to the other side of the deck. Being on wheels helped, but they were heavy, lumbering pieces of iron and steel. Edward pitched in and pushed a cannon over to starboard as water and bullets continued to rain down on the crew. The *Gentry*'s aim was improving by the minute, and the ships were inching closer.

As soon as the cannons were secure, Edward looked at Herbert, who nodded in a knowing way.

"Full and by!" The crew changed the alignment of the sails for a close-haul to the wind at Herbert's command. Herbert threw the wheel to starboard, and the *Freedom* obeyed by moving to port and closer to the *Gentry*. "Ready starboard!" Herbert commanded. The gunners loaded the cannons and readied to take aim. The *Freedom*, slowed by the change in sails, moved up behind the *Gentry*. *Freedom*'s starboard side faced the enemy's stern, but they weren't parallel. *Gentry* was already starting to turn, anticipating *Freedom*'s plan of action. The crew of the *Freedom* understood what was coming next, and knew they had only one chance. "Fire!" Herbert commanded.

Twenty cannons went off almost at once. The sound reverberated off the floorboards of the deck, shaking the ship as it did so. Crewmates with their ears perked soon heard the sound of tearing fabric. Tiny rips opened one after the other in the canvas as the balls went through sail after sail. Not all the cannonballs hit their mark, but enough did so to render large parts of the sails useless.

Blackbeard's Ship

Herbert straightened out the *Freedom* to be in line with the wind as much as possible while still moving away from Port Royal. "Broad reach the sails," he commanded.

The *Gentry* tried to turn back to give another volley and continue pursuit, but the wind wasn't helping them as it had before. Almost all its sails had holes; the ship was crippled, and there was naught the crew could do about it. By the time it had turned enough to fire cannons again, the *Freedom* was too far away, and they would not catch up again.

Other ships from Port Royal were just leaving dock, but were too far away to even bother taking up the chase.

Edward put away his spyglass and went to the quarterdeck, happy they had been able to escape with Henry and their lives. He patted Herbert on the back. "Good job, Herbert. You've proven yourself to be more than capable today, and I hope the crew realises this as well."

"You are too kind, Captain. I had a reputation to uphold. Best crippled helmsman in the New World." Herbert chuckled at his own joke.

There was significant damage to the side rails and small holes from bullets here and there, but for the most part the crew was unharmed. Henry, John, and William were helping bring the injured over to Alexandre for care, with Sam first in line with a grazed arm. Edward could hear him cursing as Alexandre applied some sort of salve with no concern for his patient's comfort.

Edward's ship was no longer pristine, with broken pieces and smaller chips of wood littering the deck. *Poor Freedom. This battle was probably the first of many. We'll need a carpenter to help you with all this damage.*

A crewman began to cheer. His friends joined him, and soon the majority of the shipmates were sharing in victorious revelry.

As each second of the hoots and hollers and pats on the back continued, Edward seethed with more anger. His knuckles went white as his fingernails dug into the quarterdeck railing, and he clenched his teeth together.

Herbert looked concerned. "Uh... Captain?"

Edward ignored Herbert. "Enough!" he shouted. The crew stopped what they were doing, their happiness draining away. "You think you ought be proud of what just happened?" Edward asked without waiting for an answer. "You think your actions are praiseworthy?" He let the question hang in the air. His nerves at public speaking were not able to creep in at all past his ire. "That battle was pathetic. You ought to be ashamed. We could have avoided that battle altogether if you had worked together on the sails and followed directions. Instead you trip over yourselves and fight with each other. I am disappointed in you all."

Some of the crew had the decency to lower their heads in shame, but others did not. The man who started the celebration was one of the men who did not.

"We wus just—" he started.

"Silence," Edward commanded with a look in his eyes that did not allow for discussion. "Your excuses mean nothing to me. If we are to survive on this ship, we will do so as a team. We cannot let what happened today happen again." His words sunk in, with the crew all nodding in agreement save the one he cut down—that one looked angry and embarrassed. "Be prepared. Tomorrow we start training for battle."

7. THE MAP AND THE WOMAN

Henry punched Edward in the arm. "You stupid git! You could have been killed up there! What were you thinking?"

Edward rubbed his arm. "Ouch! I was trying to save your bleedin' arse. If I was privy to the thanks I would get, I would've left you there."

Henry pulled Edward close and embraced him. "Thank you, Ed. You saved my life, and after I had that stupid argument with you, I didn't deserve it. I'm sorry."

Edward patted him on the back. "Don't be foolish... I'm the one who should be apologising. I shouldn't have said the things I did... I'm sorry. And if you're willing to forgive me, there is a position available on the ship for you."

Henry smiled. "First mate?"

"What? Swabbie? Did you say you wanted to be a swabbie? If that's your desire, then that's well and good, but I was going to say first mate."

"I said first mate," Henry said, his tone dry.

"Swabbie it is! The poop deck needs some shining, so get to it!" Edward chuckled.

Henry punched his arm again. "Thanks, Ed. Really."

Edward smiled. "You're my best friend. I would have fought all of England to save you. Even if your sorry arse didn't deserve it."

They laughed together as they watched the crew trim the sails. The *Freedom* was already far enough out, so they wouldn't have to worry about their pursuers overtaking them.

Sam passed by Henry with a grin on his face. He had refused to quit the crew as Henry had told him to, and now was one of the people who had saved his neck. Henry ignored him.

"So what shall we do with him?" Henry motioned to Frederick, standing across the deck from them. Edward walked over to him.

Frederick looked away from Edward's gaze. "Thank you for—"

Edward punched Frederick, sending him to the deck. Then Edward extended his hand. "Now we're even."

Frederick accepted the hand and Edward pulled him up. "I suppose I deserved that. You didn't have to save me, and yet you did. Thank you."

"We can drop you off at the next port if you wish. I won't keep you here against your will."

Frederick opened his mouth, but he said nothing for a moment. "I… I don't know what I want to do anymore. Can you give me some time to think it over?"

"Take all the time you need, but as long as you're on this ship you must earn your keep."

"Yes, Captain." Frederick went straight to work with the other crewmembers, trimming the sails to the wind.

Henry walked over to Edward and they both watched from the stern as the ships from Port Royal shrank into the distance. "So what now? Any plans?"

Edward reached into his pocket and took out the folded piece of paper, once more showing it to Henry. "A few. I want to see if anyone here is able to open the locked doors before we leave on some wild goose chase."

Henry nodded. "There's probably no shortage of people who can pick locks here. What do you think of the crew so far? Despite your reprimand, they pulled through when we needed them." He turned to look at the lot of them.

Edward was watching them too. "They're brigands and thieves. Just what we need. I hope they can follow orders…"

"It will be a test of your will, now won't it?"

"I'll no doubt have to punish some to set an example, but for now I think we should focus on making this ship fully functional. We need to find us a carpenter to fix the damage from the previous battle."

Henry folded his arms and nodded his head curtly. "Agreed."

The ships from Port Royal had abandoned the chase, and Edward commanded the third sail, the one with the Jolly Roger, changed to the new canvas. He then asked the crew if anyone was a carpenter or knew one nearby who might join them. When no one spoke up, William said that he knew a man who might join, and who lived at a port not too far away. William worked with Herbert on the heading and they made for port straightaway.

Along the way, Edward requested anyone with deft hands and experience picking locks to try gaining access to the gun deck. Many tried, but none succeeded; even the most extreme measures failed. Several men actually tried to ram the door down, but could not.

"Thanks, men, but we're done here," Edward said at last with a sigh. He leaned against the door and closed his eyes. "How is this possible?" he asked aloud. "Maybe William's carpenter will help us with knocking the walls down."

"Perhaps the locks are magical, Captain."

Edward opened his eyes to see a young boy in front of him. He was taller than most, a teenager by Edward's reckoning, but the sound of his voice was perhaps a bit higher in pitch than would be normal for a teenager of his age, and the accent was almost too formal. His clothes were baggy and layered, the top a thick calico cotton print dyed brown with a leather vest overtop, while the dusty leather pantaloons were at least two sizes too big.

"Care to explain your meaning?" Edward asked after looking the boy up and down.

"Some things in this world cannot be explained, Captain. The locks might be protected by magic."

Edward narrowed his eyes and smirked. "Sorry, boy, but I think you've read too many stories. What's your name?"

"Jim Johnny, sir."

Edward examined the strange boy closer. His face was smooth and dotted with small freckles, and he had a thin jawline and eyes the colour of the green ocean. He also noticed a few loose ends of red hair sticking out of a leather cap Jim wore. There was something odd about the boy Edward could not put his finger on.

"Yes... Well... Back to work, Jim Johnny..." Edward said with his hand under his chin.

The boy turned and ambled back to the crew cabin.

Very strange. I'll have to keep my eye on this one.

Edward's went back up to the main deck to see the *Freedom* just pulling into the port of a tiny village. The town obviously did not see much aside from the occasional merchant ship, so a frigate was drawing all sorts of attention from the villagers. Edward did not allow shore leave, as they would not be staying long. William went to find his friend, and came back an hour later with two people.

"I have brought the carpenter, Captain," William said, gesturing to one of his companions. "His name is Nassir."

Edward examined the man next to William. He was a tall black man, as tall as Edward, with muscles bigger than Henry's. His head and face were clean-shaven. A small boy, almost the miniature version of Nassir, stood at his side.

The man extended his hand to Edward. "My name is Nassir, sir. This is my boy, Ochi." Nassir spoke in a thick accent, gesturing to his son with his other hand.

Edward took the man's hand and gave it a firm shake. "William tells us you are a fine carpenter, sir. Have you worked on a ship before?"

"Yes, I have sir, many times. I am very skilled. Here is a sample of my work." Nassir removed a pack slung over his shoulder, then pulled out an item covered in cloth and handed it to Edward.

Edward unwrapped the item to reveal a figure of what appeared to be Queen Anne in fine detail. "This is lovely," he said. "If it was a bit larger I would love to have this as a figurehead. The eyes are mesmerizing. So lifelike."

Nassir smiled at the praise. "I can certainly work on one for you if you'd like, sir. There is but two small matters I must address before the deal is final. I wish to bring along my son, as I cannot leave him and I understand that this vessel will not be returning," Nassir pulled his son in close to him, as if guarding him even from the thought of leaving him behind. "The other matter is payment. Sir, I am a free man, and I will be compensated fairly for my work. If these are not problems, I will join you."

"Payment is not an issue. You will be given a fair share, just as the others."

"Edward!" Henry whispered, pulling Edward aside. "What are you thinking? He may be a free man, but that doesn't mean he should receive the same as everyone else."

"He'll be working on the same ship, won't he?" Edward replied. "He deserves as much as everyone else." He turned back to Nassir. "So, as I was saying, your wages will be the same as the other mates. Your son is another matter… We may see battle on this ship, and I am loath to see him put in danger."

"Battle?" Nassir questioned, glancing to William, and then noticing the damage to the ship.

Edward looked at William, then back to Nassir. "Did William not tell you the nature of this ship?" Nassir shook his head, and Edward glanced about to ensure there were no eavesdroppers. "We've been accused of piracy."

"Piracy!" Nassir nearly shouted. "What is the honourable William doing aboard a pirate ship?" He looked at William, but all the stoic Englishman could do was lower his gaze in shame. "I'm afraid my services will be better used elsewhere, sir," Nassir told Edward firmly and then turned to leave.

Edward pulled Nassir back by the shoulder. "Please, let me explain." Nassir hesitated, his eyes narrowed, and Edward continued in a rush. "I said we have been *accused* of piracy, not that we *are* pirates. William is the honourable man you know him as; I even owe him my life. You have my assurance that I will do whatever is in my power to keep you and your son safe, but I cannot promise that this journey will be free from danger."

Nassir measured Edward with an intense scrutiny, weighing his words. He glanced back to William for assurance, and then nodded. "If William trusts in you, I shall too. I also owe him my life. Perhaps I can repay the debt aboard this ship."

Edward smiled. "Then I welcome you to the *Freedom*, Nassir." He turned his gaze to Nassir's son. "And you as well, Ochi." He looked at Nassir once more, his expression serious. "Will you be able to fix the railings on the go? I'd like to shove off as soon as possible."

"Yes, sir. As long as the supplies are on board, it should not be a problem."

"William, please show our newest crewmate around."

William nodded and led Nassir off. Edward glanced around as the three walked about the decks of the ship. There were more than a few looks of disgust cast at Nassir, and some even spat on the deck as he passed by.

I hope my crew doesn't give Nassir any problems.

Before Edward could give the order to depart, he heard the sweet sounds of music nearby. He turned to see a musician playing the fiddle on the waist of the ship. As he played, the crew danced and sang along. Even Edward began tapping his feet to the jolly tune. When the song ended, he walked over to the musician.

"Hello, sir," Edward said. "I thank you for the tune, but we are about to depart. I would appreciate it if you could see your way back to shore."

The man turned around when Edward started talking. "Captain Edward, I presume?" He gripped Edward's hand before he could respond, and shook it with great vigor. "Thank you for allowing me to stay aboard this fine vessel! It will be an honour to serve you and entertain your crew."

The man was of average build, past middle age, but spry. He spoke with an accent which Edward thought might hail from the Provincial colonies, and there was a faint smell of alcohol on his breath.

Edward shook his head. "There seems to be some misunderstanding. I thank you for the brief music, but this is not a transport vessel. You are free to leave."

"But Captain, I have no home to return to. If you'll just take me to the next port I will be eternally grateful. I will even pay you, if that will help."

"I'm sorry, but that's not my problem. Besides, as you can see, this vessel could see battle in the future. You could be risking your life. It will be better for you to find another ship to travel on." Edward turned to leave.

The man stepped forward, grabbing Edward's sleeve. "I am used to being on ships of this… nature. Please, sir, I can be useful to your crew."

"How so? We have no need of a musician."

Henry cut in. "Edward, aren't you being a little harsh? Look at the crew, they love him." He motioned to the crewmembers who were still singing the song even though the fiddler had stopped playing.

"Captain, if I may?" Nassir interjected. William had just finished the tour of the decks when they came by again.

"Yes, Nassir?"

"On my days on a ship, ones I generally do not wish to recall, one thing was able to keep my mind on happier times. Every day, the musician on board the ship would come to our quarters and sing us a tune to remind us of home. It gave us hope, and the strength to carry on. If it wasn't for him, I would have broken, and I would not be the same man before you today. If I were you, I would allow this man to stay. You are the captain, however."

Edward watched the crew still singing the song for another moment, and then turned to the musician. "Maybe it's not such a bad idea. What's your name, sir?"

"Jack Christian."

"Well, Jack, I'm sorry for my unkindness. You may remain aboard. But don't make me regret my decision."

"I promise you, sir, you will not. We'll all be dancing together before the cows come home." Edward stared at him with an odd look. "Ah, sorry, I sometimes forget my company. I mean that we'll be the best of friends before long."

Best of friends? Hmm. "Jack, I have my first order for you. This is Nassir and this is his son Ochi. The men seem to like you. Maybe you can introduce these two to the crew."

Jack took a gander at Nassir and his son. "I can try, Captain. But I'll cook up no promises. You know how some are with Negros. Just plain don't like 'em."

"Do you dislike them, Jack?"

"No, Captain, perish the thought. Come, Nassir, let's introduce you to the crew."

Nassir held his boy's hand tight. Edward gave a reassuring nod, and he returned it. Then the Negro took his son and followed Jack to meet the other crewmembers. They stopped singing, but after a small speech from Jack and a moment of brooding, they started alongside Jack's fiddle again. It wasn't total acceptance, but it was a start.

"Smart move, Captain," Henry said as they both watched.

"This should make things easier. The sooner everyone starts working together, the better off we'll be." Edward turned to Herbert. "Herbert, sail us out of here."

"Aye, Captain." Herbert shouted orders to remove the mooring lines and move the ship away from dock. Despite their brief stay at the small port, the departure of the large ship was a spectacle. The villagers waved to the crew as they left, and children ran up the pier to see them off.

Once back on the open sea, Nassir began repairs on the railings with Ochi by his side. Jack was playing music as the crew cleaned and worked, and the sun shone on them. It was becoming a nice day.

Edward talked with Nassir about repairs to the ship. Nassir said that with the gun deck locked he couldn't fix the holes. When Edward asked about whether they could tear down the wall, Nassir expressed doubt. He admitted that the construction of the wall was like no other ship he had seen, and it might be load-bearing. They risked damage to the rest of the ship if they tore it down. He explained he only found three holes in question and none would put the ship in danger if left alone. Edward trusted Nassir and let him handle the matter.

I suppose our only way to open the ship is to play Benjamin's game. "There is another matter I'd like you to look into, Nassir," Edward said.

"Yes, what is it, Captain?"

"Could you try and make something to help Herbert, our sailing master, up and down the decks? He's crippled, so it's more difficult for him to go from deck to deck."

Nassir looked up at Herbert, who was preparing maps and instruments at a table built into the quarterdeck. He had to have noticed the odd looks some of the crew gave Herbert—so similar to the way they looked at Nassir himself. Despite proving his mettle in battle, some of the crew still couldn't quite accept Herbert. "You are a strange one, Captain. It is refreshing."

After a slight pause and an odd expression taking over him, Edward replied "My thanks?"

Nassir chuckled. "I will see what I can do for you, Captain."

With his first and second plan of action for the locks exhausted, Edward called a meeting between the *Freedom*'s senior members. He would have done it in the galley, but he needed Herbert to examine Benjamin Hornigold's map to see if he could discern anything. To ensure privacy, he ordered all the crew to stay away from the quarterdeck.

Herbert, Edward, Henry, John, Sam, and William were all present. "What I'm about to tell you"—he looked specifically at Herbert, Sam, and William—"does not leave this group. Understood?"

"Yes, Captain," they said in unison.

"When I first purchased this ship, this note was left with it." He took out the note and allowed those who hadn't seen it to read and examine it. "Parts of this ship are locked, and on one side of the note it states that if we follow the clue on the other side it will lead us to the keys. We've tried picking the locks to no avail, and Nassir believes tearing down the walls could damage the ship, so following this clue is our only option."

"What's its meaning?" Herbert asked.

"I know not, exactly. That's why we're having this meeting. I want your take on the first part: 'From two ports of two crescent moons, two and two islands north and north northwest.'"

Herbert gazed at the paper and thought for a few minutes as the others watched his face. "It must refer to some islands shaped like crescent moons, but why two? Maybe there are two islands north and north-northwest of each crescent moon. It doesn't make sense."

"Why? Are there any ports shaped like crescent moons in the Caribbean?"

Herbert laughed. "Yea, there are countless crescent-shaped ports depending on how you view their shape to be. And if we believe this ambiguous message, we'll be searching for months. I consider this is a farce played by the last owner."

"No, I'm sure he wants us to find the keys through this game of his. We only have to narrow down the choices of the ports. Let's bring out a map of the Caribbean."

They placed the map on a table built into the quarterdeck. The wind being slight, there was no need to place weights on the map to hold it down. They pored over the map, scrutinising it for clues to reveal which of the twelve possible ports were the right ones.

"Well… the ports must be good to pirates, this bein' a pirate vessel," Sam suggested.

"No, that's too much of a stretch," Edward guessed. "As we've experienced with Port Royal, allegiances can change swiftly. Unless Benjamin created this not two months ago, we wouldn't be able to say these ports are pirate havens. However, I think it is safe to assume the ports have a decent amount of sea north and northwest of them so it's possible for islands to be there."

"That leaves six." Herbert reached over the table and marked the relevant ones.

"Anywhere just colonised within the last few years probably doesn't belong," John interjected.

"Five." Herbert took one of his markers off the map.

"He says 'ports *of* crescent moons,' not ports *like* crescent moons. That would mean islands, not just ports, shaped that way." William tapped on the note a few times. "*Of* implies the whole port and island is a crescent moon shape, whereas *like* would mean it looks similar and is part of a larger piece of land."

"Three." Herbert updated the map. "I think that's as far as we'll be able to narrow it down without more information," he surmised.

One island was in the middle of the Caribbean, one in the Cayman Islands, and one close to Costa Rica. Edward pointed to the first of these.

"This one is the closest to us. We'll check north of it first. Good job, everyone. Herbert, lay the course. Everyone else resume normal duties." Edward walked over to Herbert, who was turning the ship north-northwest. "So, Herbert, how are you doing on the ship so far? Too soon to tell?"

The helmsman paused before replying with, "Well and good, Captain. Well and good."

"You're a terrible liar, Herbert. Tell me your troubles. I'm the captain, I'm here to help."

"Well, some have been ignoring my orders. In battle they were fine, and perhaps fear had a part to play in that, but since then it's changed. They should know the sailing master takes precedence over the captain in certain situations, yet they don't take me seriously. Luckily it has been small things, nothing consequential. But if we were in a storm, I fear it would be to the detriment of the whole crew if they continued to ignore my warnings."

Edward placed his hand over Herbert's shoulder. "Do not worry, friend. When the time comes, I will make sure they listen."

"Thank you, Captain."

"How is your sis— brother doing aboard the ship?"

"He's doing fine. But he's afraid of being seen, and he's unsure of what exactly to do aboard a ship, especially one of this nature…"

"Tell him not to worry. This is a pirate ship in name only—and a name bequeathed to it by others, in fact. To me, the *Freedom* is a regular ship. Tell your brother to think the same and everything will truly be well and good. And of course he can help you out like he's been doing. Maybe have him swab the deck from time to time as well." Edward chuckled.

"I'll be sure to let him know," Herbert said with a smile.

After the conversation, Edward could hear the sweet music of Jack Christian on the main deck. He left Herbert at the helm to go listen to Jack for a spell. In Jack's short time with the crew Edward had noticed that he kept the men relaxed and entertained. That in turn made them less likely to take out their frustrations on their shipmates.

I suppose my initial assessment of the man was wrong. I don't think I've been more fortunate to be wrong.

Edward listened as Jack played a tune he had heard as a child growing up, as well as others he had only recently learned, and all were a delight to hear. Before he realised it, an hour had passed with Jack not stopping his music once. Edward dispersed the crew listening, to the dismay of many.

"Jack, I think you need a break. I haven't seen you take a day of rest since you've come aboard. The crew won't revolt because you aren't there with music on one or two days."

"Ah, but Captain, this is my job. My life! I'm used to playing for long periods without rest. Besides, the crew loves it."

"I understand, but even you need to rest every once in a while. Will you force me to order you to take a break?"

Jack laughed. "I think perhaps yes. Otherwise my colleagues will pull me back in. I cannot resist the urge."

"Then I order you to take time to yourself at least once a week. And you can tell anyone who doesn't like it to take it up with me."

Jack laughed again. "Yes, Captain."

Edward left Jack to help some crewmen secure sail rigging, and noticed one of them was Jim Johnny. After the crew tied the rope down, they thanked the captain for the assistance, but Jim left immediately without so much as a thank you.

That's it! Jim has been avoiding me ever since the incident on the gun deck. I'm going to find out the secret of this Jim Johnny once and for all! Edward walked over and pulled Jim aside. "Galley, now!"

Jim tried to find a way out, but could not avoid Edward now. "Yes, Captain." And so both of them went to the lower deck and into the galley area.

Some crewmates were there, preparing the next meal. "Leave us," Edward ordered. Once the room was empty, he began his interrogation. "You will be straight with me right now or I'll make you leave at the next port, Jim Johnny!"

Jim panicked. "Uh, I don't know what you are referring ta, Captain!" Jim said in a broken attempt at a cockney accent.

"You're hiding something and I know it! Now what is it? Are you a marine spy? Answer me true or I'll see to it someone else makes you to talk."

"I… I have a condition. I can't be near captains or I get deathly ill."

"You take me for a fool?" Edward grabbed Jim by the neck and slammed him up against the wall, pinning the boy's chest down with his forearm. "You will tell me the truth or—" Edward felt something odd around his forearm and saw something on Jim's chest that shouldn't have been there on a man. *What the…?*

Then Jim grabbed Edward's arm and twisted it behind his back with ease. He tripped Edward to the ground and put his boot on the back of his neck.

Edward tried to scream, "You're a woman!" but it only came out as a muffled squawk.

"You were not supposed to find out about that." Jim's voice had resumed its normal pitch, and his—her?—accent was suddenly formal English.

The galley door burst open and the senior officers, Henry, John, and William, emerged. They all carried swords and pointed them at the young deckhand.

"Release the captain!" Henry yelled.

Jim let out a dismissive snort before releasing Edward, who rose and stood with the others. "I'll have my men lower their weapons if you promise not to do something foolish."

"Very well!" Jim said through clenched teeth.

Edward nodded to the others to put their weapons down, but they kept them in hand just in case. He walked over to the galley door and locked it.

"Take off your hat."

Jim did as commanded. Then she took a pin out of her hair, letting loose long, curly red hair that shone in the dim light. She was frowning, feminine in appearance but with fierceness in her green eyes.

The others dropped their jaws at the sight.

"He's a... she's a... It's a woman!" Henry stammered. "Did you know Jim was a woman?"

She's beautiful. Edward had to shake himself to get back to the situation at hand. "I... uh... I had my suspicions, but I didn't expect this. What's your name? Your real name?"

"Anne... Anne Bonney."

"Well, Anne, you mind telling me why you attacked me after I discovered your secret?"

"Humph! I know what your kind does to women. Either you use them for play-things or kill them at the first sign of trouble. I disguised myself as a man so I could stay aboard the ship. I warn you, gentlemen, if you try to take advantage of me, I will make it so you do not have the capacity to do so to anyone ever again."

Edward smiled. "Bold words for one so outnumbered..." She took a fighting stance. "That wasn't a challenge!"

"We need to decide what to do with her," said Henry. "She can't stay on the ship."

Edward scoffed. "And why not? She's been capable so far in doing regular duties. Let's test her mettle and see how she'll do in a fight. Then we can decide."

Henry rubbed his forehead in frustration. "Why? Why are you allowing her to stay aboard? This is foolishness."

"I agree she was foolish in attacking first. But we already have one lass aboard. What's the harm in another?"

Anne stepped forward. "You have another woman on the ship? Who is it?"

Henry glared at Edward, ignoring the question. "I swear, someday all the trouble you've visited on this crew will rain down like a storm, and then you'll be wishing you'd listened to me."

Edward laughed. "You know you wouldn't miss this for the world. William, Anne, do a little swordplay." William was sweating bullets and couldn't keep his eyes off Anne. "William, what's wrong? Have you never seen a woman before? Come now, ready yourself for a little test." Edward handed Anne a sword and William slowly unsheathed his.

The two sized each other up. William was still sweating and he looked on the verge of collapse. Anne attacked and he deflected the first blow, but then she managed to pass his guard to his neck, stopping short of actually hitting him.

"That was a lucky shot. William was distracted."

"Henry's right. William, you must at least try."

William nodded and got into position. Anne struck first, thrusting her blade at his face. He slapped her sword away with his, but didn't strike back. He stepped away and circled her. She slashed towards his gut, but as he brought his guard up she stopped short and went to knee him in stomach. He used his free hand to stop her knee. They continued fighting, but from what Edward could tell they were evenly matched.

"I've seen enough. You can clearly hold your own."

"Humph!" Anne turned away from William and handed Edward's sword back to him. He took the grunt to indicate defiance and contempt for his doubt.

"You can stay aboard on one condition: You must continue dressing as a man and no one must find out about you. Continue your regular duties and help the crew as before. Agreed?"

"Agreed," Anne responded without hesitation.

"And as for everyone here, it will be the same with the other girl. You are all sworn to secrecy about the true nature of this crewman. Understood?"

"Yes, Captain," they all said in unison.

"Now, let's all leave before the crew thinks something has happened." Edward left the room followed by Henry and John.

William lingered a few seconds, and Anne confronted him as soon as they were alone. "Do not think me an imbecile! Why did you hold back? You know I am skilled."

"Yes, I do know it. I could not strike against you without guilt."

Anne's eyes widened, fear mixed with cold rage. "Then you know who I am?"

"Yes."

"Then I order you to stay silent about your knowledge. I shall have none know of this. It is 'Jim' from now on. Understood?" Anne tied up her long red hair and covered it again with her hat.

"I saw the command on your face before you even had to say the words." And he knew the orders issued from her were higher even than a captain's.

Anne and William left the room, their bond secured, their secret hidden between the two of them.

8. FORBIDDEN

"Father, do you have to leave?" the young boy asked.

The father tucked his son into bed with a sad frown on his face. "I'm sorry, son, but I have to do this." He smiled. "I need to make enough money to feed you. It's like Davy Jones' locker in there." He tickled his son. The boy laughed and fought against it, tousling the blankets once more. The father tucked his son in yet again and got up to leave. "I'll be back before you know it."

"Father?" the boy said, expectation in his eyes.

His father turned back before leaving. "Hmm? What is it, son?"

"The song."

"Oh. Sorry. I almost forgot." The father sat down on a stool and began to sing a lullaby to his son as he did each night he was home.

Edward awoke with a start in the darkness, the recurring dream lifting his slumber. The dream always ended the same: His father left and never came back. That part his mind couldn't change, because that's how it happened in reality.

He rose from his bed in the corner of the crew cabin and lit an oil lamp. He could see and hear the crew in their hammocks, swaying with the ship. It was peaceful to see all those men sound asleep in their new home.

He walked up the ladder to the next floor. There was a lit lantern on each end, letting a little light into the darkness. *Soon, we'll open you up. We just have to find your keys, don't we, girl?*

When he reached the main deck the smell of salt air mixing with the pine of the ship greeted him. That heavenly scent made him want nothing more than to sleep up here each night, if not for the cold. The wind whipped against the ship with a howl, and water splashed the hull. Then he heard singing. It was Jack's voice. He was stumbling about, drunk.

I should help him back to his hammock. Edward walked closer, but the sight of Jack's profile and the song he was singing stopped him. *He's crying.*

Jack was singing a familiar lullaby. It was the same song Edward's father had sung to him as a boy. It was a joyful song about a boy growing up to be a great and splendid king. But the way Jack was singing it made it seem like a funeral dirge. Edward felt tears in his own eyes. He waited there until Jack finished the song, and then turned and drifted back to the crew's quarters.

Edward went out there on several occasions, and he heard the same thing each time. Sometimes Jack was singing a different lullaby, but still in the same way. Edward couldn't bring himself to disturb the man's time of grief. Despite his determination not to interrupt, he still went up to listen to Jack whenever he had that dream.

And he had the dream most nights.

Ever since the day Anne's identity as a woman was revealed, William was not far from her side. He was always watching over her, no matter where they were. She noticed this sometimes, and delivered words sending him away—but for a time. He always resumed his guard when her attention was elsewhere.

What is William thinking? He's been following Anne from the moment of her revelation. Perhaps he fancies her? I can't let this affect his performance as my boatswain. "William! Here! Now!"

William ran over in an instant. "Captain!" He saluted.

Edward leaned in for a whisper. "William, you need to stifle your affection for… Jim. The crew is starting to notice."

"Sir?" William looked confused.

"Jim, remember? The one with the secret? The crew will uncover the ruse if you keep this up."

There was a small pause as William processed what Edward was saying. "Yes, Captain. It shan't happen again. I shall do my best to restrain myself." William remained as stone-faced as ever.

"Good. Now back to work."

"Yes, Captain." William saluted and left the aft deck.

Edward watched as William passed by Anne with nary a glance. She looked up at Edward from her post and saw him watching. She gave him a grateful nod, and he returned it.

"Captain," Herbert called. Edward went to the quarterdeck to see what he needed. The helmsman pointed off the bow to a small dot in the distance. "There's Half Moon Cay."

"Excellent," Edward exclaimed. He pulled out a spyglass and looked at the island in front of them, but wasn't able to see much. "At least now we can start this blasted search. It feels more like we've been chasing the wind, and the crew is restless for some action. I fear Jack's music can placate them only so much."

Herbert had nothing to add to Edward's comments, so he changed the subject. "With your approval, Captain, I'll have us move north-east for time, then north-west, then mirror the direction on our return. That should provide us the most complete view of the area."

Edward nodded. "You are the expert here, so I will defer to your judgement, Herbert."

Herbert smiled. "Aye, Captain." He turned the ship starboard to move them north-east of Half Moon Cay and start the search.

The search was long, even with the *Freedom* sailing at full sail. Everyone available was watching the ocean, many with spyglasses or regular glasses, and the rest with the naked eye. Some men hung off the rope ladders leading to the masts, others stood atop the mast bars holding the sails in place, and a few were even in the crow's nest. No matter how much they explored, however, they were never able to see any islands.

"I don't understand," Henry complained one day. "They were supposed to be here. It feels like we've been searching for a whole month."

"Don't be so dramatic, Henry. It's only been a week or so... I think." Edward counted the days off on his fingers.

"We've been gone long enough that you've been growing a beard. You could have Alexandre shave you."

"I like it. It makes me look more distinguished, and older." Edward stroked his black chin hairs, which were, at this point, little more than stubble.

Henry rolled his eyes as he ran his fingers through his brown hair. "Well, the crew is becoming impatient regardless. They long for what we were meant to do, and someone told them it would involve riches and piracy."

"Well, *I* never told them that. I clearly stated we've been *labelled* pirates, not that we *are*. We're headed to Luna Bay next. They'll be able to have some shore leave for a few days once we arrive. Until then, we'll just have to keep busy."

Nassir approached Edward and Henry, interrupting their conversation.

"Captain," he started in his deep, accented voice, "I have something to show you." Edward nodded and Nassir led him to the aft deck.

Nassir had modified the deck railing on each side of the ship by cutting out a section and reattaching it with hinges to make a gate. The gates opened up right next to the ladder, where Herbert could grab onto a rope and shimmy up or down the decks. Someone still had to bring him his wheelchair, but Nassir placed chairs right where Herbert would land so he could sit down while he waited.

"This is ingenious, Nassir! Just what I wanted for him."

"This is nothing. It is only the first part of what I have

planned," Nassir said, but he sounded happy for the praise.

"What do you have planned?"

Nassir laughed. "I cannot say. It will have to remain a secret for now."

Edward grinned. "All right, keep your secrets then!" He turned toward the helm. "Herbert?"

Herbert wheeled himself over to the edge of the quarterdeck. "Yes, Captain?"

"Have you tried out Nassir's invention?"

In answer, Herbert opened up the gate in the railing, jumped out of his wheelchair, climbed down the rope, and sat in the chair waiting for him.

"Yes, I have tried it." He grinned. "It's amazing! And I love the chairs; they make it a lot easier. Thank you, Nassir! I really appreciate it."

"Do not thank me; the captain wanted me to make something to help you." He smiled in spite of himself.

"I'm not the master builder. You deserve the credit." Edward held his hands in the air as if backing away from receiving the praise.

"It's a great thing regardless of who thought of it. I thank you both. Now, I need to get back up there before we're blown off course." Herbert climbed up the rope to his wheelchair and manned the helm again.

"Great work again, Nassir. I'm glad to have you aboard. Even if we are scoundrels, like you think we are."

"I am starting to rethink my position on that."

"Glad to hear it. If anyone gives you trouble, point me in their direction and I'll assist in any way I can."

"Aye, Captain."

Ochi walked by with something in his hands. Nassir stopped him and asked him what he was doing.

"Kenneth wanted me to take this black powder to him," the boy replied.

Edward heard the words and turned around. Herbert's interest was also piqued. "Black powder? Ochi, let me see that bag."

Edward took the bag and examined it; sure enough, it was gunpowder. *Why does Kenneth need gunpowder, and why did he make Ochi bring it to him? Kenneth has been making trouble ever since he started the cheering after our failed first battle at Port Royal.* Edward told Ochi and Nassir he would handle the matter, and then hurried to the foredeck where Kenneth and his group were waiting by the cannons.

"Kenneth, why did you make Ochi bring you gunpowder?"

Kenneth let out a sigh as he turned around. He was a tall, nasty-looking man with crooked, discoloured teeth, shaggy hair, and a flagrant disregard for general hygiene. "Me 'n' the boys 're workin up the cannons. We wanted ta practice our shot, 'n' the boy was jus' bein' useful."

Out of nowhere Herbert appeared, jumped on Kenneth and punched him.

"Herbert, stop it! Yield, yield I say!" Edward pulled him off Kenneth.

"That cripple hit me. Get 'im, boys!"

"Stop right there or I'll hit you myself," Edward flared. "That's an order." He turned to the helmsman. "Herbert, explain yourself. Why did you attack Kenneth?"

Herbert was on the floor of the deck, holding himself upright with his hands. "You might not realise the weight of this, Captain, but I do. He was trying to use Ochi as a powder monkey. They have them on ships with cannons like this, little boys meant to bring bags of gunpowder from the holds to the cannons. So many young ones have died from accidents." Herbert almost had tears in his eyes. "It's because of that I... No one should have that kind of job, Captain. Least of all a child." There was a seething anger showing on Herbert's face, and Edward could tell this situation meant more to him than just a passing fancy.

Edward knelt down to Herbert and whispered to him, "I understand your frustration, Herbert, but you can't beat anyone who does something you don't agree with. I stopped it before anyone was harmed. I'll take care of this. If you have a problem, you come to me, all right?"

Hebert pursed his lips, but after a moment replied, "Yes, Captain."

"Now back to your post. Some of your shares will be withheld because of what you did."

"Understood." Herbert crawled back to the rope and shimmied back to the main deck.

Edward went to Kenneth and grabbed him by the scruff of the neck. "If I had known the whole story I wouldn't have been so easy on you. From now on, if you want the powder you grab it yourself, end of story. If you had done that during an actual battle I would've thrown you overboard, but seeing as you didn't, I'll be lenient and diminish your shares. Don't let it happen again. Understand?"

Kenneth managed a defiant grunt.

"I'll take that as a yes. All of you are at half shares until further notice," Edward commanded as he walked away.

Kenneth had only been a nuisance before Edward cut his shares, but now he seemed contentious and volatile. As the days passed, his mood became fouler, towards Edward most particularly. He never directly disobeyed an order, but he made a point of voicing his complaints to anyone who cared to listen. Few did care to—least of all Edward, who, so long as he did not actually cause trouble, paid him no mind.

By contrast, Frederick was being more than accommodating to Edward. He followed orders and did the required work and then some. He was a mate skilled at running things on a ship; that was why Edward had let him on board when he first started whaling.

One day when Frederick was swabbing the deck, Edward made a point of speaking with him about his stay. "Frederick, I'm sorry, I meant to take you straight to the next port, but it slipped my mind. We'll be in Luna Bay soon and you'll be free to go."

Frederick stopped what he was doing. "Are you ordering me to leave the ship?"

"No... Why would I need to order you? You're free to leave."

"Well, I've changed my mind. I'll stay aboard—if you'll have me."

"But... I thought you hated me. And why do you want to stay on a ship full of pirates?"

"You saved my life at the gallows when you could have left me to die. It helped me realise that's all you were trying to do from the start. I was wrong, and you were right. Besides, it's not so bad on board. You have yourself a fine crew, I'd say. Some have a rather... salty disposition, but it's not much different from the crew before the split in Port Royal. And I know you aren't really a pirate. I'd be happy to repay my debt to you aboard."

Edward extended his hand and grasped Frederick's. "Glad to have you with us."

Edward had also felt ambivalent towards Sam at first, but the young man's relationship with others aboard the *Freedom* improved over time. In general he was less inclined to fight and argue, and even got along with William to an extent. The two now shared a no more than passive resentment towards each other, more like rivals than enemies. Henry, however, still didn't like Sam one bit.

Edward found Sam alone one night, drinking out on the deck in the dark, and joined him.

"Having a good time?"

Sam laughed. "Aye, a pirate's life for me." He took a swig of rum and graciously passed the bottle to Edward, who accepted it and had a few sips.

"So why are you a pirate, Sam? Why stay with us?"

"I've been here since the beginning, mate. At first I thought you wus a pratter so focused on rules you had 'em up yer bung-hole. But when your *Freedom* was threatened, you took charge against that marine. No hesitation. That's why I'm still 'ere, Captain. Someday, something's gonna happen with you, or many somethings, and I wanna be there to see 'em."

"Mmm." *I don't know what it is he sees in me.* Edward continued to drink in silence with Sam for a bit longer, until he became tired. "Thanks for the drink, Sam," he said before heading below deck to sleep.

"Any time."

During the dull days of sailing, in spite of his reluctance to practice, Edward was also able to improve his public speaking abilities thanks to Henry's techniques. His nervousness was still there, and he still panicked after a time and had to stop, but that eventuality arrived later and later. He made speeches in the sectioned off dining area in front of ever larger groups. Sometimes they were discussions about their finances or supplies, and other times they were stories from Shakespeare, or the news.

The Shakespeare bits gave Henry an idea.

"You know what? We should do that."

Edward laughed at that. "Do what exactly?"

"We should have plays on the ship. I think it could help with morale, and it would be fun."

"That is a most foolish idea if I've ever heard one. These are pirates, not some high lord mollies. That's silly—and if you think I'll do more than a soliloquy, you are mistaken, sir!"

"Come now, you know it would be fun. And who's to say no one here would enjoy it? They enjoy listening to you do it."

"I'll think about it."

Henry scoffed. "No you won't."

He was right. *There's no way I'll make a fool of myself more than I already have.*

Edward, however, continued to do the readings, and improved over time. He used gestures and moved around, talking to certain people as if they were a true audience. Henry smiled as he watched his protégé.

⚓ ⚓ ⚓

Edward invited Anne into the galley for a private talk to see how she was adjusting to life on the ship. She let out her hair and untangled it when they were alone. Edward began to stare.

She's gorgeous.

"What?" Anne snapped.

Edward coughed. "Uhh… nothing… How are you adjusting

aboard the ship?"

"What do you mean?"

"Well, it must be hard, I imagine."

"Why? Because I'm a woman? Do you need me to remind you of our first encounter here?" she said, tightening her fist into a ball.

"Peace! Peace! I only meant your previous life. It must be hard to switch to pirating."

"What about my previous life? What do you know?" Anne moved closer to Edward, her finger pointing at his face.

Why is she so defensive? Edward let out a sigh. "I know nothing. That's why I'm asking. I'd like to know more about you."

Anne lowered her hands. "Oh… Sorry. I thought you… Pay that no mind. Truthfully, I don't find it hard here at all. My life at home was simple… easy, even. I like to work hard, and I have always had a romantic fascination with being out at sea. I never viewed pirates as the brigands and rogues everyone else did. If you knew the political mishaps of the privateers after the last war, you would understand why pirates do what they must."

Edward had lost focus halfway through what Anne said.

Anne explained further. "What I mean to say is that they were commissioned by the crown, but they only knew how to fight and steal. The crown left them without jobs after the war ended. They were not even given half-pay as the normal military has. It is not fair the way… the way the queen treated them."

Edward shrugged. "I guess you understand it better than I. All I know of pirates is the rumors of horrible deeds spread about."

"That is all they want you to see. And why pirates are hated so. What I cannot understand is why you are a pirate. You are young. Were you on a privateer ship when you were younger?"

Edward leaned against the galley's stove. "No, my father was a fisherman… a whaler in truth. I wanted to follow in his footsteps and bought this ship… Well, I suppose I bought it. I don't remember it exactly as I was quite drunk at the time." He laughed at the situation, which is one thing he thought he never would do. "It turned out to be a pirate ship, and we happened to be in the presence of a marine ship when we unfurled a sail that had a Jolly Roger on it. I pinned the captain, Isaac Smith, and used his life as bargaining to get us out of there. That's how we ended up in Port Royal. We've been on the run ever since."

"Truly? Well, that is unfortunate for you. I have heard the name of that captain. They call him 'The Hound' in some circles. He is an excellent tracker."

Edward nodded. "Yes, he seemed one who wouldn't yield easily." He shuffled a bit, and thought of another question to fill the silence. "So, what made you choose this ship? Hadn't you already heard about how we'd been labelled as pirates?"

Anne shook her head. "No, I found out after."

Edward folded his arms. "And it didn't bother you?"

"Well, at first I was going to leave at the next port, but when you found out my secret, things took a much different turn than I'd expected. I decided to stay because you are not like other pirates. And now that I have heard the whole story, I suppose you are not pirates at all."

"Just on the run like pirates." Edward chuckled at his misfortune. "Well, for what it's worth, Anne, I'm glad you're here with us. It's nice having you aboard."

"Does this mean you'll tell me of the other woman on board?"

"Not a chance."

"Come now. Just a hint?"

"No. You'll have to find out for yourself."

Anne sniffed and pouted. "Fine then."

Edward chuckled. "You're cute when you're angry..." He stopped, frozen.

What did I just say?

Anne blushed, and they stared at each other for a long moment, neither of them knowing what to say.

"I have to leave," Edward said quickly.

"Me, too." Anne began tying up her hair and Edward moved to help her, but it only made the process more awkward. She managed to put her hat back on, but as she was about to rise from her seat on the stove, they stopped and realised the situation they were in.

Edward was pressed up against Anne's chest. He could feel the rapid thumping of her heart next to him. His hands were around her shoulders. He closed his eyes and leaned forward. Their lips touched. They stayed there for a few seconds, the warmth of each other just registering before Anne pushed him away and slapped him. The image of another woman invaded Edward's mind. *Lucy.*

"How *dare* you!"

"I... I know. I'm sorry. I don't know what came over me."

Anne went to the door and then turned back to him. "Maybe I was wrong about you. You are like the rest of them." She whirled around and stormed out.

Edward was left thinking of Lucy, his former flame from Badobos, and of Anne. *I can't believe I did that. How could I be so stupid? But why did Anne slap me? I swear she leaned in... unless I was imagining it.* Edward couldn't know for certain, so he left the galley and headed back to the main deck.

Anne and Edward never spoke of the incident, and avoided

each other at every turn for the rest of the day. By nightfall the tension abated, but others noticed the awkwardness between them. Henry approached Edward about it when it became obvious, which didn't take long.

"Ed, is there something going on between you and… and Jim?"

"What? No, don't be silly. Let's talk about this later, shall we?" *Please take the hint, Henry.*

"All right, Ed. Let's meet an hour from now in the galley."

Their arrival at the galley frustrated the galley crew, who didn't appreciate all the impromptu meetings, but they followed the captain's orders and left, grumbling under their breath about the frequent interruptions.

"So what's going on, Ed?"

"I kissed Jim… I mean, Anne."

"You kissed Anne?" Henry said, incredulous.

"It just… happened. But now I can't stop thinking about Lucy. I feel like I betrayed her. And Anne's mad at me as well."

Henry pinched the bridge of his nose. "You're still thinking about Lucy? Edward, it's already been past a month, and it was only a kiss. You chose to leave her behind without even a letter explaining things. By now she's probably heard about what happened. Besides, you're better off without her—or Anne, for that matter…"

"What's that supposed to mean?"

"I… I just think that you can do better."

"What was wrong with Lucy?"

Henry shuffled around and scratched his face. "She hangs around with those prissy bints. It doesn't matter if she fancies you. She's the same as them. It's not as if we can return home anyway, remember?"

"I know, but I don't care for your attitude. She's different from them. And what about Anne? What's your problem with her?"

Henry shook his head. "Since when did this become a serious discussion about your love life, Edward? I thought we were discussing how this was a mistake?"

"We are."

Henry ran his fingers through his hair. "She has a smug attitude about her. She thinks she's better than others. Just listen to the way she talks. Like some high-class Englisher born with a silver spoon in her mouth."

"I disagree there as well. First off, why would she be on a ship like this if she was rich?"

Henry held his hand up to stop Edward from continuing. "Of course you disagree, but our opinions on her eligibility are moot.

Remember how we're trying to keep her secret just that? A secret? You go gallivanting about like two lovers, and questions will be raised."

"Yes, yes, I know. What do I do about it?"

"You apologise, you say it won't happen again, and you don't let it happen again." Henry emphasised the last part. He grabbed Edward's forearm and glowered at him. "Involving yourself with her is a whole mess of trouble waiting to happen."

Edward let out a long sigh and shook his head. "You're right. I'll do what you say." He still couldn't shake the thought of Lucy out of his head.

He sought out Anne later in the day. Walking up to the aft deck, he noticed her and William talking in hushed voices. When she saw him, she tried to leave, but he grabbed her by the arm, causing William to straighten in surprise.

"I wish to speak with you."

"I have nothing to say to you."

"Please." The hint of pleading in his face was meant only for her.

Anne let out a sigh and said, "Fine, but make it quick."

Edward and Anne left William standing on the deck in complete bewilderment. They returned to the galley to commandeer it from the crew, who were quite fed up with the constant shuffling by now and actually voiced their anger. Edward managed to calm them down by telling them this would be the last time. When the crew was out of earshot, he sat down with Anne to talk.

"I wanted to apologise for my actions again. I don't know what came over me, but I promise you it won't happen again."

"I should hope not."

"Please don't leave the crew."

"I shan't. But if you ever kiss me without my permission again, I will make sure it is the last thing you ever do. Am I clear?"

Edward gulped. "Understood."

Anne rose without another word and left Edward sitting at the table. He let out a breath, then stood and followed her.

After they parted ways, Henry had his own talk with Anne when she came back up to the main deck. "Hey, Jim?" She came over to see what he wanted. Henry spoke in a hushed tone. "I want you to stay away from Edward. He doesn't need someone like you."

Anne laughed at him. "Whatever makes you think you can tell me with whom I can and cannot associate? Edward can think for himself, surely. As can I. What happens between us is of no concern to you, understood?"

"Sorry Jim, but it does concern me. Edward and I have been

best friends for almost our whole lives. He hasn't been with anyone before, and he doesn't know what type of woman is best for him. I have his best interests in mind."

Anne straightened at that, her eyes narrowing to slits. "Oh, and how many women have *you* been with?" Henry pursed his lips and didn't respond. "I thought so. Edward is a man, not a boy. I understand his need for a confidant, but he does not need you to protect him from what *you* are afraid of," Anne said haughtily.

And with that, she left Henry silenced and embarrassed, standing alone on the deck.

From then on Edward and Anne continued their lives aboard the ship as if nothing had ever happened. Now and again one of them would steal an unseen glance at the other and smile. And every night, in their separate beds, they recalled the kiss that never should have been.

9. THE TWO BY TWO ISLANDS

The *Freedom* reached Luna Bay without incident, and Edward allowed the crew some shore leave for a couple of days. They restocked food, ammunition, and general supplies to last them for the next few months. John was keeping track of everything and made a note to Edward that the next time they resupplied they would be out of money.

Let's hope there will be more than just a key on those islands. Either that or we'll have to start acting the part of pirates. I don't want to, but if we're left with no choice…

Edward stayed on the ship, having no inclination to leave. He and a few crewmen kept busy by checking the ship and making sure John hadn't missed anything.

While their speaking relationship was strained, Anne and Edward always had the courtesy to greet each other in passing.

Edward watched her as she was tying up the sails. The riggers were ashore, and everyone else was too afraid to do it. *Anne certainly is intriguing. Lucy never would have done something so bold as to join a group of pirates in disguise. At least, I don't think she would.* The thought of Lucy brought him back to himself. He still felt guilty about the kiss, so he kept his distance from Anne as best he could.

After the two days ashore, the crew returned. Frederick was among them, eager to work. It was as if he had become a different person.

When everyone was present and accounted for, they left Luna Bay, circled around the island, and headed north.

As they had done with the first island, they followed a diamond course far north of Luna Bay to cover the most ground. Edward was sure they would find something this time.

They searched in the same manner as before, travelling for days until they almost lost hope, until one day an excited cry from the crow's nest lifted Edward's spirits again.

"Land ho!"

"Where?" Edward yelled as he ran to the quarterdeck railing and gripped it hard as he looked to the crow's nest for an answer.

"North and starboard."

Edward looked off to the right side of the ship, and there it was: a small island in the distance. He began to laugh out loud at the sight of it. *Finally! We found one of them!* "Herbert, turn the ship north.

Head for that island."

Herbert, along with many, caught Edward's buoyant mood. "Aye aye, Captain!"

Henry jumped up the steps leading to the quarterdeck. "Is it the one? Is that the island?"

"It must be, Henry! There's nothing else it could be. Are you as excited as I am?"

He was. It appeared that they were finally about to solve the next part of the riddle. Once they came closer to the island, however...

"What kind of a cruel joke is this? The devil himself must be laughing at us!" Henry suggested bitterly.

The island was nothing but a large sandbar. There didn't appear to be anything on it at all.

"There must be more to it... We should search the whole thing."

"For what, Edward? There's nothing there!"

"There must be something. A trip door, a secret entrance, *something*."

"Very well, we'll search."

They took a few teams and scoured the whole "island" for a hidden passageway or a clue, but found only sand. Edward and the crew returned to the ship in a foul mood, still confused as to what they were searching for and why.

They continued sailing in the prescribed pattern. Each day passing left them feeling more restless than the last. Tension mounted amongst the crew, and the captain's dark mood was infecting the others.

On their return approach to Luna Bay, John approached Edward. "C-Captain?"

"We need to rethink this whole business, John. We're not reading the map right. There's some kind of trick to it we're overlooking. I'm sure of it."

"Captain?"

"I want to have a meeting with you, William, Sam, Herbert, and Henry again. Another look at the riddle could be useful."

"Captain?" John uttered for the third time.

"What is it, John? You have your orders."

John recoiled, but went on regardless. "Captain, the c-crew is angry with what's been happening recently. Th-they would like to know what we're searching for."

"They want to know what we're doing? Call everyone together then. I'll tell them what we're doing!"

"Aye aye, Captain."

John traversed the ship and gathered everyone to the main deck, where Edward was waiting to speak to them.

"So I hear you all want to know what we're searching for."

The crowd murmured in the affirmative.

"Well, I think you should be more concerned with performing your duties than why you're doing them, don't you? Keep to task and you'll know soon enough."

A ripple of whispers washed over the crew.

"Does anyone have an objection?"

A crewman spoke up. "I think we 'ave a right to know why we're doin stuff!" Others voiced their agreement.

Edward was reaching the level of nervousness where he would soon panic. His public speaking practice sessions had not prepared him for objections. He tried to say something, but stammered while another crewmember spoke up.

"We should have a say in what we'll be doing as a crew," the man claimed. "Aye, we should vote on it," another added.

Edward's eyes went out of focus and he could feel his heart beating through his flushed cheeks. "Henry!" he yelled and motioned for him to join him. When Henry arrived, he whispered for him to take over. He handed him the paper and told him to explain the keys and the possibility of treasure.

"Very well then. We'll let you know exactly what we're here for." Henry held up the paper. "This is what we're after."

The crew looked at Henry, confused. "Paper?" someone asked.

"What? No. You may have noticed some of the doors on our ship are locked and you're unable to enter those sections. We don't know exactly what some of them hold, but this piece of paper will lead us to the keys to unlock them. And there's another reason to find these keys: treasure. There may be something more than just keys if we manage to find the location where they are stored."

"You mean you don't know where it is?"

"No, that's why we need you all to help in this. There's a riddle on this piece of paper that leads to some islands. On those islands is the treasure. So far, our attempts at solving the puzzle have come to naught. If you vote to search for them, we can hold a meeting to find out what the riddle means. This vote is a vote of trust. If you trust in the captain and me, as you have already, we will find these islands and we will find the treasure."

The crewmembers muttered and whispered to each other, debating Henry's words.

Edward came back into the conversation. "All in favor of searching for the keys?"

Edward raised his hand and several in the crowd followed. On the quarterdeck, Henry, Herbert, Christopher, and John raised their hands. On the main deck, William, Sam, Anne, Nassir, Alexandre, and Jack all voted in favor. A few more began raising their hands while nudging others to raise theirs. Anne watched this hesitant response with growing impatience and finally ran up the first few steps of the ladder before facing the crew.

"You want adventure, don't you?" she yelled, to which many responded in favor. "You want treasure beyond your wildest imaginings?" More replied to her in the affirmative. "Then raise your bloody hands, because treasure and adventure are what we will find!"

The vast majority now put up their hands, and Anne went back into the crowd. Edward smiled at her, and when she noticed she turned aside, a slight redness on her cheeks.

"All opposed?" Edward asked.

A few people raised their hands, but not enough to call the vote. Among them were Kenneth Locke and his group.

Edward stared straight at Kenneth. "The majority rules. We search for the islands." Then he addressed the whole crew. "Now we will have a meeting to see if we can figure out the riddle. If we cannot, then each of you will be called to try your wits at it."

As Edward had requested, Henry, John, William, Herbert, and Sam joined him on the quarterdeck. Edward set up the maps and everything they needed.

"Sam, do you have any new thoughts on the riddle?"

Sam took the paper from Edward's outstretched hand and read it over, front and back. "I have nary a clue, jus' as last time. I be a simple man, Captain."

Henry scoffed and said, "That figures."

Sam gave him a death stare and continued. "There is something I reckon is important. This bit about the 'wit and grit.' Maybe there be traps on the islands for both smart and dumb people."

"Well, you have a good point there, but we can worry about it later. We know from what we discussed earlier that it's two of these three islands, but we need to find out how they're connected."

They went over and over the puzzle for a good few hours with some reasonable ideas proposed, but nothing approaching a definite solution. They brought other crewmembers in, but none of them could make heads or tails of it. Impatience and irritation set in. Arguments broke out.

This is ridiculous. Can no one figure this nonsense out?

Edward turned away from the table to get away from the noise.

Maybe we're thinking about this the wrong way. It's probably something so simple it's right in front of our eyes. It has to be that. Some sort of trick to catch people off guard. Edward was deep in thought when he heard someone say something that drew his attention.

"Wait… What did you say?"

Blackbeard's Ship

Herbert spoke up. "Henry's being a fool. He thinks north means straight from where the island is pointing. It doesn't, Henry! It refers to magnetic north. That's why we have compasses." That renewed the argument once more.

The words sparked something in Edward. He went over the riddle in his head once more. "*From two ports of crescent moon, two by two islands, north and north northwest, wit and grit…*"

He jumped up and shouted, "I've got it!" causing everyone on the ship to stop what they were doing and look at him. "I know where the islands are!"

"What?" Henry said with a blank stare.

"I solved the riddle of where the islands are located. It's because of the two sides to everything. The riddle isn't just a test of how smart you are. It's also a test of how dumb you are!"

Everyone looked at him as though he had been dropped on the head as a child. "Maybe you need some rest, Edward. You're not making sense."

"It makes perfect sense, Herbert. It's the perfect way to throw us off. Everyone's first inclination is magnetic north of the islands themselves. That's what each person we brought up here kept asking which way north is. And if you keep thinking nautically, then you'll never see the true picture. It took Henry's comment of going straight from how the islands are pointed that helped me work it out. Here, I'll show you."

Edward took the map they had of the Caribbean and drew lines on it according to how each island was oriented. He used his knowledge he was learning from Herbert and drew two lines, one for north and one for north-northwest from each. Not magnetic north, but north as in straight out from the curve of the half moon formed by the island.

The lines Edward drew went out from the islands almost like a V. The first island they'd gone to, Half Moon Cay, had a V going past the west side of Jamaica. The second island, Luna Bay, had a V that went south to Panama and the Isla de la Providencia, nowhere near the lines from the first island. The final island, Slivers Isle, went southeast and intersected with the lines from Half Moon Cay.

The intersecting lines from both Vs created four points in the middle of the Caribbean Sea.

"We used our smarts to narrow it down to three islands, but after we couldn't move forward. We would have never figured it out if we didn't look at it from both perspectives. The island we were just at, Luna Bay, leads nowhere—it's something to try and throw us off the trail to the real islands. The two true ones have two lines each and they both intersect in the middle of the Caribbean Sea. Four points, two by two islands. That's the riddle, and those are the islands we've been searching for."

Everyone inspected what Edward had put on the map and considered his explanation. As they realised the logic in it, their eyes lit up like his.

"He's right! It makes perfect sense, in a foolish sort of way," Henry said.

"I have to admit, I never would have seen that. Good work, Captain." Herbert sounded a bit downhearted at not having been able to solve the riddle.

"I never would have figured it out if not for all of your help. Sam pointed me in the right direction with his remark on the two parts of the tests. Then Henry's comment about where the islands were pointed provided the rest."

Everyone began to feel excited; they had finally solved the puzzle, and soon they would be swimming in treasure.

"Let's not become too exuberant yet. We have a long road ahead of us." Edward went to the edge of the quarterdeck where the crew was still waiting. "Everyone, we've solved the riddle! This ship needs to be seaworthy before we can proceed. Weigh anchor! Release the sails! Everyone back to work! Herbert, set the course! Let's find us some treasure!"

"Aye aye, Captain!"

⚓ ⚓ ⚓

The days came and went at a quick pace. The crew was appeased, indeed happy, since their purpose had been made clear. No one knew what adventures awaited them at the islands, but the mystery heightened the thrill.

Treasure proved a fine motivator.

Then, one day, a familiar cry signaled the end of their search.

"Land ho! Dead ahead!" a crewman yelled from the crow's next.

"How many islands do you see?" Edward yelled to the scout above.

"One."

Damn!

"No... wait! I see another one... And another... Four islands! Four islands off the bow."

Ha-ha! Yes! "Excellent! Good job!" Edward saw Henry and John staring at him, looking as if they were about to explode. "As you will, gentlemen. Let it out."

Henry and John, along with the rest of the crew, let out loud whoops, and cheers erupted from every nook and cranny of the ship. Edward couldn't help but join in; having his solution to the riddle proven true in reality was almost reward enough.

Blackbeard's Ship

Almost.

When they reached the islands, Herbert took the ship between them. The four islands were almost bare; they consisted of small rocky hills covered by tall grass and a few scattered trees.

Herbert pushed himself up with his arms for a better view. "They're closer together than the map you made indicates, but it's certainly an ingenious riddle."

"I can see why people would pass these islands by," said Henry. "There's nothing on them to speak of."

"Well, Henry, let's hope you're wrong. Take her in to the port side island, Herbert. John, gather a small landing party. Tell them to bring weapons. I don't want to take any chances."

Herbert and John set about carrying out Edward's orders. When the ship had made landfall, Edward, Henry, William, and a few others disembarked on the island.

"Be on the lookout for anything out of the ordinary."

They searched the island, examining everything they saw with care. The group stayed close together; it was a small island, but they had no idea what to expect. They climbed a grassy hillside, checking the ground for a clue to their next step, but saw nothing remarkable. Then they went down the other side of the hill, which was rocky and covered in moss and vines.

"I don't understand. There's nothing here, but these *must* be the islands," Edward said to no one in particular.

"Maybe there's some trick. Do you have the paper still?" Edward pulled it out and handed it to Henry. "There must be something in the next part of the riddle about these islands." Henry sat down on a rock and read it with a furrowed brow. "'Two by two tests'. Do you think this is the test? Finding the spot on the islands where the key is located?"

Edward thought for a moment. "Nah, that's too easy. I think there's more to these islands than there appears to be. There's mention of a fifth island in there too, but do you see another island around here? There must be something else here…"

"Captain!" William called out. "I believe this is what you are looking for." He was pointing at the entrance to a cavern in the rock face.

Edward and Henry rushed over. "How did you find this?"

"I was walking along the side of the rock face and felt a cool breeze and picked up an odd smell, so I investigated. The opening was concealed by the moss and vines, so I cut them down and this is what I found."

"Genius!" Edward commented. "Let's return to the ship."

"What? Aren't we going to journey inside?"

"Not yet. We need to figure out exactly what we'll do for these tests."

When Edward and the others arrived back at the ship, the men wanted to hear about everything. The questions came one right after the other.

"Did ye find the treasure?" "Where's the entrance?" "Did ye get a look inside?" "Is it haunted?"

"Haunted?" Edward chuckled. "No. We haven't gone inside yet, so calm yourselves. I'll let you know what we're doing when we're ready to do it."

Having fielded enough questions, Edward went to the quarterdeck so he could consult first with the senior officers and then the entire crew before he proceeded.

"Find anything, Captain?" Herbert asked.

"We found the entrance to a cave, but we didn't enter. I imagine there are similar entrances on each island. But we have something else to consider. Henry, the paper, if you please?" Henry handed him the paper which held the riddle on it. "See this part about the tests? 'Two by two islands, two by two tests. Two by two crews, one of wit, one of grit. Each test gains one key for the chest. Bring the keys and find the chest in the belly of the fifth.' There's probably a clue inside each island, which leads to a fifth island where the chest is. Each island holds a cavern, and each requires both smarts and strength."

Henry shook his head. "No… The way it sounds to me, it seems like two will require wit and the other two strength."

"Maybe you're right, Henry, but we can't afford to take any chances. What if we send a group of people in who won't be able to complete the task? We don't know what's down there. They could die."

"What will we do?" John asked.

"We have to separate into four groups and have each choose an island. Each group needs individuals with a range of skills, capabilities, and knowledge. They need to be able to deal with any eventuality." He turned to Henry. "You, John, William, and I will be the team leaders. I'll take the last island, the rest of you can choose accordingly."

"So we will split the crew into who is smart and… well… who isn't?" Henry asked as he folded his arms.

"Somewhat. Everyone has their strengths and weaknesses. We have to make sure each group has the best chance of success."

They proceeded to divide the company into four parties. Each party consisted of some who could read and write, some who knew how to use a compass, some who could do math, some who possessed exceptional strength and dexterity, and so forth. Which qualities of wit and grit would actually be tested by their expedition, no one could guess at.

I'm sure everything will go smoothly. Benjamin wants us to have the keys. It won't be that hard. Will it?

Jack was to be left in charge of the remaining crew who were not to participate in the expedition. Edward trusted Jack, the men liked him and would listen to him, and he could keep them entertained with his music.

The process of choosing members for the four groups went, for the most part, smoothly. But when Edward picked Anne to join his group, William spoke up.

"Jim should be with my group, or I will join yours."

"No, William. It will cause an imbalance. I need his skills with me. You don't have to worry, he'll be safe."

William took a moment, and, seeing Edward's point, conceded.

"So I guess I'm staying here, am I?" Herbert's eyes were stuck on the deck and his chin sunk into his chest.

"What are you talking about? You're in my group. Nassir will carry you along, provided you wish to come." Herbert's face lit up. "I'll take that as a yes, but I'm sending you back at the first sign of trouble. Understood?"

"Understood!" Herbert said with a salute.

After explaining the situation to the crew, and how they would be split, they voted on the proceedings. The crew was in agreement, so they let everyone off. They began with William's group on the island they landed on. Alexandre was with him at the southern island.

The crew in the first group exited the ship by rope ladders, with some jumping from the deck to the sandy beach below. Others took their time stocking with weapons and supplies in case the need arose.

After the first group disembarked, they went with Henry's group, which included Sam, to the west island. John's group, with Frederick and Kenneth Locke, amongst others, took the north island. Lastly, Edward's group took the east island.

"Well, this is it. Stay alert, everyone."

Edward's group made their way from the ship via ladders or leaping over the side onto the small island. They took in the surroundings while they waited for the captain and the rest of the men to land.

"Captain, I'm not sure if you've noticed, but there is something odd about these islands."

"What is it, Herbert?"

"Well, there are shallow parts around the islands at the ends. The four may be connected. It's almost like a compass, they seem to be connected like a cross."

Connected like a cross? Belly of the fifth? "Maybe we'll meet up with the other groups at some point."

"It's plausible. Look in the middle of the four islands, I know it's hard to see, but the water is very shallow there. I guess we won't know what it means until we head inside our island."

"Speaking of heading inside. Nassir!" The tall Negro walked over to Edward. "Can you help Herbert down? The rest of you get his wheelchair."

After nodding to Edward, Nassir helped take Herbert down the side of the ship while another crewmate lowered his wheelchair to the beach.

It was intended that Nassir's son, Ochi, and Christina, Herbert's sister, would stay aboard ship in the care of Jack. But now that his father was actually leaving, the boy was afraid, and he desperately wanted to go with him.

Edward noticed Ochi watching his father at work. "Ochi. Come here, boy." He trudged his way over to Edward. "You scared to be alone?"

The boy nodded. "Yes, Captain."

Edward chuckled. "Now you needn't worry. You remember Jack?" Edward pointed to the fiddler. He saw him pointing and walked over. "Your Uncle Jack here will protect you while we're away."

"You can count on me, Ochi." Jack knelt down to the child's level.

"We're going to find us some treasure and your father will be back in no time. You won't even notice he's gone."

Ochi had tears in his eyes as he nodded again.

"Hey, Ochi! I have something important for you to do. See, when I leave this ship, I won't be a captain anymore. A captain is only a captain on a ship. I need someone to take over for me while I'm away." Edward took off his tricorn hat and put it on Ochi's head. "Do you think you can be captain for me? Can you keep the ship safe for me and your dad?"

Ochi's face lit up. "I sure can!" He played with the hat and then put it back on. He was in awe of that hat.

It'll be nice to let him play for a bit.

Jack took Ochi's hand. "Let us man the helm, Captain." He smiled as he led the boy away.

Edward noticed those remaining behind were talking in a group. "Keep an eye out, gentlemen, and keep the ship safe." They all replied with an "Aye, Captain."

"Captain?" a tender voice said from behind Edward.

It was Herbert's sister, Christina. *I barely noticed her; she's so quiet all the time. She rarely leaves Herbert's side.* "Yes, what is it Christina?"

he whispered so that the others could not hear.

"What will I do while you're gone?"

Hmm. "Well, you see Ochi?" Edward pointed to him. "He's captain while I'm away, but he needs a first mate to help him out. Without a first mate, the captain is lost. You think you're up to the task?"

Christina smiled and nodded her head.

"Well, you'd better hurry before he casts off without you." He pushed Christina off in the direction of Ochi and Jack and she ran up to them. He had seen them playing together before. It was nice to see they got along so well. Jack also seemed right at home with the children and was smiling and playing right along with them. *I promise I'll bring your family back soon, little ones.*

When Edward was certain he had packed everything necessary for the expedition, he disembarked. They fanned out in smaller groups to investigate every part of the island. Nothing looked promising until one of the groups found a hole beside a knocked over tree. The tree itself was gnarled, decayed, and a shell of its former self. The opening it left led almost straight down and was wide enough for several people to climb down the abundant vines covering its walls.

"It's pitch black down there, Captain. You don' mean fer us to climb down into its depths, do ye?" one crewman asked.

"That's exactly what I mean for us to do, gentlemen." Edward and his crew steeled themselves for their journey into the abyss.

10. BETWEEN A ROCK & A CURRENT

The climb was treacherous for the lot of them. The moss was slippery and some vines broke, but luckily the rock face allowed for plenty of footholds. They kept climbing down until no light reached them from overhead and all was darkness.

When Edward reached the bottom, he noticed a faint light. As his eyes adjusted, he could see they had entered a long underground cavern, and the light was coming from far ahead of them. The whole cave, save the twenty square feet of rock they were standing on, was filled with water. It was moving forward in a swift current, and seemed too deep and felt too cold to swim across. A fair-sized boat capable of holding ten to twenty people was secured to the bank with a rope. However, using the boat posed a problem.

Rocks of all shapes and sizes protruded from the surface of the water going as far as Edward could see in the dim light of the mossy cavern. A crossing could be treacherous with the current.

"Blimey, ow're we suppos'ta get by wif all those jagged rocks there?"

Anne walked up behind Edward while everyone else was gawking at the water. "You believe that to be dire? Take a closer look at the boat," she whispered.

Edward almost blushed at her closeness as he turned to the boat. What he saw caused him to dash up to the boat, examining the rear.

"What's wrong?" Herbert asked.

Edward turned to him. Nassir held Herbert in his sturdy arms, and he seemed hardly to notice the weight he was carrying. "The rudder's broken on the boat. There's no way we can steer it."

"Let me examine it," Herbert said. "Nassir, could you bring me closer, please?"

"Certainly." Nassir carried Herbert over to the back of the boat.

The helmsman made his assessment. "You're right, Captain, it's broken. It can't be fixed. As far as I know, we don't have anything with us we can use to create a makeshift one. We also don't have oars of the proper size back on the *Freedom*. We could break the ones we have, but then they would be useless to us after this."

"What are we to do then? We need to keep moving forward."

"All hope is not lost, Captain. We can use whoever goes across as our rudders and oars. It's not the best way, but it's all we have at the moment."

Edward cocked his brow. "What do you mean?"

"I'll sit in the bow of the boat issuing orders. Depending on where we need to go, ten people on one side and ten on the other can put their arms into the water to either turn or slow down the boat. It's tricky, but it should work."

"Should work, or will work?"

There was a small pause before Herbert said "It will work," with confidence brimming in his eyes. "You can count on me."

"That's what I wanted to hear. Uhh..." *What was Anne's fake name again?* "Jim...?" Edward uttered the name in a half-questioning drawl as he turned to look at her.

Anne arched her eyebrow. "Yes, Captain?"

"Gather everyone together. We need to move on."

Anne did as commanded, and Edward's group moved to the boat at her beckoning. Edward explained what they would be doing, and asked for volunteers to continue onward in the boat.

Edward wanted Anne, Nassir, and Herbert on the boat as a matter of course. Others were reluctant to join after seeing the current and the rocks, but with some persuasion, seventeen volunteered. Herbert explained what would happen and what commands he would deliver for various manoeuvres. When he finished, Edward reiterated everything to make sure it was clear to everyone.

"Now, everyone who's crossing, board the boat. The rest of you head back to the surface and board the ship." *I hope this works.* Edward watched Anne as she boarded the boat. *It will work.*

Herbert made his way to the bow and positioned himself so he could see everything. Edward was near him on the left side with Anne right beside him, and Nassir was on the right side. Everyone piled in, except the last two who waited for the order to shove off.

"Wait, what about my chair?"

"The other crewmembers will have to take it back; it's too big to take with us, and if it should fall out it would be lost. Nassir, you'll have to take care of Herbert from now on, yes?"

"Understood, Captain," Nassir said in his deep, accented voice. Edward had no doubt Nassir would have assumed the task—whether ordered to or not—with a smile on his face.

Edward turned to the crewmembers waiting at the end of the boat. "Let's shove off!" They pushed the boat farther into the water and jumped in.

The current immediately took them in its cold grasp. The crew soon realised how difficult it would be to control their course—and how easy it would be to die by smashing against jagged rocks—and it unnerved them.

"Full!" Herbert yelled over the noise of the rushing water.

Everyone put their hands into the water and did their best to hold them straight as the water pressed against them. This slowed the boat a good deal. A rock came up on their port side. "Left!" Those on the right side took their arms out of the water, making the boat turn to the right. "Full! Stroke!" The whole crew put their arms back in and synchronised their movements to Herbert's commands. They were able to move well out of the way of the rock in time.

They kept on, with Herbert issuing commands and the crew following to the best of their ability. Every time they took their arms out of the water they rubbed them to bring the warmth and feeling back. The water was not bitterly cold, but the continuing exposure did take its toll.

Edward and Anne were right beside each other, with her body pressed up against him. He couldn't turn his gaze to her, but he could have sworn when they weren't rowing he felt her touch his hand.

Herbert was successful in guiding the crew in avoiding all obstacles—if at times by the skin of their teeth—and their initial fear was subsiding. The rocks around them stood out of the water like giant moss-covered fingers. The remnants of the sea stuck to the skin like dirt under the fingernails. Salt water, seaweed, and crabs scattered between the cracks and crevices. It was almost a pleasant ride.

Then the current grew stronger.

Herbert shouted orders to everyone in a frenzy to avoid the multitude of rocks in their path. Full! Left! Right! Stroke!—the commands resounded one after another over the roar of the gushing water. But the boat creaked under the force of the current, and nothing they tried seemed to do any good.

My arms are burning! I don't know how much longer I can take this!

"Do not worry," Anne's voice said from behind Edward. "I know we can make it." The force behind Anne's words seemed to give him the strength he needed, and he was able to keep going.

Herbert continued to yell out orders one after another, until Edward felt he had used up his last ounce of strength; from the looks on the faces around him, they all had. Then, without warning, the orders ceased.

Is it over? Edward looked up, and he understood why Herbert had stopped. Two large rocks, a short distance apart, loomed dead ahead. There might have been enough time to go around them, but it would have been risky. The only alternative was to pass between them. *But will the boat fit through?*

"Herbert!"

"I know, Captain! We can make it! Arms in!" Everyone pulled together toward the centre of the boat and away from the sides.

They were moving a lot faster now that there was no resistance.

Blackbeard's Ship

The rocks were inching closer by the second.

The crew watched in helpless terror. The rocks were immense; if they hit them, there would be nothing left. A collision was seconds away, but time seemed slowed to a standstill.

Edward held his breath and closed his eyes in silent prayer.

A scraping sound from the starboard side caused several people to gasp aloud. Edward opened his eyes and saw the boat was intact. He could breathe again. He smiled at Anne and then looked toward the front of the boat.

What he saw brought terror to his eyes. They were on a collision course with another rock. The crew had no time to save themselves. It was too late.

"Brace for impact!" Edward yelled, seconds before the boat smashed against the rock.

Everything was a blur as bodies flew this way and that. Some were flung from the boat and into the water. Others, including Edward, hit the rock first and then fell. He smashed his left arm against the rock and then slid into the depths. The current took him tumbling downstream. He flailed his arms and legs in a panicked struggle to orient himself in the swift-moving water, every conscious thought vanishing save one: *Anne! Where's Anne?* After a few seconds of stumbling about, Edward was able to right himself as the current died down. He could see other crewmembers surfacing. Off to his right was a small dock, no doubt intended for the broken boat; he noticed Nassir helping Herbert and some others up onto it. Edward searched every face in desperation, but the one he wanted to see was missing.

Damn! Where is she? After another few seconds, he dove into the water again, the light from the exit giving him at least something to see by. *Rocks! Nothing but rocks! She can't have drowned; she's too stubborn for that to happen. Wait... There!* He noticed movement beside a large rock and swam over to find Anne struggling to free her leg from a crevice between the large rock and another. *There's no way we can lift the rock... No! We have to try. I won't let her die!* He moved in close beside her and tried to push the rock with his feet while bracing himself on the bedrock beneath. No matter how hard he pushed, it wouldn't budge. Anne tried to help by lifting as best she could in her awkward position.

I need more air, but she needs it more than I do. He turned her face to his, and for the second time their mouths touched. Edward granted her the last of his remaining air before returning to the surface for more.

As soon as Edward was ready he went back down. Anne was struggling to move the rock on her own. Edward gave her more air, and they continued the struggle together. They pushed as hard as they could without stopping, sometimes changing angles, but all to no avail.

He looked into her eyes, and she into his. He could see the anger, and the fear.

I'm not letting you die, Anne! Edward leaned with all his might against the rock and he could feel it budging. Then Nassir, the giant of a man, appeared out of the darkness, swam over to them and added to their efforts all the strength he had. With each push, the rock nudged ever so slightly forward—and, in a few seconds, Anne was free.

Yes! Thank you, Nassir!

They rushed to the surface at once, the murky waters providing their last resistance to salvation. When they broke through the surface, all eyes were on them. Edward and Anne were gasping for breath as they made their way to the dock with trembling arms and legs.

Edward climbed up first, and, in an instant after seeing Anne's loose hair, turned himself around to face all the eyes upon him. "My God! Is that crewman all right?" Edward thrust out his arm and pointed at the far wall of the cavern.

Everyone turned to where he was pointing. With the precious few seconds they had, Nassir took out a cap from his back pocket and handed it to Anne. She shoved her soaked hair into the wet leather before everyone looked back at Edward in confusion.

Edward shrugged. "Oh, I guess it was nothing."

Anne stifled a cry of shock. "Edward! Your arm!"

"What?" His left arm, the one that had hit the rock after the crash, was limp, and he wasn't able to move it. During his effort to rescue Anne, he had been unaware of anything wrong, but as soon as he saw his dangling arm the pain returned in full. It felt torn and broken. "No need for concern," he said with a grimace. "I'll have Alexandre inspect it later."

"Are you sure? It could be broken."

"Worry not, it's trivial at best. We have to press on." Edward walked up the wooden dock and counted the crew as he went. The cold of the water also hit him. He was chilled to the bone and his teeth were starting to chatter. "We're missing three people."

"They're lost to Davy Jones, Captain. They couldn't swim."

Edward stood straight and motionless. It was the first time anyone in his crew had died. He closed his eyes and he felt numbness in his limbs and his mind, but it was not from the cold of the water. He was weary, and when he spoke his voice was low and hollow. "We'll hold a ceremony tonight in their honour. For now, we must move on. Let us hope their deaths are not in vain…" *They died because of me. If I were stronger, if I had only been paying attention…*

"I'm sorry, Captain."

Edward turned to look at Herbert. He was holding his weight up with his arms; his body spoke more to the weight he felt than did his words.

"It was my fault," the helmsman said. "I should have noticed the danger in time. I should have had us go around those rocks, but I foolishly thought I was good enough to guide us through. I won't let it happen again."

Edward knelt down to Herbert and lifted his chin. "Those men died at my command, not yours." Then Edward turned and walked away, his body sore and his footsteps heavy—but his determination set like stone.

11. THE DOCTOR AND THE DIALS

William and the other members of his party walked down the sloping corridor into the depths of the cave. It was the very one he had found when they first landed at the "two by two" islands.

The air was stagnant and smelled of rotten wood and the burning cinders of their torches. The corridor they traveled through was wet with dripping seawater, and slick with green and brown moss.

"This is quite *l'aventure*, yes, William?" Alexandre commented.

"Yes." William seemed in no mood for talk, but that was usual for him.

They took care in watching their step, trying to avoid the slippery moss. William strode forward with purpose and was always ahead of the others, except for Alexandre.

"You are quite *rigide*, William. *Se relaxer, mon ami.*"

"I cannot relax. Not right now."

"Are you worried for your *fille*?" Alexandre said with a long, drawn-out smile. "Ah! I should not have said that. Now I have let *le chat* out of the bag."

William stopped in his tracks and turned to Alexandre with eyes of cold stone. "Cut the theatrics. What do you know?"

The other crewmembers were catching up, so Alexandre motioned to keep walking down the sloping corridor. He began to whisper in French.

"I'm an observant man, William. I know how to identify a woman in hiding when I see one. The way she walks and acts, the way she tries to mask her voice. It's all about observation. She is not the only one either. There are two more on board."

"Two?" William knew about Anne and Christina—but who was the third?

"Yes, three altogether. The third is good at hiding. I must say, even I had trouble spotting her, but I have no doubts. But enough of that. I know you are not in love; you are too formal and protective. It is obvious by your mannerisms that you were in the military; I seem to recall a high-ranking youngster named William—rather famous, too, for some... shall I say, less than reputable actions?

"And as for the girl, she's decent at hiding herself, but too protective of her red hair, and of a certain ring I've seen before. Very hard to make a forgery.

"Taking those factors into account, I deduce there is only one person she can be. I admit even I was surprised when I reached the conclusion myself. Why, having the daughter of—"

William slammed Alexandre against the stone wall. "You keep your mouth shut about who she is! I will kill anyone who threatens her safety!"

Alexandre laughed a weary, emotionless laugh, unfazed by this outburst. "My dear William, I am merely an observer. I will simply watch until her mask shatters. I enjoy the game. Where is the fun in telling everyone?"

William let Alexandre down when he noticed the crew approaching. "Remember what I said."

"Of course," Alexandre said. "This confirms one thing for me though..." he commented as William walked away. "That you remain loyal to her means you are innocent."

William walked off into the dark of the corridor, alone, ahead of everyone else, as he had five years ago.

⚓ ⚓ ⚓

William's party caught up to him and left the corridor for a large craggy dome. William had placed some torches in sconces, allowing the crew to see their surroundings better.

Twenty feet from the sloping corridor was a sharp drop to water below. There was a pegged wooden dial, almost like a large stone-mill, in the middle of the standing area. In front of the dial, five feet from the edge of the cliff, stood two cannons, ready to be fired into the darkness. On either side of the cave was a large stockpile of gunpowder and cannonballs.

The crew could see nothing else but craggy walls and ceiling. No way to cross the cliff, and, as far as anyone could see in the darkness, nothing even on the other side of the gorge.

"Is this it?" one crewmember asked.

"There's no way across," said another.

"*Pas nécessairement*," Alexandre refuted. "There must be something we can do with the cannons. Try turning the dial."

A few of the men went to the dial and began pushing. As the wheel turned, the cannons swiveled on some mechanism set into their bases. Once they reached a certain angle, they stopped moving and the wheel could not be turned any farther.

"Hmm. Now *renverser, s'il vous plaît*." At Alexandre's command, the men turned the wheel the other way, and the cannons swiveled left. They stopped turning before the cannons would be able to hit the wall.

"Aha, as I thought!"

"What? What do you see?" William asked.

"Search the walls for a target."

William examined the cannons. "You heard him. Search the walls."

Several men took torches and inspected the accessible parts of the wall. Sure enough, on both sides of the craggy dome wall hung two wooden planks with rope tied around them.

"If those are hit, they must release something so we can cross the gorge." William peered behind each cannon to the target on the left wall. They were moved as far left as they could be by the dial. "The angle of the shot is wrong. We can't hit the target. Can these cannons be taken apart?"

Alexandre sighed. "*Non, non, non.* They are fine. Leave them."

"What do you mean? They'll never hit like that. And we can't shoot the rope with our guns, it's too far away."

"*Avoir confiance en moi.* I know what I am doing. I need but a moment."

Everyone waited as Alexandre took out a stick of graphite and a piece of paper, on which he scribbled various pictures and annotations. He went at it for a few minutes while everyone watched him pacing back and forth in thought. His leather shoes made a distinct tap tap that rebounded off the cave walls.

When he finished and put the paper away there was a glint of determination in his eyes and furrowed brow. "Start the dial, *si'l vous plait.*"

William nodded to the crew. They turned the wheel, making the cannons move right about five inches.

"*Arreter!*"

They stopped as commanded. "Why here?"

"Fire *les canons* in sync and you shall see," he replied with a smirk.

William smiled in spite of himself; he thought he could see what was happening now. "Do as he commands."

"But Will, it don't make no sense to be firin' 'em. They won't hit nuthin'."

"I have a feeling we're in for a surprise. Just make sure you fire them at exactly the same time."

The crew gathered gunpowder and cannonballs from the stockpiles, loaded the cannons, and prepared to fire.

Alexandre bestowed upon himself the honour of the firing signal. "*Tirer!*"

The cannons fired with tremendous force. Some of the onlookers were able to see, or hear, the two cannonballs ricochet off each other. The impact caused one to hit farther to the left than it normally would have. But this had been Alexandre's intention. When the dust cleared, the target and the rope were gone.

The crew stood there wide-eyed and slack-jawed. Even William was awestruck by the spectacle. "How did you do it?"

"Simple *mathematiques, mon ami*. Now, the other target."

The crew immediately turned the wheel to the other side until Alexandre told them to stop. They fired the cannons once again, with similar results, and a dusty drawbridge dropped down in front of them.

They all cheered and congratulated Alexandre on his genius; even William freed himself of his black thoughts and praised him for his ingenuity. The company crossed the bridge across the gorge together.

But whatever it was they expected to find, what they actually encountered only confused them. They stood at the brink of another rocky ledge ten feet long and another gorge, which they could neither cross nor see beyond. At the bottom of the chasm, they could see water flowing forward, ahead of them.

"Will, there be another one of them dials," a crewman said as he pointed to the right side of the cave.

In an alcove along the wall was another wheel similar to the one at the entrance. The alcove almost seemed to be there to protect the dial from something. The question was: from what, exactly?

Will noticed a rope running along the ceiling. He followed it forward and it went across the second gorge, presumably where another drawbridge was. The other end went to another wooden plank target, on the ceiling this time. A matching target was twenty feet from the first, also on the ceiling.

Alexandre noticed the same thing. William issued a command: "Four of you return to the other side and examine the cannons; everyone else help me turn this."

Half of the group went to the first section, with the first dial, and a few joined William at the second dial. When everyone was in position, he yelled out to the side. "Ready?" he asked the crew at the cannons.

"Aye."

They turned the wheel as far as it could move.

"What did it do?" yelled William.

"It be moving up, Will. They be aimed at the ceiling. One is aimed a bit lower than the other."

"As I thought." William turned to Alexandre. "The second dial, on this side, will allow us to hit those planks on the ceiling. The first dial allows movement left and right, and the second allows movement up and down. Let's fire a shot after turning the cannons to the centre."

Alexandre nodded as he stood in the middle of the cave watching the planks with attentive eyes.

William cupped his hands and shouted across the first gorge to the team and the first dial. "Move the dial until the cannons are facing the centre. Then fire them at the same time."

After a moment to grasp the situation, the group at the cannons replied with an "Aye."

The crew came out from the second wheel and began to watch with William and Alexandre. They could hear the other team turning the cannons and then loading them. The sound of the blast punched their ears and reverberated off the walls.

The cannonballs bounced off each other as before, but this time it made one ball jump higher. One cannonball almost hit the plank, but the ball was too low from the ceiling.

They had another problem as well. The cannonballs were heading across the gorge, right at William, Alexandre, and the others. The cannonball hit one of the crewmen in the chest, sending him flying into the abyss with a splash. The others jumped to the edge to see if he could be saved, but he was dead before he hit the water.

"Dammit!" William slammed his fist against the stone ground.

The crew watched the water in desperate hope the man would surface again, but he was gone.

William turned to see Alexandre watching, his baggy eyes glassy and emotionless as usual, almost as if nothing had happened.

"You are a surgeon, dammit! Can you not even feign caring?"

"*Je suis désolé.* I keep a detachment from patients and others alike."

William understood, but in that moment his anger would not subside. "Come, everyone, we can mourn later. Alexandre, hide in this alcove so you aren't killed either."

"*Non.* I must stay here."

"What are you talking about? That's suicide."

"If no one watches the *trajectoire* then we won't be able to adjust the position. Do not worry. *Je serai bien.*" One side of Alexandre's mouth curled into a hollow smile.

I cannot tell whether he is insane or if he really does care. "Very well, be careful."

William and the rest went into the alcove and began to turn the dial so the cannons were aimed a touch higher.

"Move the cannons a bit to the right," Alexandre shouted across.

"Aye," the crewmen replied, and they set to the task.

"*Tirer!*"

No sooner was the order issued than they heard the loud bang of gunpowder. This time the ricochet was closer to the target, but the height still wasn't good enough. Alexandre observed one cannonball fall, without worry, as it smashed into the ground ten feet from him. He took more notes and then relayed orders to William's group.

The next shot was dead on, and the rope was released. This time the cannonball had missed Alexandre by only five feet. One target remained.

Alexandre instructed the other group to move the cannons left. He counted the seconds on his fingers and then told them to fire. He must have counted wrong, because something went awry.

The cannonballs hit each other and bounced. One shot up, hit the ceiling, and then headed down with the other to where the surgeon was standing.

"Look out!" William yelled.

Alexandre took a casual step out of the way and the cannonballs passed him before smashing into the stone floor. He made some more notes and then yelled orders to the other side again. He counted down once more.

The crew watching from the second dial in the alcove were holding their breaths from the tension. Some were sweating, on the tips of their toes, others bit on their nails, and still others closed their eyes, but every few seconds opened them again.

The cannons fired. The cannonballs hit each other. One went to the ceiling and hit the target dead on before plunging into the gorge with a splash. The rope released and another drawbridge lowered.

The crew ran over to Alexandre, jumping up and down in amazement. Alexandre himself smirked, not displeased with the adulation.

"*Pas besoin de louanges.* Let us move on before my head swells with praise."

"Come on, boys!" William yelled to the other side, and his group began to make their way across the second bridge. He turned to Alexandre. "Why did you do it?"

"What do you mean?"

"I mean, why did you decide to stay and watch the angles? We had plenty of cannonballs; we could have tried to guess at the timing. We would have gotten it eventually."

"Hmmm. *C'est quoi le mot?* Ah, yes! Duty. It was my duty, and no one else's. With all due respect, you could not have accomplished the task with guesswork. I am the only one who could have done the calculations. I am not totally heartless, William, despite what you may think."

"Perhaps not." William paused, gazing upon the sullen-eyed man in front of him with a new light. "Let us press on. They are waiting for us."

Alexandre nodded, and they both walked across the bridge and into the heart of the caves, not knowing what further trials might await them.

12. THE AMBUSH IN THE DEN

Henry and his team found themselves in a spacious subterranean room, having found the way into their assigned island's cave. They had had to rappel down a deep shaft, and had left the end of the rope tied to a large rock in case they needed a way back up.

They could see by the light from the opening that the chamber was roughly square, and the walls were smooth to the touch. At the end of the room was a wall the crew could climb up to another level. Henry couldn't see the far end of the chamber very well, but it appeared as if the higher level might provide an exit.

Up the wall on the left and right sides of the room ran thick ropes attached to the floor by heavy iron pegs. The ropes went all the way to the ceiling, but because of the angle of the room he couldn't see where they were attached.

I wonder what those are for?

"So, First Mate, what're your orders?" Sam asked with a slight mocking tone.

Henry gritted his teeth and let out a deep breath. "We continue. Be careful, everyone."

They set out to cross the room, inching forward, with Henry and Sam leading. There didn't seem to be any traps, and they were able to move at a good pace. When they reached the middle, Henry took another look around the room. He was now able to see each of the ropes went straight up the wall to the ceiling, then snaked forward to the upper ledge. Presumably, when they climbed up to the ledge, they would find out what the ropes were for.

Henry noticed something odd about the walls on the level they were on. There were little circular notches, like someone had carved them into the rock. Both walls were covered with them.

As Henry turned to start walking again, he noticed a raised section on the floor. It was too smooth and clean cut to be natural. Before he could examine it further, a crewmate who wasn't paying attention stepped on it. The raised stone pressed down, and the circular notches on the wall opened, transforming into dark, round holes.

"It's a trap! Run!"

Everyone reacted in a different manner. Some ran forward, some ran back, some ducked, and some stood there wondering what the fuss was about with foolish expressions on their faces.

Blackbeard's Ship

Bolts shot from the holes in the walls without a discernible pattern. They hit men caught unawares in the legs and they dropped them to the ground immediately. Henry had a head start and was able to reach the end of the room, along with some others, without incident. Sam took a bolt to the shoulder but kept running. He stopped, started, and watched his step as he tried to reach the far wall. Sam pulled back when a bolt whizzed by his face but another hit him in the thigh. He fell to the ground, clutching his thigh.

"Dammit! Get up, Sam! Everyone, you have to make it to this end where it's safe! Crawl if you have to," Henry yelled.

"What're we gonna do, Henry?" one crewman asked.

Henry glanced at the ropes attached to the ground. He just knew that they were somehow related to stopping the bolts from firing.

"Everyone climb to the top!"

Those who had made it all the way across steeled themselves, turned their backs on their brothers, and climbed the wall. They tried their best to ignore the screams of pain and pleas for help from the ones who could not follow them.

The crew climbing used the uneven stone as handholds and footholds. One man grabbed a raised stone, activating another hidden trap—and before he could react, a pendulum axe swung down and sliced him in two. His body crumpled and fell to the floor in a shower of blood.

"No!" Henry cried as he and the others looked on in helpless horror. They were losing men by the minute, and there seemed to be nothing Henry could do. *No! There must be a way to stop this before anyone else dies!* "Keep moving! If you feel anything move from under you, jump away or fall to the ground."

The men all seemed like they wanted to immediately jump off and not risk going any farther. "Move!" Henry's command impelled them back into action and they began climbing again.

They were climbing a little slower now, but that was proving to be a good thing. The crew checked each handhold and foothold for suspicious cuts in the stone. Once Henry found himself close to a premature end as another pendulum swung down and past him. It thrust into the stone wall, sending small pieces of rock flying everywhere with the force.

Then Henry heard the unmistakable sound of stone rubbing together to his left. He saw the horror in his comrades' eyes.

Not this time!

Time seemed to slow. Henry saw everything stand still, almost as if it were a painting. The crewman's eyes widened as he turned to see the impending doom. Henry reached over and grabbed his hand. The huge pendulum was falling, the razor-sharp axe threatening them both. He yanked the crewman out of its path, and the axe sliced into the rock wall in his place, sending chunks of rock and dirt everywhere. He was holding the crewman by one hand, dangling him in the air. He placed him back on the wall where he could find a foothold again.

How did I do that? Henry stared in amazement at his palm.

"Thanks, Henry. I thought I was a goner."

"Huh? Oh, you're welcome." Henry's eyes darted to the scene below. There were still crewmen trying to crawl to safety. *Now's not the time for questions or pleasantries.* He began his ascent again, carefully avoiding the traps. The climbers were able to make it to the ledge without further incident.

Henry could see nothing up on the ledge suggesting a solution to his dilemma; he had saved some of his men, but how could he help the rest from up here? The two thickly twined ropes he'd seen earlier hung from the ceiling on both ends of the ledge. He followed the rope once more as it snaked its way across the ceiling to the middle of the room, then all the way down the wall, where it was tied to the floor. He rushed to one of the ropes and gripped it in his large hands.

"Half of you take hold of the rope on the right, the other half grab the left one with me!"

They rushed into two lines, knowing exactly what needed to be done. They pulled hard, stretching the ropes taut, but whatever was at the other end was too heavy. They kept pulling and pulling, but nothing moved.

"Come on, you bastard!" Henry let out a grunt, gritted his teeth, and pulled as hard as he could. His muscles bulged from the strain. The rough twine dug into Henry's hand and pulled against his skin, close to drawing blood, but he kept pulling.

The bottom ends of the ropes, attached by iron pegs to what had appeared to be the floor, were actually attached to thin slabs of stone. As the men pulled with all their might, the slab near the left wall moved upward, covering the holes the bolts were firing from. Now that the sheet was moving, it wasn't hard to bring it up the rest of the way and stop the bolts on that side completely.

Now the other side. "Hold on to this side! I'm going to help the others!" Henry held on until the men with him nodded for him to let go. The weight of the stone sheet caused them to skid a little, but they were able to hold on and keep it from sliding all the way down. Henry ran over to the other group. They had moved the slab a few inches, but it seemed to be stuck halfway. Henry's added strength was able to bring it all the way up so the onslaught of bolts was completely stopped.

Henry frowned at the sight of his men who lay wounded in the chamber below. He addressed those who were still strong and mobile. "Help those who are injured back to the ship. We can handle it from here."

The terrible episode had left everyone shaken, but with the immediate danger gone they were able to come back to the here and now.

The crewmates who escaped harm helped their brothers up and carried them back to the entrance of the trap. Their boots crunched the leftover bolts as they walked, and they left pools of blood in their wake.

They'll be safe now. We have to find a way out of here so we can reach the other groups.

On the platform with the ropes there was a large gap in front of them and a drawbridge that somehow needed to be lowered if they were to keep moving. Henry searched everywhere, but he couldn't see any way to lower the drawbridge. They needed to figure out a way of keeping the ropes in place so they could proceed with exploration.

It took Henry a moment for an idea to surface. "Everyone, we can tie these ropes together so we don't have to keep holding onto them. Who's good at knots?"

"I am," Sam said as he pulled himself up with a heave. He was sweating and ragged. The bolts were gone from his shoulder and thigh, but there were two dark red holes and fresh blood running out in their place.

"Sam, what are you doing? You're injured."

Sam laughed. "Maybe this'd stop a child like you, but for me it be a flesh wound. I'm fine. I can tie the knot while you hold it in place."

The two teams pulled the ropes closer together, and they had enough slack to make a knot. Sam tied the ends together, and then the teams released their grip one by one. The now single rope snapped taut at about chest level, held by the iron pegs embedded into the rock, and everyone was free to move.

"I'll send you back to the ship if you are harmed again," threatened Henry.

"I'd like to see you try!" replied Sam.

Henry gestured toward the hoped-for exit. "We have to find a way to release that drawbridge. I don't see any rope holding it in place, so there must be a switch somewhere."

"Henry, what about that over there?" A crewman pointed towards the wall across the lower level where they'd entered.

"What are you talking about? I don't see anything."

"Come over here and look."

Henry walked over to the crewman; everyone else crowded

around them, trying to see in the dim light. By squinting his eyes, Henry could make out something made of wood which, at first glance, appeared to be suspended in the air above the entrance. Upon closer inspection, a ledge protruding from the wall held it in place.

"That must be the way to release the bridge," Sam guessed. His breathing was still heavy and he was holding his shoulder with one hand.

"Yes, but how can we get to it? We don't have any way of securing a rope to the other side."

They all thought it over, but no one was forthcoming with any suggestions.

We need a ladder or something to climb across... Henry glanced around at the room once more. *Wait, we have one of those.* "I can cross by shimmying on the top of the slab we pulled up."

"Are you sure that's safe?"

"Safe or no, it's our only option." Henry walked to the slab without waiting for an answer. He put his back to the wall, stepped onto the stone slab, and inched his way across it, careful not to lose his balance. *This is a lot narrower than I thought.*

"Don't look down," Sam said.

Henry's gaze immediately shifted to the floor below, and he lost his grip on the wall. *Oh God!* The weightless feeling hit his ears. He pushed with his toes and brought his balance back.

Sam exhaled. "I told you not to do that, you git."

Henry closed his eyes for a second and let out a sigh. "Well I wouldn't have if you hadn't mentioned it! Shut it, all right?"

Henry's body was rigid and his breathing rapid. He took his time, but no matter where he directed his gaze he could still see some of the floor. It was making him sick. His hands were against the wall, gripping with as much friction as it would allow. Then he reached the centre of the slab where the rope was attached.

I'm at the halfway point. Good. Good. I can do this.

He grabbed onto the rope and turned himself around so he could maneuver around it. He lifted one foot over and onto the other side of the rope, straddling the twine now, and he could hear some of the crew gasp. He put his other foot over and it slipped with an unmistakable scraping noise. He fell. A collective yell echoed from the crew. Henry tightened his grip on the rope still in his one hand. It burned as he fell to the top of the slab. That one last tug on his arm almost cost him his grip, but he didn't let go.

Henry was dangling in the air, and the only thing between him and death was a few fingers and a thumb. His body had twisted and contorted with the fall. He hung against the slab facing outward, and could see the crew yelling for him to climb back up, as well as the high drop right in front of him.

His eyes went wide. He turned himself around and caught his breath before reaching up and placing his right hand on the top of the stone slab. He pulled himself up, and with his left hand grabbed higher up on the rope. He inched his way back up to the top until he had both feet safely back on that small ledge of stone.

He let himself have a minute to steady his breathing. The crew had gone silent now. When his heart finally stopped pounding in his ears, Henry continued his trek across the stone slab. He reached the other side without further incident, and finally stepped over to the ledge with the lever. He took another few seconds to rest before walking over to the contraption.

Henry gripped the large wooden stick in both hands and pulled it with all his strength. It worked as expected—but as the draw-bridge began to lower, two large pendulum axes dropped out of nowhere and onto the ropes holding the slabs. One of them sliced through the rope, but the other jammed in place, almost suspended in the air. The slab Henry had walked across shot down to the ground from the rope being cut, uncovering the wall and allowing the bolts to fire once more. The other slab stopped partway.

The knot they had made caused the rope to stop in its place, but it was almost to the bottom of the floor. Henry couldn't jump to it, nor move back to the other side. "You need to pull the rope back so I can get across."

The crew's eyes went from him to the rope, and then the jammed axe ready to fall at a moment's notice. With obvious trepidation, they gripped the rope and began to pull it back as far as they could.

The second axe hovered overhead, seeming to shake a little, as if with the slightest nudge or breeze it could fall.

"You have to hurry, Henry. That axe will drop any minute!"

Without further deliberation, Henry ran to the stone slab. He moved onto it and shuffled across, his mind empty of all thoughts and focused solely on making it to the other side in one piece.

Pendulum axes began appearing out of nowhere. One of them slammed into the wall to Henry's left, inches away from him. One after the other they fell, intent on killing him. Henry was moving as fast as he could, but they kept falling faster and faster.

He reached the halfway point. *Almost there. I'm almost there, dammit!*

Henry tripped again. He fell off the slab with no rope to hold onto this time. Everyone watched in shock and terror. Henry reached out and grabbed the ledge, arresting his fall.

"Get up, Henry!" Sam yelled.

I can't die here. Not now! Ed still needs me.

Henry put his other hand on the stone slab and pulled himself up. After his back was against the wall again, an axe descended and slammed down inches from his fingers. His feet moved of their own volition. He was nearing the end, but the axe that had stopped in midair fell again, heading straight for the rope the crew was holding onto, the same rope keeping him alive.

No time for prancing about!

Henry bent down and leapt into the air. The rope was cut at the same time and the slab fell with a thud. Henry landed on the ledge with the other crewmembers. He had one foot on the edge, and the other in the air. As he tried to place the other foot down he fell backwards. Henry was flinging his arms wildly as he tilted backwards over the ledge to certain doom, when a dozen arms caught his and pulled him to safety.

When he was safely back on the ledge with them, the crew let out a collective sigh of relief. Sam even smiled.

"Nice work, First Mate," Sam said, this time without sarcasm.

"You weren't so bad yourself."

The crew's gaze returned to the floor below. The dead crewmembers they had been unable to save still littered the rocky ground along with the multitude of bolts which caught them.

I hope the other groups had an easier time than us… I hope Edward is safe.

Henry and the others crossed the drawbridge and headed, once again, into unknown territory.

13. THE WEIGHT AND THE CHEST

John, Frederick, and their men entered a cave and immediately found themselves in a narrow, spiraling corridor. The walk was endless, the cramped corridor was oppressive, and one crewman in particular was becoming quite agitated.

"What the hell is this anyway? Why we be goin' in this blubberin' cave? We be pirates. Why ain't we attackin' ships and pillagin'?" Kenneth Locke yelled in his thick cockney accent.

Kenneth and his friends were, as usual, making trouble, and made a miserable situation more uncomfortable for everyone.

"I can't believe him!" Frederick shook his head. "The captain has saved our lives, and this is what he thinks about what we're doing? He sounds more like a common thief."

"Well, we are pirates, after all, or at least that was how it was sold when we were looking for crew in Port Royal. He does have a point," John replied.

"Yea, but he makes it seem like it's something we *should* be doing. Edward hasn't actively attacked anyone. We've only defended ourselves."

"And broken the law in doing so."

"Are you agreeing with him or disagreeing, John?"

"Neither. We've all been branded pirates whether we like it or not. We must become accustomed to taking what we can to live. But that doesn't mean you have to listen to that fool prattle on. Ignore him."

"All right, I'll try. I just can't stand him."

John and Frederick decided to push farther ahead so they wouldn't have to listen to Kenneth anymore. Soon they reached the end of the spiraling corridor and emerged into a small room containing a statue on a pedestal, and a hallway on either side.

"What is this?" Frederick asked no one in particular.

"This must be the trial the riddle talked about."

John walked to the statue. It was a figure of a ship, a frigate very similar to the *Freedom*, carved in precise detail. The bow was tipped upwards, and behind it was a set of scales built into the stone. Like the ship, the right side of the scale was tipped high in the air. John could see engraved words in the stone pedestal below the ship and scales, which he read aloud.

"The eight pieces of the Spanish pride bring balance to the

scales and reveal the true path." John reached into his pocket and pulled out a few coins and placed them on the right side of the scale. The scale tipped down and the ship's bow moved down in tandem with it. The bow was now pointed down and the stern raised high in the air, but nothing more happened. "I need five more pieces of eight."

"What for, John?" Frederick asked as he pulled a few coins out of his pocket and handed them to him.

"I'm trying to balance the scales, and the message on the bottom calls for eight pieces of eight. I need two more." John turned to the group gathered behind him. "D-does anyone else have any?"

No one responded; they only stared at John and Frederick with curious looks.

Frederick decided to provide an ultimatum. "Whatever this is, it's probably important. The sooner you give John the two pieces of eight, the sooner we can move on. He'll return them after."

Two men each pulled out a coin and handed them to John. He took the coins and put them on the scales. He tried various combinations of the coins on either side, but nothing worked; no matter how he distributed the weight, the scales never balanced. Halfway through his attempts, the rest of the crew emerged from the spiral walkway, including Kenneth.

"Hurry up, old man. I'm bored here," Kenneth said.

"I'm tr-trying," John stammered.

"Shut it, Kenneth," Frederick retaliated. "I don't see you contributing." Kenneth made a defiant sound and then walked down the left corridor alone. "What does it mean? You've tried everything."

"I think it means we're using the wrong pieces."

"But how? It's standard currency."

"Yes, but these must be sensitive scales that need to be balanced with precise weight. There must be pieces of eight scattered about in this room."

A thunderous crash from the left corridor shook the room.

"What was that?" Frederick yelled as he ran in the direction of the noise.

Around the corner they saw Kenneth sitting on the floor nursing his elbow. In front of him was a large square slab of stone, studded with spikes thrust into the ground.

"W-What happened?"

The other crewmembers tried to help Kenneth up, but he shoved them away. "The damn place is alive an' tryin' ta kill me."

"You must have done something to trigger it. What did you touch?" Frederick questioned.

"I ain't touched nothin', you git! Nothin' that don't be worth takin', anyway."

Frederick, bigger and more aggressive than John, picked Kenneth up off the ground and slammed him against the wall. "What did you take, Kenneth?"

"Get offa me, you little tosspot." He struggled and squirmed, but couldn't escape. "Fine! I took a single piece of eight, all right? It was jus' lyin' there on a rock sayin 'take me please.' Whut's wrong with that?"

"What's wrong is we need that coin to leave, and you could have died, or worse, hurt someone else with your recklessness." Frederick let Kenneth down. "Now give me the piece of eight."

Kenneth spat on the ground before submitting and handed the piece of eight over. Frederick pulled a pouch from his side pocket, emptied its contents, deposited the coin Kenneth found, and passed the bag to John.

"We need to locate seven more pieces of eight like this one in this room. Obviously, they are guarded by traps, so be careful. If you find one, return to the statue and scale and give the coin to John. Understood?" Everyone nodded. "All right now, split up."

"Thanks to you, Frederick. I'm terrible at speaking in public."

"No problem. I guess that's something you and the kid share in common. He's better, certainly, but he still needs a kick."

"I'm always so nervous, especially around p-people like that. You'd think I would be more used to public speaking than to bullets… At least all those years in service weren't entirely wasted."

Frederick laughed. "You'll be used to it soon. Wait here, John. I'll be back after I help the others."

As the crew went about the search, they began to realise the whole room was a maze. The tall stone walls, straight and plentiful, seemed to have no discernible direction to them. There were hallways that led nowhere, and turns that went to dead ends. Everyone lost their way at one point, traversing places previously visited and already explored. And then there were the traps. Each one was designed in such a way that one needed excellent reflexes to avoid them, and few were left untriggered.

Frederick spotted a piece of eight at the end of a corridor and was about to walk to it when he stopped himself. It occurred to him to examine the floor, and sure enough, it was dotted with raised sections. They were distributed in a pattern, however, and once Frederick realised this he was able to step in the safe zones and grab the coin.

Luckily, no one was hurt too badly by the traps, and in no time they had found seven out of eight of the coins. They had one left to locate.

Kenneth was sauntering around the maze, but wasn't checking

where he was going despite the fact that he almost died earlier.

"Stupid git Frederick thinks he can boss me around. I'll show 'im and Edward who the real pirate is."

Full of smug swagger, he turned a corner and saw a sight most pirates could only dream about. It was a medium-sized chest filled with about one hundred gold pieces. Without wasting a moment on common sense, he bent over the chest and ran his fingers through his treasure.

Kenneth cackled with glee. "With all this gold I could buy my own ship, maybe two!"

Kenneth dug in and tried to remove a handful of coins, but before he could clear his hand of the chest, the lid closed on his wrist. With a clicking noise, the chest was locked on his hand. No matter how he tried he couldn't move the small chest or open the lid. His hand was stuck in the chest's belly with the golden coins tickling his fingers and taunting him for his greed.

"Dammit! Someone help me! I need help," he pleaded.

The crew heard him screaming and followed it to his location. He was digging at the seam of the chest, trying to open it again, but he was only making himself tired.

Frederick watched him for a moment. "What did you do this time?"

"I reached into this chest and the blasted thing locked on me arm."

Frederick laughed and the others with him joined in. "We warned you about the traps, you even triggered the first one, and now you have a chest stuck on your hand. Maybe we should leave it on you and teach you a lesson."

"Dammit, Frederick, stop flappin' about and help me!"

"Yea, yea, I'll help you. No need to throw a fit." Frederick walked closer until he noticed the last piece of eight on a rock pedestal beside the chest. He grabbed it and handed it to another crewmember. "Take this back to John. I'll be fine here."

The crew obliged and left the two of them alone.

Frederick examined the chest. "I don't see anything that will open the chest at the moment, so let's focus on removing the chest from this pedestal."

"Hurry it up. I ain't got all day."

"Would you rather I leave you here? Shut it while I work," Frederick said as he searched. "...Actually, since you not talking is a long shot, why don't you tell me why you have such a poor attitude? Even I know when to let go."

"He ain't nothin' special. I be movin' up in the world. The first chance I get ta jump ship I'm takin' it. I be the captain then. Now hurry up and pull this off me!"

They heard a loud sound like rocks moving, and the ground trembled. After a few seconds, the noise was gone and the ground stopped shaking.

"John must have solved the puzzle. And I think I found the release mechanism for this. I... just... have to... reach it." Frederick pushed a panel at the base of the pedestal holding the chest, and Kenneth was able to lift the chest off, which was a start. But when the panel was pushed, it triggered something else. Rocks shifted on the walls around them and small holes appeared. Kenneth realised they had set off a trap, but Frederick was just standing up and didn't notice. Kenneth acted on instinct and pulled Frederick around, using him as a shield.

Bolts fired from the holes. Three of them hit Frederick while Kenneth hid behind him. The bolts stopped firing, and Frederick fell to the floor with a thud.

The other crewmembers, hearing the commotion, rushed over. John went to Frederick and turned over his limp body. Warm blood still flowed from where the bolts hit.

John pulled his friend close and held him for a moment, feeling the heat still radiating from him but knowing it was too late.

"He's dead," John said, his voice sure but hollow.

14. THE FIFTH ISLAND

Edward and his group entered a long hallway after they finished their fight with the rapids. The hallway was dark save for a few torches they found and lit. Seawater dripped into the hallway from above, falling into small pools. The acrid smell of burning oil and rags and stagnant water filled the hallway as they walked.

Edward walked ahead of everyone else. The crew followed him, hurrying to catch up. Anne wanted to say something, but Edward's stern expression made her keep her silence.

Edward was numb from the pain of the icy water and his shoulder, but there was a dull throbbing at the back of his eyes. He clenched his teeth to push it away, but the pain returned whenever he thought on the dead crewmates they had had to leave behind.

At the end of the hallway stood a pedestal with a key resting on top of it and a door beyond. Edward picked up the key and examined it. *This must be for the chest mentioned on the paper.* He walked to the door and placed his hand on the knob. His hand was shaking, and he stood fixed in place for a moment.

Anne walked up behind Edward and whispered, "What is wrong?" The rest of his men were scattered behind him, according him distance.

"Nothing." Edward looked back at the crew. "What are they doing?"

"I think they know how you are feeling right now. They are concerned. *I* am concerned."

"They don't know how I feel," Edward snapped. "No one does. No one is thinking ahead. I could walk through this door and find out…" Edward paused and shook his head. "Find out Henry died." Edward's voice turned soft. "I don't know if I can face that."

"Then let us face it together, Edward." Anne placed her hand on the door handle and waited.

Edward gazed into her green eyes, and he too placed his hand, no longer shaking, on the doorknob, on top of hers. They turned the knob together and opened the door.

What it revealed made them gasp.

"How… How is this possible?" Anne stammered as she took in the sight with wide eyes.

Blackbeard's Ship

In the centre of the room beyond the door there was an island with a large stone pyramid in the middle. Water was pouring in from the ceiling and into a moat between where Edward's group was and the island. The water wasn't high enough to swim across, so from what Edward could see there was no way across. To the left and right of the room there were wooden doors and alcoves similar to the one they entered through. He thought that they would be the exits for the other groups of the crew.

"Why could we not see this when we were above?" Anne asked to no one in particular.

"It must be a trick of the eyes. At a higher angle it blends with the rest of the water. That's why we couldn't see the water pouring in, or the opening," Edward said.

"Yes, but who built this place? All this for some treasure? It must have taken years..." Anne trailed off in thought.

Before she could continue, they heard a noise from the left side of the large room. Another door opened up, and William's group walked through. Edward could see he was holding something in his hand. *Another key...?* He and his men were awestruck by the scene and did not see their friends right away. "William!" Edward yelled.

William, Alexandre, and his group all turned to the noise, and when they saw their captain they let out a cheer. William, seeing Anne, looked relieved.

The cheers went on for a few moments until Edward noticed John and his group entering through the door to his right, opposite William's group. John's face was downcast until he saw Edward and his other crewmates.

I guess everyone had it hard. We'll have to hear about what they went through later. For now, we have to find a way across.

Edward was walking to the edge of the bluff to see if there was a way across when the ground began shaking. He instinctively backed up and the tremors stopped. The other groups were searching as well and seemed just as dumbfounded. *Was that me?* He inspected where he had been standing and noticed something odd.

A small circular piece of rock protruded above the rest of the stone. Edward placed his foot on it again, and the shaking started again, but this time he held his foot in place. A slab of rock slid out from underneath the bluff the crew was standing on. *So this is the way across!* No sooner did Edward think that than the slab stopped moving about one quarter of the way across the moat. He took his foot off the stone but it did not spring back. He tried tapping it again, but nothing happened.

The other two groups noticed what he was doing and searched

the ground in front of them. They each found the pressure plates in their respective areas and pushed them down. The slab resumed its movement as they kept their feet in place, reached a point three-quarters of the way to the island, and again stopped.

That leaves one group.

Everyone stood watching and waiting for a few seconds. Then the ground shook, and the slab moved the rest of the distance across the water. Edward's face beamed at the sight. It meant Henry's group was there.

That bastard had better not be dead.

Everyone crossed the stone bridges to the island. The sun became more intense as it shone in from above. When they had all gathered at the base of the pyramid, Edward motioned to John and William, who both climbed the stairs. Before Edward joined them, he had Alexandre examine his arm.

"So how was the trial with your group?" Edward asked.

"*Il était amende,*" Alexandre said as he surveyed the arm. "This is simply dislocated." He tugged Edward's arm hard and it snapped back into place.

Edward jerked his arm away and rubbed it with his good hand. "Ah! That hurt, you blasted Frenchman!"

"You are welcome."

Edward tested his arm and properly thanked Alexandre before climbing up the pyramid. There were four sides to it, with one set of stairs for each of the leaders with keys. When they reached the top, Henry was right there with them, and they were all holding keys.

Edward let out a sigh of relief upon seeing Henry. "I'm glad everyone is all right. Did anyone suffer any casualties?" The others lowered their eyes in shame. Edward knew the answer without needing words. He too hung his head in shame and guilt over the losses.

"Let's focus on leaving, Ed," Henry offered. "We must worry about the living before we can honour the dead."

"Yes," Edward agreed as he shook his head as if to cast the guilt away for a moment.

At the apex of the pyramid, a chest sat on a pedestal, and it had four keyholes. The others nodded to Edward in confirmation, and they all inserted their keys in the locks. They turned them at the same time and heard a click. Edward slowly lifted the lid.

To their surprise, the chest contained another key, a sheet of parchment, and four gold coins. Edward took out the parchment and read it aloud. "Congratulations on surviving the trials. This key is a gift from me to you. It will open the door to a part of your ship. There you will find the details of the next challenge you must face in order to open the other parts of the ship. Good luck." Edward crumpled the parchment and threw it down with a huff. "More trials!"

"Well it's not all a loss." Henry reached into the chest and pulled out the gold coins.

Edward smiled. "Those will come in handy. John, you take care of those. Let's take the chest too; I'm sure we'll find a use for it."

Henry put the gold back in the chest, then John closed the lid and lifted the chest off the pedestal. No sooner had the chest been lifted than the ground began to quake violently beneath their feet. They almost lost their balance and had to hold on to the pedestal to keep from being thrown off the pyramid.

"What's happening?" Henry yelled over the rumbling.

"How am I supposed to know?" Edward exclaimed with a curse.

Edward could tell they were moving up. He thought back to the words of the riddle: '*The belly of the fifth.*'

The whole pyramid, and the island which held it, was rising above the level of the ocean water. After a few moments they were able to see the *Freedom* and the rest of their crew. The crew on the ship pressed against the railing, watching the spectacle unfold before their eyes.

With the island above the water now, the crew turned the *Freedom* around and docked it at the newly surfaced fifth island. They threw rope ladders down for everyone to climb up, and one by one the adventurers stepped onto the deck of the ship that was their home. The trials were over, and the crew was glad to return to the world of wood and rope and sail they were used to.

Edward stood on the deck, scanning the water and the islands, finally settling on the fifth. His eyes drifted to the key he had gained. Despite the hardship and the loss, he hoped it had been worth the trouble. No amount of gold could replace his lost men, but it could bring some help to their families.

He tested the key on the aft cabin, below the quarterdeck and the wheel, but it didn't work. Then he tried the fore cabin. The key turned with a click, and Edward smiled as he pushed open the door. The other crewmembers realised what was happening and followed him into the room whose contents no one had seen.

It was a spacious cabin that seemed to be used for weapons storage. Barrels were stocked with rifles of the highest quality. There were swords, too, each well crafted and razor sharp. But most impressive were the cannons: three decent-sized twelve-pounders that would enable them to attack from the front first, then the sides as they passed a ship.

This will be a good spot to hold meetings from now on.

Edward noticed a piece of paper affixed to the mast pole coming down through the centre of the room. He picked it up and read: "The jungle holds the next key. May this map be your guide to the captain's trial. Look at it with eyes clouded by a pirate's home. Know this: Only the captain may enter, and only the captain may leave." A map was drawn beneath the writing, which represented nothing Edward could recognise. It seemed to show a few landmarks, but nothing significant, and nothing was marked save an X in the middle of the jungle area. *I guess I'll have Herbert examine this later.*

Edward walked out of the foredeck cabin and motioned to everyone on board. "Prepare to set sail. Officers, follow me. We're having a meeting."

15. THE LOST AND THE LEFT BEHIND

"Frederick died?" The news floored Edward. The deaths of the other crewmembers had hit him hard enough, but this was something else entirely. Edward had known him from their hometown. "I cannot believe it. What happened?" he asked.

"He d-died because of a trap. I told one crewman to take his body back while we were in the fifth island. I was so angry with Kenneth after…" John clenched his teeth and fist together.

"Why were you angry with Kenneth? What did he do?"

"Oh, uh… sorry, Captain. It's p-probably best I not tell you."

"I have a right to know, John."

John recounted in detail what had happened: how Frederick had helped Kenneth, and then he used Frederick as a shield, and had the gall to brag about it afterwards. As Edward listened his expression changed from sorrow to rage. Before the tale was complete, Edward stood, grabbed one of the new swords, and rushed out the door.

"C-Captain! Stop!" John yelled, but Edward kept going.

"Kenneth Locke! Where are you?!" Edward screamed to everyone on deck, which made them all turn and stare.

"Ed, you need to stop. Killing him won't solve anything," Henry pleaded, but Edward wasn't listening.

"Kenneth! Your captain requests your presence immediately."

"Edward, this isn't like you. You can't kill one of your own crewmembers."

"Watch me," Edward shot back over his shoulder. Kenneth now approached him. "I heard what you did to Frederick."

"Whut of it? He be dead now, so whut does it matter?"

Edward gritted his teeth together, grinding them as anger washed over him. He thrust the cutlass at Kenneth.

Kenneth jumped out of the way and one of his friends tossed him a sword. Now it was a duel. The medium-sized chest filled with gold was still on his good hand, weighing him down and forcing him to use his left for the cutlass.

They circled each other and the crew gathered around, chanting for blood. Edward swiped and slashed at Kenneth, who was struggling to dodge. Using his off hand and having the other slowing him down was making him more of a target than usual, but Edward's lack of experience made the fight equal.

They clashed swords, and the clang of metal resounded over the hollering from the men around them. Blow after blow was tiring Kenneth, but Edward was still fresh, his anger driving his blade. At times Edward wielded the sword like a club in both hands; it was enough to overpower any man given his size and strength. A last mighty bash from him struck the sword from Kenneth's hand and sent it flying. The tip of the blade pierced the deck with a loud thunk.

Edward pointed his blade just underneath Kenneth's throat. He pushed Kenneth with the sword until they reached the edge of the deck.

Both fighters were sweating and taking in ragged breaths. "Now jump," Edward said, motioning the direction with his chin.

Kenneth was stunned. "Whut? Ye can't be serious!"

"Oh, I am." Edward raised his voice so the whole crew could hear him. "On this ship, we do not use another crewmember's life as a tool to save our own. What you did to Fredrick was a disgrace beyond reckoning. I banish you from my ship. You are no longer of my crew. Now jump before I cut you open. At least on this island you will have a slight chance of survival. It's more than you deserve."

Kenneth turned and placed his hand on the railing, but didn't climb up. He stood there, staring at the beach, for a few seconds. Then he whirled around and went on the attack.

Kenneth used the chest on his hand like a club, swinging it at Edward and at the sword in his hands. Edward jumped back and Kenneth kept swinging, but the chest was too heavy and unwieldy; Edward was able to dodge the blows by taking a few steps out of the way. Kenneth grabbed the chest in both hands, raised it over his head, and brought it down with all his might and a guttural scream. It missed Edward again and hit the ship, breaking a plank in two.

"I be a better captain than you!" Kenneth shouted. "Look who ya got on yer crew. A Negro and a cripple? What a joke." Kenneth was panting. The fight was taking its toll. "This is a pirate ship, ain't it? You're soft. You can never be a true captain. They will chase you and you will break. Because you're weak!" Kenneth took another swing, but Henry and William intervened and grabbed him.

"Throw him overboard," said Edward coldly.

Kenneth thrashed and writhed, trying to escape William's grip, but his strength was ebbing. He shouted obscenities and insults to Edward again and again as Henry and William threw him overboard and he fell to the sandy beach below. The crew could still hear his shouts when Edward addressed them. "If anyone has any objection to my decision, you can join him; otherwise, know this: I am the captain of this ship, and my word is law. If you disrespect me, or another crewmember, you will be dealt with appropriately. Understood?"

The crew gave a resounding "Aye, Captain!" in response.

"Now set sail. We're heading for Jamaica."

Everyone set to work, and Herbert steered the ship. No one talked to the captain for the rest of the day.

"We are gathered to pay respects to our honourable dead."

Edward was on the quarterdeck delivering a eulogy to the crew. They all stood with rapt attention. In front of them was the only body they could bring back: Frederick's. All the others were either lost to the depths or too marred for viewing. He had been cleaned and his clothes changed.

The moon reflected on the waves. A cool breeze blew over the ship. Henry was standing behind Edward with a lamp; other lanterns were scattered throughout the ship.

"Although they are no longer with us, they will remain in our hearts. Their sacrifice will not be forgotten. They were our crewmates, but they were also our friends, our family on this: our ship, our home."

Henry, John, and William had all offered to say the eulogy instead of Edward because of his nervousness, but he had told them it was his duty. He had written it himself, and had practiced to make sure he didn't make any mistakes.

"They, like us, had dreams, ambitions, families, and friends. They, unlike us, had their dreams and ambitions cut short, and now they cannot care for their families. It is our duty, as their crewmates and their friends, to take on their dreams and ambitions, and to care for their families in their place."

Edward scanned the crew. Some appeared in a fog, staring out at nothing, some at Frederick's body, and others intently at him. Over the months they had been living, working, and fighting together they had indeed become like a family, and they all felt the pain of this loss. Edward knew this, but he still felt alone in its sting.

"Do you, as crewmates, as friends, as family, agree to take on these responsibilities?"

They all replied with a firm "Aye."

"Then may they rest in peace, knowing no more worries."

Edward nodded to four crewmembers stationed near the ladders at either side. They trudged with heavy feet to Frederick's body, picked it up off the deck, carried it to the starboard side and placed it in a small boat. They lowered the boat to the water, threw a lighted torch into it, and let the current take it away. It drifted down the broadside, so everyone was able to see the burning pyre.

"Fire!" Edward commanded.

Select crewmembers stationed at the sides fired rifles three times into the air. The noise boomed then faded after each shot, and by the third shot the current had taken the boat a hundred feet off the fore.

With that, the ceremony was complete, and Edward dismissed the crew. He went to the fore cabin and stared out the windows to the shifting seas and the small boat on fire as it drifted away. A minute later, the door opened.

"I'd like to be left alone, if you don't mind," Edward said, without turning to see who it was.

"I wished to see if you were well."

Edward recognised the voice. "Sorry, Anne. I'm tired."

"I'll leave if it please you, but I have something to say first, if that is all right?"

Edward nodded.

"I do not claim to know how close you were with Frederick, but I do know you cared for him, like you care for the others aboard the *Freedom*. You are closer to everyone because of the past months, but right now you are shutting yourself off from your friends."

"Then what am I supposed to do, Anne? Those men died because of me. Maybe Kenneth was right. I am weak."

Anne walked up to Edward and slapped him. Before he could say anything, she wrapped her arms around him and pulled him into an embrace. Edward slowly pulled his arms up and gripped her tight as tears fell down his cheeks.

They stood there together as Edward let himself feel the pain he was so desperately trying to bottle up inside.

"It will be all right," Anne whispered.

And Edward knew it would.

16. THE MUSICIAN'S INCIDENT

Herbert examined the map left in the aft deck again and again, but he couldn't find anything on the ship's maps matching the location on the paper.

When Edward asked him how his search was faring, he answered first with a sigh and then rubbed his eyes. "I'm sorry, Captain. I must take a break, if it please you. I'm sure I'll be able to find out where it is someday soon."

Edward placed his hand on Herbert's shoulder. "It's all right, Herbert. I'm certain you'll solve the riddle in time. Take us into the nearest port for now. I think we all need a break after what we just went through."

"Negril is close, we should be there within the hour if the wind keeps in our favour."

Before the *Freedom* reached Negril, the crew made sure to put all weapons other than the cannons in the fore cabin. If anyone asked, the crew could say they were for defense. As it happened, the arrival of their strange frigate and its motley crew appeared to arouse little curiosity or concern.

"Perhaps this port will provide us with a little relaxation," Edward hoped aloud.

"After all we've been through, I think we well deserve it," said Henry. "How long are we to stay?"

"A fortnight should suffice. The men can have their fun, and maybe by that time Herbert will have figured out where the map is directing us. If not, we can move on. We can't risk staying at one port for too long. Not with Captain Smith still on our heels."

Henry cocked his brow and looked taken aback. "We haven't seen him in so long! What makes you think he's still after us?"

"Just… a feeling. It feels as though we're merely one step ahead of him, and any moment he'll be on us."

"You say some odd things, Ed."

"Shut up, you tosspot." He punched Henry in the arm and he smiled.

"So Captain, what will you do for your leave?" Henry asked.

"I haven't the foggiest. Inspect the local market, I suppose. I should like to buy a few things with the gold we found on the two by two islands. What about you?"

Henry waved his hand. "I'm not sure what we should be doing."

"What do you mean?"

"Well, what do we do on our off time? Back home we had jobs, then the bluff."

"How about we have an honest drink this time? ... Mostly honest."

"No more stealing my dad's rum?"

Edward laughed. "Not this time, I'm afraid."

And so Edward, on the first day, oversaw the loading of the supplies John brought in. Food made up the bulk of the supplies, including plenty of fresh lemons and limes, but some necessary gunpowder and bullets as well. The four gold pieces went a long way, so half of the remainder went into a common stock for later, and the other half was divided amongst the crew.

After that, Edward went to the local market and bought a few things for himself. He found some nice local produce he couldn't pass up, and decided he would cook it that night. He also found a nautical supply shop with everything imaginable for a sailor. He decided to buy a star chart and a guide for using it. He supposed it might be useful.

That night Edward cooked up the produce he'd bought at the market for the crew who'd stuck around, including Henry. It was a simple dish, but far different from their standard rations. He packed it full of vegetables and a little meat.

The crew sat in the sparce dining tables near the stern. The ship, resting at anchor, rolled gently with the waves. The smell of the stew and the pine evoked a feeling of being outdoors. This was their home, and it felt right eating here rather than in town.

"You astonish me, Captain," one crewman exclaimed. "This is bloody good!"

"I agree, Ed. Nice job. Where did you learn how to cook?" Henry asked.

Edward turned his head, a confused look on his face. "I never told you?" Henry shook his head. "Oh... Well, the Hugheses always had me buy the food and cook for them. I bought spices, but I only used them on my own food. Over the years I've gotten pretty good."

"I guess the captain's a pirate from birth," another crewmember joked, drawing laughs from the crowd.

They ate and joked and told stories for a few hours. In that place, they were free to talk and act as they wished without fear of being overheard.

After dinner, Edward and Henry went out as planned and had some drinks at a local bar. Jack was there as well—and just getting started, by the state of him.

Edward thought he would end up watching over Jack, but it

turned out they *all* needed someone to chaperone them. After a few drinking games, Edward was running all over the place like a madman. When Jack entered his singing phase, Edward, Henry and the whole bar joined in. Everything went well until someone bumped into Henry, and Henry in his drunken stupor took it as a slight. He immediately started a fight, which escalated until the whole bar became one huge brawl.

If Jack was good at anything while drunk, it was fighting and running away. He deftly fought four men by himself, jumping over tables, smashing chairs over backs, and throwing bottles—empty ones, of course—into faces. After that, he grabbed Henry and Edward and ran out the door. They made their way back to the *Freedom* in record time.

The next day they woke up on the hard wooden deck. As Edward regained consciousness, he felt the subtle rocking and shaking of the boat inside his stomach, and he immediately ran to the side railing to let out all he had drunk and eaten the night before.

Henry was quick to join him.

"Have a good night, boys?" Jack questioned, as chipper as ever.

"Oh yes, it was jolly until about five minutes ago."

Edward turned and slid to the floor, the railing bracing his back. "I'm never drinking again."

Jack laughed. "All men have uttered those words, but all men return to the drink. Here," he said, handing them cups filled with something dark neither of them recognised.

"What is this? It smells rotten."

Jack sat down with both of them. The morning sun bestowed a bit of heat, but the salty breeze kept them cool. "Rotten? It's coffee, lads. Have you never had coffee? It's been around for centuries, but it's only just starting to make its way across the world."

Edward and Henry took small sips of it and turned their heads in disgust. "It's so bitter! How can you drink this?"

"It does well for waking yourself up in the morning, and ridding yourself of the after-effects of certain indulgences. You grow accustomed to the bitterness."

"Whatever you say," Henry said as he stared into the blackness of the cup with a cringe.

"I discovered it in England back in my younger days. They used to sell it in bars I frequented. While I quit one addiction after another, I've always stuck with the coffee." Jack tipped his cup and guzzled some down. "It goes well with some opium, though I'm of the notion many would claim opium goes with anything."

The word "younger" struck Edward and it dawned on him how different in age they were. Jack was well into his thirties, maybe even early forties. If he had any children, they could almost be as old as

Ochi or Christina, or even Edward.

"Did you quit the opium?" Henry asked while taking sips of the hot beverage.

Jack laughed and peered deep into the black coffee. "Yes, none in this cup, I swear it. I suppose I replaced the opium with two addictions back then. I met a girl, as the story usually goes. She wouldn't have anything to do with a bum like me, but I was smitten. I stopped going to the bars, and maintained a steady job as a musician. I saved my money and persisted. Eventually I won her heart, or at least made her acquiesce to my constant advances." They all chuckled. "Those were the best times of my life." Jack finished his coffee and rose.

"Wait, what happened then?"

Jack frowned, grief filling his eyes for a moment, but then forced a smile. "A story for another day, perhaps. I have business I must attend to. By your leave, Captain?" Edward nodded and Jack left the ship.

"I wonder what happened."

Edward thought back to the time he was on deck late at night listening to the tearful songs Jack sang to himself. "I don't know."

Edward and Henry sat there on the deck and drank the rest of their coffee, wondering what Jack might one day tell them about his love and what had become of her.

⚓ ⚓ ⚓

The next day Edward asked Herbert whether he had made any progress with the map.

"Not yet, Captain. Frankly, I'm stumped. I'm sure it's another trick like the last one, but I have yet to figure it out. I've not upset you, have I?" Herbert asked anxiously. "I'm doing the best I can."

Edward chuckled. "I'm not angry, Herbert. Take your time and ask some of the other crewmembers if they have any ideas. I'm certain you'll work it out in no time. How's your…" Edward looked around to be sure no one was within hearing distance, "…sister, Christina?"

Herbert's anxious look shifted into a smile. "She's doing well. Mostly staying close to me, but she's been enjoying playing with Nassir's boy. They're about the same age too, so it makes things easier."

"That's good to hear. At least they can have a semblance of a normal life."

Before they could continue their conversation, another crewman ran up the steps. "Captain!" He was out of breath and trying to deliver his message through ragged gulps of air.

"Breathe, man, breathe."

The crewman took a few deep breaths and finally was able to say what he wanted to. "It's Jack! He's in trouble."

"Trouble? What kind of trouble?"

"He's been kidnapped!"

"Kidnapped?" Edward repeated, astonished. "What happened?"

"Last night he was taken by some men after losing at a game of cards. He couldn't pay, and they took him. He tried to fight them, but they overpowered him."

"Did you follow them? Do you know where they went?"

"Yes, Captain, I followed them to an abandoned house not too far from here."

"Gather a few people together and tell them to grab some weapons."

"Aye, Captain."

"What are you planning to do?" Herbert asked.

"I'll take him back by force," Edward declared.

There weren't many people on the ship at that moment, but they managed to scrape together five, including the crewman who had followed Jack's captors. They all concealed pistols and knives under their clothes. Edward decided to hide a sword as well, sensing that knives might not suffice.

Whoever these men are, they'll know who they're bloody well dealing with.

When everyone was ready, the crewman led the way to the abandoned and dilapidated house and around to a side entrance he had found. Edward and his men reached the entrance undetected.

Edward was the first to enter. He pulled out his pistol and held it tight as walked through an opening missing a door, cautious not to make a sound. No one was in the room, but he could hear muffled voices. The rest of them followed and took out their weapons.

They had entered the kitchen. Edward followed the voices to the main entrance. Rotted stairs in the centre led to a second floor and there was one doorway, missing the doors, in each corner. Two led back to the kitchen, and the other two, on the other side of the room, led to the living room. The voices were coming from there. Edward and the rest sneaked over to both openings and waited, listening.

"The boss will make sure he collects what you owe us. We know you have friends. Now where are they?"

There was a long pause and then a loud thud and a groan, like someone being punched.

"Answer the question!" a second man yelled.

"They're with yer mum, keepin' her warm." Jack's voice was low and almost forced with pain, but he managed a laugh.

A crack this time. It sounded like something was broken.

That's it, I'm ending this!

Edward jumped from their hiding place and pointed his pistol at one of the two large men beating Jack near to death. "I think you've done quite enough, mates. I'll be taking back my friend."

Behind Edward two crewmen also brandished their weapons. At the second entrance to the living room, the other three with Edward entered and pointed their weapons at the men.

Jack pulled up his heavy head. His mouth was filled with blood that was dripping on the floor. The two large men backed away. When they were at a safe distance, Edward motioned to a couple of crewmembers to help Jack out of the ropes binding him.

"I wouldn't do that if I were you," a cold voice said from Edward's left.

Ten men with guns and swords out entered the room. Edward immediately turned and pointed the gun at them.

The man who had spoken carried no gun. He was tall—not as tall as Edward, but an imposing figure nonetheless. He was a hardened man with a strong-jawed but ugly face.

"My name is Luke. That man owes me money for a game he played against my boys here. It's not worth dying over, gents. Lower your weapons and we can make a deal."

Edward didn't lower his gun in the slightest. "The one deal I'll agree to is the release of my friend."

"And all I'll settle for is what's owed to me. I think the way forward is clear."

Edward glanced around the room. Edward and his crew were outnumbered two to one. Edward lowered his gun and the other crewmembers followed suit. "How much does he owe?"

"Five hundred piece of eight."

Damn. How much did you bet, Jack? "I'll need time to gather the money."

Luke placed his hand under his chin in thought. "You have one week."

One week? How are we to scrape together that much so quickly? "All right, one week. But, you must promise to keep your thugs away from him. I need Jack alive and well."

"Agreed." The man stepped forward and put out his hand. "Gentlemen make a deal with a handshake."

Edward stepped forward and returned the handshake. "You'd better not break the agreement, or else." Edward stared Luke down and he could almost see the sweat on his face. He turned and went back to Jack. "Jack, how are you?"

"Been better," Jack drawled, blood dripping from his puffy lip.

"Don't worry, we'll be back to pay your debt and bring you back to the *Freedom*."

Tears fell from Jack's face. "I don't deserve it… You should leave me… I'm not worth it. I failed as a husband. I failed as a father. I couldn't protect them. What do you even need me for? I only play music, and then this happens. Leave me behind…"

Edward shook the man's shoulders. "Jack… shut it." He let the silence linger for a minute in the air as he stared into Jack's bloody red eyes. "Stay strong."

"Aye," Jack sputtered.

Edward motioned to his companions and they backed out while staring down the thugs. "See you in a week, Luke."

Edward and his five men left the house and started walking back to the ship until Henry and Sam ran up to them.

"Edward, we heard what happened. Where's Jack?" Henry asked, glancing about.

"Some thugs are holding Jack ransom because of a bad bet he made," Edward explained.

"Well, what're we waitin' for? Let's get in there and bust some heads!" Sam yelled.

Edward grabbed Sam's arm before he could run off. "We can't. They have twelve armed men, and we can't risk Jack's life. We agreed to pay his debt, and we have a week to gather the money."

Henry ran his fingers through his straight brown hair and let out a sigh. "Edward, we have another problem," he said in his sing-songy Welsh accent. "There's a marine ship approaching. It's an hour away, maybe two at most."

Edward pulled out a spyglass and scanned the horizon until he noticed the ship approaching. *Dad damn it!*

Edward paced up and down the street. The crew watched as he circled around a few times, looking at the ground as if it would provide him with answers. He stopped and shook his head, his wavy black hair swaying back and forth.

"Ready your weapons. We're rescuing Jack now," Edward commanded as he turned away from shore to head back to the house.

"Wait, Ed, I thought you just said you made a deal with them. And aren't we outnumbered?" Henry asked.

"The deal is off. We don't have enough money or enough time to gather it with that marine ship on the way. Force is our only option left. As for the numbers," Edward began, glancing to his meagre regiment, "we'll manage."

"So that's how it's going to be now?" Henry said, anger filling his every word. "Anyone who disagrees with you will die? When did we stop being just *labelled* as pirates and instead *become* them, Ed? I'm no longer seeing the line."

"One of our crew was taken, beaten half to death, and is being ransomed for some coin, and you want to talk about lines and labels?" Edward asked, waving his hands angrily. "If you don't want to join us, very well, but don't act like our hands are clean. I made the same decision when I chose to save you and Frederick from the noose. Our crewmate is in danger, and I'm not about to let one of my men die because I wasn't strong enough to do the right thing. Men died on those islands back there because of me. Not this time."

Edward left Henry standing there, frozen in place. The crew followed Edward after glancing back at Henry.

Edward pulled out his sword and returned to the back entrance of the dilapidated house. The crew joined him as they put their backs against the outside wall. He motioned to two crewmen, then to the left side of the house. They nodded and went around the building, ducking to stay away from the windows. He sent another two around the right then motioned for Sam and the remaining crewman to follow him.

Henry, pistol in hand, came running, half bent, to the back of the house. Edward couldn't voice his thanks, but a look and a nod said more than words could have.

Edward inched closer to the opening, the door long since gone. He could hear voices of the men inside. Two were having a jovial conversation in the kitchen from what he could tell. He turned and peered over the threshold and saw the two, with a third glancing out the windows.

He pulled back and held up three fingers to his companions. After they nodded, he held a finger up to his lips.

He peered over the threshold to see only two men now, the third having moved on. The two talking had moved, and their backs were showing. He crept in. Henry followed behind him. The two tiptoed to the men, standing right behind them.

Edward nodded to Henry, then grabbed the man in front of him, placing his large hands across the man's mouth. Henry did the same. The guards grabbed at the foreign limbs in an attempt to remove them, muffled shock uttered beneath warm palms. Edward slit the man's throat. Blood gushed from the wound and down his arm. He saw movement from the corner of his eye and pulled the dying man close, lifted him off the ground, and stepped back out of sight. Henry followed suit.

The man Edward had noticed coming glanced into the kitchen from the entrance hall. Edward and Henry were up against the kitchen wall, only a foot or two separating them from another enemy. Edward's man was still alive. A muted gurgle erupted, and blood seeped through his fingers. Errant arms and legs still pulled and kicked, but they were more like twitches now. Soon they stopped, and Edward bent down to slide the dead man onto the floor.

His hand was covered in warm blood, and Edward couldn't pry his eyes away from it—the last remnants of life from the first person he'd ever killed.

I had to. I had to. I had to.

Sam knocked Edward on the shoulder, forcing him out of his stupor. Sam nodded to the doorway to the entrance hall, then moved to the other side of the kitchen, to the other doorway. He reached through the doorway and pulled in another victim. He was efficient. His knife went through the skull before the man could utter a word. The only sound was shuffling and then a hard thunk.

"Garry, was that you?" A voice rang out from the far room.

Sam and the crewmate looked at Edward and Henry. Everyone's eyes were wide, save Edward. He pulled out a pistol from his belt and walked into the main room.

With no response, the man who called for his friend walked out of the far room and into the entrance hall. When he noticed Edward, an unfamiliar face, he pulled out his musket. Edward already had his pistol up while walking, and fired before the other man. The noise seemed to shake the empty house. The bullet hit the man's chest, and he fell backwards, clutching his wound and dropping the musket.

Another man ran out of the far room. He had a cutlass in his hands, and in a blink Edward had his sword out again. Another pistol rang out to his left. His eyes were drawn to the source. It was Sam. The man who was about to attack Edward fell to the floor, dead.

Edward nodded his thanks and Sam returned the gesture.

Six men, including the leader, Luke, rushed out from rooms on the second floor, each with a musket or a pistol in hand. Henry pulled Edward toward the far room as the six fired. Bullets rained down, just missing their feet.

Edward and Henry put their backs against the wall of the far room, right next to the doorway. Sam and the other crewmate had made it into the room. Jack was still tied to the chair. Edward nodded to him. He smiled back, but looked anxious.

The sound of footsteps bounded off the stairs and then went silent. Luke and his men moved to the lower level of the entrance. "Edward, I thought we had a deal," Luke called out.

"Circumstances have changed. The deal is off," Edward yelled back. "We're taking our crewmate and leaving."

"What about my money?" Luke yelled back.

Sam cut the bonds that held Jack in place and picked him up to help him walk. He took him back to the wall so that Luke's men couldn't shoot him from the other room.

The crew outside was looking into the far room through the windows. Edward noticed them and motioned for them. They nodded and went back the way they had come.

"You have a choice now," Edward said. "Your money… or your life."

There was a pause before Luke laughed. It was a loud and obnoxious sound, forced even. "As I recall, you have six men with minimal arms. We're stocked, and our pistols are loaded. I return that choice to you. You and the lives of your men, or my money."

Edward turned to his friends. They nodded to him. "There's one thing you have wrong, Luke."

"And what's that?"

"I have more than six men. Now!"

The window at the back of the entrance hall burst open under the butt of a rifle. Luke's men turned to the noise just as Edward's crew kicked the front doors down. Luke's men heard that, too, and reacted to it as well.

The distraction bore fruit. Edward and Henry ran out from the back room. Before Luke's men could choose which way to fire, Edward's crew shot at them from all sides.

When the dust and spent powder cleared, only Luke was still alive. He had taken a bullet in the leg, and he was trying to crawl away from Edward and company. Edward and his men sauntered over to him, and Luke looked up to Edward with fear-filled eyes.

"Your friend's debt is paid. We're square," Luke said, glancing about, moving with his hands and avoiding the gazes of the men in front of him. Eventually, his eyes settled on Edward. "Please, there's no need for more bloodshed. It's over. I won't come after you anymore. I swear it." Edward continued his steady approach, sword in hand, as Luke kept backing away. "Please, don't kill me. Please," Luke pleaded. Edward was not appeased. He grabbed Luke by the chest. "Please, please no…"

Edward shoved the sword through Luke's eye, and the man went limp. He pulled the sword out, let Luke go, and stood up. The sword dripped fresh blood to the ground.

"I had to," Edward whispered.

17. INTO THE STORM

On the ship, the crew's frenzied feet pounded against the deck as they prepared to leave. Those arriving with Edward joined in the frantic activity, and soon they had let loose the sails and left the port without notifying anyone.

Herbert set the course away from the approaching marine ship, and after the wind filled their sails the crew could relax for a moment. Edward himself fell to the deck out of exhaustion and Jack sat down beside him to talk.

"Thank you, Captain. No... Thank you, Edward. You saved my life."

"You're my crewmate, Jack. I'd do the same for any of you."

Tears streamed down Jack's face. "I know, but... seeing everyone there to free me—I just didn't think that would happen. I thought you would have left me, but you didn't. You truly are my family. My new family..." Jack drifted off in thought.

Edward sensed where the man's thoughts were taking him. *Those memories must be painful for him. I'll change the subject.*

"Edward?" Jack cut him off before he could say anything.

"Yes, Jack?"

"I promise you, I won't ever drink again."

Edward nodded, not having the words to reply to Jack's promise. He remembered Jack's words to him the other day. 'All men have uttered those words, but all men return to the drink.' *I hope for your sake, Jack, that isn't true.*

William rushed to the aft deck. "Captain! The marine ship is closing in at top speed." His keen eyes had been, as usual, first to see it.

Edward walked to starboard and took the spyglass from his pocket. As William had said, a ship was approaching under full sail. It was a smaller vessel and a bit faster than the *Freedom*, and it would catch up to them soon. When the ship drew close enough, Edward was able to see the markings on it.

Under normal circumstances this wouldn't cause him any concern, as they had replaced the foresail, but something told him it was bad news. "All hands about face! Hard to port! Head north, Herbert!" Edward yelled orders as he moved back to the aft deck, his coat lifting in the wind.

Herbert had already changed course; the sharp turn caused some who hadn't yet gotten their sea legs to lose their footing.

"What's wrong, Edward?" Herbert asked. "Don't tell me that ship is…?"

"Aye, it's a marine ship. I don't care if it is smaller than us, we don't have the firepower to fight against it. We're escaping before they can catch us."

"We don't even know if they're chasing after us. There's nothing marking us as enemies."

"I just have a hunch that we should be avoiding that ship. I'll not take the chance they're friendly."

Herbert turned the ship north-east to catch the best of the wind. He yelled to the crew to "Let go and haul," then turned to Edward. "Captain, I didn't mention it before because it wasn't relevant, but there's a storm coming from this direction. There are oxeye clouds on the horizon. If we keep heading this way, the storm will be upon us soon."

"This could be good fortune for us; the marine ship might turn back. How bad will it be?"

"Have you ever seen a typhoon?" Herbert asked.

"No."

"Well, you are about to."

As they approached the storm, the winds rose and soon became violent. Behind them the marine ship drew closer, but Edward was determined to outrun it. The wind lashed at the rigging and sent waves crashing against the side. Rope and sails loosened and whipped with the wind, and the *Freedom* rocked with the waves. Thunder rumbled off in the distance, foreshadowing the true storm yet to come. Despite the ferocity of the storm, the marine ship continued pursuit.

Why do they keep approaching? Edward took another look through the spyglass. Now the ship was closer and he could make out some of the people aboard. *There's something familiar about that ship.* He could see someone standing at the prow with a spyglass pointed at the *Freedom*, mirroring him.

No! It couldn't be! He moved his spyglass to see the name of the enemy ship, and confirmed it to be the H.M.S. *Pearl*, the ship Isaac Smith commanded. He ran to the edge of the aft deck. "All hands to arms! Gunners, man your cannons! Prepare for battle!" How had he found them? For that matter, how had he survived?

Edward turned to Henry. "It's Smith. Isaac Smith."

"What? He chased us here? How did he survive?"

Edward chuckled at the similarity of their thoughts and handed Henry the spyglass.

"He must have heard about Port Royal and then headed in the same direction we did. Or he has the devil's own luck tracking people," Edward said, frustration forcing him to spit out the compliment. "I don't think he'll retreat without a fight."

"Is there no other way?"

"What do you mean?"

"I can't help but think of Robert. These people are just doing their jobs. We shouldn't harm them, of all people. We've done enough killing today, methinks."

"Henry, we're not trying to harm them, we're trying to defend ourselves. They're out to harm us." Edward threw his hands in the air. "What would you have us do? Fall over and die? I know you disagree with my methods, but this is different from those thugs. We must defend ourselves."

Henry thought about it while rubbing his nose. "If you say so."

Edward and Henry grabbed some weapons from the stock barrels. Edward tucked two pistols and a sword into his belt, and carried a musket in his hands. Meanwhile, the crew prepared to fight the heavily armed marine vessel. Cannons were being loaded, guns prepped, and wills steeled.

The marine ship slowly sailed into the sights of the first cannons on Edward's side. Edward ordered his crew to fire. Immediately the marines reciprocated: cannons fired, bullets flew. The sounds of the storm winds, of explosions from black powder and splintered wood, and shouting united in a terrifying cacophony.

Cannons hit *Freedom*'s port side. They smashed into the railing, skimmed across the deck, and off the other side. Wood chips scattered across the ship. Water poured over the side and washed the splinters away. Another cannon hit the side, and another chipped away at the railings. A cannonball hit a crewman and the force of the iron ball ripped his legs clean off.

The water washed him away too.

Edward and Henry stood right among the crew, firing rifles and issuing orders. They had learned, since their last battle at sea, how to reload their muskets. Edward had to resist the compulsion to throw them away for already loaded ones. As he fired a second round he noticed the other ship inching closer to theirs. "Herbert, keep us away from their ship! I don't want them boarding us."

"Yes, Captain!" Herbert shouted over the noise.

From his perch at the helm Edward could see the other crewmembers fighting. He could see John, crouching behind a barrel, reloading his musket. When his weapon was ready, he left his cover, aimed, and fired in quick succession, all in smooth, practiced motions.

William was issuing orders to the gunners at the cannons when a bullet hit one of them in the chest. William took over and fired the cannon himself.

Sam seemed to lack the others' expertise. Either he didn't know how or was too bothered to reload, so he tossed the musket to another crewman to do it. He was firing at a rapid rate, but seemed to be firing blind. Like some others aboard, he needed training.

Anne was in the crow's nest picking off opponents with a new-model rifle she had chosen. She had taken that rifle before any could claim it and kept it in her hammock or on her person at all times. She never missed, and she aimed at the marines' legs or arms, to disable rather than to kill. Whether it was her skill, or the quality of the rifle, Edward did not know, but he suspected a little of both.

The combat went on and on, with neither side willing to withdraw. Herbert's skill, along with the violent waves, kept enough distance between the ships to prevent boarding. The two sides relied on cannons and muskets only. The wind grew in power, causing huge waves to crash against the hull and sending spray over the deck. The ships rode the waves and crashed down into the water, knocking men not used to the sea off their feet almost every time.

The cannons were hitting their mark and sending pieces of both ships flying in every direction. A number of marines, but also several of Edward's men, had fallen from cannon fire or gunshot wounds. *Dammit! We're evenly matched. We need a miracle to get us out of here.*

Then the rain started.

That's not what I had in mind! Edward reloaded his musket and turned to fire. *I have to end this!* He was startled to find himself peering, across the watery chasm between the ships' hulls, down the rifle sight at the one man whose death could end this: Isaac Smith.

He pulled the trigger knowing—feeling—he would hit his mark.

Nothing happened.

What the …? Bullets flashed by him and he ducked for cover. It was then that he noticed something odd: the noise was not as bad as before. The rain and waves and wind were roaring, but the gunfire had lessened. A lot of people were misfiring. *The rain is seeping into the gunpowder.*

Edward took a quick assessment of his crew. Some were lying on the deck with wounds. Some were fighting to keep their guns dry so they could fire. Some were running around keeping the sails and everything else in shape while trying not to be shot.

I can't let my men and my home die like this! Edward ran over to Herbert, who was being held steady by his sister Christina. "We need to flee!" he yelled over the wind. "Any suggestions?"

"None that don't involve suicide!" Herbert yelled back.

Edward gritted his teeth. "Suicide it is! Take us into the storm!"

Herbert's eyes went wide. "Are you insane? We'll all die!"

"I trust you will not let that happen. We only need to be in there long enough to shake them off, then we can escape. Hold for a moment." Edward went to the edge of the aft deck again.

"All hands cease fire!" Those who heard his order repeated it to those who hadn't, until they had all stopped what they were doing. The crew looked at Edward expectantly. "Prepare to fire on my mark! Now, Herbert!"

"Aye aye, Captain." Herbert flung wheel to port to head into the centre of the storm. As the *Freedom* moved, it came close to slamming into the marines' ship.

"Fire!"

At Edward's command, they all unleashed their weapons at once. It was like a wall of fire and iron rammed the other ship and blasted it to hell. The smaller marine vessel narrowly escaped being staved by the *Freedom*, but the damage done was enough. Edward could see Smith rise from the deck of his ship, glancing to his wounded crewmen, the *Freedom*, and the imminent storm. He shouted orders, and they began trimming and furling the sails and slowing down. The ship turned hard to starboard and left the storm.

The marines would be leaving the crew of the *Freedom* alone.

The crew who were able yelled and hooted at their victory. Even Edward had to smile and join in. He raised his hand in triumph as the rain poured down his face. But their joy was short-lived.

The real battle was only beginning.

18. BLACK BART & THE PIRATE COMMANDMENTS

The storm hadn't fully subsided two days later when the *Freedom* ran aground on an uninhabited island in the Caribbean.

No one had detected any sign of land before they hit. The impact was violent and jarring. The majority of the crew were thrown off their feet and many injured. Edward hit his head on a railing and was knocked out. He slipped in and out of consciousness for a few hours.

When the cloud over him lessened, Edward noticed he was in a bed in the crew's cabin. He tried to rise, but a hand stopped him.

"Easy, *mon capitaine*. You took a fall in the crash." Alexandre was right beside him, checking his head.

Anne, still disguised as Jim, was on the other side of him, and she placed a damp cloth on Edward's forehead.

Edward pressed a hand to his head, holding the cloth in place and trying to suppress the throbbing pain. "What's happened to the crew? Is Jack well? He was *already* injured."

"The music man is recovering. The other crew are *démoralisés*. They are lost and angry. I've done what I can for them, but we've lost five to fever and wounds. Four others were missing after the battle and storm."

Edward closed his eyes. Anne placed her hand on his and gripped it, as if trying to impart strength to him. When Alexandre's eyes lingered on the scene, impassive as he was, Anne removed her hand almost as swiftly as she had placed it.

Edward coughed. "We'll have a few words tonight as we bury them. Where did we land?"

Alexandre searched for the words. "Ahh… Herbert?" Edward nodded. "He does not know. And the *nègre* says repairs need to be made before we can set sail."

"I'll have to talk with everyone." Edward stood and started to leave.

"*Mon capitaine?*"

"Yes, Alexandre?"

"*Vêtements.*" Alexandre pointed to Edward's middle.

He followed the finger and noticed he was in his nightwear. "Damn! Where are my clothes?"

Anne laughed as Alexandre pointed to the wall. As Edward

pulled the rest of his clothes on, the surgeon and Anne moved on to help the other crewmembers injured in the storm.

Edward dressed, but left his coat behind due to the warmth. After examining the injured crewmen, he went to the top deck and was met by some of the men. They presented mixed looks; it was clear they were glad to see him up and about somewhat uninjured, but their perilous adventures had exhausted them.

He noticed Nassir's son, Ochi, lowering a plank of wood over the side of the ship. Nassir was suspended by a rope on the side, removing and replacing planks from the damaged sections. He still wasn't able to do anything for the gun deck, but it had suffered minimal damage.

"How are the repairs?" Edward asked as he watched.

"Good day Captain! Glad to see you back," Nassir responded in his deep, sonorous voice. He looked around at the side of the ship, pointing with his tool. "She is slow and steady, and would go faster if some others were helping." Nassir grabbed the plank his son had sent down and continued with his work.

"I'll find men to aid you. I'm sure there are some who aren't busy."

Nassir paused, as if he had something else to say, but he thanked Edward and continued working. Edward resumed his walk around the ship. Everyone on board appeared busy, swabbing the deck, fixing the sails, cleaning up in the aftermath of the battle.

He scrutinised the damage to the rails. Some sections were completely torn off, with splinters strewn about on the deck emphasizing the destruction. The fife rails at the bottom of the main mast were damaged as well. Luckily the masts themselves had suffered no harm beyond a few bullet holes.

"Don't worry, girl," he said aloud. "We'll fix you up in no time." He ran his hand affectionately along the railing, but as he did so a sliver of wood embedded itself in his skin. He winced and pulled his hand back. It seemed to him as if the ship were saying it was angry with him for the battle and storm. He pulled the splinter out of his hand. *I'm sorry, there was no other way. I'll try not to let it happen again.*

The first thing he noticed was the pristine water, of such clarity he could see fish swimming along the bottom. The expansive beach turned to grass, followed by palm trees and other foliage on into the centre of the island. The whole area appeared untouched, and in the noonday sun it shone like a tropical paradise.

Some of the crew had disembarked, and Edward noticed several gathered in clusters on the shore. Half of the ship rested on a sandbar, so he climbed down the side on a rope ladder and walked across the shoal toward a group loitering about. After asking them where John and Henry went, he asked them to help Nassir with repairs. The crewmen were reluctant at first, but there was no arguing with Edward's gaze.

He watched them depart, and then set out for the interior of the island. The forest was as beautiful and serene as the beach. Rocky streams wound around towering palms and fruit-bearing trees. The splashing and gurgling of the fresh water was a delicate accompaniment to the calls of bright tropical birds. The shaded path seemed worn, and he wondered whether someone had been there before him. He followed it for about fifteen minutes until he heard a rumbling sound growing louder as he walked. When, in a few more minutes, he emerged into a sunlit clearing, his jaw dropped at what he saw.

It was like a scene from an adventure story. A great plume of water rushed over a mossy forested cliff at least forty feet high and plunged straight down into a circular basin at the bottom. It turned the basin into a pond, lined with fine sand which, combined with the water's depth, made swimming and a dive from the top inviting. And there, lounging about nude in the water, were Henry, William, and a few other crewmembers.

"Oi, Ed!" Henry called out, waving to him. "How are you feeling?"

"I'm well now that I'm here. This place is amazing!"

"I know! It's a paradise. What luck to be brought here after a storm, right?"

"The devil's own," Edward replied as he took in the surroundings.

"Gonna join us, Captain?" one of the other crewmembers asked.

Edward smiled and proceeded to remove his clothes. He scrambled up to the top of the cliff and jumped, making a big splash. The water felt warm on his bare skin. He emerged from underwater and laughed as he made his way over to the others.

"We should bring the whole crew here, there's enough room for everyone." Edward ran his fingers through his wet hair, slicking it back.

"No need to tell them yet. Let's enjoy ourselves. We deserve it."

Edward laughed. "That we do…"

They swam in the lake and everyone had a try at the jump. William declined to participate until Edward forced him to; as ever, William was tense, but when he landed he actually smiled.

They must have been there an hour or more, oblivious to the passage of time. Then John's somewhat plump form burst through the brush and found them merrymaking. He was panting and out of breath.

"Good day, John, care to join us?"

"C-Captain, you must come quick!" John stopped to catch more air.

"What's wrong?"

"A marine vessel and a p-pirate ship have begun fighting on the sea in front of this island."

Edward and the others sprang out of the water and rushed to put on their clothing. They ran back toward their encampment, and as they emerged from the forest of palms they saw exactly what John had described. A marine ship and a pirate ship were fighting an all-out battle offshore. He could see each one's identifying mark atop their masts. For the pirate, it was a man on the left and a skeleton on the right, both holding onto an hourglass between them. For the marines, it was the symbol of the British navy, but Edward let out a sigh when he noticed the name of the marine ship was not the H.M.S. *Pearl.* Their archenemy, Isaac Smith, did not have the clairvoyance to know where the *Freedom* had landed after the storm.

"Wh-what do we do, Captain?" John asked.

Edward watched the ships' cannons firing back and forth. The two vessels appeared evenly matched. "Tell the crew to board the ship. We're going out there to help them." Edward walked over to the *Freedom* as the crew converged on him.

"Who are we helping?" Henry posed.

"Who do you think, Henry? The pirates!" *If they don't win, the marines will attack us. If we help the pirates, they will probably leave us alone.* "Nassir! Nassir!"

The carpenter leaned over the side of the ship. "Yes, Captain?"

"Is she ready to sail?"

Nassir spied the two ships fighting. "As ready as she can be."

"It'll have to do." Edward waved for those watching on shore to come with him. "Everyone board now! Prepare for battle!"

The crew who were still on the *Freedom* lowered ropes and ladders down for the others to climb up, then proceeded to ready the ship to leave right away. The tide had risen, lifting the ship enough so the wind filled their unfurled sails and took them out. The few left back on shore boarded a small rowboat and caught up with the ship.

Edward, on the main deck, grabbed his captain's coat, threw it on, and armed himself. The *Freedom* was in the perfect position to strike against the marine vessel; the two battling ships were moving east with the wind, and the marine ship was nearest shore. Herbert had turned the ship around so they were travelling straight into the marine ship's path. The whole crew moved into position and readied their guns and cannons. The marines only noticed the *Freedom* closing in on them when its cannons let loose at Edward's order. With the continued bombardment from the pirates on their other flank, their ship took heavy damage and rocked back and forth from the impact. Then the second volley from the *Freedom* hit them, and the crew rushed in a frenzy to try to save themselves. They soon realised all they could do was raise the white flag. The battle was over almost before it had begun.

"Cease fire!" cried Edward. "They've surrendered." Everyone stopped firing and watched as the pirates boarded the marine vessel, taking prisoners and weapons from the defeated crew.

"Orders, Captain?"

"Take us back to shore; the other crew can take over now."

"Aye aye."

Herbert steered the ship around in a wide arc so as to circle around the other two ships. As they passed the pirates' vessel, Edward noticed a tall man who appeared to be in his mid-thirties to early forties wearing an outfit similar to his. *He must be the captain.* The man took off his hat and bowed. Edward returned the honour in kind.

The *Freedom* made its way back to shore and landed on the shoal. The crew handed the sails but everyone kept guns and cannons ready to fire at a moment's notice in case the pirates were less than welcoming. They watched as the pirates ransacked the marine vessel. As far as Edward could see, the marines themselves were not harmed, but the pirates took everything they had, including the clothes off their backs. Then they let the marine vessel escape. Stripped of supplies, the marines sailed off to the northeast, back to Jamaica and less threatening territory.

After the marine ship was out of sight, the pirate ship sailed over to the *Freedom*. The closer it came, the more tense Edward's crew became. They knew they had to be ready to open fire at any moment. And, despite the larger size of the *Freedom*, the pirates' sloop, with its larger cannons and more experienced crew, could prove a formidable foe.

Instead of attacking, the ship landed close to theirs, and its captain and many of his crewmen disembarked. Edward decided to follow suit and took along several of his people—who did, however, take the precaution of carrying weapons.

Edward then noticed the extent of the damage the pirate ship had sustained. The *Fortune*—the name was proudly displayed on its side—had many holes caused by cannon fire. The crew who stayed on the ship were already working on repairs and making it seaworthy again.

Blackbeard's Ship

I guess they wouldn't be able to fight us anyway. We'd probably both end up losing.

Now that Edward was able to see the other captain up close, he noticed how enormous the man was—and how intimidating: seven feet tall, with broad shoulders and massive arms. He was wearing a tight shirt that emphasised his powerful form. His stride was straight and true—never a misstep, never a glance at his feet. He had a strong, clean-shaven jaw. His brown eyes shone with raw determination, and seemed to concentrate the force of his menacing presence.

Edward kept his hand on the sword in his belt. He swallowed hard and began sweating. *He's so huge!*

When the two groups were a hand's breadth apart, the other captain again bowed to Edward. "Salutations, my savior! I am forever in your debt. To whom do my crew and I owe our gratitude?" The man spoke with a slight Welsh accent similar to Henry's.

Edward breathed a sigh of relief. *All right, Edward, you can do this. Just breathe and focus on the captain.* "My name is Edward Thatch." He put out his hand. "And you are?"

The man took his hand. "Bartholomew Roberts."

"Ahhh!" Sam let out a yelp at the man's name and ran up to inspect him. "Black Bart?"

"Oh, my boy, I cannot bear hearing that name. So vile and ungodly a thing. The good Lord blesses my work. I prefer to be called Roberts."

"Is it true you stole gold and jewelry straight from the king of Portugal himself? Out of his own bedchambers?" Sam was smiling from ear to ear.

"Oh you heard about that, did you? It was nothing. We raided his ship and took it; as God had commanded me, I obeyed. Unfortunately, before I returned to my ship, which you see here, I was betrayed by a former comrade. He stole my second ship out from under me. I will hunt him down and he will be judged as the sinner he is! Right, men?" Roberts' crew hollered in affirmation of their captain's words.

"How did you end up here, then?" Edward asked.

"After the scoundrel Walter Kennedy left in my last ship, we went searching for him. We joined a crew sailing a vessel called the *Sea King* and were attacked by the marines you helped us defeat. The *Sea King* fled, and left us to die. We tried to escape and managed to make it here, where providence saved us with your help. Now, please, share with us the story of your arriving here."

"We were chased by some marines through a storm," Edward explained, "and eventually shook them off, but the storm blew us off course and we ended up here. Wherever here is."

"Ah, we are truly like brothers, Edward. These false prophets they call marines can try to burn us, but God is with us. He will not burn his true shepherds." Roberts grabbed Edward and pulled him close, like a chick under his wing.

"Uhh, yes, of course, sir."

"This day delivers us good *Fortune*, and like your ship's namesake, we should celebrate our *Freedom* today. Let us break bread and open the casks! Men, let us celebrate meeting another of God's children! Edward Thatch!" Bartholomew Roberts lifted Edward's hand into the air and both crews cheered and hooted.

God's children?

⚓ ⚓ ⚓

The battle-weary crews had already been more than willing to put off repairing their ships. Now Captain Roberts' words provided them all the excuse they needed. They scrambled to set up small camps all along the shore; they lit fires for cooking, and sat around eating and drinking as they exchanged stories of adventure and pirating.

Roberts had been a pirate for but a year, and already, amongst pirates and marines alike, he was a man to keep an eye on. Sam, in particular, was in awe of the man. Roberts recounted how he had saved a group of his men from being imprisoned. They had been captured on land one day, and to take them back he attacked a local member of the marines, stole his uniform, and went in to rescue them.

"I tell you, men, God was with me that day. The blue marine's uniform was so tight against my breast I thought I would pass out, or at the least be discovered."

The first mate, Hank Abbot, took over for a little of the story. A short man in comparison to Roberts, he looked quick on his feet, and a perfect complement to Roberts. He had light brown hair and thick brows and mustache. Chestnut eyes and a cleft chin made him the picture of a western colonist.

"Anyone in their natural mind would have guessed he didn't belong. His shirt and pantaloons were ripping at the seams, but no one paid him any mind; he waltzed into the prison unopposed like a calf at sundown."

Everyone laughed at the absurdity of it all. "And you have to remember," Bartholomew added, "I was in enemy territory. God may have been with me, but he did not see fit to dry my sweat."

Hank laughed as he continued. "So there the captain is… sweat dripping from his brow, face purple and arms white. He was the like of an apparition walking, but still no one says or does anything. He beats the guard with his bare hands and takes his keys, lets us out—and lo and behold, we find a storehouse of extra clothes for soldiers. I reckon we would have set the place ablaze had we put those uniforms on any faster."

"I tell you," Roberts interjected, "Hank here was shaking in his boots by the end. I wouldn't have been surprised if he had soiled himself."

"But I didn't," Hank assured them, the fire crackling as he continued his side of the story. "And we managed to escape without incident. The next day we set sail like nothing had happened. It was rumored afterward, we heard, that a bear in a blue outfit rampaged in the prison. Frankly, I don't know which should've embarrassed them more: that they had let our captain in looking the way he did, or that they thought he was a bear."

"Ah! The bear again! The crew bestowed upon me the nickname Bartholomew the Bear. I saved them and this is how they treat me!"

Everyone roared with laughter at the thought of Captain Roberts, his burly arms covered with hair, being mistaken for a bear. They laughed, too, in admiration for a man of such intimidating strength who could jest so heartily at his own expense.

And so went the festivities for most of the night. But after a time the seamen, tired from their adventures, battles, and hard work, and sedated by food and drink, fell asleep, many on the ground where they lay. And then it was just Edward and Roberts awake, drunk, and walking around the island singing pirate songs. They walked along the path to the waterfall guided by the light of the moon and there decided to sit down and rest.

As Roberts went to sit, something dropped out of his coat pocket. "Oh, there goes me Bible." Roberts tried to pick it up, but he couldn't reach it. He then tried to reach farther and fell over. Then he shuffled along on his backside over to it, picked it up, and examined it with unfocussed eyes. Edward burst out laughing.

"Hey, Bart. Bear. Bearbart." Edward laughed again at himself as Roberts turned around.

"What?" Roberts crawled over to Edward and leaned his back against a palm tree for support.

"There should be some kind of... commandments... for pirates... no?"

Bartholomew's eyes went wide. "You're... so... smart. Why didn't... why didn't I think of that?"

Roberts was on all fours, his knuckles against the earth. Edward broke into laughter again. "You... you're like a monkey right now. Maybe they should... should call you Monkey Bart."

Roberts appeared serious as he stared at Edward. He watched

him until Edward couldn't take it anymore and collapsed into uncontrollable spasms of laughter. Roberts joined in. The two of them continued merrymaking and singing for another hour until Edward fell asleep in front of the waterfall.

⚓ ⚓ ⚓

"Edward! … Edward! … *Edward*!"

Edward woke with a pounding headache. Bartholomew Roberts' impressive figure was standing over him.

"Wake up, Edward. We have much to discuss." He pulled Edward up off the sand.

"Day already? Ugh, I can still taste the rum." Edward smacked his tongue against the roof of his mouth to try to rid himself of the poor aftertaste. "What do we need to discuss?"

"The Ten Pirate Commandments."

The what?

Roberts and Edward hiked back to the shoal and discussed his idea while the both of them downed some food and water. It was midday, and the majority of the crew was already up and about, making repairs on their vessels. The wind carried with it the scent of the greenery and the salt water along with the spiced meat and vegetables they were eating.

"When you mentioned commandments for pirates yesterday, it made me think. What if there were ten commandments pirates had to follow? At least, on our own ships. Each man would swear upon the Bible to uphold those commandments, and if he went against them God would strike him down."

Did I really suggest something like that? "I don't know, Roberts. Do you think the men will hold true to it?"

"Of course they will. It's the Bible. Besides, there would be punishments for violators. I have some figured out already."

Edward was drinking from a cup containing a potion provided by Alexandre. It was supposed to help with a night of rum, but all it did was numb his tongue and make him cough profusely from the horrifying taste. *I wish I had some of Jack's bitter coffee right now.* After he was able to speak again, he let Roberts show him what he had so far.

Edward examined the list of commandments, stroking his small black beard as he did so. "Hmmm. On the third one, we should change it so the first mate receives the same shares as the captain and quartermaster."

"Why is that? The first mate ranks below the quartermaster, Edward."

"Oh? I try not to make any decisions without consulting Henry. And what about Hank? Don't you think he deserves a little better?"

"I suppose so." Roberts made the changes on the paper, then handed it back to Edward and he continued to read number four.

No boys and women allowed aboard the ship? That's going to be a problem. "Roberts, I cannot abide by this fourth rule. I already have a child aboard my ship, and we cannot kick him off. His father is my carpenter."

Roberts scratched his chin. "I see. Well, children are a concern during battle; I've had to bury many young ones because of accidents involving black powder. I suppose we can change this to keep them out of battle situations. The problem with women is relations with men, and being kept aboard while offshore. Women have died aboard my ship during battle in the past. God does not like innocent blood to be spilled. Not to mention it is bad luck."

Edward let out the breath he had been holding in. "It's just about the... relations?"

Roberts' head shot up from the page. "Edward, do you have female crewmembers aboard your ship?"

"No! No! I thought the rules should be clear on what was not allowed. So that's number four. Have you thought of more?"

"No, this is all so far. We need six more to make ten commandments."

"Let me have a look. I'll see what I can come up with."

Edward and Roberts worked together, each making suggestions and proposing changes, but after an hour they had created only two more commandments. Then Henry joined them.

"What are you two doing?" Henry sat down on one of the logs they were using as seats.

"Roberts and I are trying to think of ten commandments for a pirate ship. General rules each member should follow. We have six so far, but we're having a spot of trouble with the rest. Here, why don't you take a gander?"

Henry read the page over a few times, trying to decipher the actual text among the corrections and annotations. "It's good so far, but I have a few ideas for the final version."

Edward smiled. "Let's hear what you have."

And so Edward, Roberts, and Henry talked for the next few hours, revising the old, bringing in new, and throwing out what didn't work. In the end they settled upon eleven commandments which they decided to call the "Pirate Commandments," a name allowing them the ability to add as many as seemed necessary. These are the eleven they created:

The Pirate Commandments

I. Every man shall have an equal vote in the affairs of the moment. He shall have an equal title to the fresh provisions or strong liquors at any time seized, and shall use them at pleasure unless a scarcity may make it necessary for the common good that a retrenchment may be voted.

II. Every man shall be given fairly the basic necessities of a list on board, because over and above their proper share they are allowed a shift of clothes. But if they defraud the company to the value of even one piece of eight in plate, jewels, or money, they shall be marooned. If any man robs another he shall have his nose and ears slit, and be put ashore where he shall be sure to encounter hardships.

III. None shall game for money either with dice or cards.

IV. The lights and candles should be put out at eight at night, and if any of the crew desire to drink after that hour they shall sit upon the open deck without lights.

V. Each man shall keep his weapons at all times clean and ready for action.

VI. If any man shall be found seducing any of the opposite sex and carrying her to sea in disguise for the principal act of sexual relations, he shall suffer death. If any man makes a child work for the express purpose of battle, he shall also suffer death.

VII. He that shall desert the ship or his quarters in time of battle shall be punished by death or marooning.

VIII. None shall strike another on board the ship, but every man's quarrel shall be ended on shore by sword or pistol in this manner: At the word of command from the quartermaster, each man being previously placed back to back, shall walk ten paces, turn and fire immediately. If any man does not, the quartermaster shall knock the piece out of his hand. If both miss their aim they shall take to their cutlasses, and he that draws first blood shall be declared the victor.

IX. No man shall talk of breaking apart from the group lest he own a share of £1,000. Every man who shall become a cripple or lose a limb in the service shall have 800 pieces of eight from the common stock and for lesser hurts proportionately.

X. The captain, quartermaster, and first mate shall each receive two shares of booty, the master gunner and boatswain, one and one half shares, all other officers one and one quarter, and private gentlemen of fortune one share each.

XI. The musicians shall have rest on the Sabbath Day by right. On all other days, by favor only.

After they finished, they gathered together their crews and explained the commandments to them. They agreed that any man who did not wish to swear to uphold the commandments could leave at the next shore, and no one would think less of him.

No one took the offer.

One by one, each crewmember swore upon the Bible. The captains swore to act as an adjudicator over disputes, and the senior officers agreed to do so if the captain was involved in the dispute or indisposed.

After the ceremony was over, everyone went back to their duties. Edward's crew still had a lot of work to do on the *Freedom* to make her seaworthy again. After Roberts' crew had finished repairing their ship, they helped work on the *Freedom*.

After the repairs had finished, Edward and Bartholomew stood on the deck of Edward's ship, watching the sun sink to the horizon.

"How do you do it, Roberts? Every day, being chased by marines, hunted by everyone, betrayed by your friends..." Edward looked down at the water lapping against the ship, "killing... Do you enjoy being a captain, being a pirate?"

"Ha! That is like asking a fish if he enjoys water. This pirating business... it calls to me. When the crew and I are up to the waist in gunfire, and cannons, and storms, and treasure... there is no better adventure. This life calls to me as God does." Bartholomew paused, looking Edward in the eyes. "As for the killing, I can see in your eyes you are conflicted. Let me tell you that that is a good thing. God says 'Thou shalt not kill.' However, that did not stop God from commanding the Israelites to wage war against the Midianites. Killing should never be easy, but when it is for a righteous cause, when it is to save the ones you love, then it is just.

"You know, my child, we are not evil. Evil, good, justice, injustice... They are all made by the times, and by those who live in the times. Who is the queen that she can say we are wrong and she right? We do the same thing as she, only in a more surreptitious way. At least we aren't lying about it. And we do not steal more than we need, except by God's will. You want to know the real reason why they oppose us? They're afraid. They fear what we stand for. We're free to do whatever we want and the queen can do nothing about it."

Edward scoffed. "Except kill us."

"Our bodies, Edward. They cannot take away our spirit, or our determination, or our will." Bartholomew took Edward by the shoulders and faced him dead on. "Or our *Freedom*." Those words struck Edward to the core. "In the end, if someone inherits our will, our determination, our spirit, and gains the same *Freedom* we have, they will realise something is wrong in this world... something is wrong in a world that drives men to do the things we have to do to survive. That will is a force greater than any bullet, greater than any government. And that, Edward—that is why they are afraid."

Edward paused to contemplate Bartholomew's words. Chills ran down his back. "Your words fill my heart, but I still have doubts about this life."

"'Tis better being a commander than a common man. And better to be free than suffer in chains." Bartholomew's strong hands squeezed Edward's shoulders gently. "Give it time." And with those final words, Roberts walked back to his own ship to rest for the departure the next day.

Edward stayed, leaning on the stern railing. The fresh smell of the sea and palm trees breezed by him, and he watched the setting sun on the horizon while thinking about Bartholomew's words.

19. THE JUNGLE

The following day, the crews of the *Fortune* and the *Freedom* met one last time for a meal and said their goodbyes to each other. The few days they were together had created a firm bond of friendship, and as a token of gratitude they conferred on Edward half of the loot they had procured from the marines. It included a few items of clothing, marine uniforms, some food to help them reach their next destination, and a decent amount of money and weapons.

"Well, Edward, it appears this be our time of parting. We sail out to do the Lord's work once more. What say you join us on our adventure? You can be a part of my crew," Roberts said with a wink.

Edward laughed. "It's tempting, but we have our own adventures to complete, and I rather enjoy being captain. How about we keep that open for another day?" Edward extended his hand.

Bartholomew gripped it and gave it a firm shake. "When next we meet the seas will tremble before us."

"Aye, that they well."

Roberts turned to Henry and spoke to him in Welsh. Edward couldn't make out what the exchange was about.

"All right, men, back to the ship! We have work to do! There be sinners who need cleansing." Bartholomew and his crew went back to their ship, and Edward's men did the same.

"What did he say to you, Henry?"

"He told me to be brave and protect the crew. I told him I would."

Edward patted Henry on the back as they made their way back to the *Freedom*.

Each crew waved and yelled goodbye to the other as they boarded and prepared the ships, and the noise grew louder as they both took to the sea. Everyone watched as the *Fortune* moved farther away in the opposite direction of *Freedom*, and soon the other ship was out of sight.

"I'm going to miss them," Edward announced to Henry as they looked out at the empty sea.

"Me too, but what do we do now?"

Edward thought it over for a moment. "We still need to solve the riddle to lead us to the next key."

"Do we even know where we are? We landed at that island after being knocked about by the storm. What should our heading be?"

Dammit! I never thought to ask Roberts where we were exactly. "We'll have to head back to a location we are familiar with first."

"No need, Captain," Herbert said over his shoulder. "I found out the location from one of Roberts' crewmen. I figured you would want to sail to the closest island so I set the course right away. We'll arrive in about a week's time. We have enough food to last us until then, and we can restock at the harbour before searching for the islands."

"Well done, Herbert! Keep us steady, my friend."

"Aye aye, Captain!" Herbert replied with a beaming smile.

Over the next week the crew was in high spirits. Not only had they enjoyed the company of other men who weren't trying to kill them, but they seemed to like the idea of the commandments.

To help pass the time, Jack made music, and he even taught others how to play on some of his spare instruments. Another group had pooled their money and bought a pack of cards during their brief stop in Negril before the storm. Since then, the cards were passed around between crewmates each day. Edward allowed the card games as long as no money was being wagered, as required by the commandments.

John spent time tabulating all the items aboard the ship, including the number of cannons and the amount of gunpowder in stock. He calculated how much of everything needed to be in each location and drew up lists on which items could be checked off when purchased in port.

Nassir was still working every day on the figurehead he had promised Edward. It was now about half done. He had started from the bottom, which Edward thought odd, but it was starting to take shape.

Nassir and William had frequent talks when they were alone, or far enough away so no one could hear them. Edward recalled Nassir saying he owed William his life, and found himself wondering what had happened there.

Sam spent his days drinking and being lazy. John had to remind him of the commandments and force him into work several times over the days. He seemed to enjoy practicing swordplay with William and Anne, at least.

Edward had bought a fishing pole at Negril, and he was using it each day there was no wind for the sails. Henry made his own fishing pole and joined Edward. Today they both had their shirts off because of the heat.

"Any bites?" Henry asked as he sat down on the railing beside Edward.

"Not yet."

Blackbeard's Ship

The sun was strong and beat down on them and their exposed flesh. Having worked indoors most of his life, Edward used to be pale, but with being on the *Freedom* all summer he had gotten some colour. Henry too used to have the typical farmer tan, but now his whole body was darkening from the time out in the sun.

Edward, his black hair in waves down to his shoulders, and Henry, his straight brown hair tied back in a ponytail, sat in silence on the railing of the ship, waiting for some movement in the water. Their bodies, large and muscular, were both like that of stone statues watching the sea lapping against the ship.

But Henry's stone façade soon softened some. His eyes were downcast. "Ed, I want to apologise for the way I acted before. I know your reasons for doing what you did to those thugs in Negril. And, hell! We probably helped that town by doing what we did."

"It took you a week to come around?" Edward laughed and Henry joined him.

"Well, that—and realizing I would have done the same if it was you in there." He took a moment and clenched his fist, deep in thought. When he spoke, his tone was deadly serious. "I want you to know I'll be there when you need me next time."

Edward nodded at his friend's renewed resolve. "I believe I have an answer to your question that day, Henry. The moment we became pirates rather than just being labelled pirates was the moment I took my ship back from Smith. We were naive to think we could live normally while having that label. We have to accept it, all or nothing."

Henry didn't reply as he readied his own fishing rod, but Edward knew he had heard him. Whether he agreed was another matter.

"So Herbert still hasn't figured out the next clue?" Henry cast his line into the water.

"He's still working on it. It has a map on it, so I'm leaving it to him."

Edward felt a tug on his line and pulled back on it. The fish tugged again. He stood up on the railing of the ship and pulled as hard as he could. Henry cheered him on as others in the crew stopped to watch. When the fish broke the surface of the water it thrashed and wriggled against the hook in its mouth. Edward thought it must have been a Bar Jack of at least ten inches. Edward was jumping up and down with the excitement of it all, which was a mistake. He lost his balance, slipped off the railing of the ship, and fell into the water.

"Ed!" Henry yelled.

After a few seconds, Edward emerged from the water.

"Are you well?"

"I am well. Could you lower some rope down?"

When he climbed back on deck—his fishing pole lost to the fish and the sea—everyone patted him on the back and chuckled.

"It's bloody good you can swim, Captain," one of them said.

"You cannot?" The crewman shook his head no. "Who here can swim?" Only two out of the thirty there raised their hands. *Maybe we should teach them. It would be bad if they went overboard.* "I suppose I'm finished fishing for a while. Have fun, Henry."

"Will do, Ed. Let's see if I can avenge our captain, boys." They all cheered Henry on.

Edward had a rag thrown into his face. He pulled it away and Anne was there, smiling. "Impeccable dive, Captain. Good form."

"Har har. Thank you for the towel." Edward dried himself off. "I've seen you and William practicing fighting and swordplay on these off days. What is that strange dance you and him do?" Edward sat down and put his back against the ladder to the aft deck.

Anne joined him. "It is not a dance, but not far from it. It is a fighting art from the East. Would you like to learn it?"

"Well, I'm more interested in the swordplay, but I suppose I could try this too. Sam seems to be more tolerant of William because of it."

"Yes, they are gaining more respect for each other, but their relationship is still rocky, to say the least. If Sam was any better of a fighter, William could end up hurt."

"Well, I'm sure William can handle it, and dish it back out as well."

Anne nodded in agreement as another crewman came by to talk with Edward. "Captain, the surgeon wants to see you."

"What about?"

"I's not sure. Captain. He's doin' some sort of… experiment with grenades."

Edward shook his head immediately. "Oh no, I'm not going down there. Tell him he's on his own." The crewman left and went down to the crew cabin to relay the message.

"Whatever was that reaction for?" Anne asked with a raised brow.

Edward folded his arms. "The last time Alexandre was doing an experiment it was some sort of fire-spitting contraption. It ended up exploding and I almost lost my beard and brows. Unless I need medical attention, I'm staying away that French madman."

Anne had to stifle a laugh.

She has a cute laugh. "Yes, yes, keep laughing," Edward said, pushing her playfully.

Henry turned from his fishing and saw Anne and Edward laughing together. Edward thought he could see a frown on his friend's face before he turned back to his line.

"Captain!" Herbert yelled over the railing. "I've figured it out! Come quick!"

Edward catapulted himself up to the aft deck and ran to Herbert, with Anne not far behind. "You figured out the map? Show me!"

"It took me a while, and some experimenting, but I figured the line 'look at it with eyes clouded by a pirate's home' meant 'clouded by the sea.' I used the reflection of some water and I was able to find the location. We need to sail to Mexico, the northwestern point on the edge of the Caribbean Sea, specifically the Yucatan Peninsula."

Edward examined the map and saw Herbert had marked where they needed to go. "This is astonishing, Herbert. You're a genius. I knew you could find it." Edward gazed at the map, deep in thought. "Why Mexico, why there? There must be some significance," Edward thought aloud.

"I recall hearing a rumor the area is host to a lost Mayan civilisation. It's been left untouched because anyone who travels there never returns. Some think the spirits of the Mayans haunt it."

Edward put his palm to his face and rubbed his eyes. "Either we're caught by traps, or we face ghosts of long-dead civilisations. Oh, Benjamin, when I find you..." Edward left his threat unuttered. "What do they call that place?"

"The Forest of Burning Hearts."

Edward stared at Herbert in disbelief.

"I swear it to be true," Herbert assured him. "The descendants of the Mayans call it the Forest of Burning Hearts."

"Yea?" Edward replied, dubious. "And where did you learn all this?"

"Being in Port Royal is like being in the centre of the Caribbean. You can hear a lot of stories by being near the port and listening. Whether it's true or not remains to be seen, but knowing is half the battle."

"You say that, but you're not the one who's going into battle. Lay in the course. I'll address the crew."

"Aye, Captain. It will take a few weeks' travel, so I'll take us to a port halfway there to let everyone rest and prepare for the remainder of the journey."

"Understood."

Herbert turned the wheel to port, spinning the ship almost all the way around with the current. The crew's attention went to the helm because of the sudden change in course.

Edward addressed their obvious concern. "We've changed course to our new destination, thanks to Herbert. We now know the location of the next ship key and are headed there right now. As we voted on the last expedition, I thought it appropriate we put this to a vote as well. All those in favor say 'aye.'"

A paltry few responded in favor, with a few stragglers joining in. *What in the Lord's name?* "What's wrong? This key will open another part of the ship, which we'll need to do. Why are you hesitating?"

Fear and doubt filled their eyes. After a moment one man stepped forward. "We all be afraid, Captain. Some of our mates didn't make it back last time, God rest their souls. How do we know that won't happen again?"

"This trial isn't like the others we've faced together, so worry not. I face this trial alone. On the map it said 'Only the captain may enter, and only the captain may leave.'"

This caused more doubtful glances and fear than before. "But Cap'n, you can't! What if you die? You're headed into the unknown, how can we save you from that?"

"I won't die, and I won't need saving," Edward reassured them with a smile. "Now: all those in favor, say 'aye'!"

Many still hesitated, but the majority agreed with their captain. The course was set now.

A few moments later, Henry, John, and William all walked up the steps to the aft deck. "We've got a problem, Ed."

"What is it, Henry? The course has already been decided."

"You're planning to complete this trial alone? It's too dangerous; you have to let some people join you."

"No, I don't. I'm the captain. This is my trial, and my duty. I'll complete it alone."

John stepped forward. He was wringing a cap in his hands. "I agree with Henry. You should t-take others to help you out."

Anne, who had been observing in silence until then, spoke up. "Please listen to us, Edward. We only fear for your safety." She touched his arm almost in pleading.

Edward's hands tightened around the railing. "Must I order you to stand down? I won't have anyone else risking their life for this."

Henry raised his hand to reach out to Edward, but he pulled it back. "Understood, Captain."

⚓ ⚓ ⚓

After a short stop at the Swan Islands, the *Freedom* headed north. Herbert guided the ship along the eastern coastline of the Yucatan Peninsula to find their destination.

Anne forced Edward to start training in both the eastern fighting art and swordsmanship with her and William. His skills improved at a steady pace, though never reaching the level of theirs.

He was able to learn only a few proper stances and some simple, effective strikes and counters in the weeks it took to reach their destination.

Anne seemed almost frantic to teach him as much as possible before they arrived. When asked why, she avoided giving a true answer.

"You must learn, so it is as well to be now than later," she said when he asked.

Edward thought there was more to it than that, but wouldn't press the issue.

As the days and nights passed on the journey, the crew learned the name of the forest. More than a few gave Edward passing glances with worry painting their faces. More than once he had to turn down offers of a strong arm for the journey, or reassure other crewmen that he would be all right. For every one who talked with him, there was a group of three or four who had a stake in the proposition, and were disappointed with his answer.

As they followed the coast of the Yucatan, they were guided by the map Benjamin left. The document was surprisingly accurate, so finding the beach they needed to land on wasn't difficult. There was only one spot to land for miles around, unlikely to be found without knowing it was there. Aside from the sandy beach the map pointed to, it was rocky shores or hills as far as the eye could see.

The beach was like any other, albeit small—full of sand and small rocks, and a few crabs scattered about with birds trying to feed on them. The beach went up on an incline to a dark forest of tall trees with intertwined branches and pine needles blocking the light.

As Edward stared into the opening maw of that so-called Forest of Burning Hearts, he felt the tension rise in him. What awaited him was another trial devised by Benjamin Hornigold. If he didn't pass, it could mean death.

Edward steeled himself. *I won't die. Not yet. Not when I've come this far.*

He packed essentials for travelling through the woods: food, spare clothes, rope, camping and travelling gear, compass, sword, two pistols, and of course the map itself.

"Be safe, Edward. Come back alive." Henry put his hand out and Edward grabbed it in return.

"I will."

Anne was standing there, looking at him with steely eyes. Edward smiled in an attempt to reassure her. It was all he could do to show her it was going to be all right.

Edward took one last look at the crew. "If you're going to steal my ship, at least wait until I'm out of sight, yea?" He smiled and they all chuckled. He jumped over the side, grabbed onto the rope ladder, and climbed down to the sandy beach below.

He walked up the beach and into the forest and found a trail, which seemed to be the one located on the map. The forest was dense and the trees stood tall, their thick canopy preventing the sun from reaching him. *It will grow even darker toward nightfall*, he thought. *Herbert estimated I would need about a day and a half to reach the spot marked on the map, so I will have to find a place to set up camp.* As he walked, his nostrils detected a scent both familiar and pleasant. *These trees are the same Caribbean pine the Freedom is made of. Amazing.* For a moment he felt at home. And then he recalled the dreadful name by which this forest was known.

The Forest of Burning Hearts... A sudden chill went down his spine as he took in the sights and sounds of this strange place. From every direction he could hear noises—animal cries, he thought—and as twilight fell, they took on an otherworldly tone. He made a torch out of a stick, a rag, and some oil he had brought. He began to quicken his pace, hoping to find a good place to spend the night before it was too dark to see.

On and on he went into the shady depths of tree roots, bushes and grass, fallen pine, and mushrooms, as the chorus of animal voices echoed louder. He began to feel that the forest was taunting him; he thought he could see shapes moving to the right and left of him, and eyes terrible yellow eyes piercing through the shadows.

He panicked. *Are those animals? Are they real or am I imagining them? Maybe they're the spirits of the Mayans. Oh God, I'm going to die.* He noticed a large rock in his path, which was almost like a wall in front of him. One of the Caribbean pines was growing atop it, its roots snaking down the rock. The area in front of the rock wall was like a circle of smooth grass with the roots of trees winding their way around. *Perfect!*

Then Edward saw something move, something he knew was real. He ran to the rock and backed up against it as he grabbed one of his pistols. Large, dark shapes began to emerge from the shadows. It was a pack of wolves, seven of them—and they were poised to attack.

"Well, come on, then!" he yelled, but they stared at him, growling. "Very well. I'll take first blood!"

Edward shot at one, wounding it. The sudden loud noise caused the others to lash out. They jumped at him all at once. He dropped his pack, rolled, and threw the flaming torch at one of them. The wolves landed where he had stood not moments before. He pulled out his other pistol and fired it, hitting another wolf. That one fell, but the other five were still on the prowl.

He pulled out his sword and assumed a defensive stance. The wolves circled him. He didn't know which of them would attack next.

There's too many of them! No! Concentrate, Edward. Think about what Anne taught you. "Visualise the enemy in your mind. Breathe deep and do not rely on sight alone. Human instinct is a lost trait among us, but one that is deeply valuable as it uses all the senses. You can use it to sense your opponent's whereabouts and avoid being shot in the back." Now—breathe!

Edward filled his lungs. His blood was on fire, and he became conscious of everything around him, as if his five senses had become one. He saw everything.

He focused on each soft sound made by the wolves. Their paws on the rocks and branches. The panting from their mouths. He could, as it were, see all their movements without sight. One was behind him, limping. Another beside that one was panting and licking its lips. One on his right, waiting. One in front, pacing. And one on the left, snarling, fangs bared.

The wolf to his left jumped at him, the fangs reaching for his throat. He ducked and stabbed the wolf in the chest, rolling with it. Another wolf jumped on top of him. Edward dropped his sword, put his feet against the wolf's belly, and catapulted it against the rock.

He rose to his knees as another wolf ran straight at him; he punched it hard in the snout and it whimpered before slinking into the underbrush. Another pounced at him from the side; he kicked it as hard as he could, breaking its ribs. The second to last jumped on his back and dug its teeth into his shoulder. He grabbed it by the head and whipped it against the rock.

One more! Edward thought to himself as he turned to see it lunging at him.

With no time to counter, Edward shielded himself with his arm. The wolf tore into his flesh with terrible ferocity, boring deep into his skin, down to the nerves. He yelled out in pain.

The animal dug deeper. Edward forced himself to stop screaming and tried to pry the animal's fangs off his arm. No matter how he strained, the wolf didn't release him.

In that moment, when his pain was at its greatest, when he was pulling at the animal's snout, Edward stared into the wolf's eyes. He didn't back down, despite the wolf tearing into his arm. As his gaze, and nails, bore into the wolf, it let him go with a whimper. The rest of the pack, as well, stopped the attack and slinked off into the forest. Before he could contemplate the strangeness of it all, the pain and the loss of blood hit him all at once, and he fainted.

Away from this world, he didn't notice those who had been watching his struggle, and who now gathered around him and lifted his body from the ground. They carried him away to a place where warriors went to face their trials.

20. A SACRIFICE

Edward awoke with a start. Cold sweat was beading down his face, and he felt faint. He didn't recognise his surroundings. He would have expected to awake in the comfort of his ship, or in the jungle. Instead, he found himself in what appeared to be a small grass hut.

He noticed a cloth covering the wound on his forearm. It still hurt to touch, but it wasn't as bad as before and it wasn't bleeding. He raised his head, but he saw no one.

The hut was rectangular, with rounded corners. The floor was of hardened mud or clay, and the roof was made of sheared wood. Several mats rested on the floor, and at one end of the room there was a wooden table with a mortar and pestle, along with materials used for mixing.

Edward was about to stand, but as soon as he removed his blanket he felt a draft.

What in God's name?! I'm naked!

He rushed to cover himself again. He searched, but couldn't see his clothes anywhere. His clothes, his weapons, his pack—all gone. *Whoever brought me here must have taken my things as well, so where are they?* He stood, wrapping the blanket over his nakedness. He couldn't see anyone around through the open door of the hut, so he walked outside.

What met his eyes was a whole village of huts, a civilisation hidden here, deep in the forest. He could see the tall pines beyond the settlement's boundary. He gazed at the scene for a few minutes, and then turned back in the direction of the hut.

What he saw took his breath away.

A large stone pyramid reached above the trees and spanned an area half the size of the village itself. At the four corners of its base were four pillars of intricate design, carved in the form of animals, strange creatures he had never seen before. Steps in the middle of the pyramid went almost to the top. Halfway up the steps there was an opening with a large standing area. Nearby, to the right of the pyramid, was nothing short of a palace, made of intricately carved stone and almost as tall as the pyramid itself. Other buildings, similar in style, were scattered about the vicinity.

They did not give the impression of dwellings, but might have served some civic or religious purpose.

Edward stood, awestruck and silent. Then he noticed the village was not deserted: a crowd of people were gathered at the base of the pyramid, and on the opening halfway up a man stood, pointing at something. Edward glanced around, and suddenly it dawned on him. *He's pointing at me!* He noticed others staring at him from the crowd, and some walking toward him, spears in hand. *This cannot be good...* Edward tied the blanket tight around his waist, then turned and ran in the opposite direction. He didn't dare look behind him—it would only slow him down—but he didn't have to see his pursuers to know they intended to catch him. *This is no way to treat a guest!*

He was almost to the edge of the jungle when a figure appeared in front of him holding a spear with its point extended toward Edward, as if in warning. Edward instinctively dropped to his knees and used the momentum to slide on the ground, avoiding the spear and sliding closer to the man. Edward thrust out his hand to grab the weapon, hoping to disarm the attacker. The spear was within reach of his fingertips when, at the last second, it was yanked away.

The man lifted his foot and slammed it down on Edward's face as he was trying to slide past, pinning him to the ground and halting his ill-formed escape attempt.

"You will not escape your fate," the man said, speaking with a deep, accented voice.

He knows English? "Why are you doing this to me? What fate?" He asked, his voice muffled by the foot on his cheek.

"Silence!" the man yelled.

Two other men approached. The three conversed in a language unlike any Edward had ever heard. Then they picked him up off the ground and dragged him back toward the village.

He was now able to his captor. He was as tall as Edward, about six feet four inches, but even more muscular. He was wearing padded wooden armour over garments of tanned cowhide, loose-fitting to allow great freedom of motion. The entire outfit was ornamented with bones and carved human figures; on its sleeves, feathers of blue, red, and gold were sewn into the leather. On his head was a headdress atop which perched an eagle's skull, and from the front of which long fangs hung down the sides of the man's face. That face was formidable, with a strong jaw and a killer's eyes.

The three men dragged him to the pyramid while the crowd

watched and chanted something Edward didn't understand. He tried to pull against them and objected loudly, but he was silenced with a blow to the chest. Only when they reached the base of the pyramid did they let him go. The warrior who'd caught him prodded him with his spear, urging him up the stairs.

As Edward climbed, he looked over his shoulder at the villagers. Their dress appeared bizarre to him. Many were more or less naked, with strange adornments on their bodies; bones pierced their noses and brows, and whitewash covered some faces.

When he reached the standing area halfway up, he saw an elderly man in similar garb as the one who had captured him. But this man was not wearing armour and did not appear to be a warrior. He wore a full cowhide garment, dyed green and red and gold with many feathers attached to it. A multitude of stone figures adorned him, even more than the warrior was wearing. The warrior handed Edward to the elderly man.

"Do you speak English? I didn't know of your village. Please let me leave and I'll not—"

The warrior slapped Edward with the flat of his spear and shook his head, warning him to stop talking. The old man forced Edward to face the crowd and from his vantage point he could see the whole village.

The old man turned to the crowd and addressed them in a booming voice. They stopped chanting and listened. Edward glanced this way and that, trying to see where he might run, but there were warriors everywhere. The one who'd caught him administered a glare as if to drive the very thought of escape from Edward's mind. He was sure he wouldn't be able to fight them all off, and if he caused too much trouble they would kill him on the spot and forego the ceremony.

At the end of the speech, the crowd began chanting again; the man walked to Edward and in one swift motion tore off the blanket covering him. He tried to cover himself with his hands. *Dammit, old man! This is so embarrassing!*

The man handed Edward a cup filled with a strange-smelling liquid.

I suppose I'm to drink this, am I? I guess if I want to stay alive I'll have to do as they say. Everyone watched him as he stood there. Then one of the warriors motioned toward him with his spear, so he drank the potion down in one gulp. It tasted as bad as it smelled, but everyone cheered when Edward handed back the empty cup.

The old Mayan raised Edward's hand into the air, and the crowd cheered again, but Edward wasn't feeling so well. He was already dizzy and tired, and everything was becoming a blur.

The Mayan guided him to a raised platform, then motioned to a pair of warriors. They forced Edward to lie down on the platform—which, given his condition, required very little strength—and tied down his hands and feet with ropes. Edward wanted to struggle, but had trouble even moving a muscle.

Why am I so weak?

When they had finished tying him down, the older man performed a ritual dance with the warrior who'd captured Edward while the villagers made music with drums. The warriors who tied him down cranked wheels on each side of the stone platform, causing it to move towards the pyramid.

Edward pulled his head back as far as he could towards the pyramid and his apparent destination. The platform was heading towards a small alcove, but he couldn't see anything special about the recess in the pyramid. *Why am I moving? What is this contraption?*

The older man had kept dancing and now the younger warrior handed him a torch, which he threw into the alcove of the pyramid, starting a fire.

Ah, I see. I'm to be burned to death. Shite. Edward tried to pull on the ropes, but to no avail.

The platform kept inching towards the flames. The heat felt more intense as he moved closer to his demise. The old man continued his dance to the beat of the drums while the villagers kept chanting. Strangely enough, Edward found the spectacle morbidly captivating.

This must be why they call it the Forest of Burning Hearts.

"Hey!" Edward yelled. The man didn't respond. "Hey! Let me go!" Neither of the dancers paid any attention to him.

The heat was intense to the point of being unbearable. He only had minutes left before he was roasted alive.

"I didn't do anything to you, why are you doing this? I'll give you money, guns, anything you want!" They all ignored him as they continued the ritual.

The top of his head felt like it was burning.

"Let me out of here! You can't do this to me! My crew will avenge me!" His threats garnered no more attention than his pleading.

Mere seconds left.

"You'll regret the day you made an enemy of a pirate!" he yelled with all his strength.

The platform, the dance, the drums, the chanting—indeed, the whole ritual—halted. The older man and the warrior wore confusion and shock on their faces. Mutterings in a foreign tongue reached his ears over the crackling of the flames.

They stopped. Thank you, Father.

The older Mayan spoke to the two warriors and they started the wheels again, but this time in reverse. After the platform reached its initial position, they released the ropes binding Edward's hands and feet and helped him up. The old man examined him, turning his head this way and that, forcing open his mouth, checking his muscles. Satisfied, he said something to the warriors and they helped him, still unsteady from the drugged potion, climb down the pyramid steps.

The warrior who had captured Edward stopped them and glared. "You may have saved yourself for now, but you will never pass the tests. I will never consider you a brother." With that he let the others pass.

What was that about? What does he have against me? He looked back at the warrior, who was still glaring at him.

Wait a… Tests?

21. A LEADER

Edward was taken to a hut similar to the one in which he had awoken that morning. When the warriors had left, a young woman handed Edward his clothes. Edward had forgotten his shame, but as soon as he saw his clothes he hurried to cover himself. Laughing at his embarrassment, the woman placed a small cup on a table at one end of the hut, and then left. Edward inspected the cup warily, but it was different from the one he had drunk from atop the pyramid and smelled somewhat normal. He drank the contents and immediately felt a bit better and more alert.

Such strange medicine. I wonder how it works.

The warrior who had captured Edward earlier walked into the hut, still glaring at him. He was angry about something, but Edward couldn't think of what. *If anything, I should be the angry one. They tried to burn me alive!*

"The king requests your presence."

"And if I refuse?"

"We will resume the ceremony."

"Lead the way!" Edward declared. The warrior left the hut and Edward followed close behind. *Maybe if I try to befriend him he might turn around.* "Do you have a name?"

"There will be no talking until you speak with the king."

Well, so much for that.

Edward and the warrior walked through the village, their destination appearing to be the palace nearby the pyramid. People were going about their daily routines, although many stood watching as he passed, jostling each other to catch a glimpse of him. When he smiled and waved to some children, they laughed and ran away.

Edward did not speak as the warrior led him to the king's palace. He stepped up a flight of white and grey limestone stairs into a large, open room. The walls were decorated with murals and a variety of animal skins and weapons—probably displaying the king's own accomplishments—and the floor was inlaid with coloured limestone in patterns that appeared to represent deities or other mythological figures. He could see several doors leading to rooms within the palace on the left and right.

Against the far wall of the room was a raised stone platform supporting a stone throne. The king, the same man who had done the ceremonial dance on the pyramid, was sitting on the throne.

Attending him were four warriors kneeling on mats in front of the throne. The warrior who had captured Edward took his place on a mat in front of the king, and a servant placed a mat in the middle of the room for Edward. The servant poured him a cup of water, which he sipped.

After a moment of silence, the king began to speak in the tongue Edward couldn't understand. After he finished, the young warrior who captured him translated. "We are the village counsel. I am the king, Kinchil. This is my son, the war chief, Pukuh."

That young one is the war chief? No wonder I was beaten!

"And these are the village elders: Ixtab, Hanapu, Mulac, and Tohil."

The elders bowed to Edward as their names were mentioned, and he bowed to each in return.

"My name is Edward Thatch," he announced as he bowed to the king.

Pukuh relayed the information without expression. For the moment he seemed to be hiding his hatred of Edward. "You have come here alone to face the trials of the warrior," the king continued. "When you become a warrior, you will become one of us. Then, the trials and the ritual of rebirth will make you a spiritual warrior and a brother to the Mayans."

Pukuh paused, seemingly finished with his prepared speech. Then he added: "You will never pass the tests. I will make sure of it."

The king leaned forward and, frowning, smacked his son's face. Edward had to stifle a smile, but Pukuh did not react. Then the king spoke, and again Pukuh translated.

"First you must make an offering of water to Ah Tabai, the hunter God, and pray for the honour to participate." Pukuh picked up his cup of water, but Edward stopped him.

"Hold, hold a moment! I never agreed to this. Why must I face these trials? I should like these trials rather than be burned alive, but what purpose does it serve?"

Pukuh's eyes flared. "How dare you! It is an honour that one such as you, a weak outsider, should be considered for this! I ought to kill you right—"

Kinchil yelled something fierce at his son, stopping him. They spoke to each other for a moment, and then Kinchil reached in among the multitude of necklaces he was wearing and brought forth an object that startled Edward.

It was a key.

That can't be! Can it…?

The king addressed Edward, Pukuh still translating, while his eyes were captivated by the key. "Many years ago a man came here.

He was a brave warrior who could not be bested by any of ours. He fought and ran from us in the jungle for five days until he and I fought on the full moon of the fifth night. We were exhausted, but we fought each other with all our might. We were equals, and neither of us won that day," the king said, a small smile on the corner of his lips. "The king of the time honoured him with trials for his bravery, and he passed them and he became our brother. He called himself a pirate and gave us this key, saying another like him would come one day, and should be accorded the same honour. If he passed the tests, then he would be given this key as a reward."

Benjamin Hornigold! Edward thought back to the man who had taken his money and left him his ship in exchange.

"We have honoured that agreement with you. If you pass, you will gain this key. Does this key hold any significance for you?"

Edward nodded. "I believe it is a key to my ship. I was guided here through a note left in that ship by the previous owner."

"Then you must attempt the trials if you wish to have this key." The king put the key back around his neck, out of sight. "Now, the offering and prayer."

Pukuh picked up the cup again and poured its contents onto the ground in a line. Then he bowed down to the stone, his head almost touching it, and remained in that position. Edward did the same and waited in silence.

To whom should I pray? Their gods? Ours? I care not about either.

After a moment, Pukuh rose, and so Edward sat up as well.

"The first test is one of leadership," said Pukuh, translating the king's words. "You will choose three warriors to accompany you in a hunt. You will guide them and they will act under your orders. You will be hunting a wolf pack that has been attacking our village, and"—Pukuh stared daggers at Edward—"I will be accompanying you."

"You as in *you*, or the old man?" Edward asked, pointing at them in turn.

"You will call him King Kinchil. And no, he will not be joining you." The young warrior clenched his fists. "I will."

⚓ ⚓ ⚓

All the king's warriors were lined up, armed and carrying weapons, for Edward's inspection. The king and the war chief watched as he chose the ones he would bring with him. Beforehand, he was forced to strip and dress in the traditional warrior's garments: a suit of wooden armour and cowhide, and, on his head, a cap in the form of a wolf's head, complete with fur and teeth. It made him appear part man, part wolf. *Well isn't this brilliant. I'm to kill wolves while looking like one.*

Edward walked up and down the line, inspecting each warrior: testing his muscles, examining his eyes, assessing the weapons he carried. *This is foolishness. They all seem capable and in good shape. I'll choose at random.* He stepped back and, without thinking, pointed to three individuals in quick succession.

Pukuh's jaw dropped, and the king laughed.

"What? What is it?"

Pukuh's shock turned to anger and he clenched his teeth. "Nothing. You chose well. We leave immediately. Grab any provisions you may need, and meet at the village entrance."

"Where are my things?"

Pukuh pointed at a nearby hut. "Over there."

Edward gathered a few things, including his compass and some food. But something was missing. *Where's my sword? Dammit!* Edward went back out and made his way to the entrance of the village where the warriors were waiting for him.

"Did you bring my sword or pistols in with my other belongings?"

Pukuh spat on the ground. "That is not a warrior's weapon. We left them where we found you. You will use a spear." He tossed one to Edward.

He caught it easily enough, but eyed the primitive weapon hesitantly. "But I don't know how to use it."

"Then you are not a warrior," Pukuh said. "Will you be a leader and lead, or is that something else you are not capable of doing?"

"I'm going, I'm going." *Now the question is where? Hmm.* "The wolves that attacked me, were they part of the pack threatening your village?"

"Yes. They've attacked people in our village without cause. We used to walk with them side by side, but as of late they have been acting strange. We do not know the reason. We thought a sacrifice would appease the gods, but instead they chose another, lesser way of bringing balance. They are strange beings indeed."

"I'm certainly glad for their decision," Edward said with a smirk. "Since the wolves that ambushed me were part of the pack we're searching for, we'll begin by heading to where I was attacked." The warriors followed Edward, not saying a word.

The Mayans moved with swift and silent feet through the forest. Edward, however, did not. Every time he stepped on a rock or a twig he made a loud noise, and each time he stumbled he cursed. His companions found this intolerable and attempted, with limited success, to instruct him in the proper manner of walking through the underbrush.

Within a few hours they reached the rock where Edward had

faced off against the wolf pack. He found the wolf he had killed with his blade. He dropped his spear and bent to grab his cutlass, but before he was able to rise, the business end of another spear was pointed between his eyes.

"Never drop your weapon. The moment you do is the moment you die."

"I do not believe I'd be the only one," said Edward.

Pukuh frowned in confusion—until Edward lowered his eyes, and he followed them down to discover the point of Edward's cutlass almost jammed into the Mayan's ribs. The warrior backed off and lowered his weapon, shock plastering his face and eliciting a smile from Edward.

Pukuh shook his head. "For this trial, swords are forbidden. This is for your warrior rebirth, and you are permitted to use only our weapons."

Edward couldn't be quite sure, but there seemed to be a little more respect in Pukuh's voice than before. "Very well, I'll abide by your rules. But I need my sword when we're done."

"Understood. Now, did you wish to waste time, or do you have purpose in being here?"

"Some of the wolves who attacked me scurried off somewhere. It must have been back to the main pack, so we'll follow their tracks and they'll take us to them."

"You know how to track them?" Pukuh asked.

"No, but that's what I have you for, right? Can you ask the others which of them would be able to track the wolves, please?"

Pukuh did as he was asked and one of the other warriors stepped forward. "All of them can track, but Hukan is the best. He could track a raindrop in a river."

Hukan inspected the fallen wolf and the traces of dried blood on the ground from the wolves wounded in the fight with Edward. He led the group south, following a trail of blood. Soon they found another wolf carcass, and the trail ended.

Hukan conveyed his assessment to the warriors. Pukuh translated. "He says the trail of blood is gone, but the ground is soft around here, so the tracks are easy to follow." Edward nodded to both of them, and they resumed tracking. Hukan examined overturned rocks, broken branches, and bits of animal hair on low vegetation. When Edward thought that the trail was lost, Hukan kept moving as if nothing had changed. Even when the others seemed to have doubts about their direction, he alone proceeded with confidence.

When the day turned to afternoon, they came upon the edge of a low cliff. Small rocks were scattered down its face, all the way to the bottom. It stretched both ways for a good distance. Hukan walked to the verge, then offered his assessment to Pukuh. "Hukan says the wolves went down the face of the cliff. They have worn the ground by their frequent passage. It is not safe for us to climb down, so we will circle around."

"Very well," said Edward, "let's move on." The others turned and walked west, but Edward was fascinated by the scene beyond the cliff edge. Trees as far as the eye could see: a sea of green, shining in the noonday sun. He could hear the sounds of the forest echoing clearly even from that great distance. It was different from the night before—no longer a cry of terror, but a song.

"Come, Edward," Pukuh prodded him.

"Yes."

Edward was turning to leave when a rock beneath him crumbled, and the edge of the cliff collapsed. He lost his footing and began to fall, but Pukuh swiftly reached out and grabbed his hand. Edward held on tight, and for a split second he was safe. But the ground was still unstable, and the cliff edge broke again, taking Pukuh this time.

They both tumbled down the steep cliff to the hard jungle floor, neither of them able to stop the deathly plummet.

The world went black and the two men lost a couple of minutes of their lives to the ether. When he came to, Edward got up off the ground. His head hurt, and he had pains all over. He was sure something was wrong with his back; sharp pain lanced up and down his spine whenever he moved.

Pukuh was holding his leg, so Edward limped over to examine it. The Mayan's left leg was twisted out of place, the bone seemingly broken, but Edward was not sure. The warrior wouldn't be able to walk on it now. He was sweating and it was evident he wanted to yell out in pain, but he only grunted.

A lesser man would be screaming and panicking right now.

The other warriors were peering over the cliff edge and were shouting something down to Edward and Pukuh. Pukuh shouted something back. Then he grabbed his leg and gave it a swift jerk. With a loud crack the leg was immediately back in its proper place.

"What the hell are you doing? That's dangerous!"

"It is the only way," Pukuh said through ragged breaths. "They want to know what to do."

"Tell them to go back to the village to get help, or at least something to help you walk. We'll head east along the cliff face and wait."

"No, you should leave me here, I'll slow you down. I can't walk like this."

"I'm not leaving you behind! You could die out here, and I won't let that happen!"

Pukuh seemed surprised at such a display of concern from Edward, and merely shook his head.

"Tell them," Edward commanded.

Pukuh yelled up Edward's orders and the others made their reply. Edward already knew what they would say, as they were to follow his command. They disappeared from sight, heading back the way they had come.

Edward picked up his and Pukuh's spears and helped his companion to stand, encountering only slight reluctance from the injured warrior. He pulled Pukuh's arm around his own shoulder, and Pukuh used his spear in his free hand to help himself walk.

They followed the cliff, heading east as Edward had suggested. They spoke little, focused on arriving at their destination and avoiding further injury. The sounds of chirping birds and small forest denizens were their only companions. After a few hours of walking, with a little rest at intervals, they reached the end of the cliff. Night had fallen.

They probably arrived at the village and are explaining the situation by now. It'll be dawn before they return. "We should get some sleep. We're going to be here a while," Edward said as he let Pukuh down against a tree.

"Yes," Pukuh agreed as he eased himself down.

Edward also sat down and brought out some of the food he had been sampling through the day. He offered some to Pukuh, who refused it.

The moon shone its pale white light over the dark forest. At the edge of the cliff there were only a few scattered pines; the roots, snaking and gnarled like the fingers of an old man, were sticking out from the ground before plunging deep for nutrients. Various creatures were out and sounding their calls, long and short, loud and soft, screeching and soothing—there was no semblance of order in the jungle of the night.

After a few minutes of relative silence, Pukuh spoke up. "Why did you help me?"

Edward arched his brow. "What do you mean? Why wouldn't I?"

"I haven't been very hospitable to you. You could have left me and saved yourself, but you chose to stay with me. Why?"

Edward thought it over for a moment. "I don't really know why," he said. "I don't carry any ill will towards you. I mean, I could have done without the human sacrifice bit, but what's a few singed hairs between friends?"

"I apologise for that. We have been persecuted before by others of your kind. We protect our jungle and our livelihood any way we can."

So that's why. "Would you have left me behind? You seem to hate outsiders quite a bit."

Pukuh stared off into the dark forest and sat in silence and deep thought for a few minutes.

Thirteen Years Ago

"Pukuh!" someone yelled. "Pukuh!"

Pukuh, age thirteen, turned around. He was an athletic youth and, like his father, a great warrior who could best many of the adults already.

"What is it, Jutak? I need to go. My father is calling me."

Jutak was the same age as Pukuh, and just as spirited. A strong, muscular body made him tough for his age. He and Pukuh had been friends and rivals since they were little.

"It is for the test, yes? You take the test to become a true warrior now, right?"

"Yes, and if I am late, I will be scolded."

"Don't forget your promise."

Pukuh walked to the palace. "Do not worry. I will make sure you come with us."

Pukuh ran through the streets of the village to the palace. He went up the limestone steps and into the main chamber. There his father, the war chief, was waiting with the king and the elders. He went to his knees in front of them.

The king, an older man who could no longer speak with ease, sat on the throne with a dignity beyond his failing years. He wore many adornments celebrating his high status and his achievements from over the years.

The war chief, Pukuh's father, spoke for him most of the time. "Pukuh," his father said, his voice resounding throughout the palace, "today you take the test of a leader, the first step in becoming a warrior of this village. You will be participating in a hunt. There are outsiders near the village. You will hunt them down and either capture them for sacrifice, or kill them if they are deemed a threat. This is your decision. Make the offering, pray to the gods for success, and then we will choose four warriors to accompany you. You have our blessing on this hunt for honour."

These were the words of not only his father, but the king. He had their blessing both, and Pukuh's heart swelled with pride. "Yes, my king." He took the cup of water, poured it out on the ground, and prayed to Ah Tabai for success in his hunt.

When he had finished, the king, his father, and the elders all saw him off. The warriors lined up for Pukuh to choose amongst them. It wasn't hard for him to decide whom to take, as he had trained with them his whole life.

However, one person was missing from the group. "Fa— I mean, War Chief? Where is Jutak?"

"He, like you, is not a true warrior yet, and so cannot participate in your test. He will have to have his own someday."

"But I promised him I would take him along!"

"You will have to break that promise, then."

Pukuh crossed his arms in defiance. "You want me to be a leader and make decisions? This is the decision I have made. I would have Jutak with me."

Pukuh's father stared at his son and gave an exasperated sigh. He looked to the king for approval, and the older man gave a nod. "Very well. Do as you wish."

Pukuh's beamed. "Jutak!"

Jutak emerged from one of the nearby huts and ran to his friend. He had armour on and a spear in his hand, ready for battle. He and Pukuh smiled for joy at his being granted the privilege of joining the hunt.

Pukuh chose three others he felt would do well, the best warriors of the village.

After the hunting party had gathered supplies, they set out to track down the outsiders threatening their village. Spears in their hands, they moved with swift and silent feet through the pine forest, crossing streams and rocks and fallen branches. They went on for an hour, until they reached a large, flat, open area of rock and grass, and there they saw a party of white men setting up a camp.

With only four of them in the camp, they did not appear at all formidable. Spectacles adorned their thin faces, and their arms were small and spindly, obviously unused to physical labour. They had strange equipment and notebooks with them.

"Shall we attack now, Pukuh?" Jutak asked. "They are distracted."

"No, we shall wait for the cover of night when they are asleep. For now, we shall keep our distance."

Jutak and the other warriors nodded. They trusted Pukuh and his decisions. They ran back a safe distance and set up their watch.

Jutak was smiling. "Pukuh, are you excited?"

Pukuh laughed. "About what?"

"The beginning of our promise. You become king and I become war chief."

"It has been so long since we made that promise. I cannot believe you still remember."

"Of course I remember. And soon I'll do this test, and we'll both be on the path to fulfilling our dreams."

"Yes, yes. Continue like that all night and we'll leave you behind.

The Voyages of Queen Anne's Revenge Collection One

Get some sleep." Pukuh pushed his friend and Jutak pushed him back.

"Wake me when we're ready to leave." Jutak turned over and rested his head on a tree root.

Darkness fell, and with it the nocturnal voices of the jungle began to cry out, claiming the night as their own. Some of the group, including Pukuh, kept watch, and some slept to conserve strength. When a few hours had passed, the watchers woke their comrades, and the Mayan warriors stole into the white men's camp, silent as wolves stalking their prey. They found a few tents pitched around a fire which had burned down to its last few embers. The men were asleep; there was no sound save for the animals in the woods.

Pukuh was about to signal an attack, but something made him stop. *Something's not right.*

A loud sound like thunder broke the silence, and a nearby tree broke and splintered as if something had hit it.

Pukuh saw a man with a pistol in his hand walking closer. Five others lined up behind him, all with the same weapons.

"Pukuh! What do we do?"

"Retreat! Run!"

The warriors did not hesitate. They ran from the enemy whose power they did not understand. Had the white men been fewer, he would have attacked, but his warriors were outnumbered.

They ran through the forest, past the trees and rocks and streams, back toward their village and away from the white people and their devices. Pukuh knew they could not pause or risk slowing down, as the thunderous noises kept resounding against the trees. *I was a fool. I should have taken more care. I should have searched harder. Men like that would surely have guards in a dangerous place such as this. I've failed the test.*

A scream from beside Pukuh snapped him back to reality. Jutak was on the ground to the left, holding his leg. Pukuh ran to his aide.

"Leave me! Save yourself, Pukuh!"

"But…" He looked back and the white men were still chasing them. One was reloading his gun and was gaining on them.

"You can't take me with you. It will slow you down."

Pukuh grabbed his friend by the chest and shook him. "What about our promise, Jutak?"

"You have to live for both of us now, Pukuh." Jutak closed his eyes and recited a prayer. Pukuh's eyes were wide with horror. He was caught between the desire to save his friend and the certain knowledge that the attempt would result in both their deaths. *I can still save him! I'll carry him back myself.*

Unfortunately, Jutak made the decision himself. He finished his prayer, took out a small hunting knife, and stabbed himself in the gut. He did not cry out from the pain, but, with his final breath, whispered, "Run!" Then he went limp in Pukuh's arms. Tears streamed down Pukuh's face as he pulled up his hands, covered in the blood of his best friend of thirteen years. He rose to look into the face of the ones who had brought tragedy.

The white man and his guns.

Pukuh didn't remember, but the other warriors claimed he was filled with the spirit of the god that is his namesake. The God of Death, Pukuh, awakened in him. He killed all of the white men himself in a rage. By the end, his body was slick with blood.

Blood of his enemies, his friend, and his own.

⚓ ⚓ ⚓

Present Day

"No," Pukuh said in answer to Edward's question. "I would not leave you…" He turned his gaze back to Edward. "Outsiders have harmed this village before. I did not want that to happen again, but you have shown me you are not like them. Even though you are weak, you are honourable."

Edward wasn't sure what to say. "Thank you, Pukuh… I'm glad I've earned a little bit of your respect."

Pukuh smiled. "Only a little." The two of them sat in silence, staring at the stars. "You remind me of the pirate who came before you," Pukuh said, breaking the silence. "His name was Benjamin. Have you met him?"

As I thought! It was *him!* "Nearly. He took my money, but left me his ship. I've been chasing down the keys to open it up fully ever since. I can't even use the cannons yet because the cabin is locked. If I find him, he will feel my wrath."

Pukuh laughed for the first time since they met. "That sounds like something he would do. My father said that he was always pulling pranks, something that at his age was seen as strange. He had a youthful state of mind."

"Is he the one who taught you English?"

"Yes. At first I hated him like all white men, but that changed over time. I grew to love him, and he taught me how to speak this language."

"It seems we've both inherited a bit of what he had."

"Yes, it appears that way."

Soon they went to sleep, but they had not slept long when Edward was awakened by Pukuh jabbing him.

"We are not alone," Pukuh whispered.

"Animals?"

Pukuh nodded and pressed his back against the tree. It was all he was able to do in his condition. Edward knew he would have to do any fighting alone. He picked up his spear and readied himself. He could hear the sounds of the jungle closing in: the shrieking of birds, the snapping of branches, the rustling of leaves. Edward couldn't keep track of it all. *Which one do I listen to? Where are they coming from?*

As if hearing his thoughts, Pukuh offered some advice. "Don't listen for what you can hear, listen for what you can't. Close your eyes and distinguish which sounds are from prey running, and which sounds the predators are trying to hide."

Edward followed Pukuh's advice. He closed his eyes and concentrated on the sounds. He could hear the wind rustling through the trees. The birds flew from branches, and then there was silence to his left.

Edward turned, bent his knees, ready to spring, and raised his spear, ready to strike. A wolf jumped out from the bush in front of him. Edward thrust forward, stamping his foot. The spear lodged in the wolf's throat, spilling its blood everywhere. He pulled out the spear as the wolf dropped to the jungle floor. Then, upon their brother's death, more wolves sprang from the brush and circled the men. It was obvious to Edward they were planning to attack Pukuh first; he was injured, and they could tell. They fixed him in their sight, preparing to pounce.

They must think he's the weaker one. Are they ever in for a surprise!

The pair of wolves nearest Pukuh jumped first. Edward turned and stabbed one in the ribs, downing it. Pukuh was able to brace his spear, and the other wolf impaled itself. He dropped the spear and pulled out a knife.

"You can run, you know," Pukuh said to Edward. "I wouldn't be offended."

"You think you can take all the glory yourself? You don't stand a chance with that pitiful knife of yours. I'll pass this test by bringing you back in my arms, like the babe you are."

"Oh, so that is your plan, is it? You are to use me, then?" Pukuh slid himself up the side of the tree to where he was able to manoeuvre a bit better.

"I suppose you could say that. Save the war chief. Be a hero."

"Well, I am not about to be saved by you a second time."

The wolves resumed their attack. One lunged for Pukuh's arm, and he thrust his knife into its skull. Immediately another attacked the same arm, and yet another sprang upon his broken leg. Pukuh cried out in pain and stabbed the one on his arm again and again as Edward slammed his spear into the other's heart.

One wolf jumped on Edward's back and another attacked his

injured left arm. As Pukuh gouged the eye of the wolf on Edward's arm, Edward dropped his spear and grabbed the animal on his back, pried its fangs off his shoulder, and threw it at the tree. There was a distinct snap and a whimper as the animal's back broke.

Now only one wolf remained. It had remained aloof, watching the whole contest as if gauging the power of its opponents. It was bigger than the others—and, to judge from its grizzled fur and the scar down its left eye, the alpha male as well. It stood still, watching both men, gazing at the fierce eyes that stared back at it. Their eyes were like its own. They were the eyes of fellow hunters, the eyes of brothers.

The wolf turned and walked away—not out of fear, but out of respect.

Edward watched the wolf until it was out of sight, and then let out the breath he had been holding in. *I don't think the wolf clan will be bothering Pukuh's village any longer.*

Pukuh turned to Edward. "I would say you passed the test."

"Does that mean we're brothers?" Edward said with a grin.

"No."

Edward's smile faded. "Oh…"

"You still have one more test. And I can assure you, it is going to be more difficult than the last."

22. AN UNINVITED GUEST

Toward morning, Pukuh's companions returned and found him and Edward. They brought bandages for their wounds and a wooden crutch to help Pukuh walk back to the village. They were set on hunting down the wolf pack, but Pukuh told them what had happened and presumed that the wolves wouldn't attack again.

That, at least, is what Edward thought he told them, until he saw them burst out laughing at a certain point in the story.

"I'll break your other leg if you're making a joke at my expense."

"Worry not. I told them you screamed like a little boy only once."

They were in good spirits on the journey back to the village, and when they arrived everyone was waiting for them, cheering and crowding around. Edward assumed the attention was for Pukuh, and withdrew, but many villagers approached Edward as well. He didn't understand what they were saying, but some of the older ones cried while holding his hands, undoubtedly thanking him for helping Pukuh. The attention made him blush.

The king soon arrived and embraced his son. He said a few words to disperse the crowd and then invited Pukuh and Edward to accompany him to the palace. This time they sat side by side before the throne. Pukuh recounted, from start to finish and in his own language, the story of the hunt. Edward understood not a word of it, but felt proud nonetheless. Then, as Pukuh finished the tale, all the elders burst into laughter.

Dammit! Again? Edward flashed Pukuh a baleful stare.

Pukuh smiled as he stood and moved to the other side of the room, in front of his father. The king addressed Edward, with Pukuh translating. "You have passed the first test of leadership. Your decision to send for help, as well as your decision to stay with the war chief, has brought you honour and made you a leader in the eyes of the gods. Tonight there will be a feast in honour of your defeat of the wolf clan."

Edward bowed deeply. "You honour me too much. I'm afraid I couldn't have made it out alive without your war chief either."

Pukuh translated, and the elders returned Edward's bow. Their respect for him was evident.

But then a commotion rose outside. A warrior soon ran in and relayed a message, whereupon everyone rushed out of the palace.

"What is it? What's happening?" asked Edward, as he and Pukuh hurried out.

"There's another white person coming into the village, and he is on the attack. I hope he is not one of your friends, because he's about to be killed."

"I should hope not! I told them all to stay at the ship." Edward ran out of the palace and down the stone steps, hurrying to the village gate, where he could see someone fighting with the warriors. *Dad damn it! That* is *one of my crew! I have to stop that fool before someone dies.*

Outside the village perimeter, one warrior was lying on the ground, and inside two warriors circled the crewman, one at the front and one at the back. They both thrust their spears, aiming at his legs and chest. The crewman jumped, did a flip, and caught the spears in midair. Then he spun around and thrust one spear into each warrior's leg.

Edward's jaw dropped at the incredible sight.

The crewman stood up, and that was when Edward noticed that his hat had fallen off in the last attack, and he could see the red hair of Anne Bonney.

Anne saw Edward and her face lit up. She began to run to him as he ran to her. Before they were even close, all the warriors in the village rushed upon her at once, forming a circle, their spears pointed and ready.

"Stop!" Edward yelled. "Don't kill her!" he pleaded as he ran.

They didn't attack, but they didn't lower their weapons either. Anne did not let her guard down, but even she knew when she was beaten. Edward forced his way through the tight circle, pushed their weapons aside, and grabbed Anne close, trying to protect her. He again told the warriors to stop as Pukuh stepped forward on his crutches to intervene.

"Please, Pukuh, tell them to stop. This is my friend."

Pukuh did as he was asked, and the warriors put their weapons away but kept them at their sides. This "friend" had taken out three of their warriors with ease.

Edward let Anne go when he was sure no one else would attack, but he still shielded her.

"Why did she come and harm my people? Someone could have been killed, Edward!"

"I know, Pukuh, and I'm sorry. I tried to tell everyone to stay on the ship, but some are a little too free-spirited, it seems." Edward glanced back at Anne. She averted her gaze as she scratched her freckled nose. "I'm sure you have some warriors who are the same, correct?"

Pukuh thought it over for a moment and then nodded. "Yes, I

suppose you are right. My men shouldn't have attacked her without my orders."

"Well… I was the one who attacked first." Anne stepped forward and made a quick bow. "My name is Anne. I'm sorry; the thought of Edward in danger drove my hasty actions. I thought that I could let him alone, but when he was gone for a few days, I feared the worst and needed to find him."

Pukuh considered Anne for a moment, and then he turned and told the warriors and villagers gathered around something. All the men smiled, and the women pouted in jealousy.

Oh, what did he say now? Edward palmed his face in frustration, wondering what clever humiliation Pukuh had brought down upon him this time.

"Come," Pukuh directed. "We return to the palace to discuss what to do next." As they all walked, Pukuh explained the situation to the elders while Edward and Anne followed at a slight distance and talked privately.

"So you came because you thought I was in danger?"

"I did not think it would take so long, these tests. I feared the worst."

"I hope you at least told William you were coming here." Anne was silent. "You told someone, right?"

Anne's ears went red like her hair, and she averted her gaze. "I left a note… with John."

Edward shook his head, exasperated. "Let's hope for your sake no one else decides to defy orders and try to find me. There's a feast tonight, and I should like to attend instead of handling more of my crew."

"A feast? Why?"

"Well, the tests mentioned on the map were tests of leadership issued by the people in this village. The previous owner of the *Freedom* gave a key to the current king. I finished the first test, so they're having a feast. If I pass the next, we get the key."

"What was the test?"

"We had to find a wolf pack that had been harming the village."

"Is that how you received those wounds?" Anne asked, pointing to his arm. "You aren't hurt, are you?"

"It only aches most of the time," Edward said with a smirk. "The test is also why I'm wearing this guise." Edward motioned to his warrior outfit.

"I was hoping you would explain."

Edward chuckled. "I suppose I look rather silly, do I?"

"Yes, yes you do," Anne said with a sly grin.

Anne and Edward entered the king's palace and sat down. Once again, the king spoke and Pukuh translated. "You have the prowess of a warrior, Anne. Many of my own could not equal your skill. That is extraordinary in a woman."

"I assume you do not train women?" Anne asked.

"It is rare, but not unheard of if one shows the desire," he replied. "You wish to stay during Edward's next test?"

"If you would but grant me the honour." Anne gave a humble bow.

"You are granted permission, but if you are to attend the feast tonight you must follow our rules. This goes for both of you." Edward and Anne nodded in agreement. "You will dress in the festival clothes of our tribe. Edward will dress in garb appropriate to a warrior, and Anne will be clad in the formal dress of our women. Is this acceptable?" Again they nodded. "There is one more condition. Edward must learn a warrior dance, and Anne must help prepare the food with the women."

"A dance!" Edward exclaimed, but caught himself and whispered to Anne, "A dance? I..."

"We agree to the terms."

Edward frowned at Anne. "I have to dance? I *can't* dance!"

"I am sure you'll do well enough. Besides, *I* intend to enjoy it." Anne grinned.

The king continued: "With that settled, you may take your time and explore the village before we have to start preparing. Enjoy tonight's feast, for tomorrow your second trial begins."

After bowing to the village elders and the king, Edward and Anne set about wandering around the village. Everywhere people were walking and talking, the doors of their huts were open and welcoming, and everyone came and went as they pleased. Children playing in the streets ran up to the white-skinned strangers. The girls seemed enamored with Anne's beautiful red hair, while the boys wanted to touch Edward's beard.

They visited the other stone structures in the village Edward had noticed when he first arrived. They were smaller than the palace and the pyramid, but no less picturesque. Anne guessed they were all made of limestone, and had some kind of religious significance.

"These could relate to specific times of the year," she offered. She pointed to a statue in the centre of the room of a man holding his hands, palms up, in front of him. "Maybe when the light hits the hands it means something."

"We'll have to ask Pukuh about it at the feast."

By the time they had finished studying the temples, Pukuh had come for Edward, and a woman for Anne. They took them to do their chores before the festival, and to dress them. Anne gathered fresh vegetables and helped prepare the palace for the feast, and Edward spent the rest of the afternoon practicing a traditional dance of the Maya.

As it happened, he needed every bit of that time.

Why do I have to do this nonsense? Edward thought for the fifth time since starting. He would make it halfway through the dance before making a mistake, and then they had to start all over. Pukuh and the other warriors teaching him the dance would be joining him in the performance, so they could tolerate no mistakes.

"If you make a mistake you shame our village," Pukuh's deep accented voice warned for the fifth time.

"I know. I'm trying."

"Once again…"

When the time for the feast arrived, Edward appeared in an outfit donated by one of the warriors. It was a tight fit for his large size, but it showed off his muscles well. The men all wore the colours red, gold, blue, and purple, arranged in a specific pattern. Pukuh explained that the colours were traditional and specific to their tribe, and if he were to see another tribe's colours he could tell where they were from. Edward thought them a nice change from the bland colours he was used to wearing.

The feast was held in the centre of the palace. A long, low table was set with all kinds of food, mostly vegetables and fruit, with a little meat. Surrounding the table was a soft mat, and pillows were scattered everywhere for people to lie on.

The king was there with his wife, relaxing at the head of the table, waiting for everyone else to arrive. Edward and the rest of the men entered first and sat down. He sat to the left of the king, Pukuh to the right. The warrior next to Edward had been instructed to keep a seat open beside him.

The women walking in caught Edward's attention, and what he saw made his mouth stand open like a sail caught by the wind.

Anne was dressed in the fashion of the Mayans. Her outer garment was loose-fitting and went down to her ankles; it was tied at the waist and had a slit up each side, revealing colourful trousers beneath. The colours were red, blue, pink, and purple in a star pattern with gold trim and flowers stitched to the bodice around the neckline.

But it was not her clothing that made Edward's jaw drop.

Anne's hair was loose at the back, with her long red curls flowing down past her shoulders. Two long strands of hair fell from behind her ears down her chest, each bound with gold ribbon, and thin braids looped around from her forehead to the back, where more gold ribbon bound them together.

She's stunning.

Anne walked up to Edward, but he was rendered speechless. Everyone sat down as he stared at her. It took him a moment to realise he was still standing, and then he swiftly sat down with Anne beside him.

The king stood and recited a prayer, which Pukuh would later tell Edward was to their rain god, thanking him for their bountiful blessings. After that, the warriors performed their dance. This particular dance was another part of the ritual of thanking the rain god, intended to help bring rains and end droughts. *Obviously*, thought Edward, *the gods don't always require human sacrifice.*

But he still felt like a fool. *I think I'd rather be sacrificed than experience this embarrassment. And in front of Anne, no less!* He tried to watch her face as he was dancing around a fire. She was smiling; not laughing or smirking, but smiling.

He only stumbled a little, and no one seemed even to notice, for which he was grateful. After it was done, everyone at the feast cheered and praised the dancing warriors as they seated themselves. It was time to eat.

Everyone talked and ate together at once, and there was much laughter. The king and his queen were not in any special seat and sat as equals amongst the guests.

Anne leaned over to Edward. "This is so nice," she whispered as she glanced about. "And so unlike the dinners at..." She looked at Edward and her smile faded. "Never mind," she said as she straightened herself and filled a wooden plate with food.

Edward cocked his brow, but she didn't notice and he decided to let her be. He turned to Pukuh. "So what is tomorrow's test?" he asked.

Pukuh put his food down and then went quiet. "You will find out tomorrow."

It can't be any worse than what we've already been through. Edward decided to leave it at that. "Can you tell us more about the temples we saw?"

"Ah, those are for the winter and summer... what's the word? Solstice! When the sun is at the correct angle, it will shine on the hand of the sun god."

They talked and ate throughout the night. As the end of the feast neared, a strange, sweet drink was served. It was fermented and, while it was full of fruits, it was as strong as rum. Edward and Anne had only a little—Edward, because he knew he needed to be alert for tomorrow, and Anne, because it was her custom to drink sparingly. After a few small servings, however, Edward could tell she was more relaxed.

"My mother wants to know when you two met," Pukuh said.

Edward took the lead. "We met on the ship. I was in a port looking for some men to join my crew and she boarded. She dressed as a man because women are considered bad luck aboard ships."

Anne continued. "He later found me out. I still conceal my identity from most aboard the *Freedom*, but there are a few with whom I can be myself."

Pukuh relayed the story to his mother. She was a beautiful woman. She wore her hair in braids, and was dressed in garb similar to Anne but more ornamental, decorated with what looked like real gold. Her mannerisms and demeanor bespoke her royal status.

"When were you two wed?" Pukuh asked, sipping his drink nonchalantly.

Edward and Anne both registered mild shock on their faces and then sat up straight. "We're not married," they said together.

"We have only just met," Anne asserted.

"We barely know each other. Only a few months now," Edward added.

They glanced back and forth at one another and around the room. Everyone was smiling at their shyness.

"Yes, yes, I understand," Pukuh reassured them before he translated for his mother.

After a moment of discomfort, other questions followed, and Edward and Anne soon relaxed again. Many asked them about the ship, how it was to live on it, what they did there, and what it meant to be a pirate.

"I suppose I've never really thought about it," Edward said. "I've always learned a pirate was someone who killed anyone without mercy and took whatever they wanted from hard-working citizens. Now, though, in our situation, I can see it in a different light. We don't have to follow any rules that we do not wish to, and we can travel wherever and do whatever we please. It's freedom, like the name of our ship."

Pukuh, being the primary one who understood English, was momentarily speechless in contemplation of the words. He stared at Edward until someone snapped him out of it and asked him to translate.

After a long night of celebration, people retired to their homes. The guests thanked the king and queen before departing, and many of them hugged Anne and Edward as they left.

"So, where will we be staying tonight?" Edward asked Pukuh.

"We have prepared a place for you in the palace. Come, I will show you the chambers we have for guests."

Edward and Anne bowed to the king and his wife, thanking them for their hospitality, and then left with Pukuh for the eastern section of the palace. Passing through the large limestone arches, he took them to a medium-sized room equipped with everything they would need. It held a bed consisting of a cotton mat and a dozen pillows, a divider for privacy, and a separate section for bathing, with a limestone tub and a fire to heat the water. The room even had a mirror on a wooden stand in one corner.

"So is this for Anne or for me?" Edward asked.

Pukuh scratched his head. "It's for both of you."

"Both of us? But... but there's only one bed!" Edward stammered in embarrassment.

"Yes. You do not want to share it? Aren't you two... how do you say it in your language? Special friends?"

"Ah! N-no! You've got it all wrong! We're not s-special friends, or anything!"

Pukuh smiled and patted Edward on the back. "I'm sure it will not be a problem for one night. The woman has already made her decision." Pukuh motioned to the bed.

Anne was already lying in the dozen pillows, curled up and fast asleep. Edward turned back to Pukuh with a look of defeat on his face. "Very well. I guess you win. Have a good night, Pukuh."

"You as well, Edward. You'll need it for tomorrow," Pukuh said cryptically, and walked out.

Edward let down a dark cotton sheet which acted as a curtain for the opening to their room. He took off his shirt and walked over to the pillow-strewn bed. A few blankets made of thick cotton lay in a heap on one side. He covered Anne with one blanket, and then set up a few pillows on the opposite end for himself.

"Thank you," said a voice from beneath the pillows.

Edward glanced over to her. "So you are awake. I thought it was odd for you to fall asleep so soon."

"It was easier that way."

Edward mumbled in agreement as he made his bed and lay in it. A comfortable silence descended between them. They could hear the hum and click of bugs and birds from outside, and a cool breeze blew over them from a window.

"I never had a chance to mention it, but do you know you scared me when you first showed up?"

Anne turned around to face Edward. "Scared?" she asked.

"I was afraid, and a little angry," he said with a chuckle. "I didn't know what they would do to you. I know you're strong, and I know you can beat anyone you face, but I was still scared. I didn't want anything to happen to you."

Anne blushed. "I'm sorry... I was scared too. That's why I had to come." Anne placed her hand over his and looked deep into his dark eyes. "How do you feel now?" Anne sidled closer to him.

"How do I feel now?" Edward shifted and they were closer still.

Anne moved herself even closer to Edward. "Yes, now."

Her red hair was lying out on the pillows and flowing over her shoulders. Her beautiful green eyes were gazing back at him. Those eyes were like the ocean, and they, too, called to him. He gripped her hand while keeping his eyes fixed on her, and then he leaned in and kissed her.

"Does that answer your question?"

Anne flashed a coy smile. "I thought I told you not to kiss me without my permission."

Edward smiled. "Sorry. It slipped my mind."

Anne kissed him back for a brief, sensual moment. "We should sleep. You supposedly have a big day tomorrow." Then she turned over and pulled her blanket over her. Edward thought he saw her wipe a tear from her eye.

"Good night," Anne whispered.

"Good night," Edward replied. Thoughts of home, and the woman he'd left behind, were far from his mind.

⚓ ⚓ ⚓

Edward woke to a cold wind blowing on him and the golden sun rising on the horizon. Instead of soft pillows and a warm bed, he was lying on cold limestone. Instead of a ceiling above him he saw open sky.

Where am I?

He arose, and immediately felt the surface on which he had lain start to shift with his movement. Shock and fear moved his feet to keep his balance, and the surface became level again. He stood on a large, square slab of limestone, and, to judge from the landscape, it was somehow perched high in the air. It was not one solid piece of stone, but a multitude of large stones held together by something. A spear lay at his feet, and when he turned he saw Pukuh standing on the other side of the square, his own spear in hand.

"This is the second test. Prepare yourself." Pukuh ran to Edward. His eyes were fierce, as they had been when the two of them fought the wolves.

He was ready to kill, and ready to die.

23. A WARRIOR

Pukuh attacked with incredible speed. It took everything Edward had to dodge his spear, a task complicated by the ground shifting under their feet as they moved. The platform tilted precariously and Edward could feel his footing start to slip. He ran to the other side and the stone platform leveled out.

"What are you doing, Pukuh?! Are you trying to kill me?"

"This is the second test. You must defeat me in mortal combat."

"That's absurd! Why must we fight? What does this have to do with being a leader? I cannot believe Benjamin would participate in this test."

"This is the same test he and my father had when they were younger. The location has changed, but the fight was the same. He happened upon our village by accident, and my father, then the war chief, fought him to protect the village. Now we duel here, twelve years later. The test of a warrior."

"Where are we?"

"This is on top of the pyramid. This stone slab will not fall, but if you fall off it you will die. Now, take your weapon and fight me!" Pukuh kicked the spear over and Edward picked it up.

Very well, if it's a fight he wants I'll give it to him!

He gave the spear a swipe in the air and prepared a defensive stance.

"Defense will not work here, Edward!" Pukuh ran at him again in a bull rush, swifter than a wolf with blood on its lips.

Edward sidestepped and slipped behind Pukuh, trying to hit him with his elbow. Pukuh dropped and tripped him. Edward had to use both hands and feet so he wouldn't fall off the slab. Pukuh seemed secure and sure of his balance.

How is he doing that? And with a broken leg, no less!

"Rise, Edward."

Edward pushed himself to his feet and readied himself.

Pukuh's right. I can't win this by being defensive. If I start running around, I'll likely fall. He looked over the side of the pyramid.

"What is wrong, Edward? Afraid of heights?"

Edward took a closer look at Pukuh. His legs were trembling despite his stability, and he was pouring sweat.

It's amazing he's able to move like that, but there's no way he's fully recovered yet. Maybe I can force him to surrender.

184

Edward inched forward and used the back end of his spear as a blunt weapon. He kept jabbing at Pukuh's torso and pushing him back. Pukuh dodged the blows or deflected them. When he had had enough and countered, Edward went in to strike his leg. It was a clean shot right on the broken area.

Pukuh suppressed a scream of pain and then slammed his own spear into Edward's arm on the same spot where he had been bitten by the wolves. The nerve endings were raw, and the strike was hard, opening the wound even deeper. Edward also suppressed a yell.

Dammit! Bastard!

"Do not think I am the only one injured here, Edward." Both men were short of breath and sweating.

"Edward!" he heard someone yell from behind him.

It was Anne. She was on the roof of the palace. He had been too concentrated on surviving to notice earlier, but many villagers, including the king, were gathered there to watch. The warriors on the roof had taken a bow from her hands and were trying to restrain her, but they were having difficulty.

No! I don't know what they'll do to her if she tries to interfere! "Anne! Stop!"

"Edward!" she yelled as she fought against the many trying to hold her down. "Let me go!"

"Anne, please stop!"

She finally stopped struggling, her eyes still fixed on him in worry.

"I'll be fine," he told her. "I promise."

The warriors let her go. She pursed her lips and nodded to him through heavy breaths. The king laid his hand on her shoulder and stared into her eyes for a brief moment before motioning for the fight to continue.

Edward turned around and Pukuh rushed him again. He tumbled out of the way. Pukuh back-flipped to the opposite end of the slab, slamming his weight down onto it. Edward's side shot up into the air, sending him flying.

It was immediately clear to Edward that he was going to fall past the edge of the fighting grounds to his death. He caught a glimpse of Pukuh's face; its expression was one of great sadness.

No! We'll pass this test together! No one dies today!

Just as he went over the edge, Edward thrust his spear into the crack between two of the stones. It wedged in far enough to allow him to hang off the spear shaft, and his weight pulled his side of the slab down and caused Pukuh's side to shoot up.

Edward was able to hang on, but he couldn't climb at that angle. He could only wait for Pukuh to fall back down onto the other end, which would level the stone and allow Edward a chance to climb back up.

Pukuh landed, but slipped on his broken leg and rolled down the slab towards Edward, unable to stop or right himself. He was sliding across the stone like rainwater, and within moments he fell off the end of the slab next to Edward.

No!

Edward reached out and grabbed Pukuh's hand just before he fell out of reach. The collective gasp of the onlookers on the palace roof could be heard all the way across the intervening space. Their war chief's life was now hanging by a thread.

But it wasn't over yet.

Edward was hanging onto the spear with his injured arm. He had put too much strain on it, and the pain was ripping into him. He was desperate to hold tight, but his hand was starting to slip. The fight to hold on was sending waves of pain through his arm and his whole body. His fingers wanted to release from the struggle, and his hand was giving way.

Not today. We will not die today!

He screamed, a scream less of pain than of determination. He swung Pukuh up and onto the limestone arena. Pukuh was able to secure a foothold this time and scrambled to the other side to level out the square. Once it was stable, Edward released the spear and climbed back up. Covered with sweat and gasping for air, he stood up and faced the spectators.

"I refuse to fight!" he declared.

"Fight or die, Edward! Those are the only choices!" Pukuh said with equal force, as he clutched his shaking legs.

Edward turned to Pukuh, but yelled so everyone could hear. "No! There is always a choice. We are allies. Killing each other only weakens us," he said. "If these are supposed to be tests of both leadership and fighting skills, then the two must go hand in hand. As a fighter I have already shown my prowess against the wolves. Now, as a leader, I will not continue this fight." He turned to the king, Pukuh's father. "I know you can understand me, King, and I know you made the same decision years ago when you faced Benjamin. Fighting is only good when you have something to protect. Benjamin wasn't your enemy, and your son is not mine." Edward threw his spear down off the edge of the arena, and the noise of it clattering on the stone below resounded like a clap of thunder punctuating Edward's words. "I will not fight."

The villagers were speechless. In a way, Edward had committed treason. No one knew what the king was about to do.

"You are quite right, my boy," the king announced in perfect English with an accent not unlike Edward's own. "Benjamin came to me in peace, and I was too much of a fool to see it. He took the same stance you have taken, and I spared him before striking the final blow. By being prepared to die, he made me change my ways. He would not bring harm where no harm was due. When we parted, I vowed never to speak his language—*your* language—again, until his successor arrived." The king had a wide grin plastered on his face. "I congratulate you. You have passed the test."

Edward bowed to the king and smiled to Anne. She beamed with pride and hooted along with the villagers in celebration of his victory. He turned to Pukuh and bowed to him, as well, before joining him in the centre of the arena.

"Congratulations, brother." Pukuh held out his hand.

Edward grabbed Pukuh's forearm. "Brother." Edward brought him close in a quick embrace, which he returned. There was a moment of silence before Edward looked around the platform. "Uh…" he said with a dumbfounded expression, "how do we get down?"

With their fight finished, a warrior opened a hole through a loose piece of limestone, allowing the two brothers passage out. Pukuh and Edward were able to climb down the hole to stone steps at the back of the pyramid, which was how they had brought him up in the first place.

They immediately went to the palace, where the king announced that they would perform the ritual of rebirth for Edward. He extended the invitation to Anne as well, and she accepted joyfully. The rite would be performed at a dome-shaped structure called a temazcal, north of the village, which, Pukuh explained, was made of stones from a nearby volcano. There the participants would cleanse themselves for an hour after the battle, and Edward and Anne would be reborn as Mayan warriors.

When they all arrived at the site, the king prayed in front of the temazcal—Pukuh later told Edward he was asking the gods to allow them to enter it. He also summoned the guardian spirits of life, earth, and fire to assist in the rebirth.

When the prayer was finished, they entered through a small doorway. The interior was spacious and warm. In the centre was a stone pit, where a low fire burned beneath a bowl of stones and herbs wafting a delicious scent of mint into the room. Circling the pit were rings of stone at different levels like an amphitheatre on which the participants would sit.

After everyone was seated, the king, who also acted as the village shaman during rituals, poured water from a carved stone vessel onto the rocks. Fragrant steam filled the room. Speaking in his native tongue while his son translated, he told stories of the gods and of the path of a warrior. His words were passionate and lively, and Edward and Anne were eager listeners. At the end, he told those present to release all worries to the temazcal with a warrior's shout.

All joined as brothers and sisters in a great shout of liberation, which was heard all the way to the village.

When Edward and Anne least expected it, the king poured cold water on them to finish the ceremony. The two of them yelped at the unexpected shock of cold, and everyone laughed and gathered around them. As they all embraced, the king prayed to keep their new brother and sister safe as they walked the warrior's path—the path of Ah Pukuh, the God of Death.

Edward and Anne left the ceremony feeling refreshed and rejuvenated.

On the walk back, Edward recalled the trials he had been through, and the last one his crew had faced. He had seen so much, and gained new friends, but he couldn't help but think of the future, and the rest of the keys they needed to find.

"Let's pack our things, Anne. We must return to the ship."

"You are leaving so soon?" Pukuh exclaimed. "We were to have another feast."

"I'm sorry, Pukuh, but we can't. We finished what we came to do, and my crew is waiting for us. It's already been four days. They're probably restless with worry, missing two crewmembers. I hope you understand."

"I do. We will gather some supplies for you to take back. We shall await you at the village centre."

They walked back together, but when they reached the village, the warriors and Pukuh headed one way and the king accompanied Edward and Anne to the palace. They climbed the steps side by side, without distinction of rank, as equals, friends, and brothers.

"I am truly glad you arrived, Edward. It is like seeing Benjamin in his youth once more."

"What was he like?" Edward asked as they ascended the stairs.

"He was a brave warrior, and he loved everyone he met. Anyone whom he called a comrade or a friend was like family to him. To anyone who tried to harm a member of that family he showed no mercy. He told tales of his adventures, which paled in comparison to those I experienced with him. I imagine he became quite the pirate, as you will one day."

"Maybe that's why he made these tests," Edward reflected. "To make a crew like the one he had himself. Through the trials, we grow stronger." Edward gazed at his hands—scarred, but stronger than they had been a few months ago. "Or maybe it's just a fool's game."

The king laughed. "Perhaps both, young one. He enjoyed playing games, but they always seemed to have a deeper purpose."

Edward and Anne returned to their room and packed what they had brought with them. They then left the palace and headed to the centre of the village where everyone was waiting.

Nearly the entire village had turned out to greet and say goodbye to them. As they passed among the people, many hugged or shook their hands, and shoved food and clothing into their packs, as if they were family. Children ran up to touch Edward's beard or Anne's hair one last time, and Edward picked up one of the boys and carried him on his shoulder as he walked through the crowd.

It's astonishing how kind they are. I hope we can return someday.

They reached the front of the village, where Pukuh was waiting for them with all the warriors as well as the king and queen. Piled on the ground was a large stock of food tied up in bundles, as well as a few stone weapons, spears, and daggers.

"It pains us to see you leave so quickly, my friends. Is there anything I can do to persuade you to stay longer?" the king asked.

"I wish I could, but we need to depart before the crew starts to worry, which I'm afraid they are already doing. Someday we will return, and then you will meet my whole crew, and we shall have a great feast."

The king chuckled. "I long for the day." Edward and Anne both hugged the king and queen, thanking them again for their hospitality.

Edward turned to Pukuh. "Well, brother, I guess we'll meet again in a few years?"

"With your permission, I would like to join you for a time."

"What? But you're the war chief, aren't you? You can't abandon your responsibilities, can you?"

"Please, Edward. We have no need of a war chief who doesn't know the ways of war," he said with a grin. "I would join you for training, so I might better myself for my village. Besides, there are many capable warriors here to protect my home while I am away. Of course, the decision is yours to make, as you are the captain."

Edward could see the man was quite serious. He even had a bag packed. Edward looked to the king for approval. "Is this all right with you? He's not only your son, but your greatest warrior."

"I'm afraid Pukuh is following the tradition I created twelve years ago. I did the same as he wants to do. As then, you may choose to take him or leave him."

They're all prepared for it. It would be nice to have him aboard. We'll have another fighter with us.

"Very well. Who am I to break with tradition?" Edward smiled, looking at the beaming faces of Pukuh and his father. "I'll allow you to join, but remember one thing: I'm the captain. If you're my crewmate then my word is law. Aboard my ship, I am king." Edward held out his hand.

"Understood, Captain." Pukuh grasped Edward's hand, sealing

the bond.

The king placed his hands on top of theirs. "In this," he proclaimed for all to hear, "the pact created twelve years ago between Benjamin and me is renewed, unweakened by the passage of time. This is an honour to our village and to our people." The king lifted their hands in the air, and the people began to cheer and shout. Then he reached into his cluster of necklaces, brought out the key which Edward had now won the right to possess, and handed it to him. Edward accepted it with a bow of gratitude to the king, and then placed it around his own neck.

Edward, Anne, and Pukuh departed to the sound of the villagers cheering and shouting wishes for their good fortune. Edward listened to the echoes of that sound with a mixture of gratitude, joy, and sadness as it faded behind them and was swallowed up in the deep silence of the pines.

For a time, as they trekked through the forest, they did not violate that silence. A while later Edward spoke.

"I hope you're prepared for this, Pukuh. Have you ever been on a ship? Did your father tell you about what pirates do?"

"My father has told me at length of the adventures he had with Benjamin. I know full well what I am becoming, and I know it is an experience that will benefit me."

"As long as you are aware."

They had walked for a few hours when they reached the spot where Edward had fought the wolves for the first time, and Edward found his sword still near the body of the wolf he had killed with it. His pistol still lay on the smooth rock he had slept on. He went and picked up both weapons.

"My father told me those things that spit fire and rocks are not as accurate as a good bow," said Pukuh.

"Yes, but they're powerful, and on a ship when you're being boarded they can be quite handy."

"I'll stick with my spear."

They resumed walking, but Edward stopped short. "Oh, yes... Anne, you should probably change."

"What?" Anne asked, her brow cocked.

"It dawned on me that you're still wearing women's clothes. I know we aren't there yet, but you need to be accustomed to being a man again."

"Oh, perhaps you're right." She folded her arms as they kept staring at her. "Do you plan to keep watching while I change? Get going! I'll catch up."

"Yes, ma'am!" Edward said as he and Pukuh hurried away.

Pukuh was smiling. "Are all your women like that?"

"No, she's one of a kind."

24. THE REVELATION

Once more disguised as a man, Anne hastened to catch up with the other two. When darkness fell, they stopped and set up camp and a fire to stave off the cold. Pukuh had brought along a few bedrolls, so all three of them were able to sleep in relative comfort.

Pukuh eyed the darkness just outside their firelight. "We should not all sleep. The forest is dangerous at night."

"Who wants to take first?" Edward asked.

"I shall," Anne offered as she set up her bedroll.

Edward gazed at her in her masculine attire, a far cry from her appearance at the village. *She looked so striking in that dress. I hope she didn't throw it away.*

"I shall go after," said Pukuh. "Edward, you will take the last."

"Very well. If anything goes wrong, wake us all up. Don't try to do anything stupid."

With everyone in agreement, Edward and Pukuh crawled into their beds, but their sleep was short-lived.

Anne woke them a few hours into her watch. "I hear noises in all directions. I think we are being surrounded."

The men moved with caution as they tried to rise without a sound. Pukuh threw Edward a spear and he caught it deftly. They could hear the noises now, too. Anne produced two daggers, one in each hand.

The sounds were coming closer. Whoever or whatever it was either wasn't good at hiding, or wanted to be heard. Branches gave way with a violent snap, night birds flew away, bushes rattled.

On every side of them wolves appeared. There must have been at least twenty of them altogether.

"There're too many of them, there's no way we can kill them all," Edward said with gritted teeth.

"With that attitude, you might as well offer your throat to them as a gift," Anne said. "We shall make it out of here, Ed. We just have to work together."

"She is right. Let us put our backs together so they cannot divide us."

They did as Pukuh suggested and made themselves as one. Each had weapons raised, ready to strike when the wolves attacked.

But the wolves did not attack. They didn't even growl. They stood in silence, watching.

"What are they waiting for?" asked Anne.

"I don't know." Edward tried to discern exactly what they were doing.

There was no escape—the wolves far outnumbered them—yet nothing happened. Then Edward noticed one of the animals moving towards them. It was the leader of the pack, the old wolf who had walked away from their last encounter. It was large and strong, and Edward could tell by its deliberate approach this animal had a lot of pride.

He's not attacking. He knows if he comes closer I could strike him down. Why is he continuing? He could have jumped at me by now.

The wolf stopped, lay down on the ground, and gazed steadily at Edward. He put his weapon in one hand and bent down.

"What are you doing, Edward?" Anne exclaimed.

"Trust me." He put his empty hand towards the wolf's mouth, so close the wolf could have bitten off his fingers with ease. Instead, it licked them. Edward moved closer and the wolf rose. He patted it on the head and scratched behind its ear. "It's all right, they aren't here to fight. I think they're here to protect us."

Anne and Pukuh watched in amazement as Edward knelt beside the alpha male. It was being completely submissive to him.

"Pukuh, I think we have been invited into their pack. Or I'm now seen as their leader."

Anne looked astonished by Edward's command of the wild animals.

Pukuh glanced at the other wolves with a furrowed brow. "Are you sure they are docile?"

"They haven't attacked us even though we've lowered our guard. Is that not proof enough? Now we can all rest."

At a gentle push from Edward, the wolf stood up and went back to the rest of the pack. Some of the wolves then dispersed to form an outer circle of sentries, and some stayed close in as bodyguards.

Pukuh peered about. "I think we should still take turns with the watch."

Edward agreed and told Pukuh to wake him when he was to take over, then lay down in his bedroll and made himself comfortable. Anne was still standing and staring at him.

"Anne…"

"Huh… What?" she answered in a daze.

"You can sleep now."

"Oh… yes. Good night," Anne mumbled as she crawled into her bedroll. She lay awake for some time, staring into the darkness, the possible dangers far from her mind.

How did he do that?

Anne kept asking herself that question, but she could find no answer.

⚓ ⚓ ⚓

The wolves had kept up their watch for Edward and his companions. As the morning light began to penetrate the forest canopy, Edward saw the alpha male walking to greet him. He pulled out the last bit of dried meat he had and, after taking a little for himself, gave the rest to the wolf. Then, with a wave of his arm, he sent the pack back into the depths of the woods.

Edward woke the others, and they packed up their things and prepared to walk once more. They would be home aboard the *Freedom* within a few hours.

"I still cannot believe it."

"Can't believe what, Anne?"

"You commanded a wolf as if it were a simple house pet. It's… unprecedented."

"I guess it was kind of odd. But Pukuh and I showed them our strength a couple of times already. That one with the scar too. I guess he felt, since I bested his pack, he should join the stronger one. Right, Pukuh?"

"Wolves are honourable spirits; they would not take the killing of their pack lightly. It would make sense that either he would kill you or join you for protection."

"See?"

"I suppose that makes sense," Anne said, but Edward could tell that she was still skeptical.

They walked down the path once more after eating a little to keep up their strength. The jungle was bright despite the dense canopy, and the sounds seemed less ominous than when Edward had first entered. It was a pleasant walk all the way to the ship.

They emerged back at the small hill and sandy dock where they had landed. "There she is, Pukuh. The *Freedom*. Isn't she beautiful?"

"It is as I remember," he said as he walked down the slope.

"Not quite the same. This time it's a new crew and we'll be able to make our own adventures. Come, Anne—I mean, Jim! Let's board. Pukuh, you have to remember to call Anne Jim. No one can know she's a woman. It'll cause trouble."

"I understand, brother. I will keep the secret."

The crew noticed them approaching and they all gathered along the side of the ship. Some let down a rope ladder, while the rest of them cheered and shouted greetings. Edward and Anne returned the greetings and climbed up to the deck. Pukuh was close behind them.

Henry was waiting on deck. "Welcome back, Captain. Was it a

success?"

Edward smiled as he took the key from around his neck. He lifted it into the air and everyone cheered once again. "I'd say it was a success. We also have a new crewmember. He's a native of the village where I stayed."

Henry looked over Edward's shoulder at the newcomer. Pukuh was greeting everyone as Anne introduced him. "Are you sure he'll be a good fit aboard the ship? What can he do?"

"He's a warrior, so I imagine we'll have to train him in how to work on a ship, but I don't think there'll be any problems. He's strong; even now he has a broken leg, yet you would never be able to tell. I'll tell you all about what happened later. For now, let's find out what this key opens."

Henry grabbed Edward's arm before he could leave. "What about Jim?"

"What about Jim?"

"He disobeyed a direct order. Aren't you going to punish him?"

"He went out of concern for me; I can't fault him for that. I wouldn't punish anyone who did that," Edward said, folding his arms. "It was dangerous, but it turned out all right in the end. Come, let's go."

Henry folded his arms and frowned as he watched Edward head aft.

Edward first went to the aft cabin and tried the key, but it didn't open. Next he went to the cannon deck. He put the key in and turned it, and the lock opened with a click. Edward smiled. He pushed open the door and walked in.

The spacious room was clean and well kept, and the smell of Caribbean pine almost stung the nose. On the port and starboard sides each were fifteen twenty-two-pound cannons, lined up and ready to deploy. Beside each one were large cannonballs stored for immediate use. On either end of the deck, as well as in the middle where the main mast came down through, were storage areas with more cannonballs and black powder. At the stern of the room was another door, but it had a lock on it as well.

If this follows the pattern of other frigates, that would be the captain's cabin, though the bow end still remains a mystery.

Everyone rushed in and examined the cannons, admiring their beauty. They appeared brand new, never used. Everyone was excited, especially the gunners who, because of insufficient cannons, had to rotate shifts during battle. Now they would all be able to fight at once.

With these, we now have fifty-three cannons aboard the ship. We'll be a lot more dangerous in battle.

"What're these things?" A crewman examined the cannons' firing mechanism with a confused look.

"What is it?" Edward asked.

"These cannons 'ere 'ave some sort o' string on 'em that moves this." The crewman demonstrated the mechanism on top of the cannon.

It was like a flintlock on a gun, but it was attached to the cannon and stuck when the string was pulled. Edward had never seen anything like it.

"It's to fire the cannons, I suppose. Quite the clever addition," Edward said as he stroked his beard. "This will make it safer for you, I imagine?"

The crewmate examined the cannon again, and then nodded. "Yes, Captain. We'll be more accurate, too."

"Good, that's what I like to hear."

"Captain?" A crewman was standing on the other side of the mast, pointing at something.

Edward walked over. He already had a fair suspicion of what he would find, and he was right: another piece of paper, with instructions for obtaining the next key. Edward squinted and frowned as he examined it.

This is just gibberish!

It was a set of letters, but they didn't spell anything or make any apparent sense. Edward turned the paper over.

Finally, real words!

"In the centre of the Navassa Island the decoder for the cipher can be found."

Apparently they would have to sail to this Navassa island to find out what the script on the other side of the note meant. Edward thought Herbert might know where to find it.

Edward was headed for the ladder when he was stopped by Henry. "Ed! Come quick! We have trouble!"

"What kind of trouble?"

"British Navy trouble."

Damn! "All hands, prepare for battle!" He yelled as he emerged from the lower deck.

"Here," Henry said, handing Edward a spyglass. "You know more of ships than I do. Can you tell what class it is?"

Edward peered down the spyglass at the approaching ship. It had three masts, with a forecastle and quarterdeck at the bow and stern respectively. "I think it's a fifth-class frigate, same as us. I guess it's a bit of providence we now have as many guns, if not more."

The crew were frantic to get ready for battle: gathering weapons, preparing the first wave of cannons, checking and rechecking everything just in case. William, Henry, Herbert, Pukuh, and Edward were the only ones not rushing about. In perhaps ten minutes they would be in battle, but they needed a clear plan.

"You think it's Smith again?" Henry asked.

"He's been at us for six months now so he's probably the only one who would travel this far to catch us."

"But how did he find out where we were headed? How can he be so good at tracking us?"

"I haven't a clue." Anne once said they called him "The Hound" in the marines. *Maybe he can smell us? No, that's foolishness.*

"He's one lucky bastard, that's for sure."

"William, can you suggest any strategies for the battle?"

William had been listening the whole time, but was waiting for orders before offering an opinion. "Just one: Hit them with everything, and then do it again."

"I like that plan." William nodded. "All right. Herbert, we'll be counting on your skills here. Are you up to it?"

"I won't let you down, Captain."

"Good. Everyone to arms! Prepare broadside volley!"

Edward went to a gun hold and grabbed two pistols, a sword, and a few daggers. Everyone hid behind barrels or railings for cover from the rain of bullets soon to be upon them. Edward's gaze turned to the opposite end of the ship, where he saw Anne, watching him, holding a pistol in one hand and a dagger in the other. She nodded to him and he smiled back.

Pukuh appeared beside Edward. "So I guess I am to learn the hard way how to be a pirate?"

Edward considered him for a moment, and then said, "I want you to stay below deck."

"What? Why?"

"You're in no shape to fight. I won't have you dying in the first battle of your career."

"And what about you?" Pukuh grabbed Edward's wounded arm. He winced and brushed him off.

"Don't do that, dammit! Look, I'm saying this as your brother. Don't make me say it as your captain. I can still fight with this, but you can't move well with your leg broken."

"Very well. I will stay out of battle—for you, brother."

"Thank you." Edward knew the Mayan's pride was hurt, but he couldn't have him die under his care. He wouldn't be able to look Pukuh's father in the eye if that happened.

The navy ship was approaching at a steady pace with the wind, bobbing up and down on the waves. On the side of the ship was the name H.M.S. *Pearl.* On the bow stood a man dressed in a blue navy uniform with several medals of commendation on the breast and shoulders. Edward could see him through the spyglass. There could be no mistake.

It was Smith.

Herbert concentrated on the approaching ship, gauging its distance as it sailed closer and closer. "Not yet," he whispered under his breath. "Not yet... Almost there... No... Now! Fire starboard!" he yelled.

All the gunmen on the top deck simultaneously dropped their linstocks into the cannons and let loose a barrage on the other ship. At the same time, a crewman relayed the signal to those on the gun deck and they pulled on their strings in quick succession, one after another, setting off a continuous sweep of explosive fire from stem to stern.

The *Pearl* countered immediately, and cannonballs shot towards the *Freedom* at lightning speed. They ripped through the hull, shattering boards, sending pieces of wood flying everywhere. Some crewmembers were struck by the wood; one man died from a stray shard in the eye, and another had his legs shredded by a cannonball.

"Fire at will!" Edward yelled. The crew raised their rifles and muskets and began to fire. The screams of men and the loud bangs of guns filled the air. The blowing of the wind and the calls of the gulls were swallowed completely by the terrible sounds of combat. In the minds and senses of all present, only the battle existed.

After the ships passed each other, Herbert went hard to port to turn the *Freedom* around, tacking into the wind as he did so.

"Transport the wounded below deck quickly!" Edward yelled. He reloaded his rifle and ducked behind cover. The salt air filled his nostrils with the smell of blood and burning black powder and danger. The smell invigorated him, but also sickened him. His thoughts were flying this way and that, never focusing on one thing for long.

We have a fore cabin filled with cannons. We'll be heading straight for the Pearl soon. We can attack them twice!

"Gunners in the fore cabin! I want those cannons set to launch in one minute!" Edward was bounding up the ladder to the quarterdeck while some rushed in to do as he commanded. "Herbert, I want you to head straight for them. We'll fire a volley at their bow."

"Aye aye, Captain."

"When we are as close as possible I'll yell the order to fire, and then I want you to swerve the ship so we can fire a port-side volley." Edward went to the railing overlooking the lower deck to watch the approaching ship.

"Captain?" Herbert asked.

"Wait for it."

The ship came closer.

"Captain..." Herbert's voice was more urgent.

"Not yet... Now! Fire forecastle!" he yelled, and a crewman relayed the order.

But Edward had waited too long. Two of the shots missed, and the ones that hit did little damage as they glanced off the curved wood of the *Pearl*'s hull.

Bollocks!

To compound the misfortune, Edward's hesitation had resulted in the *Freedom* turning aside too late. Instead of making a close pass, the two hulls scraped together, damaging both, and brought the ships to a standstill. The marines threw grappling hooks over to pull the two vessels together and lock their movements.

Edward yelled, "Fire port!" and a volley of cannonballs bombarded the *Pearl* as they were preparing to board the *Freedom*. The navy gunners retaliated in kind.

The close blast of cannons erupted in the middle of the two ships. Wood and smoke shot up from between them. The force rumbled across the ships like an earthquake.

A gangplank was dropped and secured across the gap between the ships by the marines. Edward pulled out two of his pistols and ran to the nearest ladder as marines began to cross the gangplank to his ship. Fifteen ran over, then twenty, and all had pistols and swords drawn, ready to meet their sworn enemies—ready to die, if need be.

"Kill any who try to board!" Edward yelled. "Have at 'em, men!"

The two groups clashed above the gap between the ships. Swords rang out and the blast of guns and cannons echoed like cracks of lightning in the middle of a hurricane.

Two marines swung on rigging ropes and landed next to the ladder. They both ran at Edward, their swords ready to slice him open. He backed up and shot the two of them at point-blank range. Their blood and brains splattered against the deck.

Edward felt sick, and not just from the carnage. He felt pain growing in his left arm; his exertion had opened the wound, and it was bleeding again. The loss of blood and the sway of the ship nauseated him. As he stared at the dead bodies of the two marines lying in front of him, the face of Robert Maynard flashed into his mind—Robert, his old friend, who wanted to join these men in battle against him, a pirate.

He retched on the deck.

Edward shook his head violently.

Keep yourself together, man! Your crew depends on you. They're the enemy, that's all they are. They're not Robert.

He pulled out his sword.

Ignore the pain! Ignore the nausea! Keep fighting!

His eyes scanned the main deck. The two crews were fighting with each other in a writhing mass of bodies. Amongst the barrels, the masts, and the ropes, they clashed with swords and shot pistols.

Edward could see William fighting, but he seemed to be disabling his opponents, not killing them. He could see Sam laughing and smashing in skulls and slitting throats, completely at home in the anarchy. Edward also saw Henry fist-fighting and taking on more than he could handle, as usual. Then John came to his rescue, killing one marine by firing his rifle and another with his bayonet. Here, in battle, he seemed a different person, his eyes filled with determination and the cold detachment of one used to death and killing.

Then Edward saw the man he was searching for: Captain Isaac Smith.

There he is. He's *the one who caused all this, and the one who can end it.*

At that very moment Smith cut one of Edward's crew down.

"That's enough, Smith! It's me you're after, is it not?"

Smith smiled. "Well if it isn't young Edward Thatch the supposed non-pirate. You look a touch pale. Don't tell me you're sea-sick."

"Hardly!" Edward jumped on the railing and ran down it, sword drawn. He jumped off and aimed a vicious cut at Smith, causing him to back off. Edward kept up the assault and slashed at the man relentlessly, but each stroke met Smith's blade.

"Is that all you can muster after all this time apart? I expected more!" Then Smith went on the offensive.

Each strike was more accurate and more deadly than the last. Edward put up his blade to try to parry, jumped this way and that, and almost had to run to avoid being hit. The difference in skill was as clear as a spyglass.

I have to distract him.

"Who taught you how to fight, Smith? Your mother?"

"No, my father." He kept attacking Edward, but with the talking he was a little slower. "Your crew looks a little more capable this time around, and a full set of cannons to boot. Stolen, no doubt. Pirate scum!"

"It's a rather humorous story. I'd be glad to tell it if your men weren't dying around your feet." Edward laughed and Smith's eyes wandered around.

Perfect!

He slashed at Smith and grazed his arm. Smith sidestepped and countered, hitting Edward in his injured arm. He screamed out in pain and tried to run as he held his arm close, but Smith was right behind him.

Edward ran around the mast pole, only to run into another marine. The man knocked him down and Edward fell flat on his back. The marine jumped on top of him, his sword coming down to Edward's throat. Edward grabbed the marine's hand, stopping the sword inches from his neck, but dropping his own sword in the process.

The marine grinned wickedly and pushed his free hand on top of his sword hand, trying to drive the blade down and ending Edward on the spot. Edward made a desperate grab for his last pistol from his belt, but the marine seized his arm. He fought to aim the pistol, struggling clumsily with the marine for control of the weapon.

The sword blade was centimeters from Edward's neck, and his injured arm was having trouble blocking it for much longer. With all his strength he forced the pistol closer and closer to the marine's face. Soon the marine's sword began to cut into Edward's flesh; the blade was trembling from the strain of Edward trying to push it back, and he knew he wouldn't be able to hold it off much longer. He pulled his knee up and hit the marine in the groin with all his might. The man coughed in pain and his strength seemed to wane, giving Edward the break he needed. He pulled the pistol up to the marine's chin and fired.

The shot of gunpowder burned Edward's ear, and his head rang and everything became a blur. The dead marine lay on top of him, blood pouring from his neck. He pushed the man off him and rose to his feet, gripping some rigging to help himself up. The ringing disoriented him and the edges of his vision were turning black. He saw Smith standing in front of him, now holding a sword in each hand. He was saying something, but Edward heard nothing.

Smith went in for the kill, his blades crossing over his head and swiping down in a vicious arc.

Then someone ran between them and stopped Smith in his tracks. Edward could barely hear the ting of blades clashing.

Who is that? Anne!

Edward shook his head and the ringing and dizziness began to subside. Slowly his hearing returned. He was able to hear all the terrible noises, and Anne's shocking words that instantly made them all stop.

"In the name of Anne Sophia Stewart, princess of Denmark, princess of Norway, and daughter to Queen Anne of England, I command you to stop this attack!"

25. THE PRINCESS AND THE PIRATES

The words fell as a command. The revelation stunned those close by into silence. As others noticed the sudden stop in violence, they too joined and the words were passed to everyone in turn. Weapons were lowered, and the silence was all the heavier for all the tumult just preceding it. None knew what to do or what to think, only that they had to stop whatever they were doing.

Anne removed her hat and let out her red hair before presenting to the astonished Captain Isaac Smith a necklace holding a signet ring.

Smith stood, unable to move or speak, shock and disbelief plastered on his face. After a moment, with all eyes on him and on Anne, he dropped his swords and knelt down.

"We are at your command, Your Royal Highness."

The rest of the marine crew followed suit and dropped to their knees. The crew of the *Freedom* watched in disbelief and awe the scene unfolding before them.

Anne's the princess?

Some of the pirates moved to start the attack again. "All hands cease fire!" Edward commanded, which the crew reluctantly obeyed. Most were still confused—including Edward himself.

She can't be the princess. This must be some kind of trick. She must look like her. I'll… I'll play along with it, until we can sort this mess out.

"You and your men are to leave this ship and return to England," Anne commanded.

Smith's gaze shifted to Edward, then back to Anne. "But, Your Highness…"

"I issued you orders, Captain. Any action not involving steps to put those orders into effect will be considered an act of treason." She stepped forward and lifted Smith's chin with her finger. "You would not think to commit treason, would you, Captain?" Anne's demeanor and accent had taken on a menacing and cold perfection that was sharper than any knife.

Edward watched her in amazement. *She's really acting the part.*

"No, Your Highness. I will follow your orders immediately." Smith stood up, saluted, and walked away. "Men, we leave."

The crew of the *Pearl* still gawked at Anne, utterly stunned.

She stood with her hands on her hips, her hair blowing in the wind, and she was looking down on them with the cold, haughty eyes of a princess, eyes boring into them more than any words could. They all rose to their feet and walked back to their own ship. Anne dismissed Smith, who followed his crew. They rushed to remove the grappling hooks tying the ships together and soon were sailing off to the east.

After the *Pearl* had left, Edward walked up behind Anne.

"That was bloody brilliant, Anne! Where did you learn to act like that?" Edward turned her around to face him. To his surprise, she was on the verge of tears, and shaking with anger.

"I cast my lot with pirates, and this is how it turns out," she whispered. "I guess I can never run from my past, can I, Ed?"

"What are you talking about, Anne? It was all an act, wasn't it?" Edward noticed she was wearing the ring now. He pulled her hand up and looked at it. He realised with a shock what it was: a signet ring bearing an engraving of three feathers encircled by a crown, below which were the words, *Ich Dien*, "I serve." That ring was bestowed upon the heir apparent to the throne of England. The queen had no sons, and all her other children had died at an early age. It being in her possession meant Anne was the heiress presumptive to the throne of England.

"It can't be true!"

"I am sorry, Ed. I am sorry!" Anne ran to the fore cabin, with William close on her heels.

Edward's crew gathered around him, bewildered and seeking direction.

"Is she really the princess?" "What are we to do with her?" "Wasn't that Jim?" "What do we do now?"

"Everyone, stop! Clean up or something. Have Alexandre examine the wounded. Get the ship out of here!" Edward pushed through them to the fore cabin.

Anne was sitting in a corner, her back to the door. William stood near her, sword in hand. Anne's head was almost lying on her knees, slumped, defeated. The sight broke Edward's image of her even more than the revelation had done, and something like sadness pulled at him to see her in such a state.

"Leave us," he ordered William. William didn't move, but tightened his grip on his sword.

What does he think he's doing? Is he going to fight me?

"It will be all right, William," Anne said without looking at him. "I'll be fine."

William bowed, though her back was turned, and left. On his way out he glared at Edward, as if to say, "If you dare hurt her, I'll kill you." Edward simply nodded as he left.

"So what you said wasn't a lie? You are the princess, truly?"

"Yes, Edward. It became harder and harder to reveal to you

who I was, and I imagined if I did you would make me leave. I knew you would not hurt me, but I did not wish to leave. I still do not wish to leave." Anne turned around to face him. She was crying.

Edward went to her, kneeled down, and embraced her. "Anne, it doesn't matter who you or your family were. Now you're a part of this family."

"You… you mean I can stay? I can stay with you?"

"Yes, of course."

Edward's calm acceptance made Anne cry all the harder. They held each other for what seemed like hours: she in his arms, letting out her emotions, and he comforting her.

"At least now your posh accent makes more sense," Edward said with a chuckle.

Anne laughed and wiped her eyes. Edward was happy he could at least see her smile again.

Noises from outside the cabin had grown louder as the seconds passed, and Edward could ignore it no longer. "I'm sorry, Anne. I have to check on what's happening." Edward walked over and opened the door to the main deck.

The whole crew was standing outside, with William in front of the door, blocking access with his sword. The men were making a great commotion, yelling and screaming.

"What is this nonsense? Stop this at once!" yelled Edward.

The majority ceased their commotion, but one crewman, Frank, decided to be the voice of the mass. "We have with us now a golden opportunity. The princess of England is aboard our ship. With her we can demand a ransom from the queen in exchange for her safety."

"You're a fool if you think your plan will work."

"You can't see the potential in this plan, Captain? We would be richer than any pirates alive. What do you say, boys?"

The crew cheered and yelled.

"Silence!"

Everyone immediately became quiet as Edward stared them down. "What would you do then, hmm? When we've gotten the money and given them the princess, you think they will go lightly on you? You think they will let you walk away? They'll chase us to the ends of the earth to make an example of us. It would be no different if you asked for a pardon in exchange. The mere thought that the marines were at your mercy would need to be purged from everyone's minds. Once the bargaining chip is handed over, they don't have to hold to any agreement."

Frank faltered but for a moment. "Then she should leave. She's a danger to us all. Not only is she bad luck, but those marines will chase us down to retrieve her anyway." Once again the crew shouted their agreement.

Edward walked into the crowd. "This is one of our crew you're talking about. We've been together for the past six months. You've cleaned together, you've eaten together, you've laughed together, and you've fought together. She is a part of our family now. Would you willingly cast aside your own brother, your own sister, your own son or daughter, just for some coin, or because you're afraid? If you aren't willing to die for the people you stand next to, then maybe you shouldn't be on this ship. I want each of you to think long and hard on this, because if you aren't willing to die for your family aboard this ship, then you don't deserve to be here. When we land at the next port, make up your mind and then leave if you want to. As for me, I am allowing Anne to stay here as long as she likes."

"Aren't we going to vote on this? According to the commandments we have that right."

Edward grimaced at the man who spoke up. "According to the commandments, you have the right to vote on the affairs of the moment. Affairs of the moment are where we are heading, division of shares, and other business which does not involve who *I* choose to have aboard *my* ship! Another commandment states that to leave the ship you need one thousand pounds, though I am disregarding it for those of you who wish to depart due to this. Would any like to object to my fairness today?"

No one could challenge Edward. No one who looked into his eyes could want to. The crew saw in them an implacable authority that had grown, in the months they had served under his command, to equal the authority of his legendary father.

Edward waved his hand in dismissal. "Now back to work. We're heading back to the Swan Islands. Herbert, take us south."

"Aye, sir."

The crew shuffled off and went back to work. They were not feeling their usual enthusiasm; men shot sidelong glances at each other, probably wondering how many would stay and how many would leave when they reached the next port—wondering which of their brothers would be willing to die for them, and which would let them die for profit.

As Edward stood watching the crew resume their tasks, Henry walked up to him.

"We need to talk."

"Things are a little hectic right now, Henry. I don't have the time. I... oh, my head!" Edward felt a sudden stabbing pain, and brought his hand to his forehead. His vision blurred, and the earlier dizziness returned in force.

"Ed, are you all right? Ed? Edward!"

But Edward was already beyond words, and fell to the deck, unconscious.

⚓ ⚓ ⚓

Edward drifted in and out of consciousness over the next few hours. He had been taken to his bed near the ladder in the crew's quarters. When he finally woke up, he pulled himself upright and noticed Anne nearby, watching him, and William off in the distance.

"Welcome back," she said with a sad smile.

"What happened?"

"You passed out yesterday on deck."

"Ah! Yesterday? I've been asleep for a day?"

"You were injured during the battle and lost a lot of blood. Alexandre took care of you. I wanted to be here when you awoke, so I have been changing your bandages and feeding you water."

"Thank you, Anne."

Anne twisted her mouth and looked down. "I... I should be the one to thank you. You defended me."

"You're special to me. I defended you because of that. I'd do the same for everyone in the crew."

"Hmm..." Anne's eyes narrowed.

"What?"

"You say I am special, and yet you would defend everyone in the crew. That's not very special now is it?"

Edward began sweating. "Well, you're a different kind of special. I'd say you are more special."

Edward rested his hand on Anne's. She gripped it tight. They both smiled as they held hands.

"So... so how's the crew been while I've been out cold?"

"They are well. There have been some arguments. It is obvious what they are about." Anne released Edward's hand and looked off, dejected.

"It matters not; those people will be able to leave soon. They shouldn't be a part of this crew anyway if they're going to act like that. What else has been happening?"

"The crew is worried for you, but they will not draw near to me. Mostly because William glares at them so much. And Henry still wishes to speak with you. He wants to have a meeting with all the senior officers."

Edward frowned. "I should like to get it over with now." He started to rise, but Anne stopped him.

"Alexandre said you shouldn't be walking so soon. You need to have something to eat and then some rest to let your body recover. I shall bring the others here."

"No... no wait!"

Anne ignored him and walked away and up to the top deck, with William following close behind.

She's strong. Stronger than me. As soon as this is all over and things are back to the normal way they were, she'll bounce back.

Edward lay there, waiting patiently for them to return.

Henry came down the ladder with John, William, and Anne close behind, and they all walked down to the end where Edward was waiting. Anne said some words under her breath to William and she started to leave.

"Wait, Anne, don't leave. You're a part of this discussion as well."

Anne turned around and glanced at Edward, and then at Henry.

Henry shook his head. "Ed, I don't think she should be involved in this."

"Whatever you have to say I'm sure you can say in front of her."

Henry sighed. "Who am I to go against the captain's orders?" Anne sat in a hammock on the other side of Edward while Henry and John sat down in chairs.

"So what is this about, Henry?"

Henry let out a sigh. "I think Anne should leave."

Edward was shocked at the bluntness of his statement. "Explain yourself, Henry, but know this: Anne stays as long as she wants. I'll not change my mind."

"I had a feeling you'd say that. She'll be a danger to us at some point. Maybe not now, but down the road it will cause trouble for us."

"I already told you, I know they will chase us. I'm willing to fight to keep our crew safe and whole."

"Whole save for the bullets in them," Henry replied with a scoff. "If you would take a moment to separate your feelings from your common sense, you would realise the risk is too great. The reason why you want to keep her around is you fancy her."

Edward clenched his fists. "That's not true. I would do that for any aboard the *Freedom*, no matter how great the danger."

Henry turned his gaze to John. "John, you've been with us from the beginning. What's your assessment of the situation? What do you think our rival Smith will do once he returns to England?"

John jumped from his seat with a start. Beads of sweat began to form on his forehead. "W-well..." He glanced back and forth before clearing his throat. "S-Smith doesn't like to lose. He'll no doubt call on the navy for help, possibly even the qu-queen herself." Anne shuddered at the mention of that title. "Th-they'll bring the full might of the British navy down on us. When they find us, we'll be tried as enemies of the state. And found guilty, of course. No matter if the p-princess claims otherwise." John looked at Anne. "Sorry."

Anne shook her head to try to alleviate his guilt.

"And you, William? What do you think?" Henry asked.

William looked at everyone in turn and then finally at Anne. He hesitated until she nodded approval. "I believe John's assessment to be correct. My apologies, Your Highness."

The tension rose as silence settled on the room. Everyone waited on Edward. He was the captain. No matter what was said, he was the final authority.

I can't just tell them this is my order and they have to follow it. Henry's anger will build if I don't do something.

"Henry, what would you do if I were being attacked?"

Henry cocked his brow. "Huh? What kind of a question is that?"

"It's relevant. What would you do if I were in trouble?"

"Ah! I see what you're doing. Well, I would save you, obviously. And I know you'll say because of that, we should save Anne."

"Yes, I am. What if I had thought saving you from the gallows was too great a risk?"

Henry's face registered shock. He obviously hadn't drawn that connection. He certainly had to remember how, at the time, he'd said that Edward should have left him to die.

Edward continued. "I didn't think about the risk. All I cared about was saving you. I think you would have done the same, because we're brothers. Besides, you knew from the beginning we would be chased by the marines because of being pirates. How does this change anything?"

"Don't sidestep the issue, Edward. You are right that you saved me, but you decided to save me after you heard I was captured. Right now we're talking about our future safety. She's a liability, and you're a fool if you think otherwise. Smith is one thing; the entire British navy after us is another." Henry's penetrating gaze was equal to Edward's.

Edward turned away from Henry and muttered something under his breath. As he talked his voice kept rising in volume. "I am captain of this ship. If Anne wants to stay, then she stays. If you aren't willing to accept that, then I make you the same offer I did back when I offered Herbert a position. If it's such a problem to you, you can leave. Our dream was freedom, and I don't see how you can abide by denying someone else that dream."

"Tch," Henry spat. "I'm not leaving. But don't expect me to risk my life for her. When the inevitable happens, I'll be there to save your arse like usual, and then I'll say I told you so." Henry left with a scathing glance at Anne, his feet stomping loudly until he reached the top deck.

John was next. "I pr-promised your father I would be by your side when you needed it. I won't break that promise."

Edward nodded to John and he also left.

William shrugged. "I will protect the princess, no matter the cost. I have made mistakes in the past, and I do not intend to repeat them. If she wishes to stay, I cannot go against that, but I won't leave either."

Anne nodded to William, and he went back to the other side of the ship to keep guard of the ladder. It was only Anne and Edward now.

"I am sorry, Edward. I did not mean to cause a fight between you and Henry," she said, her eyes downcast. "Maybe I should leave… They are right. I am putting everyone in jeopardy."

"It doesn't matter. Henry will come around eventually. Besides, I want you to stay. Making you leave goes against what this ship stands for. Making you leave goes against what I stand for."

"*Freedom*, huh?" Anne said, staring at the floorboards. She seemed almost nostalgic about something. "Thank you, Edward." She smiled a little. "Ed."

Edward smiled and held her hand again.

⚓ ⚓ ⚓

As the days progressed, many in the crew became more vocal about their opinions. The debates intensified, and if not for the presence of Edward and the other senior officers, fistfights would have broken out. The crew was split between those who would stay and those who would leave.

They had to be reminded several times of the fact that if they had a quarrel it would have to be decided by a duel.

Anne was feeling isolated. Some who supported her as a crewmate were walking on eggshells around her with no real reason. They saw her as the princess now, not as a common pirate. That attitude was better than those who were outright against her, but still.

The only thing keeping Anne's detractors from taking her captive was the other half of the crew willing to protect her.

"So, William, I guess I had the wrong idea about you," Edward commented one day.

"Explain your meaning."

"I thought you were infatuated with Anne, and that's why you wanted to protect her, but I suppose that's incorrect. If I had to guess, by the way you avoid any marine's gaze, and by how well-mannered and highly trained you are, I'd say you… must be…"

William responded with a blank stare.

"An indentured servant!" Edward smiled. "Am I right?"

"No."

"What? I was wrong? Then what are you? Ex-marine?"

"Yes." William never lost his blank expression, but Edward thought he could see a twinge of anger.

"Ah! That makes sense. You're still loyal to the monarchy. Will you turn me in to the authorities?"

"I have not decided."

Edward's jaw dropped, but William's expression was as still as stone. "Haven't decided? Should I consider myself lucky?"

"I have my reasons to stay away from the marines. You saved my life, and the princess likes you, but if it comes down to her or you, I won't hesitate to bring you down. You seem to be different from most pirates, though, so I haven't decided what I'll do yet."

"Thank you… I think."

William went almost nose to nose with Edward and, despite the latter's height advantage, seemed to look down at him. "Know this: you walk a fine line here. The moment you think of crossing it is the moment I take matters into my own hands."

Edward returned the look in kind. "I understand."

William nodded and walked away.

Later that day, Edward had a talk with Herbert, as the matter of having women aboard concerned him as well. "Herbert, I think after the crew is allowed to leave we should tell everyone about your sister."

"Aye, I thought it might come to that."

"Is Christina comfortable with it?"

"I already told her about the possibility, and in truth she would enjoy it quite a bit if she could stop pretending to be a boy." He smiled. "I cut her hair short the day before we set out, and she cried so much I thought we would drown before I finished. I'm sure she'll want to grow it out again."

Edward laughed. "Soon she will be able to."

The next day Edward had a brief talk with almost everyone in the crew. He asked each man to express his opinions and feelings freely. Some were vocally against Anne staying, and said so much with very harsh words.

"That bitch has no place on a pirate ship." "She's a woman and a princess; it's likely the gods have cursed us." "I can't stay on a ship with a woman!"

Edward tried to reason with the crewmen who had decided to leave, but their hate and superstition blinded them to his words. Those vocal against Anne had made their decision and Edward could not change that.

Some crewmen were still undecided, so Edward presented them with the same thoughts he'd left with Henry. He talked about the name of the *Freedom* and what he believed it meant to be aboard it.

Edward even had a chance to talk with Alexandre when he was receiving a checkup. "And how do you feel about having a woman on board, Alexandre?"

"Nothing has changed, *Capitaine*. I've always know Jim was a woman."

"What? How?"

"I believe I have shown you my *pouvoirs de déduction*? I noticed things."

"Hmm… I suppose that makes sense. I remember you could tell Henry had broken his nose simply by looking at him. So, you're fine with Anne being aboard?"

"*Oui*. I never had an issue with women aboard ships. Anne is also a princess. This makes things… interesting. I will enjoy watching the events unfold."

"I don't know whether that's a good or bad thing, but I'm glad you'll stay with us."

Edward then approached Jack.

Jack rubbed his chin in thought. "Well, I knew about the superstition concerning women on a ship, but I didn't realise people took it so seriously."

"Neither did I. So, will you be comfortable staying?"

"Why, of course. I don't mind her being aboard. And, if I remember correctly, she always enjoyed my violin. I like those who appreciate fine music."

"Well, I'm glad you're staying. The days would be even duller without you."

"I'll do my best to lighten the mood, Captain."

And then Sam.

"A woman on a pirate ship! What were ya thinking, Captain? And she's the bloody princess! This is a bloody big mess." Sam ran his fingers through his straight black hair in frustration.

"She's been quite useful. She did save our lives in that last battle by revealing her identity."

"Heaps and mounds that does us when we'll be drinkin' salt water all the way to Davy Jones' locker."

"So you're to leave as well?"

"I be stayin'."

Edward arched an eyebrow. "But you said…"

"Aye, I know what I said. If I was afraid o' danger, I would'a left a long time ago. I'll hafta get used to it, is all."

Edward laughed. "That's good to hear." He turned to leave.

"Captain?" Edward turned back. "I know ya care fer her, so I 'ave a little advice. Don't let anyone near her 'less you trust 'em. Not everyone aboard here is like you."

Edward responded with a stern look and a nod.

I know, Sam. I'll protect her.

Within a week of Edward's talking with the crew, the mood aboard ship seemed to shift, with less bickering and more willingness to adapt to the new situation. But many still wanted nothing to do with the woman and the trouble she would bring, and they weren't afraid to make their feelings known.

The *Freedom* was heading back to the Swan Islands, the same place they had stopped on their way to finding the last key. Edward addressed the crew once more as they neared port.

"Those of you leaving today will have all weapons confiscated. You will receive as much compensation as we can afford for your work, but the weapons remain. If you've already made your decision to leave, bring your belongings to the main deck to be inspected."

There was a small outcry among those intending to leave. They didn't want to be searched and to have their arms taken away.

"These are the terms. Abide by them, or be thrown off with nothing."

At that they all stopped complaining and reluctantly gathered their things to leave. In total about fifty people were leaving the ship, almost a fourth of the crew. *That's better by half than I'd expected. We'll still need to replace them, but at least we won't be a skeleton crew.*

"Now, search them."

The remaining crewmembers were reluctant to follow this command, but with a stern glance from Edward they obeyed. Nearly a third of those leaving were found to have concealed weapons among their possessions. By the time the search was complete, the ship was pulling into port.

Their former crewmates disembarked in silence. Those men had made their choice, and would never again set foot on the deck of the *Freedom*. Edward wished them well and provided them as much as he could spare from the common stock for their work to that point.

"Anyone else?" Edward asked when the last one left the ship. No one spoke. "Good. Turn the ship around. We're leaving."

"We're not going to stay, Captain?" Herbert asked.

"No. Head southwest until we're out of sight of the islands. We'll decide our next destination soon. We don't want them to know where we're headed. They could harbour some ill will towards us."

"Aye, Captain."

Edward turned his gaze out to sea once again. The salt air filled his nostrils—that sweet smell that brought the nostalgia of his youth. He let out a long sigh as he stared into the emerald waters.

Father, I know I can't be a fisherman like you. But if you were here, would you be proud of me?

"So, where are we headed now, Ed?" Henry brought Edward back from his reverie.

"I don't know. We need some new crewmembers. Pirates, of course. Where do you think we should go?"

Henry shrugged. "You expect me to know?"

"Herbert, do you have any ideas?"

"Well, there is one place I know of. I haven't heard much about it recently, but it's close by. The Cayman Islands. The Grand Cayman, specifically."

"All right, we'll try there first. Set sail for the Grand Cayman!"

26. THE SMELL OF BLOOD

The voyage to the Grand Cayman wasn't a particularly long one, but to Edward the weeks felt like months. They were especially monotonous, with the crew finding little to do, and the heat being so oppressive. The sun was rising earlier and setting later each day, and on deck there wasn't much shelter from its glare.

Edward held a thick, twisted strand of rope in his large hands as he and some others helped trim and tie down the sails. He had already spent time moving some barrels out of storage up to the top deck and others back down into storage, and, before that, doing general maintenance with Nassir and his son. He was always eager to learn every bit of what it was to be a sailor, and that meant he had to have his hand in everything going on aboard ship. During these long days on the empty sea, his only wish was to keep busy, however exhausting the work.

How did my dad do this every day? Edward thought as he fanned himself on the top deck. Seeking relief after working the sails, he lay in their shadow, shirtless, exposing the skin of his muscular chest to the warm breeze.

"You aren't much of an imposing presence right now," a sweet feminine voice rang from outside his vision. Edward sat up to see the only possible owner of that voice. She handed him a cup of water and sat down beside him.

"Thank you. It's tough to be captain-like with this heat. The air is so heavy today." He took the water and downed it in one gulp, then gazed at her, sitting next to him.

She was wearing a loose shirt that exposed her arms, and her trousers were rolled up almost to her knees. Edward couldn't help but stare at her bare legs and shoulders. Her soft skin with a healthy colour from the sun and freckles here and there caught his eyes and wouldn't let go. He could feel his heart starting to beat louder and faster in his ears.

"What's wrong, Edward? Is there something on me?" Anne asked as she checked herself.

"Uhh, no… No! Sorry, I was thinking about how you don't seem exhausted from all this work."

"I learned a lot of Oriental disciplines in my training. Many of them talk about controlling everything in your body using your mind. They say some of the more learned among them, masters who have trained all their lives, are able to break rocks with their bare hands and stand on burning coals without injuring themselves. Some say they can even evade bullets through concentration."

"Are you saying you aren't exhausted because you keep telling yourself you aren't?" Edward arched his brow in disbelief.

"Essentially," was all Anne gave.

"How is that possible?"

Anne thought about it for a moment. "The body has built-in limiters to protect us, but it's all in the mind. If you can break those limits, with your conscious or unconscious mind, you pass from the realm of normal human ability. If you tell yourself you can do something so often that you believe it with all your heart, it is bound to change what you can actually accomplish."

"And so that's how you can keep going without tiring? You tell yourself you can?"

"At its simplest, yes, but otherwise it can happen naturally in extreme circumstances. It also helps that I am used to exerting myself."

"Have you been able to do other things that way? Like dodging bullets or something?" Edward laughed even as he said it, skeptical of the whole thing. To a simple fisherman's son, this was like a penny-book fantasy.

Anne didn't seem to hear him. Her eyes were staring straight ahead, wide and glazed over as if she were lost in a daydream, remembering.

⚓ ⚓ ⚓

The smells of sulfuric gunpowder and coppery blood mixed with the salty air, filled her nostrils, and made her gag. She knew she would never become accustomed to it, but it was different this time.

This time the she had killed the man that lay in a pool of his own blood. She felt sick. Anne had never taken a life, and though he was a pirate, he was nonetheless a human being.

It was not so easy for her to justify.

"You'll pay for that, bitch!"

"We're gonna have our way with ye before we get a ransom coin."

"You'll pay with yer body and yer blood."

The crew was closing in on her. She had only a sword left with which to defend herself. The captain made his way to her through the crowd, brandishing his own sword. His tall, imposing figure made him look more beast than man, and his rage-filled eyes pierced her like those of a hawk upon its prey.

Calico Jack was what the marines called him, after the cotton print clothes he habitually wore. He was known by another name, as well: Mad Jack, the most wanted pirate in the Caribbean.

"Stand down, little queen. Don't make me cut your arms off."

She did not back down. She wasn't naive; she knew what they were saying, and what they would do. She would rather die, rather kill herself then and there, than let them have their way.

She attacked the giant in front of her. He swatted her away like a fly. She could taste blood in her mouth, but she kept attacking. She fought until she could no longer lift the sword in her hand, and then she fought some more.

When she was on the verge of collapse, and her world was starting to turn black, she could see the twisted faces of the pirates before her—their yellow, rotten teeth, scarred faces, greasy matted hair, hunched backs, jeering, lewd smiles, demonic eyes—and she could feel them closing in on her weary body with hideous intent.

No, I will not let it end like this!

She forced her eyes open and, summoning a strength and speed she didn't know she still had, lunged at the captain with her sword, cut his face from his right eye down to his mouth, then leapt high and kicked him in the chest. She cut down everyone in her path, all the way to the edge of the ship.

Everything around her felt slow, or she was moving faster than anyone or anything else. She could see the bullets they fired flying past her; it was almost as if she could reach out and pluck them right out of the air…

⚓ ⚓ ⚓

"Anne? *Anne!*" Edward shouted, waking Anne from her thoughts. "Anne, are you well?"

Edward was clutching her arm, shaking her. His eyes were wide with concern.

"I am well, Edward. I apologize, I seem to have been lost in thought. What was your question?"

Is she truly well? Edward stared at Anne, prompting her to repeat that she was in good health. "How are you able to do something like that? It seems impossible."

Anne provided herself one last shake to clear her head. "Well, part of it is training, and part of it is instinct. Recall what I mentioned before? Instinct is something lost to humans because we have become lazy. If you train yourself so that when you fight you attack without thought, then instinct can aid you. It might even be possible to control its more unbelievable manifestations. I can help train you, too."

Edward sighed. Any thought of work exhausted him even more.

He lay back down on the warm wood of the deck. "Maybe some other day," he said, making it sound more like "That will never happen."

"That was not an offer! We start tomorrow." Anne left no room for dissent. She was smiling a beautiful smile, making any feeble objection float away like mist.

She got up to leave, but Edward stopped her. "Speaking of training, talk with William. When we gain some new crewmembers I want to have everyone learn from you two. We need to become more organised, and better at fighting as a group. That last fight should have been an even match, but we'd have been dead in the water if not for you," he said with a nod in her direction. "And, on the topic of water, we should train everyone to swim as well."

Anne had her mouth half open as if she wanted to say something. After a second, she turned from his gaze.

"Now I know something is wrong. Why are you hesitant? You never had a problem training the crew before." Edward stood up.

"... Now that everyone knows who I am, they are fearful even to be near me. You may have turned them away from trying to ransom me, but I remain a woman in their eyes," she said as she casted her eyes downward. "Either they are afraid to hurt me, or they think it unlucky to be around me." Edward had rarely seen her so dejected.

First, her real family, and now this one. How am I to show everyone they may treat her the same as anyone else aboard?

Edward scratched his head in frustration, and then it hit him. "I think I'll take you up on that training, but let's do it right now." Edward walked down the poop deck ladder.

"But... I thought you were exhausted?"

Edward turned and smiled. "Not too exhausted to beat you."

Anne looked taken aback at first, but she caught onto what he was doing. "Oh is that so? We shall see about that, Thatch."

She smiled and followed him down to the main deck, where they sparred with each other, holding nothing back, for the whole crew to see.

⚓ ⚓ ⚓

It was the third day of travel, and the second since Edward had resumed his training with Anne. Each day she became more aggressive to help with his reflexes, but it was taking its toll on his body.

If this kept up, Edward would have to see Alexandre. He'd prefer to avoid that; he didn't want to feel as if he was risking his life each time he sought medical attention.

Now Edward was resting on the foredeck. The sun wasn't as

strong today, the clouds letting through just enough of its rays to provide subtle warmth. He listened to the faint sounds of Jack's music and the ocean lapping against the boat. The salty, humid air made his wavy black hair sway like the folds of a sail.

I quite enjoy this. It's a pirate's life for me, I suppose? Edward chuckled to himself at the thought.

"This is a strange thing, the sea," a deep, accented voice said from behind him, and Edward turned to see Pukuh approaching, spear in hand. He was a sight to behold: bone piercings, wooden armour and leather undergarment, animal feathers, and tattoos all over his body—a mere glimpse of him could elicit fear. He needed some normal clothes, Edward decided.

"Good day, Pukuh," Edward said. "What do you mean?"

"I would often look upon the sea as a child, thinking back on the adventures my father told me he had with Benjamin," Pukuh replied, gazing out at the endless blue surrounding them. "It has a strange pull to it, don't you think?"

Edward knew what Pukuh was talking about; he could feel it, but he couldn't help thinking his feeling was different. "I've always wanted to be on the sea, but I didn't choose the life of a pirate. I was forced into it."

"Benjamin claimed many were, and I imagine the same is true today. My father told me Benjamin had chosen the life for the excitement, and for that he is stranger than any other."

"What was he like?" Edward asked, curious about the one who had, however inadvertently, bequeathed him the life he found himself living.

"I only truly know what my father has told me," Pukuh replied. "When he left with my father I actually hated him because he was an outsider and took my father from me." Pukuh chuckled, a wisp of nostalgia in his eyes. "When my father returned, stronger than ever and with so many adventures to share that filled his face with joy, I could not fault the man that brought this about. My father said Benjamin was an odd man who didn't listen to any conventional wisdom, choosing instead to suit whatever fancy called to him at the time. He was dangerous, a warrior without peer, and an inspiration to his crew. He was not afraid of anything, and inspired fear in his enemies. My father admired him as well, which I always found odd: a king admiring a pirate." They both laughed.

"I suppose that is a bit odd."

"Yes, I thought the same until I met you."

"Until you met me? Why?"

Pukuh leaned his back against the railing. He looked to the many crewmembers tying ropes and running about, some talking and others working. "You may not have chosen this life at first, but you are like Benjamin: you do not fear it. You could have run, you could have tried to escape from the other ship a few days ago, but you didn't. It was the same with the wolves. You stood your ground, almost pushed for the fight, even. You chose the warrior's path at all times."

"But I had to. I couldn't have done anything to escape."

"Maybe so with the wolves, but not with the marines. You had the same size ship, yet you only thought of fighting. And as I understood the story from the other crewmembers, you chose it from the beginning as well. When you thought you would lose your treasure, you fought instinctively to protect it. You aren't afraid to spill blood—or lose it. A true warrior and a true pirate." Pukuh patted Edward on the shoulder and then got up and walked away.

Edward opened his mouth to make an objection, but as he thought it over he realised Pukuh was right. At each turn, he could have run away from this life, disappeared, and become a sailor at some other port, his dream fulfilled. Instead, he'd chosen at all times to fight.

Does that mean I really did choose this life? The life of adventure and constant bloodshed? Edward's heart raced at the thought, and the possibility began to scare him.

⚓ ⚓ ⚓

Edward descended into the lower decks, limping on one leg and breathing staggered breaths. As he entered the crew's quarters, he saw Alexandre at work in one corner. The small desk at which he sat, made for him by Nassir, was bolted to the side of the ship. Edward could see numerous objects on and around it: medical equipment such as gauze, needles and thread, various knives, and other things he didn't recognise, scattered sheets of paper, covered with scratches and scribbles, weighted down by miscellaneous items including a gun, and more contraptions, small and large, that he knew better than to ask about.

He moved halfway into the room before he stopped.

Maybe if I leave I'll be able to let it heal on its own, he doesn't need to see it. No, no, it's fine.

Edward wanted nothing more than to turn around and escape the possibility of more pain, but a familiar, French-accented voice from the dimly lit corner stopped him.

"Your leg is dislocated and you have several bruised ribs," Alexandre said matter-of-factly from his seat, his eyes still focused on papers. "Fighting with Anne again?"

"Yes, you're right. I don't suppose you'll tell me how you knew without even looking up?" Edward dragged himself to a chair beside the desk and sat down. The smell of sulphur and black powder pervaded the air, mixed with ether and other odd scents. *How can he work in this?*

"The timing of your step was off, indicating a limp. You wouldn't be walking on it if it were broken, so dislocated. Your breath is ragged, and you coughed when breathing in, so bruised ribs. Looking at you makes it all too easy."

"You're as stunning as ever, Alexandre, and I see your English is better every time we talk."

"Yes, well, I have had my practice. Come, sit down." Alexandre got up and motioned to a chair on the other side of the table.

Edward sat down and Alexandre examined his leg further, twisting it this way and that. "Lost again?"

"Oh, yes."

"It shows, *mon ami*. You two have been practicing more often of late." He quickly pulled on Edward's leg, snapping it back into place for him.

"Ah! Blimey Frenchman!" Edward yelled, but the pain was gone in a moment. "Thank you. And yes, we have been. The more I work with her, the easier it is for the crew to accept her."

"Noble. I noticed, despite your riveting speech, their hesitancy about having a woman aboard. Not to mention the queen's daughter. Your fighting her as if nothing were out of the ordinary would of course make some hesitation dissipate. Now lift your *maillot*."

"Lift my what?"

Alexandre sighed. "Shirt, lift your shirt, man. I learned from you *rosbifs*. The least you could do is learn a little French."

Edward lifted his shirt and apologised.

Alexandre examined the bruises on his chest, eliciting winces from his patient. "I will apply some ointment. It will help with the bruising on the outside and cool the inside."

"Thank you." Alexandre went back to his desk, opened a couple of drawers, and took out some herbs, which he threw together into a mortar and ground with a pestle. "So where did you learn medicine?"

"Why the sudden interest?" Alexandre stopped for a moment and added a clear liquid that foamed on contact.

"I realised how little I know about you. Our first meeting was rather rushed, if you recall."

"*Oui*, I remember," Alexandre replied. "I have been all over the world, the old world and the new, learning from many, and gathering much practice. This," he said, pointing to the mortar, "I learned from a shaman in the north of Asia. It uses oil from a local plant and leaves that is applied like a... *coller?*"

Stick? A sticky ointment? "A paste?"

"*Oui*, a paste. Now, lift your shirt again." As soon as Edward did so, Alexandre applied the white substance over his ribs, producing more winces until he was finished. Alexandre put gauze over it and a wrap to keep it in place. "There, *tout fini*."

This feels so odd. It's tingling and cold, but the bruises don't hurt anymore. "That's amazing. I don't even feel it anymore. Thanks, Alexandre!"

"You are welcome," he replied, returning to his desk. He grabbed a different ointment in a stone jar, which Edward was already familiar with, and walked back to him.

Edward pulled up his left shirt arm, revealing the red mess, which used to be an even uglier red mess, of a scar. It was healing, slowly, and if not for Alexandre and the treatment he'd received from the Mayans, he probably wouldn't have an arm at all now.

"I told you before not to spar while you are healing, but you won't listen to me no matter what I say, will you?"

"I should say… no." Edward laughed as Alexandre finished applying the ointment.

"So how is Pukuh's leg?"

"It was not broken, simply a bad sprain and dislocation which he set himself with you present, I understand, so it has already healed."

"Well, at least one of us is all better. Thanks again, Alexandre." Edward rose to leave.

"Ah yes, here." Alexandre picked up and handed Edward a pistol.

It was modified and had something different in the barrel from the pistols Edward was used to. "What's this?"

"If I can't stop your practice fighting, I can try to stop the real thing. When we met, I was testing this pistol. This is the completed version," he said, motioning towards the pistol. "It has rifling and uses custom bullets. They take a long time to make, but they are more accurate and have longer range than regular pistols. You'll need only one bullet to kill, if you take proper aim."

"I could definitely use this. Can you make me a matching one?"

"*Certainement.* But, as I said, it will take time."

"I should like to know as soon as it is ready, if you please." Edward started to leave, but stopped himself. "Alexandre, why did you join us? And, for that matter, after being through all these battles, why have you stayed? You know the risks, and this obviously isn't the usual ship to be on if you want to explore the world."

"It is the same as I mentioned at our meeting. I want excitement. This world is dull, but you've proven to be more than adequate entertainment. I shall enjoy seeing your descent."

Descent? "What do you mean?"

"You are a pirate, but so far you've only had to defend yourself and attack those who attack you, or whom you consider evil already. Soon, you may run out of people you can steal supplies from. You will need to go on the offence to survive. At that time, I will be able to see an answer to a question that's been puzzling me."

Edward stared deep into Alexandre's eyes. The blank stare did not wholly conceal an unsettling glint of excitement. He believed he knew what Alexandre's question was, and he knew he didn't want to acknowledge it. But—despite it making him sick to his stomach— he had to ask.

"What question?"

Alexandre smiled, and Edward cringed as the smiling mouth asked, "Do you enjoy the smell of blood?"

Edward spun around and left without another word, terrified by the man who knew so much from just observing. That he was able to know exactly what Edward wanted to know was amazing; that he was excited to know the answer to the question was horrifying.

What made Edward sick to his stomach was that some part of him was excited too.

27. THE BODDEN TOWN BANDITS

"We are close to the island now, Captain. I hope it's still the safe haven for pirates I've heard it is. You remember what happened when you thought Port Royal was safe?" Herbert turned himself around in his wheelchair. The creak and clank of the wooden joints made the wheelchair seem likely to break, but it stood fast, as it had for years.

"How could I forget?" *Henry almost died because of Frederick. No, not Frederick, rest his soul. The magistrate was at fault, but I don't want anything like that happening again.* "We can't take any chances this time. The more discreet we are the better."

"That's well and good," Henry said as he walked up the steps to the foredeck, "but how do we remain discreet when we need at least twenty-five, maybe forty, crewmembers?"

"So few? I thought we lost more."

"Yes, well, a lot of those who left were freeloaders, and while we were at sea John had plenty of time to reassess how many we need aboard. Operating with a skeleton crew has shown us we can work with less."

"See, Henry? It all works out in the end." Edward smiled.

"You don't have to tell me, I'm with you."

"You have to agree all's well that ends well, eh, chap?" Edward said as he smacked his friend's back.

"Edward, I'm agreeing with you. Yes, it's good they left."

"Be as contrary as you want, some good came out of this mess."

Henry wiped his face. "I hate you."

"Aww, love you too, mate." Edward punched Henry in the arm.

Herbert, watching this exchange, just shook his head, but Edward noticed a smirk on his face.

After Edward and Henry had finished laughing at their own foolishness, Edward realised for the first time the oddity of seeing Herbert on the foredeck. "Herbert, why aren't you at the helm?"

"Christina's taking over for a bit. She wants to feel useful aboard the ship, and I've been teaching her a little of how to read the sky and manage a ship of this size."

Edward frowned. *It will be dangerous for her if she's on deck when a battle breaks out.* "If she's going to be on deck then she would do well to learn how to defend herself. She won't be forced to fight, as per the commandments, but she should at least be prepared so she can stay alive. Either she learns to fight as well, or she stays below deck."

"Understood, Captain. I'll let her know her choices." Herbert turned and climbed back down to the main deck with his chair in tow, his massive arms straining with the effort.

"What are you thinking?" Henry asked, his anger apparent.

"What's your meaning?" Edward replied casually.

"Having her trained to fight?" Henry's eyes were fierce and he gripped Edward's arm. "Are you mad?"

"What of it? If Christina is to be above deck working, then she has to be prepared to fight, even if it's mentally."

"She's a fifteen-year-old girl, Edward!" Henry yelled, which caused everyone on the foredeck to stop and stare, hoping to watch the expected argument. Edward gave them stern looks and they went back to work. Then he leaned close to Henry and talked in a harsh whisper.

"Don't you ever talk back to me on deck. You've done it before, but it has to stop. This is my ship, and I'm the captain. If you have an objection to the way I do things, then we can discuss it in private. We don't need dissention in the ranks. Are we clear?"

"Clear as the wide sky." Henry turned to leave. "Captain."

Edward watched him walk away, and then noticed some were still staring. "Back to work!" he barked. They all rushed to obey his order the second time. Then Edward went to the front of the deck and gazed out at the open sea. He stood there brooding for a while, until his anger wore off and was replaced by melancholy.

⚓ ⚓ ⚓

The next day Edward was at the helm with Herbert. On the distant horizon a land mass was taking shape. It was the first of the Cayman Islands, and it was a welcome sight to a weary crew.

"So where are we landing?" Edward asked Herbert.

"We will be landing in Bodden Town, but that's not the official name."

Edward raised his brow. "Not the official name? Why?"

"Well, the islands around here are owned by the British, but because they're such convenient stops for transients they've been settled mainly by thugs and rogues. The government doesn't like to officially acknowledge its ownership of the land, and so hasn't bothered to name any of the settlements."

"So why is it called Bodden Town?"

"Because of the Bodden family."

"And why is it named after them?"

Herbert almost seemed to be tiptoeing around the subject. "It's because… they own the town."

Edward palmed his face and his voice took grew agitated. "How can they own the town?"

"Outsiders call them the Bodden Town Bandits, but it's worse than it sounds. The family controls the trade and all the activities on the island through force. They have an extensive network throughout, and have their hands in everything. It's quite the lucrative business, I hear."

"And how does the family feel about people who encroach on their territory?"

"As long as it's business, it's fine, but you have to defer to them first. If you don't, then… well…"

"Herbert?" Edward prodded.

"You're silenced."

Edward sighed. "Don't you think we would have been better served had we been told this before we arrived? This makes things difficult." Edward stroked his short black beard, deep in thought.

Herbert waited for orders, but they never came. "Do… do you want me to change course?"

"No, no. Stay steady, this doesn't change our plans. We simply have to be even more careful."

Edward was still brooding and stroking his beard when John walked up to the aft deck to check on things.

"John! Perfect timing. Come here."

"Yes, Captain?"

"I want you to tell everyone who's been tasked with finding potential crewmembers to keep a watchful eye, even amongst the rogues. Tell them to seek out individuals, no one in groups. This town seems particularly lawless."

"Understood, Captain," John said as he went about his task.

"I should like it if we can have some peace while here. We've had enough trouble of late as it is. I'm going to find Nassir to talk over the *Freedom*'s needed repairs. Keep her steady," Edward ordered Herbert.

"Aye, Captain."

Edward walked down to the main deck. People were running this way and that, some carrying rope or barrels of wine, some swabbing the deck, and others practicing swordplay or checking weapons. Some saluted or called out to him as he passed, and he greeted them in return.

He located Nassir on the gun deck, checking the sideboards while his son watched from nearby. He had a puzzled look on his face, as if something was not quite right.

"What's the problem?" Edward asked as he approached.

Nassir and his boy Ochi acknowledged Edward's presence, and then Nassir went back to the sideboards. His deep, rumbling voice sounded troubled. "There is no problem, but that is the problem."

Edward cocked his brow. "You are speaking in riddles."

"Yes, that is exactly what this is." Nassir was rubbing his hand over the pine boards. "There is no damage in this area of the ship."

"None? What about the battle we just had?"

"Yes, there is recent damage, but not from before. Nothing old."

"But... I remember you saying it was damaged. Back when we met Bartholomew Roberts. You said you couldn't repair it for some reason."

"Yes, it was the same reason I didn't want to try breaking open the locked sections: This ship was built like no other ship I've seen and I didn't want to risk permanent damage by cutting into the wood from the outside. Now that I can see it from the inside, however, I can tell that the damage in this area is new. The old damage would have shown signs of rot, but there is none."

"Hmm, that is odd..." Edward scratched his head and thought about it for a moment. "Perhaps we were merely lucky it didn't rot. We should take it as a blessing."

"Perhaps," Nassir repeated, still doubtful.

After another moment to ponder, Edward moved on. "I wished to speak with you regarding the repairs. How bad was the damage, and how long will it take to fix?"

"The battle was not long, and so the repairs will not take long, provided we have sufficient supplies and manpower."

"Confer with John for and supplies any provisions you may need. I should like to see the repairs completed as quick as possible. We may not be here long."

"Aye, Captain," Nassir said as he bowed.

Edward patted a smiling Ochi on the head and nodded to Nassir as he left. *Quite the head-scratcher indeed. But I have more important things to worry about.*

⚓ ⚓ ⚓

The *Freedom* eased into the harbour as the crew raised the sails and readied the lines to secure it. Edward watched the preparations, issuing orders as needed. He wore his full outfit—tricorn hat, black coat, breeches, and tall boots. He appeared older than his years, with his black beard now being rather large, and his maturity evident in his command. He addressed the crew, telling them to stay out of trouble and keep a low profile—the less trouble they made, the longer they could stay—but otherwise to enjoy their leisure time.

Edward asked Anne and Henry to join him for a drink at the local tavern before they set to work on recruiting. It had been a while since Edward was able to relax, and he meant to as soon as possible.

The crew put out a gangplank, and Edward was first to disembark, with Anne and Henry close behind. He sauntered down to the harbour with some of his crew following after. Those on the ship threw rope down and those on the pier lashed it to pegs, securing the ship, while Edward was met by the harbourmaster.

"Name?"

"Edward Thatch."

"Business?"

"My business is my own. If it is a matter of coin, then my quartermaster John will oblige you. Now if you'll excuse me, I'll be on my way." He went around the man and strode off, with Henry and Anne following him.

The harbourmaster ran up in front of him again. "Stop. Stop, I say!" The man placed his hand over Edward's broad chest. "The brothers Malcolm and Neil Bodden request the presence of all... prominent travelers such as you. My associate will guide you to their house." He pointed to a young Negro in a servant's suit.

"My apologies, but you can tell the Brothers Bodden I refuse. I do not know them and so I have no business with them. You can tell them if they want to speak with me then they can come see me themselves."

The harbourmaster was left speechless and flustered. He motioned to the other man, who nodded and ran off.

"Do you think that was wise, Edward?" Anne asked as they started walking down the harbour towards town again.

She was wearing a simple, leather jacket over a loose white tunic, tight-fitting trousers, and comfortable boots. Her hair was tied in a ponytail in the back and loose in the front. Now that she was known to be a woman it afforded her a more comfortable choice of apparel. Edward stared at her, dumbfounded.

"Edward?"

He coughed and raised his eyes. "I told them the truth. I have no business with the men. We've just arrived and I wish to relax. They can't expect people to do business the moment they arrive. I mean, look at this place!"

Past the harbour there was a sandy beach with the salty sea lapping against it with each oncoming wave. In the distance, palm trees and green grass holding loose coconuts and various flowers went as far as the eye could see, swaying in the wind like sails.

Straight from the stone steps Edward, Anne, and Henry had walked up, there was a local market with vendors hawking fresh fish, produce, and other local delicacies stretching far to the left and right on the cobblestone roads. The smells were heavenly and a welcome respite from the old biscuits, dried meat, and soft cheese they were used to at sea.

In front of them the main street went all the way to the end of the small town. Strewn about the street there were patches of green and palms growing from them, left untouched from the making of the road. It gave a feeling of earthiness and brightness to the dark stones.

Some of the houses and businesses going up the street were made of wood from the local palm trees, or thicker imported woods of lighter colour. All the houses in the town were one or two stories high, and none unkempt or in disrepair. The setting sun bestowed a magical hue of gold and the place felt like a painting come to life.

"It doesn't feel like the locals are too fond of visitors," Henry said as he peered this way and that.

As they walked along the streets, they became aware of people standing in doorways and at windows, watching them. Whether it was direct and blatant staring, or more subtle glances, the whole town seemed curious about, or suspicious of, the newcomers. Men with cigars blew great puffs of smoke from their mouths. Others held newspapers that covered their mouths but left their eyes showing. Still others stole glimpses from behind decks of playing cards. All but the children playing in the streets eyed them with one thought.

They all stared at the three strangers, expecting trouble.

"What of it?" Edward scoffed.

Though the air was thick with tension and the town eerily quiet, Edward wasn't fazed. He sauntered down the main street with his back straight, his coat flapping in the wind, his face expressionless as stone. He walked until he found the first bar, and went inside.

A gang of toughs, full of bravado, potentially even some pirates, were stationed in the seats as if they had them on permanent reserve. Everyone in the bar was laughing and drinking, but when Edward, Anne, and Henry walked in, they all stopped. They owned the place, and the young man standing tall amongst the veterans was like an insult to them. No one moved, but their eyes followed the newcomers.

Edward went to the bar and sat down on a stool. "Rum, please." Seeming pleased by his choice, the rest of the patrons went back to their carousing.

On the outside Edward was calm, but he knew if they all fought, he and his companions would lose. He was the one who had warned the crew to tread lightly. He had to be an example for them.

Henry sat and ordered rum, like Edward, and just as Anne was about to sit down, someone smacked her on the behind. "Be a good wench and fetch me a beer!" an overweight man in a dirty tunic yelled, provoking the laughter of his friends.

Anne's face flushed red and hot—not with embarrassment, but with rage. "Stay calm, Anne," Henry warned.

"I am calm." Anne's words sifted through grinding teeth and she sat down with a hard plop on the stool.

But the man mistook her flush and decided to push his luck further. "Aw, come now lass, don't be cold. Let me buy ye a drink and you and I can head to the back and I'll show you the pleasure a real man can provide."

Anne let out a long breath, then turned to the thug. "No, thank you." The perfect pronunciation—so out of place where they were—made her stand out even more, which further goaded the thug.

"Oh, ho, we have a prissy little bint here, don't we?" the fat man said, eliciting laughter from those in his entourage. He grabbed Anne's arm. "Come on, lass, don't knock it 'till ye touch it."

Edward was silent through the whole incident, but he downed his rum in one gulp, rose to his feet, spun around, and smashed the glass on the fat man's head. The man fell to the ground, screaming and bloody. The more he tried to grab at the glass in his eyes, the worse he made it. His friends jumped up, as did everyone else in the bar.

The only things keeping them all at bay were Edward's cold stare and his stature. At six feet four inches, he was taller than any man there, and his second in command, Henry, was almost as tall and just as powerfully built.

"So much for not making trouble, eh Ed?"

"I suppose I can't control my temper like you can, Henry." They both raised their fists to prepare for the twenty-some men, and a few women, about to pounce on them. Anne stood between the two of them and prepared herself as well, nodding to each of them to signal she was ready.

But just as pandemonium was about to break loose, two average-looking men sauntered through the door, followed by several well-armed men of more intimidating build. They were twins, dressed in matching outfits of the finest silk, and Edward could easily guess who they were by their superior air and lack of weapons. At the sight of them, the whole room fell silent.

"The Brothers Bodden!" Edward announced.

The brothers assessed the scene before them. "Any trouble here with our newcomers, boys?" asked one of them in a faded Scottish accent.

Everyone went back into their seats and to their drinking, quiet now.

"Good," the other brother said in similar accent.

The fat man was still writhing on the floor, his companions trying to silence him. He motioned to the table and one of the men under the Boddens' employ went over and shot the poor fellow in the head, silencing him for good.

"You must be Edward. We heard from our associate you would only come if we invited you ourselves." His brother continued, "Well, here we are. We have business to discuss. You will come with us."

"And if I refuse?"

The Bodden Brothers' men instinctively pulled out their pistols and surrounded the three pirates. The brothers chuckled. "You wouldn't want to do that," one of them said. They smiled at each other and walked out the door.

Their thugs prodded Edward and the rest to follow, and they all left the bar, heading up the main street. The local residents stared at them but gave their procession a wide berth. When they reached the end of the long, sloping cobblestone road, they arrived at a large metal gate in a tall, thick stone wall. The gate opened onto a stone path leading to a large whitewashed house.

Like the gate, the house was made of fine materials and a higher quality design than the other houses and businesses in town; it was built of imported wood, and had two stories and several rooms. On a balcony some women were sitting at a table sipping tea, tended by Negro slaves. The whole estate might have been a high-class inn or a manor house for a wealthy family back in England.

Edward, Henry, and Anne were led up the path and into the house. The interior was even more extravagant than the exterior had suggested. They were taken through a large ballroom up to the second floor, and ushered into a study.

The walls of the room were lined with shelves holding numerous books, weapons and relics, including a Scottish coat of arms. At the back was a large wooden table with several papers strewn about where all of them sat down.

"Now that you are on this island," the brother seated on the left began, "it is best we explain the rules to you."

"Brother, manners!" chided the brother on the right. "Introductions first, business after."

"Yes, yes, it always slips my mind. I am Malcolm Bodden, and this is my brother Neil. We know the captain is Edward Thatch; our boy told us that much. Who are the beauty and the beast with you?"

"What do you say, beauty, beast? Care to give your names?" Edward asked.

"No," Anne and Henry said in unison with the same nonchalant attitude.

Edward shrugged at the brothers' questioning look.

Malcolm, on the left, started again. "No matter. Now, the rules.

Blackbeard's Ship

Things are a little different here in our town—and I do mean ours, because we own it. Any and all business is to be done through us, or our associates."

Neil picked up after Malcolm. "Don't trouble yourselves about fights or anything of that nature. We realise that the heavy supply of booze we bring in daily, as well as the… groups we attract, are responsible. There's really nothing that can be done. Simply enjoy yourselves."

Malcolm piped in. "And don't die in the process." The two brothers laughed at their own joke, but Edward, Anne, and Henry didn't see the humour. "So, fellows, do you have any business you hope to accomplish here?"

Edward thought about it for a second. "As you put it, we're here to enjoy ourselves and not die in the process, of course—but then, that's a full-time business. Your men seem to have rather itchy trigger fingers. Should I be worried?" Edward stared the two down as he leaned back in his chair.

The tension was evident on the brothers' faces, but they tried to laugh it off. "Perish the thought! Our men would never seek to harm our guests." Malcolm said. "… Unless you cause us trouble—or don't relinquish our share."

"Your share?" Henry asked.

"Yes, we were about to discuss that. If you plan on selling anything…"

"Spices, clothes, slaves," Neil interjected.

Malcolm smiled. "The usual for your types… All that is taxed by us."

This was Anne's territory. "How much?"

"Twenty percent," Malcolm stated.

"That is ludicrous!" Anne almost jumped up out of her seat, but Edward restrained her.

When Anne had calmed herself, Edward spoke with the brothers. "We understand the rules now. Is there anything else, or can I and my friends resume drinking and causing a ruckus in your town?"

The brothers laughed again. "Yes, our men will escort you out. Enjoy the town, and remember: we're watching, always."

Edward, Anne, and Henry left without another word, and were soon on the main street, heading to the ship.

28. THE PRINCE & THE PAUPER

Pukuh watched as Anne, Edward, and Henry all left the ship to explore the town. The thought of being on solid land once more enticed him, and so he made his way to the gangplank.

"Uhh, Master Mayan, sir?" a voice from behind said tentatively.

He turned to see who it was. "You are the one they call John, yes?"

"Yes."

"You may call me Pukuh."

"Yes, of course. Do you plan on travelling into town like… that?" He gestured to Pukuh's clothing.

"What is wrong with my warrior clothing?"

Some other crewmembers who were listening laughed, as if he were a fool for even asking.

"W-well, there's nothing wrong with it, but you might attract unwanted attention from the locals, is all."

Pukuh made a spitting sound. "Let the white people stare. I have no shame in wearing what I have earned from the gods." He turned and crossed the gangplank.

Pukuh looked back and noticed John praying, possibly to those same gods, that he wouldn't get into, or cause, trouble.

Pukuh's first stop was the local market stationed right above the harbour. A straight street led up the hill, all the way through town, and he could see Edward and the other two walking up it. On the left and right was the market street with many people littering the small available area. The noonday sun was shining down on him, and several people were buying and selling and walking around.

The street was lined with stalls. Fruit, vegetables—both local and exotic—fresh fish and fishing equipment, and even weapons and ammunition could be bought there. Almost everything imaginable was for sale.

Pukuh stood out like a beached whale with his nut-brown skin, bone piercings, tattoos, and leather warrior's outfit decorated with eagle feathers. The locals, in their conventional tunics and trousers, stared at the strange sight, and some of the women actually cowered at his approach. But Pukuh was indifferent—even oblivious—to the attention.

The market fascinated him. Examining some of the local produce, he saw foods he had never seen before. There was a brown, ball-like thing that sounded as if it had liquid in it when he shook it, as well as a hard round fruit with stripes of alternating light and dark green. They didn't seem too appetizing to him. He noticed some apples and took one, and began to munch on it as he walked.

"Oi, you have to pay for that!"

Pukuh turned back to the vendor. "Pay? I have no cacao beans on me."

"Cacao beans?" The man raised his brow and had a confused look in his eyes. "This is no trade. I'm talking about this." The vendor pulled out a coin from his pocket and showed it to Pukuh.

"Ah yes, my father mentioned something like this." Pukuh pulled a purse from off his belt. He opened it and tossed a gold coin to the vendor. "That should suffice, I hope?"

The vendor's eyes bulged at the sight of the gold, as did those of others close by. "Yes, yes, that's quite enough!" He laughed, and Pukuh turned to leave. "Wait, hold a moment. I can't let you go just like that." He filled a bag with apples and some other fruits and handed it to Pukuh.

"Thank you," he said, taking the bag.

After that, everyone around tried to sell things to him, scrambling to find their best wares and foods to present to him. He declined them all politely, but he was becoming annoyed, so he went off down a side street leading away from the market.

"I didn't realise those shiny coins were so valued," he remarked aloud.

"Hey stranger, you want to have a good time?"

Pukuh turned his gaze to the voice. The owner was a woman standing in front of a white house of several floors with a red door. A few other women were standing close by. They all wore ordinary clothing, but were showing off their legs and shoulders.

He walked over to the woman who had spoken. "Mmm, you look different," she purred. "You have money?"

Pukuh showed her the gold coin. "What does this mean: 'good time'?"

"Why don't you come in and I'll show you?" She grabbed his hand and pulled him in through the door.

After about ten minutes, he hurriedly came back out. He didn't say a word to them as they pursued him, yelling profanities. Back out on the streets, he shook his head. *What kind of a world is this that forces women to do that for trade?*

He continued a short distance down the street and noticed an establishment with several people inside, talking and drinking. The swinging doors creaked as he entered through them, and immediately all eyes were on him. Pukuh sat down at the bar and flashed a gold coin.

"I would like a drink."

The barman wasn't fazed by Pukuh's odd appearance, but several customers took notice. The barman noticed their curiosity, and then said to him, "We don't serve your kind here. This is a civilised establishment, and I don't want any trouble."

"I am not here to make trouble. I wish to have a drink. My father told me there is something called a beer I must try."

"I already told you I'll not serve you." He leaned in and whispered to Pukuh, "You'd best leave now before my regulars do something."

Pukuh glanced around the bar and noticed everyone still watching him. He scoffed and left the bar without another word. A few of the patrons followed right behind him.

"Hey, foreigner!" a man yelled.

Pukuh turned to see three ragged, ill-smelling, thuggish-looking men approaching. "What is it? I have no business with you common white men."

"Common white men?" They surrounded Pukuh. "Who do you think you are? You look like a savage, but the gold you carry says otherwise. I suggest you give it to us before we take it."

Pukuh assessed the situation. There were three of them—a short man in front, a fat man on the right, and a muscular man on the left. He was surrounded. Not very good odds, were he someone else.

Pukuh jumped high and kicked the short man in front, sending him flying backwards. Pukuh fell to the ground, but swiftly pushed himself back up. The other two men grabbed the Mayan warrior as soon as he stood. He slammed his fist into the elbow of the fat man on the right. The bone broke with a muted snap, and he let go with a scream. The muscular man on the left punched him in the jaw. He rolled with it and kicked the man in the groin. The brute doubled over, clutching his manhood.

The short man in front had recovered quickly from the kick and attacked him with a knife. His bag of fruit still in hand, Pukuh grabbed it in both hands, swung back, and smashed the hard fruit into the man's chin. The bag hit him with so much force he nearly flipped in the air before falling to the ground with a thud.

The fat man, still cradling his broken arm protectively, pulled out a gun with his other hand. Pukuh jumped and rolled to the side as the sound of thunder roared and the bullet flew past his face. The man's eyes went wide as his last attempt at defense was thwarted. Pukuh dashed to the fat man with the spent gun. All in one motion, he picked the fat man up by the neck, lifted him off the ground, and slammed him back to the stone.

With two of his assailants unconscious and one still doubled over in pain, the fight was over. Pukuh had a bead of sweat rolling down his forehead, which he promptly wiped from his brow. Recalling Edward's words to stay out of trouble, he grabbed what was left of his bag of fruit, went back to the main street, and walked back to the *Freedom*.

As Pukuh approached the ship, he saw a few crewmen swabbing the deck, and a few others cleaning barnacles off the hull.

"Is the one called John still on the vessel?" Pukuh asked

The closest crewman laughed when he noticed Pukuh's garb. "He be below decks."

Pukuh nodded to the crewman and headed down to the crew cabin, where, amongst the swinging hammocks, he found John cleaning the floor.

"John?"

John jumped at the sound and then stood up. "Y-yes?"

"I would like a change of clothes."

29. WHAT MATTERS MOST

"Edward, what are we to do? The brothers have a monopoly on everything. I imagine they will want compensation if we start trying to recruit people. And what about the tax?" Anne spoke in a whisper as they walked down the street.

"We don't have to worry about the tax," Henry interjected. "We've nothing to sell. As for the recruitment, we didn't mention it and we know nothing of their rules concerning it. Ed, you should have told them about it."

"No, Henry. This way, our plans remain secret, and if they do find out, we can feign ignorance."

"What's your plan, then?" Henry asked.

"Unfortunately, I don't have any ideas yet, so I'd like the two of you to search the town, find our men, and tell them not to ask anyone about joining until I give further notice."

Anne stopped Edward before he could leave. "Where are you going?" she asked.

"I should like to see what John and the others have to suggest. Return to the ship when you're done."

They watched Edward walk away towards the ship, lost in thought.

"Is he always like this?" Anne asked.

"As long as I've known him. When he makes up his mind, there's usually no changing it. He's less quiet and shy than he used to be, but still the same Edward. When his father disappeared, I couldn't stand to see him crying, so I started talking and playing with him. We fight a lot, but we've stayed friends."

Anne kept gazing at Edward's back as he disappeared into the distance.

"I want to apologise for what I said to you before, back after Edward kissed you," stated Henry, "and also for my wanting you off the ship. I've come to realise you aren't like I thought." Henry made her face him directly. "But remember this: If he's harmed because of you, you'll never have my forgiveness." Anne nodded and Henry walked away. She opened her mouth to say something, but didn't follow through. "I'll handle the left side of town," he said. "You handle the right. Meet you back at the ship." He waved as he went into the nearest bar.

Anne stood there. She couldn't see Edward any longer, but she could see the ship down the slope. She clutched the ring between her breasts and thought about the terror coming for them, wondering whether she would have the strength to protect him when the time came.

⚓ ⚓ ⚓

"So, any suggestions?"

The few members of the *Freedom* left on the ship all sat at the dining tables below deck past the crew cabin. Alexandre, John, William, and Sam all listened, not saying a word. Edward waited.

"Nothing at all?"

"I have *une* question."

"Yes, Alexandre?"

"Why am I here?"

Edward glared at him. "You're here because I'm your captain and I asked you to be here. I need ideas on how to solve our problem."

Alexandre slumped forward in his seat and sighed. He wanted to make it evident he wasn't excited by any of this.

"What if we brought people to the ship?" William suggested.

"That's what we's trying to do, mate," Sam mocked. "You have anything more to add?"

William gave Sam a stern look. "I mean, bring them based on a common interest. Such as drinking or a game of cards. Then we have the whole ship to talk in without unwanted listeners."

"How will we know which people work for the B-Bodden Brothers? Anyone in town could be under their employ." John was sweating, as usual. He wiped it from his forehead and kept himself small, which was hard for such a big man.

"You have a point. How are we to distinguish friend from foe in this town?"

"Not like we can jus' walk up to the blokes and ask 'em outright," Sam chuckled.

"It's a risk we'll have to take. We can always tell the Boddens that their people asked to join us."

Alexandre groaned.

"Something to share, Alex?"

"You are inviting your own downfall if you think that will work."

"Then what do you propose we do?"

"Sit, *mon ami*. I have a plan which, I believe, even lesser minds such as yourselves will be capable of carrying out."

Edward sat down. "This had better be good."

"Never fear. It will be."

⚓ ⚓ ⚓

William walked into the room they had reserved in the small, two-story inn on the main street. "Is everyone in place?" Edward asked when he entered.

"Yes, Captain. Our keenest eyes are in place and ready to keep watch on all the entrances."

"I still do not understand why we are here," Anne complained. "You did not explain it properly."

"We're going to watch the comings and goings at the Boddens' villa. Whoever leaves the villa will be followed to see where they frequent, and to find out who are their usual contacts. We'll take a week to do this in shifts, while the rest of the crew does upkeep on the ship. As soon as we know who's with the Boddens, if they try to mix in with anyone we bring aboard we'll be able to kick them out."

"I wish to follow people rather than stay here. I don't believe I could stay awake during this," Anne said, stifling a yawn.

"No, Anne. William's going to do that. You're with me tonight. We'll sleep in shifts." Edward watched the door of the villa intently. "Oh, there's someone leaving! William, get down there quick!"

"Yes, Captain!" he said, as he went out and down the stairs.

Anne plopped herself on the bed. "Edward, this will be such a bore," she said with much pouting. "My talents are being wasted here; I am much better at tracking. What is the purpose of it anyway? There are other places we can pick up crewmembers, other towns on the Grand Cayman, other islands in the Caymans even. Why this town?"

"We landed here first, and we need to repair the *Freedom*. Besides, it's a nice break for the crew, and they need it."

Anne stared at Edward as he gazed on the Bodden house and the gate before it. "There is more to it than that, Edward Thatch, I am sure of it. I just do not know what it is."

"Whatever do you mean? I have given you the reason, what more do you wish to hear?"

"Very well, I merely hope this does not come to blows. I don't think that would be the nice break the crew would want or need. I do not wish anyone to be harmed." Anne placed her hand over Edward's. "I do not wish *you* to be harmed."

"I won't be harmed. No one will. These brothers aren't the fighting type." Edward noticed someone entering the Boddens' so he made note of their appearance.

"Let us hope you're right. They are not so different from us. They are bandits—and we are pirates." Saying the word made her smile for a brief second, but the smile was quickly replaced by a frown. "Does it ever get easier?"

Edward looked at Anne and let the question hang in the air. "No…" He turned back to the villa. "It never gets easier."

⚓ ⚓ ⚓

The days and nights were long for everyone that week. Waiting and watching wasn't natural to a rough gang of seamen, and they were restless. Jack was keeping the cleaning crew happy with songs, ballads, and tall tales. John had bought Pukuh a regular set of clothes for seafaring. Pukuh brooded about it in silence, as was his way, and it was plain to all he hated wearing it.

Edward and Anne were feeling the effects of long hours spent sitting in chairs throughout the day. Having each other's company helped; they were able to talk and laugh and tell stories during the night, and they took turns sleeping during the day.

"So what is it like, being a princess?" Edward asked one evening.

"Humph. It is not so glamorous as one would think. Many gatherings with people of high class, all of them namby-pamby nobility who had not done a decent day's work in their lives. Not my type of people."

"Judging by the company you're mixed with now, that much is evident."

Anne laughed, but it sounded more cynical than happy. "My fondest memories are not of being with my mother, but with the Bettys in the kitchen. Either I was helping them prepare a meal, or talking with them. After a while, they treated me like a normal person instead of someone who would off their heads at the slightest misstep."

"So what is your mother like? You don't talk much about her."

Anne hesitated for a moment. Edward felt she would still prefer to avoid the subject. "She is a strong woman who has lost a lot. I am the one child that has survived to adulthood, and because of that she was too protective of me. She is highly intelligent, and a strong commander; she takes an active role in war and in politics. When her mother once told her the queen does not have much power, she retorted, 'But I will.' She has a defiant attitude towards anyone who opposes her, and does not hesitate to do whatever is necessary, no matter how dire the situation."

"She sounds a lot like—"

"Do not *dare* finish that sentence!" Anne almost screamed as she turned in her chair to face Edward. "I am nothing like her." Anne set her gaze back to the street and continued her watch in silence. Edward thought to apologise, but decided against saying anything. For a few hours an awkward silence pervaded the room, and when normal conversation resumed, her royal status was not brought up again.

The other watchers at the inns were too preoccupied with memorizing faces and tailing the bodies attached to them to think about anything else. Exhausted and irritable, they longed for the week to end so they could rest again. Their brains were so full of faces and descriptions that even their dreams were invaded by floating heads and words.

While those in the inns were watching people, William and the others were gathering information. They acquired a list of the names of known associates of the Boddens. It was extensive, containing over two hundred souls. It included informants, toughs, and those running businesses owned by the Boddens, any or all of whom might be feeding the brothers information or helping with their dirty work.

And all of whom needed to be avoided.

After completing their reconnaissance, the senior members of the crew met back on the *Freedom* to discuss their findings.

"Every one of these businesses is controlled by the Boddens by one means or another," William reported to Edward. "Either they own it outright, own it under the table, or exact a fee for a permit to continue operating. The ones that pay a fee aren't exactly loyal to the Boddens, so the brothers employ several informants who seek to fill their purses by frequenting the bars and businesses in search of new tidbits of information. Those are the ones we want to avoid," he said, glancing around the table to ensure his words were heard. "Then there are the cutthroats who do the Boddens' dirty work. They collect the fees from the businessmen and frequent the bars the rest of the time. Some of them will probably end up mixed with the crowd we bring in. We don't have to worry if one or two see what we're doing; they have not the intelligence to tell the brothers what they've seen, especially if they are burdened with enough spirits."

Edward thanked William. "It will be a lot easier, knowing who we're dealing with."

"You are welcome," said Alexandre, stressing each syllable and smiling at Edward, who ignored him.

"Good work, everyone. Rest up, for tomorrow the town won't have the chance to sleep with our revelry!" The group responded with yawns and low hoots and groans. Edward laughed. *They'll be better tomorrow. You've lost, Bodden Brothers, wait and see!*

Throughout the following day, Sam and the other crewmembers brought in many people from all around town for an afternoon and night of booze, singing, dancing, and games. Edward appointed guards from among the crew and positioned them at the docks to stop anyone from coming aboard, or even near, the ship if one of the regular crew wasn't with them. The crew who had watched the Boddens' home spotted their men and swiftly booted them from the ship as well, keeping prying eyes away.

As night drew closer, the party grew more raucous, and some fought and caused trouble. Edward and Henry kicked out any who became too violent. The senior members aboard the *Freedom* also talked with some of the potential recruits, and by nightfall they had managed to enlist twenty men.

The day had been a success. But the night destroyed it all.

Accompanied by fifty of their strongest men armed to the teeth, the Bodden Brothers themselves broke through the barricade of guards and forced their way onto the *Freedom*. Everyone aboard stopped what they were doing and stared at the intruders. No one moved.

"This gathering is over." "Clear out and go home."

The two of them had issued their orders, and in an instant most of the people from the village obeyed. It didn't matter that they were on a ship with almost four times as many hands. They were, simply, afraid.

It should be me whom they fear more.

"You are beginning to become a nuisance, Edward Thatch," said Malcolm. "We think you should leave," Neil added.

"And what is this all about?" Edward stalked straight over to them. Several of the bodyguards pointed blades and guns in his face, but he paid them no heed. He stared daggers at the brothers and they backed up instinctively, despite the guards.

"You have two days." "Finish your business and be gone, or else."

They rushed down the gangplank and headed back into town,

leaving their threats lingering in the air.

⚓ ⚓ ⚓

Edward slammed his fist on the table in frustration. Everyone nearby jumped at the sudden display of anger.

"Damn those Bodden Brothers! We can't bloody well do anything without them interfering!"

"Don't become angry over it," Henry suggested. "There's nothing that can be done."

"Nothing? Nothing!" he replied through gritted teeth. "Are you suggesting we give up?"

"We're not giving up. We tried our best. We can stay and run a fool's errand, or leave and seek help elsewhere. We've survived this long without the necessary crewmembers. We can last a little longer."

Edward paced while the senior members and several of the other crewmembers were sitting and watching. No one said a word, but their faces said everything: concern, frustration, defeat.

"How many stayed of those we gained?"

"O-only five, Captain," John said.

Edward paced some more and wiped his face. "Five! Five out of twenty. That's not good enough. We need crewmembers."

"And why do we need to recruit them here, Captain?"

"Because, Henry, it *has* to be here."

"But why?" Henry stood to face Edward.

"Because they're taking away our freedom!" Edward yelled.

Everyone within earshot of Edward's voice was listening intently.

"All our lives we've been pushed, we've been beaten, and we've been told what to do, Henry. Even you," he said, pointing at his friend.

"What are you talking about?"

"I'm talking about this world, Henry," he replied with a flourish of his arms. "They all want us to follow their rules and do what they say. They have from the very beginning. Your parents wanted you to keep on being a farmer and take over the business. They hated me and our talk of being fishermen because it wasn't their plan. They didn't care about your freedom, and they would have been ruling your life even after they died. That's not the way I want to live.

"When I finally accepted this ship as my own, and I took that first step towards freedom, it was a feeling I hadn't experienced before. And you know what? Because we're here today, and this is happening to us, I know why I fought that marine captain, Smith, right from the beginning: because he too threatened my freedom.

"I make you a promise today, Henry: I will never let anyone take my freedom away. When I lose my freedom it will be on my own terms, in death or otherwise."

When Edward had finished speaking, a hush fell in the ship. The whole crew was staring at him as if stunned. Anne had a soft smile on her lips. Henry distractedly ran his fingers through his hair. Any doubts surrounding their staying filtered into the ether.

"Very well, Ed. You win. We can't let them do this to us. But what are we to do? The Boddens own this town. How are we to do anything about that?"

"I don't know."

Henry rolled his eyes and heaved an exasperated sigh. Edward sat in thought for a moment. He looked at all those gathered around, watching him, their leader, the man whom they would follow almost without question, each of them battle-hardened warriors, pirates, and sailors unified together in a terrible force to be reckoned with.

"Henry, you said the Boddens own this town, right?"

"Yea, I did."

"Then to hell with it. We're pirates. Let's steal it from them."

30. FREEDOM VS. THE FAMILY

"Everyone with me? To arms, men! It's time to take this town for ourselves!" Edward pumped his fist in the air, and those gathered cheered. Henry and Anne looked shocked.

"Ed, this is madness. Shouldn't we think this over a bit more?" Anne asked.

"There's nothing more to think about. We have enough people to take over their little mansion by force. I'm surprised no one else has done it already."

Henry shook his head. "I guess nothing we can say will stop you?"

"No."

Henry shrugged his shoulders to Anne. Following Edward, they all went to the main deck. It felt like an army, with the clatter of so many boots on wood. *Edward's* army.

Edward went to the fore cabin and reached into his arsenal. He took two cutlasses, two pistols, a third pistol which Alexandre had made for him, and a musket. He also saw a weapon he had never seen before.

"What is this monstrosity?" he asked of no one in particular.

"That… is a blunderbuss," Anne replied as she grabbed a sword and the rifle she loved so much. "It fires lead shot. It is excellent in small quarters."

"That's mine!" Henry claimed as he grabbed the blunderbuss from Edward's hands. "I think you have enough weapons."

Edward tried to reach for it again. "You can never have enough weapons. Give it back. I want it!"

"Enough, children. We are on a mission, remember?" Anne said.

"Very well. You can have the blunderbuss, Henry, but I get it next time."

"Deal," Henry said as he chuckled with his new toy in hand.

Edward went back out as men poured into the fore cabin to grab their armaments. He went to the helm and found Herbert right where he wanted him.

"What's happening, Captain? Why does it look as if everyone is preparing for war?"

"Because we are. We're going to attack the Boddens and take this town for ourselves." Before Herbert could ask any more questions, Edward gave him a set of instructions to carry out after the crew left the ship.

Herbert smiled. "You can count on me, Captain."

"Good to hear it."

Edward turned to the crew on the main deck. Some who had not been with the group below deck were wondering what was happening. He explained the plan, and then chose just over one hundred people to take with him, leaving about sixty on board to guard the ship and to carry out the orders he had entrusted to Herbert.

Nassir and Jack stayed behind to take care of the children and guide the remainder aboard the *Freedom*. William was to guard Anne, and Sam was... well, he was going to be Sam. Pukuh changed back into his warrior's clothing and had his spear and daggers ready. He also brought along a bow and arrows. Alexandre asked to join as well, and brought a pistol, along with his medical supplies, in a small leather bag.

Once everyone was prepared, Edward issued some final instructions and led the group out. They marched up the main street, all one hundred and some of them, armed to the teeth. This time, bystanders looked at them not with suspicion or contempt, but with fear. They sensed what was about to happen. The cigar smokers, the newspaper readers, the card players—all retreated to their homes and shut their doors and windows. Some ran away, and some even ran to the Boddens' home.

By the time the company reached the top of the hill, the town was virtually deserted. When they walked up to the mansion's iron gate, Edward stood in front, Anne and Henry at his sides, and raised his fist in the air to signal his crew to stop.

Guards with muskets and rifles appeared on the balconies of the house's second floor. The Bodden Brothers strolled out the front door and stopped, staying far away from the gate.

"What are you doing, Thatch?" "This doesn't seem like a friendly visit."

"It's not. I'll give you one chance, brothers. Surrender and I promise to be lenient with you."

They both looked at each other and burst out laughing. "You can't touch us." "You'll never make it past the gates." "Boys." They nodded to their guards, who aimed their muskets at Edward and his crew.

"Men." Edward signaled his crew.

They walked off to the sides, leaving the street outside the gate empty except for the figure of Edward. The Boddens were confused at what they were seeing. Edward turned, pumped his fist in the air, and walked off to the side with the others.

After a few seconds, thunder sounded from the shore. The Boddens' eyes grew wide as they realised what was happening, and they ran back inside the house.

Metal crashed against metal as the iron gate was smashed off the stone wall by cannonballs. It flew back, almost hitting the house, and fell to the ground with a grating crash, the cannonballs embedded between its beams.

"Attack!" Edward yelled.

He pulled out his musket and fired at one of the guards on the second floor of the mansion. The bullet hit the guard in the chest and he tumbled over the balcony to the floor below. Edward ran to the stone wall which had held the gate and put his back up against it.

His crew fired at the guards on the balcony before they realised what was happening. Only a few managed to survive the onslaught.

Anne and Henry joined Edward at the stone wall. Guards were pouring out the front door and the side of the building. The crew divided into those who would stay outside and those who were to invade the house.

Edward, Anne, Henry, and William were among the invaders. Pukuh, Sam, and John were in the defense group.

Edward nodded to his group and then went out past the wall as he drew two pistols. The guards hiding behind pillars at the entrance popped out and fired upon Edward. He ducked and rolled out of the way as Henry and Anne fired their guns at the two guards, taking them down.

Edward rose when two guards ran around the corner. He fired his pistols at them. He hit one in the arm, and the other went back behind cover. He ran to the door and drew one of his cutlasses.

"We need to head inside. Anne, Henry, William, you're with me. The rest of you split between the left and right and head in the back way. Ten of you, with us!" They all rushed to follow his instructions. "Blunderbuss, would you do the honours?"

"Gladly!" Henry said with a smile.

Edward went up to the door and kicked it down. Five guards were lying in wait for them. Henry fired the blunderbuss in the middle of them all, then dropped to the ground. Two of the guards fell and three jumped out of the way. William and Anne headed inside and took them out with their pistols.

The rest of Edward's group headed inside to finish off the rest of the Boddens' guards. Outside on the main street, the thugs loyal to the Boddens made their stand. There were twenty of them so far, and more were coming by the minute.

"So, savage, what say we clean these streets?" Sam offered to Pukuh.

"If you can keep up with me, white man, I will award you a gold piece," Pukuh replied, his deep accent contrasting with Sam's cockney.

Sam laughed. "You're on."

Pukuh, barefoot and wearing his own clothing of leather and feathers, ran to the men gathering on the streets, spear in hand. Those who saw their death approaching fired at the Mayan. He jumped and rolled out of the way.

Sam took out a rifle and shot it at the men on his side of the street. He hit one of the rogues in the chest, dropping him. He pulled out twin pistols and ran to catch up with Pukuh. The thugs focused on Sam now, pointing their muskets and shooting at him. He ducked into a side street for cover.

John, still at the end of the main street, loaded his rifle and fired it at the crowds, downing one man with a shot through the head. He reloaded while Sam and Pukuh did the dirty, close-quarters work.

Pukuh stabbed a man through the heart, then jumped into the air and kicked another in the face. A third man pulled a gun on him and fired at close range, but Pukuh pulled another man in front and used him as a shield.

Sam, having expended his ammunition, drew his cutlass and held it in two hands like a club, but it was no club. They came at him like moths to a flame, and he laughed, in a frenzy, as he hacked and chopped.

Inside the house, William had a bullet in his shoulder from protecting Anne, but insisted he could keep going. Henry was down with a bullet in his leg. Several others were injured and in need of medical attention.

"Where are the Boddens? We've searched everywhere," Edward said between deep breaths.

"I saw someone go into a secret door over there," Henry announced, pointing to the wall beneath the stairs leading to the second floor.

"Sit still and put this in your mouth," Alexandre ordered Henry as he gave him a piece of wood to bite down on. He began removing a bullet lodged in his leg.

Edward went to the place Henry had pointed out. It was a small oval alcove with a three-pronged candelabrum on a shelf with some books. He examined the alcove, but couldn't find anything like a door.

"I have seen something like this before. There are doors like this in Buckingham Palace," Anne said as she walked past Edward.

She put her thumb to her teeth as she considered what to do. She grabbed hold of the candelabrum and tried to pull on the sides, but nothing happened. Then she pulled back the spines of the books one by one. On the third one there was a sound like a lock opening, and then a hidden door in the alcove opened from the right to the left. Inside was a staircase leading down.

"Excellent work, Anne! Everyone loaded and ready?" Those who were fit to join him nodded. "We're finishing this."

Edward had a musket in his hands, ready to fire, as he went down the stairs. It was a long, winding corridor with candles lit in small alcoves along the sides. It went down a fair distance and it took the group a few minutes to reach the bottom, but they didn't meet any resistance along the way.

At the bottom, another corridor branched off to the right. Edward had everyone stop as he inched around the corner. Immediately he was met with rifle fire. He jumped back and the bullets missed him, hitting the wall.

"All your guards above are either dead or too injured to fight, brothers," Edward yelled. "Come out peacefully and we can end this." No answer. He whispered to one of his crew, "You have a grenade on you?" The crewman replied by pulling out four, and Edward took two for himself. "Good. On my mark, we throw them, then rush in." The crewman acknowledged his understanding as they lit the long fuses of the grenades. When the fuses had burned to within an inch of the end, Edward nodded and they both threw them down the hallway and into the other room.

"Grenade!" one of the Boddens' men yelled. Rapid stamping of feet and thuds were heard, followed by four distinct explosions.

"Now!" Edward yelled. He went around the corner and down the short hallway.

Smoke filled the small room. Edward shot a nearby thug in the neck. He fell to the ground, convulsing and clutching his bleeding throat. To his left, the guards were coughing from the smoke and trying to gather their wits about them. The rest of Edward's men, including Anne, killed the remainder of the guards amidst the confusion.

When the dust cleared, Edward was able to see the whole room. It was square and not much higher than their heads. There were boxes and bags filled with sand which the Boddens' thugs had used for cover, but they were now broken and torn from the grenades. At the end of the room there was a large iron door with no visible mechanism for opening it.

Near the door was a large copper cone with a copper tube leading up to the ceiling and through the stone wall surrounding the iron door. *I wonder what this does.* Edward tapped on the cone with his knuckles, causing a tone to travel through the tube.

He heard a voice through the strange device. "Who is this?" "Is that you, George?" "Are they dead?"

Edward recognised the voices of the Boddens through the device. He replied, "No, this is Edward Thatch. You've lost, now surrender so we can end this."

It took a few minutes before one of the brothers talked again. "All right, we surrender. We're opening the door now."

Edward smiled at his comrades. The iron door swung open a crack, but then stopped. He walked over and opened it up more.

The door had barely opened halfway when Edward found himself staring down the barrel of a cannon.

On instinct he pulled back, and the cannon fired, the sound of thunder deafening everybody. The cannonball hit the door and ricocheted into the room, but it embedded itself in the far wall without injuring anyone.

When the ringing in his ears had receded somewhat, Edward pulled out his cutlasses. The cannonball had opened the door wide, and one of his crew had thrown a grenade inside. The thing exploded and filled the inner room with dust.

Edward ran in, and was met with two small cannons, manned by the brothers. Edward saw one of the brother's hands lowering a linstock towards the cannon.

Edward's body reacted, knowing what to do long before he could form the words in his mind. He turned his body to the side and fell backwards. The sound of the cannon erupted and an iron ball shot out towards him. He could feel the force of the ball on his stomach as it passed inches away from him, tearing at his insides like a dozen punches.

The other brother lowered the linstock into the cannon. Edward was still falling as the second cannonball passed over his chest this time. The speeding ball, like a giant bullet, transferred its power through the air and hit Edward in the chest. The cannonball passed over him and hit the iron door, ricocheting off and into the square room.

Edward landed on the ground on his back, and then got up with unsteady feet. He noticed his hand was trembling and his stomach and chest ached with pain and pressure. He shook his head and turned his attention to the brothers, who sat motionless beside their smoking cannons, paralysed with astonishment. He strolled over to the brothers and put one blade to each throat. "This battle is over!"

31. THE CROSSED SWORDS FLAG

The first thing Edward did was take the Boddens upstairs to stop the fighting outside. After the Boddens sent their men away, Edward's crew stayed and guarded the home.

Edward, with his newly taken authority, told the Boddens how they were to run the town from now on. He would allow the brothers to keep managing their business, but he was to have a cut of the profits.

They would first lower the rates at which they taxed the citizens. The town was to become a safe haven for pirates, but protecting the local businesses was to be the brothers' job and that's what would allow them to tax. Edward didn't want the brothers administering false protection and using extortion like they had before. They would also have a full militia paid and trained so that something like what Edward just did wouldn't happen again.

They were also to keep records of everything taxed and traded, and confer twenty-five percent of their earnings to Edward.

"If I examine the numbers and find something doesn't add up, you'll find yourself sleeping with Davy Jones, understood?"

"Yes, sir," the brothers said in unison.

With that business finished, Edward released the brothers so they could start repairing their home and carry out their orders. He and the rest of the crew, aside from a few left to guard the mansion, headed back to the *Freedom* for further instructions.

Edward and Anne helped Henry limp back to the Freedom. They had found something to bandage the gunshot wound in his leg with, but it wouldn't fully heal for some time.

"Are you sure you can trust them to keep their word?" Henry asked.

Anne gave a short derisive laugh. "Did you see their eyes? They are too afraid of us now."

"I don't think they'll betray me," Edward replied. "I'll send letters every once in a while to remind them who their boss is."

Over the next week, the crew of the *Freedom* helped fix the gate on the Boddens' property and tended to the wounded. The crew kept order in the town until the guards still alive were healed. Edward also gathered new people for the crew over the week, which wasn't hard given their impressive display. Men flocked to the *Freedom* by the dozen after they took over the town.

Edward introduced the new recruits to the ship's officers, laid out for them the rules for living and working aboard the ship, and had them speak to John, who compiled a list of their skills and prior experience so they could each be assigned suitable work. He then explained the pirate commandments to them and had them sworn in, as the others had been.

Edward wanted to speak with Henry about their next course of action, namely sailing to Navassa Island and continuing with the journey to unlock the next section of the ship. But before they could even begin to talk a voice interrupted them.

"You folks are mighty strong. It be a fool's game challenging the Boddens like ye did, but ye won."

Edward turned to see an older gentleman standing there, leaning on the port-side railing. "Oh? Then why did you join us fools, old man?"

"Because after I saw your power, I knew you could help me out. And by that I mean we can help each other."

Edward walked over and leaned on the railing. The man had salt-and-pepper hair and beard, and eyes like an old trickster. His cheeks and stomach were full, like they had once been taut and muscular, but were now sagging, perhaps from nothing more than laziness.

"And what, pray tell, does a man like you need help with?"

The old man flitted his eyes this way and that suspiciously. "Perhaps we should discuss this in private."

They took the old man to the fore cabin and emptied it of everyone else. The three of them sat down at a table placed there for meetings, and the man, who went by the name Bill Hastings, related his tale.

"So you and your friend had a dispute over how to spend some gold, and now you want our help to retrieve it before he does?"

"That is correct."

"And how much gold is it?"

"One thousand Spanish doubloons of the finest quality."

Edward looked at Henry for a moment, and then both of them howled with laughter. Bill was shocked and became flustered. When the laughing didn't seem close to stopping, he finally became angry.

"What do you find so amusing in this? We're talking about gold here! You take me for a fool?"

Soon the laughing stopped and Edward wiped a tear from his eye. "No, it is quite the opposite, sir. It would be you who would take us for fools if we were to believe your story. What is it? We sail to the place where the treasure is and your group attacks us and steals our ship? Or maybe there is—"

A gold piece, round but irregular, fell into Edward's lap before he could finish his sentence. It had inscriptions and pictures on it showing that it had been minted, if poorly. He examined it to make sure it was real.

"Where did you find this?" Edward asked as he passed the coin to Henry, who inspected it as well.

"I told you, it's part of the one thousand me and my companion had. We lived similar lives to yours, and that was our last payday. The details don't matter, the only thing that matters is I can show you where it is, and I'll let you have ten percent."

Edward yawned in apparent disinterest. He strolled over to Bill. "Hmm... Even if I did believe your tale, I wouldn't settle for such a meagre share. Without us you have nothing." He walked past him and headed for the ladder.

"Fifteen," Bill said without turning around.

"Thirty," Edward replied.

Bill spun around. "That's extortion! There's no way you're getting thirty for my life's work!"

Edward shrugged. "We're pirates. And remember, we are protecting you and stealing from your friend too."

Bill gritted his teeth and clenched his fists. "Twenty! Without me you've nothing either."

Edward paused for a moment, walked back over to Bill and put out his hand. "Twenty it is then." Bill stood up and they shook on it together, sealing the bond. "Now, where do we need to go?"

Bill smiled. "First we need to head to my home and retrieve the first part of the map. It's in George Town a few hours west of here." Bill started to leave, but Edward stopped him.

"First part of the map?" Edward asked.

"Yes. I have one part, and my friend has the other. We'll secure mine, and then we'll grab my friend's. And—oh yes: I don't want my friend to think ill of me, so would you kindly pretend you have me hostage?"

"Pretend to take you hostage! Sir, you are trying my patience. Maybe I really will take you hostage."

"Oh, pish posh and a bottle of hops," Bill said with a wave of his hand. "This is easy, you boys'll do fine." And without another word, Bill turned and left.

Edward sighed and rubbed his eyes in frustration, to which Henry shrugged. "You brought this on yourself. You never had to accept the deal." Henry and Edward went back to the main deck.

"Yes, well a lot of good your advice will do me now. You were silent the whole time."

"Well, silence must be golden, because I'm the one with the doubloon." Henry held up the coin between his fingers.

"Give me that." Edward held out his palm.

"What, this?" Henry taunted with a grin.

"It's mine."

"This little coin? No, you must mean this peso." Henry threw him a copper piece.

Edward's gaze went from the copper, then back at Henry, his eyes full of contempt. Henry twirled the gold coin, smiled again, and ran off before he could try to grab it. He let him go, and went instead to Herbert.

"Herbert, we have a new heading. George Town, on the west side of the Grand Cayman. You know of it?"

"Aye, Captain, I know of it."

"Keep her steady then."

Henry walked up the ladder to the stern, still holding the gold piece, talking to no one in particular. "Well I guess I'll deliver this to John to deposit, since our friend hasn't claimed it."

"Keep it." Bill joined them at the stern deck. "Consider it a token of good faith." Henry nodded to Bill and headed to the main deck to seek out John.

"Very well then," Edward said. "I merely hope that faith isn't misplaced."

"Oh, it isn't, Captain. Worry not. We'll all be better off. You'll see."

It took them less than half a day to reach their destination. They disembarked at George Town and Bill led Edward, Henry, and William, all of them armed at Bill's behest, along a path leading through open fields to his house beyond the edge of town. The three asked Bill why he was at Bodden Town to seek help with his venture, and he replied: "I came because I heard the rum was good, and that pirates frequented the place. But mostly because of the rum."

Edward and Henry were growing less impressed with the man the more they learned about him.

When William was told the story of how they came to be on this journey, his response was on par with his usual: indifference. This time, however, there was a hint of disbelief. Edward told Henry later that he thought they were called idiots despite no words being uttered.

"Yes, well, if William was saying that, he does have a point. Everywhere we go things end badly for us. We search for the keys and we all risk our lives. We search for crewmembers and we fight bandits at their game and ours. I wouldn't be surprised if other pirates show up, we fight, and then don't gain anything in recompense."

"You exaggerate. It won't end like that. If anything, our fortunes are due for reversal and this will be the greatest payday we've ever had."

"We will see," Henry said, clear doubt in his tone.

"Here it is," Bill announced as they approached the small, two-story, wooden house where he lived alone. They could tell immediately that the door had been broken in.

"Everyone quiet," Edward whispered as he drew his Alexandre-made pistol.

The others drew their weapons as they approached the door, Edward and Bill on the left, Henry and William on the right. On the silent count of three, William kicked open the door, and they all rushed in, guns pointed and ready to shoot at… nothing.

There were plenty signs of a break-in. Tables and chairs were flipped and strewn about, objects were broken, books were torn and thrown to the floor, every cupboard and storage space was emptied.

"Are any valuables missing?" William asked.

"Not that I can see. There's money left on the nightstand." Bill pointed to his bed in the corner and a wooden stand beside it. "A trifling amount, truly, but still there. Why?"

"Because they were here for something specific," William said.

Something specific? "The map!" No sooner did the words leave Edward's mouth than Bill rushed up the stairs to the second floor.

In a spot near the middle of the room, a few loose floorboards concealed a small sunken compartment. Bill had kept it covered by a carpet, which was now rolled back, the floorboards pried up, and the compartment was empty.

"It's gone." Bill's voice was dead and his face drained of colour.

"Dammit!" Edward kicked a nearby chair, breaking it. "Now what?"

Bill trudged down the stairs and sat on the bottom step. "What can we do? My friend Theodore must have been here. Maybe he even had people helping him." He shook his head in frustration. "But it doesn't matter. We have no way to reach the treasure now."

"You two have an excellent friendship, I must say," said Edward, "both plotting to steal the other's share at the same time!"

"We're a regular pair," he said, his eyes fixed on the floorboards.

"Can't you remember anything from the map? Even the starting point would give us something."

"What use will that be? We won't know where to head once we arrive."

"If Theodore is there then we can follow his tracks, or the tracks of whoever was with him."

The glint returned to Bill's eyes and he jumped up. "You're right! If we leave now we can still catch them!" He ran out the door, and the others raced to catch up with him, their vigour renewed and their minds filled with the hope of treasure.

They were, for the moment, incapable of imagining the danger awaiting them.

⚓ ⚓ ⚓

The island they sought was northeast of the Grand Cayman by a half day's travel. Bill remembered the riddle he had written on his half of the map: "Nor'east of seven mile the treasured island lies." He seemed very proud to have thought of it himself.

"That's too easy," Herbert said when he overheard it. "You live in George Town, and Seven Mile Beach is directly north of it—that riddle isn't likely to fool anybody."

Bill was offended. "Well... not everyone can read a map like you can."

Herbert rolled his eyes before setting the course.

After a half day's travel, the crewman on the crow's nest yelled "Land ho!" and everyone's gazes turned eagerly toward the bow.

Edward, along with many of the crew, moved to the prow to view the island through a spyglass. Anne joined him and leaned over the side of the ship, her red hair swaying in the wind as she tried to catch a glimpse of the island.

"What do you see, Ed?"

"Not much. The whole island is covered in a thick forest, and from this distance it's hard to judge its size. Other than that... Wait, I think I can see a ship."

"Where? Let me see!" Edward handed the spyglass to Anne. A ship was indeed anchored at the island, but it was too far to make out its size or its flag. "I wonder who they are." She handed the spyglass back to Edward, smiling from ear to ear.

"You seem happy."

"Oh! I suppose I'm simply excited." Anne walked back to the main deck.

"All right, everyone! Back to work. This ship won't sail itself. Prepare for battle! We don't know if that ship is friend or foe." Edward followed Anne. "Why are you excited? It may be dangerous."

"I suppose it is as you said a few days ago. I feel free now more than ever. I do not have to hide, I have nothing to fear, and I can live my life the way I want. And it is all thanks to you, Edward." Anne leaned up to Edward and kissed him on the cheek, causing everyone around them to stop and stare and whisper things like: "The princess and the captain?" "Anne kissed 'im!" "Lucky bloke!"

Edward grew red in the face and yelled to them all to get back to work. But the warmth of the kiss, and the feelings it evoked, lingered. He couldn't focus on the task at hand until a shout brought him out of his thoughts.

"Cap'n! You should see this!" one crewmember yelled.

"What is it? Is the other ship shoving off?"

"No! Look at the flag, Cap'n!"

Edward took the spyglass out again and stared at the ship. He could see its flag flapping in the wind; he had already guessed it would be a pirate flag, and his suspicions were now confirmed. It had a large skull, but instead of crossed bones below the skull it was crossed cutlasses.

Henry stood beside Edward amidst the commotion, and he had a smug smile on his face. "Don't you even start!" Edward said.

"I'm one for three," Henry said.

Edward scratched his beard. Had Henry's prediction been right? Would they have to fight these blackguards and gain nothing out of it?

"This means nothing," Edward said firmly, then turned to the crewman who had called him over. "So, what of it?"

"Cap'n, that's the flag of John Rackham, Calico Jack, the ruler of the Caribbean Sea."

Edward's jaw dropped at the mention of that name. His focus shifted to the helm, to Herbert, who had joined Edward's crew to avenge himself upon this very man.

Are you to take your revenge today, Herbert? Is it within your power to accomplish?

More worryingly, is it within mine?

Edward did not know the answer, but he had a feeling he would soon learn it.

32. THE HUNTER AND THE HUNTED

"Captain, I want to go ashore! No, I *must* go ashore!" Herbert demanded.

"You realise it will be dangerous," Edward warned.

"I don't care. I've been waiting years for this. If I can't face him now, then I can't face him ever."

"You could die."

"I'm willing to take that risk. And I'll do this whether you let me or not!"

That's a good answer, Herbert. How can I refuse such conviction? "Very well, but you stay in the middle of the group—and if there is a fight, no one is going to be able to protect you. Understand?"

"I won't need to be protected," Herbert replied with a sinister look in his eyes.

Edward turned to the deck and addressed the crew. "All hands prepare to engage the enemy! We'll show them what it means to be real pirates!" The crew roared in approval.

Anne motioned for Edward to come over, and then led him to the forecastle at the furthest point on the ship away from Herbert. "I do not want you doing this, Edward."

"What? Why not?"

"Some have already mentioned it, I am sure, but this man is Calico Jack. He is dangerous. It is better to stay away from him."

Her words were curt and perfunctory, as if she was reading the newspaper, but her mannerisms told a different story. She had her arms wrapped around herself almost like she was protecting herself from a cold breeze. Edward saw in her eyes something he had never seen before, something he never thought he would see: fear. The sight almost made him rethink his decision.

But he couldn't.

"My apologies, Anne, but I've made a promise to Herbert. I can't back down now. Besides, we'll watch each other's backs, right? We have nothing to fear in that case."

Anne gave him a smile, but he could tell it was forced.

I'll have to show her there's nothing to fear. Calico Jack is a man, and all men bleed.

Edward guided the crew to land the ship on the beach, and half of them went to shore to fight the enemy. As he ran with them to confront the group of pirates on the sandy ground, Calico Jack's men didn't pay he or his crew any heed despite the noise. It took Edward a moment to realise why.

They were drunk, the lot of them.

The only men of Calico's crew sober were those on the ship itself. They were desperate in trying to rouse their comrades to awareness, but it was no use. The enemy fired one shot with the cannon, which missed by a heavy margin.

They surrendered themselves to Edward and his crew immediately after.

Edward and the crew on the beach gathered the enemy crew together and bound their hands with rope. "And this, gentlemen, is why we don't drink while on duty." Those in the landing party laughed as Edward turned to the group of captives. "Who's in charge here?" After a few seconds of silence, one of them raised his bound hands. Edward stared in surprise at the intoxicated man sitting on the ground, went over to him, and knelt down. "Where are your senior officers?"

The man smelled of the strong stuff, and his eyes were unfocussed. He seemed unsteady even sitting down, and before he spoke he hiccupped. "Nah, all de senior occifers went inta the bush. We was supposed ta be protectin' tha ship, but…" He raised his hands, motioning to the scene before him, and then burst into a fit of laughter.

"Which way did they go?" Edward asked. But it was no use, the man was too far gone. Edward grabbed his cheeks in a vice grip and shook him a little. "Which way did they go?"

"Itsh a secwet," he slurred, and started laughing again.

Edward released his grip on the man and he almost fell over. *I need to talk with someone who isn't tanked.*

The sound of shifting sand and the creaking of wood came up behind Edward as Herbert wheeled himself up beside the captain and the drunken man. "Maybe this will loosen everyone else's tongues," he said as he shoved a pistol into the man's temple and fired. Blood sprayed everywhere, and the man fell dead onto the sand.

"Herbert, what the hell are you doing!" Edward grabbed the pistol out of Herbert's hand, but it was already spent.

Immediately one of the other captives stood up. "I'll tell you where they went! Please don't kill me!"

"I'm getting results," Herbert growled, wheeling himself over to the man who had spoken.

"They went into the jungle. If you head straight in for about five minutes, you'll see a path. We arrived an hour ago, so you should be able to catch up if you hurry."

Edward shook his head. *No point in arguing over dead enemies.* "Well, this is it!" said Edward. "You ready to kill this Calico Jack?"

"It's not him," Herbert replied as they moved away from the men tied up.

Edward stopped. "What do you mean, not him?"

"It's Gold Division Commander Gregory Dunn's ship."

"Gold Division? What's that? Who's Gregory Dunn?"

"There's gold trim on the ship's flag. It denotes the Gold Division of Rackham's pirate crew, for which Gregory Dunn is the commander. I noticed it as soon as we landed. It's all right. Golden Arm Dunn will do for today." Herbert wheeled up to the edge of the jungle and peered in.

"Why do they call him Golden Arm?"

"I'm not exactly sure, but I believe it's because he's in charge of acquisitions and manages the monetary side of John's operation. They say he's a coward, and leads a bunch of them too, but they're good fighters in a pinch. I wouldn't take them lightly, Captain. This is one of Calico Jack's men, after all."

"Worry not; I won't do anything rash, like you." Edward folded his arms and glared at Herbert, but knew he wouldn't back down— not this time, not over this. "I'll gather some others to join us. You wait here."

Edward went back to the members of his crew guarding the enemy pirates and told them to search them for any weapons, or anything that could be used as one. He then went back to the ship and gathered together the senior officers and some of the better fighters to take along with him and Herbert. Half of the crew would stay behind to watch the ship and the hostages.

Pukuh, William, John, Anne, and Henry took the chosen fighters down to the entrance of the forest and waited. Edward gave some final instructions to Jack, who would be left in charge while they were away.

"Keep an eye on Dunn's men. We don't want them trying anything while we're gone," he said to Jack. "Make sure no one drinks. I don't want what happened to the other crew to happen to us." He laughed along with Jack, and then whispered: "And keep an eye on Christina. Without Herbert here to protect her, I fear for her safety. Maybe bring Nassir up here with her, all right?"

"You can count on me, Captain. I've been taking the combat lessons along with everyone else, so I'll use force if I have to."

Edward thought he could hear Jack say "I won't fail this time," under his breath, but he couldn't be sure so he ignored it. "Good man. I'm counting on you."

"It's good to hear Herbert has a chance to avenge those who wronged him." Jack gazed at Herbert on the beach. He was pushing himself up the sand to the entrance of the forest.

Edward could see in Jack's eyes a determined focus which he'd never seen before. He felt there was more to it than him simply being happy for another crewmate's revenge. There seemed to be hope buried deep down in those eyes.

"It's not going to be so easy. We got lucky. This is the first step, really; the hard part comes next." Edward patted Jack on the shoulder. He felt like saying more, prying a bit more, but he couldn't. He had a job to do. "Take care, Jack."

"Take care, Captain."

Edward went back down to the beach, and the group he had told to wait had gathered at the edge of the jungle. Pukuh, William, John, Anne, and Henry were all there, along with about fifty other crewmembers, all decked out with weapons.

Pukuh was wearing his traditional warrior's garb: eagle-skull headdress, feathers down to the wrist, bones across his chest. Edward smiled. "I recall you saying there were two types of warrior classes you could be a part of, yes? Jaguar and Eagle? Why did you choose the Eagle?"

"Because my father was a nobleman and he was also an Eagle warrior," Pukuh explained. "And because the eagle is freer than the jaguar. It can soar the skies to its heart's content, as you sail the sea."

Edward felt a twinge of embarrassment. His paean to freedom had been making the rounds. "I understand the appeal in that," he said. Then he turned to the rest of the group. "Everyone ready? Keep a sharp eye as we move through the brush. The rest of that crew is out there somewhere."

Edward took the front, accompanied by Anne, Henry, and Bill. John and William were close behind, followed by the rest of the company, with Herbert and Pukuh guarding the rear. A few minutes into the jungle they found a well-trodden path wide enough for three or four to walk abreast.

"Bill, it seems like these pirates were the ones who ransacked your home and took the other section of the map. That means either you and your friend think very much alike, or that he's in danger."

"I know." Bill looked solemn. It was a blow to him.

As they walked, they could hear the sounds of the jungle on all sides. The hooting of birds, the chattering of monkeys, and the rustling of the trees in the wind blended with the breaking of twigs and branches from the footsteps of the crew.

Since his time spent in the Mayan woods, Edward had been trying to enhance his hearing, but had a difficult time. It was not so easy here as it had been then. Eventually, he gave up trying.

They're at least an hour ahead of us. I shouldn't have to worry right now.

"Look, Ed!" Anne said, pointing to a patch of mud.

Edward made a motion to stop everyone and then he knelt to examine the mark. It was a boot print. "Tracks." He looked ahead and saw they followed the path for as far as he could see.

"Now we know they were headed this way. If we keep following, then we won't need a map. Can you tell how many there are?"

Anne searched for other prints, as well as trampled vegetation and broken twigs and branches along the trail. "I can't tell exactly, of course, but it appears to be at least as many as we have here, if not more. They were travelling at a leisurely pace. We can catch up if we pick up our pace."

"Hmm, more than us won't be a problem if they're cowards, as Herbert claims."

"It will be a problem if they ambush us," Henry warned.

"Very well. Let's split the group. John, William, each of you take fifteen men and go out one hundred paces from us on either side. Keep pace with us as best you can. We'll stay on the path, and if we get a scare we'll send a signal to attack."

"What will that be?" William asked.

"I don't know... How about the sound of an eagle?"

"I've never heard the sound of an eagle," one man said. A few others confirmed that they hadn't, either.

"Truly? You have never heard an eagle? Well, it matters not. If you hear a screeching sound over and over, come running to help us."

"I think we should at least hear the sound of an eagle before we plan on using it." They all nodded in agreement.

Edward sighed. "Pukuh?"

Pukuh put his hands together and made a series of high-pitched noises in quick succession.

"But that sounds like everything else in the forest!" "I'll not be able to hear that!" "Pick something else!"

"Enough! How about I just yell 'help'? Will you be able to hear that?"

"That's much better." "I like that." "I feel safer now."

"Is everyone satisfied?" They all nodded. "Good. Now back to the task at hand. If they want to ambush, they'll do it from the jungle, so we can outflank them. When you hear us yell for help, come back to the path and attack the enemy pirates. Now get going."

"Edward, have you had any formal education?" Anne asked as they started walking again.

"What kind of formal education?"

"Military."

"Oh, no. But my father did serve in the Nine Years' War. He taught me how to play chess and different things like that. It must be from that."

"Your father must have been a very smart man. I am sorry that he has passed."

"What are you talking about? My father is alive!" Edward snarled, glaring at her. Those hate-filled eyes had never before been directed at her, and she began sweating. "I… I am sorry, Edward. I thought… Henry said…"

"Calm down, Edward," Henry interjected. "I'm the one who told her he disappeared. It was a natural assumption after all these years."

Edward stared down both of them, and then walked away in a huff.

"Sorry about that, Anne," said Henry. "I should have told you. His father was all he had when he was younger. Edward won't accept his death. He's not mad at you, but just give him some time."

Anne's thoughts were elsewhere. "All right," she mumbled, as everyone continued walking except her. She stood there, the vision of those eyes piercing her to the core. So many emotions rushed over her in that moment. *But why do I feel it so much? Is it because it was directed at me? Am I simply more sensitive to it?*

Pukuh touched her arm. "We must keep moving."

She came out of her daze. "Yes." She started walking again.

"You are close to him?"

Anne regarded Pukuh for a moment. "Yes, I suppose I am."

"Then it is clear you would be affected by his stare. It was one of emotion rather than intimidation. The large one, Henry, was not affected because he's seen it and felt it before."

Anne nodded at the logic. "You are right. How do you know of this power he has?"

"In your tongue we call it the Eagle Eye, the eye of the hunter. Something only a rare few possess, it is in many legends we tell. My father has seen it in one man, besides Edward."

"Who was that?"

"Benjamin Hornigold, the previous owner of the ship *Freedom*."

Anne was even more shocked than before, if possible. She stopped once again, and Pukuh with her. "*Freedom* was Benjamin Hornigold's ship?"

"Yes. My father travelled with Benjamin for a short time when I was a child. Do you know this man?"

Anne was rendered speechless. *Everyone who knows anything about pirates from ten years ago knows that name! I thought the name* Freedom *was just a coincidence… What star was Edward born under that he would be the next to inherit the Golden Horn's ship?*

"Miss Princess?"

"No… No. I am not familiar with him."

Pukuh eyed Anne curiously, but didn't press the issue.

Blackbeard's Ship

They ran to catch up with the group and kept walking together. Anne stayed at the back with Pukuh the rest of the way. They kept a good pace, following the obvious tracks left by the enemy pirates. They kept walking for a half hour until the tracks abruptly ended.

Edward knelt down. "They must have travelled into the woods after this point."

Henry glanced about. "Everything's gone quiet. What happened to all the animals?"

Before anyone realised what the lack of sound might mean, the enemy crew jumped out from behind bushes and trees. The surprise caught everyone off guard, not the least of them Edward. He took a sucker punch square in the jaw, thrown by the captain of the other crew, and went flying. His brain was so rattled by the force of the blow that he couldn't think straight.

What hit me? It felt more like a sack of rocks than a fist.

He got to his knees, then picked himself up off the ground and saw the Gold Division Commander of Calico Jack's pirate crew, Gregory Dunn, stalking toward him. It was then that he knew the real reason for the man's nickname, The Golden Arm.

Dunn's right hand, from the balled fist to below the elbow, was covered in solid gold. The upper arm appeared more muscular than its left counterpart, no doubt because of the added weight and extra use. The elbow looked raw and damaged from the perpetual shifting of the hard metal on the skin.

How is that even possible?

Dunn had a smile on his face. Edward gritted his teeth and brought himself to his full towering height. He called for help, and soon the sound of reinforcements could be heard in the distance.

Edward drew his twin swords. *Let's see how you are on even ground!* Edward focused on the enemy in front of him. No one else mattered to him. His head, though ringing with pain, was clear.

Dunn pulled out his own sword and put up his right arm as a guard. Edward attacked, but Dunn blocked one stroke after another, either with his golden right arm or the cutlass in his left hand. Every few times Edward attacked, Dunn countered, but he was able to parry the sword and Dunn's fist out of the way. At first Dunn was far from hitting him, but then the sword strokes became subtly more accurate. Then the golden punches nicked his side. Both the enemy's sword and arm kept inching closer to Edward.

He's reading me! I have to become unpredictable.

Edward began to call upon his training in hand-to-hand combat and varied his stance, stepping in and then pivoting on the balls of his feet. He combined his twin blades into one for a slice, and then separated them to jab at Dunn in different areas at once.

He seemed to be gaining the advantage when a pounding weight slammed into his gut. It was the golden arm. It seemed to appear out of thin air, and it hit him harder than anything he had ever experienced. He fought the urge to double over, but was overcome with the pain. He coughed as air and spit forced its way out and he began collapsing forward. As he fell, Dunn punched his jaw again, and Edward went reeling onto the jungle floor.

Dunn went behind Edward and forced him to stand by pulling the blade of the cutlass across his throat. Then he yelled to the crowd still fighting: "If you don't want your captain to die, cease fighting." The words soon broke through the tumult and everyone stopped what they were doing. "Good. Now drop your weapons. Boys, surround them."

Dammit! If I weren't so weak, this wouldn't have happened. Edward was quick to blame himself, but as he looked at his crew it appeared they, too, were on the verge of defeat. Despite his strategy of out-flanking them, Dunn's crew, with their numbers and training, were winning against Edward's mostly inexperienced troupe.

Anne watched on in horror. Her eyes met Edward's, and all he could do was stare back at them.

I'm sorry, Anne. You were right. But I'll find a way out of this.

"Kill them!" ordered Dunn.

"No, wait! Stop!" Edward yelled with outstretched hand. "We have the rest of your crew at the beach! If we don't return, they die!"

Dunn paused. "Very well. Boys, stay your weapons. Where do you suggest we go from here, Captain? We seem to be on even footing—at least as far as captives are concerned." He laughed at the implied insult to Edward's fighting abilities.

I can't believe I'm so weak, and he's that strong. It was as if he were toying with me.

Edward thought quickly. "Let's work together. We'll find the treasure and split it in half. There will be more than enough for us both."

Dunn mulled it over for a moment before ducking behind Edward. The sound of a rifle shattered the quiet of the jungle. A bullet sped past Edward, so close he felt air tremble as it passed his ear.

"Who fired that?" Dunn yelled. "Who's fool enough to risk his captain's life?"

Edward knew who it was even before he was found. The enemy crew closed in on Herbert at the rear of the crowd, took the pistol out of his hands, and pushed his wheelchair toward Dunn.

"And who are you, that you would try to kill me in that state?" He cackled. "You're a fool to think you can hit anyone with a pistol at that range. You can't even walk. How did you expect to run away?"

"I would never run—unlike you, you little coward! I'll kill you!"

Herbert grabbed a knife out of one of the pirates' belts and tried to throw it at Dunn, but Dunn's mates stopped him. They took him out of the wheelchair and tossed it aside, breaking it. They threw him on the ground and pinned down his arms, one of them stepping on his neck.

"Feisty one, do you know who I am? I'm one of Calico Jack's generals! You don't even know who you're dealing with, do you?"

"I know who I'm dealing with!" Herbert mustered all the strength of voice he could with the boot on his throat. "You don't remember me, but I remember you. You were a coward back then too. Always running around, wiping the boots of your master. You've moved up in the ranks, but trash is still trash."

Dunn cocked his brow as he re-examined Herbert. After a moment his eyes opened wide. "Oh, ho! I remember you now!" Dunn guffawed. It was high-pitched and grating in Edward's ears. "You're the little boy who became a cripple after the accident with the powder. That was so many years ago now. Captain had high hopes for you. Too bad he doesn't accept cripples in his crew and tossed you aside. If I'm trash, then what does that make you?" Dunn cackled again as Herbert struggled to free himself. "Now... no one makes fun of me and lives to tell the tale. Men, exact punishment! I'm a touch occupied over here. Make it slow and painful." His crew nodded and kicked Herbert while he was on the ground.

"Stop. Stop, I say!" cried Edward. "You can have the gold, all of it! Leave my crew alive and I'll even help you bring it back to your ship."

Dunn let the beating continue for a little bit longer, and then told the crewmen to stop. "We have a deal." He let Edward go and stepped away.

"Edward, what are you doing?" Bill whispered forcefully.

"Would you rather have your treasure, Bill, or your life?"

"My treasure!"

Edward sighed. Dunn told the three who had beaten Herbert to join him. Herbert was bloody and already bruising. Edward went up and knelt next to him. He took out a handkerchief, wiped the blood from his face, and turned his head to the ground to allow his lungs to clear.

"How... could you... Captain?" Herbert said through ragged breaths and coughs full of blood. "You promised you would help me with my revenge."

Edward couldn't look into Herbert's eyes, those sad eyes filled with bloodied tears. "I know, Herbert. I'm sorry. I have more to think about than your revenge right now. The lives of the crew, including yours, are on the line. I'm sorry." Edward rose and walked away.

"You promised me! You traitor! You betrayed me like Rackham!" The tears streamed down his face as he yelled, his voice strained with pain.

Dunn spat on the ground. "Shut him up."

Edward lunged with lightning speed and grabbed the Golden Arm's shoulder in a vice grip. Edward's anger flared and he felt as if it could crush the smaller man's bones in an instant. Dunn's crew pulled their guns and swords on him, but he didn't care. His eyes saw only the enemy before him. Dunn waved his men off. "Never mind, leave him alone."

Edward released his grip, and then he, Dunn, and three of Dunn's crew set off down the path toward the treasure. Edward could hear the cries of Herbert as he walked deeper into the jungle. His heart sank deeper and deeper as the sound faded away.

33. THE PREDATOR AND THE PREY

Dunn took the lead, followed by one of his crew, then came Edward, and then the other two men in the rear with guns trained on their captive. Dunn held the top and bottom halves of the map together, puzzling over the strange instructions. He settled on a direction and the group set out.

This jungle was a stark difference from the one Edward had been in on the Yucatan. Instead of the tall pines, there were palms of all sizes. Thin trunks stuck out of the green grass at odd angles and led to long and wide leaves of the fullest green, with coconuts just beneath them. The ones on the tree were mostly green, and many brown ones were littering the grass beneath.

The sounds were similar, but also very different, from the Mayan jungle. He could hear the sway of the palm leaves brushing against each other in the breeze. He also heard different bird calls he didn't recognise, and the screech of lizards as they crawled up the trees.

The odd group of travelers walked down a natural path of grass or muddy sand left undisturbed save for the tracks they were leaving behind.

"So how did your arm become golden, anyway?" Edward asked bluntly.

Dunn's men stopped short, stared at Edward in alarm, and backed away from him. Dunn turned around and punched Edward in the gut. "That's how. Now shut it and keep walking."

The crew pushed Edward forward even as he clutched his stomach. *That right arm of his is a nuisance.* "Touchy subject, I guess. What does the map say?"

"Didn't I tell you to shut it?"

"Very well, I won't talk. Just trying to make this less of a bore."

Edward kept walking the path with his enemy, being pushed and prodded all the way despite his willingness. He thought back on the look Herbert had worn before he left with Dunn. Those eyes pierced him deep in his heart. Edward furrowed his brows at the enemy captain in front of him. *I'll find a way.*

They walked through the jungle until the path ended and stopped at a rift in the earth. The gorge went as far as they could see, east to west, through the whole island. In the gorge, they could see water running over jagged rocks at the bottom. On the other side, the island and the forest continued on, but there was no path. The rift was too large to jump across, and they couldn't walk over the jagged rocks.

"Oi, Blackbeard! We need us a bridge. Grab that log over there and lay it across."

Blackbeard? Is that supposed to be an insult? Edward stroked his beard as his gaze turned to the log. He saw it, moss-covered and slick-looking; it didn't seem strong enough to support a normal-sized person, let alone Edward. "You expect to cross that?"

"No, I expect *you* to cross it. There's a tall tree you can tie some rope to so we can swing across."

Edward grabbed the log in both hands and lifted one end. He shifted and swiveled it around until it was right by the edge and let it drop to the other side. He inched to the edge of the gorge. It had to be at least fifty feet to the bottom, and the rocks below looked sharp enough to kill.

Edward felt a slight pressure of something hard in his back. It was Dunn, prodding with his golden arm and holding a pistol in his other hand. "Move."

"Will you provide me the rope, or do you expect me to procure that on the other side as well?"

Dunn put his pistol away. He grabbed the rope from one of his crew and then shoved it at Edward. "Here, now make haste. You know what's on the line."

"Yes, better than you." For Edward the treasure no longer held any real worth, except as the means of procuring the safety of his crew.

Edward stepped up on the log, positioning himself sideways with his feet pointed outward, and shuffled along it inch by inch, keeping his eyes on the far end. A gust of wind blew in his face and threw him off balance, but he managed to right himself.

"Faster! We're losing daylight!"

Edward turned his head to look at Dunn. "I should like it if you'd stop distracting me. That would help me go faster." He turned his head back, but glanced down at the rushing water by accident. He couldn't take his eyes off it. The wind blew in his face again, he lost his balance, and this time he wasn't able to regain it. He slipped off the log, and the others gasped. His body scraped along the mossy bark as he fell. Then, at the last instant, he thrust out his arm and wrapped it around the trunk.

Dangling in the air, he took a deep breath, hoisted himself up, threw his other arm around the log, and pulled himself back up on top of it. This time, instead of standing up, he shimmied across on his stomach.

When he reached the other side, he paused to catch his breath, stood up, and searched for a place to tie the rope. He saw a tree close to the edge of the gorge that appeared sturdy enough to hold it. He climbed the trunk and secured the rope near the top before climbing down and throwing it across.

One at a time, Dunn and his men swung across the chasm to the other side, while Edward was told to wait far enough away so he couldn't do anything to them. Last to cross was Dunn, who did it with one hand, refusing any help. The other men took down the rope while he studied the map again, holding both pieces in his one good hand. He kept looking at the map in confusion, turning it this way and that for a good few minutes before putting it away in frustration.

"Do you need help?" Edward offered.

"No, I've got it under control!"

They followed Dunn northeastward through the jungle. With no path, they had to hack their way through thick vines, bushes, and leaves blocking their way. The five walked for about twenty paces, then changed direction, going forty paces north, forty southwest, and ten south, at which point they emerged from the jungle at a spot somehow familiar.

It was a gorge like the last one, except the water at the bottom of it flowed in the opposite direction. Edward took one glance at the gorge and then smiled to himself.

"This is the same spot where we were before," he stated.

"Are you saying I can't read a map? This is where we were supposed to go!"

"Easy," Edward said in an attempt to calm Dunn. "Look over there. It's the log we used." He pointed to the undeniable proof in front of them.

They all walked over and confirmed it to be true. They had gone in a loop. The question was whether or not this was intended by the instructions. *I don't think Bill or his friend is clever enough to come up with something like that.* "Let me see the map."

"What? You think we're headed the wrong way? I followed it perfectly."

"Then you won't mind me checking it to make sure. If you're right, then I'll admit it and we'll continue."

Dunn seemed to relax his guard, and handed Edward the map. He needed but a moment to solve the riddle, but he read it a few times to make sure, because it seemed too simple to be true.

The Golden Arm must not be good at puzzles, this is so simple. I guess I have to hand it to Bill and his friend. They were able to stump someone.

"Follow me."

Dunn folded his arms and snorted, but followed Edward back into the jungle. They went through the thick brush again, but this time their route was different: forty paces north, twenty northeast, and forty east, at the end of which they reached a wall of rock.

"Here we are. Now we have to climb over this and we'll find a path. It says so right here at the last part. Some of the numbers were there to throw us off."

Dunn still had his arms folded, but he accepted what Edward said without objection. "What are you waiting for? Climb up and tie some rope for us."

Edward sighed and began climbing. This part was a little easier than the last; there were plenty of crevices for his hands and feet, and no slippery moss to deal with. He went at a slow pace, making sure not to release a good position before testing the next. He reached the top before long and secured the rope to a boulder so the others could climb up.

Once again they climbed one by one until Dunn was left by himself. He could only pull himself with one arm, and stubbornly tried several times, but he didn't know the proper way to do it.

Eventually Edward yelled down to him. "Either tie it around your waist, or wrap your legs around it and use your right arm pressed against your chest to pull yourself up." The Golden Arm swallowed his pride and did as Edward suggested. He put the rope between his legs, pulled himself up with his good hand, and then pulled it tight to his chest with the right so he wouldn't fall as he went higher.

Dunn finally reached the top, though at a snail's pace, and Edward put his hand out to help once again, but Dunn knocked his hand away. "You take me for a fool, Blackbeard? Get him away from me." The other crewmembers pulled Edward back, and then one helped their captain up from the ledge. When he was safe, they let Edward go.

As Edward had predicted, a path was right in front of them. They all set off down it, but this time Dunn walked beside Edward. The familiar sounds of the jungle returned, but Edward thought he heard an odd rustling behind them and turned around.

"What is it?" Dunn asked.

Edward observed the thick forest for a moment, but he couldn't see anything or hear anything more. "Nothing… Just my imagination, I suppose."

The minutes rushed by with the exertion of walking, but Edward grew tired of the silence. Despite being men of similar background and from the same crew, there was not much rapport between them.

"So what happened between Herbert and John, anyway?"

Edward was a little surprised Dunn didn't berate him or punch him. "He must have told you his side already. What good will telling the same story do?"

"I've not heard his side of the story," Edward explained.

There was a short pause before Dunn spoke again. "He and I were never on the best of terms, even back then. I was in my teens, and Herbert, being the younger, received special treatment from the captain. He took a shine to Herbert because he could see potential in the boy. No matter what I did, he was always praised. He was always the favorite." Dunn's voice had an edge of pent-up irritation.

So Dunn was envious.

"After the accident, the captain didn't want to have a cripple aboard and so he was left at Port Royal. Then it was my chance to shine. I worked harder than ever, and without competition I came to where you see now," he said, tapping his chest with his golden arm. "I'm part of the greatest pirate crew in the world today. You rookies won't ever understand without seeing it firsthand. I can't even hold a candle to the captain's flame. If you thought I was strong, then you don't even know what strength is. You and your crew are weak," Dunn scolded.

He's right, we are weak. We need to be stronger if we're to face what's coming. I need to be stronger.

Edward heard the rustling noise again, but once again when he turned to look he saw nothing and heard no other noises. *I know I heard something this time, I'm not going mad. I should be on guard.*

As they kept walking the path, Edward glanced behind and to the sides in search of the source of the mysterious sound. After walking for another twenty minutes, they reached the end of the path, and nothing they saw seemed to indicate what they should do next. After a moment of perplexity, Dunn pulled out the pieces of the map again.

"What does it say to do next?" Edward asked.

"It says to look up." They stared at each other for a second, and then both looked up into the green canopy above them, having no idea what to expect.

High up, hanging by a rope from a tree, was a large wooden and metal chest. Its sides adorned with elaborate carvings of fine craftsmanship, there was no denying it was an object of worth, and no doubt to any that this was what they had come to find. The two of them smiled, and Dunn pushed Edward toward the tree from which the chest was suspended, motioning for him to climb. "Go on then, get me my treasure!"

Edward pulled the Golden Arm close to him. "You remember our promise, Gregory? I give you this gold, and my crew and I—*all* of them—leave safely."

"I'm a man of my word, Blackbeard. Just keep your cripple away from the captain—and me, of course."

Dunn handed Edward a knife. Edward didn't say a word or make a motion of agreement. He turned and walked to the tree.

That is something I will not do, Dunn. I already made one promise.

He climbed with caution, almost to the top, and it made the tree bend down with his weight. He took it slow, inching forward toward the rope holding the chest.

Those on the ground tried to goad Edward into moving faster, but he continued forward at his own pace. Finally he was able to place one hand on the rope while supporting himself with his legs wrapped around the tree trunk.

How did they put this up here in the first place?

Hanging in that precarious position, he used the knife to saw through the heavy rope, but the fibers were not easy to cut. The chest began to sway. Edward put his weight into the cutting down to the final thread, and with one last slice the chest fell to the jungle floor. Edward had to drop the knife and grab onto the tree, which sprang back when relieved of its burden.

The chest opened on impact. Hundreds of coins spilled out and covered the ground with bright flashes of gold. Despite the exuberant response of hoots, hollers, and pats on the back between Dunn's crew, they didn't presume to touch any of the gold. Their commander, however, almost dove into it; he grabbed fistfuls of the doubloons and let them run through his fingers like a parched man finding clean water.

He soon shook himself out of his manic obsession, however, ordering his men to gather up the coins and put them back in the chest as he turned to see Edward descending from the tree. And as soon as he touched the ground, Dunn pulled out his pistol.

"Not a step closer, Blackbeard!"

"What… What is this? We had a deal, Dunn! The gold in exchange for my crew and me. You mean to dishonour our arrangement?"

"Oh, I intend to honour it, but do you? I see the lust in your eyes. You were waiting for this moment to take our lives and steal the chest for yourself were you not?" he asked, though in his eyes no answer would change his mind. "It ends here. You won't take my gold, as I'll take your life."

"You're mad! You're blinded with…" Edward stopped. He was hearing the strange noise again, but this time it was in two places—and after a split second two huge forms burst from the bush and canopy.

A gargantuan jaguar leaped out from behind the trees, landed on one of Dunn's men, and crushed his head in its powerful jaws. At the same time, what appeared to be a giant eagle swooped down and struck at Dunn's head. He swerved and jumped back just in time to avoid the strike, but his pistol was broken by the beak of the animal. It was no beak, however, nor was the eagle truly a bird.

Pukuh had jumped from a tree, attacking with his spear. In his warrior's dress, he was like an animal in motion, striking fear into the hearts of those around him. Of equal fear-inducing fortitude was the jaguar. With yellow fur and black spots like a leopard, it had two large fangs on the top and bottom rows of its large mouth. It must have been at least three hundred pounds of pure muscle. Dunn's group didn't know of which to be more afraid: the real jaguar or the man-eagle. As for Pukuh, he was focused on the jaguar, and the jaguar on him. They each knew where the true threat lay; the others were just prey.

Pukuh pulled out another spear he had strapped behind him and tossed it to Edward. He pulled his own spear from the ground, crouched down low, and stared at the jaguar, which returned his gaze as they began to circle each other. Edward grabbed his spear off the ground and circled in the opposite direction, also facing the beast, which growled and hissed at them as they sought to corner it.

"Just like old times, eh, Pukuh?"

"Yes, but this beast is not tamed so easily. It must be killed, or we must leave its territory."

"Right." Edward gripped the spear tighter and crouched lower, imitating Pukuh.

"We'll leave this in your hands!" yelled Gregory 'Golden Arm' Dunn.

Edward turned his head to see Dunn and his two remaining crewmembers carrying away the chest full of gold. They had seen an opportunity to escape, and they were taking it.

"You damn cowards!" Edward yelled back.

"Look out, Captain!"

Edward turned back in time to see the fangs of the jaguar closing in on him. He turned his spear sideways, dug his feet in, and pushed its shaft against the animal's front paws. The animal kept trying to force its way forward on its hind legs, snapping at Edward's face and trying to free his claws. It took everything Edward had to hold on to his spear as they struggled and pushed each other back and forth.

"Keep him still!" Pukuh said as he tried to strike at the jaguar— but he hit only air, or almost nicked Edward.

"I can't!" Edward growled.

He pulled in a deep breath and pushed the jaguar forward and off him at an angle. He arched the spear and slashed the animal across the chest as he forced it off him. After the jaguar fell it rolled back to its feet in an instant, unfazed. The cut had been too shallow.

This time it sprang at Pukuh, swiping and striking. He jumped and rolled out of the way, the jaguar missing him by inches. The pressure was intense, and Pukuh barely kept up. Edward tried to jump into the fray again and managed to lure the jaguar away from Pukuh.

Sweat rolled down Edward's and Pukuh's faces and their breathing became heavy. The exertion of keeping the jaguar off them was taking its toll. "I don't know how long I'll last like this, Pukuh."

"We can win, brother! Follow my lead."

Pukuh ran to the right of the jaguar, leaving Edward to the left. He thrust his spear out, inching closer to the animal but not striking. Edward followed suit, and the beast wasn't able to follow both. It backed up from them and tried to claw at the spears, but missed. It kept backing up until it hit a stand of trees. With nowhere to move, it was just where Pukuh wanted it.

"Now!" he yelled.

Edward thrust his spear forward with full intent to kill. The jaguar leapt upwards and dodged the blow. Pukuh then followed with blinding speed and stabbed the creature in the neck. Blood seeped from the open wound in huge spurts, and after some futile pawing at Pukuh's spear, the huge beast fell limp with a bitter groan.

Edward and Pukuh both collapsed on the ground, physically and mentally exhausted. Nearby lay the body of the slain member of Dunn's crew, a stark reminder of how close they had come to death.

"We seem to have trouble with wild animals, you and I," Edward said.

"Yes, I suppose they feel threatened by other wild animals encroaching on their territory."

Edward laughed. They sat there for a minute until Edward thought back on Calico Jack's pirate crew. He stood and brushed the dirt off him. Then he noticed something shiny near the mauled man's body. He walked over, lifted the body, and beneath it found ten golden doubloons.

"What is it?" Pukuh asked as he peered over Edward's shoulder.

"A taste of what we can have." Edward picked up the gold pieces and pocketed them. "We need to head back. There'll be a battle once Dunn reaches the shore."

"Yes, he is unpredictable. Also, the cripple seems to want to kill him. It will complicate things. Do you have a plan?"

"No, but I'll find a way to end this today. For Herbert."

34. HONOURING THE DEAL

Edward and Pukuh ran back along the jungle path as quick as their tired legs would carry them, dodging brush and jumping over logs, trying to catch up to Dunn. "They won't be able to travel fast with the chest in tow. Do you have any guns with you?"

Pukuh scoffed as he ducked under a branch. "No, those are not a warrior's weapons. A coward's, maybe."

Edward laughed. *I should have expected that.*

They soon reached the cliff, but the rope had vanished. Edward started to climb down the ledge, but Pukuh stopped him. "This way is faster," he declared before jumping to a tree a few feet away. Like a monkey he jumped from tree branch to tree branch, finally grabbing a low angled palm and letting himself gracefully down to the ground.

There's no way I can do that.

Pukuh, as if reading Edward's mind, reassured him. "You will make it. Come down."

"No, thanks, I'd rather not break my arm."

Edward, knowing he could not compare in agility with the Mayan, went back to the ledge and clambered down. When he reached the bottom, Pukuh was grinning coolly at him.

"What? I would have died attempting that, and you know it."

"Whatever you say, Captain."

As they continued on the path, they had to slow down, as the fight with the jaguar had taken its toll on Edward. He was breathing in heaves and sweating through his shirt. They hurried on beyond the path and into the bush again until they reached the gorge with the rapids at the bottom. Edward stopped running and sat down to catch his breath. He couldn't see the log they had used before.

"They must have broken the log to stop us."

"They will fail. Come, I'll show you how I crossed."

Pukuh led Edward along the edge until they reached a tree leaning far out over the gorge. He pointed to a thick vine suspended between the tree and another on the other side.

Looks safe enough.

Pukuh climbed up first, followed by Edward. They both suspended themselves on the vine, climbing out over the chasm, holding on with their legs and arms. As they went farther, the vine sagged more and more.

274

"Uhh, is it supposed to do that?"

"No… Perhaps hurrying will do us good."

They moved faster, but that seemed to make things worse. Edward looked back to where they got on the vine, and what he saw made his thoughts turn grim. The vine was starting to thin and appeared about to snap.

Before Edward could warn his friend, it broke and they fell. Luckily they were holding the part of the vine still attached to the tree on the far side of the gorge. They held on tight and swung forward, landing safely, if roughly, on the other side of the gap.

Edward stood up and dusted himself off. "Why is it every time we're together I always end up in mortal danger?"

"You chose the life of a pirate, and I am the one who puts you in danger?"

"Good point. Let's keep going."

Edward and Pukuh continued the chase until they reached the spot from which Edward had set out with Dunn to find the treasure. He and Pukuh found no one there. They concluded that when Dunn returned he took them back down to the shore. Pukuh could see their footprints heading back, and Edward could see the still-fresh bloodstains on the path where Herbert had been beaten. His wheelchair was gone as well, which hopefully meant he was still alive.

Herbert, I promised you revenge, and I hope I can deliver on that promise.

"The tracks are still fresh. We might be able to reach the shore at the same time they do."

Edward nodded, and they took off running. They went on for half an hour before the path ended, never catching sight of their quarry. Edward slowed down as they reached the edge of the forest.

"I don't hear sounds of fighting. That means either we're just in time or too late."

The forest ended abruptly, and there were several bushes and fanning leaves before the sandy beach. Edward and Pukuh hid behind some of the bushes. Now they could see both crews on the sand of the beach, each with their captives in tow. Jack appeared to be conversing with Dunn in the centre of the beach, trying to negotiate a mutual release. Of Edward's crew, about eighty were on the ship, some of them pointing rifles and cannons at Dunn's crew, ninety were on shore guarding the hostages, and the other group of fifty were still held by Dunn. Edward's crew outnumbered Dunn's by fifty; they could take them in a fair fight, but under the circumstances couldn't risk harm to Edward's senior officers.

"Pukuh, I want you to sneak aboard the *Freedom*. I'll remain on shore to distract them and try to bring the rest of the crew on our side. I want you to tell the gunners to fire when I give the signal. No one is aboard their ship and they aren't ready to depart. We can win if we play our cards right."

"What is this 'playing of cards' you talk of?" Pukuh asked.

"It... it's an expression. It means... when two people are playing a game with..." Edward shook his head. "I'll tell you later, we don't have time. Go give my orders to the crew and everything will work out."

"Yes, brother." Pukuh went farther down the shore, closer to where the *Freedom* was anchored.

Edward waited until Pukuh was gone and then came out of hiding.

"Already started without me, Dunn? Shame on you. Not only are you a coward but you have no manners."

"You! How did you survive?" Dunn asked, his brows furrowed.

The Golden Arm was at least as shocked as everyone else. Elated cries of "Captain!" and "Edward!" reached him from all sides. Henry and Anne wore bright smiles of relief.

"The report of my demise by our pirate friend here was somewhat premature. As you can see, I am perfectly safe. I can take over here, Jack, thank you. Keep everyone on their toes, eh?" Edward said as he glanced toward the ship.

Jack nodded and grinned before he went back to the crew guarding the tied-up pirates. Jack whispered some words to them.

"You bastard, how did you win against that jaguar? And where is your dark friend?"

"I won because I fought. You lost because you ran. My friend died because of that animal." Edward gritted his teeth to give the appearance of anger over his lost crewmate.

"And you say *I* lost? Ha! I'm still alive."

Not for long if I can help it.

"If you want to keep living I suggest you let my crew go. We had a deal, remember?"

"That hinged on the fact of me gaining the gold, but do you see a treasure chest here? No. I have four dead crewmen and nothing to show for it."

"You lost the gold on the way back?" Edward arched his brow, trying to remember if he'd noticed it along the way back, but he knew the answer. "That's what you get for your greed, but our agreement was met. I led you to the gold and gave it to you. What happened after is your fault."

"I've lost four crewmen, including the one you killed here on the beach, and you've lost one. I think it's fair that we take three of yours in compensation."

"Look behind me, Dunn, and then behind you," Edward said, pointing for emphasis. "I have more armed crewmen than you, and the ones from your crew are tied up while mine are simply un-armed." Edward grabbed Dunn by the chest and pulled him in close. "You start fighting now and you'll be the one who dies. I suggest you take the offer I gave you before and we can all leave safely." He released Dunn, pushing him away.

Beads of sweat ran down Gregory Dunn's forehead, leaving streaks on his dust-covered face. "Yes, maybe it would be best to keep to our arrangement. We'll let all the hostages go and then head back to our ships."

Edward nodded, and both of them turned and told their crews to free the captives, who then moved to rejoin their own crews. They exchanged hostile glances that threatened a fight, but Edward's stern eye curbed any thoughts of attacking. John wheeled Herbert past Edward in his half-broken wheelchair. Herbert kept staring at the ground, dejected and looking the worse for his wounds.

With the crews back in their proper places, Edward and Dunn nodded and walked away from one another, their business concluded. But Edward was not finished with the Golden Arm. He motioned for one man to toss him a sword, and then gave the crew on the ship the signal to fire with a swipe of his hand.

"Attack!" he roared.

A loud blast of cannon fire broke through the silence, followed by several more. The cannonballs hit the beach with thunderous impact, shooting sand into the air, then rolled along the ground, crushing and maiming several of Dunn's men. Edward's crew rushed over to the enemy as the cannon blasts stopped, and the sounds of a ground battle soon replaced the thunder of the cannons. Swords clanged, guns blazed, and screams echoed along the beach.

Through the commotion Edward sought his prey. This time he would win against him, and Herbert would have his revenge. He cut through the others in his way, and soon found Dunn shooting a pistol and taking out a cutlass, his back turned. Edward came up behind him and attacked, but Dunn saw it out of the corner of his eye and dodged.

"You call me the coward and yet you attack us while our backs are turned?"

"No different from you, ambushing us in the jungle. Call me an opportunist."

Their swords clanged together with mortal intent. Dunn was serious this time, but Edward had learned from their previous fight. After the battle with the jaguar, he faced a foe that was all too human, and all too predictable.

"I guess this means our arrangement is broken and we won't

spare your crew," Dunn said through rapid breaths.

"I think you have it backwards, Gregory. My crew will leave here today, as will I. At no point did I agree *I* would spare *you* in our arrangement."

Edward slashed and thrust at Dunn, but couldn't reach him no matter how he tried. Dunn used his golden arm deftly, blocking and parrying Edward's sword.

That arm is mine!

Dunn went to punch Edward with his golden arm, and Edward grabbed it, pulling him forward. He flipped Dunn to the ground, jumped on his back, and wrapped his legs around Dunn's neck and arm, making him drop his cutlass. Edward pulled the golden arm back, placed his sword at its elbow, and thrust the blade down with all his strength.

Dunn screamed out in pain as Edward dug the blade in deeper. Blood spurted from the gash and washed over the sword, Edward's hand, his trousers, and the sand. He kept pressing into the elbow as Dunn tried to escape from the vice grip he was in. Edward rose to his feet, stepped on Dunn's chest, and pulled the arm with all his strength.

Others heard the screams and watched in terror as the golden arm was being torn off. Blood splashed everywhere as Edward's muscular arms pulled hard. The whole time he wore a smile on his face that kept all, his own crew included, far away from the centre of the horror.

The din of battle died off and the sounds of Gregory Dunn screaming and the crunch of shattering bones replaced it. With one final pop Edward ripped the golden arm from Dunn's body, then raised it above his head as a symbol of their victory.

His crew yelled and cheered with excitement, and the other enemy pirates surrendered and dropped their weapons. Their commander was defeated. The Golden Arm was no longer.

Dunn's crew surrendered without further fighting. Edward's crew gathered them all together on the shore between the ships. Dunn himself was becoming weaker and weaker from loss of blood. Edward propped him up on his knees and he sat there, listlessly swaying in the wind, waiting for the end.

"Herbert! Where are you?" Edward yelled.

Herbert wheeled himself to the front of the crowd and over to Edward and Gregory Dunn. "Here, Captain."

"I'm sorry about before, I…"

Herbert cut Edward off. "No, Captain, I'm the one who should apologise. I know you were thinking of our safety first and foremost. I'm sorry for what I said."

Edward gave a small, sad smile and squeezed Herbert's shoulder. "Well, here's the chance for the first step in your revenge." Edward claimed a pistol from a crewmember, which he then handed to Herbert. "This is your job."

Herbert took the pistol and Edward backed away. Herbert moved closer to Gregory Dunn, the Gold Division Commander of the Calico Jack Pirates. He took aim.

Dunn laughed weakly. "So this is it, then? Killed by the cripple John loved?"

"Shut up! You don't know anything! He doesn't love anyone. He's a pirate! He used me, and when my usefulness ran out, he discarded me. It would have been the same for anyone."

Dunn laughed again. "It's you who don't know anything, boy. You were like a son to him, and I was the tool. All of us still are… He doesn't care about us, but you he did. Now, though, if you pull the trigger"—and he nodded toward Edward—"*he'll* be the one who pays. You don't know the hell you'll wake by taking out your petty resentments on Mad Jack. You'll all die for this! You'll all pay for angering the King of the Caribbean. You'll—"

Herbert pulled the trigger. Gregory Dunn jerked and he fell to the sand, dead. The Gold Division Commander was no longer, and the first step in Herbert's revenge was complete.

Edward passed Herbert and stood next to the corpse, facing Dunn's crew and addressing them. "Return to your captain and tell him what happened today. Tell him we killed his Golden Arm because he crossed us. Tell him we're coming for him, and that there's a new King of the Caribbean."

Everyone within hearing of his voice stood watching Edward in awed silence. Then someone called out: "What do we call the new king?"

Edward looked down at the corpse of Dunn, then raised his head high and scanned the eyes of the vast company, friend and foe alike, gathered on the beach.

"My name is Edward Thatch, but you can call me Blackbeard."

35. THE ARM SWORD

After their victory, Edward sent a few crewmates back to the trail to search for the gold Dunn lost on his way back to shore, but they returned empty-handed. There was no sign of the chest or the remaining gold pieces.

Edward thought he knew what happened. It had probably been dropped into the gorge. With the rapids and jagged rocks at the bottom, there was no way they could check. The treasure was likely lost to them. Edward sighed.

As compensation, Edward's crew ransacked Dunn's ship for supplies and anything that could be sold. Cannons and gunpowder, spices and food, as well as a good supply of clothes and weapons— all were taken. They left enough for the other crew to survive on, but no weapons were spared. They even found a few hundred pieces of eight in the captain's quarters.

A few members of Gregory Dunn's crew were willing to swear allegiance to Edward in exchange for freedom. Among them was Bill's friend who had also vied for the treasure, Theodore Hammersmith by name, who had a tale to tell.

"And so Bill, when I couldn't find you, I went to these men for help. They said they would help me, but they overheard me talking about treasure and gold and so they kidnapped me instead to find the treasure. They tortured me something fierce, but I never told them nothing. Why, you might as well call me Stone Lips."

Bill had a look of teary admiration on his face.

"Oh? So how did they find Bill's home and his half of the map if you were so tight-lipped?" Edward asked.

Theodore, better known as Ted, had a confused expression for a moment, and then burst into feigned tears. "Oh, they tortured me night and day, Bill, night and day." Edward sighed and covered his face. "I may have let slip that a map was in your home. Oh, but you must forgive me my momentary weakness, Bill; I'm so sorry. But see what fortune has brought us! Someone has delivered us a knight in shining armour to save us from the cruel oppression of Gregory Dunn. How did you ever meet such a man?"

"I met him while on… a business trip. I returned home to my house robbed and the map gone, so I thought the worst. I immediately asked them to help me, and through memory I navigated them to the island. It was a good bit of providence I was able to put together what had happened to you. I knew you were in some peril and had to be saved. I'm glad Edward was here to help, or else we might not have found you." They hugged each other in an obvious display.

These two...

"It's such a shame. All our hard work gone like that."

"I know, but at least we have our lives." It was obvious both of them were upset and holding back their anger.

Edward reached into his pocket and pulled out the ten doubloons he'd found. "Dunn dropped these in his haste."

Bill and Ted reached out at the same time to snatch the gold from Edward, who pulled his hand out of reach.

"Hold out your hands. Both of you."

They smiled falsely to each other as they opened their hands. Edward placed four gold pieces in each of their hands, and left two in his own. He lifted it for both of them to see.

"Twenty percent," he explained, to avoid a dispute arising. *I wouldn't want to shatter the stories these boys told. That would just be a shame.* "This is my cut for helping you both."

Once again, Bill and Ted smiled to each other in the most insincere way Edward had ever seen. "Well, I suppose that's only fair," Ted said.

"Yes, only fair," Bill agreed.

Edward went back to the ship and handed John the two pieces of gold. Henry noticed and went to talk with him.

"So I guess that's our twenty percent?"

Edward chuckled. "No, we actually have three. Remember?"

Henry smiled when he realised what happened. "So I guess in the end you got what you wanted in the first place—thirty percent."

Edward had a devious smile. "Not only that, but we have the Golden Arm's arm. If it's made of solid gold, we'll be rich!"

"I can't say I enjoy the thought of having a dead man's arm, nor using it for profit, but I suppose it's better than attacking innocents."

"I'll drink to that."

With their business finished and Edward's ship filled with people and supplies, they shoved off the island and headed back to the Grand Cayman. The return trip took a little longer than the way there. Night fell three quarters of the way through and so they decided to hoist the sails and let the crew have some rest.

Edward awoke in the middle of the night, the dream shaking him awake him as it was prone to do, and decided to take a walk. Lighting the lantern near his bedside, he gazed upon his crew packed tightly into the hammocks around the cabin, all sleeping soundly. He thought back to when he had first received the *Freedom*, to how he couldn't think of it as his home, no matter what, despite his desire for a ship. Now, amidst the sweet smells and those familiar wooden floorboards and the crew, he couldn't think of a place he'd rather be.

He went up to the main deck and noticed Herbert gazing at the full moon. He looked solemn, almost reflective.

"So?" Edward said as he joined Herbert at the railing on the port side.

"So?"

"How's the wheelchair? I saw it was damaged during the ambush."

"Nassir fixed it. There wasn't too much damage."

The wind was blowing and the sails flapped with each gust. The ropes swayed and the masts creaked. It was a beautiful night, and the moon's light reflected on the rippling waves.

"How do you feel, now that you've taken the life of one of Calico Jack's crew? You don't seem very happy."

"I am. At least, I think I am. I don't know how to describe this feeling. Satisfaction? Contentment? I feel like I've taken the first step in the journey I started eight years ago. You've made it a reality for me, Captain. And for that I'm grateful."

"You're welcome. But you have to remember that your life is more important to me than revenge. If a situation like that comes up again, I may end up doing something you don't like."

Herbert shook his head in shame. "I know. I was so filled with rage I couldn't see what you were trying to do. I've had time to think, and I know it won't happen again. I know now you'll fulfill your side of the agreement, and I'll keep mine as well. I have to be patient and wait for it."

"So what will happen when it's all said and done? Will you leave the crew? Live a peaceful life with your sister?"

Herbert looked confused. "No, Captain. I'm with you to the end. You've brought me this far, and it would shame me to leave you when you've helped me with my goal. I'll help you achieve your goal as well."

"My goal?"

"Yes. Don't you have a goal in mind? Why did you become a pirate?"

Edward thought about it for a time and then smiled. "I want to always be free."

Herbert smiled along with him, and then took another look at the large silver moon off in the distance. "I'd like that too."

As the sun broke over the horizon, they landed at the Grand Cayman once more. Bill and Ted left the *Freedom* together. They went off to drink and spend their new gold pieces.

The crew unloaded some of what they procured from the other ship and sold it at a good profit. They resupplied the ship with enough food and other necessities and then headed back to Bodden Town to sell the rest.

"Why Bodden Town?" Anne asked Edward.

"Merchandise we sell in Bodden Town will be taxed, and that tax will come back to us bit by bit. We'll be making more this way in the end. It's just good business."

Anne smiled a knowing smile and nodded in approval.

Having landed in Bodden Town, Edward headed straight to the Bodden Brothers' home. He took a few of the crew with him; it had been a few days since the fight and the agreement, and he wanted to make a strong impression. He also brought John as he would be best to check over the ledgers and make sure the brothers had everything in order.

The newly repaired gates were opened for him, and the brothers were swift to greet him. They hunched over in unconscious submission to him.

"Mr. Thatch! What brings you back so soon?" asked Neil.

"Had we expected you we would have prepared a meal," Malcolm added.

Edward walked straight to them. "No need for pleasantries, brothers. I returned to make certain our arrangements were being carried out, and to sell some supplies we've acquired."

"We'll make sure you receive the best price for the goods."

"We'll send someone down to organise the sale right now." Malcolm waved to one of the servants, who hurried down to the harbour immediately.

"Now as for the other matter, please step inside. We've drawn up some ledgers, which you can inspect. This way, please."

Edward nodded and followed them into the opulent house. They went into the second-floor study and examined all the pertinent records. Edward's name was at the top of the list of partners alongside the brothers'. Twenty-five percent was accorded to Edward and the rest shared between the brothers, as he had stipulated. Already he had amassed a good amount of coin.

John, after taking a bit of time to check everything in the ledger, nodded in approval, confirming everything was in order.

"The town is growing at a rapid pace, especially when you factor in all the merchant and pirate ships visiting the harbour," Neil said.

"It's becoming a popular trade spot. Before you arrived, we were working on plans to expand the housing supply to accommodate more permanent residents," Malcolm added.

"I'm surprised you haven't done so already. Have you started construction yet?" Edward asked.

"No, Mr. Thatch, not yet," Neil said.

"Good. I want you to make the houses small. Keep them cheap to maintain and live in. Cater to pirates and lower-class citizens. Spread the word to the surrounding islands and towns that Bodden Town is the place to be for profit and avoiding the authorities. Do that, and in less than a year, you should have twice as many people here."

The Boddens smiled at the prospect. They liked the idea. "It will be done, Mr. Thatch."

"Now, is there anything else you need?"

"Yes, I'm in search of an appraiser. I have some gold I want melted and minted."

"If it's an appraisal you need…" Neil started.

"…we would be happy to provide that service," Malcolm finished.

Edward turned and took a large bag from one of his crew. It was slick with blood at the bottom. He reached inside and took out the arm of Gregory Dunn.

The brothers' jaws fell open and they stared at the severed limb in shocked silence for several seconds.

"Where… did you…"

"…find that… thing?"

"I took it from a man who crossed me. I wanted to see what I could sell it for. What do you think?"

Edward handed the arm to the two brothers and they reluctantly took it. They examined it by weight first, with each of them lifting it and giving it a gentle toss in the air.

"This is solid metal."

"Solid?" Edward questioned with a raised brow.

Neil nodded. "Though how it was fused to his arm is beyond our reckoning."

They cleared their worktable and pulled out some tools for a more thorough examination. They used a magnifying glass to examine the whole arm, and paid particular attention to the spot where metal ended and flesh began.

"This is an alloy, not pure gold, if it's even gold at all."

"It's much too strong. You say you fought the man?"

"Did you hit the arm with your sword at all?"

"Yes, several times I struck it with my blade."

The brothers turned to each other, then back to Edward. "Come look at this." Edward joined the brothers on their side of the desk. "Do you see any spots here where you hit it with your blade?"

Edward examined the whole arm up and down several times but couldn't find a chip, a scrape, or any damage at all for that matter. *Dunn used the arm as a shield. He must have had the arm for years and practiced with it all the time. How is it there's no damage showing at all?* "That's impossible," he mumbled.

"Yes, but it is clearly true."

"This metal is like no other we've ever seen. You could quite possibly sell this for a fortune."

Edward stroked his beard as he examined the golden arm once more. "I have a better idea."

⚓ ⚓ ⚓

For the next two months, the *Freedom* remained moored at Bodden Town, where the crew was set to working on two projects: the cleaning of the ship, which had been neglected during the hunt for the treasure, and the building of new housing in the town, under the direction of Nassir.

Many of the builders were, at first, opposed to a Negro leading them, and Edward would have given them a talking-to, but Nassir stopped him. Nassir showed them his skills as a carpenter and his capacity for hard work, and, by his example, turned them around on his own. In the end, in spite of some continued grumbling, they were all working side by side with him and the rest of the crew.

Edward finished making arrangements with the Boddens concerning how funds would be distributed and what they should do next for the town. They started sending out messenger ships to let other islands know of the wealth in Bodden Town, and they soon saw the results as more and more ships appeared in the harbour.

Edward had the best swordsmith in Bodden Town create a cutlass out of the metal from Gregory Dunn's arm. It took the whole two months of their stay, and cost a good amount of coin; the swordsmith had never worked with a material of such hardness and strength. When finished, it was the finest piece of art Edward, and many aboard the *Freedom*, had ever seen. The hilt had a hand guard made of silver and steel, ornamented with an eagle design, and the shining, golden blade was of such quality that it took on an edge sharp enough to cut clean through six inches of solid oak as if it were paper.

"So the Golden Arm lives on still. It's rather fitting we should be in possession of this after we killed him."

"I imagine we'll have more to remind us of victory over Calico Jack later," Herbert said to Edward as he piloted the ship out of the harbour. "His commanders are… unique, to say the least. They all have their quirks and oddities."

"Oh, such as?"

"There's the Silver Division Commander, Lance 'Silver Eyes' Nhil. He works as a scout for John."

"Let me guess, his nickname is for his eyesight?"

"Yes, they say he has supernatural eyesight and is an excellent marksman. Before he was a pirate, he took part in competitions around the world and tested rifles for several arms manufacturers. He's the best there is. He's also said to be an unflinching optimist. No matter how bleak things are, he and his crew never lose their morale. That's won them a lot of battles."

Edward chuckled. "And is there a Copper Division Commander?"

"Yes, Grace 'Copper Legs' O'Malley. She kept her name, but she's actually married to John Rackham. She's the messenger and judge in the pirate crew. If the other divisions get out of line then she takes swift action to deliver punishment. She also has a pair of greaves and boots made of copper, apparently of her own invention. I'm not sure what they do, but I can imagine it's something dangerous if she's named for them."

"Both of them will chase after us now that we've taken out one of their commanders. I'll be relying on your knowledge to help me take them down, Herbert. We're in this together."

"I know Captain, and I thank you. I'll give you my best in anything you need. Where to next?"

"Next? Next we're off to Navassa Island. There's a key we've been neglecting."

"Aye aye, Captain. Next stop: Navassa Island."

36. THE PAST AND THE RELAPSE

Five Years Ago

Rachel felt the cool morning breeze on her face and pulled a strand of her long chestnut hair behind her ear as she watched the sun rising. No matter how often she had seen the day begin, the beauty of that golden-red ball inching over the edge of the world never ceased to enchant her.

"Good day, wife," a man said as he walked up behind Rachel and wrapped his arms around her.

"Good day, husband," she said, holding her husband Jack's arms close to her. The aroma of coffee sitting on a nearby table mixed with the scents of the cool breeze and morning dew. Rachel closed her eyes as she leaned back into his chest. "I could get used to this."

Jack laughed as he rested his head gently on top of hers. "Every morning I come out here, and every morning you say that. I would think you would be used to it by now."

She smiled. "That's the thing about dreams, love. You never get used to them."

"Well, if this is a dream, let's pray we never awaken."

They stood there, wrapped in each other's warmth, taking sips of the coffee together. They watched from their back porch as the sun rose over the horizon. They listened to the birds singing from their treetop perches, and the faint sounds of the sea.

"Are the kids still asleep?" asked Jack.

"Yes. They won't be up for another few hours." Rachel turned and gazed into his eyes. Jack knew what they both wanted at this moment. With his arm around her shoulders, he led her indoors.

They came back out when the children woke up. Rachel made breakfast as Jack prepared to leave for work. Their two children, Maximilian, ten, and Jessica, nine, sat at the table.

"Good morning, Father. Good morning, Mother," they both said.

"Good morning, children."

"What did you two dream about last night?" Jack asked, as he always did.

Maximilian spoke up first, excited. "I was at sea, and this big monster whale broke the boat in half!"

Jack lifted the young man in his arms. "Whoa! And what did you do then?"

"I... I bopped him in the 'ead and told him to stop."

"You sure showed him," he said with a chuckle. "Jessica, what about you?"

"I dreamed I was a lion, and then I went 'roar' and all the other animals were scared."

"That sure is a scary roar. Why don't you do that again? I don't think Mother heard it."

Jessica did her best imitation of a lion roaring as Jack and Rachel smiled. Jack loved these hours before his workday began, when he could relax with his family. Living a modest but comfortable life in his little house, in the small village of Hastings, he was truly happy for the first time in his life.

After playing with the children some more, Jack finished off his breakfast and set out. He held classes teaching others how to play, read, and write music. He enjoyed the work, and on this day the time went by like it was nothing.

"And so that will conclude today's lesson. Katie, remember to practice those chords I showed you for next time, and all of you remember to study the sheet music tonight. Whoever can name and play all the notes will receive a treat." Jack packed his things, including his violin, into his bag. He said goodbye to his students and to their parents who picked them up.

On his way home, Jack gazed at the setting sun in the distance. It was late. He could see the various shops and offices down the dirt road, the passing horses and carriages, the men and women dressed for their daily business, the children still playing in the streets. He smiled as he headed back to his home where his wife and children would be waiting.

Their one-story home with the fence and apple tree in front was as he had left it. The leafy branches and green grass swayed in the wind and sent to him the sweet smell of spring. As he approached, however, the smell turned foul and stung his nose. It made him stop in his tracks and it was then that he noticed the golden sun on the horizon wasn't the only source of light and warmth.

His house was alight with a blaze inside, and smoke wafted on the wind.

Jack dropped his pack, a discordant, muffled ring like a cry sounded in the twilight. Whether the cry was from him or his clanging violin he knew not. His feet and his mind raced towards the gate, throwing it open and rushing past a few onlookers in front of his house.

He burst the door open, and then was forced back by the leaping flames. He threw his arm up to shield himself from the fire and looked in horror at charred bodies in the center of their kitchen. Tears streamed down his face and he paced in front of those few feet where he could stand, not knowing what to do as the fire raged within.

The smell of their bodies, the burning hair and flesh, a cloying, sticking ulcer, reached the back of his throat and he retched himself while stumbling away from his burning home.

Two of the men, the bystanders who were watching outside, picked him up to his feet. It took him a moment to look up at them and recognize who they were. Marines of the royal navy. Jack furrowed his brow, his mind already broken, and now befuddled. Why were there marines in front of his house? Why were they doing nothing to help?

The marines took him a few steps, where another man dressed in uniform waited. He looked up to see a man he knew, George Rooke.

"George? What…? What's going on?"

George Rooke, aged thirty, was an impressive figure with dark eyes and slick black hair, clean-shaven and strong-jawed, with the toned body of a marine official who kept himself in excellent condition. He wore white gloves with his black uniform and was immaculately clean in every way, as if he had an aversion to dirtiness.

When Jack had known him, he was a recruit in the marines, but now he wore the badges of a rear admiral. It had been ten years since they'd last met.

"Hmph" George scoffed. "Don't play dumb, Jack old boy. You knew this day was inevitable. You couldn't run away with my bride-to-be and think I wouldn't track you down, could you?" George looked down upon Jack with a smug smile on his face.

Jack's eyes grew wide with fear. "What did you do?"

George's smile grew wider. "I rid the world of the filth you and that whore created." George bent down and placed a hand on Jacks shoulder. "If I can't have her, no one shall. Nothing personal, she was spoiled goods after all. You understand don't you boy?" He said with a wink. "Good day, Jack."

George Rooke turned around and left, his work done. After his men roughed Jack up for good measure, they followed right behind him.

Jack was left, broken, bloody, watching his life burn away in front of him.

⚓ ⚓ ⚓

Present Day

One night, on the way to Navassa Island, when the moon was shining, Edward went for a walk on the main deck. Approaching the stern, he heard a familiar sound, and he found Jack Christian, drunk and singing a sad lullaby. Jack had not kept his promise.

"Jack."

Jack turned around and smiled from ear to ear. His hair was disheveled and it seemed as if he hadn't shaved in weeks, and his eyes were red from tears. He held a bottle in his hand and the stench off him was strong. He was unsteady on his feet and swaying from the drink.

"Cap'n! Join me for a drink!"

Edward slapped Jack hard, knocking him to the ground.

"Whut was that fer? That hurt, you bastard!" he yelled and tried to stand, but ended up merely flopping around. "I'll get you in a minute."

"Stop fooling around, Jack. What about the promise you made?"

"Whut about it?"

"You promised to stop drinking, yet here you are with a drink in your hand," he said with a wave towards the bottle. "Give me the bottle." Edward put his hand out, but Jack drew back. He pulled it close to his face and sipped at it while he watched Edward from the corners of his half-opened eyes. Edward reached for it again and again, but Jack kept pulling it away. Edward ended up fighting him for the bottle, and he won, but received a few kicks and punches for his trouble.

Jack was thrashing this way and that after Edward took the bottle. "Give it back!" he screamed.

"No."

Tears rolled down Jack's face. "I need it. It hurts, Cap'n. It hurts too much. I can't take it."

"You're stronger than this, Jack. You don't need it."

"No! I do need it! Give it back!" Jack wailed, stretching out his hand. He kept repeating it again and again. His voice went from a yell to a whisper as Jack clutched Edward's leg, begging him for the bottle.

It was a pitiable sight, and Edward couldn't take it. He wasn't strong enough to deny his friend his vice when he was like this, no matter what happened to him.

His bottle back in his hands, Jack smiled as he downed half its contents and started singing again. Edward walked away, his head bowed, hands balled into fists, and tears stinging his eyes.

37. THE THIRD ISLAND

It took a week and a half to arrive at Navassa Island, and the crew sang sea shanties with Jack and trained with William and Anne to relieve the boredom of an otherwise uneventful journey. The new crewmembers consisted of pirates from other crews, some seamen from fishing boats, and former merchantmen who knew their way around a ship. They soon learned this was a different type of crew, and they could expect to see a lot of combat.

William showed them how to use muskets and other flint-locks; they learned how to load, how to aim, the proper time to use each weapon, how and when to take cover, and how to follow orders. Anne taught them hand-to-hand fighting and the use of close-quarters weapons. Many navy officers used longswords, but Anne taught with the cutlass, a smaller blade that was more practical in the confined space of a ship.

One day, when there was no wind and travel was at a standstill, almost the whole crew was able to have dinner together. They broke out the best foodstuffs: salted meat, cheese, and biscuits were the mainstay, but since they had just left Bodden Town, they had some unspoiled fruit and vegetables as well. With Edward's permission, they drank light rum and water. The crew quickly became animated, with everyone telling jokes, eating, and playing games. Some played cards and others arm-wrestled, while the crew working in the galley brought out food at varying intervals.

Edward was sitting with Henry and John. Anne joined them. "It certainly is lively now, is it not?" she said, smiling.

"Yes, I was just saying how we've gained quite the crew," Edward agreed.

They all observed the merrymakers. Pukuh was having a drink with Sam, hesitantly trying rum for the first time. Ochi, Nassir's boy, was with Christina, Herbert's sister, and a few of the men. They were showing her tricks with coins and cards, and she laughed at the magic on display. William was even having a little to drink with Nassir, Alexandre, and Herbert, who sat at a table together, eating and swapping stories.

"I would not want to be anywhere else," Anne said.

"Hear, hear!" Henry raised his glass and the rest of them joined.

Anne leaned toward Edward as they talked and placed her hand on his under the table.

The festivities continued well into the night. A bond was formed over that meal, a sense of belonging—of family, even—which affected even the new members, and remained strong as they reached Navassa Island.

The island was small and uninhabited. Rocky shallows prevented the ship from landing near shore.

"If we sail any closer we're liable to run aground, Captain."

"This is well enough. We'll take a longboat ashore. William, you're with me. Henry, are you coming?"

"I suppose I shall."

The three, joined by a couple of other crewmembers, jumped into one of the dinghies, lowered themselves into the water, and rowed to the rocky shore.

The island was small and quite plain, with gentle rolling hills covered only in grass and scrub. From the top of the first rise one could see the other side of the island without need of a spyglass.

"So what are we searching for?" Henry asked.

"There's supposed to be something that will help decode the gibberish of the last clue left by Benjamin. It's supposed to be in the centre of the island."

They all walked to what seemed to be the right place, but there was nothing to be seen. They searched the ground, combing through the grass, but to no avail. No paper with a cipher, no secret code, nothing.

"Was it already taken?" asked Henry.

William answered immediately. "This island doesn't see any activity. The location would be a prime spot for traders, but the rocky shore means it is bypassed. The probability of it being taken is slim at best."

Henry turned to Edward. "You said it was in the centre of the island, right? What if it's buried?"

"That would make sense." Edward directed a couple of the men to return to the ship to retrieve some shovels.

"Captain, I found something," William said.

Edward went over to William. He was pointing to a patch of grass. "What is it?"

"The grass in this area is patchy and there are rocks upturned, as if it was dug up. If we dig here we may find what we are looking for."

"Good job, William. I knew those keen eyes would come in handy." Edward patted William on the back.

When the men returned with the spades, they dug in the spot William had pointed out. They made a wide circle to cover plenty of ground, and they took shifts—necessary, because they only had two shovels. As Edward was taking his break, he heard someone yell

Blackbeard's Ship

from the hole.

"Ed, I found something!"

Edward ran back to the hole and Henry tossed up a triangular stone to him. On each of its three sides there were inscriptions. Edward helped Henry and another crewmember out of the hole.

"What's on it?" Henry asked, wiping sweat off his brow.

"I'm not sure, but this must translate the message on the paper we found. It's covered in dirt, so let's head back to the ship and we can clean it off and examine it." Edward tried to sound calm, but he was excited and eager to find out what the message was going to be.

On the boat ride back, Edward washed the stone with ocean water, revealing that the inscriptions consisted of letters of the alphabet. On each of the stone's three sides were two sets of letters, one to the left and one to the right. To the left was a section of the alphabet with the letters in alphabetical order: A-I on the first side of the stone, J-R on the second side, and S-Z on the third. To the right, however, was a seemingly random ordering of the same letters of the alphabet.

It must mean the left side is what was on the paper, and the right is the true meaning. Brilliant! With this we'll be on our way in no time!

While rowing back to the ship, all Edward could think of was what they would find at the next island, and what part of the *Freedom* would be opened when they found the key.

Back at the ship, ropes were lowered to them, they secured the longboat, and the ship's crew pulled them up. Edward immediately jumped off and went to the crew's quarters where he kept the paper left by Benjamin Hornigold.

Having procured some parchment, a quill, and a bottle of ink, he went to the nearest table. Several of the other crewmembers who saw his urgency followed him, curious to see what he had found. He started from the beginning and copied down the translation on the parchment. But, as he went along, his excitement turned to confusion, and then to anger.

Gibberish and more gibberish! It doesn't solve anything!

The frustration of finding clues that meant nothing, and of pursuing wild goose chases to find still more nothing, was building inside Edward. He gripped the stone triangle in both hands. He was shaking with rage.

"Uhh, Captain?" one of the crewmembers called.

Edward shot to his feet and hurled the stone triangle at the wall. Fuming and breathing through flared nostrils, he turned to the gathered crew and shouted, "Back to work!"

Everyone saw the look in his eyes, and the crew scattered quicker than if someone shot a pistol in a chicken coop. William, Henry, and Anne remained.

"There was no need for that, Edward," Anne said as she walked over to him.

"Yes, there was! That damned Benjamin is taunting us with his riddles and tricks! He creates these trials, which are supposed to test us, and it ends up killing some of our crew and injuring others. And he treats it as some game!"

Henry chimed in. "Yes, and you've been playing the game up till now. You were excited up to the point where it wasn't going your way. If you don't like it, then why even participate? We have the important areas unlocked, why not quit now while we're ahead?"

"We can't quit!"

"Why not?"

"Because it's still his ship!"

Henry looked confused. "What do you mean, it's still his ship?"

"He sold the ship to me knowing full well we would have to do this. He sold us part of the ship and it was as if he said 'It's up to you to find the rest.' He still owns the parts of the ship we haven't unlocked, and until we do it's not really my ship." Edward had calmed down and was no longer shouting. "This ship is still his, and if we truly want to own it, if we truly want to have our *Freedom*, then we have to play the game." He let out a sigh. "I was just a little frustrated. But I'm not giving up. I will beat his game, and this ship will be mine."

"Take a few breaths, and we'll try to figure this out together." Anne stroked his cheek in a soothing manner.

Edward closed his eyes, nuzzled into Anne's hand and gave it a kiss. "It's all well and good, I'm fine now. I'll grab the stone and we'll see if there's some trick to it."

Edward turned to where he'd thrown the stone triangle, and saw William there, bent over, examining it. He had two pieces in his hands.

Two? Oh no…

"Is it broken?" he asked, as he knelt down next to William.

"Not quite. It appears this was meant to be broken apart."

Edward's mouth fell open and he cocked his brow, so William handed him the pieces to examine. In the centre of one there was a triangular hole, and on the other a peg of the same shape meant to keep them together. He could see an inscription of numbers on each of the sides of the triangle. The side with A-I had the number 3, J-R had 1, and S-Z had 2.

Wait a minute!

Edward dashed over to the table, where Anne and Henry were reading the gibberish on the paper.

There are three paragraphs. The numbers must correspond to the paragraphs. What about the other half of the stone?

Edward inspected it.

They have numbers 1-3 as well.

Edward examined the paper again. He kept repeating the word "three" over and over in his head.

"That's it!"

"What's it?" Henry asked.

"The three faces of this stone triangle have 1, 2, and 3 on them respectively. There are two sides to it, and both sides have the numbers on them. There are three paragraphs we need to decode, and each paragraph has three lines. The left side of the triangle relates to the three paragraphs, and the right side to the three lines for each paragraph. We have to arrange the two sides of the triangle to correspond with the paragraph and the line."

"How are we to rearrange them?" Henry asked.

Edward showed them the broken stone and smiled. "If I hadn't gotten angry we wouldn't have found this out. All's well that ends well, eh chaps?"

Henry and Anne both chuckled and shook their heads. They all sat down and worked at the paper. Now that they knew what to do with it, translating it didn't take very long. The message was short and plain. It contained instructions to find the next island, with no more riddles.

South of Jamaica,
East of Providencia,
Northwest of Barranquilla.

The Lone Island
Holds the next
In the line of keys.

One entrance, one exit
Two corridors of tests
Two enter, two leave.

"That's fairly straightforward, wouldn't you say?"

"I believe so, Henry. I'm still curious what the two entering and two leaving part means," Edward said, stroking his beard.

"It could be people. Maybe this is a trial for the captain and first mate?"

"That makes sense, similar to how the first trial was for the whole crew. This will test the leaders of the crew themselves," Anne added.

Edward nodded. "Yes, but it doesn't necessarily have to be the captain and the first mate. In the second trial it was very specific in that it was for the captain only. Why wouldn't Benjamin do the same here if that was the case?"

"Well, we can figure that out later. For now, let's sail to the island," Henry said, putting an end to the debate.

"Right. I'll fill in Herbert."

Edward and the others dispersed and went back to work. Herbert set the course south-southwest to their destination. He used the three positions from the clues to triangulate and give an approximate location of the island. After a quick stop for more supplies they headed for the island.

The journey took a couple of days, uneventful except for the hot weather and a particularly bad storm along the way which, thanks to Herbert, they rode out without serious trouble. But on the morning of the third day they sailed into a sudden mist, which Herbert thought odd.

"This shouldn't be here. There's been no change in the air, and it's a hot day, not humid, so any fog should evaporate. Strange," he said with a furrowed brow.

"Hmm," Edward mumbled as he stroked his beard. "Eyes forward! There's strangeness afoot!" All hands aboard kept sharp eyes on every inch of the water. The fog wasn't thick, but caution seemed warranted. The wind was slight and the ship slow. No sound broke the eerie quiet other than the rocking of the waves and the seamen going about their business.

A crewman's voice came from the crow's nest. "Captain, off the stern! A ship!"

Edward turned and pulled out his spyglass. Sure enough, a ship was trailing behind them, a grey shape just visible through the mist. Edward studied it through the glass, recognised it by its shape, and cursed under his breath.

How does he keep finding us? Damn him to Davy Jones' locker!

"What kind of ship?" Herbert asked.

"Frigate. It's an old friend who would love nothing better than to have me in irons. Run us to the wind, Herbert. Maybe this mist will help us lose him."

"Aye, Captain," Herbert said as he moved the ship farther to starboard.

"Let all the sails fly, gentlemen! Make this ship live up to its name!"

They went much quicker with the wind full in the sails. Edward turned to take another look at the ship behind them. It was gaining on them still. The fifth-rate frigate named the H.M.S. *Pearl* moved like a vessel of a lighter class. It knew these waters, and, like the commander on board, shot straight to its target.

The minutes passed like hours as it drew closer and closer. Then the mist broke, and Edward could see, dead ahead, the island that was their goal.

"There, Herbert! Head around the island!" Edward went to the edge of the deck. "Get ready to fight, you scallywags!"

The island was not quite an island. More of a small mountain, it had high rocky cliffs covered by moss, grass, and a few trees here and there. It did not appear habitable, nor was there a spot to land on.

The *Pearl* was gaining on them as they tried to round the island. Herbert had the *Freedom* hugging the shore as close as possible to the mountainous island while avoiding the rocks. The *Pearl* was closing in on the port side of the ship, and it wasn't long before a familiar sound erupted from it.

Cannonballs flew toward the *Freedom* one after the other. Some hit the water, others the cliffs, sending chunks of rock hurtling towards the crew. A few hit the ship, causing damage and injuring crewmen in their wake.

"Return fire!" Edward yelled.

The cannons on the top level erupted almost all at once, and those on the lower followed soon after. The *Freedom*'s volley did more damage than the *Pearl*'s had, making holes and breaking railings. The *Pearl* had the clear advantage, however. Anything shot was bound to hit the island, if not the ship itself, and the falling rocks were the most dangerous and unpredictable part of the attack.

Sweat beaded on Edward's face as he searched for some way out of their vulnerable situation. He noticed a sort of inlet to starboard, an opening to the island, big enough for a ship to enter. "Herbert! Into the island!" Herbert nodded as he threw the wheel to starboard. The sudden shift in direction knocked some of the less experienced seafarers off balance. Edward held to the railing with one hand and grabbed Herbert's chair with the other to keep it from rolling or tipping.

The *Pearl* followed soon after, and because it was already pointed in the right direction, it ended up right beside the *Freedom*. The two ships were almost close enough to be able to board.

And then something strange happened.

As they entered the inlet, a strong current took both ships and began pulling them forward, limiting their maneuverability, and forcing them into the island's interior, side by side. Overhead a rocky ceiling covered them as they moved into the hollow of the island itself.

Neither ship took this surprising turn of events as adequate reason to hold fire. The cannons never stopped, and rifles began firing as well. Edward could see Smith staring across at him with a satisfied expression.

Bastard. You chase us across half the Caribbean and think it will be easy for you? I'll show you the terror of a Thatch!

"Captain, eyes forward!" Herbert yelled.

Edward's glance shot to the prow. Ahead of them loomed a huge rock, splitting the tunnel in half and permitting the passage of only one ship on either side. Edward knew the division of the tunnel would increase the speed of the current, and once a ship went in, there could be no turning back.

So this is what's meant by "two enter and two leave!" Two ships, not two people. This is a trial for the crew. Or is it crews?

"Captain, what do you want me to do?"

"We have to go through on the right side. There's no other way. There's no room for two ships, so the *Pearl* will have to take the left."

No sooner had Edward spoken than he noticed, seemingly oblivious to the looming threat, the *Pearl* drawing even closer to the *Freedom.*

That fool! He intends to kill us all! Well, then, if he wants to play that game, we'll play.

Edward grabbed the wheel from Herbert. He pulled the wheel to the port side, aiming the *Freedom*'s prow at the *Pearl*. The two ships were in a dead heat with each other, but still far enough away that no one dared to board for a direct assault.

Edward stared down Smith as both ships headed towards the rocky pass in front of them. Neither crew cared to carry on the battle now. They were focused only on their imminent destruction and on the two men who appeared ready to lead them to it.

All Edward and Smith cared about now was the game.

The two of them were an even match. Neither backed down from the other's challenge. The ships moved ever closer to the rocky divider. The crews were running around and frantically yelling.

Closer.

Sweat beaded on Edward's forehead.

Closer.

A few more seconds. Closer.

The H.M.S. *Pearl* turned hard to port, and out of harm's way, which made Smith turn away and yell at whoever changed the course. Edward flung the wheel to the starboard side.

Freedom turned at a forty-five-degree angle to the oncoming wall. The current pushed them further into the cavern of the island. The ship's momentum slowed as it shifted with the current, but the wall was imminent. The crew collectively held their breath, or clenched their teeth, waiting for the collision.

The current pulled *Freedom* forward just as it touched the wall.

Blackbeard's Ship

The grating noise of scraping wood on rock rumbled over the rushing of the current. The noise lingered until the current righted the ship and took her fully in its grasp.

"You could have killed us!" Herbert yelled.

"It was a gamble, and I won. Otherwise we both would have died for certain. There's only room for one ship in each tunnel, and if this is anything like the first trial, we'll need him to complete his side to escape here."

Herbert sighed. "So what happens now?"

"One entrance, one exit. Two corridors of tests. Two enter, two leave," Edward recited. "We'll meet up with them again at the end of this island's gauntlet. We both entered and will face the tests, but only one of us will leave here alive."

38. A SHIP OUT OF WATER

The current took them deeper and deeper into the tunnel at an alarming speed. Herbert was throwing the wheel this way and that to avoid smashing against the rocks, as the frequency of twists and turns increased.

"How is this possible?" Edward yelled as he grabbed the railing at the next bend.

"The inside of this island seems to be pulling in wind somehow. It's filling the sails and causing the water to flow," Herbert replied.

"Furl the sails!" Edward yelled to the crew in response.

"It's either that or something supernatural, like that mist," Herbert yelled over the frantic voices of the crew, who were rushing this way and that to pull up the sails and secure the rigging.

Something's certainly not natural about all this… Benjamin's work, no doubt.

Even after pulling up the sails, the ship was still speeding through the tunnel inside the island. Edward focused on the path ahead of them. The ship was heading straight towards a sharp ninety-degree turn in the rock tunnel.

"Herbert, we're going to crash! What do we do?"

There was a moment's pause from the navigator. "I don't know!"

Edward panicked. *What do we do? What do we do?* The craggy wall of doom was inching closer with each second.

Alexandre appeared from the main deck. His eyes were wider than Edward had ever seen them. "Herbert, turn the ship on my command. Captain, have every crewmember grab grenades and throw them into the water off the port side at the same time."

Edward stared at him. "What will that do?"

"Do not ask questions. Trust me!"

Seeing Alexandre's determined expression, Edward turned to the main deck. "All hands grab grenades and stand at the port side deck!" The crew looked at him the way he had at Alexandre a few seconds before.

"Don't stare at me like a bunch of gits! Get movin'!"

The crew scurried like lizards across the deck to where the grenades were cached in sealed boxes. Some crewmembers brought their fellows up from the lower deck, and everyone took grenades, as instructed.

Blackbeard's Ship

Edward had the gunners position themselves in front of those holding grenades. Each gunner had a linstock in his hand, ready to light the fuses of the grenades. When everyone was ready, Alexandre yelled to Edward to start. "Light those grenades, everyone! Go! Go! Go!" Everyone pushed the fuses to the linstocks and waited for the next command.

The ship turned and its port broadside was now facing the wall of the tunnel. It was still being carried by the current, and if they did nothing it would smash into the wall.

"Now! Throw those grenades!" Edward yelled as he threw his at the wall ahead of him. It bounced and fell into the water along with dozens of others. Mere seconds remained before the ship would smash into a wall of rock.

"Hit the deck!" Edward yelled as he jumped away from the side rail to the floor of the ship.

Everyone followed suit. A thunderous explosion and a crash of waves erupted from the port side. Edward thought that the ship had smashed against the rocks, but the underwater explosion of dozens of grenades had sent up huge waves between the ship and rock wall. The waves slowed the ship and cushioned the impact enough for them to survive.

After the explosion, everyone rose to their feet as the current continued to carry the ship deeper into the island, although slower than before. Edward assessed the damage. There were some bruises and scrapes, but nothing serious. He went over to Alexandre, who was still with Herbert at the helm.

"How did you know that would happen? And for that matter, how did they stay lit in the water?"

"As I have told you, *mon ami*, I observe, and therefore I see what others do not. It was a simple deduction. As for the underwater trick, I did a little experiment with the fuses. I used several different chemical treatments to make them work while underwater. This was the field test."

"This was a test? You're mad!"

Alexandre shrugged. "*C'est la vie.*" He and Edward paused after his remark, and then they both laughed.

Herbert kept his eyes on the tunnel ahead, and shouted: "All hands brace yourselves!"

Edward's and Alexandre's heads spun around toward Herbert, then toward the bow. They grabbed the railing when they saw, dead ahead, the water was gone from their path. The *Freedom* was about to slide over a small gap which the rushing water was falling into, and onto stone. Some grabbed safety lines while others wrapped their arms around the railings or other sections of the ship. Then they could no longer hear or feel the rush of water around the ship's hull. The ship moved past the water and slid onto the smooth stone path with the speed of the current. At the end of the slide they passed from the small, cramped tunnel into an open room.

The room was a large, square cavern within the island. The walls were covered with patches of moss, and water dripped down from cracks and stalactites. There was no flowing water in the vicinity and no visible exit.

When the ship stopped sliding forward, it tipped to the side, but stopped on the angle of its keel. Some supplies and weapons on deck slid off and fell to the rocky ground below, but no one went with them. After a little getting used to the tilt, it was possible to walk. Edward looked back to where they had come from. He could see the rocky ramp that had brought them into the room. He noticed that the floor of the cavern was perfectly smooth.

"Thanks to the way *Freedom*'s keel is shaped, and that smooth surface," said Herbert, "there's probably only minor damage to her." Herbert's sister was now wheeling him on the deck; the tilt of the ship would make wheeling himself too dangerous. "If our keel broke we'd be dead even if we got out of here. But then, leaving does appear to be a problem."

"Yes, it does. I can't see an exit, can you?" Edward asked. Herbert and his sister both shook their heads. "We should check everywhere around here to make sure. There might be something hidden that can't be seen from here."

Edward took John, Nassir and his son Ochi, Anne, and several other crewmen with him, and climbed down the side of the ship by rope. Edward, Nassir, and Ochi inspected the keel for damage. Once satisfied it would be all right, they began looking around.

The cavern was almost a perfect square, with a floor too smooth and walls too straight to be natural. The ceiling, however, had craggy rocks and stalactites hanging from it. In the corners were large mounds of piled-up rocks, perhaps debris from the process of smoothing the floor and walls.

Edward noticed above the corner where he was standing, on the ceiling, there were large rocks shaped like a semicircle with a hollow middle. Each corner had a similar rock formation, located far above the mound of rocky debris on the floor.

"What do you make of those, John?" he asked, pointing at the ceiling. "Do you think that's an unusual rock formation?"

"They certainly seem man-made, Captain."

Anne was kneeling on the ground, inspecting the rocks in the front right corner. "Ed! Come look at this! Here, in between the rocks, you can see something at the back."

Edward knelt down beside Anne and peered into the spot she was looking at. He could see something at the back made of wood.

"What is it?"

"Let's find out, shall we?" Anne said, starting to move some of the rocks away.

Edward and some mates joined in and began removing the piled-up rocks and putting them aside. As they worked, the other crewmembers cleared the other corners. When they removed the topmost layers of debris, they found the same apparatus in each of the four corners. There was a large hollow wooden cylinder fashioned around a rock sticking out of the wall. On the end of the wooden circle there were four holes that could hold something in them. At both ends were metal grooves and stoppers, meant to stop the wooden part from being spun in a certain direction.

The process of clearing the rocks was sweaty, tiring work, and the air in the cavern was muggy. "I wonder what those are for," Edward asked, mopping his forehead, catching his breath, and grateful to be sitting down at last.

"They look like they can spin around," said Anne, also perspiring but not the least bit breathless. Edward couldn't help but admire her beauty even then. "They could be pulleys for use with ropes, but the purpose of that down here eludes me."

No sooner did the words leave Anne's lips than a great rumbling noise rose through the floor. Everyone sprang up, startled. The noise grew louder as the room shook violently. Cracks began to appear on the walls, and the shaking became so strong the crew could not keep their footing.

The wall in front of the ship began to crack and crumble near the ceiling, and fell three quarters of the way down before an abrupt stop. On the walls to the left and right, chunks of rock fell off, revealing four hidden compartments. Finally the shaking stopped, and everyone was able to rise from the ground. Edward, after reassuring himself no one was hurt, asked those on the ship what lay beyond the newly formed opening.

"It be water, Captain, and another tunnel. That be our way out," one crewman relayed back.

The problem is moving our ship up there. Whatever is in those compartments in the side walls must be the key.

Edward went over to one of the compartments and was able to see four iron poles and an incredibly long and thick bundle of rope. He picked up one of the iron poles to examine it. Before he could get a good look at it, the pole slipped out of his fingers and fell to the ground. With the impact, an explosion erupted inside the pole. It sounded like a gunshot and caused the pole to fly across the room, almost hitting a few people on the way.

"What in God's name was that? Everyone be careful with those iron poles!" Edward admonished. "They're dangerous." None sought to argue with his brief assessment.

Edward left the other poles alone for the time being and examined the rope. The rope was in a neat, untangled coil, but it was much too long and thick to be of any use to them on the ship. It was the same for the other three compartments that opened.

He picked up and examined one of the poles with caution. On one side, several holes went along the length of the pole with small plugs in them. Inside the holes he found black powder. Peering down the length he thought he could see flint attached to a long strand of rope.

That's what caused the explosion. It must work the same way as the cannons on the Freedom. Pull the rope and it moves the flint and ignites the black powder. How does this tie in? We have strange iron poles, the huge rope, and a system of pulleys—but what to pull? I suppose we can pull the ship, but how, and where?

Edward looked up to the loops of rock on the ceiling.

Maybe…

He turned to the crew. "Let's bring this to the ship, I want to try something."

While the crew worked to haul the rope on board, Edward went below decks and returned with a large iron javelin from the *Freedom*'s short-lived whaling days. He tied the rope to it and attempted to hurl it up into the hole in the ceiling.

He pulled back his large muscular arm, spread and bent his legs to maximise his potential strength, then released the javelin with all his might, almost falling with his great heave of a follow-through.

It fell far short of its mark.

Sam chuckled. "And you're supposed to be the smart one?"

Edward frowned. "It was worth a try. Do you have any bright ideas of how to get the rope into those holes?"

Sam just shrugged, and after a few moments of perplexity all round, John came forward. "One thing your father used to do was have a cannon shoot a javelin towards a hard-to-kill target. That was why he preferred metal to wood: it was sturdier."

"Let's try that then. Someone set up the cannon." Edward pulled the rope with the javelin back onboard. The rest of the crew packed gunpowder into a cannon of suitable size, and Edward pushed the javelin deep inside, packing it tighter. Once it was ready, he had one of the gunners aim it at the hole. The cannon fired and the javelin shot straight and true—for the most part—right to the mark, and then the rope fell to the floor as the crew on the ship held onto the other end.

"This will work. I want four teams down on the ground to tie that rope to the pulleys in the corners. Cannoneers, get the javelins from below deck, and repeat this procedure for the other three holes with the other rope we found in the compartments. Everyone else, start removing everything you can from the ship. We need to have the ship as light as possible."

Herbert raised his brow. "What are you planning?"

"We have to lift the ship into the air to move it over that wall. We'll use the pulleys to do it."

Herbert shook his head. "I hope you know what you're doing."

The crew who manned the cannons were able to shoot the javelins through the four rock semicircles in the ceiling after a few tries. Once the rope was lowered to the floor of the cavern, the crew on the ground tied them to the four pulleys.

The rest of the crew went about removing anything not tied down to the ship. A multitude of hands and enough rope allowed them to clear the ship within an hour. The hardest part was the cannons, which required several people to handle, and if they weren't careful, it could damage the ship during transport. They decided to leave the cannons on the gun deck and only remove those on the main deck and foredeck cabin.

Once everything was unloaded, the crew took the end of the rope not tied to the pulleys and snaked it through the gun deck of the ship. They made sure to weave it in and out of the port and starboard holes, which were used for the cannons, to help disperse the weight. Then they tied the rope together around the mast pole to secure it all.

"Do you think it will hold?"

Herbert scanned it over. "I don't know. The rope seems strong enough, and the weight should disperse enough now that we've removed all the cargo. If it doesn't hold, the keel is sure to break this time."

"Well, I don't see a better way. It's the only thing we can do."

The teams on the floor inserted the iron poles into the holes on the side of the pulley, and left a supply of gunpowder near each. When turned, the iron poles locked into place. Edward's theory was that if all the poles were fired at once the force would cause the cranks to spin, and move the ship up. When everything was set, Edward gave the order and the rope triggers were all pulled at once.

The simultaneous explosion of the poles sent out massive flares as they went red from the heat, and the force of it propelled the cranks forward and the ship upwards. The rope went taut and the wood creaked and groaned across the ship. Edward and the crew gritted their teeth in suspense. The ship moved up, slowly but surely, and within a few seconds stopped and hung suspended in the air. The crew let out a collective breath.

Edward instructed the four groups to fill each pole once more with the gunpowder. They had to repeat the process three more times before the ship was well above the rock wall they had to cross. The top mast was a hundred feet below the ceiling when Edward called the crew to a stop.

The whole crew was staring at their ship, their home, hanging in the air, moments away from ruin. One misstep, one hitch, and it would be destroyed. The attitude was somber, but they couldn't dwell on what ifs. Now was a time of action.

We've come this far. Now how do we move it into the water?

Everyone looked around for a clue as to what to do next. Edward was staring at the ship, and he noticed it was swaying slightly from the move upwards.

Hmm. That could work.

He turned to Herbert. "Herbert, from what you saw of the water, was there a current?"

"No, Captain."

"Good. Everyone, listen up! We need to move the ship into the water. To do that, we'll need excellent timing—and luck. What I need is to have everyone grab the rope from each of the pulleys, and start pulling on it. Those in the back of the room will be trying to pull the ship back in unison, and those in front pull the ship towards the water in unison. Hopefully we can get the ship to start rocking back and forth. Then, when we have enough of a swing, we'll release the pulleys and the ship should move into the water."

The crew eyed him like he was mad.

Edward sighed. "Does anyone else have a better idea?"

No one spoke up, so Edward began implementing his plan. He used hand signals to indicate to the two groups when to pull. At first the ship moved only slightly, but the more the men pulled the more the movement became a rocking motion.

As they continued, Edward could see the ship getting closer and closer to passing over the rock wall and then the water. Farther and farther it went over the line dividing the rooms. The stress of the situation transferred to the crew; the ever-looming threat of their home being in constant danger and the weight of the ship in their hands made their sweat hit the smooth stone ground like rain.

The ship moved back as far as it could, almost hitting the back wall, and Edward knew this was the moment. When it went past the halfway point of the room, he yelled "Now!" to release the pulleys.

The crew heard the order, and they hit the release mechanism at the perfect moment.

Save one.

The release mechanism on the front left pulley jammed, and the ship buckled to the side as it moved forward and down. If the rope wasn't released soon, the ship would smash against the wall.

Blackbeard's Ship

The ship was falling. Edward's ship, Edward's *Freedom*, his home, his crew's home. It was going to crash, and he could only watch as it did.

No!

Edward pulled his golden blade from its sheath. He planted his feet and reared his arm back. His arm, long and muscular, tightened and bulged as he drew all his strength into it. He threw the blade at the rope. It spun in the air almost like a top, the golden blur flashing in the torchlight.

The crew watched on in horror, every second passing with a thousand grim thoughts on top of a thousand others, making it seem to last for hours.

Edward let out a howl like a lion's battle cry, his eyes fixed on the sword.

The blade hit the rope, slicing through it like butter. The ship fell with a thunderous crash, and from both sides great waves surged up and soaked some of the crew. When the water cleared, the crew could see that the *Freedom* was in the water, and mostly unharmed.

Everyone cheered and released the tension they held within. Some grabbed drinks, others hugged their mates, and still others yelled and fired pistols into the air.

Edward went to Anne, pulled her close, and kissed her with unrivalled passion. He had his arms wrapped around her waist and nearly lifted her off the ground. After a split second of obligatory shock and outrage, she reciprocated with abandon, pulled him tighter, and kept her mouth pressed to his. The room grew silent, and, hearing the sudden hush, Edward and Anne turned their heads to see everyone staring at them, whereupon the whole crew burst into cheers and laughter once more. They were all in high spirits, and for a little while all thoughts of being trapped inside an island with a formidable enemy left them.

When the celebrating was done, the crew threw grappling hooks to the ship and boarded again. They brought aboard the cargo and iron poles, as Edward had an idea for making use of them. It took them another hour or so to have everything back to normal again.

"All right, everyone, now that we're all back on the ship we need to move on. We have a job to do, and there's one more trial to go before we have to face off against Smith. When that's over, then we can celebrate." The crew all crowded close to their captain, nodding their approval. "Now, let's move it! We have a battle to win!"

39. A CAPTAIN'S RESOLVE

They had to use oars to move the ship forward, as no wind was breezing through. It was similar to the first tunnel, but without a deadly current threatening them at every turn.

"I much prefer this relaxin' ride," Sam said.

Edward frowned. "Keep your wits about you; we don't know what tricks Benjamin might still have in store for us."

"Right," he said, as he glanced warily from side to side. "If you don't mind me askin,' Captain, who is this Benjamin ya be talkin' about?"

"He's the one who sold me this ship. The truth of the matter is, I don't remember him. I was drunk at the time. I must have showed him where I had my life savings, and then he left me this piecemeal ship."

"Sounds like this ship is only jus' beginning its adventure." Sam smiled and then laughed. He never seemed to be afraid of anything.

Looking at him, Edward thought it odd for the man to be a pirate. He was only a few years older than Edward himself. Edward knew how he himself was turned to this life, but not how Sam came to the same fortune—or misfortune, depending on outlook.

"Now I'll ask you a question. How did you become a pirate?"

Sam's blithe exuberance changed to thoughtfulness as he took a moment to consider the question. "I jus' always been. I never put thought to it, but I wanted to do something different, so I joined your fishin' group. Then, with all that's happened, I figured I 'ad no choice in the matter. Stayin with ye seemed like a good way to be entertained, and I haven' been disappointed yet."

"You've been a pirate all your life?"

"Fer as long as I can remember. I had powder or a cutlass in my hands since I wus a boy. Is all I know me whole life."

"How many people have you killed?"

Sam scratched his head. "Must be at least a hundred or so."

Edward couldn't help but feel somewhat sad for one who had lived this life since childhood. He would never have had a chance to play, to have friends as Edward had. He may not even have known his parents. Yet when Edward imagined himself having grown up as Sam did, he felt a strange excitement. He preferred to ignore that feeling.

"We only kill to survive here. If we can take a ship without killing anyone, we'll do so."

"Sometime you 'ave to show a little blood before they understand the consequences." Sam smiled and his eyes glinted.

"True."

Herbert called down from the helm. "Captain, you should take a look at this. Straight over the bow."

Edward turned his attention to the front, where the tunnel opened up into a massive dome-shaped room, with about two-thirds cut off at the left by a flat rock wall. In front of the *Freedom* there was a tall wooden barrier and a wall of rocks blocking the view of what lay beyond. "Let her swim!" Edward commanded. The crew stopped rowing and pulled in the oars. The ship floated forward until it hit the wooden barrier and bounced back a bit.

The rocks on either side of the barrier were large and round, with steps carved into them leading to a pedestal on the top of each. Edward felt safe in assuming that these rocks would show them how to open the wooden barrier, and much to the surprise of his crew, he stripped down to his trousers and dove off the starboard side into the cavern's icy water. He swam to the rock, climbed the slippery steps to the summit, and found, as he had expected, the next puzzle in Benjamin's game.

On the pedestal he saw a horizontal wheel with pegs all around it, almost like a ship's wheel, making a sort of circular tabletop. The points of a compass were painted around its edges, and a small wooden ship sat in the centre. There was also a metallic arrow pointing due north.

From his high vantage point, Edward could see past the wooden wall blocking his ship. A short distance beyond the wall he saw a miniature ship that looked like the *Freedom* sitting motionless in the water. It had full sails, and even miniature cannons and crew. It was surrounded on all sides by random sets of curved wooden barriers. The barriers were all over the water and seemed to make a maze, but it was disjointed. Some parts appeared to define a path, but it didn't have enough continuity anywhere to suggest a true maze. Near the centre, all the wooden barriers were absent.

That central area is probably where we need to send the model ship, but how to do it? I could jump into the water and move the ship myself, but that would be too easy. There must be something preventing us from doing just that.

Edward looked across the wooden wall to the other rock on the opposite side. On the top of it was a wooden pole sticking out of the rock, which he guessed to be the lever of a switch.

"Someone bring Herbert here with a few other crewmembers," he yelled back to the ship, "and get a couple of crewmen over to that other rock."

Herbert leapt overboard and proved himself a powerful swimmer. Nassir followed and helped Herbert up the steps to where Edward was, and Sam joined them. Two others stationed themselves at the second rock and awaited orders.

"I think what needs to happen," Herbert said, pointing to the replica ship, "is that boat over there needs to be moved to the middle of the maze for the barrier to be removed."

"I figured that much out myself," Edward said, to which Herbert responded with a look of irritation.

"So let's move it then!" Sam said, making to dive into the water past the rock.

"No, wait!" Edward grabbed him by the trousers, holding him almost suspended in the air.

The surface of the water roiled and broke, and crocodiles leaped out at Sam one after another. Their powerful jaws snapped at the tasty flesh about to offer itself to them. Edward pulled Sam back and threw him onto the wheel. Sam was wide-eyed and breathing heavily. The crocs were waiting and watching with only their cold beady eyes above the water.

Well, I guess we know why we can't move it ourselves.

"By the devil's beard, that was close! Thanks, Cap'n. Ye saved me life."

"Don't mention it. I knew it would have been too easy if we could do that," he said. "I wish to find out what that switch does before anything else." Edward motioned to the group on the other side to flip the switch, and together they pushed and pulled the large wooden pole as far as it would move.

When they flipped the switch, the fragmented walls of the maze sank into the water and another set of walls of equal incoherence replaced them.

It must be that both sets together are the full maze. This will make things tedious.

Edward reached out to turn the wheel and see what it would do, but before he could start it, the ground began to shake and rumble. He and the others grabbed the wheel to steady themselves. He searched for the cause of the quaking, and what he saw made his heart leap into his throat: the rock walls of the channel *Freedom* floated in were starting to close, and they would soon crush the ship and anyone aboard. Edward shot his gaze to the other rock. "Turn it back, quick!" The crew complied, and the maze shifted back, but the walls threatening the *Freedom* kept moving.

"Dammit! Move the wheel! We need to find out what it does."

As they turned the wheel, the crew on the ship was going mad. People were shouting and running. Some jumped off and into the water, trying to swim to safety on the spherical rocks. Others tried to contain the panic and calm the others, but to no avail.

Blackbeard's Ship

"Get yourselves together, men!" Edward yelled, his voice echoing off the walls. "You are members of my crew, and I will not tolerate such weakness! Put the ship broadside and fire the cannons at the wooden barrier to break it. Now get back on that ship and get to work!"

With a clear task to accomplish, and reassured by the words of their leader, the crew calmed down. The crew onboard help those who'd jumped off back aboard, and then placed oars into the water. Using the oars, they turned the ship so its broadside was facing the wooden barrier. They loaded the cannons and fired, trying to break the wooden barrier apart. The gunners kept firing again and again, but the large iron balls only made dents in the thick wood.

Edward gauged how fast the walls were closing in. They had ten minutes at best. "How's the miniature ship?" Edward asked.

"The wheel moves the red arrow of the compass on the table and opens up panels in the ceiling of the dome to let wind in," Herbert said as he pointed above. Beams of light shone in at different spots along the rock face of the dome. "This wind fills the sails on the miniature ship and allows it to move through the maze. Wherever the red needle of the compass is pointing is where the wind will blow."

Edward looked at the wheel and the compass once again, and took notice of the needle and the location of the holes in the ceiling. He nodded in silent agreement with what Herbert said.

"After we flipped the switch," Herbert continued, "a wooden box opened up at the centre of the maze. That's where we need to put the ship, I imagine. The problem is that at this angle it's hard to see the full maze. Not to mention only half the maze is showing at a time."

Herbert commanded the direction of the wheel, dictating the way the red arrow of the compass moved and in turn the direction the wind was blowing. They also had to switch back and forth between one setting of the maze and the other depending on what they needed to see.

The cannon fire was doing nothing to break the barrier, and the walls were closing in on the *Freedom* with each passing second. It was taking too long to complete the trial. Edward shouted: "Cease fire! Turn the ship back around! The walls are too close!"

The crew stopped the cannons and rowed the boat back to its original position. They only had a few minutes left before the walls would reach the ship and start to crush it. Fear was beginning to sculpt the lines of Edward's face. He watched as the miniature ship reached another dead end.

Dammit! We won't make it in time!

He turned back to the *Freedom*. "Throw me some grenades!"

The crew threw him grenade after grenade until he had six, and then a linstock for lighting them. He lit the grenades and threw them all in the water. They exploded a moment later with a thunderous boom and a splash of water. Edward drew his golden sword and, when the explosion subsided, put the blade between his teeth and dove in. He swam with the current made from the wind, peering this way and that, but the murky water made it impossible to see anything. The water chilled him to the bone; every stroke sent pain through him.

There was a flash to the left, an open jaw, and razor sharp teeth. Edward gripped the sword in his hand and thrust it deep. His arm was slow in the water, but the blade went through the croc like it was paper. Blood filled the water.

He had to come up for air. He splashed around, taking deep breaths. The crew was yelling to him; the rock walls were still edging closer and closer. He turned back.

He was at the edge of the maze. "Edward! To the right!" someone yelled, but it was too late.

The jaw snapped shut on Edward's stomach, and his whole side was engulfed in pain worse than the icy cold. He was losing blood and the creature wasn't letting go. He could see the croc's companions closing in faster, excited by the blood.

Edward stabbed the bold one right between the eyes. He swam and grabbed onto the nearest barrier of the maze and pulled himself up. The dead body of the crocodile still hung off his side. He pried the jaw open and threw the body back into the water. The other crocs savagely ate the dead one as soon as it fell.

Edward could see the hungry eyes of hundreds of them teeming in the water. The pain in his side throbbed. He hoisted himself up onto one of the walls of the maze, then leaped from wall to wall to avoid the creatures. The crocs followed him out of the water, snapping and making a terrible hissing noise from their open jaws as they swam toward him.

Edward was paying so much attention to where he was he didn't look where he was headed. He was closer to the ship, but now he didn't have anywhere else to jump. The water was too murky to see where the submerged wood was, and the hissing beasts were closing in on him.

"Flip the switch!" he yelled.

Slowly the other sections of the maze rose as Edward was lowered into the water. The crocodiles moved even quicker than before. He leapt to the raised sections, trying to put distance between himself and the bloodthirsty animals.

He stopped at the model ship now located in a dead end of the maze. He put the sword in its sheath at his side and picked up the ship off the water's surface with both hands. It was heavy and awkward in his wet hands. It was also hard for him to see where he was jumping now. Sweat and saltwater poured down his cold face. He kept up his pace, moving closer and closer to the centre of the maze. He called on the crew to pull the switch twice more as he jumped from wall to wall. The crocodiles were gaining on him.

And the walls were still closing in on the *Freedom*.

Edward was at the point where he could no longer move forward. The centre of the maze was right in front of him, and uncountable pairs of hungry eyes were right behind him. He jumped into the water with the ship still in hand and kicked his legs as quick as they would go. The crocodiles slipped past the wooden barriers, closing in on him at the centre. He reached the centre and pushed the ship into the wooden box.

Another wall closed on the wooden box and the whole thing lowered into the water, maze and all. Anything blocking him from the crocs also departed into the deep. The eyes closed in on him from all sides. He pulled out his sword, took a deep breath, and let himself sink.

Come on, then!

The crocs were only feet away from Edward when hundreds of iron balls began to fall into the water like rain. The multitude of bullets pelted the crocodiles around him, causing the water to turn red. Edward surfaced to see the crew alive and well, firing rifles on the beasts. They fought with all their determination to keep their captain, their friend, their brother, alive.

In mere moments, all the crocs were dead.

After it was done, Edward swam over and climbed up a rope ladder let down for him. "Thank you everyone, you saved my…"

Anne stopped him before he could finish. She placed her hands over his mouth. "It is we who owe you thanks, Ed. You saved our lives; we were merely returning the favor. We are family. How could we do any less?" She looked at the crew and they nodded in agreement with smiles on their faces.

Edward closed his eyes and smiled as well.

They turned the ship around and picked up Herbert and the others. The rock walls once threatening the *Freedom* had closed completely, and the wooden barrier was open like a gate, parted down the middle. When Edward asked what had happened when he put the ship in the box, they told him how the wooden barrier opened and allowed them to paddle out. As they headed to save him, the wall on the left side of the dome had fallen, but revealed another wall just like it.

I think I know what's happening. "Crew, listen up!" They all gathered around him. "On the other side of that wall is our enemy, Isaac

Smith. He's chased us all across the Caribbean for the past ten months and more, and he thinks he's got the better of us. I know we have the hardier crew, the superior ship, and the greater heart. We can win against him and end his terrorising of us today!" The crew roared approval. "And whatever happens, I want you all to know that you are the best crew anyone could ask for, and the best family a man could have." He smiled and put his hand out, palm down. "To *Freedom* and family!" Everyone reached out to put their hands on top of his, or on the shoulder of another crewmember.

"To *Freedom*… To family!" they repeated, as they lifted their hands into the air. To some of them, those words meant more to them than all the jewels, all the gold, all the treasure in the world.

They certainly did to Edward.

Now, as they all stood together on the deck of the *Freedom*, the earth began to shake and rumble once again, the second rock wall fell into the watery depths inside the island, and the H.M.S. *Pearl* stood revealed. The enemy ship turned towards them.

"All hands prepare for battle! It ends here!"

40. NO REGRETS

The *Pearl* and the *Freedom* approached one another. Their battle would soon begin. In the dome of the island, it felt as if they were the only two ships in the world, caught in an eternal battle in the centre of the earth: one representing justice and order, the other freedom and anarchy.

There could be only one victor.

Edward rushed to don the clothes of a captain: his tricorn hat, leather long jacket with white tunic beneath, black pantaloons, and leather boots. Fitting himself for battle, he tucked four pistols into his trousers and strapped two cutlasses to his sides, one of them the priceless weapon forged from the Golden Arm. In his hands he held a rifle, and to his back he strapped another in case he didn't have enough time to reload.

Having completed his preparations, he noticed Henry heading below deck.

"Henry, what are you doing?"

Henry stopped and turned to face Edward. He looked tired and worn, his eyes baggy and his brows sagging.

Henry let out a small sigh as he ran his fingers through his hair. "I cannot participate in this battle. I tried to fight them last time, but I can't kill these people, Edward. Every time I do, I see Robert's face."

"But… these marines aren't Robert," Edward pleaded. "I've said it before: he would understand."

"Would he? Would he really?" Henry snapped back, the fire returning in his eyes. "You think he would understand us killing marines? People like him? You think he would understand us stealing? You think he would understand us becoming pirates?"

"Henry…" Edward called, reaching out towards his friend.

"No, Edward!" Henry said, pushing away Edward's hand. "Robert wouldn't understand that. I'm fine when it's people like the Boddens, or those thugs that kidnapped Jack. I understand that and have learned to deal with it. But not this," he said, slowly shaking his head and closing his eyes. "Every time I try, I feel sick inside. Whatever comes, I'll see you at the end of this battle. I hope you don't lose yourself, Edward."

Henry turned and descended below deck, and Edward watched him leave. Edward gripped his rifle tighter and turned to the oncoming ship.

The ships drew abreast of each other.

"Fire!" Edward yelled. The crews on both ships let loose their cannons and guns. The smell of gunpowder filled the subterranean dome. The two ships circled each other as they fought. Cannonballs smashed through wood; splinters flew everywhere. Both ships had about the same number of crew, the same number of cannons, and the same strength. They were too evenly matched, and it was clear to Edward that neither could gain an advantage. He turned to the aft deck.

"Take us in close, Herbert!" Herbert nodded and flung the wheel to the side. "All hands prepare to board! We're taking the fight to them!"

The ship pitched hard to starboard and they pulled in the oars, letting the ship's momentum carry it. The marines saw this and duplicated the maneuver. Edward climbed up the main mast and grabbed a rope. Others did likewise at the different levels on each mast, waiting for the two ships to come closer together. When they were close enough to board, Edward yelled "To victory!" and swung off the mast to the other ship.

He landed in the middle of the main deck with a thunderous crash and a fierce grin that kept everyone at bay. Fear was evident in their eyes, and they thought twice about approaching.

Their hesitation would cost them.

Before anyone could make a move toward him, Edward pulled out and fired two of his pistols at the same time. Then, in one swift motion, he threw them away, spun around, and drew and fired another two. He had shot four marines in less than five seconds. Rising to his full height, he pulled out his two cutlasses.

The marines attacked him at once with their swords. Within moments, Edward noticed one person lagging. He weaved through the other marines' swords and slammed his shoulder into the weak link, pushing through the circle of death. With the other crewmembers boarding as well, the marines couldn't all focus on Edward. With several marines' attention moving to his crew, he found himself with more manageable numbers.

The sounds and smells of battle filled the dome. The two ships stood hull to hull, now locked together by hooks. Hundreds of men fought on the dual battleground.

At the foredeck of the *Freedom*, Anne and William were fighting several men, but neither side was attacking with weapons. The marines because they knew who Anne was, and William and Anne because they didn't want to harm marines.

William stood in front of Anne. Two of the marines went for his arms to disable him, but William kicked the first one in the chest, then grabbed the second one's arm and twisted it back. A third attacked him with the butt of a rifle. He threw the second man into him, knocking them both over.

Anne kicked a marine in the temple, knocking him unconscious. Another jumped her, pinning her down. She rolled with him and flipped him overboard. A third tried to lock her arms when she stood up. Anne twisted around, took the marine's arms with her and threw him into a group, knocking them all over.

"I don't know how long we can keep this up, Your Highness," William panted.

"We'll do it as long as it takes; I do not want their blood on my hands," she replied.

John, on the poop deck of the *Freedom*, fired his rifle at a marine trying to swing across from the other ship. The bullet hit the marine in the arm, and he released his rope and fell into the water. Another jumped over in front of John and charged. He thrust his bayonet deep into the man's chest. Yet another man jumped at his back when he wasn't paying attention. Nassir appeared out of nowhere and bashed the man on the head with a large block of wood.

"Thank you, Nassir!" John said.

"Do not mention it," Nassir replied with a quick smile.

One man jumped on Nassir's back and put him in a choke hold. He elbowed the man's chest, causing him to fall to the deck, clutching his ribs. Nassir swung with the large block of pine and hit the man in the face, knocking him out.

Back on the *Pearl*, Sam and a group from the *Freedom* were making their way across the stern. Sam swung his cutlass like a club at the first marine he saw and hit him in the neck, dropping him instantly. He fought without sparing a thought for technique or finesse, swinging wildly at anyone in the path of his blade. A marine attacked him from behind, and Sam spun and backhanded the man on the cheek, laughing like a hyena.

Pukuh was on the *Freedom*, spear in hand, dispatching men left and right as a paragon of an Eagle Warrior. One man lunged at him with a sword. He sidestepped and hit the man's nose with his elbow, breaking it. Another man attacked from the left. He thrust his spear into his chest. One more pointed a pistol at him and fired. He jumped into the air, flipped, and kicked the man in the face, landing on top of him. Those who faced Pukuh had fear in their eyes, some for the first time ever.

Edward, on the *Pearl*, was now confronted by two large men, each with swords as big as they were.

"Those don't seem standard issue, fellows." Edward made sure to keep his distance.

"We call 'em the whale killers," the one on the left said.

"We used to be sailors, but found the game was too easy," the other said.

"Well, it seems we have something in common. The name's Edward, but you can call me Blackbeard."

The one on the left spoke up again. "Catchy. I'm Donald, and this is me brother James."

James gave a slight bow. "Now that introductions have been concluded, let us have at it, shall we?"

The one called James lifted the huge whale killer over his head with both hands and threw it down at Edward, who jumped out of the way just in time for the blade to smash a hole into the deck of the ship. The wood cracked and splinters flew up as if a cannonball had ripped through it. Others in the marine crew saw the brothers fighting and gave them as wide a berth as possible.

And then a clear voice resounded over the din of battle.

"Stand down, men. That one's mine."

Isaac Smith walked down the ladder from the aft deck. There was blood on his sword, and a cut on his cheek. One of Edward's crew swung down on a rope and dropped in front of him. Smith kicked him in the face, sending him to the deck, unconscious. "So you call yourself Blackbeard now?"

"It's grown on me. Come to try to capture me again?"

"We're not here for you, Thatch. We came for the princess."

"I don't think she wants to leave with you, Smith."

"We'll see how much of a choice she has once you and your crew are dead."

"I'd like to see how you manage that."

Smith, sword already in hand, went to meet Edward. He raised his blade and swung it straight down. Edward used his two cutlasses to block it, but this allowed Smith to get in close and knee him in the stomach. He bent over in pain, and Smith uppercut him with his elbow, sending him staggering back.

Edward raised his head to see a blade being thrust straight at his eye. Instinct took over and he moved his head to the side and out of the way. The strokes of Smith's blade thrust and slashed at him in rapid succession, each blow aimed at his vital organs with surgical precision. He had to use everything in him to avoid the blade: his swords to parry, his legs to jump out of the way, and the weaving and bobbing of his body to dodge. He noticed the blade Smith was using was long, and as they moved it was difficult for Smith to maneuver in tight quarters. Edward led the captain around the mast, avoiding the strikes the whole way. He climbed backwards up the ladder, and left an opening for Smith to attack on purpose.

Smith struck downward; Edward smiled and moved out of the way, and the blade went past him and bit into the wood of the ship.

Smith struggled to pull it out but could not. Edward laughed and kicked the captain in the chest, sending him flying backward down the ladder. Smith flipped and fell onto the main deck, and Edward leapt down the ladder to finish him off. But Smith was quick to regain his wits and took a pistol from the belt of a fallen comrade.

Edward was running towards him, both cutlasses forward. Smith aimed his pistol at Edward. It could have been over in an instant for either of them.

"Hey, Smith!" a man yelled from the other ship.

Smith turned to see Henry jumping through the air, heading straight for him. It was too late to react. Henry had a rifle in his hand, but he held it like a club. He swung the rifle hard and the butt of it hit Smith across the cheek and nose. His nose broke on impact and he fell to the deck once more.

Edward went behind him and put his golden cutlass to Smith's throat. "Marines, stand down!" he yelled. "If you don't want a head-less captain, stop fighting!" He bent over and whispered to Smith: "This remind you of something, *Captain*?" He emphasised the last word, making Smith grit his teeth in anger.

The marines all looked at their captain, with Edward's sword one whisker away from fulfilling his promise, and Henry with a rifle pointed at Smith's gut for backup. They stopped, as commanded, and threw their weapons down.

It was over.

The pirates gathered the marines in the centre of the ship and bound them. Smith was put in with the group as well.

"Please don't kill my crew. You can take my head if you want, but leave my crew out of this. They were following orders."

"And why should I listen to you? You wouldn't listen to us in the beginning, and now here we are." He put the blade to Smith's neck once more, making him wince at its sharpness. "I'm not going to kill you, despite how you wronged me. Nor will I kill anyone else. We're done here." He turned to the *Freedom*. "John, tell Alexandre to bring over medicine and other supplies."

"Aye aye, Captain."

Edward turned his attention to Henry as the threat died down. "You saved my life, Henry," Edward said.

Henry clenched his jaw and looked away from Edward for a moment. "I'm sorry," he finally croaked. "I thought only of myself when you were all putting your lives on the line... I forgot what was most important."

Edward went up to his friend and smacked his shoulder. "I forgive you, old friend. I forget sometimes, too."

Edward and Henry clasped hands. The crew yelled loudly in triumph. This was the victory they had been wanting and waiting for.

Anne walked over to Edward, but he could tell by the restrained smile on her face something was wrong.

"What is it, Anne? We won."

"I know. I cannot help but think this is not the end. They were after me, Ed, and this will not stop them. They will keep chasing us."

"And we'll beat them each time they do," he replied, gripping her shoulder before pulling her into an embrace. "Come, let's go back to our ship and leave this cave."

Anne nodded and they walked together back over to the *Freedom*.

Edward consulted Herbert about how to leave the island. Herbert pointed to a square hole in the dome that appeared big enough for a ship to fit through. Light was pouring in through it, but water was flowing in from it as well.

The only issue was that the hole was two hundred feet up the dome.

"Hmm… That water is flowing towards us from the ocean, but the exit is up too high. We might be able to climb up, but we'll never leave with the *Freedom* as is. What do you think, Herbert?"

"I don't know how to get the *Freedom* up there. It doesn't seem possible. I examined the room as we were battling and I wasn't able to see any switches or tricks usually accompanying these trials," Herbert surmised. "And heading back isn't an option… We could wait for the water coming from the exit to fill this interior area, but at the rate it's falling we would run out of food before that happened."

"This is quite the predicament." Edward contemplated the dilemma for a bit when a thought occurred to him. "We're forgetting something. The key for the ship! Where is it?"

Edward could see nothing that might be holding a key—no pedestal, no out-of-reach niche that might be holding a chest. He looked at the openings in the ceiling, and then a glint of light struck his eye. In the centre of the dome a key was suspended in the air on a long chain. Edward climbed the rope ladder to the crow's nest, and then up the rest of the main mast. He guided Herbert in moving the ship until the key was within reach. He grasped the key and it pulled free.

The next step in the game was complete, and soon the whole ship would be his.

From his high perch, Edward noticed something else. The openings in the ceiling which had provided the wind to move the miniature ship through the maze were on both sides of the dome; the side where the H.M.S. *Pearl* had been waiting had similar openings to theirs. Edward recalled that manipulating the openings had caused slight changes in the wind inside, and to the flow of the water.

I wonder...

Edward climbed down and went to the starboard side. The crew was guarding the marines, and Alexandre and the military doctor were tending their wounds.

"Smith, did you have to solve a puzzle using a wheel to create wind and currents?"

"Yes, we had to navigate through a maze made of stone walls almost as tall as our ship," he said. "We had to relay orders to those manning the wheel to change the wind's direction. Why do you ask?"

"Because that is how we leave here."

Smith smiled. "Oh, aren't you the clever one."

Mock me all you want. We won.

"Have you puzzled out how to leave?" Herbert asked over the railing.

"I have an idea, but first I want to find out what this key leads to."

Edward went to the nearest locked door, to the stern cabin. He put the key in, it turned, and he opened the door and stepped inside. What he saw astonished him.

The stern cabin's decorations were opulent, to say the least. A large chandelier hung from the ceiling, and a red carpet covered the centre of the floor. At the sides were shelves built into the ship itself, filled with a great variety of books protected by glass. From the rarest fiction to all manner of nautical books and maps, it was a treasure in and of itself. The wood-panelled walls were perforated here and there by small windows to admit light and allow sight to the outside. Installed around the whole room were oil lamps of the finest quality, along with decorations of pistols and swords. In the middle of the room was a large, wooden, oval table with several chairs around it. On the far end of the table there was an ornate, high-backed chair with red upholstery trimmed in gold. It was, no doubt, the captain's chair for meetings.

He found the next clue for the game on the table in front of the captain's chair. It was in the form of a letter sealed with an imprint of a golden hunting horn. Edward didn't open it, but instead slipped it into his pocket. He left the cabin, locked the door behind him, and went to talk to Herbert.

Edward's idea for their escape involved the use of the wheels atop the pedestals. He placed several crewmembers at each, and had them set the compasses to point north so the wind was blowing towards the exit. As soon as the compasses faced north, something large clicked and the wheels fell into the rock and disappeared. More rock at all heights on the walls receded and water began gushing in from above. The water was coming in from the ocean and filling the interior of the island at a rapid rate.

"Everyone back on the ship!" Edward yelled, but the crew needed no convincing to rush back to the *Freedom*.

The crew glanced left and right, staring warily at the water pouring in, but after the shock subsided, their faces were brimming with joy. The water flowed into every crevice of the island and caused the ships to rise with it.

Herbert was astonished. "Whoever created this is brilliant! The placement of the openings is perfect."

"How could someone construct such a thing?" Edward exclaimed.

Herbert could not help bursting into laughter. "It would have taken years."

Edward, Herbert, and the crew gazed at the spectacle in front of them in awe. The water began causing eddies and a chaotic flow of the current, and Herbert came back to his senses.

He ordered men to furl the sails, and others to man oars, then yelled for the crew on the *Pearl* to do the same. For an hour, he masterfully directed the crews in shifting the ships away from the waterfalls, and circling the centre of the island, where the waves and current was the most stable. Through skill, and a little luck, the two ships avoided smashing into each other or the rock walls of the island's belly.

When it was over, the currents subsided, and the water had reached its peak. The exit was now level with the water *Freedom* and *Pearl* were floating in.

"Let's go!" Edward commanded.

Herbert ordered the crew to lower the sails of *Freedom* and *Pearl*, and the wind inside the island pushed the ships into the tunnel exit.

Anne came up to the deck with Edward and Herbert, and gave Edward a kiss. Anne and Edward held hands and gazed into each other's eyes as they passed through the short tunnel, exiting the island once and for all and entering the light of the world once again.

They didn't even notice the terror around them until it was too late.

"Captain. We have a problem," Herbert said.

"What is it?" Edward asked, but there was no reply. He followed Herbert's astonished gaze and thought he was seeing a mirage. Ships were at various distances from the island, ringing the horizon. Edward ran to the main deck, with Anne following on his heels. His mouth opened wide with shock as sweat poured down his face.

There had to be over a hundred ships approaching from every

direction. Edward took out a spyglass and examined the flags. They were royal navy ships of varying classes and armament.

"This can't be happening," Edward whispered.

Before Edward could even think of a plan, four ships of equal size, all of them larger than the *Freedom*, surrounded the pirates. They flew the flags of the three divisions of the navy, White, Red, and Blue. The fourth ship was flying the general flag of the navy, the flags of the naval divisions, the flag of Denmark, and finally the British flag at the top.

Before anyone even realised it, four men jumped onto the starboard side of the *Freedom*, one of them in the lead, the others close behind. All of them wore ornate uniforms with an abundance of medals on their chests and insignias of rank on their shoulders.

At the rear, on the leader's left, was a well-built man wearing a white suit and white gloves. Clean-shaven and immaculately groomed, with slicked-back black hair, a strong chin and pleasing features, he would be considered handsome by many. He projected an air of something like smugness, or perhaps disgust, to the pirates in front of him. He held his gloved hands in front of him, palms out, as if disdaining to soil them through contact with the world or even his own clothes. He was the youngest of the four, but his perfect poise suggested a dangerous power like a coiled snake ready to strike at a moment's notice.

He was Sir George Rooke, the Admiral of the White.

The man in the middle was elderly and rather frail-looking, with grey hair, a full grey beard, and a furrowed face. He wore a deep red suit with more decorated medals than those of his fellows, and carried a cane of ornate design. His carriage belied his fragile look: he held his gaunt body erect, took in everything with a glance—nothing escaped the wrinkled slits of his eyes—and was quick in his reactions, almost to the point of precognition.

He was Sir Cloudesley Shovell, the Admiral of the Red.

The man on the right, clad in deep blue, was both tall and rotund in the excess, suggesting a greater-than-normal appetite. He had a round face with several rolls under his chin, and a large moustache curled up across his cheeks. He wore a bulky powdered wig reaching down to his shoulders. In one hand he had a chicken leg, from which he ate heartily as he glanced about with nonchalance bordering on malaise.

He was Sir Strafford Fairborne, the Admiral of the Blue.

In front of these three was a man dressed in black and gold. He, of all of them, was the least to be trifled with. Clean-shaven but for a well-trimmed goatee, with chiseled features and a superbly formed body emphasised by his fitted uniform, his extraordinary physical power was unmistakable. But his eyes were the key to him: in them a lion lay in wait, too self-possessed to search for prey, but ready to move with infallible precision and speed should it appear. His whole bearing seemed to create, in whatever setting he might find himself, a still point of invulnerable calm—and, for those with reason to fear, of danger.

The man was Prince George of Denmark and Norway, Duke of Chamberland, Lord High Admiral, husband to Queen Anne.

Edward knew who these men were by the ranks on their shoulders, even though he did not know their names. There was no mistaking the four most powerful men in England, and no mistaking the fact that Edward Thatch now had absolutely no way to escape. The *Freedom* had been defeated before its captain and crew even realised the situation they were in.

"Father!" Anne stood immobile, rooted to the deck in shock.

Prince George ignored his daughter and stared straight at Edward. "I trust you know why we are here?"

Edward stood to his full height. "Aye," he replied. "What will happen to my crew?"

"If you cooperate with us, you will all have a trial in Great Britain. If you make things difficult, you can guess what will happen."

Edward's eyes darted left and right in a last desperate search for a way out, but it was futile. Four battleships surrounded the two smaller ships, the *Freedom* and the H.M.S. *Pearl*, and beyond them lay over a hundred warships in the distance.

"Father, please let them go. I joined them willingly. They did not kidnap me," Anne explained.

"They are pirates, my dear, sweet Anne. In what world would we ever let them go now? They will be tried, and the world will see justice served to the criminals who kidnapped you. Then life will move on. Now come with us."

"Let's negotiate something here!" Edward said. "I'm sure we can make a compromise that would benefit everyone."

Prince George responded with a dry laugh, but before he could say anything, one of Edward's crew spoke up. "I can't let you do that, Captain." It was Jack. He had a rifle in his hands and was pointing it at George Rooke, Admiral of the White. "I cannot allow this man to live."

"Jack! Put the weapon down, you fool! Do you not see the situation we are in?"

"I understand, Captain, but that man…" He stared at Rooke with an intensity of malice none could understand save him. "That man…" He couldn't utter the reason for his hatred, but everyone could see that he was trembling and on the verge of tears. "He's a dead man!" he yelled, and fired.

In the instant the gun went off, George Rooke disappeared

from sight. The bullet went past where he had stood and hit the side of the *Freedom*. Immediately Rooke was in front of Jack. His eyes went wide with shock, and then he gritted his teeth in anger as he thrust the rifle's bayonet forward. Rooke sidestepped and kicked the gun out of his hands, sending them up into the air with the force. Rooke delivered another kick to his face which sent him flying to the mast where he hit it with a thud. He fell to the deck unconscious.

The *Freedom*'s men pulled their weapons on the admiral. The other admirals all pulled out their weapons.

"Stand down!" Edward yelled. For Edward's crew, his words carried a force not to be resisted, and all of them immediately put their weapons away.

Edward turned back to Prince George and knelt down on the deck. He prostrated himself before the powers of the British navy, bowing his head before them.

"I beg of you, please allow my crew to leave alive. For this favor, I offer myself to you."

Prince George looked beyond his daughter to the tall, proud man begging for the lives of the crew he loved.

"And why should we release them and take only you? Who are you that your life can substitute for all of theirs?"

Edward looked up to the man before him, his eyes speaking the resolve in his heart. "I am Edward Thatch, the dread pirate Blackbeard, and I am the captain of the ship known as *Freedom*. Surely I alone could serve as warning to other pirates that dare cross the British Navy?" he questioned. "Consider this the last wish of a dying man."

"Well said." The prince turned to George Rooke. "Rooke, stand down. This fight is over."

Rooke nodded. Holding his gloved hands fastidiously in front of him, he went back to the side of the other admirals.

"Edward Thatch... Blackbeard," Prince George declared for all to hear, "I hereby arrest you for the kidnapping of Princess Anne Sophia Stewart, daughter of the Queen of England. You will be imprisoned, tried, and put to death as the mastermind behind the kidnapping. The ship will be confiscated and the crew released— save one." He looked at William.

William hung his head in shame as he walked up beside Edward. Edward turned to him, but William shook his head. He would go willingly.

"Father, please!" Anne begged, but her words and tears went unheeded.

Prince George waved for one of the ships to come around. The battleship drew up beside the *Freedom*, and the crew placed gangplanks between them. Several marines came over and, at Prince George's instructions, bound Edward and William in irons.

"May I have a few words with my crew?"

"Of course. Men." Prince George motioned to his men and they backed off.

Edward turned to his crew. He saw the confused and stricken looks on their faces. Some had been there since the beginning, all the months at sea, through all the battles and trials. Others, though their time aboard was short, knew they had experienced the greatest adventure of their lives. They all looked at him standing there, ready to die, and felt an unbearable sadness.

Edward gazed upon them all—from Alexandre, tending to Jack, yet looking up to him, to Pukuh, the stoic warrior who understood more than any other his resolve.

"Ed, there must be some other way!" Henry pleaded.

"Sorry, Henry, but there isn't. This is all we can do. Use this freedom the prince is giving you to live full lives. Don't do anything stupid while I'm gone." Edward smiled for the last time to his crew. "Goodbye."

And with that he turned and walked away.

He heard voices crying his name and his title behind him as he walked toward the gangplank. Tears fell from the eyes of many on that ship as they watched their captain, the man who had brought them together and fought for them to the very end, go to his death.

Anne stood beside the gangplank. Her eyes had never left Edward's face. He walked over to her. The marines put up their guard, but Prince George motioned for them to stop. "I won't have another chance to say this to you, Anne, so I'll say it now." Edward leaned in and whispered something into her ear, and then walked across the gangplank to the marine battleship.

Anne's eyes widened and she stood, stunned and motionless. Her father moved close to her and spoke softly. "Do not let him see your tears, my dear. Do not make him regret his decision this day." Then he led her across the gangplank.

The naval crew took Edward to the ladder leading down to the brig of the battleship. "Take care of my *Freedom* for me," he said to Prince George. The prince nodded as they took Edward below. He went down into darkness.

The final words Edward had whispered to Anne lingered in her mind and heart. They resonated and grew until she couldn't bear it any longer. She fell to the floor of the battleship in tears.

"I love you too, Edward!"

THE END

BOOK TWO OF
THE VOYAGES OF QUEEN
ANNE'S REVENGE

BLACKBEARD'S
REVENGE

PROLOGUE

The sun sent a gift of heat and light down in waves upon the open sea. Storm clouds advancing from the east, and the growing winds, were the only reprieve from the scorching.

"Cap'n, there be a storm brewin'," the helmsman said over his shoulder.

A tall, well-built man sauntered up beside the helmsman, a distinctive snap sounding as he thrust his one wooden leg to the lumber of the ship. A pipe was in his mouth and he blew great puffs of smoke into the air, carried off by the rising winds. His dark, grungy, salt-and-pepper hair was held in by a tricorn hat and covered his wrinkled, piercing eyes. The hair did not cloud his vision as he peered at the clouds. The man let the sea air into his nostrils with an almost animal ferocity.

"Aye, but she be a storm of man, not the Lord." After taking another puff of the weed and eyeing the east, he turned his attention to the crew. "Hoist the sails! A guest is comin' and he's not the type to be left waitin'."

None questioned the peculiar message from their captain. The crew was fully aware of his perception and long since past wondering how he divined his knowledge. And, as if to reward their blind faith, a ship approached from the east.

The ship, a second-rate ship according to the British Navy's standards, flew no flag and carried no mark of distinction to any country or man. Nearly one hundred guns over three decks and with a crew of over seven hundred souls made the ship fearsome to behold. A ship so large should be hard-pressed to manoeuvre delicately, but it moved as deftly and gracefully as a swan in a pond. The second ship sailed next to the first ship so close they appeared as one from afar.

If the second ship moved like a swan, then the captain was a falcon. He gracefully jumped across the railings to the waist of the first ship. As he passed, the crew of the first ship removed their caps or bent their knees. The second captain paid the crew no heed and headed straight to the helm where the first captain still stood.

"Leave us, Bertram," the first captain ordered the helmsman. "These old sods need to have a conversation."

"Aye, Captain." Bertram locked the helm and left.

The second captain threw the first captain a bottle of aged

scotch.

"You come bearing gifts?" The first captain asked, then took a long swig of the scotch while walking to the middle of the quarter-deck. "So, am I in the presence of the Lord of Gifts today? Or Stormbringer?" The first captain gestured wildly. "Benjamin perhaps, or Albert? The Red Hand, or the Golden Horn? Or what is it you're called these days? … John? … Jack?"

The second captain raised his eyes for the first time, showing his aged face. "What about in the presence of a friend?" The man smiled, showing more wrinkles. He was well groomed with short black hair and a few grey hairs peeking through. His eyes, though softened in the presence of a friend, were just as piercing, if not more so.

The first laughed heartily. "Of course!" He grabbed the second man and the two hugged each other tightly. The first eventually pulled away and held the second at arm's length. "You are always a friend, and always welcome."

The two sat leisurely and passed the scotch and weed back and forth. Once the introduction was complete, the crews lost their formality and reserve and mingled together, swapping stories and alcohol like best friends reunited.

When the weed was spent and the scotch, like the stories, nearly depleted, the first captain decided to start business. "So, Benjamin, what brings ye here? Not playing dog today, are ye?"

Benjamin laughed bitterly. "No, not today. I've arrived to ask a favour if I may be so presumptuous."

"Speak and it shall be done. You know I can never refuse the Golden Horn's will."

"Even if the Gold is tarnished?" Benjamin cast down his eyes.

"Tarnished Gold is still Gold, no?" the captain said with a laugh hoarse from age and too much pipe.

Benjamin's smile was melancholic. "I suppose so." He took another swig of the scotch before passing the bottle back to the captain. "Have you heard news of my successor?"

Despite the din of the two crews, despite the storm which now surrounded the horizon, despite all the noise, the word *successor* caused a hush to spread over the two ships. Those drunk instantly sobered, and those laughing became silent. All eyes turned, and all ears perked, towards the two captains.

"I never thought I would see the day." The captain opened the scotch bottle and finished the remainder in one great gulp.

"You know of whom I speak?"

"Aye, I heard 'bout a fledgling youngster causin' a stir in the New World and Old. Uses your old ship, fer God's sake, of course I know who yer talking 'bout." The old man laughed hoarsely. "Need me to show him how things were done in our age?"

"No, he's running errands right now. I need him to remain unspoiled before he's ready to hatch, but my sources tell me the Black Plague is moving on the boy as we speak."

At the mention of "Black Plague" the first captain held fast for a moment before solemnly setting the empty bottle on the deck with a clang. "That is bad news. The egg is liable to be broken if the Plague ain't stopped."

"Exactly. Thus, I am asking you to stop Plague. I am asking you, William Kidd, the Tsunami, to do this for me." Benjamin's nonchalant demeanour belied the gravity of his request.

The crews, mainly silent until then, began whispering amongst themselves on the events unfolding.

"You're askin' for a lot," Kidd replied.

"I would not ask anything of you I believed you could not accomplish."

"Aye, even at yer boldest, yer reasonable. So, what do ye want me to do? Kill him?"

"No, just keep him occupied until the egg is ready, or cripple him, whichever you prefer," Benjamin smirked.

"And how will I find this egg of yours to keep an eye on him?"

"I have someone on the inside. They can provide you with updates on his whereabouts."

Kidd nodded, rose and strode to the edge of the quarterdeck, overlooking the crew. "Ready yerselves, boys! Soon we see if a Tsunami can stop the Plague. By the Sound of the Golden Horn!"

"By the Sound of the Golden Horn!" The crews repeated, raising their glasses and bottles before drinking. The old hymn was the battle cry from the olden days when all the world's best pirates followed Benjamin Hornigold, and it meant Kidd's crew approved of the deal struck.

The two crews separated soon after, knowing full well a great battle would soon happen between William Kidd, one of the Pirate Warlords who fought in the War of the Horns, and Edward Russell, one of the Immortal Seven, the Admiral of the Black.

1. CATCH TWO & TWENTY

Six Weeks Ago

The guard kicked a large plate of food, or something akin to food, into the prison cell. The plate clanged as it skid through a slot at the bottom of steel grates and across the dingy stone floor.

The guard's lamp illuminated the food and the men in the cell. The prisoners closest to the grate—rough, filthy men—shielded their eyes from the faint light. Satisfied, the guard moved on, leaving the lamp in the corner opposite the cell, illuminating just enough to eat by.

The prisoners' bodies were caked with dirt, bones exposed due to lack of muscle and fat, and their beards and hair unshaven. Bruises covered their bodies from beatings, white and red disfigurement peppered their flesh from the hot iron, and long bloody messes covered equally long scars on their backs from the lash. Craven sinners rotting in desolation in their communal hell.

Despite their ravenous hunger, none dared to move. *He* hadn't taken his share yet.

A man of above average stature and build slowly rose. His once-tanned skin was now lightened by lack of exposure, his strong arms were thinner from poor food and exercise, and his wavy black hair and long black beard matted with grease. Though his form was diminished, his spirit was not. His eyes carried the same strength as a year ago, and kept the devils of the prison at bay.

Edward Thatch sauntered to the plate of food and took his share, along with some for two others. Edward took what he needed, then sat back down in the dark of the cell. After he was seated the frenzy began, the strongest and fiercest fighting for their pathetic morsels.

Edward handed a share to an old man, and another to a young boy. Together the three ate in reflective silence after the fighting in the cell stopped.

The prison was made of hard grey stone hastily assembled with no regard for comfort. The stones were misshapen and set haphazardly, making sitting and sleeping a chore. Water leaked in from God knows where, causing an incessant drip, drip, sound every few seconds which lent to the dank atmosphere and stagnant smell. No fresh air could creep its way down to the basement and through the sweat and odour from thousands of days of compounded sweat and faeces.

"Can you tell me another story, Edward? Please?" the boy asked, as he had almost every day before.

The child's small frame belied his imaginative and intelligent mind. He was not yet aged enough to grow facial hair, but the blond hair on his head was long and shaggy from the years he'd spent in the dungeon. He was born in this prison and protected by his mother until she died. He had heard stories about the sun and sea and the outside world, but never saw them firsthand.

"Perhaps later, Edmond. A year has passed since I last laid eyes on the sun and my beloved. I feel I need time to reflect." Edward slowly ate the mouldy bread and gruel.

"Now, are you referring to the vast and untameable ocean, or your beloved Anne?" The old man on the other side of Edward spoke up.

The grey-haired gentleman possessed a beard longer than Edward's, a sharp nose, and keen eyes not yet dulled by his old age. When Edward arrived, the elder was nearing death's door, not having the strength to fight for his portion of food and relying on leftover scraps. Edward fought for the old man, and now he had a little skin on his bones and more strength to lend to his wisdom.

Edward chuckled at the old man's penetrating question. *Maybe both, Charles.* Edward's mind drifted to Anne, his love. The last time Edward had seen Anne was after he was captured and forced into the brig of a battleship. A fleet of warships from the British Navy descended on Edward and his group of pirates aboard his ship, the *Freedom*. The fleet was there to 'save' Anne, the daughter of the Queen of England.

Anne's father was gracious enough to take Edward but freed his crew as a last request. And, by Edward's estimation, it was only due to Anne's pleading to her mother that he was imprisoned instead of being executed. During his prison term, Edward had had a hard time deciding which would have been the worse fate.

Another man, large in stature but too thinned by malnutrition, also laughed, but haughtily. "That's all ye have left: stories. No use thinkin' bout them no more. We ain't leavin' here, least of all a little shit as you."

Even through the long hair and beard the man showed his yellow and grungy teeth in a sneer. His face and body were square in appearance, and in his prime he might have taken the appearance of a wall when standing.

He sat with his hands draped over his knees as he gestured to their surroundings. "This is the hell of hells. No one sent here will ever be let free because of our 'crimes against the state.' Any who think we's gonna be leavin' here is a sorry sod indeed."

"No one asked you, Simon." Edward, sitting cross-legged, turned his scornful gaze to the middle-aged man. Most would flinch and think twice about what they said after Edward's stare, but not Simon.

"Yea, well I's tired of hearing talk about the outside. Talk of the like is no use to us here. Jus' brings back bad memories."

"There's no harm in allowing the boy to dream."

"There's always harm in dreamin'. See where dreamin' got you. We all heard the story: You wanted freedom, so ye fought against the marines and ye ended up here. Nothing good never came from dreamin'."

"You're wrong, Simon. The realisation of the dream was the cause of our downfall. If I hadn't tried to achieve my dreams then I wouldn't have ended up here, but because I did this is the inevitable cause. And if you only dreamed of your revolution, instead of being a fool and lighting a bomb, you wouldn't be here."

Simon rose from his seated position and Edward followed suit, meeting him in the middle of the small cage. "Who're you callin' a fool, you dunderwhelp!"

At Edward's six-foot-four height, the top of Simon's head barely reached Edward's chin. "Careful what you say, Simon. I might break your other arm this time. Remember how long the first one took to heal?"

Prisoners in other cages whispered amongst one another at the beginnings of the fight. Several in Edward's cage also goaded the two on. The guard heard the commotion and smacked his club against the bars.

"What did I tell you twos 'bout fighting? Stop this nonsense or the both of ya get ten lashes."

Edward and Simon didn't turn their attention to the guard, but both knew he would follow through on his threat if they didn't sit back down.

"You heard the man, Simon. Sit down before you're hurt," Edward said.

Simon spat on the ground before turning back and sitting back against the wall. Edward nodded to the guard and he too sat down again.

Before the guard moved on, a noise echoed down the dark hallway near the stairs. The guard ran to investigate, his keys and weapons clinking and clanging as he moved. When the guard reached the foot of the stairs, he jerked back with muffled "Oof!" and dropped to the stone floor with a crack, knocked unconscious, or dead.

A dark figure jumped on top of the body and started rummaging around for something until another, taller figure stepped out of the stairwell.

All the prisoners with enough strength pressed their faces against the iron bars to catch a glimpse at what was happening.

"Hurry up, Princess," the taller one scolded. "We need to be outta here before they're done pissin'."

The first one grabbed the keys off the belt of the unconscious guard and turned to the taller one. "You think I'm not aware, Sam? Who was the one who created this plan? Now we need to find Edward's cell, so help me search."

Until now, Edward had had merely a passing interest in the event. One or two ill-formed attempts at escape happened during his year of imprisonment, and both failed. But the keywords *Princess*, *Sam*, and, of course, *Edward*, piqued his interest now. He also felt sure he'd heard those voices before.

Edward ran to the cell bars. "Anne?" he yelled.

At the calling of the name, the two figures snapped their heads around and ran over to Edward's cell. The small one passed the keys to the tall one and grabbed Edward's outstretched hands.

Edward could see the face of the one he loved in the faint light. Anne's curly red hair glistened from under her hood, and her ocean green eyes glittered from newly forming tears. She kissed Edward's palms and held them close to her face as if she were trying to impart, or take, every bit of warmth she could.

Despite Edward's dark reverie, he could not help but be brought out of his gloom and into Anne's light. She was as an angel in front of Edward. Every second felt like eternity as if to accentuate the horribly long time Edward and Anne had been torn apart, and yet eternity was not enough.

"What are you two doing here?" Edward finally asked, pulling himself back to earth.

Sam, working the keys one by one, spoke first. His straight black hair and smooth, pretty face had not changed in the year since parting. "We're here to save ya, mate! This be a prison break." Nor had his confidence bordering on arrogance changed either, apparently.

"Oh, is that why you stole the keys? I assumed you would become a guard for a moment." Edward's comment was full of sarcasm. Sam stared at Edward with eyes as cold as stone at midnight before continuing with the multitude of keys. "I mean *why*. Why are you both here?"

"Is not the action and reason the same? We wish to see you free, my dear, sweet Edward."

Edward pulled away from Anne's soft cheeks and sat back down against the back of the cell. "You had better leave before someone catches you then. I'm not leaving."

"What d'ya mean yer not going?" Sam said, losing his place with the keys out of shock.

"I think the words are fairly clear, are they not? I do not wish to join you, so please leave, unless you want to become a cell mate."

Sam turned to Anne and threw his hands up in the air, exasperated. "What now, Princess?"

"Work the keys, I'll handle this," Anne instructed with gritted teeth. "Edward, as much as I'm sure you've grown accustomed with your new surroundings, your family and I went through much trouble to be here, so, please, forestall any objections and join us."

"Why bother when the end result will bring me back here sooner or later?"

"So you believe what we are doing is futile? You believe freedom is futile?"

"I've enjoyed a lot of time to think here, Anne, and despite my bitterness over what has happened, I see no future for me on the sea. If I escape here, I will be hunted down and imprisoned again, or worse, killed. If I am captured at present, then what else can be done to me?"

"You feel there is no future for you? For us?" Anne held Edward's gaze, but Edward turned away. "No, I do not," he replied. "At least, not one ending without pain."

Anne's face fell. The sound of hastened footsteps at the stairs caught Anne's attention, so she ran to the edge of the stair opening with a knife drawn. When a large, well-built man emerged, Anne threatened him with the knife, but then lowered the weapon and began speaking with the man in hushed tones. Edward was not able to make out who the man was because of the little light, but judging from the closeness Anne shared, and his build, Edward had an idea.

The man walked over with Anne at his side, and when he reached the cell he lifted his hood so Edward could see his face. "Now what is this I hear about not wanting to leave?"

In front of the cell a man of Edward's age, twenty or one and twenty years, stood tall and large. He was shorter than Edward, but more toughly built, especially being well fed. His straight brown hair was tied back, and his strong jaw, like his crossed arms, were set as stone.

"Henry! You, as well?" Henry, Edward's childhood friend, had joined Edward on his first flight of freedom as whalers before they were accidentally branded pirates.

"Yes, I am here, as are two others of the crew. And John is waiting for us with horse and carriage as well. Will you stop being foolish and join us now that you are fully aware of the gravity of the situation?"

Edward crossed his arms in mirror to Henry, in direct defiance.

"No. As I told Anne, I do not see the point in being captured again. I'm choosing to end the cycle here. Leave me be before you are forced to join me in my torment."

Henry considered Edward's words for a quick moment before laughing almost too loudly. Edward thought Henry to be mad, and from the looks on Anne and Sam's faces so did they.

"Apologies, Henry, but I do not see the humour in this situation," Anne said.

Henry looked at Anne, but pointed to Edward. "He's lying," Henry proclaimed. "You would have noticed if you'd known him as long as I. He's still acting chivalrous for our sakes. He's been so long here he doesn't think anyone can escape, and wants us to leave before anything happens."

"I'm not lying, Henry. You don't know me as well as you think. Run while you still can."

Anne nodded, the three ignoring Edward's pleas. "So what do you propose we do?" Anne questioned with one hand in the air, palm up.

"We force his hand." Henry sat down on the stone, folding his legs to get comfortable.

Anne grinned and joined Henry, and Sam shrugged his shoulders and made a sarcastic comment before sitting as well. The three faced the cell, watching Edward with nonchalance bordering on indifference.

"What are you doing? You must make haste before the guards find you."

The trio didn't move an inch, their bodies and faces becoming as the stone in the prison itself.

Edward stood up. "I don't want to go with you, don't you see? We are no longer friends, comrades, or family."

None responded despite the biting remarks Edward made.

The noise of several footsteps sounded against the hard stone stairs, signalling guards on the way.

Edward jumped to the bars, gripping them hard until his knuckles turned white. "You must flee, now!"

The three did not react, and simply gazed at Edward, calling for action with their eyes. Sweat trickled down Edward's face when two armed guards descended from above.

The guards, their muskets pointed at the three, shouted orders to clasp their hands behind their heads. Henry, Anne, and Sam all relented to the orders, and then rose at another command. One guard guided them away in front, with the second forcing them forward with his musket.

The three were about to be resigned to a fate Edward would not wish upon any, their freedom stripped and their spirits ripped from pain and anguish.

Deep down, in his heart of hearts, no matter what Edward said, he wanted to be free as well. For most of his life, Edward suffered an oppressive, unloving step-family, so even when he was branded a pirate and chased across the Caribbean, even when the world was at its bleakest, he was still free on that ship with those he cared about. Because of the consequences of his decision, his heart and mind struggled for and against the freedom he desired.

But today... today, the heart won.

"Take me with you! I want to be free with you, my family!" Edward shouted, his words resounding across the floor and then some.

Anne, Henry, and Sam smiled.

The guards were momentarily distracted by Edward's outcry, and the three took that chance to strike.

Anne spun around, gripped the muzzle of one guard's musket, and thrust it upwards. The musket smashed into the guard's nose, breaking it. As the guard clutched his nose, taken aback by the blow, Sam jumped around Anne and punched the guard square in the jaw, knocking him unconscious.

Henry held the other guard in a headlock. The guard dropped his musket and struggled to pull Henry's massive biceps away, but it was no use. The guard elbowed Henry in the ribs again and again. Henry endured as long as he could, but lost his grip and the guard broke free.

The guard pulled himself away and drew a deep breath. The man was about to cry out for his comrades on the upper floor when Anne whipped out a knife and flung it at the guard. The knife hit the man in the back of the head, his cry turning into a grunt as he fell to the floor dead.

With the guards dispatched, the trio ran back to the cell together, Anne and Henry grabbing each of Edward's arms in a desperate embrace.

Henry beamed at his best friend in all the world. "Let's set you free, brother."

2. GAMMOND CASTLE

"That's the key. Yes, that one," Edward confirmed, guiding Sam to one key among the multitude.

"How can ya tell? They all look the same!" Sam said, but he did not doubt the validity of Edward's statement, as he stuck the key into the lock.

"I've been here a year. I had to occupy my mind somehow."

Sam turned the key and it opened with a click. He pulled back the door and all the prisoners tried to rush out at once. Sam and Henry pushed the door closed again as Edward tried to calm them and keep their rabid grasps from his friends.

"What are you doing?" Edward yelled above the clatter in his cell. "Quiet!" Edward commanded, silencing the prisoners.

"We cannot take them with us. We can escape with you, and maybe one other," Anne explained coldly.

Edward considered Anne for a moment. Anne must have planned his escape for months, maybe even the whole year since he was imprisoned. Edward glanced at the boy Edmond and the old man Charles. *I can't leave them.*

Anne placed her hand over her eyes in frustration and shook her head. "I didn't plan for this. What do you suggest?"

"We free all the prisoners. The storm will be too much for the guards to handle. Besides, I will not leave without my belongings. The warden has my sword at his hip, so I will kill him and retrieve it."

"You would kill an innocent man?" Henry said in shock.

Edward turned his back, revealing the scars of previous beatings. "You think an innocent man could order people to do this?" Edward glanced at his cell mates, all of them itching to leave. "We do not have the time to argue, we lost too much from *my* stubbornness."

Anne sighed. "Fine, let us free them all."

As Sam was readying to open the door once more, Edward turned to the group of cutthroats and revolutionaries of varying ages in his cell. "You will all wait until the other prisoners are released. If we all leave as one then we will overwhelm the guards. They will stand no chance if we work together."

"For once, we agree on sumthin'," Simon declared. "If any try to skip before we are ready, I'll be breakin' their legs."

Sam opened the door, and instead of the rush as before, the prisoners left in an orderly fashion, warily glancing at the leaders of the escape when passing. Edward moved to the back, where Edmond and Charles sat motionless, but wide eyed.

"Today you will realise your wish, Edmond," Edward said, making the young boy smile. "Let's move, old man." Edward lifted Charles up and pulled the old man's arm over his shoulder for support. Edward carried Charles to the door, where Sam, Henry, and Anne waited. "Here, Sam, help this man, will you? I'll take the keys."

Edward and Sam swapped their cargo, with minor grumbling from the latter, and Edward took his first step from the cell that had been his home for a year. He left the cell to embrace his friend, Henry, and his love, Anne. The embrace was short, but more than sweet.

"I take the geezer and they get hugs. A little unfair, ain't it?" Sam asked no one in particular. "No offence, old man."

"None taken, my boy."

Henry and Sam guarded the stairs with Simon while the other prisoners were being freed.

"Anne, I will need your help with one prisoner. He's almost as stubborn as myself, and I think you're the only one who can convince him to leave here." Edward stepped to the cell opposite the one he was in and unlocked the door, letting all those inside out, save one who didn't move.

"Who?" Anne asked as she joined Edward in the cell. She studied the figure of a man not unlike Edward. The prisoner had the same shaggy hair and long beard, a trademark of those present for an extended length of time. Anne's eyes widened when the man looked up at her. "William!" Anne ran to William and knelt down, placing her hand on his cheek. "I thought you had been executed!" She embraced William tightly for a second. William had been Anne's protector, her confidant, and a great friend.

Edward left them to their reunion as he freed the prisoners from their cells.

"Not quite, Your Highness. By the grace of your mother, Queen Anne, I was spared the guillotine and the noose."

Anne scoffed lightly at his remark. "Then, by my grace and Providence, I shall rescue you from this crucible. We will escape from here, together." Anne grabbed William's hand and tried to lead him away, but he didn't budge. "What are you doing, William?

We must make haste!"

"I am sorry Anne, I cannot. I will be of no use to you."

"What are you saying? Do not tell me your time here has made you weak."

William turned away; he could not face those eyes. "Prison has made me more aware of my faults, and I must atone for my weakness. I failed in my charge, and this is my punishment."

Anne reared back and slapped William hard. "All the more reason you need to be my protector! Fulfil your broken oath to me, not as royalty, not as your princess, but as my friend. Your punishment will be to keep me alive and regain your lost honour!" Anne rose and turned to the cell door. "Don't think you can take the easy way out because you feel you failed my uncle." Anne strolled away, leaving William with her words.

William's mouth was wide open. He rubbed his cheek where Anne had slapped him. After a moment he clenched his teeth and rose to his feet. Without saying a word, he joined Anne outside. Anne grinned to herself.

Edward finished unlocking the cells, and a total of fifty-eight criminals were ready to fight, comprised of thirty-five men and twenty-three women, eleven mentally ill whose minds were on the brink, and sixteen elderly and children.

"Do you know where the armoury is located?" Edward asked Anne.

"Yes, up the stairs and across a hallway," Anne replied.

"Take those who can fight to the armoury, and keep the elderly and children away from combat as much as possible," Edward commanded as he went the opposite direction of the stairs, instead heading deeper into the prison.

"Where are you going?" she asked.

"I am freeing more prisoners," Edward replied, jangling the keys as he travelled further into the darkness.

Edward had heard stories of those trapped in the deepest level of the prison. The prisoners said to be the worst devils in existence, or at least British existence, were sent there. Some considered these in league with Satan and practitioners of dark arts.

Edward thought they were just stories conjured by an overactive imagination, but upon seeing those in the darkness he had his doubts.

The stench of disease and filth hit Edward, and the smell was so vile he could scarcely breathe. He inspected the room, and could see the grates of eleven cells in the square room, five on either side and a large one at the back. Edward could feel the intense scrutiny of beady eyes, which caused his skin to crawl and itch uncontrollably.

Edward tried the keys on the closest cell. When he opened the door the prisoners rushed upon him, knocking him to the ground. Most ran away up the stairs, taking their chance to escape, while three lashed out at Edward viciously.

"Stop, stop I say! I am here to free you!" Edward yelled, but repeated himself another two times before the attack stopped.

"You mean to free us? Why?" one of the three asked.

"I cannot escape on my own."

Another tall man laughed. "The boy means to use us as decoys, methinks. No matter, this will be a golden chance, let us seize it." And without further deliberation, nor a helping hand to Edward, the three left.

Edward rose and began opening the cells once more. None attacked Edward like the first time, but some appeared on the verge. As the prisoners passed, Edward pondered what horrible deeds these prisoners could have committed.

Coming out of the second cell, a hunched-over, shifty-eyed man was being led by a pregnant woman. The man was muttering something under his breath about Poseidon and Davey Jones, but Edward could not catch the rest.

In another cell, three men passed by in tandem. The first man had no ears, the second's eyes were bandaged, but the third seemed perfectly normal. The second man thanked Edward for all three of them, stating the third's tongue was cut out.

In yet another cell a large woman with a missing eye and arm passed by with six other men following behind. The men seemed to fear falling behind the woman, but also afraid of leaving with her. After a few threatening leers from the woman, the men followed compliantly.

Several men and women were disfigured and diseased with leprosy and boils, as well as odd ailments and afflictions like frostbite. Many had also descended into madness, or were committed because of madness, so Edward decided to keep his distance.

Edward left the large cell in the back for last. He could see a man with a mask made of some type of metal. His hands and feet, unlike those of the other prisoners, were bound to the ceiling and floor respectively.

"Hold a moment, friend. I will free you in but a moment," Edward reassured him, to no response.

Edward first freed the man's limbs while examining him. The mask the prisoner wore covered the whole face, but slits left the eyes, mouth, and nose exposed. Edward found no visible signs of fusing, and the mask looked like one continuous piece of metal. *How is this possible? How was this affixed to his head?*

After Edward freed him the man stayed motionless, but whispered something under his breath. "What?" Edward asked.

The man glared the coldest malice at Edward. "The mask."

Edward inspected the mask once more from all angles, but couldn't find a spot for a key, no lock, no seam to work. "I see no way to remove the mask."

The man grabbed Edward and slammed him against the stone wall. After a moment, the man released Edward, screamed in anger and left the cell. "Anne, you will pay for this!" the man in the metal mask yelled as he quickly jumped up the stairs of the prison.

He must have meant Queen Anne. Who was that man? Edward shook his head. *No time to dwell.*

Edward ran back up the steps to the level of the prison his former cell was on. Anne, Henry, Sam, Charles, and Edmond were waiting for Edward. As he drew closer to the stairs, the sounds of battle could be heard echoing against the stone.

Anne noticed Edward approaching and stepped towards him. "I showed the prisoners to the armoury and things are escalating quickly."

"If ya thought it hell down 'ere, Thatch, ya'd best see upstairs," Sam cackled.

Edward ran up the stairs to the main level of the castle, his companions following closely behind, and found himself in the right corner, farthest from the drawbridge. If a castle could be called plain, this one qualified. The castle had a bailey in each of the four corners, with one large open courtyard in the centre, and a tall keep at the back. The perimeter had high curtain walls, making interior and exterior defence easily manageable.

The castle used to be owned by William III before his death, and ownership fell to his successor and sister-in-law, Queen Anne. Not wishing to bring unpleasant memories of her brother-in-law's death, Queen Anne converted the castle to a prison. The Queen quickly filled the prison castle with political prisoners, dissenters, and other enemies of the state.

Edward and his group stationed themselves behind stone columns and a waist-high barrier around the inside of the bailey. From above, on the curtain walls, guards popped in and out of cover trying to shoot the escapees with muskets. Below Edward, on the main level, the fifty-plus escaped prisoners fought off guards attempting to enter from the courtyard on Edward's left as well as guards rushing down the stairs on Edward's right. The prisoners raided the armoury to better fight the guards on the curtain wall.

"How is the best way to the keep?" Edward shouted over the gunfire, yells, and curses uttered from the unstable men he'd freed.

"The safest way is through a door at the top of this bailey. There isn't much cover on the baileys, but the walkways along the walls are thin so we cannot be overwhelmed with numbers," Anne yelled back. A bullet ripped into the stone column Anne was standing behind, so she ducked down further.

"What of our escape?" Henry asked. "We cannot use the latrine hole anymore."

"The way out is through. There are two release levers for the drawbridge in the front baileys. Both need to be thrown for it to be lowered."

"Then we 'ave no choice but to split up." Sam forcefully pushed Charles, the old man, down below the stone wall to avoid the bullets.

"First we need to acquire weapons, and then move to the top level," Edward said as he drew a deep breath and plunged into the chaos.

Edward dashed from column to column, ducking below the waist-high stone wall when he needed to pass between. Edward slowed down as the concentration of bullets increased, eventually stopping at the right corner of the bailey. Sam, Charles, Henry, and Anne were all following behind.

When Edward glanced back to make sure his friends were unharmed, he had to do a double take. "Where's Edmond?" The expressions on the faces of his companions told Edward they did not know the answer. Edward shifted his gaze rapidly until he saw the boy running between the fighting prisoners.

Edmond carried several weapons in his arms and more draped over his small frame. As Edmond's gaze moved to the sky a stray bullet hit near his feet, causing him to stop short. Edmond toppled over, fully exposed for the guards to see.

"Edmond!" yelled Edward. He took a quick glance from behind his cover before running out to save the boy. Edward bobbed and weaved through the mess of prisoners and bullets raining from above. Edward's heart beat like waves before a storm as the surrounding sights and smells invigorated him.

The stench of body odour and disease from the prisoners was lessened with the fresh outside air and mixed with the familiar smells of gunpowder and blood. All that was missing was the salty ocean air Edward so missed, instead being replaced with the fresh grass and newly tilled earth of the countryside.

Edward reached the young man in a flash and, after taking Edmond over his shoulder, grabbed the weapons and brought the boy back to safety. Edward dropped the weapons and plopped Edmond down below the stone barrier.

"What were you thinking, Edmond? You could have gotten yourself killed!"

Edmond's eyes filled with tears. "I saw the sun, Edward, that's why I fell. It's so beautiful."

Edward peered past the column he was hidden behind and saw a sliver of the sun through the opening of the bailey.

"You are right, Edmond, the sun is beautiful. But you have yet to see the sun as it sets and rises upon the sea. Now that… that is a sight to behold. You must be careful, or you won't live to see it. Understand?" Edmond nodded, wiping his tears away.

Edward grabbed a musket and a sword from the pile of weapons and signalled to his comrades to take their pick. While his friends equipped themselves for battle, Edward searched among the prisoners. "Simon!" Edward yelled. After a moment, Simon's eyes found Edward, and he ran over.

"Whut is it, you git? Can't ye see we're a tad busy here?"

"I am well aware," Edward answered. "We need to reach the top level of this bailey and split into two groups. There is a lever at the front of the castle to release the drawbridge. I want you to lead half the people on this side, and I will lead the others to the opposite side."

"You lead the way, and I'll make sure these rats follow." Simon started to rise, but Edward stopped him.

He handed the keys for the prison cells to Simon. "Take these and free the prisoners in the front bailey. We'll need their help."

"The bastards'll make good shields," Simon asserted with a heartless laugh.

Edward ignored the comment and peered at his crewmen, who nodded to his silent question of their readiness. Edward rushed for the stairs to his right with his friends following behind. Four prisoners were at the foot of the stairs, stopping the guards from descending, but their own ascent also prevented by those same guards.

"We're at a stalemate here, and the more time we waste, the sooner reinforcements will arrive. Does anyone have any ideas?" Edward asked.

"I 'ave one," Sam answered. "I need a bag of powder." Sam

handed Charles to Henry and took a bag of powder from the young Edmond. "I learned this on the last ship I was on," Sam explained as he cocked a pistol and set it in the bag full of gunpowder along with musket balls. "The crew turned on the captain, and 'e was holed up in his cabin, so 'e made a few of these to clear out the chief bastards outside his door. When you 'ear the boom, run up the stairs." Sam took the bag and hurled it up the length of the stairs.

Once the bag landed, the shock caused the cocked gun to release, striking the flint and exploding the powder in the bag. The explosion didn't hurt anyone, but the pieces of the gun and musket balls flying from the bag certainly did.

Edward's crew and four prisoners ran up the stairs and shot down those hurt by Sam's makeshift grenade. After, the prisoners attacked the guards now exposed along the curtain wall walkways. The only guards left were those on the opposite side of the bailey, and the reinforcements advancing across the walkway between the southeast bailey Edward was on and the northeast one where the drawbridge lever was.

Edward and his crew moved to the curtain wall of the bailey. When Edward rose from cover he could see through the opening in the bailey to the lower level where the majority of the prisoners were still fighting. The keep, where the warden was, was between the south baileys, rising high above the rest of the castle.

"Anne, are you able to kill those guards on the other side of the bailey?"

"Consider it done." Anne turned to William, they nodded to each other, and William ran to the south end of the bailey, knowing what to do without words.

Anne and William went into a sprint across opposite ends of the bailey's walls. When they reached the end, where the guards stationed themselves along the west wall, they both pulled out twin pistols.

Anne turned to face the line of guards. The guard's eyes widened. Anne let loose her pistols. The guards rose, but a moment too late. One bullet hit a guard in the back, the other bullet pierced the leg of the second.

William used his momentum to drop and slide into the walkway. William shot his pistols. Two guards fell. One guard was left with a musket in hand, ready to shoot Anne. William jumped up. The guard aimed. William plucked a musket from a dead guard's hands. The guard pulled down on the trigger. William shot the guard in the back. The guard's arms flew out. The bullet hit the stone on the wall two inches left of Anne's ear.

William dropped the musket and ran to Anne's side. She rose and thanked William as Edward and crew joined them in front of the walkway to the keep.

With the guards removed, the prisoners were able to move more freely, and, having heard the plan from Simon, the captives moved up the stairs to the top of the bailey. Edward waved a group of them across to the entrance of the keep. Reinforcements along the roof of the keep were being kept at bay with well-timed, albeit ill-aimed, musket shots.

In front of Edward were large double wooden doors with reinforced iron latticework and large iron hoops for handles. Edward pulled on one, but it wouldn't open. "The door must be barred. How will we enter?" he asked the group of twenty behind him.

"Watch out!" Anne yelled as she pulled Edward away from the doors.

A stone larger than Edward's head, beard included, fell to the ground with a loud crack. Ten feet above the double doors was an opening for siege defence, covered by a square wooden board on hinges.

Edward stroked his long beard. "That will work. We need someone to open the door from the inside." Edward turned to the prisoners. "Were there any ladders in the armoury?" The group shook their heads. "What are we to do then?" Edward questioned, mainly to himself.

"We make our own ladder," Anne declared. "Firstly, keep muskets on the opening and fire if it moves in the slightest." A few of the men complied. "Five of you move in front of the door and get down on all fours." Anne's words were met with confused expressions and tilted heads. "Now!" she commanded. The order was immediately carried out with minor backtalk. "Four more, climb on top and balance yourselves in the same position."

As the human ladder was being made, the guard throwing rocks poked his head out to attempt another throw, but was forced back by a few musket shots. Anne helped more prisoners onto the pyramid until just one man was on the top. After some time, the shaky masterpiece of filth was completed.

"Beauty," Sam said with his usual snark. "Now what, Princess?"

"Boys, you can stop firing." Anne climbed the pyramid.

Once at the top, Anne knelt down and kept a keen eye on the opening. When the guard pushed open the board to throw another rock out, Anne leapt into the air and gripped the wooden board. With a deftness all her own, Anne used her momentum to jump into the opening and kick the guard back into the keep, closing the wooden barrier behind her.

The men who formed the pyramid fell from the force of Anne's jump. "Ready yourselves, men! When she busts through that door we are storming that keep," Edward proclaimed.

Various muffled noises could be heard from behind the stone and woodwork of the keep. Screams of fighting, falling, and dying, and shots from guns and muskets filtered through the stone to the ears of the prisoners. The noises started from the spot Anne entered the keep and made its way down to the double doors.

As the noises grew louder, the prisoners grew tense with anticipation. Grips were made firmer, sights steadier, and wills steeled.

The door shuddered with a sudden whack, causing some to jump, then the sound of wood and iron scraping was heard. With another swift crack, the double doors burst open and a guard fell backwards through them, unconscious.

Anne ran across the threshold, bullets following in her wake. She gripped her left bicep with her right hand, and blood dripped in a thin stream from her forehead down her cheek.

Edward ran to Anne and held her against his diminished frame. "Charge!" he yelled.

The prisoners with Edward ran into the thick of battle, catching the guards unawares. The mass of greasy-haired and dirt-caked people yelled as they travelled up and down the spiral staircase in the first part of the keep.

"Are you well?" Edward asked of Anne, still gripping her tightly.

"Yes, I am fine Edward," Anne replied, pushing him away. She released her right hand and examined the wound, which was still seeping blood.

William too examined both sides of the wound before ripping off a strip of his tattered shirt and wrapping it tightly over Anne's forearm. "The bullet cleared through the other side, so you will not require surgery."

"Good. Now, Edward, we must quickly retrieve your belongings from the warden and free more prisoners to our cause."

"Agreed, but are you sure you're well? Will you be able to continue?"

"I will manage. Let us secure your freedom."

Edward, his musket in hand, advanced into the spiral tower heading up the right side of the staircase. The sounds of battle could be heard from below, and silence above. Upon moving to the next level, Edward was met with seven prisoners and, thanks to Anne's efforts, three unconscious guards.

This level had several arrow slits and weapon stores for a siege, as well as the wooden opening Anne used to enter and a large pile of rocks. Another staircase led to the roof, with arrow slits along the wall. To Edward's right, the west door leading to the warden's office stood undisturbed.

"Beyond is the warden's dining chambers and holding chamber for new prisoners. A stone enclosure on the left is the warden's office."

"Yes, I remember well when I was first brought here. That was the last time I saw the sun and the sea." Edward approached the door and touched the ring-shaped handle.

"Wait!" Anne yelled. "What are you doing? Guards are no doubt beyond the door, waiting for someone to open it."

"Yes, of course I considered that, Anne," Edward said, puffing up his chest.

Anne smirked, her brow raised.

"Alright, I didn't," Edward admitted, his head held down in shame. "But this is the only way through."

"Yes, well, we should force the guards to fire at nothing, then retaliate when they are reloading." Anne turned to the group of prisoners standing around. "Clear out of the way unless you want to be shot." The men complied with Anne's request without a word. Anne, William, Sam, Charles and Edmond all moved to the sides.

Anne nodded to Edward, and he waited for the company to assert their readiness. Edward swiftly opened the door and pulled until his back was against the wall. A barrage of bullets flashed past, lasting for all of two seconds.

After a silent moment, the prisoners retaliated and shot the guards in the room. Many were behind cover of one piece of furniture or another, but three foolish enough to be in the open were the first to fall. As Edward was about to take his shot he saw a man sticking a linstock into a large cannon.

The iron cannonball burst from the cannon, clipping a prisoner on the chin, snapping his neck, before crashing into the wall of the tower and sending stone chunks flying.

Blood splattered on Edward's face before he kicked the door closed, and bullets rained on it for a full minute. Edward looked at the dead man's body, blood draining from his neck and pooling on the stone. Edward didn't want to think on how that easily could have been him. "Did anyone get a good look at the room? We need to disable the cannon before the guards reload."

Above the sound of the guns being fired, the prisoners shouted descriptions of what they saw. "Near abouts twenty men, less three." "Table 'n chairs." "Tapestries." "A chandelier," Anne yelled last.

"What's a chandelier?" Edward asked.

"A chandelier is a large decorative candle holder hanging from the ceiling."

"How large is it, where is it situated, and what is holding it up?"

Anne closed her eyes to picture the scene. "The size is five to ten feet at its widest, located in the centre of the room above a long table with marines on either side, and held on an iron chain with a metal clasp."

"Do you think a musket shot could break the clasp?"

"I suppose so."

Edward turned to William and handed him his loaded musket. "Can I count on you? I know taking the time to aim is a big risk, but you're the best shooter we have aside from Anne."

"Hey! I resent that," Sam ranted, his and William's rivalry apparently still intact after a year of separation.

William, always sparing in his use of words, simply nodded, providing as firm an answer as any man could give. Edward did not doubt William's ability to complete the task in the slightest.

"Once the chandelier drops I want you to run in and shoot every last one of those guards. Understood?" Edward's question was met with loud grunts, which he took for agreement. Edward held the handle and, with a swift tug, pulled the door open.

No blast of bullets came as before, and in that second of hesitation William took his chance. He rolled forward and landed on one knee with his musket aimed high. He took one short but deep breath as his eyes locked onto the metal clasp holding the chandelier, and his arms followed immediately afterwards.

William shot his musket. The guards returned fire. The clasp of the chandelier broke, and the ostentatious candle holder fell. The seven guards around the table looked up a second too late. The crystal and gold smashed the table, sending shards of crystal and pieces of wood everywhere. The ends of the table shot up in the air, hitting a guard on the chin. The table collapsed to the ground with a thud.

Edward jumped into the room, using the confusion to his advantage, and let loose a pistol shot, hitting a guard in the stomach. The guard manning the cannon left his station and slashed at Edward with a sword. Edward jumped out of the way and kicked the man in the groin. The man doubled over and fell to the floor. Edward drew his sword and thrust it into the guard's back. The man let out a painful gasp of air before a death rattle.

When Edward turned around, the room was cleared. Bodies of guards littered the floor, their weapons strewn about, but three of the prisoners had also died.

Edward saw the large table split in twain, with one half upended from the broken chandelier. Opposite where Edward had entered, a door led to the west side of the castle. The warden's room was on the left wall, the wooden door closed.

Edward gave the door a kick. The door shook from the force, but didn't open. With the exertion from fighting, Edward was already out of breath and sweating.

"Sam!" Edward leaned on a chair. "Get the door, would you?"

Sam settled Charles in a chair. "Ye may be me captain, but I ain't yer servant."

"Open the door, Sam."

Sam, pistol in hand, reared back his leg and thrust it at the door. The door busted off its hinges and fell into the room. Sam entered the room, pistol forward, but he couldn't see anyone.

"I think the warden jumped ship." Sam laughed.

Edward entered the room. Boxes, shelves, and barrels full of prisoner belongings filled the walls. Papers, weapons, clothing, and other miscellaneous oddities plagued the small room, demanding space. A table in the centre of the room was full of peculiar items as well, with a lit candle and stacks of papers with quill and ink to the side.

"I didn't see the warden running," Edward said as he glanced about. "He's mad, but not a coward."

"Right you are, my boy," a voice rang from behind him.

Before Edward could react his golden sword was pulled in front of him and racing towards his neck. Edward's instincts kicked in and he grabbed the arm holding the sword, stopping the advance. Edward's other arm was bent behind his back, and the person attacking him forced Edward into the corner of the room.

The warden of the castle prison, Warden Balastiere, was the one now holding Edward's life in the balance. "I caught ye, caught ye good I did," the warden taunted in a manic, crazed voice.

3. THE GREAT ESCAPE

The warden rested his head on Edward's shoulder.

Sam, Anne, and Henry instantly tensed with the sudden turn of events and pulled their weapons on the pair. Those in the dining chambers approached to catch a glimpse of the scene unfolding. Edward stood stock still, the warden at his back, his hands held up to stop his friends from shooting.

"Get off him!" Henry yelled.

The warden laughed and shook his head wildly like the madmen he imprisoned. "No, no, no, that won't do. Cannot do that. No. I'm the warden, see? I issue orders here." The warden's breath was hot on Edward's ear. "I tricked you. All these years, playing the fool in front of you prisoners, for this payoff. You would not believe the delight I'm feeling..."

The thunder from Anne's pistol rebounded in the small room. The bullet sped through the warden's forehead. He collapsed in a heap off of Edward's back.

The crew and prisoners first glanced at the source of the sound, then to the warden as he fell, and then back to Anne and the smoking pistol. Everyone stared at Anne with shocked expressions, most notably Edward.

"What?" Anne said with a shrug. "He kept prattling on and on. We do not have time for such nonsense. And besides, the hostage trick is old." Anne turned and left the room. "We have what we need, let's move on."

Edward took one last glance at the warden, silently thanked Anne for her marksmanship, and returned to the dining chamber. "Right."

Anne ran to the west wall and kicked the door open. The west keep tower was a mirror image of the one on the east side. Weapons, stone stairs, an opening with rocks to throw, all there save for guards to use them.

"The guards must have been called down to the bottom of the keep or to the east side as reinforcements," William surmised.

Anne examined the western side of the castle through an arrow slit. "The bailey is clear too."

"That makes it easier for us." Edward headed down the stairs.

Edward, Anne, Sam, Henry, Charles and Edmond, and the remaining three prisoners out of seven, all ran down the stairs to the east side's set of identical double doors. The muffled sounds of gun-shots and shouts could be heard from below, a small reminder of the battle being fought in the castle prison.

Edward pushed the doors open slowly on the off chance Anne missed something. A slight breeze was blowing across the castle walls imparting cold air on the small group as they trekked silently across the walkway.

The group moved into the depths of the west side of the castle to where the remaining prisoners were kept, and met no resistance along the way. The west side of the castle was eerily quiet, until they descended into the prison hold.

Through some sort of transference, the prisoners on the west end knew something was amiss. They were yelling and hollering obscenities so fierce and foul that Edward cringed. He could make no distinction between the mentally competent and unstable.

Edward did not spend any time dwelling on the situation. He took his golden sword and began slashing at the locks and bars. They cracked open with the force of the mysterious golden blade. The metal of the cutlass was far superior to the iron locks and bars.

Even so, Edward was in a weakened state, and after a few locks were broken his arm was tired from the strain.

"Here, let me take over," Henry offered. "You rest." Henry took the golden sword and continued freeing prisoners, eventually descending steps to do the same for the more dangerous ones.

Edward sat down, leaning against the wall of the prison, and closed his eyes whilst rubbing his arm. As much as he detested the prison, he felt oddly tranquil against the familiar stone wall.

A hand caressed his shoulder. "We're almost there, Edward," Anne said, her words bringing Edward strength.

Edward kissed Anne's hand. "I'm already there, Anne."

A flood of the oddest criminals ran up the steps, most notably a man both taller than Edward and larger in build than Henry, a hulk of a man with long chains dragging behind him from his arms and feet. A smaller man was atop his hunched shoulder, guiding the large man forward.

Henry returned from the deep soon after the large man passed by. Edward rose back up from his rest. "Ready?" Henry asked, of-fering the golden cutlass back to Edward. He accepted the weapon and nodded.

When Edward, Henry, and Anne returned to the main level of the bailey they could see the freed prisoners raiding another weapon storehouse on the north end of the courtyard. After loading up on weapons, some headed up the stairs, while others advanced to the inner courtyard through the east door. Sam was sitting down, munching on salted meat with nary a care in the world, beside

Charles and Edmond.

Edward strode up the stairs and his crew followed soon after. Despite Edward's ragged appearance he was the image of a fearsome sea captain in his familiar black leather coat that reached to his knees and a tricorn hat.

"Forward, men! Release the drawbridge so we are rid of this prison!" Edward yelled to as he pointed his golden sword. The prisoners responded with hoots and hollers, and followed him to the north of the castle.

As Edward made his way across, the guards in the courtyard fired at him. Edward ducked down, but continued moving forward, while other prisoners retaliated.

Edward could see in the courtyard a wide open space with stables for horses, stations for the guards' quarters, and wagons of supplies. In the centre was a large fountain surrounded by a cobblestone road for horse-drawn carriages. Everywhere in the courtyard prisoners were fighting with guards, either out in the open or behind cover taking pot shots at each other. The courtyard was a mess of bodies, but Edward knew the prisoners outnumbered the guards.

Guards flew up the stairs of the northern bailey and met the prisoners as they reached the end of the walkway. Edward ducked below the bailey's inner curtain wall while the prisoners with muskets shot at the few guards and continued on.

Edward was about to descend the stairs, but noticed Anne climbing the outer curtain wall with a rifle. "What are you doing, Anne?"

Anne ignored Edward for a moment and searched the northwest field in front of the castle. When Anne found what she was seeking, she took a few deep breaths and fired the rifle.

"I signalled our transportation," Anne stated, jumping down from the curtain wall. "In the event we cannot escape as originally intended, the cavalry will pick us up." Anne dashed to the stairs and started her descent.

"Who is in this cavalry?" Edward asked, following Anne.

Anne turned and grinned. "You'll see."

In the lower level, the guards were being beaten to death by the prisoners. The security was lax, and Edward suspected the guards were spread too thin to gain control again.

Edward handed his sword to Henry to free the last of the prisoners in the northwest bailey before he followed Anne to a small alcove with the drawbridge lever. When Edward and Anne reached the alcove, the sudden dismay over what they saw sent chills down their spines and a wave of hopelessness washed over them.

"The lever is broken," Anne observed.

The wooden lever was cracked at the base and the mechanism

underneath completely broken apart. One of the guards had had the forethought to break the lever sometime in the middle of the escape.

"Is there a moat? We could jump in and swim across."

"No, the moat was considered unnecessary and dried up after the castle was turned into a prison. We could take the original exit through the latrine hole, but I am afraid the old man Charles would not make the drop without injury and the hole is too small to carry him."

"What about rope?" Edward offered.

"I saw none in the armoury." Anne paused in contemplation, her hand on her chin, biting her thumb. "There is no other way. Someone must climb over the curtain wall and shoot the chains holding the drawbridge in place."

Edward ran his fingers through his hair. "Now the question is who."

"I can!" Edmond offered with glee, and without waiting for an answer he ran up the stairs of the bailey.

"No! Edmond, wait! It's too dangerous!" Edward yelled after him, but the young boy paid no attention.

Edward and Anne ran after Edmond, who was already at the top of the steps as they reached the bottom. As quickly as Edward and Anne could manage, one being physically weak and the other injured, they ran up the stone steps to the top of the castle. Edmond was atop the wall and making his way to the middle where the drawbridge was.

"Edmond, get down from there," Edward commanded.

"I'll be fine, Edward!" the boy asserted with the bravado natural to youth.

Edward let out a grunt of frustration and climbed the curtain wall along with Edmond. Edward tried his best to catch up with the youngster and stop him, but the little one gained too much of a head start.

Edmond was at the middle of the curtain wall when he stopped and peered over the edge. From the corner of his vision, Edmond noticed Edward trying to walk across the edge of the wall to catch him, and when Edmond turned further he could see the sun.

The bullet ripped past Edmond's cheek. He lost his footing and fell over the curtain wall, heading to the rocky ground below. Edward leaped towards Edmond, his arm outstretched. Edmond extended his own arm in an attempt to make contact. The tips of their fingers touched and slipped apart, and Edmond continued to fall. Edward watched, the horror in his heart mirrored in Edmond's eyes.

Like a flame flickering as it is being blown out, grasping for life,

Edmond's hands tried frantically to grab onto something. The boy's fingers found the drawbridge. Edmond held fast to a slight, over-hanging lip of wood, either from a design flaw or the loosening of the mechanism over the years.

Edward let out a sigh on seeing Edmond's falling motion cut short. "Are you well, Edmond?"

Edmond, after a few breaths and a securing of his grip, laughed from the heart. "See? I told you I'd be fine." Edmond grinned. With Edmond's added weight, and the jolt of the fall, the slight opening of the drawbridge became larger. Edmond was able to see into the small gap. "I can see the chains." Edmond felt around his body while hanging from the drawbridge, but all his weapons he had been carrying had fallen to the ground. "Toss me a gun, Edward," the boy demanded.

Seeing no other way, Edward motioned for a pistol from Anne. She passed one on and he let the pistol fall into the outstretched hand of the young Edmond.

Edmond reached the pistol into the small gap only his hands could fit into and fired at the chain holding the drawbridge. The side Edmond was on lurched forward and the chain was severed. While Edward retrieved another pistol, Edmond moved inch by inch across the drawbridge to the other side. Edward moved as well, staying low to avoid being shot, and when Edmond was ready Edward dropped the pistol into his hand.

"Now, you must be careful because the drawbridge is going to—" Edward started to say, but he was cut off by the shot of the pistol.

The drawbridge fell to the ground with Edmond hanging onto the edge. The rocky moat and grassy edge were closing in by the second. Edmond turned his head to see where he was headed, the gut reaction overpowering the mind's knowledge. The thick and heavy wooden planks could easily crush the boy in two, and was nearing its promise. Edmond pushed away from the drawbridge with his feet, leaping backwards off the planks. He landed on his back, hard, and rolled away as the drawbridge crashed loudly in front of his feet.

"Edmond!" Edward yelled.

Edmond was on the ground, his small frame heaving with coughs and spasms of pain, but he was eventually able to give a thumbs-up. After a few seconds, Edmond rose from the ground and then began looking around.

What is he searching for? Edward pondered, watching the boy intently.

Before Edward could ask, his eyes caught something around the bend of the sloping road. Two somethings, in fact. They were carriages, each drawn with four horses, travelling at break-neck speed. The driver's and passenger's faces were obscured, but Edward had a fairly good idea of whom they were.

Edward ran back to the bailey, down the stairs, and into the courtyard with Anne following as the carriages raced into the castle. The drivers pulled the carriages around the whole of the fountain while firing upon the guards, save one passenger who threw knives and a spear. After closing the whole circuit the carriages stopped close to the exit.

Edward ran to the front carriage with Anne, Henry, and Sam still carrying his charge, Charles, behind him. The driver and passengers of both carriages pulled back their hoods, revealing their faces. "Herbert, Nassir!" Edward exclaimed.

The one called Herbert was a young man with glasses, and a strong upper body. In quite the contrast, his lower body was small and thin. He normally was in a wheelchair, navigating at the helm of the *Freedom* with unparalleled skills.

Nassir was a large, middle-aged negro with a shaved head and a thick African accent. His eyes were dark, and could contain boundless fury, but he was a kind man. He worked as carpenter aboard the *Freedom*, doing necessary repairs after each battle and in between. His experience was a valuable asset in keeping the ship afloat.

Edward's gaze turned to the second carriage. "John, Pukuh!" More comrades of his former life, arrived to save him.

"Captain," Herbert said, "your chariot awaits."

4. THE CHASE

Edward, Anne and William joined the second coach with John and Pukuh at the reins, while Henry, Sam, Edmond and Charles entered the first. As quickly as they arrived, and before any other prisoners jumped aboard, the carriages were sent back out the castle.

The sounds of battle cries, gunshots, and death throes could be heard a ways down the road before being overshadowed by the sound of the wheels against the earthy ground.

The carriages passed by small rolling hills with light grass and eventually into a forest with a wide road and well-worn path. Poplars decorated the entrance of the forest and quickly turned to birch and beech. The trees passed Edward's vision in a blur before he could catch glimpse of the branches.

Edward's face was beaming as he gazed upon the outside world for the first time in a year. *I wonder what the expression on Edmond's face is.*

"Happy to finally be free?" Anne asked, directing her question to both Edward and William.

"I am happy when you are, Your Highness," William replied with a slight bow.

Edward cringed. "William, don't bow until you shave. Being formal looks… odd… when you have a beard as full as mine." William ignored the comment.

Edward held Anne's hand. "I too am filled with joy, but I will not truly be free until I have the *Freedom* back," Edward said, referring to his ship. His free hand glided over his coat pocket, to the letter left by the previous owner. *No, not yet.* Edward moved his hand away.

"We have a plan to retrieve the ship as well. For now, we can rest until we return to the inn we reserved." Anne leaned her head back and closed her eyes.

"How is your arm?" Edward asked, leaning forward to inspect. The wound had long since stopped bleeding, but Anne's arm was caked with dried blood. Edward also noticed she was as pale as a summer cloud, and sweating.

"I will be fine. Rest, Edward," she insisted.

I will let Anne alone. She needs this more than I.

Edward opened the carriage door and peered outside. He stepped onto a metal lip covering the wheels, then closed the door.

Edward carefully stepped up to the coachbox, where Pukuh and John sat.

Pukuh, a six-foot-four muscular Mayan warrior, sat stoically, staring at the road ahead. He was intensely tan with long, deep brown hair which swayed in the wind. His strong jaw and fierce eyes painted the pure picture of a fighter. War Chief of his Mayan city where his father ruled as King, Pukuh left with Edward to learn more about the world so he too could be King one day.

"Brother!" Pukuh exclaimed joyfully, pulling Edward in for a hug. After a few seconds Pukuh pushed Edward back and examined him, his mouth a hard line. "You look weak."

Edward laughed. "Nice to see you too. I assumed you would have returned home after what happened."

"In fact I did. The crew were defeated, body and spirit. Henry and Anne both brought most everyone back together with much difficulty. Some are still missing, but all here are loyal to the man who gave them *Freedom*."

Edward smiled. "Good to hear. John, how are you holding up?"

John, a plump man with glasses, held the reins of the carriage and focused on the road ahead, as well as on the companion carriage. John was of nervous disposition when stressed in conversation, but on the battlefield no man was as calm. John had joined Edward from the beginning when Edward wanted to be a whaler. He had called Edward's father captain once, on a whaling vessel as well, before Edward's father disappeared.

"Oh, right as rain Captain. We have you back, and now our *Freedom*'s all we've left to st-steal."

Pukuh's head shot up and he peered to the road ahead. "What's wrong?" Edward asked.

"We are soon to be joined by others," Pukuh replied, his brow low and his eyes and body shifting to see his unknown 'others.'

"More of the crew?" Edward asked.

"No, we are not to meet any on this road." Pukuh pulled out a spear but kept it hidden.

Edward leaned back and knocked on the door to the carriage. William opened the window of the door with a questioning expression. "Someone is approaching. Pass me a musket, if we have any. Prop open the door so I have some cover."

Anne opened her eyes, still heavy as they were, and rose from her seat. "No, we may be able to talk our way out of this. Get inside." As Edward complied, Anne pulled up the cushion and revealed a storehouse of weapons and clothes. Anne donned a red longcoat of impressive make.

The ride went undisturbed for several minutes until the horses slowed. The noise diminished as the carriage eventually drew to a halt, leaving the clop of the restless horses and the sounds of animals in the forest for them to hear.

Edward opened the window of the carriage and could hear people talking with Herbert. He started to rise, but Anne stopped him.

"Wait, Edward. I shan't need more than a moment."

Anne counted off the seconds in her head before she opened the door of the carriage and strode out in a huff.

What is she doing? Edward began following Anne, but was stopped by William.

"I believe it would be more prudent to let Her Highness handle this for now," William recommended, to which Edward yielded and sat back down.

"What is the meaning of this delay?" Anne yelled.

In front of Anne were thirty men on horseback, the local militia of the town closest to the castle, on horseback. They had no special uniform, but carried swords and an assortment of flintlock weapons at their hips.

"We stopped you because…"

"Because why? We are travelling a road passed by travellers every day? Because you assumed we were common merchants and wished to purchase our supplies? Out with it, man!"

The militia man was fearful that Anne was someone of importance, and if he knew the truth the conversation could be quite different. "The castle Gammond down yonder sent a raven telling of a riot needing reinforcements."

Anne rubbed her palm over her eyes and let out a heavy sigh. "Then what, pray tell, are you doing wasting time with us? Not only are you delaying our journey, but you are allowing criminals to run free in the prisons. Off with you before you ruin anything else!" Anne pointed to the road leading to the prison.

Edward, cupping his ear with his palm, listened to the whole conversation. *Anne's speech sounds too natural to be rehearsed. Remnants of her mother's influence, no doubt.*

The militia men were flabbergasted at Anne's commanding tone. Better than ask questions and provoke ire, the leader turned his horse and galloped off with his men following closely behind.

After passing, Anne lowered her finger, but kept the scowl in case any chose to glance back until she entered the carriage again. She let out a sigh and wiped her forehead to clear perspiration.

Once again, Edward considered asking Anne if she was all right, as Anne was uncharacteristically nervous, but he decided to let her alone.

"Take us away from here, John," Anne commanded.

The carriage lurched forward and before long they were back to the same speed as before. The trees passed in a blur from the window of the carriage, and the noise heightened with the wheels spinning on the rough dirt.

"That went well, I would say," Edward said to no one in particular. The comment, however, was rather short-lived.

A gunshot echoed over the rumble of the wheels and the carriage veered sharply. "They pursue us! Counter their advances!" Pukuh yelled.

Anne darted out of her seat and opened the compartment once more. She pulled out weapons and handed them to Edward and William. The men promptly opened the doors and leaned out, peering through the window.

Edward could see eleven men on horseback chasing them, with a newcomer leading the charge wearing the uniform of a guard from the prison. *He must have told the militia to chase us, but where are the other twenty?* Edward glanced to the second carriage. Herbert moved the carriage to the other side of the road, Henry and Sam also aiming at the militia.

The guard fired the first volley, with the militia quickly gaining their wits about them. The bullets rained upon Edward and his crew like a torrent.

Edward shot his musket. The militia retaliated tenfold. Edward retreated into the carriage and gripped a pistol. The guard caught up to Edward's carriage and latched onto the door. Edward shot his arm and the man let go with a cry of pain as blood spurted from his fingers. Edward unsheathed his cutlass and slashed the man's throat open. The guard fell from the horse, clutching his mess of a neck.

The militiamen were gaining on the carriages. Henry and Sam kept firing, but, being farther ahead, their bullets missed the mark more often than not. Henry shot a man, felling him from his horse.

Two men jumped on the back of Edward's carriage. One climbed to the top while the other went around the side. Edward pulled a pistol out and aimed it at the man through the window of the door. The man grabbed the pistol and pulled it forward. Edward tried to pull his pistol back, but was too weak. The man slammed his fist into Edward's elbow. It snapped and he released the pistol with a shout of pain. The man grabbed Edward's arm and tried to pull him off balance. Edward stabbed through the door with his cutlass and impaled the man.

Meanwhile, William, on the roof of the carriage, was having similar difficulty. William's punches and kicks were slower than he was used to, and the power was a fraction of their normal ferocity. The only saving grace was that the man was more a brawler than a fighter.

The man threw wild swings, a variety of uppercuts and hooks aimed at the head and body. William blocked them easily and returned punches to the ribs and chin. The man pulled in close and clinched William, pinning him while delivering small punches. William was tiring quickly, his stamina running low, and needed to end the fight. William pushed the man off. The man was sent to the edge of the carriage, but stayed balanced and moved back to the fight. William dropped and kicked the man's legs out. The man fell like a lump, hitting his head on the edge of the carriage. William wrapped his legs around the other man's legs and spun over the side of the carriage. At the last second, William grabbed the door and hung onto the carriage while the man slipped off to the ground, unconscious.

William climbed back in as bullets swarmed on him. Edward was holding his left arm close as he fired a pistol at one of the militiamen trying to climb Henry's carriage. The bullet missed, five inches from its target.

Another horse galloped beside Edward's carriage. The horse moved like the wind, spurred on by its rider, to catch up. The man on horseback aimed a musket at Anne through the carriage's open door. William, the first to notice the imminent danger, leapt and covered Anne with his body. The rider fired. William jerked as the musket ball hit true. Pukuh threw his spear into the gunman's chest before he could reload.

Anne pushed William off and sat him down in the carriage seat. He coughed from the movement and blood spurted out onto the princess's coat and splattered her cheek. The bullet must have punctured William's lungs.

"My apologies, Your Highness."

"We cannot keep this up," Anne said.

"It is a flesh wound," William protested.

"No, it is not. We need to devise a new tactic."

Edward was about to offer a suggestion when a militiaman galloped up on the left side of the carriage. He had a pistol aimed at the group. Out of nowhere Pukuh kicked the man in the chest and swung into the carriage box. The man fell off his horse and onto a rotted tree which broke and fell on top of another man.

That leaves two men still pursuing us. We can make it.

"The men behind us were killed by Henry and Sam," Pukuh said, as if reading Edward's mind.

The three let out a collective sigh, but were well past worse for wear.

Again reading their expressions, Pukuh delivered mood-changing news. "Ten men are ahead of us on horseback, blocking the path. We will reach them soon." He held a spyglass, no doubt the catalyst to his knowledge.

Ten men on horseback waited in a line along the road, muskets pointed and ready to fire at the oncoming carriages.

When the prison guard had informed the militia of who the carriages belonged to, ten had pursued from behind while another ten must have rushed down a side road to gain ground and attack from the front, and the final ten were nowhere to be seen. Edward thought they might have moved on to the prison.

If the initial news lifted their spirits, then the second piece of information sent them back down doubly so. The three were silent while pondering what could be done to escape.

Edward considered the problem until an idea presented itself. "Do we have grenades?" he asked of Anne.

"Yes, twenty in each carriage."

"What about powder?"

"Three small kegs, again, in each carriage."

"Excellent." Edward leaned out the side of the carriage, still holding his arm close. The pain was dulled with all the excitement, but Edward knew it would be back later twofold. "John, take us up close to the first group."

"Yes, Captain," John replied, clutching a bloody shoulder with one hand while holding the reins in the other. He let go of his shoulder, pulled out a whip, and urged the horses to move faster and catch up.

"What do you have in mind?" Anne asked, having an idea of the wheels turning in Edward's head.

"I will explain when we are close to the other carriage." Edward, still leaning out of the door, watched as their carriage gained on the other, and Herbert, noticing the attempt, slowed their carriage down. When the two carriages matched speed, and Edward had gained everyone's attention, he laid out his plan.

John held the reins while Pukuh helped John into the carriage box. John had enough slack on the reins to hold them when leaning out the door. On the right carriage, Henry and Nassir helped Herbert into the carriage, with Nassir holding onto the reins in a similar fashion.

Sam pulled out all the grenades and the powder kegs and tied them together at the fuses into one large cluster. Anne did the same in their carriage.

John and Nassir whipped the horses, sending them racing towards the blockade. A few of the men, seeing no one in the coach seat, wavered in their focus. As the carriages approached without slowing, the men in the blockade lowered their aim and looked at each other as if wondering, "Are we going to move?"

Edward and company leaned out the sides of the carriages and fired upon the men, hitting a few and causing the others to move their horses away. After the carriages passed by, the militia followed in pursuit.

Edward and the crew moved out of the carriage box and to the front. They mounted the horses, with Nassir and Herbert, Edward and Edmond, and Sam and Charles all doubling up on one horse apiece. After everyone was safely on a horse, the harnesses on the animals were cut so they were not connected to each other or the carriages.

The carriages slowed to a stop while the crew escaped. The militiamen spurred their horses faster to try and catch up. As the militiamen were passing the carriages, the fuses on the grenades reached their end.

The blast of the grenades was deafening and blew the carriages apart, sending pieces of wood and iron flying. A piece of wood lodged in the neck of one man, another hit in a horse's stomach. A piece of the iron wheel pierced all the way through a young man's eye to the back of his skull, and iron balls left in the powder kegs punctured one man and his horse like a honeycomb. The blast itself tore a man's leg apart and killed his horse. After the ordeal, hardly any remained unscathed.

Edward looked back at the militiamen. Those unharmed ceased pursuing and helped their comrades, pulling the injured to the side of the road and away from the burning wreckage. Edward noticed his crew also glancing at the carnage.

Saved from the prison, Edward could finally start the plan to retrieve his *Freedom*.

5. REUNIONS

"So the *Freedom* is in Portsmouth?" Edward asked.

"Yes," Anne replied simply.

"Under heavy guard?"

"Most certainly."

"Well, bollocks. I suppose you have another plan?"

"Yes, of course. But we can discuss this later. Winchester is ahead." Anne pointed to the town ahead as she spoke.

The town of Winchester lay in front of them. The growing town was home to fifteen thousand souls and a large local militia whom Edward and crew already had the delight of encountering. Two roads crossed through the middle of Winchester. One, the main road, travelled alongside a small river leading north to London and south to the aptly named Southampton, amongst other locations, and the crossroads led west to Salisbury and east to the Gammond prison.

The square in the middle of the crossroads hosted a large market every day save Sundays, and shops and inns dotted both main roads, with the less reputable businesses relegated to side streets and back alleys.

Night was upon the crew when they arrived, and the only light was the moon rising and lanterns carried by the guardsmen. "Halt! Who goes there?" a militia man asked.

Anne jumped from her horse and ran to the man, nearly falling into his arms with tears in her eyes and hysteria in full force.

"Oh, heavens am I ever glad to see you, sir! My friends need medical aid. We were ambushed on the road, sir, by most foul brigands. We managed to escape with the help of your comrades on the road, but my friends were injured in the initial attack, so please let us through so we may find a surgeon."

"By Jove, my lady, yes. Bring your friends this way. I will show you to the nearest one."

The guard ran forward and Anne followed on foot, pulling the horse behind her. The crew were escorted five blocks down the main road to a normal home, by all appearances.

After a vehement knock, a light appeared behind the curtain and eyes could be seen glancing at the large company gathered in front of this man's house. "What?"

"Gelson, open the door. These people need your assistance," the guard yelled.

The door was opened without another moment's notice, and the man Gelson poked through. His hair and short bear was grey, though he was not an old man; his body was small but toned, and his wide eyes seemed sharp.

"Do you have any idea what time it is?"

"Come now, Gelson, these gentlemen and lady were attacked and need to be healed, and I need to return to my post. I trust you can handle things from here?"

"Yes, yes." Gelson waved the guard off, and the man walked back to the gate of Winchester. "You may leave your horses in the street, and enter when you are ready. I will gather my tools."

Henry, John, and Sam took the horses to the street next to the man's house while Anne and Edward helped William inside. Nassir carried Herbert, and Edmond helped Charles inside the home of the surgeon.

The room was wide open with no doors save the one for entering and exiting. The surgeon's bed was in the far right corner, sectioned off by short stairs and a railing separating the two levels. Cots and seats for patients were on the opposite corner.

Closer to the entrance, a desk stood at the front right, papers and notebooks strewn on top, with a large window showing the Winchester road. On the left was an operating table with dried blood on the floor nearby, an apparatus unfamiliar to Edward, and a similar window facing the road.

Edward lay William face down on top of the table. There was a faint smell of blood in the air, and something else Edward couldn't place his finger on like a lemon approaching decay: Sweet, lemony, but causing a sting in the back of the throat.

On the back left side of the room various tomes were on the floor, and strewn about a shelf and a desk. On the back right side, another shelf held jars of pickled animal parts, various liquids of unknown origin, and another desk with the surgeon's instruments on top.

In the middle of the room, for an inexplicable reason, two iron poles spaced about one metre apart were affixed ceiling to floor. The poles felt fairly sturdy and no amount of pulling or pushing made them budge, but none save Gelson knew their purpose.

Edward speculated that Alexandre, his surgeon while aboard the *Freedom*, would have loved Gelson's home. Alexandre was an eccentric man at the best of times.

"Thank you for your help. Mister Gelson, correct?" Anne asked.

"Please, call me Nathan. Now, what has happened to this gentleman?" Nathan inquired while walking to the operating table hosting William.

"He received a bullet in the back."

"Fascinating," Nathan commented, lifting up William's shirt and examining the wound. "And you?" Nathan turned his gaze to Anne.

"I have a bullet wound through the arm which needs stitching, and my comrade has a broken arm."

"And what of the gentleman unable to walk?" Nathan asked, pointing to Herbert.

Herbert laughed. "I don't think you can fix my legs, Mr Gelson, unless you're a miracle-worker."

"I will operate on this gentlemen firstly then," Nathan proclaimed while gesturing to William.

Nathan turned on the apparatus near the operating table. Pieces of metal and a yellowish liquid were in a clear bottle with a fire burning underneath. The steam from heating was then filtered through water and then to a tube with an opening at the end. Nathan positioned the opening of the tube over William's mouth and told him to breathe.

"What is that?" Edward asked.

"I call it funny fumes. Makes people laugh and oblivious to pain. I happened upon the recipe one day when I was testing a liquid toothache reliever. By itself, the liquid would burn the gums. I decided to try making the liquid a steam, and discovered the liquid produced a gas when in contact with the iron from my fillings which relieved pain."

The image of burning gums and teeth made everyone listening cringe, save an oblivious William who chuckled uncontrollably.

"See, funny fumes. Great for parties."

William had a smile showing at the corner of his lips and in his eyes. William smiling, and even laughing, was entirely foreign and uncomfortable for Edward to see.

Nathan took a thin knife and made an incision into William's back. He removed the pieces of the iron ball and sewed the wound shut without a peep from William. Henry and Sam held William down throughout, but it felt unnecessary.

Amazing. Perhaps this man is not as dull as I assumed.

"So how did you received such injuries? Do you happen to be street performers? Injuries such as these would seem to happen often by my reckoning."

Edward let out a sigh. *Perhaps not.*

"We were ambushed on the road by brigands in an attempt to take our horses," Anne replied, being the experienced confidence woman.

"Ah, how unfortunate. You should be wary at night, young ones, and keep your wits about you at all times. Consider me: I could spot a rogue any day."

Anne failed to completely suppress her amusement at this. "We will keep that in mind," she assured him as she replaced William on the operating table.

After Anne took hold of the fuming tube she closed her eyes as Nathan went to work. He sewed up the open wound and secured a fresh cotton bandage over it. After he was done, Anne removed the tube and opened her eyes, fully alert.

"Edward, you simply must try some of this!" she exclaimed, holding the tube. "My arm felt separated from my body and I could barely feel anything. What an incredible sensation." She took another whiff and began laughing uncontrollably.

"I think I will pass," Edward said, holding up his hand in protest.

"There is no need to operate on you anyway, my boy. Let me take a look at you." Nathan examined Edward's broken forearm, which was bruised and turning purple where the break occurred. "Yes, this does not need surgery. However, the bone is dislocated. If we do not fix the placement the arm won't heal properly." Nathan led Edward to the two iron poles. "Fully extend the broken arm and grip the iron bar. Then, push your shoulder against the opposite pole. Be sure to keep a tight grip."

Edward did as instructed. He closed his eyes at the pain shooting through his forearm. *What is the purpose of this nonsense?*

Edward received his answer sooner than he expected. Nathan reared back and punched Edward's forearm. Edward let out a scream which echoed through the whole home, and then fell, clutching his arm.

"Now your arm should heal properly."

"Dad damn you, you barnacle-covered son of a bitch!" Edward yelled.

Nathan laughed and shrugged his shoulders. Anne rushed over, dragged Edward to the gas machine, and placed the tube over his face.

Edward took deep breaths of the gas and his pain subsided. He closed his eyes and felt just as Anne described. His pain and arm were not part of his body, like he was floating in the air.

While in that dreamlike state, Nathan fastened a sling around Edward's arm. "I must tell Alexandre about this," Edward noted between deep breaths. "But knowing Alexandre, he will probably blow it up somehow." Edward laughed uncontrollably.

Later, Edward received instructions on how to recreate the gas, Anne paid Nathan, and the group left for an inn Anne had reserved. A few men of the militia and townsfolk still stalked the quiet streets in the middle of the night, making walking out in the open tempting fate, so Anne guided them through side streets to reach to their destination.

"So, speaking of Alexandre, why didn't we go to him for help?" Edward asked.

"Alexandre is at Bodden Town, and said to pick him up when we are ready."

"Tch." *That is something he would say.*

Edward and his group reached the back entrance of the inn without being stopped or spotted. They entered through the kitchen where those slaving over a hot fire glanced up and greeted Anne like they were the best of friends and didn't bat an eye at the odd troupe behind her.

The wafting smells of roasting meat and potatoes enticed Edward, William, Charles, and Edmond, and reminded them of the great hunger built over the time of their imprisonment. Anne's beckoning and the noises from the dining hall pulled Edward from the food and further into the inn.

He was not prepared for what would happen when he walked through the swinging doors of the kitchen to the dining hall.

At first, the noise continued as normal. The crew of the *Freedom* were jovially laughing, talking, pinching the servers, eating and drinking to their fill. But one person turned to see who entered and his jaw dropped instantly.

"Captain!"

A hush drew like a wave over the inn and all eyes turned to the entrance of the kitchen. In utter silence, the crew processed the face before them.

"It's the Captain!" "Edward!" "Blackbeard!" "Captain Thatch!"

The gathering in the large inn rushed to Edward and pulled at him all at once. Hands tried to grab Edward, or his beard; others hugged him and patted him on the shoulder. Eventually he was lifted into the air and carried around on a few of the men's shoulders. Edward was passed a drink, and cheers were shouted all around. Some had tears in their eyes, others the widest of grins, and still others were in shock over the whole affair, as if witnessing some dream.

Anne leaned against the wall of the inn, watching the crew with a wide smile on her face.

"Reminds you of old times, eh?" Henry asked.

Anne chuckled. "Yes, but there is still work to be done." Edward's face was full of joy as he greeted his crewmates by name, hugging or shaking hands. "Perhaps we can wait until tomorrow." Anne pushed Henry playfully. "Let's have some fun, yes?"

The crew were in high spirits and the festivities continued well through the night. Drinking, games, stories, and reunions were exchanged with the captain they loved so. William was also a source of much talking and greetings from the crew. Through William's calm exterior, Anne believed she could see happiness deep in his eyes.

The roast and potatoes cooked in the kitchen was served, along with a house ale. The smell of the ale overpowered the food, and thankfully the sweat from the crew as well.

Edward was also able to reunite with Nassir's son, Ochi, and Herbert's sister, Christina. Both had grown since Edward last saw them.

Ochi, now fifteen, had experienced a growth spurt and was almost up to Edward's shoulder, which is to say between about five ten and six feet tall. He resembled his father too, becoming broad in shoulder and with strong arms.

Christina, now sixteen, had grown out her strawberry blond hair, which framed her face and made her more womanly than before. Her brother had taught her how to sail a ship over the past year.

Edward was also shocked and delighted to hear that Ochi and Christina were dating as well. They were young, and of different colour, but the bond they'd developed on the *Freedom* and the year afterwards was strong. *They are happy together, and that is all that matters.*

Despite their injuries, the fervour of the crew managed to keep Edward awake until the last. But, as with every good thing, the revelry ended.

The following morning, Edward awoke with a terrible aching in his head, and his arm was pulsing waves of pain with each beat of his heart. His eyes slowly opened to the room he must have chosen at some point through the night. Anne was also under the blankets of his bed, opening her eyes after a long night of raucous behaviour.

Edward's mouth was dry, so he smacked his tongue to bring back some moisture. "Did we…?"

"No, we did not," she replied, knowing his stream of thought. "For one thing, our clothes are still on." Anne pulled the blankets off them both, revealing their dirty, smelly clothes from the night before.

"Right." Edward examined the room, noting the bottles of rum and glasses scattered on the floor. "For the record, I would enjoy remembering our first time."

Anne smiled as she snuggled closer to Edward. "I concur."

"So, I noticed only half the crew are here. Was this all you were able to gather?" Edward asked, his eyes closed and his left arm wrapped around Anne's shoulders.

"The rest of the crew are at Portsmouth, ready for when we arrive, where the *Freedom* is docked."

"And Jack is with them?" Edward asked of the American musician aboard the *Freedom.*

Edward remembered the last time he saw Jack. A demon from Jack's past had showed up, Admiral of the White, George Rooke, and Jack tried to kill him for retribution over something, but failed.

Anne opened her eyes, a sad expression on her face. "Jack… is having some issues."

Edward opened his eyes this time, darkness filling his mind. "Where is he?"

"In town. Jack has been at a tavern at least as long as we have been here, perhaps longer. I tried to bring him back, but I cannot bring him out of his pity." Anne raised herself up. "I think only you would be able to help Jack recover at this point."

"You may be right." *Jack, what happened? How could you fall so low?*

Edward recalled a conversation he once had with Jack. The man had explained how he was an addict, and the one thing which had brought him out was his love for a woman, but he never disclosed what happened to her. Edward knew the incident involved George Rooke somehow.

Edward rose from the bed and stripped. A piping hot bath, complete with rose petals floating in it, had been drawn by phantoms from the inn staff, which Edward took immediate advantage of.

After Edward lowered himself in, Anne rose and gathered his clothes. She took off the golden sword and left the hat on a seat, but took the coat, tattered shirt, and ripped pantaloons with her.

"I'll give these away and buy you a new outfit. I shall be back."

"Oh! Wait!" Edward yelled. Anne backed up, clothes in hand. Edward rummaged through the pockets until he found the ever-important letter left by Benjamin Hornigold. Without that letter Edward would not be able to follow the clue to the next key for the ship. "Could you set that on the table? Also, first the carriages, then the weapons, then the inn, and now clothes? Where are you acquiring all this money?"

"Some was donated by the crew." Anne took the letter and grinned devilishly. "And, when I left the palace this time, I... collected my inheritance early, selling it to a few merchants here and there."

Edward laughed. "You truly are a pirate at heart."

"It is the company I keep, after all. Spoils the bunch and all that," Anne said before passionately kissing Edward and leaving the room.

Edward took his time cleaning himself and thinking over his next course of action. *I want Jack with us again. He is a part of this crew and I'm sure he is equally missed by everyone else.*

The hot bath was more than welcome after the stay in prison. Edward washed away the grime from a year past in the rosewater. By the end of his bath, the water was well past clear and it lost its sweet smell.

Anne returned with new clothes and Edward knew what he wanted to do about Jack.

The clothes were very similar to what Edward wore before: white tunic, baggy pantaloons, and black leather coat. After cleaning the tricorn hat, Edward once again wore an outfit befitting the captain of a ship.

After Edward dressed, he pocketed the letter from Benjamin Hornigold and went downstairs, allowing Anne to bathe and change. A few of the crew were in the dining hall and greeted him. They too were feeling the effects of the night before, and ordered food to break their fast. Ham, fried eggs, and sausage were brought to Edward along with a cup of coffee and another of water.

The black liquid, bitter in taste, also brought memories of Jack to Edward's mind, coffee being Jack's favourite drink after a night of excess. The crew stared at Edward as he gazed into his drink, knowing what he was thinking.

The crew ate in near silence until more people joined the dining hall. By mid-morning the whole crew was out and being fed, talking and playing games of cards. When Anne entered the hall, fresh and rejuvenated by the bath, Edward talked with her about his plans to see if they coincided with hers.

Anne's red hair, still wet from the bath, glistened in the sunlight along with her oceanic green eyes. Edward could lose himself in those eyes like the sea he loved so. "So how long do we have to retrieve the *Freedom*?"

"Two months. The British Navy will start using *Freedom* as a marine vessel once all the paperwork is cleared."

"And what kind of travel time can we expect with a group this large?"

"Near one and a half weeks for travel to Portsmouth. Less if we split up, and we should. We'll stand out too much with this many people."

"All right then. Will you travel with the crew to keep them in line and set things in motion?"

"I'm fine with that, but are you expecting Jack to be resistant?"

"I don't expect any issues with Jack re-joining us, but we'll need him sober by the time we enter Portsmouth."

"I will stay and help," Henry said, walking up behind Edward.

"I be stayin' too," Sam added, walking down the stairs.

Edward cocked an eyebrow. "Why do you want to stay, Sam?"

"I 'ave a feeling somethin' fun is gonna happen." Sam said with a smirk.

Anne turned to Edward, fear in her eyes. "I think we should stay with you."

Edward laughed. "Don't let Sam's nonsense scare you. Nothing bad will happen." As soon as Edward spoke the words, he felt a chill from head to toe. *Suddenly, I have a bad feeling about this.*

"I will trust in you three then. Will you tell the crew what's happening?" Anne asked.

Edward nodded and stepped onto a small elevated stage at the front of the inn. He laid out the plan to the crew, leaving out the parts about stealing *Freedom* and anything which could implicate them to the inn staff. The crew made their objections and Edward simply stated he would be late by a week or two at the most to allow Jack enough time to withdraw the alcohol from his system. With the decision made, Edward descended the stairs and the crew prepared for departure.

Henry smiled widely. "I see your skills in public speaking have improved, my young apprentice."

"What are you talking about?" Edward said, exasperated.

"You spoke to the crew as if you had been speaking in public forever. You even answered questions without a hint of your nervousness," Henry said, referring to Edward's previous apprehension with public speaking, and Henry's attempts at helping Edward overcome his fear.

"Of course. I long ago lost any anxiety with speaking to crowds."

Henry wiped away a fake tear. "The apprentice... becomes the master."

Edward sighed. "Let's recover Jack." He stopped short. "Wait, I forgot one thing."

Edward sought out Charles and Edmond in the dining hall. The old man and the child were sitting together, eating with the crew.

"So, old man, this is it. You have your freedom now, so what will you do?"

Charles, appearing much better than he did in the prison, scratched his balding head. "I suppose I could head to Southampton, I have family who can support me."

"I will arrange for some of my crew to help you travel. Would it be too much to ask you to take Edmond along with you?"

"What?" Edmond yelled, rising from his seat. "I want to go with you, Edward. I want to have freedom on the open sea too!"

Edward pitied the boy, because he understood Edmond's desire. "I'm sorry Edmond, but you cannot join us. Especially for those reasons. You need to find your own *Freedom*. Just because my *Freedom* is on the seas doesn't mean yours is. I want you to join Charles and learn from him and then, maybe in a few years if you still feel you want to join us, I will allow it."

Edmond pouted and sat back down. "Fine."

Edward patted the young man on the head, then said goodbye to Anne and instructed her to escort Charles and Edmond to Southampton.

Henry waited at the door of the inn while Edward spoke his goodbyes to Anne. He watched with an unconscious frown on his face as Edward and Anne kissed. Anne ruffled Edward's wavy black hair and handed him a coin purse before sending him on his way.

"Ready?" Henry asked as Edward approached.

"Yes. Do you know the way?"

"Follow me," Henry replied confidently.

The two trekked through the streets of Winchester with the sun shining down upon them, allowing them a better view than the night before. The morning dew was still filtering in from the forest and carried with it the smells of fresh cooking from the market. The aroma mixed sweetly in Edward's nose before he could sense smells natural to the town, like livestock, horses, mud and moisture.

On the long cobblestone road, many were going about their business, some with child, some alone, and others Edward noticed were carrying notebooks. When Edward pointed out the many young men in similar uniforms, Henry mentioned Winchester College. The college was a prominent boarding school for boys, and accounted for much of Winchester's growth.

Halfway to their destination, Sam came running after them, offended that Edward and Henry didn't wait. The three then travelled further into town. Beggars frequently approached Edward to see if he carried coin, drawn by his dress. Edward kept his hands in his pockets at all times to protect his money and the letter, arguably the more important of the two, from being taken. They arrived at their destination well before reaching the square with all those delightful smells.

Henry stopped in front of a lively tavern and the three entered together. Inside, the place was packed with people even at this hour. There was loud music being played from a piano, and the people inside were equally loud in their festivities. The delightful smells of the town immediately fled in the face of the smell of sweat and ale inside the tavern.

Lounging on a couch in the corner was Jack Christian. Edward remembered a gentle Jack, with pleasing features of short brown hair, light hazel eyes, and fair, clean-shaven skin. However, this Jack was growing thick stubble, dishevelled hair, and his eyes were sullen with bags underneath. His normally fair skin had turned to a deathly pallor due to the drink, despite the appearance of euphoria on his face.

Edward didn't want to stay any longer than he had to, so he walked straight over to the man. "Hello, Jack."

Jack moved his whole body to see who called him. He didn't stand up, but he grinned and extended his arms. "Captain! You, you're here to see me, my brother," Jack said, his American accent distinguishing him from the British locals.

"That's right, and we're here to take you someplace special. Up you go." Edward took hold of Jack's hand and pulled him up off the couch.

"Special?" Jack asked listlessly, glancing back to the table full of booze in confusion and want.

"Yes, very special. Henry, Sam, are you going to make my injured self carry Jack?" Edward inquired, spurring Henry and Sam to take Jack.

Blackbeard's Ship

The drunks at the table—his "friends"—wanted Jack to stay, but Edward and crew were able to tear Jack away after some coaxing. Some patrons and the barman eyed Edward and his companions suspiciously as they left.

Jack was carried out of the tavern and the four began the trek to Nathan the surgeon's house. Jack drifted in and out of awareness, asking questions of Edward a few times, but most were incoherent. The group elicited gaping from passersby as they walked down the main street.

When they reached the house, the door was quickly opened after Edward knocked. Nathan stood in the doorway. "Ah, I think I remember you. Patient of mine?"

Edward sighed. "Yes, we were here yesterday."

"What did I treat for you?"

Edward was dumbfounded, as the sling was still in plain view underneath the coat he wore. "Broken arm," he replied simply.

"Ah, yes, yes. Please, enter. Someone else need treating?" Nathan questioned, stepping aside to allow the group to enter.

Henry and Sam took Jack to the operating table and lay him down on it face up. "Our friend here is addicted to alcohol and God knows what else. We need him clean, and I understand the process can sometimes be rather… messy, without assistance."

"Well then, how interesting. I will see what I can do." Nathan used thick leather belts to secure Jack's chest, arms, and legs to the table.

"Are the straps really necessary?" Henry asked.

Sam laughed. "Have ye never seen an addict without the fix fer long? Jack old boy 'eres gonna be thrashin and screamin fer sustenance 'for long."

"I'm afraid your English-impaired friend is correct. Those symptoms are all part of the substances being removed from the system. There is not much we can do but provide comfort and ensure he does not die."

The door to Nathan's home opened loudly and three men stepped in. The man in the middle wore gentlemen's clothes of a puffy white neck tie, red blazer with gold buttons, a red long coat with gold trim to his knees, and pantaloons reaching below the kneecap with high socks. The two other men wore simpler clothes of white tunic and black vest, with long black pantaloons.

"What ails you gentlemen?" Nathan asked, approaching them.

"We 'eard some blokes was tryin' ta take away a man who owes me money, and I fancied seein' who had the gall," the man in the middle said. "The name's Thomas Blunes, and you must be the famous Blackbeard."

The man in red was a man of plain appearance in every other department. Average-sized nose, white teeth, brown eyes and hair, and medium build with a height just shy of six feet, and middle age made him indistinct. Edward reckoned Blunes craved attention, judging by his demeanour and flashy outfit.

"Oh, I am some dreaded man named Blackbeard, am I?" Edward feigned.

"Ye can play the fool all ya like, but the build fits. Not many so tall as you 'round these parts. And word has it Gammond prison suffered a riot the day 'afore, near the 'ole lot of prisoners escaped. Your name was all over the papers when you was jailed a year ago. Not much a stretch, truly." Edward tensed. "Don' worry, mate, I care not about you, until a bounty be on yer 'ead, that is." Blunes moved closer and pointed to Jack. "This man owes me a gambling debt, and I will be repaid before I allow him to leave Winchester."

Edward sighed. *Oh course he does. Why would he indulge in only one vice?* "How much?" Edward questioned, reaching for his coin purse.

"Sorry, mate, but I've arrived at an idea what will pay me back tenfold."

"What do you propose?"

"A fight. You 'gainst the reigning champ of underground fightin' in Winchester. Yer name is huge, 'specially with news of the escape. People will place bets on the man who kidnapped the princess, then you throw the match."

"In case you didn't notice, I'm injured. There won't be much of a fight."

"I'm sure you'll provide a good show until you lose, and besides, I only need yer name."

"So I lose this match and Jack's debt is paid?"

"I'm a man of me word. Ye do this and he's free to go with ye." Blunes extended his hand.

Edward took Blunes' hand and shook it, sealing the deal without hesitation.

Blunes went to the nearby table, removed some paper from his pocket, used a quill to write an address down, then handed the paper to Edward. "Two weeks, The Den, eight o'clock sharp. And be sure to bulk up to at least make the fight look good, ya?"

"Right." *This shouldn't be too hard.*

6. THE DEVIL OF THE DEN

During the two weeks, Edward began training with Sam and Henry, and was provided a diet regimen by Nathan which would help with stamina and muscle building. From Edward's lack of food in prison, he'd lost most of the fat on his body, so gaining back muscle was easy.

Edward simply returned to the basics so he could hold his own and make it appear as if he wasn't throwing the match. Early morning runs around Winchester, sparring with Sam, more running, sparring with Henry, and running again was the typical day for Edward over the two weeks.

Jack had a severely more difficult time. In the beginning, the detoxification was minor: Anxiety, yawning, but with difficulty to sleep, and sweating. But not long after, body aches, nausea, tremors, and even hallucinations set in. To Jack and his friends, combining those was like some sort of punishment from God himself. Edward and company tried their best to make Jack comfortable.

"Edward, please, this is cruel. You must allow me a little bit to take away the pain," Jack pleaded after a few days, tears in his bloodshot eyes.

"I am sorry Jack, you know I cannot. The most important thing I learned from being saved from prison is to wait and hope. If you hold out a little longer this pain will be gone and you will be back to your old self."

Jack could say nothing after seeing his captain's eyes. Jack closed his eyes to the pain and waited for it to subside. Throughout the detoxification, Jack never again asked for his precious alcohol.

At the end of the two weeks, Jack was through the worst and was cleared for release from the shackles. Nathan recommended constant supervision for the next while, and even afterwards not to let Jack alone when on shore.

Edward noticeably changed over the two weeks' training. Although he was not quite back to his old self, and his broken arm was still, well, broken, he was considerably more fearsome and would no doubt produce the effect Blunes desired at his 'Den.'

"Jack, you and Sam prepare some horses so we are ready to leave. Henry and I have some business to take care of and then we'll head to Portsmouth." Edward handed the coin purse to Sam and then left to the Den.

"You can count on us, Captain," Jack reassured Edward as he left.

Sam tossed the coin purse in the air. "So… want ta toss a few back with me, mate?"

Nathan and Jack both smacked Sam in the back of the head as he laughed at his own cruel joke.

Edward and Henry ran to the location Blunes wrote down on the sheet of paper, causing those in the streets to stare. After reaching the street, Edward and Henry travelled past a few worn houses until reaching a warehouse district. Edward continued walking until he found one with the number thirteen painted over two large wooden doors, matching what was written in the sheet. The warehouse resembled an old weapons manufacturing plant.

Edward and Henry walked up to two guards at the front of the warehouse. "Password?" one of the guards asked.

Edward took out the paper from Blunes, but there was nothing indicating a password for entrance.

"We were invited by Thomas Blunes, but he didn't provide a password."

The guards laughed. "Then it's simple: you're lying. The boss would have given you a password if he wanted you here."

"No, he certainly wanted me here. I am Blackbeard."

The guards were serious for a moment, then burst into laughter once more. "You? Blackbeard? What a joke."

"I'm telling you, I am Blackbeard and there is no password."

The guards stopped laughing abruptly. "What did you say?" one of them asked.

"I said, I am Blackbeard."

"After that."

"There is no password?"

"Tch." One of the guards opened the door. "Welcome to the Den, *Blackbeard*."

Edward shook his head as he went through the door. As he was passing he could hear the guards talk amongst themselves. "The boss really needs to make a new password." "I keep asking him what he wants the password to be, but he always says the same thing." Edward rubbed the bridge of his nose in frustration, and travelled further into the Den.

Edward entered and immediately noticed a table to his right with a young scantily clad woman sitting behind it and a guard standing behind her.

"What can I do for you gentlemen?" the young lady at the counter asked in a sickeningly sweet high pitch.

"I'm Edward Thatch, Blackbeard. I'm here for a fight."

"Changing rooms are behind me. Mr Blunes will call you when

we're ready for you."

Edward thanked the woman and walked around the counter to a hallway. There was a door on each side of the hallway, so Edward opened the left door and headed in.

Inside, a man of Henry's build, six feet tall, wide, and muscular was sitting on a bench. He appeared to be Russian, from his prominent chin and eyebrows. When Edward entered, the man stood, his expression pure fury.

Another gentleman with a cotton towel around his neck looked Edward's way. "Blackbeard, I presume?" Edward nodded. "Your room is next door."

"Yes, thank you." Edward closed the door, the large man glaring at him the whole time.

"I'm guessing he's the person you are to fight," Henry surmised.

"Yes, I would say," Edward agreed as he went to the next room. "I would also say this fight will hurt."

"Yes, well, you're the one who decided to do something foolish again."

"Breaking into a prison is far more foolish than this."

Henry grinned and shrugged his shoulders.

The room they entered was plain in appearance with a low bench in the middle and a table with a rolled cotton strip for wrapping wounds, a wick for lighting, and a bucket of water.

A man standing in the middle of the room turned around. "Thomas Blunes," Edward pronounced. "To what do we owe the pleasure?"

"I need ta read ye the rules, and make a wardrobe suggestion."

Henry cocked an eyebrow. "Wardrobe suggestion?"

"More on that later. First: the rules. There are no rules. See? Easy. Fight with anythin' you can, make a good show, and throw the fight."

"And the 'wardrobe'?" Edward asked, wary of what was forthcoming.

"I have something flashy and fear-inspiring to make you stand out and make my regulars want to bet on you." After Blunes helped Edward with his image, he took Edward to the entrance hallway.

Edward wore a cloak and baggy breeches reaching to below the knees and thin shoes meant for manoeuvrability. His chest was exposed, which had filled out some since two weeks prior, showing his muscular abdomen.

"This won't work. I'll appear a fool."

"Nonsense. Remember, no smiling, jus' stare straight at the crowd," Blunes advised.

Blunes took a light to long strands of wick set in Edward's beard. The wick burned slowly and was meant for smoke, which surrounded Edward's face and lent him a ghastly visage.

After Blunes was satisfied, he pushed Edward forward and into the warehouse. On all sides a large crowd occupied the warehouse. Men and women of all stations stood arm to arm, shouting and jeering at the lack of a fight. Past them a large iron-barred cage stood in the middle of the warehouse, with guards holding the people at bay to allow the fighters passage to the cage.

Edward strolled forward, staring at the audience, the smoke wisping and billowing around his face. As Edward's eyes met the men and women, the silence his stare elicited spread like a wave around the crowd, starting at the entrance and making its way around. In the silence, Edward's gaze instilled fear. Some of the women wept, others fainted, and the men turned away, wiping sweat from their brows.

Blunes was beginning to sweat as well. "Tone it down, kid, you'll make them want to bet on the other fighter. Forget it, I can turn this around."

When Blunes and Edward reached the cage where Henry waited, the two stepped up to a stage, staring at the crowd below. "Ladies and gentlemen, tonight we are visited by a devil. He intends to show us the meaning of reaping what thy sows." Blunes lifted Edward's arm in the air. "The Devil Blackbeard arrived to take the soul of Hammons this night!" he yelled to the awed crowd. "As the dark messenger himself, Blackbeard knows the wages Hammons' sins must pay, and he will collect!"

Blunes continued to rile up the crowd as Henry, wearing Edward's coat and tricorn hat, examined and ensured the cotton bandage was tight around Edward's knuckles.

"I assumed you would be against this, Henry, but you never objected to the fight these whole two weeks past."

"Well, this seemed the only way to help Jack," replied Henry. "We certainly couldn't muscle our way out with the four of us. Besides, what's the harm in you being beaten to a pulp? You'll pay Jack's debt and learn your lesson in doing foolish things at the same time."

"I see no love was lost over our year apart."

Henry smirked and then took the wick out of Edward's beard as his opponent entered. He was met with jeers and shouts of damnation from the crowd.

"Looks as if Blunes' plan worked," Henry said, glancing at the muscular man and the crowd.

Blunes introduced the other fighter as Hammons the Hammer and brought him into the iron cage. Edward entered the cage, and the opening was locked behind him. Edward and Hammons were locked together in a prison for two.

Edward took in deep breaths. The smells of sweat, cheap ale, and blood crept into his nose along with the metal of the warehouse. Edward filtered away those senses, and focused on the man across from him.

Give them a good show.

A sharp ding of a bell indicated the start of the fight and Edward advanced towards Hammons.

Hammons took the initiative and rushed at Edward, fists flying. Edward pulled back and pushed the fists aside with his left hand, the good one. Hammons kept pushing Edward into his own pace from the start. Edward was backed into the wall of the cage. Hammons kept up the pressure and delivered blow after blow to Edward's head and chest.

Edward was having issues because of his injury. He had to block and jab with his left hand at the same time. *Damn this useless arm of mine!*

"Get off the wall!" Henry yelled, as riled up as the crowd.

Easier said than done. Edward kept bobbing and weaving, weaving and bobbing, blocking and jabbing, but he couldn't see a moment to escape the onslaught. Hammons reared back and delivered a right hook. Edward could easily see the fist approaching his temple. He pulled back, letting the wild swing follow through, then countered with a left cross.

The left cross, named for the fist crossing over the opponent's arm, was powerful because the opponent's momentum was used against him.

Edward's cross punch was brutal, and caused Hammons to trip and fall backwards. Edward jumped off the wall to the middle of the ring. The crowd turned wild.

Hammons quickly rose to his feet and continued his assault. Edward pushed back this time; he delivered jabs in quick succession to keep Hammons at bay. Hammons threw punches at Edward, but missed due to his poor reach.

By the time the bell rang once more, allowing the fighters a break, Hammons' lip was bloody and his eye was starting to swell.

Edward sat on a stool in the corner provided by Henry and drank some water. Henry wiped Edward's brow with a towel.

"Blunes wants another similar round and then you can start losing."

"Right," Edward acknowledged between deep breaths.

The bell was rung again and the second round began. The second round went much like the first, with Edward dominating the fight with quick jabs and a few well-timed crosses. Edward did end up taking a few hits; his ribs were hurting and his eye was feeling puffy.

That should be enough. Edward eyed Blunes as Henry cleaned him up and gave him water again. Blunes nodded.

"Don't lose too quickly, and protect the arm."

"Right." *I'll defend until the middle of the round, and then let Hammons punch me a few times.*

After the bell, Edward strode to the centre with confidence. Hammons ran up to Edward and delivered a right hook followed by a left hook to the body. The combination came so quickly Edward's instinct took over and he pulled up his arms to guard. The left hook hit his broken arm hard, and the jolting pain reminded Edward forcibly of Hammons' nickname: The Hammer.

Edward suppressed a scream. Whatever had been healed over the past two weeks was instantly wrought asunder from Hammons' punch. Edward's vision began fading from the pain, but he forced his eyes to stay open. He blocked an incoming punch from Hammons and fought back wildly.

Hammons stepped back and sneered at Edward's pathetic attempts. Hammons had known from the beginning Edward was injured, from Edward's plain-to-see bruise on his right arm to his affinity for blocking with his left arm.

Hammons took his time, working Edward over with lighter punches, whittling him down little by little. A jab here, an uppercut there, every hit meant to bring out Edward's weak and exhausted body.

The next round was like a blur. Edward was in too much pain to be able to fight back. He threw a left hook to Hammons' head, but he moved out of the way and punched Edward in the jaw, sending him to the back of the iron cage.

The sound of the crowd was deafening in Edward's ears, but loudest of all was a ringing noise which wouldn't quit. Sweat poured down his face, along with blood from a cut over his eye and a broken nose. Edward scanned the high walkway around the inside perimeter of the warehouse and saw Thomas Blunes, smiling.

Damn it, Jack. How did you rope me into this? Edward glanced at Henry. *I guess you were right Henry, I learned my lesson.* Edward's slow moving gaze turned to Hammons, who was stalking towards him, his massive arms ready to strike. *But I would do it again! Come on then!* Edward gritted his teeth and pulled up his heavy left arm in defiance of his weariness.

The two fighters were about to start again when screams rose from the entrance. The crowd was fleeing from something. Edward peered to the source of the noise and saw something worse than the beating he was receiving.

Twenty militiamen entered the warehouse on a raid and began arresting people in the crowd, with some of them heading towards the ring for the ultimate quarry.

Henry ran into the ring and pulled Edward out, helping him to stay up. As the two left the ring, crazed people running in front of them, they were met by an armed official.

Henry kicked him in the chest and the man fell over in a heap. Henry grabbed the official's gun.

Men and women crowded each visible exit. Edward noticed movement above on the walkway. Thomas Blunes was opening a window and jumping through, cursing as he did so.

"Look," Edward pointed.

Henry looked at where Edward was pointing, then glanced around. "Do you see any stairs to get up there?"

Edward tried to find stairs to the walkway, but he couldn't see any. Edward searched for another escape route and noticed a ladder near an exit at the back.

"There."

Henry followed Edward's outstretched hand, then rushed to the ladder, pulling Edward along in a near drag. They weaved through the crowd of people trying to run away from the militia, pushing and shoving those smaller than him out of the way.

When Edward and Henry reached the ladder, Henry pushed Edward up the steps. Edward's grip was feeble and the exhaustion of the match was settling in. He'd lost his boost of resolve from the last round and was running on empty. Edward climbed one rung at a time, trying to speed himself, but his shaking arms and legs made things difficult.

"Hurry Edward! They're gaining on us!" Henry yelled, pushing his friend further up. Henry let out an exasperated grunt and pushed Edward up using his shoulder. With the added help the two were able to reach the top of the ladder in less than a minute.

From the high vantage point, Edward and Henry could see the whole scene: The large iron ring in the centre with the crowd rushing to the closest exit, and some fighting against the local authorities. The militia barred the main entrance, and more slipped through the back, trying to block off all exits. Soon the whole warehouse would be blocked and the spectators suppressed at gunpoint.

Henry and Edward went to the open window Blunes had used to escape not moments ago. Henry helped Edward up and out of the window and then jumped up to start pulling himself through. The militia noticed and fired upon them, eliciting more screams from the crowd below. The bullets hit the window, causing the glass to shatter over Henry's head, and then he let out a scream.

Henry lost grip of the window ledge and began to fall. Edward grabbed Henry and pulled him back up inch by inch. Once Henry was high enough, he pulled himself over the edge and onto the roof.

Edward's eyes were focused again despite their puffiness. He lifted Henry's shirt and examined the wound on his back. "Good, the bullet missed the spine. Do you think you can walk?"

Henry pushed himself to his knees. "I think so. Help me up." He extended his hand and Edward helped Henry up to his feet; he was able to stand, albeit shakily. "How about you?"

"The danger has rejuvenated me; I'll be fine."

To Edward's left, a wooden board connected the warehouse to another building. "There!" Edward pointed. "Let's go that way."

Glass shattered as bullets ripped through more windows nearby, aimed to hit Edward and Henry. The two ducked down, glancing into the warehouse again. The militia were rounding up everyone they could and chasing after the escapees.

Edward moved forward, crossing the wooden plank with ease. Henry was moving slowly and he limped with each step. "Hurry, Henry!" Edward yelled. Henry shuffled across the plank, peering to the ground forty feet down. "Don't look down! Focus on me," Edward commanded. Henry trained his sharp brown eyes on his best friend as he took the last few steps across.

The militia were crawling through the window when Henry crossed over. Edward kicked the wooden plank over the edge and it fell to the ground below with a snap. More militiamen climbed to the roof and opened fire. Edward grabbed Henry and helped him move forward this time.

Edward and Henry hurried around the side of a rooftop entrance to escape the gunfire. Another plank led straight across to the next building. The two crossed once more and removed the plank so none could follow. The next building Edward and Henry were on had a flat roof and no discernible way into the building itself.

Suddenly, on the far building over, in front of the one Edward and Henry were on, a head popped up out of nowhere. When the person saw Edward and Henry, he stood up.

"Captain, this way!" Jack yelled, waving at Edward.

Edward, having no time for astonishment, moved to the ledge with Henry. Unlike the prior buildings, there was no wooden plank to bridge the gap.

Damn and damn again! Edward searched, but could find no other means of travel across. *I guess there's no other way then.* Edward pulled Henry back a fair distance, then pulled Henry up and over his shoulder, carrying him. The pain in his arm, as well as the injuries from the fight, flared, but Edward pushed it to the back of his mind.

Henry groaned in pain. "What are you doing?"

"I'm jumping across this ledge."

Henry considered what he wanted to say for a moment. "Please don't kill us," he pleaded, in no position to argue with Edward.

Edward bent his knees and focused intently on Jack. He took deep breaths as he tested his legs. Edward ran as fast as he could to the edge of the roof with Henry draped over his shoulder. He planted his foot down on the ledge, bent down, and jumped off. At the apex of his jump, Edward slowed and fell. He pushed Henry off of him at the last second. Henry fell and rolled onto the roof, but Edward slammed into the wall of the building and clutched to the edge for dear life.

Edward's grip was precarious at best, and his fingers were shaking with the effort he was pouring into holding on. Edward was already low energy, and this pushed him to the limit. One by one his fingers slipped. Before Edward and Henry were about to be wrenched from their perch, Jack grabbed onto Edward's hand and pulled him up.

Sam was on the roof as well, helping Henry into the trapdoor. Jack helped Edward move into the hole and shut it afterwards.

The four were in the attic of an abandoned building. A small lantern with a faint light illuminated the empty space.

"We should be safe here until things die down," Jack assured them, sitting down on the wooden floorboards.

"How did you find us?"

Jack scratched his head. "Well, I asked Sam and he eventually told me. We went to the warehouse and watched the match. After the militia arrived, I noticed you heading to the roof. I'm acquainted with the owner, and I knew the approximate location you would head to, so I entered this building in the hopes we could do just this."

Caught up with Jack's succinct explanation, Edward noticed Nathan treating Henry. "Not that I'm ungrateful, but, Nathan, why did you follow my crew?"

Nathan removed the bullet from Henry's back, then glanced at Edward before examining his surroundings. "I thought I was at home. Where are we?"

"You're... we're... never mind. We are at your home, in your attic."

Nathan was shocked. "I have an attic?"

Sam pulled Nathan back to Henry's open wound. "Focus, mate."

Jack stepped closer to Edward. "Captain, I want to thank you for your help over this past week. I can't thank you enough for what you did."

"I don't need your thanks, Jack. I know you would do the same for me. I need you to promise me this sort of thing will not happen again."

Jack was silent for a moment as the shadow of tears filled his eyes. "I'm sorry, Captain, but I don't know if I'll be able to keep that promise. I was in a dark place, and you brought me out, but I feel as if I'm on the edge... I need help to stay on the right side."

"Then we will all be there for you. The worst thing you can do is believe you are alone and without a family, Jack. I don't know the details of how you lost yours, and we're not a replacement by any means, but you have us now and always." Jack nodded, the tears flowing from his eyes now. "And I know not how the Admiral of the White is involved, but if you desire revenge, I will make it happen." Edward extended his hand to Jack.

Jack took Edward's hand firmly in grasp. "I will have his head, and then I will tell you my story."

"You've got a deal," Edward said.

7. THE PORTSMOUTH PILLAGING

"Do you know where we were supposed to meet?" Edward asked, a hood covering his face.

"Now, I knew I was forgettin' sumthing," Sam replied with a laugh.

"I know where we were to stay, follow me." Henry advanced his horse to the front of the line.

Edward and company reached Portsmouth in a week and a half. With their injuries, and taking care to avoid the authorities, they were forced to move slowly. There were a few scares along the way, and Edward refusing to shave his particularly massive beard, for which he was well known, didn't help.

Portsmouth was inundated with rain, the overpowering smell of mud and wet horses filling the air, but Edward could still smell a faint hint of the sea air. The horses' hooves clopped and splashed through the pools of rain. Being one of the busiest ports in England, Portsmouth didn't let the rain stop its commerce, and Edward had to guide his horse around the dense crowds.

Portsmouth had several dry docks for repair of ships, and most notably for warships. Because of its strategic position leading directly into the English Channel, Portsmouth also possessed one of the largest naval bases. Edward's ship, the *Freedom*, was being held somewhere in that dock.

Not much longer now, girl. We'll be out at sea soon.

The horses trotted slowly through the streets, over the cobblestone ground, along the edge of the Paulsgrove and Fareham Lakes, and stopped in front of a large inn. The name on the sign read "The Coast and Jib," with a picture of a triangular sail behind the words.

The group tied their horses at the stables in the back and entered the inn from the front. The pleasure upon leaving the wet outdoors and entering the dry indoors, with a crackling fire and the smell of roasting meat wafting from the kitchens, was immeasurable.

The innkeeper and bouncer stopped Edward and company as soon as they entered. "I am sorry, messieurs, this inn is filled with a party. If I am not mistaken the Cobb Inn and the Sea Wench have vacancies."

"We're part of the party," Edward assured the man.

Anne was sitting at a table in the dining hall drinking ale and laughing at one of the stories being told when she noticed Edward and the innkeeper talking, so she sauntered over. "Everyone, the captain is finally here!" she yelled to the crew.

The crew rose from their seats and crowded the entrance. The innkeeper and bouncer moved out of the way, knowing enough to see Edward was telling the truth. Edward walked into the inn, causing the same reaction as a few weeks prior. Everyone wanted to talk with Edward and ask him questions at once, not allowing him an inch to move nor a moment to breathe.

When the crew saw Jack, many hugs, smiles, and laughs were also brought his way. Jack returned them all in kind, the warmth of kinship strengthening his resolve to abstain from his vices. When he was offered ale or rum he declined politely and the crew, remembering their senses, switched to water.

The middle of the day still held the darkness of rain clouds overhead. The sombre atmosphere, and the ramifications from the night before, meant the crew had a somewhat quiet lunch, much to the delight of Edward, Henry, Sam, and Jack. They hadn't eaten much on the way to Portsmouth due to the clandestine trip.

"The date of departure for the *Freedom* was changed to five days from now," Anne said.

Edward was shocked by the suddenness and urgency brought on by the statement, despite Anne's calm. "Are we able to steal *Freedom* back by then?"

"Of course. Everything is prepared, we should be able to take the *Freedom* without a hitch. We have a diversion planned to help us out of the dock, but leaving the harbour is the problem."

"So, we don't have a plan for escaping the harbour itself? Far from being ready, wouldn't you say?"

"Rarely is anything perfect. We can only plan so much," William pointed out, sitting down beside Edward. After the month since being in prison, William was clean-shaven and resembled his old self. "Luck is also part of any plan."

"William! You shaved. Now I can look at you straight," Edward jested.

"Well, someone has to be presentable from this lot."

"You mean someone must be a pratter, right mate?"

William eyed Sam coldly, but he was unfazed. "You should do the same, Edward. It will make passing unsuspected easier," William suggested.

"No," Edward said flatly.

"Why not?" Anne asked.

Henry smacked his palm to his face and muttered, "Here we go again."

"I will not shave this beard because this is a symbol of what the marines and the government has turned me into. Blackbeard is now a name by which I am well known, and to take away the beard is to take away that name. I will use that name and this beard to strike fear into those who made me this way." By the end of his speech, Edward was standing and all eyes were on him. He sat down, embarrassed, and stroked his beard. "I will trim my beard, but no more."

Anne grinned. "I guess there is no way around it then. The beard stays."

"So, back to stealing *Freedom*, why can't we steal her after she's left the harbour? This harbour is filled with Navy ships waiting to attack us when we try to leave."

"The issue with taking the *Freedom* after she has left the harbour is twofold: Firstly, we have no idea where the *Freedom* is headed. Try as I might, I could not divine where she will be stationed. Secondly, ships are expensive. If we wanted to take the *Freedom* we would need a ship of our own, and of close rank to the *Freedom*. I still have quite a sum of money, but not enough for the size of ship we need. Not to mention if we did engage in a battle the *Freedom* would be harmed, and there is a chance we could accidentally sink her."

Edward nodded. "Understood. We leave tomorrow to take the *Freedom* then." Edward took a swig of some rum. "Anne, would you be so kind as to tell our distraction about the plans? I imagine they are in another inn?"

Anne moved from her seat. "Yes, our friends are at an inn down the road. I'll let them know." She left with William following her.

"Tell them I'll be over later to catch up!" Edward yelled to Anne as she left. Anne waved back to let Edward know she heard him. Edward finished his rum and approached the front of the dining hall. "Crew, may I have your attention please? I have an important announcement to make." The crew eventually ceased their jesting, story-telling, and rabblerousing to listen to Edward. "You've all journeyed a long way to be here, and I know all of you made sacrifices for this group of friends I have the pleasure of calling my family. I cannot tell you how proud I am to have you as my crew, as my brothers."

The men yelled a loud "hear, hear!"

"I am also proud to tell you tomorrow is a special day, so you'd best sober up and sleep well. Tomorrow, for the first time in over a year, we set sail!"

The sun was peeking out over the horizon, providing warmth to Portsmouth and offering good fortune for sailors. The previous rain washed away the filth and the clean smell of salty sea air breezed over the city.

Edward's crew travelled through the streets in the open, heading to the ports occupied by the marines. The only people up at this hour were other sailors heading to the wharf to fish or take merchandise from this port to another. Edward's group passed in a triple line behind William, the passersby staring at them with adoration in their eyes.

The crew were dressed as marines, with William dressed as their captain, and Henry beside him as a lieutenant.

William wore a more decorative outfit, not typically worn at sea, but one used for ceremonies. The coat was dark blue, almost black, with gold buttons along the front and gold trim. Underneath, he wore a white waistcoat which puffed around his neck, and on his head he wore a tricorn hat with matching blue colour and gold trim. Epaulets with his rank insignia were on the shoulder.

Henry wore the more traditional dark royal blue coat with gold buttons and gold trim. Beneath the coat, he wore a white tunic which was form-fitting instead of puffy like William's. Most of the crew wore something similar to Henry, but without the gold. Those in the back, who were supposed to represent the lowest ranked, wore civilian clothing, albeit cleaner than the crew was normally used to.

The inn was close to the port, so it didn't take the crew long to reach the wharf. It contained five ships, two in dry dock for repairs, two in open docks, and *Freedom* in an enclosed dock for supplying.

The costumes the crew wore were so well done that none questioned their appearance, despite its suddenness. William guided the group to the enclosed dock holding the *Freedom*. It was a large wooden structure with an open front leading to Fareham Lake.

The crew passed through a corridor which opened up to the closed dock. It was of simple and economical design, merely consisting of the dock itself surrounding the sides of the ship, and an open front for easy departure.

The *Freedom* was floating there, a fifth-class frigate with fifty-three guns and three masts, swaying with the rise and fall of the tide. The fortress home, made of Caribbean pine, was like a dream come true for its former—and soon to be current—crew.

Before setting foot onto the *Freedom*, the crew stopped for a moment to admire the beauty of their ship, their home. Some of them pushed Edward forward and he was jostled out of his silent reverie. He took a few tentative steps up the gangplank and onto the waist of the ship, listening to the familiar sound of his footsteps against the wood. Edward leaned against the railing as he examined his ship.

Blackbeard's Ship

The main mast in front of Edward was broad and strong, with fife rail at the base, main top at the middle, and crow's nest at the top. Edward examined the stern section with the quarterdeck, holding the wheel, and poop deck above the stern cabin. At the bow, the *Freedom* had a forecastle deck above a bow cabin, facing the open harbour. Everything was as Edward remembered, bringing back the nostalgia of his previous adventure. Even the smell of the Caribbean pine mixed with the sea air and reminded Edward of the acrid gunpowder, the iron, the battles and adventures, and the lazy days at sea.

Edward turned to the crew with a wide smile on his face and motioned for them to board. The crew shared the same happiness over finally being able to return to their true home.

When Edward's back was turned he heard a voice ring out behind him. "What is going on here?" Edward ignored the voice and continued preparing the ship with the crew. *Stick to the plan. Regardless of who arrives, look as if you belong.* But that voice sounded so familiar.

"Henry?"

Edward's eyes widened. *How does this man know Henry's name?* Edward turned to see who had entered, and his jaw dropped at the sight. His best friend from his home island of Badabos, Robert Maynard, was standing there in a full marine uniform and holding a musket.

Robert had not changed in the almost two years since Edward saw him last. Blond curly hair, smooth features, blue eyes, five foot ten inches, medium build with a toned body. When Edward and Henry set out to be whalers, before being branded pirates, Robert began his training to join the marines.

When rumours started circulating around about a pirate named Edward Thatch, Robert had searched around for the truth of the matter, eventually ending up in Portsmouth just miles away from where Edward was imprisoned.

We can still salvage this as long as he doesn't see me.

As if hearing Edward's thoughts, Robert turned his gaze to meet Edward's eyes before he could turn away. The shock of recognition was painted on Robert's face when he saw those eyes. To anyone else Edward could have been passed off as someone else, but from Edward's and Henry's best friend, no disguise could hide them.

Knowing the futility of continuing the charade, Edward stepped down off the ship back onto the dock. He walked up beside William, who was still ranting at the marine in front of him and trying to salvage the plan.

"What are you doing, soldier? Return to your post and prepare this ship for departure," William commanded, oblivious.

"William, you can stop. This man knows who I am, and if I

know him, he's already made his decision on what he is about to do. Isn't that so, Robert?"

William and Anne glanced at Edward and then at Robert with confused expressions.

"I always believed in your innocence, Edward. Always," Robert said, his back straight, but his eyes still in shock.

"Until now?" Edward asked. Robert didn't answer. "What say you forget what you saw, for an old friend?"

Robert's eyes filled with anger. "How dare you put me in this position, Edward? You too, Henry. If we were any bit friends you would know I cannot do what you request."

Edward closed his eyes and sighed. "I know, but our distraction should be here soon, and you need make a decision: Either cause your two best friends to be captured and imprisoned, or give us *Freedom*."

Robert, not having witnessed the transformation of his friend as Henry did, was even more shocked by the betrayal and devious nature of what Edward was doing. "What happened to you, Edward?"

"People such as yourself happened," Edward replied coldly.

The sound of a cannonball being fired rang out across the harbour. Robert, Edward and the crew turned their gaze to the sound. The distraction had started.

Edward used the opportunity and punched Robert hard in the face, knocking him to the ground. Several crewmen grabbed Robert and stuffed his mouth with cloth while tying him up. The utter hatred in Robert's eyes towards Edward and Henry was overwhelming. Henry turned away, but Edward stared straight at Robert. Edward would not recoil from what he was doing, what he was becoming. He owed Robert that much.

After Robert was tied up, Edward turned away. "Let's go," he commanded.

The crew boarded the ship, but Henry lingered, glancing back and forth between Robert and Edward. Eventually he too boarded the *Freedom*.

Robert writhed and thrashed on the ground. Rage filled his eyes as he struggled against the bonds. He eventually managed to spit out the gag.

"What happened to our promise, Edward? Henry? Weren't we to meet again when our dreams were fulfilled?" Robert yelled as the ship was pushed out. "What happened to being a whaler? What happened to your dream, Edward? Huh? What happened?" Robert screamed as he lay on his side, the bonds keeping their hold on him.

Edward, watching from the poop deck, replied, "Dreams change."

8. THE COST OF *FREEDOM*

Freedom was pushed out of the dock and into Fareham Lake. The wind was in their favour, heading southwest and allowing them to travel through the lake with ease.

"Set sail!" Edward yelled. The sails were let out and *Freedom* began moving. "Close-haul us south, Herbert. Let's help the *Fortune* and get out of here."

"Aye, aye, Captain!" Herbert replied, sitting in his wheelchair at the helm.

The men of the *Freedom* removed the marine disguises. Edward donned his captain's clothing, and William and Henry both removed their commanders' vests, leaving their white tunics on.

Pure pandemonium enveloped the docks. Citizens were clambering left and right, running out of their houses and trying to move as far away from the water as possible. The marines were trying desperately to man their ships, and failing due to the ship circling and firing on them in the harbour.

Edward's friends, the "distraction" he mentioned earlier, were pirates met long before Edward was imprisoned. On the right side of the other ship's black flag was a picture of a man holding the top of an hourglass and on the left the skeleton of Death held the bottom of the hourglass. The ship's name was the *Fortune*, and the captain's name was Bartholomew Roberts.

Edward and crew had met the giant Welsh Bartholomew and his crew after being caught in a particularly violent storm and landed on an uninhabited island. The *Freedom* had helped the *Fortune* out of a troubling situation with marines, and the crews became fast friends.

There, Edward and Bartholomew created the Pirate Commandments, a code each man on board must swear by and uphold. Bartholomew was a devout Christian and the idea for the commandments had struck Edward when he noticed the Bible Bartholomew carried.

In Fareham Lake, the *Fortune* was firing cannonballs at the marine ships in the harbour. *Fortune* was circling around to send another volley when the *Freedom* let out its sails. The *Fortune* fired all their cannons at the marine ships, and sailed ahead of the *Freedom*.

"Ready port and starboard cannons!" Edward commanded. When travelling south, port faced the marine ships. Starboard, however...

"Why are we firing starboard, Edward? There are no ships," Henry said, still in shock from what they had done to Robert.

"If we destroy those buildings, the soldiers who are about to show up could be slowed by forcing them to help the citizens."

"Those are innocent people, Edward! How can you justify attacking them?"

"Oh, so you are fine with attacking the marines then?" Edward said, his utter calm piercing Henry to the core. "And what about the prison guards? The thought of saving me was enough to justify killing them, so think of this as the same, and set your mind at ease." Henry was dumbstruck with Edward's cold comments, and ceased his objections.

The *Freedom* arrived at the first of two marine ships. "Fire!" Edward yelled. The cannons let loose on the marine ship at dock and at the buildings across the lake. The ship, a frigate like the *Freedom*, was blasted once more as the crew tried to board and counter. The buildings were hit directly, the cannonballs ripping through their feeble structure, sending them falling apart to ruin. The inhabitants nearby ran from the chaos screaming.

Henry knew some of those men, women, and children would die, and the realisation haunted his step. He could not move as he watched the anarchy unfold before his eyes.

The marines returned fire against the *Freedom*, and the second ship attacked the *Fortune*. A few of the cannonballs hit the *Freedom* directly, sending splinters of wood flying, and injuring some of the crew.

Soldiers entered from the west, opposite the marines ships, and also fired upon the pirates. Bullets rained down on the two crews, but they kept fighting.

Before the marine ships could be manned and the sails let loose, the *Freedom* and *Fortune* both passed by. The two ships, *Crown* and *Ruby*, quickly brought their crew aboard and lay in a pursuit course for the pirate ships.

The *Fortune* and *Freedom* were approaching a small canal before their exit of Portsmouth. Two obstacles stood in their path: At the mouth of the canal were the army's defence line of cannons and two dozen men, and to the west, the marine ships in dry dock, unharmed as of yet. The docks were filling with water and the ships were being loaded with men and readied to deploy.

Edward unsheathed his sword for display, standing with one foot on the quarterdeck railing and holding onto a rigging line with his other hand. "This battle isn't over yet, men! Let's show them what real men are capable of." The crew's morale was boosted and they shouted their agreement.

Blackbeard's Ship

The scene, if gazed at from above, would be akin to a small skirmish, a light battle between a few ships and nothing more. But, when viewed from the harbour or on one of the ships, it was hellish.

The *Fortune* was feeling the brunt of the attack as it led the charge through the canal. The soldiers stationed at the small fortresses fired their cannons on the pirates, and the *Fortune* repaid them in kind.

The *Freedom* was passing the dry docks when one of the marine ships, the *Reserve*, left the dock and headed straight for *Freedom*'s stern. "Fire starboard!" Edward commanded. The bombardment didn't deter the *Reserve* as most of the shots missed or glanced off the front. "Brace for impact!"

The *Reserve* slammed into the tail of the *Freedom*, sending her off course. The jolt and resulting spin sent a few unlucky men of the crew to the floor of the ship. The two ships were then locked together side by side in the middle of the wide canal.

The marines sent over grappling hooks over the side of the larger *Freedom*. Men in blue uniforms swung over on ropes to the enemy ship and attacked. The starboard broadsides of the two ships fired at will upon each other, opening holes, breaking cannons, and breaking bodies.

"Cut those lines!" Edward yelled as he used his golden cutlass to cut one of the grappling hooks off of the *Freedom*'s starboard railing.

Pukuh threw a spear at a marine swinging across. The spear hit the man in the chest and he fell to the sole of *Freedom* with a thud. Pukuh unsheathed a knife and ran to the starboard railing, jumping and rolling over and through pirates and marines, and cut one of the hooks keeping the *Freedom* pinned.

William kicked a marine in the sternum. The marine coughed once and fell over unconscious. William gripped the rope of one of the hooks and pulled with all his strength, bracing himself against *Freedom*'s railing. The hook went slack, and William threw it into the water with a grunt.

Anne, up in the crow's nest, aimed her powerful rifle at one of the hooks. The bullet hit straight through the middle of the rope. The twine unravelled and snapped with the strain.

Sam didn't pay attention to Edward's orders and jabbed at two marines with his cutlass, using the blade like a fencing sword. They deflected the blows. Sam took the cutlass in two hands and reared back to strike. The marines concentrated too hard on the jabs and were caught unawares. Sam knocked the swords away from the marines, bent his knees, turned the sword around, and swung the other way. He sliced open the marines' stomachs and they fell, dead.

The *Fortune*, noticing *Freedom*'s trouble, turned the ship around after destroying some of the cannon fortresses at the mouth of the canal. The second ship in dry dock, *Assistance*, was just emerging as the *Fortune* rammed her.

Herbert's sister, Christina, was watching the scene unfold and relayed the information to her brother. Being her clever self, she told Herbert to turn the ship hard to port. Christina could see what the *Fortune* was planning to do and how *Freedom* could help.

The *Fortune* pushed *Assistance* into the side of the dock. *Assistance*'s stern swung out and hit the other side of the dock. With the pressure of the *Fortune* on the other ship's bow and no way to move, the wood beams on the bow snapped.

Water immediately filled the hull of the marines' ship, and it began sinking with each drop. The crew jumped off and into the water, or swam out the hole if they could. The few marines at the broken bow jumped onto the *Fortune* and fought the pirates of Bartholomew's crew, but were easily dispatched.

The *Fortune* moved from the decapitated *Assistance* and its starboard broadside was now facing the tangled mess of *Freedom* and the *Reserve*. Herbert, under Christina's instruction, turned the ship hard to port, causing the *Reserve* to be parallel to the *Fortune*.

Bartholomew Roberts, seven feet tall, with burly arms and chest, smiled at the sight before him. "God is truly with us, and *Fortune* favours us this day, men! Fire starboard!"

The *Fortune* fired all her starboard cannons at the *Reserve*. The large iron balls ripped through the hull of the *Reserve*, killing, maiming, and destroying with each shot. With the *Freedom*'s volleys opposite *Fortune*, *Reserve* was sufficiently pumped full of holes. The *Reserve* took on water and after *Freedom*'s crew released themselves from the grappling hooks the *Reserve* retreated.

Freedom joined with *Fortune* and the two ships continued to the mouth of the canal. The *Crown* and the *Ruby* were in pursuit, damaged, but not as badly as the *Reserve* and *Assistance*. The enemy ships were far behind now, and being a weightier class than the *Fortune* and the *Freedom* they were at a disadvantage with speed.

The final obstacle was at the mouth of the canal. More soldiers and backup gunners had arrived since the *Fortune* helped the *Freedom* out. The gunners manned and aimed cannons along the harbour at the two ships.

"Forward unto *Freedom*!" Edward yelled, his cutlass high in the air, and the cry was heard across both ships.

Bartholomew repeated the charge, "Forward unto *Freedom*!" to his crew. Others among the crew chanted the simple but effective war cry. The two crews quickly became in sync with each other and the sound of the battle cry could be heard by the army at the mouth of the canal as the ships approached.

"Attack!"

Cannonballs flew through the air, bullets drove from their guns, men cried out, and pandemonium ensued. The two groups warred with neither side giving up, but the ones standing still were forced to lose. In a few short minutes the *Freedom* and the *Fortune* passed through the mouth of the canal and left the army behind. The cannons kept sounding off, and the marine ships kept pursuing, but the ships were too slow to catch up.

After the pirate ships passed the threshold, and they were a safe distance from the cannons and muskets, the crews of the two ships erupted in a cheer of unparalleled joy. Their captain, whom they went to such lengths for, was now free, and they were a family again.

Edward grinned as he turned his gaze to the *Fortune*. He saw Bartholomew Roberts on the quarterdeck of his own ship, clapping and smiling. Edward took off his tricorn hat and bowed deeply to the man who was, without a doubt, the sole reason they were able to escape today. Bartholomew returned the bow in kind.

The ships separated, as had been the plan from the beginning, the *Fortune* heading northeast to wherever the wind would take them. The *Freedom* was headed southwest, then back to the Caribbean, performing repairs along the way.

At least, that was the plan, before tragedy struck.

After they had separated from the *Fortune*, Anne ran to Edward with a grave expression on her face. "We have twenty-two injured and three dead."

"Poor souls. We will conduct a funeral service tonight in their honour. John?" Edward said, turning to the quartermaster. "Make sure the names of the men are written down so we may send their families some coin." John nodded.

"Edward, you should see the men," Anne suggested, pulling his attention back.

"Yes." Edward's face was solemn as he treaded to his fallen friends.

A crowd surrounded the bodies. Edward touched shoulders and pulled others aside so he could reach the centre. Edward mentally prepared himself for when he saw the bodies, but it was far worse than he imagined.

Nassir was knelt down, clutching a body, tears streaming down his face. The body was his fifteen-year-old boy, Ochi. He had taken multiple bullet wounds and died from his injuries.

The only sounds were the hissing wind, the flapping of the sails, and the slow sobs of Nassir. No one could offer words of consolation to Nassir; the crew could only watch the awkward spectacle and search for words which would never be uttered.

Someone pushed through the crowd to Edward's side. Christina emerged beside him to view the scene. Her eyes widened in disbelief at what she saw, and then slowly narrowed as the truth and shock sank in. The young man she had grown so close to was dead in front of her. She caressed a carved wooden rose around her neck.

Christina tried to take a step, her eyes focused on Ochi, the crew's focused on her, but she collapsed into Edward's arms. Edward eased Christina to the floor of the ship, holding her close as she watched Ochi's lifeless body. Tears fell silently down her cheeks, her fingers still on the carved rose.

Fingers quickly turned into a fist, and silence into screams.

9. RESOLVE

Nassir peered from his sorrow to see the crew around him, watching. He saw Edward and his eyes filled with rage. Nassir set his son down and rose up to his full height. "You are the cause of this!" he yelled to Edward.

Anne, beside Edward, took charge of the situation. "Nassir, please, how is Edward the cause of this? Did he shoot the gun?"

"No, but he caused the gun to be loaded. He is equally at fault for this!" Nassir pointed at Edward.

Edward gently pulled Christina off of him. Still in grief, anger was far from Christina's mind. "As Anne said, I did not kill your son. We are here today because of me, and I am partly to blame as my weakness caused these men to die, but none were forced to be here."

Nassir reared back and punched Edward in the face, sending him to the deck. "My son is dead and you blame him? Blame me?"

Despite Nassir's anger, Edward remained calm. He slowly lifted himself back up, but stayed sitting. "I am not blaming anyone but myself. I was merely stating that everyone is here of their own volition and knew the dangers. I do not believe I am the one you should be focusing your anger on. However, if this will help you ease your pain…" Edward closed his eyes, waiting for what was about to happen.

"Now you mock me?" Nassir punched Edward again and again, but Edward did not fight back. Anne, along with many others, could do nothing but turn away at the bitter display. Nassir's punches slowed and weakened until he gripped the clothing on Edward's chest and shook him. Edward hadn't moved since Nassir started. "Ochi, my son!" Nassir cried, sobbing into Edward's chest.

Jack pulled Nassir off Edward and embraced him silently.

Several minutes of agonising silence passed. Jack consoled Nassir, Anne consoled Christina, and the crew watched mutely, unable to help those who were hurting the most.

"We will perform a funeral service tonight," Edward whispered, rising to his feet.

"I do not want my son to burn. He will be buried in NiTalaa at my home of Calabar. If you do not take me I will go myself."

"We will take you, Nassir."

Henry emerged at Edward's call and, with Jack's help, Henry

took Nassir to the crew cabin. Anne took Christina down as well, and she stayed with them for a bit. Edward went to the helm to tell Herbert the news.

Herbert was still unaware of what had occurred as the crowd, and his height disadvantage in his wheelchair, had prevented him from observing the scene. "What happened?"

"I'm sorry to be the one to tell you this, Herbert, but Ochi has passed in the fight."

Herbert's eyes, so similar to his sister's, at first held disbelief, but quickly grew wide with urgency. He abandoned the helm, climbed down to the waist, then crawled to the lower decks.

Edward manned the helm as some of the men returned to work and others wrapped Ochi's body. The earlier victory was marred by the tragedy, and morale was low.

That night the *Freedom* was let to drift and held a funeral service. The two crewmen who passed on were put in a small boat on the starboard side. Ochi was wrapped in cloth and placed on a wooden platform beneath the quarterdeck.

"We are gathered here to honour and remember the dead," Edward said. "They lost their lives defending us, and our being here is thanks to their sacrifice. They are gone, but we remain. Their dreams remain, their families remain, their regrets remain."

Christina and Nassir were at the front, holding each other, and Herbert was holding Christina's hand. Nassir dried his eyes, but Christina still wept for her significant other.

"We, as a crew, as a family, must fulfil their dreams, we must take care of their family, and we must fix what they regret, so they may rest peacefully." Edward stared intently at the crew. "Do you accept these responsibilities?" The crew responded with "Aye." Many of them had been part of the crew from the beginning and remembered a similar eulogy from Edward. "With your acceptance, these three will surely be able to rest peacefully."

Edward nodded to the crew stationed at the sides of the ship. Before lowering the boat, the Mayan Pukuh placed corn and a piece of jade in their mouths. Afterwards, he uttered a short prayer to his gods to tell them of the men's arrival. The corn was food for the journey, and the jade was the price of passage. The men lost their lives in combat, considered a sacrifice, and would be allowed into heaven in honour, according to Pukuh's beliefs.

The crew lowered the small boat into the water and threw in a torch. The bodies burned as others in the crew fired muskets into the air. Three shots and the service was done, but the fire lingered on.

The pain lingered on.

Blackbeard's Ship

Over the seven weeks of travel to NiTalaa the morale of the crew was at an all-time low. Jack did his best to bring cheer with music, to no effect. The trip felt longer with the sombre and melancholic mood over the crew.

Ochi and Christina were but children, and to have them ripped apart was unbearable for the crew, but even worse to watch was the slow deterioration of Nassir. He spent every waking moment immersed in work on the ship. He worked alone, fixing as much as he could and restoring the ship to pre-battle condition. Through his constant work he took little sleep and as the weeks passed he developed bags under his eyes, and lost a dangerous amount of weight.

Christina did not have the benefit of a job to lose herself in, so she spent most of her days either sleeping or in the bow cabin weeping over Ochi's body. Anne and Herbert tried their best, but Christina was inconsolable.

Herbert too was troubled deeply by the loss, and by his inability to do anything to help his sister. Herbert had cultivated a great friendship with Nassir and Ochi through the past year, and the two were like family to him. He did not allow himself to feel grief, only empathy and sorrow over his sister's condition.

One day during the journey, Edward entered the bow cabin, mainly used for weapons storage, to pay his personal respects to Ochi. The small cabin was the only suitable location for Ochi to rest on the journey to Nassir's homeland.

Three cannons stood at the front of the curved cabin, and barrels of muskets on the sides. Spare hammocks for accommodations were also swinging in the air. On a pedestal of boxes, Ochi's wrapped body lay.

In front of the pedestal, Edward saw Pukuh kneeling down in silence. The noise of the door roused Pukuh and he turned to greet Edward with tears in his eyes.

"I'm sorry, Pukuh, I will return later."

"No, brother, stay. The dead should be mourned together."

Edward sat down beside Pukuh, a bottle of rum in his hands. He poured a little out on the floorboards of the *Freedom* and took a drink from the bottle. Edward muttered his own silent prayer, despite his not knowing anything about God, and then sat beside Pukuh in silence.

Edward stared at the wrapped body in front of him. The cloth was damp with decay, and the smell surrounding the body was foul and stung Edward's nose causing his eyes to water. Edward hadn't seen a body like this before.

The dead should not be kept in such a way. I wish we had another option, but I have to respect Nassir's wishes.

After a few moments, Pukuh broke the silence. "A father should never lose a son in such a way."

"Mmm," Edward mumbled in agreement. "If I was stronger I could have stopped them from dying." His gazed was fixed on the ground.

"Where death is concerned, strength has no part. All men die, this is fact. You say right when you say to Nassir his son chose to fight. The only choice we as men and women have is where we choose to lay our life on the line. Losing our lives in battle is tragic, but honourable. Ochi did what he could, and nothing more. You are the same. Trust in me, I felt the same before."

Edward contemplated Pukuh's words, then took another drink of the rum. "Thank you Pukuh." Edward left the room. *Thank you, but you're wrong, Pukuh. I will become stronger, and I will stop my family from dying. No matter the cost.*

When the *Freedom* reached NiTalaa, at the port of Calabar, the crew departed with Nassir to bury Ochi. Another service was held on the outskirts of town where the graves were marked with crosses made of tree branches. The crew took turns digging the grave in the hot overbearing sun.

Having no work to tend to his grief, and no exhausted sleep to take him away, Nassir mourned for his son once more. After the Calabar service, the crew left Nassir, Christina and Herbert alone at the graveside. The crew waited for hours at the dock before the three returned. Nassir wanted to talk with Edward, as did Christina. Edward spoke with Nassir first in the bow cabin.

The faint smell of decay lingered in the air, lending an eerie feeling in the small room. Nassir was haggard and tired. His usually well-groomed appearance was overtaken by stubble on his head and face. His well-rounded cheeks were hollow and his form diminished, the opposite to Edward's recovery from his stay in prison.

"I am staying in Calabar, Captain. I need to… think over things."

Edward opened his mouth to say something out of his gut reaction, but then simply nodded his head. "I understand. We'll call this a temporary leave to allow you rest. You will be returning, yes?"

"I will say maybe."

"We will return after a few months and see how you are feeling, how does that sound?"

Nassir nodded to Edward's suggestion and left the room, preparing to say his goodbyes to the crew. Edward followed and made the announcement. The crew became depressed but sympathetic for Nassir, and wanted to have a feast before he left, but Nassir declined. The ship set sail before night fell, the crew watching and waving to Nassir as he became smaller the more the ship floated away. Eventually, Nassir was no longer visible, and many in the crew felt they would not see him again.

Herbert and Christina stayed on the *Freedom*, and after their departure, Edward finally had his audience with Christina. Once more in the room filled with the faint smell of the dead taunting the recent victims of catastrophe with the sickening essence.

The beautiful girl was finally past the shock of the recent events, but was still visibly affected. Christina's strawberry-blond hair was dishevelled and her normally sparkling blue eyes were dark and bloodshot. Her frame was small and at the point of breaking standing before Edward.

"What did you want to talk to me about, Christina?"

"I want to be taught how to fight."

Edward could have expected a lot of things, but not this. "No," he said simply.

The young girl was on the verge of tears from frustration. "Why not?" Her mouth curled into a tight frown as her lip quivered.

Edward turned away from Christina; her grief-stricken face was too much to bear. How she had changed from the days when she and Ochi played on the ship. "Because I cannot risk losing you. Think about Herbert. What would he do if you were lost to him?"

"I am thinking of Herbert!" Christina shouted and anger seeped into her words instead of sadness. "Who else will protect him against those awful marines? I am the only one who has the right!" she yelled in her ire.

Edward heard the anger in Christina's voice, saw the rage in her sky-blue eyes. She reminded him of his love from his hometown of Badabos before he met Anne, Lucy. Edward could never say no to those eyes. Christina was breaking him. "There is more to what you are saying than you're telling me. If I am to approve this, I want to know the real reason you want to fight so much. I know why, but I want to hear this from you."

Christina crossed her arms. "I want revenge. I will make those bastards pay for what they've done. I want to make our enemies fear me the same as you."

Edward nodded, extending his hand. "I want the same."

Christina shook his hand, and the deal was struck.

10. THE BERMUDA GATEWAY

Two tragedies in a row took its toll on the crew's minds and many were fatigued. The loss of the crew members and Nassir leaving lowered morale, but time healed old wounds first. Mourning was over, and the crew learned to cope with the loss.

Edward felt a distraction was in order, so on their way to the Caribbean he decided now was the time to solve the next riddle. Most of the *Freedom* was locked by keys left scattered about by Benjamin. After each successive door was opened, another clue was found inside the room for the next key. The game Benjamin left, while trying, difficult, and sometimes deadly, was intriguing to all in the crew, especially Edward.

The remaining sections locked were a door on the berth deck, and two on the gun deck, one on the bow and one on the stern. The locked door on the stern gundeck was assumed to be the captain's cabin, but the others were a mystery.

Edward stood on the quarterdeck, leaning against the wooden planks at the stern. From his pocket, he retrieved the letter he reclaimed from the warden of Gammond prison. The simple white print was adorned with a golden wax seal of a classic hunting horn, the sign of Benjamin Hornigold. Edward touched the simple but elegant design before breaking the seal and opening the letter. The letter read as follows:

The Devil's Triangle
25° and Three Shots in the Dark
The Limey's Parallel Lights the Way

Edward pondered on the letter. *The Devil's Triangle sounds familiar, and twenty-five degrees could mean latitude, but three shots in the dark is a mystery and the final line is nonsense.*

"Herbert, what do you make of this?" Edward asked, handing him the paper.

Herbert set a wooden pole in the spokes of the wheel to stop it from moving while he examined the paper. Herbert adjusted his glasses and moved some hair behind his ear during his review.

"The Devil's Triangle is most certainly the Bermuda Triangle, an area between Bermuda, Puerto Rico, and Florida forming a triangle. The twenty-five degrees is a latitude point, and I imagine the three shots in the dark could mean cannon shots, or maybe gunshots. I'm not sure about the last line, though."

Edward took the paper back, reviewing it with cocked brow while stroking his beard. "Adjust our heading now, we will unravel the mystery of the last line on the way. Benjamin may have us on a fool's errand, but he was no fool. Whatever the last line means, it is of some import." Edward addressed the crew while Herbert adjusted the course. "Everyone, please move to the waist." Once the crew gathered, Edward explained. "As you all know, there are several locked sections of the ship, and we're searching for the keys." He held up the paper. "This next clue will lead us to a key, but we are having some trouble deciphering the final line." Edward read the line out to them. "Any ideas?"

Sam immediately spoke. "A Limey is slang fer British marines. 'Cause they bring limes aboard their ships."

"Good Sam, good. So what is the parallel of the British?"

"The French?" "Indians?" "Jews?"

Edward held up his hand to silence the crew. "French is the most logical parallel to English. So what is the light of the French?"

"The food?" "The language?" "The whores?" "The smell?"

Edward pinched the bridge of his nose. *This is getting nowhere.* "Alright, John, Anne, Henry, Sam, please join me in the meeting room. Jack, play us some soothing music please."

Those addressed replied with an "Aye, Captain!" and went about following the orders. The crew returned to work either swabbing the deck, fixing the trim on the sails, or other menial tasks. Jack pulled out his violin and played some upbeat and warm classical melodies.

With the relaxing sounds of music, ocean water lapping against the ship, and salty air blowing around the *Freedom*, the crew were settling into a better mood.

Edward and the ones he'd named headed to the cabin below the quarterdeck. Edward commanded the anchor to be dropped and Herbert to join them. Herbert climbed down and entered the war room with everyone else.

The cabin was lavishly decorated with a chandelier above Edward's head and red velvet carpet below his feet. On the sides of the room bookshelves held dozens of nautical books and a bevy of fiction to choose from. Windows at the back let in light and were augmented by oil lamps. Decorations of paintings, swords, and pistols were scattered about on the walls. In the middle of the room stood an oval table with expensive chairs front to back, and one ornate high-backed chair at the back in the middle.

Edward sat in the gold-trimmed, high-backed chair, and read the clue aloud. Afterwards, he ensured each one had a chance to examine the paper. "Herbert says the Devil's Triangle is another name for the Bermuda Triangle." At the mention of the Bermuda Triangle, Sam visibly tensed. "The twenty-five degrees relates to the latitude inside the triangle we need to be, and the three shots in the dark are assumed to be cannon shots."

Sam couldn't hold back any longer. "Captain, ye don't mean ta head ta the Triangle, do ye?"

"Yes, Sam, travelling to the Triangle was implied."

"The Triangle be dangerous. Horrible things happen to sailors travelling there," Sam claimed, uncharacteristically fearful.

"Well, with the name Devil's Triangle, I assumed…" Edward said with a smirk. "So, anyone have any ideas?" Edward tried to change the subject to something he considered more pressing.

The group offered suggestions on what they assumed the French light could mean, with the most logical suggestion being made by John. He supposed the parallel could be the Grand Royal Coat of Arms of France, but how that would light the way was beyond the group. After some time of deliberation, they decided to take a break and play a game of cards.

Edward, not one with much experience in games of chance, but a quick learner, put up a good fight. Sam was caught cheating and laughed it off. Anne and Henry had some playful banter and competed more against each other than the rest of the group. Herbert and John were by far the biggest winners, and Herbert was surprisingly competitive.

In the middle of the game, the door to the cabin opened and a gust of wind rushed in, the air of the sea invading the air of the old books and burning oil lanterns. The wind caused the paper and the cards to fly off the table. The group were trying to catch the cards when their eyes caught the clue flying away to the open door. They all lunged for the paper at once, but it escaped their grasp and flew to the door.

Christina was at the door, and she caught the paper before it flew off. She was wearing loose-fitting pantaloons ending five inches below her knees, a loose white tunic, and a leather vest overtop with the rose pendant showing. Her hair was tied into a ponytail, and she appeared decidedly better than a few days prior.

Christina peeked at the paper as she approached the table. Everyone was still piled on top of one another. "What are you doing?" she asked.

"Trying to catch that, thank you," Edward said as he took the paper back and folded it into his pocket.

Christina laughed as she circled behind Edward's seat. "Was that the riddle for another key?"

"Yes, and, as we've yet to find the solution, losing the paper would be devastating."

"You know, I'm really good at riddles. Would I be allowed to look?" Christina asked with a sweet grin.

Edward eyed Herbert, and Herbert nodded. "Alright, do you need to see the paper again?" Edward asked, reaching for his pocket.

"You mean this paper?" Christina was holding the riddle in her hands. She smiled coyly at Edward.

Edward smiled back at Christina's deviousness, and also at her happiness. Edward was glad to see Christina in good spirits.

Christina read the riddle over again as Edward explained what they figured out so far. Christina took a few seconds, then her face lit up. "What if Limey's Parallel means lemons?"

"Lemons?" Edward inquired, incredulous.

"Yes, parallel means side by side and lemons and limes go well together."

Edward, not wanting to dismiss Christina's suggestion outright, tried to reason with her and lead her to the conclusion herself. "So how would a lemon light the way?"

Christina touched the rose around her neck as she thought. "Ah, I know how! Don't move!" she instructed, and without any explanation she ran out of the cabin.

Anne and company peered at Edward in wonderment, almost asking him if he knew what was going on. Edward shrugged his shoulders and sat down. After a minute, Christina returned with a knife and a lemon.

Using the knife, Christina sliced a lemon open, threw one half into Edward's hand, and squeezed out the juice of the other half. Christina used her finger to wet the paper with the lemon juice. This piqued curiosity, so the others shifted closer to watch. Christina wet the whole of the paper with juice.

At first nothing happened, but after a moment the lemon juice penetrated the thicker stock paper and dots appeared on the paper. Soon, the whole paper was covered in small dots.

Edward picked up the paper. "Amazing! How did you know lemon juice would do this?"

Christina grinned at his adulation. "Well, I didn't. I read in an adventure book once about an ink which goes hidden after being written and the only thing that can bring the writing back is lemon juice. The scene stuck with me because of the ingenuity."

Edward laughed. "Maybe we need you to join us in more of these meetings." Christina smiled again even more widely. "Now let us see the familial combination in action. What do you make of this?" Edward handed the paper to Herbert.

Herbert too carried his joy on his face, delighted his sister was happy again. He scrutinised the paper at different angles to better see the dots. On the page, three circles surrounded specific dots, with a line connecting them in a triangle. In the corner, a time—one a.m.—was written in the mystery ink.

"I believe this is a star chart, with a time for when we can see them. With this, the latitude, and the location, I believe we deciphered the riddle."

"Excellent!" Edward left the cabin immediately. "Crew, we solved the riddle and are on our way to unlocking the next part of this ship," Edward yelled to the men. The crew cheered. "And we owe our thanks to Christina!" More cheers and hoots rose above the din. Christina and company left the cabin. Edward picked Christina up and held her on his broad shoulder. "Three cheers for Christina Blackwood."

"Hip-hip-hurrah! Hip-hip-hurrah! Hip-hip-hurrah!" the crew yelled, caught in the fever of praise to the young lady.

Christina was nearly in tears, but unlike in the past long while, the tears were not of sorrow, but of joy. She carried a wide grin as she sat on Edward's pedestal-like shoulder.

Another seven weeks passed as *Freedom* sailed to the Bermuda Tri angle. Edward and crew resumed training with Anne and William. For most of the crew, having slacked in the past year, training felt like starting anew.

Edward also wanted Anne to do more personal one-on-one sessions with Christina. Anne was reluctant at first, but when she saw Christina's determination she quickly approved. Christina showed much promise, and her quick mind helped in her growth.

Henry, ever since the escape from Portsmouth, was downtrodden and lethargic most of the time. Edward could see Henry was angry as well. At first, Edward attributed Henry's mood to the loss of the crewmates and the general temper aboard *Freedom*, but Henry's disposition lingered as time passed.

Edward approached Henry when he was alone one day. "Henry, are you upset about anything?"

Henry smiled, but to Edward it felt hollow. "No, nothing at all, Edward. We're safe and we're free. What would I have to worry about?"

"You were rather distraught with our escape, as well as running into Robert. I am too, but you must understand, tying him up was for his benefit. If Robert let us leave, he would have been in as much trouble as us. If Robert ran off for help we either would have fought him on one of the ships, or been captured before we could leave. There really was no choice in the matter."

Henry kept that same smile. "Of course. I understand completely."

Edward considered Henry for a moment, skeptical, but unsure of what to say. "If there is anything you wish to talk about—"

"Yes, I will come to you," Henry said, cutting Edward off.

The trip carried on with Henry appearing less agitated, but whether mere acting or him actually coming to terms with his feelings, Edward did not know.

Sam, on the other hand, increased in uneasiness and agitation the closer the ship came to the Bermuda Triangle. Any little chop in the waters or high wind would trigger sweats, and the slightest loud noises caused Sam to jump.

Edward attempted talking with Sam, but all Edward could rouse out of him was, "Something… happened there, but you would not believe me." Sam would not say another word on the matter, but it was apparent that the travel weighed on him heavily.

When Herbert took the *Freedom* into the Bermuda Triangle, the rest of the crew became as agitated as Sam. Many of the older crewmates had heard stories of unbelievable happenings in the triangle, and their nervousness passed to the younger men. Even Edward couldn't help but be on edge.

Through various calculations, and compensating for magnetic variations in his compass, Herbert brought the *Freedom* to the specified latitude. The sails were furled and the *Freedom* was left to drift. As the night wore on, the wind deadened. The calm was eerie.

Herbert, using the star chart as a reference, guided the gunners to aim the cannons at the specified stars, which also happened to be in a triangle pattern. When the time indicated on the chart came, Herbert would command the gunners to fire.

The entire crew stayed awake for the event, all of them armed, eying the horizon, shifting at every sound. Sam had several weapons at the ready and was sweating profusely.

The night was cold, colder than normal due to the humidity in the air. Edward shivered and thought he could see his breath in front of him.

Herbert watched his overly complicated moon dial, which Edward had no chance of learning how to read, until the time was one hour past midnight. "Fire!" Herbert commanded.

With the slightest hesitancy, the gunners fired their cannons in the direction of the stars.

The crew tensed as the iron balls flew through the air. Edward gripped his cutlass, John and Anne aimed their rifles, William clenched his fists, Henry held a blunderbuss, and Sam held twin pistols with whitened knuckles. All eyes followed the cannonballs until the iron disappeared into thin air. Poof. Gone. Not even a splash sounded.

"Did everyone else see that?" *Or should I say* not *see that?*

Before any could respond, an unnatural fog emerged from where the cannonballs vanished. A great howling of wind ushered the fog around the *Freedom*, and soon the entire area around them was covered in pale white.

Edward shivered, partially from the cold night and partially from the supernatural spectacle. *What is this devilry?*

The fog shielded the crew's vision to twenty feet off the rail, and the howling gusts sounded like a woman's shriek. Even the most hardened man now carried a weapon in hand, and a sweat-soaked brow above the eyes.

While the crew was caught unawares, a ship struck the bow of the *Freedom* and jolted the crew. Men fell to the deck from the quaking, and shots were fired into the air. Edward ordered calm, and ran to the bow to see the ship.

The ship scraping along the side of the *Freedom* was a small merchantman, the name *Patriot* emblazoned on the side. It had no weapons, and the civilian crew on board seemed just as frightened by events as Edward's crew.

The merchantman did not slow as its port splintered *Freedom*'s wood. The ship eventually lurched to the side and separated from *Freedom*, then sailed off into the fog once more.

Edward's lips were a hard line, and his anger rose. "Hard to port! Follow that ship. It has some explaining to do," he snarled.

Before Edward's men could gain grip of their senses and take action, another ship came up beside *Freedom*, this time a sixth-class frigate with the name *Le Pandore*. It appeared to be in pursuit of the *Patriot*, but upon seeing *Freedom*, pulled up its sails and slowed itself as quickly as it could.

The crew of *Le Pandore* were waving as if greeting friends. Edward's crew lowered their weapons, but out of confusion rather than familiarity. Edward also noticed that the fog had dissipated, and the merchantman *Patriot* was almost past the horizon and out of sight.

Le Pandore turned around and eased itself up next to *Freedom*, then sent over grappling lines to hook the ships together. A gangplank was set for the crew to cross over, and the captain of *Le Pandore* was the first to step onto the *Freedom*.

The captain was a shorter man, a little over halfway between five and six feet, wearing a tall black top hat, a red vest with coattails, a white tunic with bow tie, and itchy grey cotton pantaloons. His face was of French perfection, and with high-set eyes and long chin and nose, he was handsome in his own way.

Blackbeard's Ship

"Benjamin Hornigold, where are you, my old friend?" he yelled in a light French accent as he boarded the *Freedom*, searching but not finding the man he called out for. "This is no time for a prank, dear fellow, friends are here."

The sails flapped in the silence pervading the guest's declaration.

Sam, his mouth agape and stepping closer to the captain of *Le Pandore*, trembled at the sight of the man. He held out his hand like he was reaching for something too far away.

"Father?" Sam questioned, staring dead in the eyes of the captain.

The captain peered at Sam with a raised brow. At first, his expression was pure confusion, but it quickly changed to recognition and then shock.

"Sam?" he asked incredulously. The man ambled over to Sam, and Sam met him.

Sam held out his hand to shake, but the captain pushed aside his hand and embraced him. "It is good to see you, my son."

11. THE GHOSTS OF THE ISLAND BEYOND TIME

The crew observed the spectacle with mixed shock, confusion, and awe. No one knew what to make of the situation. When Sam and the mystery captain parted, Sam introduced him to Edward and the crew.

"Everyone, this is Dominique You, the Captain of *Le Pandore* and a man I call my father."

Dominique bowed with a flourish of his top hat. "A pleasure to meet you all. Though I am not Samuel's real father, I consider him my son, and I thank you for taking care of him." Dominique rested a hand on Sam's shoulder. "I thought we'd lost you, and I have many questions, but we can catch up momentarily. I am at a disadvantage, as I do not recognise the crew, but I know the ship intimately. Who, pray tell, is the captain?"

"This man here," Sam replied, pointing to Edward.

"Edward Thatch." Edward extended his hand.

Dominique took Edward's hand and shook firmly. "Might I also ask the year?"

Edward raised his brow to the odd question, but after what happened, he didn't know what was odd or not. "The year is seventeen-oh-seven."

"Ah, well I understand now. What Samuel here may have been reluctant to impart to you is the nature of where we are from, or should I say when? No matter. We are from the year eighteen-thirteen."

The *Freedom*'s crew laughed nervously at the statement, but Dominique was unfazed. He and his crew kept straight faces, and the laughter soon stopped and turned to awkward silence.

"Surely you jest?" Edward asked.

"Not so, Sam can attest to the truth of our words as well. He was part of my crew until the age of ten in the year eighteen-ten, yet now he is here before me at the age of twenty and some. That... fog we travelled through brought us here to seventeen-oh-seven."

"I fell overboard in a storm 'ere in the Devil's Triangle, and when I awoke I was in the year sixteen-ninety-six. That's why I am fearful of this place. Strange things happen."

To the crew, slack-jawed and bewildered, "strange" was a severe understatement. Even William carried an expression of pure disbelief plastered on his face.

Dominique laughed nonchalantly. "Yes, strange things indeed. Now, if you do not mind, can we continue chasing our quarry? I will stay aboard and we can discuss more while my crew leads the chase. Have your helmsman follow us."

Edward shook his head to clear the momentary confusion. "Yes, I believe further explanation is in order." Edward ordered Herbert to follow *Le Pandore* while Captain Dominique ordered his crew to continue pursuit. The grappling hooks were released and the ships were soon sailing once more.

Captain Dominique joined Edward, Sam, and the senior members of *Freedom*'s crew to talk in *Freedom*'s war room in the stern cabin. Dominique wanted to hear their story before he told his. Sam relayed what he had been doing the past eleven years and how he ended up on the *Freedom*, and Edward continued the story with a hint of Benjamin's game and the keys and their dealings with the British, while omitting certain sensitive details.

"Ah, well that explains this then," Dominique said as he pulled out a key from his pocket.

Edward's jaw dropped for the third time that evening. "Is that…?"

Dominique laughed. "Yes it is. I met Benjamin Hornigold one year ago in my time. Before he left he wanted me to hold onto this key, but never explained the meaning. When you meet a man such as him, and he asks you to keep something safe, you keep it safe."

"So, I guess Benjamin wants us to help you then?" Edward questioned, more to himself.

Dominique nodded. "I am chasing the ship the *Patriot*, which is carrying one Theodosia Burr Alston whom we mean to capture."

"And what is the purpose of capturing one woman?" Henry asked, wary of the supposed time-hopping captain.

Dominique paused, considering his words. "I hope you gentlemen understand if I keep the details light, as we don't know what could happen. Agreed?" Edward nodded for Dominique to continue. "In eighteen-thirteen, a war is raging between North America and the British Empire. Alston is a spy for the British, and because her father is the Vice President, the second in charge, of the North American colonies, she has access to sensitive information. Her father was arrested and suspected of treason due to her exploits."

"Hmm, the year has changed, but we have a common enemy." Edward rose from his seat at the head of the war room table. He extended his hand. "We will help you capture Alston, and you will give us the key we seek in return, agreed?"

Dominique returned Edward's gesture. "Agreed. The *Patriot* is heading to Charleston, and, as they are not aware of the mishap which has occurred with our date, they will continue as if nothing is the matter."

"How long will travel to Charleston take?"

"From where we are? A week at most."

"What happens when we catch this woman? What will you do with her?" Henry challenged.

Dominique had a crooked smirk as he glanced at his men then back to Henry. "If possible, we come back here to return her to my time and put her on trial. Is this acceptable to you, sir?" Dominique asked while mockingly bowing his head.

Edward held his hand up to silence Henry when he seemed poised to respond angrily. "This is acceptable," Edward reassured Dominique. "Now, we must hear all about your exploits in the next century, provided you approve?"

Dominique laughed. "I don't see the harm in talking about myself. I'm not so special. I would enjoy hearing more detail of this game you play as well."

Edward regaled Dominique with stories of their adventures and the trials left by Benjamin and how the *Freedom* arrived in the Devil's Triangle. During travel, Sam talked with Dominique and nearly spent every waking hour with him. He admired and looked up to the man like he was his flesh-and-blood father.

Although Dominique was an agreeable and cheerful man, Henry bore some misgivings about the whole situation. He kept a close eye on Dominique and tried to listen to all his conversations. After a few days of travel, Sam caught on to what Henry was doing and told him off, almost sparking a fight between the two. Edward would have none of it and met with Henry alone.

"Why are you bothering our guests, Henry?" Edward asked.

"I don't think we should trust Dominique."

"And why shouldn't we?"

Henry cocked his brow. "Do you really believe he is from another time? This whole story reeks of a fable."

"What about Sam, then? He confirmed the tale."

"Sam was but a boy when he was with Dominique. What if this is simply a jest which went too far, and now Dominique is keeping up appearances?"

"Why lie to us then?"

"To gain our trust, of course. He sees a familiar ship, but an unfamiliar crew, save Sam. Sam was a babe when he was lost, so Dominique thinks if he upholds the tale he wove years ago he will have an easier time getting what he wants from us. Dominique could have told us anything about the ship he's chasing, and because of Sam we are more likely to believe him."

Edward nodded, stroking his beard. "I do admit the story is

hard to believe, but their story doesn't matter to me. Sam trusts Dominique, so I trust him, Henry. End of discussion."

Henry snorted. "In that case, don't turn to me when you find out we've been lied to."

"Good to know who I can rely on these days," Edward said as Henry walked out of the war room. *What is this mood he's been in recently?*

A crewmate knocked on the door to the war room, and after Edward beckoned him inside, he told Edward that Herbert wished to see him. Edward went to the quarterdeck to see Sam, Herbert, Dominique, and Dominique's helmsman. Sam had a pallor like none Edward had seen before.

"What is the urgent issue, Herbert?"

Herbert glanced at Dominique. "From what we surmise, our ships have been going in circles the past three days. We have not left the Triangle."

Edward's brow cocked. "How has this happened?"

"We don't know, my boy. Something about the air is foul, and I fear that this is the work of the Devil in his abode. Some force does not want us to leave."

Herbert ignored Dominique's ramblings. "I have been keeping a track of our movements each day, and we have been moving forward, but when I recheck our status on the morrow, we are somewhere different. The first day I chalked it up to a mistake I might have made, or a malfunction of my instruments, but Dominique's helmsman confirmed it.

"What do we do, then?"

Herbert shrugged his shoulders. "The one thing we can do is keep moving and hope whatever is the cause dissipates."

Sam wiped sweat off his brow. "Ain't there somethin' that can be done? Each day 'ere is like tightenin' a vice on our knickers. We go'n circles enough somethin' bad's gonna happen."

Dominique patted Sam on the head. "Fret not, son. We shall find a means of escape."

"Dominique is correct, Sam. This is but a temporary setback."

"Land ho!" a crewman screamed from the crow's nest.

After their eyes darted to the crewmate, all eyes scanned the bow for the land. Herbert and Dominique both pulled out spyglasses and peered into them.

"How…?" Herbert sputtered before dropping his spyglass and rummaging through papers on his lap. "We've been in this area before, and there was no island," Herbert commented. Beads of sweat formed on his temple and ran down his cheek, a physical indicator that Herbert was out of his depth and had no scientific explanation for what was happening.

Edward placed his hand on Herbert's shoulder. "Land us on the island, Herbert. I intend to find the cause of this mystery, one way or another."

Herbert nodded slowly. "Aye, aye, Captain."

The two ships approached the island, the wind picking up and almost guiding them straight for the beach. The island was surrounded by fog which blotted out the sun when they neared. When they were close, Edward could see a ship berthed at the beach, and he guessed correctly the vessel was the *Patriot*.

"I have a feeling we were not the only ones who became stuck in the Triangle," Edward commented to Dominique.

Even as the ships closed in on the beach, there was no activity upon the *Patriot*, and when the sails were furled and secured no signs of life presented themselves. The island itself was unpleasantly silent and barren. Edward could only see the beach of sand and flat grass for a hundred feet, then the fog became so thick it made a wall.

Edward sent a search party to the *Patriot*, consisting of Anne, Christina, William, and a few crewmates from both *Freedom* and *Le Pandore*, but they returned soon after with confused looks.

"There are none aboard, Edward. The ship has a ghastly silence within, as if the crew were plucked away in the midst of great activity," Anne yelled from shore.

"Thank you, Anne. Stay there, we will be searching the island next," Edward replied, then he turned to Dominique. "I will take some of my crew to the island. Could you stay in case something happens here? If we are attacked, we need at least one of our ships able to retaliate."

"I would be happy to oblige. I thank you for your assistance today, Edward. I know my son has been in good hands from the way you have offered yourself so fully to our cause."

"Sam is my family as well. When one of my family needs help, I will not hesitate to stand by him. I would do the same for any in the crew, no matter the cause."

"Well spoken."

Edward gathered the crew together and they set out in teams to explore the island. Edward and Henry, Anne and Christina, William and Sam, and John went into the island along with the majority of the crew, with Jack and Herbert and *Freedom*'s remaining crew staying behind.

Edward commanded the teams to remain at most ten feet apart due to the fog. As the crew walked further into the island they were still able to see the people close to them. Edward was walking with Anne, and Henry and Christina were ten feet ahead of them.

The grass was wet with dew and the smell of fresh rain saturated the surroundings. Aside from the crewmates talking, and the grass being trod underfoot, it was silent on the island.

"So, what do you make of this, Anne?" Edward asked.

Anne pursed her lips and gazed around at the fog and the unnaturally flat terrain of the island. "I am reminded of one of the first things I said to you: There are some things in this world that cannot be explained."

Edward nodded in recognition. "Yes, I remember. That was when you were still pretending to be a man to hide your identity. You were referring to the locks on *Freedom* being magical as an explanation for why they could not be picked, were you not?" Anne nodded. "So, you believe Dominique is from the future?"

"I don't think I'm the authority on what is happening, but I believe in the possibility. I have seen many things which, if I told you, you may not believe. What do you think of Dominique's story?"

"As with many of the wonders we have seen, I don't particularly care. Perhaps he is from the future, perhaps Sam, Dominique, and his crew were tortured into believing this fantasy, or perhaps they are insane. Our goal is this Alston woman, and that will bring us one step closer to the key I seek. That, and helping Sam's family, are all I care about."

"Perhaps that is the best way to think of this occurrence. If we cannot explain what is happening, what is the use in pondering over it?"

"Exactly." Edward smiled to his lover, but when he opened his eyes his happiness faded. His head darted back and forth. "Where is everyone?"

Anne spun around, searching for their friends. "Hello? Christina? Henry?" she yelled. Anne looked at the ground. "The fog is thickening, I can barely see the grass beneath our feet."

Edward joined in yelling for their comrades, but no matter how loud their plea, there was no reply. Edward and Anne were alone.

"Come," Anne commanded. She grabbed Edward's hand and pulled him into a run.

The two ran forward across the grass through the pale mist, yelling as they went. The island turned colder with each passing minute, but the exertion kept their bodies warm. The silence of the island became oppressive, with the only sounds being the soft crunch of their boots against the moist grass. They ran for what felt like ages, cold sweat passing down their faces and exhaustion taking over.

Edward thought he heard a voice behind him, a voice he hadn't heard in a long time, and the suddenness of it loosened his grip on Anne. Her hand slipped from Edward's, and she disappeared into the vapour.

"Anne?" Edward called. "Anne!"

"Hello, Ed."

Edward turned, the same voice from before beckoning him to its source. Edward saw the face of one he never thought he would see again, and it brought tears to his eyes.

"Dad?"

"Don' gimme that look."

William stared down at Sam, daggers raining from his pupils.

"Stop it," Sam commanded, to no effect. "Dad damn ye, William, stop starin' at me! Yer face is like a Catholic priest during a Sunday sermon: ye could make the most hardened man's sugar stick go limp with a glance." Sam waved his arms and turned to walk away.

William gripped Sam's clothes at the back. "I specifically instructed you to stay close to the others. We are now separated because of your ineptitude. Do not make the same mistake and go off on your own."

Sam pulled his clothes away forcefully and let out a sigh. "Fine, fine, dammit. I'm following orders now, your majesty." Sam cackled. "No… your majesty's dog."

William gave Sam another look, but this time Sam laughed it off and began walking again, with William following closely behind. The white wall on all sides seemed as much a physical barrier as a wall, shutting out most of their previous sight and sounds. William's normally silent footsteps were as loud as a person talking, which made Sam's dragging feet deafening in the void.

Several times while walking gradually forward, William placed his hand on Sam's shoulder, but Sam kept shrugging it off. After a few occurrences, Sam snapped.

"William, put yer hand on me one more time and I swear…"

"Well, if you insist. I thought you could use the support, however, as I noticed the fog closing in on us."

"What?" Sam spun around, staring at the ground. As he confirmed what William said, perspiration formed on his forehead. "Dammit, dammit, dammit." Sam's eyes flitted back and forth, and he kept running his fingers through his straight black hair. After a moment, he looked William up and down. "How can you be so calm at a time like this?"

"I feel you carry enough hysteria for the both of us. Hold yourself together, man."

"We're goin' ta die here, in case ye hadn't noticed."

William placed his hands behind his back, straightening his spine. "If we were going to succumb to the fog, it would have happened already. We have been breathing it in since before we landed on the island."

Sam didn't have a response, so instead he paced around in a small circle, making audible groans growing in volume. As the grunts reached a crescendo he covered his face with his hands and wiped vigorously, finishing with a flourish.

"Why did ye join me anyway, mate?"

William arch his brow. "Could you repeat that?"

"Why did you come wit me when ye coulda went wit yer princess? We both know ye don't care fer me none, so why?"

William paused for a moment. "Contrary to what you may believe, I do not hate you. While we may disagree on methods of accomplishing tasks, we are part of the same crew. Camaraderie builds trust, trust keeps us working as a team, and teamwork keeps us alive."

"Do ye hear yerself, mate? Yer such a ninny I can't stand it. Git the stick outta yer butt sometimes, would ye?"

"The fog is touching you."

Sam jumped and circled around frantically until he noticed William grinning on the verge of laughing. "Oh, very funny, ye git. Come on, let's..." Sam paused, peering behind William.

William's gaze was drawn over his shoulder when Sam yelled, "I see a woman!" before rushing past William and towards the figure he'd noticed. William reacted just in time to begin running before Sam disappeared into the mist.

William could not see the woman Sam noticed, and because of the headstart Sam had, he could barely see him. William was fast on his feet, and routinely proved himself to be the most agile amongst the men aboard *Freedom*, but conditions were stacked against him: Thick fog which was becoming denser, Sam's natural agility, distance advantage, and changing his direction, all made William gradually fall behind. No amount of yelling for Sam to slow down helped, and Sam was beginning to disappear. First his arms, then his head, then all William could see was Sam's back.

William leapt into the air and reached for Sam, his fingers inching closer. The white smoke was overtaking Sam's clothes. William gritted his teeth as he fell. His fingers grazed the fold of Sam's tunic, and then William fell to the ground.

The force of falling caused William to close his eyes for a moment, and when he opened them again he was no longer surrounded by fog, and he could see Sam as clear as day in front of him.

William rolled over, rose to his feet, and a brick building greeted his eyes. After glancing about at the whole mansion in front of him, he recognised where they were. "London," William muttered.

Sam turned around, not noticing William before now. "How did we... what's happenin' right now? William? William!" Sam yelled, bringing William out of his stupor.

"This is Kensington Palace. Though I do not know how we have been transported here."

William and Sam examined their surroundings. To their left, a hundred feet away, was the palace itself, a two-and-a-half to three-storey mansion of red brick. The front of the building extended two hundred and fifty feet, and had several annex buildings on the sides going farther back. William noticed that fog surrounded the palace, allowing sight of the gates and perimeter, but not beyond.

"There she is!" Sam pronounced, pointing.

William followed Sam's finger to see a woman glancing about in the same bewildered way as they were. Sam ran towards her, and William followed behind briskly.

With the sound of William's and Sam's footsteps, the woman turned to face them. She had short black hair tied into a bun, with curls spilling down her forehead. Her red cheeks and small facial features could only be described as "dainty." She wore a simple white travelling dress flowing to her ankles.

Her eyes widened at Sam's forceful approach, but before she could back away Sam grabbed her by the arm. "Whut's yer name, woman?"

"What is the meaning of this, gentlemen? Are you part of the King's guard?" the woman asked.

"Answer the question!" Sam demanded.

"Sam, release her!" William said.

"But—"

"But what? What if this is the woman your father seeks? What will you do with her? We are stuck in an unknown area, we do not know how to leave, and we may need her if this occurrence is by design. Whatever you plan on doing, it can wait until we find our way to exit this illusion."

"Tch." Sam threw the woman's arm away.

William turned to the woman. "I apologise for the actions of my comrade, miss."

"Thank you, sir," the woman said with a curtsey. "My name is Theodosia Burr Alston. From your speech to your friend, I judge that you too were unfortunate enough to land on an island covered in fog, and now you find yourself here?"

"Yes, and if you were on the ship known as the *Patriot*, you will know us as the crew of the *Freedom*, which you hit a few days prior."

"Yes, yes, I recall that happening. My apologies for not stopping to introduce ourselves, but we were being chased by pirates, and entered the Bermuda Triangle in an attempt to escape. At first I thought the fog that appeared a blessing, but I fear now it is the opposite." Alston paused for a moment. "Are you with the pirates who were chasing us?" Alston asked Sam.

"No, but my father is the captain. Once we get outta here, I'm takin' ye ta him."

Alston turned to William. "You look to be an upstanding gentleman, so I will tell you this in the hopes you will do the right thing: I am on a diplomatic mission of aid to the United States of America. The ship I travel on carries medical supplies for soldiers."

William considered the woman's words for a moment. 'United States of America' was confusing to William, but he quickly gathered that it represented the North American colonies who were at war with Britain in Dominique's explanation. Alston's position from Dominique's account, however, was not the same. "We were told differently," William said eventually.

"I assure you I am telling the truth, but, as they say, actions speak louder than words. Let us find our way out of here, you can judge my actions until then, and we will see if you believe me trustworthy." Sam snorted, but William and Alston ignored him.

"I have one question which may seem odd but will help with another matter. What year do you believe it to be?"

Alston peered at William queerly. "The year is clearly eighteen-thirteen…" Alston glanced from William to Sam, who in turn looked at each other. "Is it not, gentlemen?"

"Before we delve into that subject, we should examine our surroundings. If this is an illusion, we need to find the source."

"And if it be real?" Sam asked.

Then we have far bigger problems than simply finding our way out of here." William allowed his words to sink in. "This way," he commanded.

William guided the others to the side of the long brick building. Though one would think the home to the royal family would be swarming with guards, the grounds of Kensington Palace were surprisingly empty. Coupled with the fog just in the distance, there was a haunted feel to the mansion.

Despite the emptiness, William was no less cautious in walking about the premises. He stepped behind tall decorative bushes and trees as much as possible and peered out behind them to ensure the coast was clear before venturing further. At two-thirds of the way across the side wall, William approached the wall and touched a specific brick, pushing it into the wall.

The brick being depressed caused a portion of the wall to open, creating an entrance. "Inside," William suggested, pointing the way.

After Alston and Sam entered, William followed and flipped a wooden lever to close the opening behind them. After a moment, their eyes adjusted to the dark interior.

They found themselves in a small, plain corridor with a low ceiling and no windows. Lanterns posted every twenty feet provided soft illumination. The only discerning features were the brick walls and wooden floorboards.

"Where are we?" Sam asked.

"We are in a secret tunnel known only to a close few to the royal family. They are meant to be a way to quickly escape in an emergency. These corridors connect to almost every room in the palace." William grabbed a nearby lantern and began walking through the corridor. "Follow me."

William led the group through long corridors and winding staircases for fifteen minutes. Every so often he opened a door a crack to check if there was anyone in the room, but throughout the whole search they could find no one.

The inside of the tunnels felt unused and smelled of rotting wood and stale air. Cracks showed on the brick walls, and cobwebs found their way inside as well as in each available corner. The sound of scurrying tiny feet, animals running away from their approach, could be heard far in front of them.

When they reached the royal apartments, William could hear noise in the King's bedchambers. He opened the door a small amount, as before, but could not see anything due to the poor angle.

Sam moved up beside William, who was just then lowering the lantern, and Sam knocked it with his knee. The lantern swung forward and hit the secret door, causing a clinking noise.

The three looked at the source of the noise, and their eyes widened. Before they could react, the secret door was flung open. A middle-aged man in military dress stood in front of them.

"William, we've been waiting for you. Come on in, son." The handsome middle-aged man was military advisor to William III, and former First Lord of the Admiralty, Edward Russell. He was also known as one of the immortal seven, who helped convince William III to take the throne through a show of force. He had jet-black hair slicked back, and dark eyes. Though he had been nothing short of jovial when speaking to William, William could not help but think the man a snake in disguise. Edward Russell turned his eyes to the other two next to William. "Who are these people, William?"

William was still in shock, but quickly regained his composure. He knew exactly *when* this illusion was taking place now. "These are friends. May they join us?" he asked with a bow.

"Of course, my boy," Russell said, opening the door wider to allow them entrance. "Oh, but before that, it may be prudent to leave your weapons in here. The King's constitution is on the brink currently, and he could not handle the sight of weapons right now, I'm afraid."

William paused for a moment; he recalled having a similar conversation with Edward Russell in the past. The memory of the fateful day when he failed in his charge rushed back to him, haunting his movements.

"Are you well, William?" Russell asked. "You look pale."

"Fine. Perfectly fine," William said, then he took the sword and pistol from his belt and lay them on the floor of the corridor before entering the King's bedchambers.

Sam reluctantly followed suit in removing his weapons, and gave the man a glare as he passed over the threshold. Alston had no worry of weapons, and entered behind Sam, though with reluctance.

The King's bedchambers were lavishly decorated with red and gold touching all furnishings. At the back of the room in the middle was an extravagant bed with oak canopy, and the King sitting up in it.

William walked over to the King and knelt down next to the bed. After a few seconds, he urgently beckoned the others to join him. Sam and Alston played along and knelt down next to the bed.

The King laughed, which sent him into a fit of coughs. "William, you and your friends may rise. You know you do not have to be so formal."

"Yes, Your Majesty... I just..." William shook his head and rose to his feet. "I would like you to meet Mister Samuel Bellamy, and Miss Theodosia Burr Alston. Though Samuel's appearance is ragged, he is a loyal man, and Miss Alston is a visiting dignitary from the New World colonies. Mister Bellamy, Miss Alston, I present to you King William III of England, Scotland, and Ireland in this year of the lord seventeen-oh-two," William said, staring at the two of them.

"Ah, good, good. Thank you for bringing them personally. Gentlemen, and lady, we welcome you to our house. We apologise for the secrecy, but you can appreciate that for a King to have audiences such as this is not normally possible." Sam and Alston nodded woodenly, causing the King to laugh once more. "Oh dear, our grace has rendered you speechless. Rest assured, you may speak freely and your words will be taken with the strictest confidence. William has apprised you of our inquiry, yes?" the King said with arched brow.

"Yes, Your Majesty. I told my friends here how you wished to know the thoughts of the public on the War of Succession," William said, glancing to Sam and Alston.

"So, Mister Bellamy, may we start with you? You are a London native, yes?" the King asked.

Samuel glanced to William and then to the King, and after wiping sweat from his brow he nodded. "Well, sir, the people are... with the war... they..." Sam trailed off, then shook his head and ran his fingers through his black hair. "Sorry, Your Majesty, I'm gonna just talk as I normally does if it pleases you?"

"By all means. We would not have it any other way," the King replied.

"The people don' care 'bout the war. It be a battle over a title that means nothin' ta them. Tha people only care 'bout gettin' food on the table and hopin the war doesn't make it ta their shores. Sir, kids die in tha street every day from not bein able ta eat, and those with a roof o'er head don' fare much better."

William's fist was in a ball, and his jaw was locked. He expected Sam to be Sam, but not to take it in this direction.

The King nodded. "We suspected as much, but we were not aware the poor was as much a problem as you describe. We thank you for your candour. And you, Miss Alston, how do our western brothers feel about the war?"

Alston jumped when her name was called, but quickly collected herself. "The west is currently with you, Sire. The territories siding with Britain are ready to go to war."

"That is reassuring, but your use of the word 'currently' concerns me. Could you elaborate? Also, we must say your accent is interesting. We did not expect such change over such a short period of time."

Alston peered at William and Sam. They had a dire look in their eyes from Alston's 'currently' slip, as they both recalled Dominique mentioning a war between the North American colonies and Britain in his time.

"Well, Sire, to be perfectly frank, the colonies feel similarly to your people here. It is only whispers currently, but over time those whispers could turn into shouts. Shouts for independence. I have seen first-hand what war does to the young, and the old. I do not know if His Highness has participated in war, but I am sure you can imagine the horror, and the grief on the faces of young widows, sons, fathers, and mothers. None deserve that news. None." Alston's lip quivered, and she wiped tears from her eyes. William was watching her intently.

The King was gazing at his bedsheets in a peculiar way, and after a moment he looked up at the three, then to Edward Russell. Russell nodded, silently answering the King's unspoken question.

"Once again, we thank you both for your honesty. We will take your words to heart in the coming months. May we also be candid with you?" Sam and Alston nodded. "We are planning on speaking with Louis XIV to negotiate peace terms. We acted in anger, starting this foolish war."

"Sire!" William spurted, getting lost in the illusion of his memories.

The King held up his hand. "We speak the truth, William, my boy. The people deserve better than a war built on names and titles and lands. The people deserve a better ruler than one quick to anger. The people deserve peace."

The King's words sent chills up William's spine, and he noticed the others had goose flesh. William was reminded that he saw the man in front of him not as a King, but a man who had faults and loved his people. From the looks on Sam and Alston's faces, he thought they felt the same.

"Now, if you will excuse me, Sir William, Mister Bellamy, Miss Alston, I have more matters that need to be discussed with Mister Russell." The King gestured to a door to the right of William, and after a bow, William, Sam, and Alston left through the door.

After closing the door behind him, William laid his back against it and let out a sigh. Seeing King William III alive and well, regardless of it being an illusion, was almost too much.

Alston spoke up after a moment. "I believe some explanation is in order."

William slowly opened his eyes and stood up straight. "Yes, you deserve as much after that." William stroked his chin. "As I tried to rush in telling you, the man in there is William III, King of England, Scotland, and Ireland up until the year seventeen-oh-two. This... illusion... seems to be drawn from my memory from six years ago, just before his death."

Alston's eyes widened at the mention of the year. William and Sam gave her a moment. "So, that fog took us to the year seventeen-oh-seven?"

William and Sam nodded, but then Sam glanced to the side. "Wait. What if we were taken to the year eighteen-thirteen?" Sam asked William.

William furrowed his brow and stared at Sam. "You do not really think... No, we can worry about this later. For now, we still need to find our way out of this place."

"I still have more questions, gentlemen."

"Yes, of course."

"As you have not asked me a question regarding my words with your King, I will assume you know of how North America is at war with Britain?"

"Yes, we heard as much from the pirate chasing after you," William replied.

"Then why have you pledged to help me if I am technically against Britain?"

"I am not loyal to Britain. I was loyal to that man," William said, pointing to the King's room. "William III raised me as if I were his own son. I owe him a great deal, and I love him. After my conversation with him, an assassin killed him and framed me for the murder. I am loyal to the one whom I think is fit to wear the crown as William III did: with honour and dignity." William turned to Sam. "I feel that if Anne so chose it, she could lay claim to the throne. Her mother is not fit to rule. If we are in the future, or you, Miss Alston, are from the future, perhaps the reason why our brothers to the west want independence is due to mismanagement by Queen Anne."

Sam laughed heartily. "William, yer so cold. I like this side of you." After another laugh petered out, Sam became inquisitive. "Wait, so who killed the King and frame ye?"

"Over the years, I have wracked my brain trying to find the answer, and I believe it was right in front of me this whole time. The man who opened the secret entrance on us, Edward Russell, is the most likely culprit. I recall him taking my weapon from me before I talked with the King, the same as now, and in my haste I forgot to retrieve it when leaving, as I exited via a different route. When I returned to retrieve my weapon, the King was dead, my sword piercing his heart, and several "eye witnesses" were found to corroborate my involvement." William shook his head. "Right in front of me this whole time."

Sam still had a puzzled look on his face. "How long from when you left the room to when the King was killed, would ye say?"

William gazed at the ceiling as he thought. "I returned after thirty minutes, and he was not far gone, so possibly twenty minutes after I left."

"Well, what are we waitin' fer, then? We may 'ave some time left, so let's get back in there and save him!" Sam yelled, reaching for the door.

William grabbed Sam's hand. "I already told you, this is not real. This has already happened. We are simply watching the events unfold as in my memory."

"I ain't dumb, ye ninny. This ain't jus' yer memory. We weren't here in yer memory, and somehow we 'ad a conversation with his kinglyness. Heck, if ye believe me father and this one 'ere," Sam said, pointing to Alston, "then it ain't such a stretch that this could be real, and we could change things. Even if it wus jus' a chance, don' ye want ta take it?" Sam pleaded.

William paused for a moment to consider Sam's words, and appreciate the fact that the man whom he thought cared the least for him, or anything in general, actually cared a great deal.

"No. Even if this is real, I would not change what has happened." Sam was speechless, but it was clear he had a question on the tip of his tongue. "If I save William III, it will drastically change the course of events in history, and in untold ways. We could be delaying a war perhaps, but what if a larger war erupts because of it?

"The greater reason I will not act is for the sake of Anne and Edward. Anne and Edward will never meet, nor will many of the crew onboard the *Freedom*. I have never seen Anne more happy than on *Freedom*. Also, if Anne or myself were not a part of the crew, Edward would not have been able to survive some of the trials he has faced up until now. I have grown to believe in Edward and feel that he will come to do great things.

"You may think that I treat my position as a job, and I need to relax, but I am the way I am because I love the family that we've built on *Freedom*. I would not risk that for anything in the world."

Sam smirked. "Even me?"

William laughed. "Even you, Sam." *If this is real, I am sorry, my King. I love you, but I've found my family, just as you wanted. I hope that is some solace.*

After a moment, William noticed movement in his peripheral vision. The fog was moving closer to the palace, and at an alarming rate.

"The fog is growing. Quickly, hold hands so whatever happens we are not separated."

The two complied and held fast their hands together. As the fog grew thicker and closer, it seeped in through the windows and doors, eventually filling the room. William, Sam, and Alston closed their eyes as the fog, and silence, overtook them.

When William opened his eyes, he was not on the island again as he thought might happen. He, Sam, and Alston, were now on a ship in the middle of the night. They could see a little boy and a middle-aged man dressed just like Dominique You standing on the port side, gazing out to the stars.

12. THEODOSIA BURR ALSTON

Edward opened his eyes and he was free of the fog on his vision and mind. He could see the island in its entirety, an enormous flat-land of grass with nothing special, save the mysteriousness. Edward could also see his crew, and others he did not know, scattered about. Some were waking from their trance just as Edward, and others were still in a daze.

Edward noticed Anne, and he ran to her. He wrapped his arms around her tightly, and she pulled him close.

"I was so worried," Edward whispered.

"As was I," Anne replied. Anne parted from Edward, a look of concern in her eyes. "Are you well? What did you see in the fog?"

Edward shook his head. "It doesn't matter. You?"

"I feel the same. I am simply glad to be back. We should help the crew," Anne stated, glancing about, and then she noticed the shore. "Edward, *Le Pandore* and *Patriot* are gone."

"What?" Edward shouted, turning to the shore. He could see it with his own eyes: *Freedom* was still on the beach, but the other ships had vanished at some point. "I will go to *Freedom* and find out what happened. Could you tend the crew, please?"

"Yes, of course," Anne replied, then she went to work.

Edward ran to the *Freedom* and climbed up a rope ladder to the deck. When he boarded, the crew hastily approached him and bom-barded him with questions about his and the others' wellbeing, as well as what happened after the fog caused them to disappear.

"Please, please, I will answer your inquiries later. I have more urgent matters to attend to." The crew heard his tone and gave him space. Edward approached Herbert at the helm. "What happened to Dominique?"

Herbert adjusted his glasses. "After the fog overtook you, the *Patriot* suddenly started attacking *Le Pandore*, then left shore. Dominique took his crew in search of it. That was an hour or so ago."

"Damn it, now how are we to find him? He still has the key."

"Not so." Herbert lifted a key in the air. "Dominique exchanged the key for the paper Benjamin left."

Edward cocked his brow. "What does he plan on doing with Benjamin's riddle?"

"Dominique said Alston won't be able to spy on the Americans

431

in our time, so after they took the *Patriot* back they were planning on following Benjamin's instructions to return to their time and strand Alston here." Herbert tossed the key to Edward. "Should I have stopped him?"

Edward regarded the key warily. *Something about this doesn't feel right.* "We'll see, Herbert."

"So Dominique You told you I am a spy? That could not be further from the truth." A voice sounded from behind Edward.

Edward turned to see a woman with black hair tied into a bun, standing next to Sam, William, and Henry. "Glad to see you're safe, men. And you must be Theodosia Burr Alston, I presume?"

"Yes, you presume correctly."

"So, according to you, what am I to believe?"

Alston curiously glanced to William, who nodded to her. "I am on a mission to bring medical supplies to soldiers at war with Britain. Dominique wanted my ship, and the medical supplies aboard, not me."

"Captain," Sam spoke up. "We dunno who this woman is. Ye can't believe what she says."

Alston had a sad look on her face. "Mister Bellamy, we all saw the same thing back there. Dominique pu—"

"Shut it, you bitch. I won't have you lie about my father. Ye don't know whut ye saw." Sam lifted his hand to strike Alston, but William stopped him.

"Captain, I promise you, Alston is telling the truth. She is an honourable person through and through. If what happened to you on that island was anything similar to what we experienced, you will understand why Sam is acting this way." Sam lowered his fist, but appeared angry and dejected.

Edward considered all that was said, and pondered on how he could solve the riddle of whom he could trust. He smacked the key from Dominique in his hand as he thought, and that was when he had an idea. "Sam, don't let your emotions sway your judgement. We have but one way to prove if he was lying or not." Edward lifted the key up for Sam to see. "Dominique supposedly left us the key we were seeking, so all we have to do is test it out. William, Henry, could you help the crew back to the ship?" William and Henry both nodded and left to complete the order.

Edward travelled to the gun deck of the ship and used the key on the bow cabin, with Sam following behind. The key rattled in the lock, but nothing happened.

Sam's anger subsided, but his disappointment was visible on his face. Edward was disappointed as well, as he too wanted to trust the man Sam held faith in.

Edward and Sam went to the stern of the gun deck, passing all the cannons and spare iron balls, heading to the next locked door, the supposed captain's cabin. Edward attempted to unlock the cabin, but he received the same results. Another nail in the coffin.

Sam let out a sigh, but waved Edward away when he tried to comfort him.

The two continued to the berth deck and tried the key once more on the lock at the bow end, but that door would not open either.

"The key is fake," Edward declared solemnly, turning to Sam.

Sam was broken. His eyes flitted back and forth, like he was trying to find the pieces of himself to bring back together. "No, we... we jus' have to try again. Why would he give us a fake key? There be no point, Captain. No point."

Edward shook Sam's shoulders lightly. "Let's ask Dominique why, shall we?"

Edward turned away from Sam. Sam seemed to still be holding onto the delusion surrounding his father figure, but Edward's mind was made up about the man.

I know Dominique has the real key! Now he's trying to abscond with it and his precious medicine.

Edward marched to the main deck and addressed the crew. The ship was now filled with his crew, as well as the unknown men and a few women from the island, presumably from the *Patriot*. "We are setting sail to chase after *Le Pandore*, men. Dominique tricked us and left us a false key, but I mean to take the real one from him." *If he even has a real key. No! I can't think like that. He must have it. He must.*

The crew was confused at first, but didn't question their leader's guidance and prepared the ship to leave port. Feet stamped quickly across the wooden floorboards and hands stretched the rope ladders as men released the rigging and let loose the sails.

Alston approached Edward, calm as could be. "So, you trust in my words?"

"When we catch up to Dominique we will find the truth of the matter. I will reserve judgement until then."

"I have nothing to fear, my words are true." Alston smiled brightly, with an almost angelic serenity despite the insanity of the situation, her white dress swaying in the wind.

Sam shuffled to the quarterdeck in a daze, his hands shaking, the complete opposite to Alston's calm. "What will we do when we catch up to 'em, Captain?"

Edward stared Sam in the eyes. "We will make Dominique tell us the reason for his actions, and his answer will determine what we will do."

"No." Sam shook his head. "No, this isn't right. I won't let you hurt him!" Sam pulled a pistol on Edward Thatch, pointing it straight at his captain's face.

The crew stopped what they were doing and focused on Sam. The crazed eyes, the pistol drawn. This was unlike the Sam they had known for so long. Gone was the laughter, the blithe attitude towards anything and everything. This wasn't Sam.

"Sam," Edward said, his hands raised, "lower your pistol."

"Why the fuck should I?" Sam replied, teeth gritted, pistol shaking. "You 'ad the good life, Thatch. You never been a kid livin' on the streets in England. Starvin' half the time, eatin' rats and stealing the rest. I took my share of beatings. More'n that, I reckon. I was due for fortune or death, either one, n'then Dominique saved us, Captain. Provided a home and a family when none wanted us. What would you know about havin' it bad?"

Edward slowly lifted his shirt, then pointed to a large misshapen scar on the right of his stomach. "Want to know where I got this, Sam?" Sam didn't reply. "I was a year with my uncle-in-law and his family when this happened. Being me, I was always able to push my uncle-in-law's buttons. My uncle's disposition could have been because of the booze too, but I think he simply wasn't fond of me, because he never beat his own kids, nor his wife. Only me.

"Henry lent me a toy the day I got this scar. I was so happy I couldn't wait to return home and play with the wooden knight. Heaven forbid I should be happy once in a while after my father left me. When my uncle saw me playing with the toy, it set him off something fierce. He picked me up by the neck and slammed me against the iron furnace. My uncle held me there while I screamed, and didn't release me until my aunt ran in and yelled for him to stop. He stopped, but not for good.

"The point is, I know more than you think, and I certainly didn't have a good life.

"When my father left, at first I kept wondering why he left, why he didn't return, why, why, why. Then I was angry at him, so angry I *wished* he was dead like everyone thought. But he's still my father and I love him. If and when I see him again, I'll be able to ask him why, and then his answer will dictate what I do afterwards.

"But I'm not a fool, he may be dead and I might never be able to ask him why. You still have a chance, Sam. Don't let this opportunity go because you're afraid of the answer."

Sam still held the pistol with a trembling hand. He was on the brink.

Alston stepped between Edward and Sam. "Everything will be alright." She stepped closer to Sam. Her caring eyes told a story in themselves, and Sam couldn't look away. "Whatever happens, you will never lose your true family. They will be beside you until the end." Alston stepped closer once more, and embraced Sam.

Sam was paralysed. Frozen from this stranger's action. Sam appeared as if he would crack like glass with the slightest movement. Edward took the pistol from him, lifting him from his catatonic state. Sam collapsed into Alston's arms, but she held him up and carried him away to the lower decks.

Edward stood on the quarterdeck, staring at the pistol. The tension was lifted, but the blow to the crew's morale lingered. The men were concerned for Sam's wellbeing, and likely questioned their next move. If *Freedom* set sail, the crew may be forced to face Sam's father figure in battle.

Edward could understand the general mood aboard the ship, as their feelings were being mimicked in himself. "Set sail, men!" he commanded. "Do not worry for Sam; we will find the truth and set him free," Edward recited, channelling the Pirate Priest Bartholomew Roberts.

The crew accepted Edward's words and returned to work, releasing the rigging and pushing the *Freedom* from the beach and away from the Devil's Island once and for all.

"Where are we heading, Captain?" Herbert asked.

"Back to the origin of the fog, where we first shot the cannons into the night sky. Are you able to return us there without Benjamin's paper?"

"Of course. Without the fog wreaking havoc on us, it will be child's play," Herbert replied with confidence.

Edward chuckled. "Sorry I ever doubted you," he said, patting Herbert on the shoulder.

"Edward?" Anne said, stepping up beside Edward. "Are you well?"

"Yes, I'm well. I can appreciate why Sam did what he did," Edward said, gazing off to the horizon.

"But you feel that Dominique is our enemy now?"

"I hope beyond hope I was correct about the man from the start and he is our ally, but I fear I misjudged."

"I fear we all did," Anne replied.

Edward shook his head. "Not all. Henry saw through the lies, but I chose not to listen." Edward pointed to Henry, hard at work with his fellow crewmates in preparing the ship to leave port.

"And I am sure that will not happen again?"

"Not likely. He and I are destined to butt heads until we die, I'm afraid." Edward chuckled.

Anne grinned at Edward's jest. "Here, let me take the pistol back to storage," she offered, hand extended.

Edward was taken aback as he'd nearly forgotten he still carried the pistol. He handed it to Anne and she walked away, but stopped after a few steps. She inspected the pistol and turned around.

"This is empty, Edward."

"I know," he replied. Anne smiled and left.

Alston returned from the bowels of the ship and rejoined Edward on the quarterdeck. At the same time the sails were lowered and the ship was leaving the island.

"The gentleman has much to think about, but he will be right as a trivet soon, I wager."

"You have my thanks. That was a delicate situation, and I don't think I could have handled it as you did."

"I have seen far worse." Alston peered at the horizon as the ship chopped up and down with the waves. "Young men on the battlefield for the first time panic easily. Seeing their friends and family die, losing limbs, shock is common. Your mate has been through a lot himself. In the fog we…"

Edward held up his hand to stop Alston from continuing. "We all seem to have seen something personal and intimate in that fog. If Sam doesn't want to share what happened, I do not wish to know."

Alston was slightly taken aback, but recovered. "Yes, I should not be so insensitive. I am sorry."

"That is quite alright. Now, could you tell me what your job was in the war if not a spy?"

"Nurse, but in the middle of battle the title can mean many jobs. As I stated earlier, the ship I was on carried medicine for American troops, some of which I would have personally delivered to the frontlines. Now, because of Dominique, many could lose their lives from rot and disease." Alston's gaze moved to the waist.

Edward felt hot with anger. This was his mistake, his blunder. Edward would ensure Dominique would be caught and pay for what he did.

"You were told my name, but I never received yours, sir."

Edward laughed. "My name is Edward Thatch, and I am no sir. Truly, you may think no better of us than Dominique. We are also pirates. People have taken to calling me Blackbeard these days, for obvious reasons."

At the last name, Alston's eyes widened.

"What?" Edward asked. "You know me… from the future?"

Alston nodded, her eyes soft again. "Your cognomen is well known. Truth be told, you were known to be an evil man who inspired fear in many."

Edward chuckled. "And what do you think?"

Alston considered Edward for a moment. "I believe your enemies would fear you greatly, but in your eyes I see you care deeply for your men, and they you. William is a testament to your character. You are not evil."

"Thank you."

"Would you enjoy hearing of some of your exploits?"

Edward laughed. "Perhaps it is better I don't. None should know their future. It removes a level of choice to the affair."

"True. And the ability to choose is *Freedom*, after all," Alston said with a smile.

Edward returned the smile, then focused his attention on guiding the ship again. "Ten points to starboard. Close-haul those sails, men, we've a ship to catch!" he yelled.

As the hours passed and approached the fated time of one o'clock, fortune seemed to favour the *Freedom* and its crew. The wind pushed them faster than ever, and from Herbert's approximation it had only started after *Le Pandore* had already arrived at their destination.

Herbert, hands on the ship's wheel, glancing to Edward and across the bow, spoke with confidence. "If Dominique's goal is to return to his time, then *Le Pandore* has been waiting in the same spot for one o'clock. The advantage they had in speed and the headstart are meaningless now."

Just as one o'clock approached, the crew of the *Freedom* could see *Le Pandore* on the horizon. Edward watched through a spyglass as the *Freedom* approached. He could see smoke erupt from the side of the ship, then after a few seconds the sound of cannons rushed to his ears.

Edward watched for fog, but none came. Either by a mistake on the crew of *Le Pandore*'s part, or by providence, Dominique was stuck in this time.

Freedom quickly approached the enemy ship, and *Le Pandore* turned around to let loose its cannons again, this time aiming for *Freedom*.

Edward took a moment to appreciate his mistake. Alston had been telling the truth. Edward eyed Sam, who held a defeated expression on his face.

Edward felt Sam was unable to fight, having grown up with the people they were about to fight against.

Edward approached him. "Sam, go to the crew cabin. You aren't fit to fight."

Sam was ready to object, but Edward's eyes silenced any questions.

"Herbert, bring us next to *Le Pandore*. I don't want her escaping."

"Aye, Captain," Herbert replied.

"Prepare to board, men. It's time to fight!"

As if reading Edward's mind, *Le Pandore* opened her sails in an attempt to leave. Before she was able to move an inch, the *Freedom* caught up and sent grappling lines over. The crew of the *Freedom* tied the lines down, securing the two ships together.

Blackbeard's Ship

"Attack!" Edward yelled as he jumped the gap between the two ships.

Edward landed on the waist, with his crew joining him after. One of Dominique's men attacked Edward with a knife aimed at his face. Edward swayed to the left and punched the man hard. The man fell to the deck, the back of his head hitting dead-on, knocking him unconscious.

Unequalled rage filled Edward. Edward was back to his old form, his broken arm now healed, muscles taut, and well-fed, he was a force to be reckoned with once more. Edward had placed smoking wick in his beard before the battle, and the light of the moon reflected on the smoke, making him appear otherworldly.

Edward rushed after Dominique, cutting down foes on his way to the Frenchman. A shot here, a stab there. The crew of *Le Pandore* tried to defend their captain, but each fire was a miss, and each cut was deflected.

Dominique, seeing Edward advancing on him, descended into the lower regions of the ship. "Come back here, Dominique!" Edward yelled as he followed the man into the depths.

On the waist of the *Freedom*, William defended against counter-boarders. One man jumped over, standing precariously on top of the railing. William upended his legs. The man fell, hitting his head on the side of the ship before landing in the water. Several others made an attempt to cross, only to be stopped by William.

John showed his normal prowess in battle on the *Freedom*'s poop deck. John noticed an enemy heading towards Anne. He shot his musket at the enemy's back, killing him before he could even get close to Anne. In front of John another man touched down, ready to fire a blunderbuss. John grabbed onto the blunderbuss and the two fought for control of the weapon. John kicked the enemy in the nether regions, causing him to loosen his grip. John took the weapon, and shot point blank into the man's face. The man died instantly, his head a red mess, blood pooling beneath him where he fell.

Pukuh took the fight onto the enemy ship. One man aimed a pistol at him, but Pukuh threw a knife into the barrel. The man fired and the pistol exploded, useless. Pukuh kneed the man in the chest, knocking the wind out of him. A second charged with a sword. Pukuh kicked the man's sword into the air, then stabbed him with his spear.

Henry and Anne, in a rare display of camaraderie, fought back to back. Anne fought with her eastern fighting style, and Henry with his fists. Men attacked the two left and right on the bow of *Le Pandore*.

On the left, a man attacked Henry with a sword while another struck with a kick. Anne grabbed the first man's sword arm, holding him. Henry stopped the second man's kick and punched him in the face. Anne struggled with the first man's sword. Henry turned and punched the man with the sword in the chest causing him to double over. Anne took the loose sword and stabbed the man who'd tried to kick Henry in the chest.

Christina was only suited to use knives at her current level of strength. She stayed on the *Freedom* repelling invaders. Anne had taught Christina several weak points on the human body, and to apply her weight to her strikes. Men jumped over to the *Freedom* and she swiftly cut their Achilles tendons or the backs of their knees while other crew members finished them off. Christina's anger seethed as she fought, allowing her temporary reprieve from the blood and gore around her.

Edward, now in the bowels of *Le Pandore*, couldn't see two inches in front of his face. The darkness of night combined with the dark interior of the ship caught Edward off guard. His eyes were trying to adjust to the dark, with little success.

My only hope is that Dominique is at the same disadvantage.

A flash of moonlight reflected into Edward's eyes. He ducked down as a blade passed over his head and lodged into the wood of the ship. The owner didn't bother retrieving the blade and ran.

Edward advanced slowly, his sword poised in front of him. He could hear the sounds of battle above, and cannons firing nearby. To his right, he could see sparks flying from the gunpowder as the gunners fired their muskets at the *Freedom*. With each musket blast Edward caught a glimpse of the surroundings. Bullets from the *Freedom* broke through *Le Pandore*, letting in some pale light, but not enough to see by.

With each flash of light, Edward thought he could see the shadow of Dominique moving through the ship. Edward's eyes were slowly adjusting and he could see better with each passing second, but not well enough.

Someone attacked him with a sword. Edward deflected the blow and countered, but missed. The enemy blade flashed forward, nicking Edward in the stomach. He swiped his blade across, cutting the person's arms. The blade dropped as the man screamed, but the sound was drowned out by the surrounding din. Edward thrust his blade in the direction of the screams, hitting something solid.

He examined the body. *Not Dominique.*

To starboard Edward could see the faint light of a lantern. It was of little use in this darkness, but Edward picked it up regardless and an idea sparked. He tossed the lantern to the ground and the oil leaked out, starting a blaze which would soon threaten the whole ship. Edward ran forward to another lantern affixed to the main mast in the middle of the gun deck. He once more threw the lantern to the ground, starting another fire. Edward kept doing this until a good portion of the deck was ablaze.

Now able to see clearly, Edward searched for the Captain of *Le Pandore*. He could see men abandoning their stations to stop the fires. The sounds of fighting still filled the area, now mixed with the crackling of the fire. Edward noticed a door at the stern, which, he surmised, led to the captain's cabin.

Edward entered the cabin. The barrel of a pistol was pointed straight at Edward. Dominique pulled the trigger as Edward's instincts made him drop to the floor. The bullet flew over Edward's head. Dominique ran forward, stamped his feet on each of Edward's arms, and pinned him with a sword in his face.

"You couldn't leave well enough alone, could you?" Dominique sneered.

"I need the key, bastard," Edward replied.

"Then consider this all part of the test. You've done well so far, but if you want the key you'll have to kill me first!" Dominique noticed the fires licking at the bow and looked up.

"That can be obliged!" Edward snarled as he kneed Dominique's nether regions. Dominique's power left him, and Edward was able to free his arms. He slashed at the back of Dominique's leg.

Dominique fell. Edward pushed himself back through the doorway and rose from the floor. The fire was filling the area with smoke and crackling sounds as the flames inched closer and closer to the stores of gunpowder.

Dominique stumbled to his feet, and, using his sword like a cane, closed the doors of his cabin. Edward ran and kicked down the door. Dominique had opened a starboard window and was climbing to the outside of the ship. Edward ran and slashed at his feet, but missed by a hair.

Edward sheathed his cutlass and followed the fleeing man through the window. He saw Dominique climbing the stern and quickly followed, using the window edges to prop his feet, and the rigging rope for grip.

When Edward reached the gunwales, a crewman of Dominique's pointed a pistol at Edward. He grabbed the man's arm and pulled him overboard. The man screamed and tried to grab Edward and pull him down, but gripped only air as he plummeted past.

Edward saw Captain Dominique heading down to the waist of his ship, still using his sword as a crutch. The deck was absorbing the fire from below and would soon be ablaze as well.

Edward ran and jumped high in the air, landing both feet on Dominique's back. Dominique fell to the floor with a groan and rolled from the blow. He tried to rise, but he was weak from his injuries.

Edward grabbed Dominique by the coat, dragging him to the port side. Because of the rapidly spreading fire across the ship, many in the crew abandoned fighting, and indeed the ship itself.

"Lay down a gangplank," Edward commanded.

Pukuh covered Edward's back. "Your labour has borne fruit, brother!" he said over his shoulder.

"Aye, this battle is over. Their ship will be lost to fire soon. Make sure our crew are returned safely."

"You may count on me," Pukuh replied with confidence.

A gangplank was dropped across the two ships, allowing Edward to bring Dominique across to the *Freedom*. After finishing their respective fights, *Freedom*'s crew returned to their home by jumping over or traversing the gangplank. The crew of *Le Pandore* were no threat to the *Freedom* anymore.

In short order, the fire started on the gun deck of *Le Pandore* reached the waist, and was burning the ship apart. Bowlines burned, the sails caught fire, and the wooden boards broke as they were turned to ash by the blaze. Explosions boomed from the gunpowder on the gun deck, spreading the fire further and blowing apart the wood. Soon the flames would reach the hold, where the bulk of the gunpowder lay, and would blast the keel apart.

Edward threw Dominique to *Freedom*'s deck, then ordered the crew to cut the lines once everyone was safely over. Herbert eased the *Freedom* over to the *Patriot*. The remainder of *Le Pandore*'s crew surrendered, having seen the battle on their flagship.

The original crew of the *Patriot* boarded to man it once more and *Le Pandore*'s crew were tied up. Edward was able to see the medical supplies in the lower deck of the *Patriot*, once more confirming Alston's story.

Time to finish this.

Edward returned to Dominique, who was on his knees on the waist of the *Freedom*, his hands tied behind his back. "Where is Sam?" Edward asked, but no one answered. "Someone get Sam." One of the crew went below deck to fetch Sam.

"So, what now?" Dominique asked calmly.

"Well, we'll kill you. I thought that rather obvious. But first…" Edward sauntered over to Dominique and rifled through his pockets until he found what he was searching for: The key to the next part of the *Freedom*, and the paper holding the old clue.

Dominique smiled crookedly. "Congratulations. The pawn advances once more. Benjamin always knew how to pick them."

Edward cocked his brow. "What do you mean?"

"You think you're the first? You are just another player in one of Benjamin's games."

Edward's mouth was a line, and his eyes cold. "You're wrong."

Dominique cackled with genuine mirth. "And what makes you think you're not, eh?"

Edward kept a calm face while Dominique continued to laugh. When Dominique stopped due to the stares sent his way, Edward replied, "Because, we're fighting against Benjamin, and..." Edward grabbed Dominique by the neck and held him up in the air. "I'm the King." Edward dropped Dominique and he fell in a heap.

Sam was brought up to the main deck by one of the crew. His hair was dishevelled and his eyes baggy. He ambled over to Edward, in front of Dominique.

"Sam, my son. Let me out of these bonds. Help me. Am I not your father?"

"I saw..." Sam stated softly.

"Saw what?" Dominique asked.

Sam stared into his father's eyes. "I saw the day I wus lost at sea in an illusion on that island. I didn't want ta believe it, but I remember now. Someone pushed me into the Devil's Sea, and only you and I wus on deck tha' night, Dom."

Edward handed Sam a pistol. Sam pointed the pistol with shaking hands at the captain he'd considered a father.

Dominique chuckled. "You think I pushed you? You were a child, you experienced a traumatic event. You aren't remembering correctly."

"I remember perfectly!" Sam yelled. "I jus' want to know why."

Dominique smirked. "A privateer ship is not fit for a kid, but look at you now, you're a strapping young lad. Together, we could rule these seas. What do you sa—"

"Enough!" Sam yelled, and then he pulled the trigger.

The sound of the gun travelled across the ship and out to the ocean, piercing the ears of the three crews present. The wind blew the smoke away as the pistol fell to Sam's side, and the body of Dominique You fell to the deck of the *Freedom*.

Sam walked sullenly back to the crew cabin to rest. The crew watched him as he stepped sluggishly down the ladder and disappeared below deck.

Edward picked up Dominique's body, walked to the edge of *Freedom*, and threw him overboard. It fell with a splash and floated off into the waters of the Triangle.

"Bind the rest of Dominique's crew, and move them to the *Patriot*," Edward commanded, then went to test the new key.

The two doors on the gun deck didn't open, so the key had to open the door in the crew's quarters. The berth deck, the lowest deck before the hold, was lined stem to stern with beds and hammocks for the crew. On the stern, past the crew quarters, was the mess hall and kitchen. On the bow was a locked door, which opened with the key from Dominique.

Fifteen members of the crew gathered to see the mystery room being opened, excited to see the outcome of what the riddle and fighting had brought them. The crew was rather disappointed with the results, however.

The room was a simple brig, a prison aboard the ship for holding prisoners of war or punishing crewmates. The front part of the brig was an open area with some chairs bolted to the floorboards and the remaining two-thirds separated by large iron bars extending the height of the room. The brig itself held a long iron slab for laying or sitting on, but nothing else. All in all a bit disheartening, given the previous treasures left by Benjamin in other rooms.

The crew behind Edward groaned audibly, making Edward laugh. "Come now, we only have two more keys to acquire and we've unlocked the whole ship. Besides, a brig could be useful in the future." Edward's words cheered some of them up.

"Captain, look!" one of the crewmates said, pointing to something on the wall in the brig.

Edward turned and noticed a piece of paper stuck to the wall. *That must be the next clue.* Edward entered the brig and retrieved the square paper. As he grabbed the paper, the door was closed and locked behind him.

The crew laughed and pointed. "In jail again, Captain. Whatever will you do?" one of them jested.

"Har har, very funny. Now please open the door," Edward requested.

The crew stopped laughing and searched for a key, but couldn't find one. "There ain't no key, Captain."

After Edward panicked for a moment, he pulled out the key that opened the door to the brig, then tested it on the ship's prison door. The door opened with a click and Edward was able to leave. The crew let out a sigh of relief and apologised for the jest. "No harm done, mates." Edward tossed the key to one of the crew members. "Take the key to John, he'll want to put it with the others."

"Aye Captain." The crew quickly dispersed as Edward ambled to the main deck while reading the next clue.

In the Gulf the North East Triangles Point the Way.
Four points, four points, three points, three points.
Undo and See.

I didn't think it was possible for these to make less sense. Edward turned the paper over, and found a map on the back. It had no names of countries or landmarks, but even Edward, with his limited knowledge of maps, could see the image of the Gulf of Mexico. *Well, at least we know which Gulf the clue mentions.*

When Edward reached the top once more, Theodosia Burr Alston was waiting for him.

"I am told I cannot return to my time, or perhaps it is you who are not able to return to your time. Is this true?" Alston asked, a distressed expression on her face.

"I do not know. We will try to recreate the events of our meeting tomorrow night. For now I think we should sleep."

Alston nodded. "Yes, you are correct, sir. I hope it works; the soldiers need those supplies, or you may need to return home." Alston studied the crew of the *Freedom*, battle-weary and tending to their injuries. "But, perhaps, the greater need is here," she muttered to herself.

Before Edward could question what Alston was thinking, she rushed across a gangplank to the *Patriot* to talk with the crew. Before long she returned with several women and some of the medicine and bandages from her ship.

"Miss Alston, this is too much. You need these supplies more than we do."

"Nonsense. These men were injured recovering these supplies. A portion belongs to you by rights."

Edward frowned. "I fought Dominique for my own reasons, and we wronged you. If anything, we owe you…"

Alston raised her hand, silencing Edward. "Before entering the fog, Dominique was upon us. The fog, and your ship as distraction, allowed us to escape. Inadvertently, you aided us, so let us say we are even."

Edward paused for a moment, a smile on his face. "Deal."

The following morning, the crews of the *Freedom* and *Patriot* rested, and in the afternoon shared dinner together on the *Freedom*. Edward made a rule that none were to ask anything about the future, and the crew of the *Patriot* would not tell anything of the past. The only one who needed to hold back was Alston, being the most learned of the group, and unfortunately she was not able to keep her promise.

During the night, a few hours before the appointed time in the morning, Alston secretly approached Anne on the waist.

"Miss Bonney, may I bother you for a moment?"

"Yes, of course. What do you need?"

"I must tell you something of dire import. I cannot tell the details, but if you wish your lover to stay alive, you must keep him from Ocracoke Island and Charleston after this."

Anne was shocked, and couldn't help but ask more. "What happens there?"

"As I said, I cannot tell you."

"Why are you telling *me* this?"

"I owe you and your crew my life. And if you tell a man not to do something for fear of his life being in danger, they tend to rush headlong into peril to spite," Alston said with a smirk.

Anne grinned as well, but when Alston started to leave, Anne stopped her. "I must ask you another question, which will seem odd, but I need to know the answer."

"I will do my best to answer," Alston replied.

"What happens to Queen Anne?"

Alston eyed Anne suspiciously. "Why do you wish to know about Queen Anne?" Alston shook her head. "No matter, if you have any connection to her, telling you anything would be dangerous."

"Please, I must know," Anne begged.

Alston frowned. "I will tell you only this. The Queen began acting strangely after her daughter's death by pirates. The Queen later died under suspicious circumstances after an attack on England. George I succeeded her."

Anne was troubled by more than one thing Alston mentioned. "When does all this happen?"

"I am sorry, I will not provide dates. I've told you too much already."

Anne nodded and let Alston leave. Questions swarmed Anne's head, too many to make sense of. Alston could never guess Anne Bonney was actually Anne Sofia Stewart, daughter to the Queen, and the knowledge that her mother would be killed weighed heavily on her heart and mind.

As one o'clock approached, Edward had the crews separate and say their goodbyes in case they were able to recreate the event of a few days prior. Herbert guided the crew once again in lining up the cannons perfectly, and the crew shot precisely when the moon hit the time of one o'clock.

The cannonballs disappeared as they did before, and fog appeared suddenly, filling the night air. In mere moments to fog was so thick they could barely see the *Patriot* a hundred feet from them.

"Alston!" Edward yelled. All Edward received back was a muffled reply. "Alston, can you hear me?" Edward screamed.

Edward heard a thunk beside him on the deck, and noticed a crewmate had fallen unconscious. Edward took a step, but his knees became weak and buckled underneath him. He was kneeling on the deck, and becoming increasingly sleepy. Edward peered across the ship and noticed everyone aboard falling unconscious from the fog. Before long, Edward could not keep his eyes open, and he too fell to the deck with a thud, the world going black.

Blackbeard's Ship

Edward awoke with a pounding headache. With great effort he sat up. Edward regained his senses slowly and remembered what happened.

Edward pulled himself to his feet and searched the horizon, but couldn't see another ship anywhere. The *Patriot* was no longer.

Edward walked to Herbert at the helm, and had to grip the railing to keep himself upright. "Herbert, did you manage to stay awake?"

"No, Captain. I don't think anyone did."

Henry, John, and Anne walked up to the quarterdeck. The crew were waking up one by one and talking amongst themselves, speculating on what had happened.

Edward, Henry, John, and Anne also discussed what might have happened, with no solid theories presenting themselves. Eventually, when the crew became restless and concerned over the event, the four agreed on a course of action, even if it was not the best way to deal with the situation.

Edward addressed the crew. "Men, I know what has just happened must have you questioning a lot of things, but we will not find answers to the questions we seek. Whatever happened, whatever the cause, it is over now. The senior crewmates feel that the best we can do is leave the Triangle as quickly as possible and move on."

Cries from the crew swarmed Edward. "What about what happened on the island?" "Was those crew from the future?" "What caused all the fog?"

Edward soon had enough. "Silence, men!" he bellowed. The crew went quiet, and Edward sighed. "I am sorry, I cannot answer your questions, no one can, and that is why I think it best that we forget about it for now. Whatever caused the fog and made the island appear is still out there, and we are in danger every second we remain in the Devil's Triangle.

"Each of us had an experience like none other on that island. I am not saying we cannot discuss what happened, but for now we have to leave here."

Edward's words calmed the crew, and they seemed to understand what he was saying, but curiosity still stopped them in their tracks.

"It was an illusion," one of the crewmates said. Edward looked to the source and saw Sam there. Sam glanced at the crewmates gathered about. "What 'appened here wasn't real. The time travel, the island, the fog, it wus all in our heads. I wus tricked as a young pup into believin' this fantasy 'bout another time." Sam stared at

Edward, and Edward smiled.

One crewmate scratched his head. "But whut 'bout the key?" he asked Sam.

"Shut it!" Sam hollered. "Now back to work."

The crew shrugged their shoulders and went back to their stations, unfurled the sails, and worked to bring the ship out of the Bermuda Triangle.

Sam winked to Edward, and Edward laughed.

"Do you think the crew will accept that?" Anne asked.

"Since it came from Sam, I think it will do for now. At least we are on our way out of here," Edward replied.

"Agreed."

The crew did not speak of the events in the Bermuda Triangle that day, but it became a hotly debated topic in the mess hall. None could really say whether what happened was real or not, and they would never find out. However, all could agree that entering the Bermuda Triangle was not something done lightly, if at all.

13. THE CURE

"So Captain, where are we headed?" Herbert inquired.

A few days had passed since the events in the Bermuda Triangle, and the *Freedom* had just left the area. Focus had been on the shortest distance rather than a solid direction, and so there had not been a discussion on where to go next until now.

"We're short on crew, are we not?" Edward asked, and fortunately John was coming up the ladder to the quarterdeck to be able to answer.

"Y-yes Captain, we are rather short. We have about one hundred and fifty to one hundred and sixty."

"How many should we have?"

"Two hundred and ten should do, Captain," John declared with uncommon confidence. He knew his numbers, and Edward trusted his judgement.

"Any ideas on where we can acquire some crew members, Herbert?"

"The closest would be Bodden Town. Not only would we be able to stock up and receive funds from our benefactors there, but Alexandre is supposed to be there as well."

"Let's head to Bodden Town, then. Can you take a look at this, Herbert?" Edward handed the paper containing the clue to the next key for *Freedom*.

Herbert examined the riddle in detail, along with the map on the back. "I am sure you uncovered that the map shows the Gulf of Mexico?"

"Yes, that part was easy," Edward replied.

"Well, the next location is probably in the north east of the Gulf itself from the paper's meaning, and these triangles must point to a more exact location."

"Good, good. Anything else?"

"That's all I have for now, but I will ponder the riddle. You might want Christina to inspect the paper. She was swift in uncovering the previous riddle."

"Yes, I planned to," Edward said.

After Edward and Herbert's discussion concluded, Sam descended a ratline to the quarterdeck. A week had passed since the fight with Sam's less-than-adequate guardian, and he appeared in better spirits.

"Hello Sam, how are you holding up?"

Sam brushed Edward off immediately. "I be fine, and I don't need yer pity."

Edward glanced at Herbert. "Well, sorry for asking."

Sam was exasperated. "A week ago I killed a man who might have been from over a hundred years in the future who I considered me father. How do ye think any would feel?"

Edward scratched his head. "Well, when you put it that way…"

"Ah, I'll be fine. The bastard had it coming," Sam said, with a spit to the floorboards.

"This event has made me question the nature of your true father."

"Never knew 'im. I think 'e wus from this time."

"How do you know?" Edward asked.

"Jus' a hunch," Sam replied, with no further explanation. His gaze turned to the bow deck. Anne and Christina were sparring. "Lookit them go," he said admiringly.

Edward watched as well. The two women were graceful and deadly in their dance. Christina was a quick learner, but Anne possessed years of experience and training.

Edward remembered Anne's concern over the anger Christina displayed during their training, and Anne was teaching Christina to meditate and keep a calm and level head. Christina had had difficulty at first, and often lost focus when sparring.

Edward, looking at Christina now, thought she was doing much better. *The true test will be when we face marines again. She will have a harder time holding back then.*

But now Edward noticed something off. Anne was slowing down and breathing heavily. She abruptly cut the match short and made her way to the berth deck to rest.

Edward approached Anne to see what was wrong. "Anne, are you well?"

She waved her hand in dismissal, a habit picked up from Henry. "Don't be silly, Edward. I'm fine, I am merely tired from all the recent fighting and the hot sun and I need rest. Now leave me be."

"Alright." Edward stepped aside. Anne continued to walk slowly to the ladder nearby on the starboard side.

Christina wandered to Edward's side. "Is she well?"

"I don't know. What have you observed?" Edward asked, watching Anne.

"She's been progressively slowing and cutting off our sparring more frequently as of late. I didn't pay Anne's condition any heed until recently. She's been sweating more, which isn't normal for the level of exertion she's used to, and today her hands and legs were shaking. See?" Christina pointed to Anne as she was descending the ladder.

Edward noticed Anne's legs were wobbly as she stepped down the ladder to the next deck. Before he could comment, Anne disappeared with a series of thuds.

"Anne!" Edward yelled, drawing the crew's attention

Edward rushed down the ladder to the unresponsive Anne. Edward checked her breathing and the pulse on her neck and forearm as Alexandre once showed him. Christina was beside Edward, and the crew were concernedly watching on.

"Is she well?" Christina asked, panic fringing her voice.

"She is breathing and her pulse is normal, albeit elevated." Edward examined Anne. "She has some bruises and scrapes from the fall, but as far as I can tell nothing serious." Edward picked Anne up, took her down to the crew's quarters and lay her on a bed.

With Christina's help, Edward removed Anne's vest and rolled up her shirt sleeves to let cool air reach her body. Christina let out a cry of shock. "What?" Edward asked. Christina pointed to Anne's upper left arm, her bicep, which was red with purple bumps oozing pus.

"Anne must have been shot in the battle against Dominique. The wound must have gotten infected. Oh Anne! Why didn't you tell me? Stubborn woman!"

"You two are perfect for each other," Christina said.

Edward saw Christina's expression change from a frown to a grin. He smiled back. "Yes, we are quite a pair." Edward rose. "I will tell your brother to make haste to Bodden Town. We need our friend the doctor."

⚓ ⚓ ⚓

"Nose: stuffed," Alexandre said aloud, making a mental note. While looking in a mirror, he wiggled his nose, wrinkles drawing creases around his eyes. Alexandre poked and massaged the area around his eyes and face. "Redness and pressure on the eyes and forehead." He then took a deep breath, as best he could. "Difficulty breathing."

He continued to breathe heavily in the silence until there was a knock at his door. "*Entrer.*"

The door opened to reveal Edward Thatch and Henry Morgan. Upon entering, their jaws opened slightly and they frowned.

"What in God's name are you doing?" Edward asked.

Alexandre was hanging from the ceiling of his apartment by a rope tied to his legs. "I am performing a simple experiment." His body dangled slightly back and forth as Alexandre moved and gestured while he talked.

Edward sighed. "We don't have time for this. Henry, cut him

down."

Henry nodded and went to find a chair to stand on. After procuring one he went about the task.

"We need you on the ship. Anne is sick."

"Well, it certainly took you long enough, *messieurs*. I was beginning to grow bored," Alexandre said, his stuffed nose mixing with his accent to cause his voice to take on an odd tone.

Henry shook his head as he sliced through the twined fibres. "And we wouldn't want that, now would we?" Henry made one last cut, and Alexandre's legs were free.

Alexandre fell to the floor of his apartment, rose slowly and shook his head. "*Merci*." He went to the back of the room and grabbed two small bags, and then walked to the door. "Come now, *messieurs*. We have a patient to help."

Alexandre couldn't suppress a small grin at the corner of his lips, which Edward and Henry noticed. The two also grinned, shrugged their shoulders, and took their friend back to the *Freedom*.

"Hmm." Alexandre examined the wound on Anne's bicep. After a thorough examination he said, "I believe she has an infection."

Edward rubbed his face in exasperation. "You observations are as astute as always, Alexandre."

"A simple *blague mon Capitaine*. I know how lesser minds sometimes enjoy humour to ease the seriousness of an issue."

"I appreciate the attempt."

"Well, we can cure Anne, this much is certain. She has been fighting the infection too long, and it has spread too much as a result. If we do not cure her soon she may die." Alexandre delivered the news as if he was reading the newspaper.

Edward's eyes bulged and his jaw dropped. Christina gasped and gripped Edward's hand, probably more for her own benefit than his. "You know of a cure, yes? We can save Anne, can we not, Alexandre?" Edward pleaded.

"Bring the Mayan, would you? I need his assistance." Edward asked a crewmate, who then ran off to find Pukuh. Alexandre pointed to John. "John, here." John jumped at the pointed finger, but stepped closer to the surgeon. After Alexandre wrote something on a piece of paper, he handed it to John. "I need you to return to my abode and retrieve a bottle of elixir with this name." John nodded and made his way up the ladder of the swaying ship.

Pukuh stepped into the crew quarters and to the foot of Anne's bed. "Yes, witchdoctor?" Pukuh questioned.

Alexandre sketched a picture of a leaf and seed and showed it to

Pukuh. "Are you familiar with this plant?" Alexandre asked.

"Yes, this plant we use in my village for food and medicine."

"We need the plant, Mayan. Tell Herbert to take us to your village." Pukuh nodded, not insulted by Alexandre, and left to tell Herbert the course.

"So the plant will cure Anne?" Edward asked for reassurance.

"Yes, if we procure some soon. Anne is strong, *Capitaine*, she will not succumb to this so easily."

"I know. She's too stubborn for that."

Over the next week, Edward spent the majority of his time with Anne. He was either trying to keep her cool during the day, warm during the night, or still when fever dreams gripped her. In the rare moments when Anne was awake and lucid, Edward talked with her about where the *Freedom* was headed. At first, Anne was able to reply with relative lucidity, but after a few days she was in a constant haze.

The crew visited to check on Anne and on how the Captain was holding up from time to time. Edward didn't eat, and drank only when he was helping Anne to drink. Twice a day Alexandre applied the salve John retrieved from his house in Bodden Town, cleaned the wound, and replaced the bandages. Pukuh prayed daily for Anne. John read the news from Bodden Town from the past weeks. Herbert told of the weather and condition of the *Freedom*, as well as some bad fishing jokes he said Anne always laughed at. "She was probably humouring me more than I her," he told Edward. Henry brought food and drink, and forced Edward to eat as best as he could force Edward to do anything.

The crew took shifts to keep sailing through the night instead of dropping anchor. Christina and Herbert took shifts commanding the helm, with Herbert taking the night and Christina taking the morning. Christina fought Herbert for the night shift, but he insisted on the night due to it being more difficult, and she eventually complied.

The night before *Freedom* arrived at Pukuh's village, Anne was asleep soundly for once, and Edward was ready to join her. He was kneeling down, his hand holding hers, resting his upper body on the bed.

"You can't leave me, Anne, not now. As your captain I order you not to die." Edward closed his eyes, and he could have sworn he heard Anne say, "Aye, aye" before he dozed off, exhausted.

Christina happened upon Edward when he started talking with Anne. Christina watched the scene and delivered the "Aye, aye," posing as Anne. After Edward lay asleep, Christina draped a spare blanket over him.

The next morning, Edward awoke with the blanket lying on the floor of the ship, the cold air hitting him. He took the blanket, trying to remember when he had gotten it, and covered Anne's sleeping body. Edward kissed Anne's forehead, told her he would be back, and walked up to the top deck where the night crew was still busy, wearily furling the sails.

The ship landed on the familiar shore Edward once descended on to retrieve the gun deck's key. The last time, Edward had met with Pukuh's family and the village he called home, quite possibly one of the last Mayan settlements still in existence. Pukuh had joined Edward to learn about the world and return a better warrior, and a better king, so he could follow in his father's footsteps.

Pukuh was on the waist and had a few bags packed with supplies. Pukuh and Edward had earlier agreed that only the two of them would need to go. Too many would slow them down and they weren't there for pleasure. Alexandre recommended not taking Anne along as stress could agitate her condition.

Edward noticed one more bag than there should have been. "What's in the third bag?" he asked Pukuh.

"That is for the little girl. She claimed you allowed her to join us," Pukuh replied.

Little girl? "Do you mean Christina?" Pukuh nodded his head. "Well, she was lying, I said no such thing."

Pukuh smiled. "Hmm, interesting."

Christina sauntered up to the waist and joined Edward and Pukuh. "Good morning, Captain."

"You can't join us," Edward asserted flatly before Christina could even ask.

"What? Why?"

"You'll slow us down," Edward replied, slinging a pack of supplies over his back.

"I promise I won't. Or at least, I won't slow you down as much as you will."

Edward raised his brow. "What was that?"

"We've been a few months at sea, but you're nowhere near the strength you were before being imprisoned. I know I could keep up with you in your state."

Edward laughed. "I see what you're trying to do. You can't goad me into letting you come to satisfy my pride." Edward threw a rope ladder over the port side.

"I want to help, Edward. I care for Anne too." Christina pleaded softly, all eyes on the pair.

Edward gazed at those sky-blue eyes, then to the crew, then back. He let out a sigh, then turned to Herbert. "Herbert?" he asked.

Herbert shrugged. "If she wants to join you, I don't see the harm. You are just collecting a plant, after all."

Edward folded his arms, internally debating some more while eyeing Christina. "Alright, hurry up," he ordered at last, waving his hand. Christina gathered her pack and joined them at the starboard railing. Edward pointed his finger at Christina sternly. "You had better not slow us down," he warned.

"I won't," she promised.

The three descended to the sandy beach below, moved up an incline, and into a forest of Caribbean pines. Once in the forest, a natural path with little vegetation could be followed most of the way. The tall pines rose around them and created a canopy blocking the sun. The sounds of animals created ambiance for their trip.

"Ready?" Pukuh asked.

After securing their belongings, Pukuh and Edward went into a quick jog, with Christina following closely behind. For the first half of the day, Christina was able to keep up and didn't tire, but come midday she was sweating and slowed down. To her credit, Edward slowed down as well, and despite what he claimed earlier, they were having a competition of pride.

Edward refused to take a breather, and Christina refused to ask for one. By the time the two had slowed to near walking, sweat pouring down their faces, and glaring at each other, Pukuh decided to end the rivalry before one of them collapsed. He suggested taking a break to rehydrate and eat.

Edward stared daggers at Christina, and she at him. "Tired yet?" he asked.

"I could do this all day," she replied.

Pukuh chuckled as he watched them bickering. "You act as siblings."

"Perhaps in another life," Edward postulated with a laugh.

After Edward and Christina were rested as could be, Pukuh started again and set a slow pace. The three travelled at a good pace, despite having to slow down. Normally, the trip to reach Pukuh's village would take a full day and a half, with rest overnight. At the rate they were travelling they would reach the village before nightfall.

The group soon reached a large flat area with a smooth rock and slight hill. On top of the ten-foot-high rock the roots of a tree were snaking down, searching for nourishment which was not present.

"This brings back memories," Edward said between short breaths.

"Yes, this was where you flailed about against the beasts of the forest."

"What happened?" Christina inquired.

"I fought a pack of wolves the first time I arrived."

Pukuh grinned. "Strange, does 'fought' mean 'flailing about' in your language? Ah, the mysteries of you people never end."

"Did you win?"

"Barely. I was heavily injured and fainted."

"I carried Edward to the village because he was too weak. He is still weak, but I will not carry him this time."

After taking another short break, the journey continued. They were not far from the village now, and daylight was dwindling. When they reached the edge of the forest that night, Pukuh stopped suddenly, motioning for the other two to be quiet and duck down.

"Something is not right," Pukuh muttered as he handed his pack to Edward before heading to the village.

Edward and Christina backtracked and hid behind a large pine tree. Edward tried his best to watch Pukuh, but he was like a shadow in the dark. Dressed as he was in his original warrior outfit of eagle feathers and well-fitted leather armour, he was in his element as War Chief.

Pukuh dashed to the closest home, a hut made of mud and clay with a straw roof, similar to most others in the village. He sneaked into the village and sought out the cause of his unusual feeling. In a half hour he was back to where Edward and Christina hid themselves.

"What's wrong?"

"My village has been taken by white men. Before we can retrieve the medicine we will need to free the villagers."

"Where is the plant located?" Edward asked.

"The fields are on the other side of the village, behind the pyramid." Pukuh gestured to the pyramid in the centre of the village, where the Mayans held rituals. The huge structure, along with a few other large stone buildings, marked specific points of religious significance.

"Christina, you should head back to the ship. This is too dangerous.

Christina's mouth made a line. "No, I will not leave. I am not some useless child."

Edward sighed. *We don't have time for this*. "Fine, harvest the plant we need and head back to the ship as fast as you can. Do not stay here, you could be hurt and Anne needs the medicine as soon as possible." Edward took out Alexandre's drawing of the plant from his pack and handed it to Christina.

She nodded as she accepted the drawing, confidence evident on her face. "You can count on me, Edward, I won't let you down."

"Pukuh, I need you to howl like a wolf. I think we'll need some help with this."

Pukuh nodded, knowing full well Edward's stream of thought. Pukuh let out a great howl which sounded like a real wolf. He kept calling until he heard a return call off in the forest.

"Christina, whatever happens, do not be afraid."

The three waited in silence for ten minutes, watching the forest for any movement or sound. Suddenly, without warning, a wolf stepped out from behind a tree. He was a big one, the leader of the pack, with a scar down one of his eyes.

Christina hid behind Edward as Edward stepped forward and knelt down. He glared at the wolf with his fierce eyes as the wolf stepped closer, fangs bared. *You remember me, don't you? I am your master.* The wolf stopped growling and went up to Edward's legs, pushing his head into Edward's hand in deference. *Yes, that's right.*

More wolves, all different sizes and shades of grey or brown, emerged from hiding after the leader's display. Twenty wolves in all joined the three humans.

"Christina, I want you to take one of the wolves and make your way around the village to the field. We will start attacking the guards here, which will draw away anyone guarding the field. Wait until they leave, find the plant, and return to the ship."

As if able to understand Edward, a reddish-grey wolf moved beside Christina and let its fur touch her fingertips. Christina jumped at the sensation.

"Don't be afraid, the wolf won't hurt you." Edward took Christina's hand in his and caressed the wolf beside her. The animal panted, staring up at Christina with grey eyes. "See? Everything will be fine. This one will protect you," Edward reassured Christina while commanding the wolf.

"Whatever you say, Edward." Christina said without much confidence. She set out around the perimeter of the forest with the wolf following beside her.

Edward turned to Pukuh. "Now, let's free your village." Pukuh nodded and the two trekked into the village.

They ran to the nearest hut with the wolf leader sticking beside Edward. Some of the wolves followed or advanced into the village to hide on their own. Edward peered out from around a corner of the hut.

He could see down the main road of the village, a wide swath made between the houses leading all the way to the large pyramid in the centre. He noticed a fire at the base of the pyramid and people gathered around. He also noticed several sources of light moving slowly about the village.

"The white men at the pyramid are guards, they have all my people trapped there. I was not able to see inside, but my fa... the King is probably in the castle. I noticed a flickering light."

"We should free the villagers first so they can fight with us, then help your father," Edward suggested, to which Pukuh nodded in assent.

Edward passed the huts to the closest source of light. He could see a man walking between the huts. A shadow zipped by and then the man fell to the ground with a thud. Another man close to Edward heard the thud and moved closer to inspect. Edward sneaked behind the second man, covered the man's mouth, and sliced his neck. The man squirmed and twitched, releasing a moan, then fell limp in Edward's arms. Edward pulled him back between the huts before moving forward.

The night was dark and the pines surrounding the village afforded no protection from the cool wind blowing through. The scents of the pine, similar to the *Freedom*, along with dust and stone, filtered through to Edward's senses. A faint smell of burnt gunpowder told Edward a battle had happened here a few days past.

Edward and Pukuh made their way silently forward to the centre of the village, quickly approaching a large fire with thirty-plus men guarding all the villagers. The wolves were nowhere to be seen save for the leader at Edward's side.

Edward and Pukuh reached the last hut before the bonfire. The hundred and fifty or so villagers were sitting in front of the pyramid. Some of the white men were napping, others were roasting food on the fire, and still others kept their guns pointed at the prisoners. Two other bonfires were alight along the front of the pyramid. All the men were talking loudly and jovially to let the villagers know they were still awake, and still in charge.

That would soon change.

"So what is the plan, brother?" Pukuh asked in a low voice.

"I don't see any other way than to charge in headfirst."

"I am liking this plan," Pukuh smiled.

"Just… let me…" Edward turned to the wolf, and pointed to the men at the bonfires.

"Are… are you communing with him?"

"Trying to tell him to attack," Edward replied, still gesturing with hand signals he believed the animal might understand. After a moment, the animal turned and strutted away between the huts again.

"What did he say?"

"What?"

"The wolf, what did it say back?"

Edward pinched the bridge of his nose. "Are you daft, man? The wolf isn't psychic."

Pukuh frowned. "I distinctly recall Benjamin stating he could speak with animals."

"I think you were on the receiving end of one of his practical jokes, my friend."

"I do not know. He was very convincing," Pukuh replied, a dubious look on his face and his arms folded.

Edward sighed. "We strike on the count of three."

Edward stepped to the edge of the hut and counted out to three on his fingers. On the third, Edward dashed out with his cutlass forward. The guards only realised what was happening when Edward and Pukuh were upon them.

Edward sliced the chest of a man napping on the ground. Pukuh stabbed another with his spear who was turning around.

The wolves pounced on the guards. One man lifted his musket at Edward. The pack leader jumped over the fire and ripped out the man's throat. The musket fired into the air as the man struggled weakly before dying.

Edward fought with another man for his musket. Ordinarily, Edward would have easily overpowered the small man, but he was fatigued after their day-long trek through the forest. The man twisted and pulled and pushed for supremacy. Edward lifted his foot and stomped hard on the man's toes. The man's grip loosened. Edward jerked the musket forward and the barrel hit the man in the nose. The man released the musket, clutching his broken nose. Edward shot him in the chest.

When the villagers finally gained grip on what was happening, they rushed in to help. The warriors used their fists and legs to subdue the enemy before them. The Mayans once more fought alongside the wolves like their ancestors had before, as the legend goes.

When Edward killed the last guard near him, he found Pukuh. "Let's save your father."

"Onward, to the palace."

Edward and Pukuh ran past the villagers and the warriors killing the guards, and rushed to the steps of the limestone palace.

Christina stood at the edge of the forest, and ducked between some pines. She made her way to the back of the village and could see the fields. On the right side, nearest the pyramid, Christina noticed large corn stalks, then to the left of the corn was squash or possibly pumpkin, then tomatoes and other vegetables, and other things Christina didn't recognise at the far end.

The plant didn't appear to be big, but the picture could be deceiving. Christina examined Alexandre's drawing by moonlight. Once she was confident she could spot it, and reasonably sure that the field was clear of enemies, Christina and the wolf entered the farmland.

The smells of the plants, vegetables, and freshly turned soil ignited Christina's senses. Living on a ship had its advantages, but fresh produce was not one. Christina forced herself forward, lest she pick one of the corn stalks or tomatoes. The smell of lantern oil and sweat also helped bring Christina back to her mission.

She scanned the different plants by the subtle and pale light she was afforded, trying to discern which was which. Alexandre's drawing being exceptionally detailed was a boon, as Christina knew nothing of plants, especially the medicinal kind.

I hope none of these are poison.

As Christina was inspecting the plants, she heard footsteps behind her. She turned around to see a fat man with a musket reaching down for her. Before she could react, the wolf struck and suddenly blood spurted from the man's neck. The wolf released the man and backed away. The man gripped his throat with one hand, still alive. Christina lunged at him, pulled out her daggers, and thrust them into the base of his neck. He fell backwards with Christina on top of him. When he hit the ground she fell off him and onto some plants.

Christina quickly rose and pulled her daggers from the corpse. Her face and clothes were spattered with blood. The wolf appeared again in front of the body, and Christina pet it in thanks. The wolf panted, baring its tongue and bloody fangs, in delight. "I think I will name you Shadow. No, wait, too obvious. Tala… yes, I'm fond of that."

Christina went back to the plants and examined them as best she could, taking as much time as she felt she could spare. She narrowed it down to two different plants with the same features in the little amount of light. Even with daylight, She suspected she would still have issues differentiating them.

I don't have time for this. Christina took her pack off her back.

Christina emptied her supplies onto the ground until the pack was empty. She filled the pack with the two types of plants, root and all, taking what she hoped was more than enough to be able to cure Anne.

After Christina had filled the pack to the brim, she strapped it onto her back and ran into the forest, Tala following closely behind. As Christina passed the village she could hear the sounds of battle and war cries still raging.

I hope Edward is well.

Christina ran through the forest, the rush from the previous fight still pushing her on. Once Christina's energy wore off, she slowed down to a jog. She and the wolf pushed themselves the whole night to reach the ship as quickly as possible. Christina took a few short breaks, and shared some dried meat she'd pocketed before.

Christina was long past tired, pure determination driving her legs forward. She herself didn't know how she was still moving, but kept advancing for as long as her body would allow. Anne's life depended on Christina, and she would not let her, nor Edward, down.

When morning approached and Christina was close to the ship, something caused her and the wolf to stop in their tracks. Tala instantly began growling, pulling her front paws down and lifting the hind in an attack stance. Christina was too shocked at first and stood in stunned silence at what she witnessed.

You must be joking.

In front of Christina and Tala was a black bear. Fur dark as jet, beady eyes, large paws with sharp claws, and deadly teeth greeted them. The bear was a medium-sized male, three hundred pounds and much larger than Christina or Tala.

Before Christina could take a safe route around the bear, Tala lunged forward. Being predatory, Tala saw a threat despite there being no cause. Christina flung her hand out at Tala a moment too late. The two animals began fighting.

Damn. Alright then, time to test my skills!

Christina removed the pack, pulled out her daggers, and jumped into the fray.

14. THE KING & BLACKWOOD

Inside the palace's main room, the light of the moon shone on a white man with a grey moustache. The man held a musket and was standing above the King, who was bound and lying on the stone floor. The old man leaned down and gripped the King by the cheeks, pulling his face forward.

"We've been fighting for days, I've taken control of your village, and I am losing my patience. I will ask you one last time, tell me where the gold is, or I will burn this village to the ground," the old man threatened.

The King spat in the old man's face. "There is your gold."

The old man backed up and cleaned his face with a handkerchief as a younger man kicked the King in the chest. "There is simply no reasoning with you, is there?" He turned to one of his subordinates. "Grab one of the villagers. Maybe killing his people one by one in front of him will loosen his tongue."

Before the man could fulfil the order, a gunshot sounded outside. The guards nearest the opening of the palace peered outside to see what the commotion was about.

"The villagers are putting up a fight," the young man reported.

"The men can handle a small uprising," the greying man said.

"I don't think so, the villagers have help." The young man pointed.

The older man walked over to catch a glimpse of what the younger man was talking about. "Well, those savages are making a right old mess of things, aren't they? We've work to do." The old man took his younger companion and the King away, leaving guards to cover them.

Outside the palace, Edward and Pukuh were ascending the limestone steps to the top. They could see the light of lanterns or a fire flickering between the stone columns.

Before reaching the top, Pukuh stopped Edward and motioned for him to move off the steps and onto the side. Pukuh went to the right and Edward to the left.

Edward peered over the edge of the stone building blocks. He could see two men facing the stairs with their muskets pointed for-

461

ward, with another two men behind them. Edward and Pukuh stealthed their way to the top level of the palace, through the columns, and into the large palace room.

Pukuh threw his spear into the chest of the guard on the right. After a blood-curdling thunk, the man fell, dead. All eyes moved to the noise. Edward used his cutlass to impale a man through the chest from behind. When he drew the cutlass out the man fell face down and bled profusely onto the limestone. Pukuh used his knife to slice open a third man. Blood splattered over Pukuh's body as the man lost control over his limbs.

The last man fired his musket at Pukuh. The shot hit the Mayan warrior in the arm. Pukuh clutched the wound with his opposite hand. Edward swung his blade horizontally against the shooter. The power of the blow tore the musket to pieces and sliced open the shooter's stomach.

Edward rushed to Pukuh. "Are you well?"

Pukuh lifted himself off the floor. Blood seeped through his fingers. "I am fine. We must go. The only way out, aside from the steps, is to the roof."

Edward helped his friend walk forward, Pukuh showing the way to the roof of the palace. The two passed through several stone corridors and up a winding staircase until reaching the roof. Upon emerging they could see Pukuh's father and another older white man at the edge.

As Edward and Pukuh crossed the threshold of the stairs, they were greeted by two young men and musket barrels staring them in the face.

"Please, gentlemen, join us," the older man said. "Oh and drop your weapons, if you would be so kind."

Edward and Pukuh dropped their weapons to the ground, and they were prodded forward, closer to the edge of the palace roof. Pukuh's father was at the edge, on his knees, with his hands bound behind his back.

The wind blew coldly on the tall and open viewpoint Edward and Pukuh were perched upon. The two could see the entire village from where they were. From the pyramid, the tip of which reached the palace roof, to the religious stone buildings, and the many huts where the villagers lived.

The old man peered below, to where the fighting was nearing an end. His men were almost all killed and the villagers were freed. "Such a shame, they were good men... Oh well, more gold for me." The older gentleman with the long moustache moved closer to Edward and Pukuh. He lit a pipe and smoked, blowing a pungent yet sweet smell in their faces. "Strange bedfellows you have here, King. Who is this young chap?" he questioned, pointing to Edward.

"My name is Edward Thatch, also known as Blackbeard. I owe this village much, and I could not sit by and watch it be overtaken by anyone."

The old man whistled. "Seems we have a celebrity here, and our fortune doubles. There is a bounty on your head, pirate. We can turn you in after we are done here."

Bounty? No matter, I'd love to see how you will escape here, old man. "Speaking of your business here, what is that exactly?"

"Oh, I am glad you asked." The old man pulled on the rope tied around the King's hands, lifting him up. He then pushed the King out to the edge of the roof, precariously teetering on the brink. "Legend tells of a treasure of gold in this forest. We stumbled upon this village on our search. A Mayan civilisation still standing after all these years, with this much wealth in architecture? It must be where the gold is. If you know where the gold is, tell me now, or your King and benefactor will be taking a trip."

Edward and Pukuh both jerked forward on instinct with the threat. The men with the muskets pushed the barrels into their chests hard. Edward and Pukuh calmed themselves, but didn't give the old man any information. Edward couldn't tell the old man anything because he didn't know of where any gold was, or even if the old man was right.

"I see one of you is injured. So between the three of you, we have two natives who know the location, and one bystander. Can you guess which one of you is expendable?" the old man asked with a sneer. "Johnny, let our bearded friend rest his legs."

One of the younger men nodded, then backed up a few paces. He pointed his musket at Edward's leg and fired.

The bullet seared through Edward's thigh and he fell to the ground with a yell. Edward gripped the wound as it bled onto the stone roof. Johnny pointed a pistol at Edward's head, keeping the threat active.

"Now, the next one goes through his head. Which one of you will tell me where the gold is, hmm?"

Pukuh eyed his father intently. The King nodded to his son. "Alright, I will show you what you seek," Pukuh hissed through gritted teeth.

"Don't, Pukuh," Edward whispered between deep breaths. "Don't let this bastard win."

"We do not have much choice in the matter, Captain." Pukuh eyed Edward intently. "Follow me," Pukuh commanded, walking back to the stairs of the palace.

Edward stood and did his best to stay on his legs. He leaned on Pukuh for support as the two made their way slowly to the stairs.

The old man pulled the King back onto steady ground. "Now,

your warrior here is clearly more reasonable than you are."

"You should have tied my legs too," the King scoffed.

The old man's eyes narrowed, and then he looked down at the King's unbound legs. The King reared back and kicked the old man in the chest, shoving him backwards over the edge of the roof. His body hit the stairs and tumbled down to the ground below. Each sickening thud sounded loudly through the whole village and drew all eyes. He was dead on the first step, and by the last his body was a mangled mess.

When the two younger men watched their boss fall off the roof, Edward and Pukuh grabbed their weapons and fired. With those three dead, Pukuh's village was freed from the white men who tried to take their treasure.

Edward, with his arm around Pukuh's shoulder and hopping on one leg, walked to the King. The three peered over the edge of the palace roof to the scene below. They could see the bloody and broken body of the old white man at the bottom of the palace stairs, and all the villagers gathered around.

Edward laughed. "Nice work, Sire. I didn't expect that at all."

"You did not receive my message?" Pukuh asked.

"Is that why you were staring at me? I told you, Pukuh, I don't have such a power. Stop thinking foolishness. Benjamin tricked you."

Pukuh folded his arms. "I don't believe you."

Pukuh's father ignored the exchange and instead overlooked his people who were gathered at the foot of the palace. "My son, and our brother Thatch, returned to save us!" he yelled over the side. "You owe them your thanks."

The villagers cheered and screamed their thanks to Edward and Pukuh. The two of them waved and smiled at the praise. Their timing could not have been more perfect, and they were able to help avert disaster, and hopefully on their own ship as well.

Their legs were heavy and tired beyond all concepts of fatigue, yet, through willpower alone, the pair continued to move forward, slowly. The one, shaggy fur matted with blood and gaping wounds everywhere, dragged one useless hind leg behind the three others. The other, on two legs, with bloody wounds and deep cuts, inched forward on a broken leg, the bone sticking out the back.

Christina breathed deeply, producing ragged, exhausted sounds. Her vision was doubled, and the world spun. She relegated her sight instead to the ground beneath her, watching as she forced the foot she could use forward.

A bit farther, she told herself.

Christina's animal companion, the wolf she'd named Tala, was beside her, in equally bad shape, or worse. Christina leaned on Tala and on a stick in her other hand.

The bear had done a number on the pair, but it now lay dead along the trail of the woods. Tala and Christina were a good team. They attacked together, with Tala drawing the bear's attention while Christina attacked it from behind. The two managed to kill the bear, but with the state they were left in, the gains scarcely outweighed the losses.

Christina missed her step and tripped over a branch. She fell to the ground, her body heavy and her mind on the verge of shutting down. She forced her face forward, focusing her eyes ahead. She could see bright sunlight in front of her which could mean only one thing: the beach.

Christina pushed with her weak arms, trying desperately to rise, but she could only extend her arms halfway before they wobbled fiercely and collapsed. Nevertheless, Christina would not stop. She knew the crew was depending on her to bring the medicine back, and she would not let them down.

Christina once more pushed on her feeble arms to gain leverage. When she was about to fall again, Tala suddenly appeared underneath her chest and helped to lift her up. Christina was able to stabilise herself on her hands and knees, but she could no longer muster the strength to stand up now that she had fallen this far.

This is all I need. I can do this!

Together, with one arm wrapped around Tala, Christina and her wolf companion were able to keep moving forward. The clear goal in front spurred Christina onwards, and Tala instinctively sensed the mood, picking up the pace to help her ahead.

Christina and Tala passed the threshold as a pair, emerging into the noonday sun and falling forward onto the sandy decline of the beach. They fell and rolled over on their broken bodies twice before stopping and sliding on the sand.

The hot sun beat down on them. Christina's vision was on the sun high in the blue sky, and she did not possess the strength to move even her head anymore.

This is far enough, right? Please don't die, Anne.

Tears rolled down the sides of Christina's face as she drifted into unconsciousness. The plant medicine in the pack still on her back was there for the taking; her only hope was the crew would see her and find the plants for Anne.

"We have to hurry," Edward said as he tried his best to run, the wound on his leg hampering his abilities.

"I know," Pukuh replied. With the bullet wound on his arm, and the constant moving over the past days, even he was beginning to tire and slow down.

"I have a bad feeling about the bear corpse we saw." Edward turned his head, but he could no longer see the body.

"The bear had bite marks and strikes from daggers. Christina and the wolf with her killed it," Pukuh assessed.

Edward stared at the ground. "Yes I know, but there is so much blood on this trail now, I fear we will find Christina's corpse soon."

"Your fears are unfounded. Look, we are at the opening now." Pukuh pointed forward to the entrance of the forest.

The floundering light of the sun was on the horizon, giving a golden glow to the trees and understory. When the pair passed the threshold of the forest they could see the *Freedom*, with much of the crew on the main deck walking and talking and waiting. When one of the crewmen saw their captain and the Mayan warrior on the beach, he informed the crew. The crew yelled and waved at the returning men.

On the way to the ship, Edward noticed two spots of sand dyed red with blood, but whatever caused the blood stains were gone now. *Christina and the wolf?*

The crew threw down a rope ladder for Edward and Pukuh to climb back to the top deck. The two were surrounded by the crew and bombarded by questions about what happened.

"Enough, enough! Where is Christina? How is Anne? I will answer your questions later, but right now mine are more important."

The crew cleared the way to the ladder of the berth deck. Edward entered the crew cabin where Anne was still lying down in bed with Alexandre in a chair next to her. Anne's fever hadn't broken yet, but her bandage was fresh with a green tint underneath, and a cup stood beside her bed.

Alexandre turned to greet Edward. "Welcome back, Captain. I applied the medicine to Anne's bandage and also made her drink some. The rest is up to her now."

"Good, job Alexandre. I'm sure she'll pull through. You are literally a life-saver."

"I try."

"Where is Christina?"

"In a bed over there," Alexandre replied whilst pointing to the stern of the crew cabin. "She and her wolf are resting. Their injuries were severe, but they will recover."

Edward kissed Anne on the cheek and checked on Christina. She was in the middle of the ship on a bed. Sitting next to her was

Herbert on one side and the wolf on the other. Herbert was distraught and weary.

"Captain! What happened out there?"

"I'm sorry, Herbert. She was supposed to gather the medicine and then head back to the ship as quickly as possible. Some treasure hunters took over Pukuh's village, but Christina should have been able to escape without harm. On the way back, we saw the corpse of a bear on the trail. Christina could have killed the bear, with help."

"A bear?" Tears welled up in his eyes. "How could this happen? First Nassir's son, and now my sister. When will this end, Edward? At what point will you stop pointlessly endangering others?"

Before Edward could defend himself, Christina's slender fingers touched Herbert's. "Stop," she said softly.

"Christina!" Herbert exclaimed as he pulled her hand close.

"I am glad I went," she stated slowly. "I saved Anne, which was worth all the pain. Don't blame Edward for a decision I made and would make again if I had the choice. Now, let me sleep," Christina commanded before closing her eyes once more and drifting into sleep.

Herbert was silent for a moment. "I'm sorry, Captain. I was upset. My sister is the only family I have left. I can't lose her."

"Christina is strong, probably stronger than you think. She will not die so easily. And don't forget, she is our family too. I will protect her when she needs me just as she will protect us when we need her."

Herbert nodded and continued to watch over his sister.

Edward examined the wolf. She was also very injured, but with bandages covering the wounds and cleaned fur. Edward petted the wolf, but she remained asleep. *You did well to protect Christina. I hope you are alright with being on a ship for a while, as we cannot stay for you to recover.*

Edward left the crew cabin and returned to the main deck. He saw Pukuh telling the tale of what had happened to them at his village, much to the delight of the crew. Jack was providing music for the story, changing the tempo depending on what was happening.

Henry advanced to Edward. "Once again, you somehow turned something simple into an exercise in risking lives."

"Oh, and how did I cause treasure hunters to find Pukuh's village? Do you even care I'm still alive?"

Henry pursed his lips. "I'm glad you're safe, but there was no reason Christina should have been put in danger. She walked an untold length with a broken leg and severe loss of blood. Even Alexandre was shocked at the sight of her."

"I was quite worried for her, I'll have you know. She insisted on gathering the herb while we liberated Pukuh's town. Afterwards, she was to leave immediately. How was I to know a bear would be waiting on the trail?"

Henry rubbed his temples. "You could have *ordered* her to return to the ship, to stay put, any number of things, but you let her out of your sight when she was your responsibility. You talk of wanting to be stronger so you can protect them, then when they're hurt it's not your fault. Do not try and shirk your mistake off on a sixteen-year-old!" Henry stepped close to Edward and whispered with rage in his voice. "If you care so much for your so-called family, take better care of them." Henry left before Edward could formulate a response.

Edward watched as the crew talked and celebrated well into the night, thinking over what Henry said.

15. THE BROTHERS BODDEN

At Edward's behest, the *Freedom* returned to Bodden Town. During the week and few days it took to arrive there, Anne's fever broke and she regained her strength day by day. She was able to talk, eat properly and walk around.

"Christina fought a bear?" Anne questioned skeptically.

"Yes, no jest, she fought a bear and killed it to bring you this medicine," Edward replied as he grabbed one of the dried leaves and began chewing on it. He frowned from the bitterness, but didn't stop chewing.

"I will be sure to thank her. And I owe you thanks as well. I faintly remember you by my side as I dipped in and out of wakefulness."

Edward's cheeks reddened, though the colour was obscured by his beard. "Yes, well, I was worried."

"How are your's and Pukuh's injuries? I notice you have a bandage on your thigh." Anne said, pointing to Edward's leg.

"Just a flesh wound," Edward assured. "I can barely feel it."

Anne looked unconvinced, but didn't press the issue. "Help me up, I wish to see Christina."

Anne extended her hand, which Edward took and pulled as Anne shifted and rose to shaky legs. She used Edward's shoulder as a crutch as she made her way through the crew cabin, past all the swaying hammocks, and to the bed hosting Christina and Tala.

Tala was lying on top of Christina and was roused out of light slumber by the noise of Edward and Anne approaching. The animal panted, wanting to be petted. For a wolf, she became rather docile around Edward and Christina. Tala moving around woke Christina, so she sat up for Anne and Edward.

Christina's wounds were still healing, but the worst was behind her. She had deep gashes on her back, arms, and legs covered by cloth, and her broken leg, set now thanks to Alexandre, would take a long time to fully heal.

"Anne, I'm so glad you are awake and well," Christina said while petting Tala.

Anne laughed. "I have you to thank. I was informed you were through a fairly traumatic experience, and by your appearance you were in as bad a shape as myself."

"I would have fared much worse if you hadn't trained me."

Blackbeard's Ship

Edward stayed for a bit, watching the two young women talk with beaming smiles, before heading up to the top deck. According to Herbert, they would land at Bodden Town soon, and Edward had business there now that Anne wasn't in danger.

The first time Edward landed in Bodden Town, the town was being run by the Bodden Brothers, Malcolm and Neil, Scottish twins also known as Bodden Town Bandits. Edward muscled his way through taking over the town and became a shareholder in the settlement. He also wanted the brothers to make the town safer for the townsfolk, and turn it into a pirate hub. Edward's direction had seemingly opposed goals, but he knew the brothers were up to task.

Edward hadn't seen the brothers in over a year, and felt he needed to make an impression in case his influence had slipped away over time. He took Sam, John, Henry, and Pukuh with him to see the brothers.

The port of Bodden Town was bustling in the afternoon, with ships constantly docking and weighing anchor. The town had doubled in size since Edward was imprisoned, and the harbour market was teeming with merchants and buyers.

Edward and company entered the overly active market, passed by the people walking to and fro along the harbour, and up the main street. The main street went up a slight incline all the way to the Bodden Brothers' mansion.

The streets were more active than Edward recalled as well. More people were sitting outside the local businesses and engaged in their daily routine. The town had no shortage of regular townsfolk, but Edward also passed taverns and inns occupied by rogues and pirates alike.

Edward also noticed people he assumed were in the Boddens' employ walking about the town, acting as guards. They wore white outfits with black pants to distinguish themselves from the rabble. Edward appreciated seeing the guards.

At the top of the small incline, Edward and company reached an elegant two-storey white mansion with a high wall around the perimeter. An iron gate in the middle faced the main street and two guards stood in front. At Edward and his group's approach, the guards hefted their weapons and stepped up to him.

"No entrance for guests without appointments," one guard asserted.

"The brothers will make an exception for me," Edward declared, not stopping.

The guards planted their hands on Edward's chest, forcing him to stop. He glanced at the hands and then back at the guards. Edward stared daggers at them.

"I am Edward Thatch, the one known as Blackbeard. The

brothers work for me, and thus you work for me. Remove your hands, or I will remove them from your body."

The guards' faces turned pale and they immediately moved away. "We are terribly sorry, sir, we did not know. The brothers have been expecting you for some time, ever since word of your escape reached here months ago." The guard opened the gate for Edward. "The brothers are in their study. I trust you know the way?"

"Yes, that will be all, gentlemen." Edward waved them off as he passed the gate.

Edward's friends followed him to the mansion, past two large columns and through the white door to the interior. The expansive mansion was opulent, with a large ballroom at the entrance, chandelier on the ceiling, alcoves in the walls, chairs for reading, and servants at beck and call.

Edward strode up one of the curved staircases in the ballroom and through a set of large wooden double doors into the brothers' study. Along both sides of the walls, more alcoves held different relics, weapons, and books.

The brothers themselves were at a table on the far end of the long room, perusing some documents. When the brothers noticed Edward enter, they dropped what they were doing.

"Mr Thatch." Malcolm, short but stout and muscular due to his Scottish heritage, wore a suit of red silk. He was not attractive, but not ugly in any sort of way, simply average.

"We've been expecting you," Malcolm's brother Neil continued. He had the same appearance as his brother, what with them being twins, but wore a blue suit.

"I heard, and can I expect you understand the reason I am here?"

Malcolm started: "We suspected you would be inclined to claim some of the moneys we accumulated over your year's absence," And Neil continued: "That you need more men on your crew is also within our powers of insight." Malcolm took over once more: "We also believe you are here to make an unnecessary show of power, what with your muscle behind you." Malcolm pointed to Edward's company. "Though, as stated, completely unnecessary." Neil and Malcolm, together since birth, were able to finish each other's thoughts. "We kept the bargain struck many moons ago, and you are free to see and reap the benefits, which are substantial." "Given the untouched accumulation."

Edward approached the table at the brothers' behest. They produced a ledger showing the values of his and their stock over the year. Several pages were filled with notes from various debits and credits, but the brothers skipped to the final page, showing the most recent balance.

Edward glanced at the figure and his eyes widened in shock. He had never seen such a sum before, nor did he know what he could do with all that money. For a simple whaler's son, the amount was too great to think about. Over six thousand pounds filled Edward's reserves over the past year alone. The prospect delighted him, and from past notations, the rate of propagation would only increase in the future.

"John, would you inspect this, please? I want to make sure everything is in order."

"Yes, Captain."

John examined the contents of the large ledger month by month. As he examined the different deposits and adjustments, Edward and the brothers discussed what had happened over the year he was gone. Bodden Town continued expanding with low-cost housing to build the population along with creating and maintaining a local militia. The brothers ensured the men were trained, obedient, and organised so the militia could function autonomously from the brothers or Edward if need be. The militia made sure pirates and thieves understood the townspeople were off limits, and in exchange their goods received fair trade. Bodden Town was slowly turning into a more respectable Tortuga.

John finished his assessment. "The numbers are sound, Captain."

"Good work, John, and you too, brothers."

"Thank you, Edward." "Your praise is much appreciated."

"Our ship needs re-stocking, so, working with John on supplies and new crew members for us would also be appreciated. I would also take five hundred pounds of my stock for personal use, and one to three thousand can be redistributed as you please. Consider it an investment, and with it I want an equal share in this venture. I want thirty-three percent of the shares, to be exact, as opposed to the previous agreement of twenty five."

"Consider it all done," Malcolm confirmed.

"I'll await you back on the ship, John," Edward said, leaving the work to be done by John and the brothers, in many ways better suited to the task than he.

"Brother, you forgot," Neil chided. "Oh, yes I suppose I did. Edward, a moment please?"

Edward turned back around to the Boddens. "Yes?"

Malcolm began. "Two things: Firstly, not long ago, a man dressed in black was here asking about you. He never provided his name, and, so far, our sources have not been able to find any information on who he is, but you should be on alert."

"Why?" Edward asked, his curiosity piqued.

"Something about the man felt off, as if sickness and death followed in his wake. He's dangerous, and you should avoid him. Yes, even you Edward, Blackbeard. We managed to point him to Tortuga, so you should have nothing to fear for the moment."

Normally I would laugh at such a notion, but with the way the brothers are talking, maybe I should heed their advice. "And the other matter?"

Neil picked up for his brother. "We were wondering if you could take care of some local toughs. We would have the militia handle the brigands, but they are attending to other matters at the moment. One of the pirate gangs is growing bolder, and their villainy is affecting the townsfolk. If the famous Blackbeard were to make an example of them, others would be deterred from such actions. Here is their captain's name and where he is staying." Neil scrawled a name on a piece of paper and handed it to Edward.

Edward raised his brow. "I would be glad to help, but didn't you say someone dangerous was searching for me? Isn't throwing my name around asking for trouble?"

"This action is no more than you have already done," Malcolm surmised.

"And besides, you will be doing this to pirates, who themselves don't want their names spread," Neil added.

"And, were you not leaving soon after this? This is not your home, so the town is not in danger. The *Freedom* is your home."

Edward nodded. "True. Alright, we'll take care of those pirates then. John and you two can figure out supplies."

"Re-supplying won't take long, Captain," John reassured him as he and the brothers began working on a list.

Now, down to business.

"You see, I'm talking about an unwritten rule this town has, one I've helped establish. You aren't understanding the rule, thus why I'm here," Edward said, sitting down in a comfy chair and holding a glass of rum.

Edward and crew were on the second floor in a reserved room for Miles Miller, also known as Miles the Murderer, the murderer-turned-pirate who was causing trouble for the Bodden Brothers. The room was large and long, with a nice bed, hardwood table and chairs, billiards table, and a massive picture window overlooking the street below.

Miles was on the ground, blood spilling from his mouth. Sam had taken pleasure in beating him into submission. Miles was known for his murders and ruthlessness, but on his own he was nothing special.

Blackbeard's Ship

"You broke those rules, and now you must be punished."

Sam kicked Miles in the chest, causing him to flip and fall on his back. Henry and Pukuh had subdued two other crewmates Miles had with him.

Miles coughed up blood, and tears filled his eyes. "What did I do?"

Edward laughed. "Well, your moniker is Miles the Murderer. You tell us."

"They wus whores, why's it matter?"

Sam kicked Miles' chest again, producing a scream of pain and a distinct crack of his ribs breaking. "Who they are or what their profession is doesn't matter, Miles. You broke the agreement each outlaw has when in Bodden Town. Don't make trouble, and trouble won't be brought to you."

"What will you do to me?" Miles asked through ragged breaths.

"Get him up," Edward commanded Sam, who picked up the bloody and weak body of the pirate Captain Miles. Edward took Miles from Sam, lifting him off the ground by the chest. "We will make an example of you, so no one does what you did. Don't worry, you *should* survive." Edward grinned devilishly, causing Miles' eyes to fill with fear.

Edward pulled the ragged body of Miles back and threw him at the large picture window. Miles crashed through the thick glass and fell down the two storeys to the street below. Townsfolk glanced at the body, then up to the broken window of the inn.

Edward returned to the inn's pub area. Edward's crew stood above the many unconscious members of Miles' pirate crew. Broken tables, chairs, bottles and glasses littered the floor of the inn. The innkeeper stood behind the bar, with several of his wait staff hiding in fear. The staff's eyes were on Edward and as he approached they pushed themselves even further against the wall.

"Send the bill for repairs to the Bodden Brothers, would you?" Edward asked with a smile. The innkeeper nodded mutely.

When Edward exited the inn, the citizenry focused on him briefly before moving on about their business. Edward walked over to Miles. His body was broken, but he was breathing.

"You managed to survive. Good, because I have one last thing to tell you." Edward turned over Miles' body to face him. "Pay attention." Edward forced Miles' weary eyes open to gaze at the terror of Blackbeard manifest. "Don't fuck with my town again." Edward left with those parting words, and Miles blacked out.

Miles was no longer called a Murderer after that.

16. MYSTERY IN THE GULF

With the help of the Bodden Brothers and their network, the *Freedom* was restocked with a full crew again in less than a week. The new mates were all people who had been screened before for the militia, but the brothers didn't hire for being too rough. Edward felt they would be a perfect fit for his crew.

Before setting sail, Edward had the new crewmates swear by the pirate commandments made by him and Bartholomew Roberts. If they would not swear, Edward released them from the crew.

Edward also split a generous sum of the money from his shares of the Bodden's stock amongst the crew for their hard work, which was fed back into the town at the local market and taverns and whorehouses before leaving.

Once headed out to sea, Edward had Herbert point *Freedom* towards the Gulf of Mexico, their next destination, although specifically where in the Gulf was a matter of debate.

"So, Herbert, have you had some time to think over the riddle left by Benjamin?" Edward asked.

"Yes, actually. I believe I figured out the answer," Herbert said, obviously irked about something. Before Edward could inquire, Herbert discussed the reason for his ire. "That smug Alexandre claimed to have solved the riddle within a few seconds of hearing the clue, and he had the audacity to give me a clue."

Edward sympathised with Herbert, knowing firsthand how irritating Alexandre's arrogance could be. "What was his clue?"

"What has four points and what has three points?" Herbert questioned before yelling orders to trim the sails.

Four points, three points. Edward decided to read the riddle again.

In the Gulf the North East Triangles Point the Way.
Four points, four points, three points, three points.
Undo and See.

Four points. Four points. Edward pondered. *Compass? Cross? X? Those seem too obvious. A square or rectangle? Maybe. What has three points which is related to those?* He could only think of the Father, the Son, and the Holy Ghost for the cross, or a triangle relating to the square. *What would either have to do with this?*

"All I can think of is either a Cross and the Holy Trinity… or a square and a triangle."

Herbert was surprised. "The religious significance is intriguing, but I believe a square and a triangle are the most likely fit."

"How does a square and triangle fit with the riddle?"

"May I?" Herbert asked, his hand extended. Edward handed him the paper and he went to work.

Herbert first folded the paper in half, making a rectangle, four points, then folded the rectangle in half making a square again, four points. Herbert folded the square from one corner to the other, making a triangle, three points, and then repeated the process, three points. After showing Edward the finished product, Herbert unfolded the paper—undo and see.

On the paper now was the outline of four squares, with each square having four triangles pointing to the middle. The triangles in the northeast square pointed to a specific location on the map. The Northeast Triangles Point the Way.

"Incredible," Edward said. "Good work, Herbert. Take us straight there!"

"Aye, aye Captain."

Over the next week, the new crewmates were acquiring their sea legs and familiarising themselves with the veterans. Edward was learning the names and making his presence known as the captain.

Anne fully recovered from her fever and returned to work aboard the ship. The new members were apprehensive having women aboard at first, but after an incident involving a punch from Christina, and some broken fingers from Anne, they realised the two were not to be trifled with, and better sailors than most.

"Already putting the new men in line, I see?" Henry asked Anne one day, soon after she'd returned to active duty.

"Well, one has to teach the young ones manners or they are likely to rebel. Spare the rod..." Anne started.

"Spoil the child," Henry finished and they both chuckled.

After a moment, Anne's expression turned serious. "Is everything well, Henry? You have not been yourself in many days past."

Henry waved his hand in dismissal. "Don't trouble yourself. I'm just tired."

"Henry, from our time spent together before freeing Edward, I can tell when you are lying. Tell me your problems."

Henry opened his mouth, shook his head, and his mouth made a line. "I need to deal with my own problems, Anne. I will not burden another with this. If you'll excuse me?" Henry left, not waiting for a reply.

Henry's mind turned to his friend, Robert Maynard, and what he and Edward did to him. Henry also reflected on other innocents whom the crew of *Freedom* sacrificed to escape Portsmouth. The memory of the houses turning to rubble, and the thought of those caught in the middle, still made Henry sick to his stomach.

Christina's leg was still healing, and probably wouldn't be better for another few weeks, but the wolf, Tala, healed quicker and was often seen exploring the ship. Edward found it a bit disconcerting, but Tala appeared docile and did well with the dried meat normally available.

"So, can I keep her?" Christina asked Edward as they were feeding Tala one day.

"How are we to keep a wolf aboard? We should take her back to Pukuh's village. Wolves aren't meant to live amongst humans, they're dangerous."

"So says the one who used a pack to save a village."

"Hey, don't use logic and wit against me, Missy." Edward sounded upset, but he was grinning. "Alright, I'll allow Tala to stay for now, but any trouble and she's gone. And she's your responsibility."

Christina nearly jumped out of her seat with a hug for Edward. "Thank you, Edward, you're the best captain ever!"

Edward sighed. "I'm the only captain you've had."

Christina stuck her tongue out. "Well, go ahead and ruin the compliment then." Edward ruffled her hair and started to leave, but Christina spoke again, in a more serious tone. "Thank you Edward, for all you've done for me and my brother. Despite what he said earlier, he admires and trusts in you. We've been through some rough times, he and I, and you've given us hope. Despite losing family along the way," Christina turned away from Edward and wiped a tear off her cheek, "you've allowed us the chance to avenge them. Thank you."

Edward smiled. "I will do my best to live up to your expectations."

"I'm certain you will," Christina affirmed in her sweet voice.

As Edward reached the top deck he heard a lively "Land ho!" from the crow's nest. Herbert turned the ship to face the island dead on. Edward went up to the bow for a better view. He pulled out his spyglass and peered to the island beyond.

The island was small and round in shape, with no trees and a large structure in the middle. The structure was made of stone, from what Edward could tell, and rose higher than any building he ever saw. As they approached the island, the crew was truly astonished by the size of the monstrosity. The tower must have been at least four chains in height, or two hundred and sixty-four feet, which was taller than the tallest castles.

The ship landed on the sandy beach and the crew descended onto the island. Edward instructed them to bring weapons and all available supplies for any situation they might encounter. They entered all of these trials unprepared and always paid for it, but hopefully this time would not be the same.

The breeze of salty air flew through the fresh grass and passed over the old stone structure. The beautiful day on a quaint island in the middle of the Gulf of Mexico was not lost on the crew. They took their time to enjoy the sights while they had the chance.

"Here we be again, eh, Cap'n?" Sam questioned, striking up a conversation.

"Yes, there is almost no end to Benjamin's trickery."

"Two keys and you be free of 'im." Sam laughed.

"That is the hope, at least. You never know, Benjamin could show up and demand his ship back once we've opened the final room."

Sam laughed even more at the notion. "Well, the only way ta make *Freedom* yer own ship is ta rename her."

"Rename the *Freedom*? I wasn't aware you can rename a ship."

"Of course ye can. The ship is yers, or at least it will be after we secure all the keys, like ye said. Ye can do whatever ye want," Sam reassured him as he continued to walk up the beach and onto the grassy part of the island.

Hmm, rename the ship? But, *Freedom* fitted so well with what they were trying to accomplish.

"Are ye coming, Cap'n?" Sam inquired, glancing over his shoulder.

Edward shook himself out of his contemplation and joined the crew at the foot of the tower. Edward passed through the stone archway into the dark of the tower and was handed a lantern by Anne.

The room the crew entered was open and spacious, with a note of stale water in the air. The walking area was relegated to a single strip of stone around the perimeter, as the centre of the room was hollowed out, with a hundred-foot drop to water below. Edward could make out the remains of a sunken ship at the bottom.

"Captain, look on the left," a crewmate exclaimed.

Stairs made of stone on the left of the room led up to the next level. Edward decided to move to the steps with caution.

"Let's move to the next level, but be careful, there may be traps," Edward cautioned the men following behind him.

Edward approached the steps on the left side of the room, placing his foot on the first step slowly and deliberately. Nothing happened. He stomped his foot harder across the whole of the step, but nothing bad happened. He did the same thing for the next three steps, first testing and then tempting, but no traps were sprung.

Edward moved to the next level, and soon determined what had happened. On the next level half the floor and ceiling were covered in spikes, except for a walkway in the middle leading to the other side. Dead bodies, now nothing more than skeletons, could be seen impaled on some of the spikes.

Someone had been here.

The room smelled of stale air and decay from the dead bodies. Little air flow caused the smell to permeate the room. Though it was prevalent in the room of the tower, it nonetheless faded over time and did not sting as it did the first time Edward smelled a decaying body. The fact that the bodies had decayed completely meant some time had passed since it was entered.

When Edward realised someone had been here before his eyes widened and he rushed through the walkway between the spikes and up stairs on the left side with little regard for traps. Anne and Henry were worried for his safety and yelled for Edward to slow down, but in the next room they saw more dead bodies and another completed puzzle, and they were able to grasp what Edward saw.

The crew followed Edward through a fourth room, the last one, and up the final set of stairs to the roof of the tower. In the centre of the roof was a pedestal with a chest on the top. Edward opened the chest with shaking hands as the crew flooded the roof to join him. They went up behind Edward, waiting for the final nail in the coffin.

"The key is gone," Edward confirmed, his voice shaking like his hands.

17. THE STRAW

Despite everyone deducing what happened before Edward voiced it, the words produced no less shock upon the crew.

Edward held up a piece of paper, which he had retrieved from the chest.

"What is that, Edward?"

"A letter left from the person who took the key, confirming he took the contents of the chest."

"Is the letter signed?"

"Yes, by a Daniel Richardson, but that could be anyone." Edward nearly threw the paper over the side of the tower in frustration, but Anne stopped him.

"Any clue is better than no clue. We will find him. We must."

Anne read the paper.

I reckon whomever is reading this is either the rightful owner of this key, the snake who set up this trap, or both. By now you shall see that I have taken the key for myself. Its use may be unknown to me at the present, but it is now mine. If you are in need of the key, no need to get torn up about it as I've found it fair and square, and paid a pretty price in slaves to do so. You lost this hunt.

Do not come after the key, or misfortune will surely follow.

Daniel Richardson.

"Might I have a *regarder* at the paper?" Alexandre asked as he made his way through the crowd.

He sauntered over, a small smirk on his face unreflected in his dull eyes. As he strode across the tower roof, his long coat swayed in the wind. He took the paper from Edward and examined it thoroughly: bending, smelling, and eventually licking the paper.

"This is wood from the American Chestnut Tree and the ink is produced in Canada, so Northern America, possibly Maine or New York." Alexandre smacked Edward on the arm. "Not so lost now, *mon ami?*"

Edward's jaw dropped. "How could you possibly know these things?"

"You saw my methods, they should be self-explanatory. The smell of the paper and the taste of the ink are the determining factors."

Anne took over. "Perhaps we will rephrase: How do you know from the taste and the smell they are in fact those types of paper and ink?"

480

"Over the years I studied many things: ink, papers, soil, plants, along with their defining characteristics. I travelled the world and saw many, so I am able to know with absolute certainty where the paper and ink are made."

"So the man we are searching for is in New York or Maine?"

Alexandre palmed his face. "*Non, non.* Only this note is. The man himself could very well be anywhere now. Judging by the fading of the paper and ink the message is at least two to three years old. You noticed the decayed bodies below? Some time has passed since the key has been *pris* from here. I provided a starting point: America. The rest is up to you."

Edward peered at the paper, smacking it against his hand while he thought. "Thank you, Alexandre. You helped us once more. I believe we should head back to the Bodden Brothers. Their information network could be of great help to us in our search."

"Aye, aye, Captain!" the crew responded favourably.

"And so, your surgeon, Alexandre, believes this man to be from New York or Maine?" Malcolm asked whilst holding the paper note Edward found.

"*Non,* I mean, no. The paper itself is from New York or Maine, but the man we are pursuing may not be there any longer. We don't know. He must have had a crew, we could be talking about a sailor, a captain more specifically, or someone rather prolific. In the letter it mentions a number of slaves he sacrificed to get through the trials, and we saw a number of bodies. The whole endeavour would have cost a great deal."

"More from Alexandre?" Neil ventured.

"No, the last part was from my own deductions. Alexandre concurred."

The brothers nodded in contemplation. "We will put our eyes and ears to the task." "We will see what we can find out about this Daniel Richardson."

"Thank you brothers. You know where to find me."

Edward and crew waited for a week in Bodden Town, but the brothers were only able to procure the smallest bit of information on the elusive Richardson. They were able to determine that he was a slaver who may have operated a ship taking slaves from Africa to America.

"Unfortunately, our information network only spreads so far on this island." "You may have better luck with a friend of ours: Aaron Cook." "Cook lives in Tortuga. You can take this letter of introduction to him." "We sent a notice ahead of you, so by the time you arrive he should have an answer for you, if any." "But, if he does not, then we are afraid you will not find this man without years more searching."

Edward wasted no time in leaving Bodden Town, and the crew were all for the change in scenery. *Freedom* had travelled back and forth to Bodden Town a few times in the past month, and while relaxing for the crew, they wanted to move forward.

The path to Tortuga led east of the Cayman Islands, where Bodden town was, north over Jamaica, and on the north of Haiti. Along the way, Edward noticed Henry staring longingly to the south, in the direction of Jamaica, and their home island, Badabos.

"Thinking of home?" Edward asked, joining Henry at the starboard railing.

Henry breathed deeply, staring at the clouds along the south. "Yes, it has been too long."

"Not long enough if you ask me." Edward turned around and sat on the railing.

The sun stood high in the sky and wind was in their favour. The sails flapped lightly, as did the rigging lines. The crew was in good spirits now and Edward could see smiles on their faces despite working in the hot sun.

"You don't ever think back on those days? The days before we were forced to start running all the time, before we started killing all the time?"

"Of course I do, I would be lying if I said I didn't. But this life is better. We have family who cares for us, we have *Freedom*. We may have to defend our *Freedom*, but that doesn't make us less free. If anything, we are freer than anyone else. No one can tell us what to do."

Henry chuckled. "Oh, so that's what freedom is? Sounds a bit childish to me, but what do I know?"

"Explain your meaning," Edward commanded, his anger rising.

"I mean exactly what I said. Your notions of freedom are childish, and are becoming tiresome." Henry rubbed his face in frustration as he stood up from the railing. "I'm sorry, I shouldn't have said that. I don't wish to debate with you, so can we stop? I didn't mean what I said."

Edward rose as well, facing Henry while folding his arms. "No, you did mean what you said, and I can't let this go. You think what we're doing is childish?"

"No, but the way you justify your actions by saying you're fighting for freedom, when in reality you're satisfying your own rebellious nature, is childish. Sugar this life how you want, we are outcasts."

"Outcasts?" Edward responded. A crowd of the crew had gathered to watch.

Henry, sometimes as hot-headed as Edward, could not back down now. "Yes, you call this freedom but we've been shunted from society for our reckless behaviour. This is no freedom. *Freedom* cannot be foisted upon someone. We've simply changed prisons."

"How are we imprisoned? We have the whole world to explore! The ocean is ours."

Henry stepped forward to Edward, the two of them didn't even notice the crew watching. "Only the size of the cage has changed. What if we wanted to land in England, or Port Royal, or some other locale owned by the British? Do you think we would have a whole lot of freedom there?"

"Alright, Henry, if you're so smart then how does one actually attain freedom?" Edward spoke with a tone which made it sound like he was calling Henry an idiot.

Henry laughed derisively. He couldn't stop now. "I don't know, Edward, why don't you try ruling the world? That's a good start. Or maybe we can ask your father when we find him? Maybe he found his freedom out here somewhere, what with him not returning and all."

Edward levelled Henry with a thunderous punch to the jaw. Henry held a hand to his jaw, his eyes wide. Edward grabbed Henry by the chest and exacted a pound of flesh from him, blow by hideous blow. The debt Henry took with his words was far too great.

Anne heard the commotion and ran to the top deck to see Edward still punching Henry without end. The crew was trying to tear Edward away but they were like flies before his rage.

"Why don't you keep talking about my father, you bastard? Say something else," Edward yelled, ignoring the men pulling him back.

"I'm sorry, Edward," Henry cried.

Anne ran in front of Edward, pulled back her fist, and punched him. Her fist, whip-like in motion and with pinpoint precision over years of training, landed perfectly on the temple, knocking Edward unconscious in one blow.

"Take him to the crew cabin," she ordered while pointing to the ladder. She then grabbed Henry by the chest and dragged him into the stern war room cabin. She nearly threw Henry onto the oval table in the room. "Start talking. Why was I forced to knock Edward unconscious and why did he assault you?" Her long red curls bounced with rage as she pointed and stared daggers at Henry.

Henry pulled himself together after taking a breather, but was still distraught. "I was arguing with Edward and made a comment about his father, which I shouldn't have."

"Damn." Anne placed one hand on her hip and she bit the thumb of the other. She had seen Edward's anger over his father's disappearance before, but not to that extent. Henry must have truly struck a nerve. "I will speak with Edward and do my best to calm him. Be prepared to apologise if you wish to remain on this ship."

"Thank you, Anne," Henry said as he deflated onto one of the chairs around the table.

Anne went down to the crew cabin. Several crew members watched her as she passed, but none stopped her due to the glare in her eyes. They gathered at a distance from Edward and were waiting and watching to see what he would do, but parted for Anne.

Edward awoke from unconsciousness a while later, his head foggy and his anger below boiling. He sat hunched over on a chair, staring at the floorboards. Edward was chewing on the Mayan leaves, a habit he picked up during thoughtful times.

When Edward noticed Anne he did not rise. "I want him off the ship."

"I am not your cabin boy. If you wish your best friend to leave this ship, you will dismiss him yourself. Although you would be a fool to do so. More fool than when you beat him near to death on the waist."

Edward rose to his full height, causing William, standing nearby, to tense. "What did you say?" He stood a full foot over her, but she did not back down.

Anne pointed her finger threateningly in Edward's face. "You heard me, you big brute. Henry said something he regrets, as all people do, and you cast him out? Only a fool would do such a thing."

"Do you know what he said about my father?"

"Yes, words. Words only have meaning if you let them. Words only make you angry if you let them. Do not let meaningless words anger you."

"But…"

"Quiet! If you cannot find your own fault in all this, and understand how Henry feels, then maybe you were never friends to begin with." Anne turned and walked away. "Meditate on this, and then apologise for your foolish actions, or lose Henry forever," Anne warned over her shoulder before herding the people out of the crew cabin and back to work.

Edward fell back into the chair, defeated. He pressed his thumb and forefinger against his temples to try to dull the pain. He reflected on what he had done as tears fell from his eyes.

Edward entered the war room. Henry pulled his head up at the noise, and at the sight of Edward he rose.

"Edward, I'm sor—"

Edward raised his hand. "Don't. Just… don't." Henry sat back down as Edward grabbed a chair and sat in front of his friend. Edward frowned as he sat hunched over in the chair. After a moment, he smiled wistfully. "You remember the first thing you said to me after my father disappeared?"

At first Henry was caught off guard at the question, but a smile formed as he realised where Edward was going with his story. "I said 'He's in a better place now.'"

Edward chuckled and ran his fingers through his wavy black hair. "Robert pulled us apart after I scrapped with you. I still believed my father left me on purpose, not that he could have died. I was so angry because I thought you meant he was with another family, but I understood later, and we made up."

"I remember how you shut yourself in your room for weeks and wouldn't talk to me."

"I was pretty stubborn back then."

"Back then?" Henry asked with a smirk which caused both men to laugh.

"I pushed you, and I shouldn't have hurt you. I'm sorry, Henry."

"I'm sorry too, Edward, I shouldn't have said what I did."

"I know you mean it when you say you're sorry, but I will need some time to forgive you for what you said. So what do you say we act as if a few months have passed, and become friends again? It's been a long time since we were friends." Edward extended his hand to Henry.

Henry shook Edward's hand in agreement, then rose and hugged him. After a moment they left the war room laughing together. When the crew saw Edward and Henry back to normal, smiles abounded, not the least of which was on Anne's face.

None could think their peace would so swiftly and irrevocably be broken in the near future.

18. THE DAY THE DEVIL KNEW FEAR

Edward and crew landed in Tortuga after a few days' travel. The island was ruled by pirates and their ilk. Having no specific ruling class the island was claimed by rogues for their trade. If one journeyed to Tortuga, an unspoken rule was to travel in a group and hold weapons, as thefts and other acts of villainy were commonplace.

Freedom landed on the south end of the small island. Many ships flagrantly displayed Jolly Rogers, and others hid them for fear of a marine raid. The rest were merchant ships not afraid of the treacherous acquaintances surrounding them.

The harbour was a main hub of trade and money flow, with a few businesses thriving on the stolen booty for profit. The area around the docks was a mess of activity, and from the ship Edward could see the mass of bodies moving to and fro in the mercantile apex.

The true town of Tortuga was two miles north of the hub and surrounded by a wooden wall for defence, but security was sorely lacking at times. The merchants who frequented Tortuga were the ones who supplied the men for the militia, but when the pirates became too wild the militia would be taken out until the issue was resolved. Raids, pirate attacks, marines from the British or conquistadors from Spain had all tried their hand at taking over or destroying Tortuga, but the town always managed to return from the brink larger and more festooned with felons.

Jack watched from the sidelines as Edward asked for volunteers to see the man they were after in Tortuga. Ten minutes after Edward left with Anne, William, and John, Jack decided to visit the harbour.

Jack's feet seemed to move under their own accord, and he soon found himself in front of a tavern. He looked at the tavern for a long moment before deciding to head inside.

As Jack was entering, Edward and the others were leaving. Jack overheard them talking about entering the town now that they had a better idea where Aaron Cook was.

Edward noticed Jack entering the tavern, but Jack didn't meet his eyes. Jack wasn't sure what he was doing at the tavern himself, so he didn't wish to be questioned by Edward right now.

Jack examined the tavern. He could see rough men downing

rum as if it was water, men in various types of clothing and colour playing a game of cards, and others showing off weapons of various sizes as if they had to compensate for something. The smells of blood, sweat, alcohol and various other things filled his nostrils, and Jack felt at home.

Jack walked to the bar table and sat in an old chair. "Whiskey, if you please, sir."

The bartender nodded and handed him a small glass which he filled generously. Jack paid and thanked the bartender, and the bartender left to tend to his other regular patrons.

Jack stared at the drink in front of him. The liquid had a brown, almost chestnut colour. The smell was strong and brought to mind a warm spice mix of cinnamon and nutmeg, as well as a hint of chocolate and toffee. Jack sniffed the mixture slowly as he turned the drink in his glass, its sweet promise tempting him.

Just a touch, Jack thought, *enough to wet the lips*. Jack tipped the glass up, but stopped just shy of the liquid making contact.

Jack set the glass back down and pushed it away from him before he had a second thought. The bartender asked him if anything was wrong, but Jack reassured him that he was fine. Jack sat and stared at the glass, thinking on the past for a time, and then the future. His thoughts drifted to his love, his wife, Rachel, and his kids, Maximilian and Jessica, and the man who killed them, George Rooke.

I made a promise. A little bit won't hurt. But the Captain saw me, he'll know. No he won't. We'll just have one glass, that's all. No!

Jack went back and forth in his mind, but eventually all the voices drowned out and it was just him and the drink. He pushed the glass back and forth in his hand as the time passed.

Someone came up beside Jack, but he didn't look up from the drink. "Ah, thanks fer the drink, mate," the man said as he grabbed the drink in front of Jack and downed it in one gulp.

Jack's mouth opened and he looked at the person who stole his drink. Sam sat down next to him, smirking in his trickster fashion.

"Samuel. To what do I owe this pleasure?"

"Wanted a drink. No better place, right? Barkeep, another!" Sam shouted.

The barkeep came over and filled Sam's cup again. This time Sam decided to sip and savour the drink instead. Jack and Sam sat in silence for a while.

"So, how have you been coping since… the incident?" Jack asked.

"Fine," Sam said, taking another swig of the drink.

"I heard what happened to some of the crew, some of the things they saw in that mist. I'm glad I didn't have to experience that. I can only imagine what I would see."

"We all have shit we gotta deal wit. It's how ye carry on that matters." Sam lifted the glass and glanced at Jack. "This ain't the way, mate."

Jack hung his head in shame. "I know." Jack ran his fingers through his hair. "Edward sent you, didn't he?"

"Ran back to the ship a'soon as he saw ye enter," Sam confirmed. "Wanted someone ta watch ye. I volunteered."

Jack laughed. "Maybe we both could learn something from Edward. He chooses to deal with his problems head on, always moving forward."

Sam knocked back the last of his drink. "He 'asn't hit the wall yet. All us broken souls git there, you know better'n most." Sam stood up from the chair. "When he's drownin' we'll need ta be there ta help him surface."

"Right," Jack agreed, then joined Sam. The two left the tavern and headed back to *Freedom* to await their captain's return. As they walked, Jack patted Sam on the back. "Thanks, Sam."

Edward, Anne, John, and Henry passed through the open gates of Tortuga, and were met with a glimpse of how Bodden Town might have been under different rule. Townsfolk gallivanted about, talking and drinking and singing together without a care in the world. Others fought without anyone to stop them, and some made wagers on the outcome.

"I suppose this is to be expected in this locale?" Anne asked, gaping.

"Business as usual, perhaps?" William added.

"They are rather, e-enthusiastic," John nervously stuttered.

Edward eyed the various villains warily. "Stay close."

They moved in a tight-knit group to the nearest tavern, a seedy building made of rotting wood full of bullet holes. The tavern was occupied by gentlemen of questionable repute—and one man also full of bullets, dead on the floor. When Edward asked the bartender, he directed them to a green house on the west side of town.

"I don' know how Aaron comes by his intelligence as he never leaves his home, but his information is true as can be. He's the man you're huntin' for," the bartender confirmed.

Edward thanked him, and they left to find the green house. Edward and company passed by other taverns and businesses selling weapons and stolen merchandise as well as people walking the streets of the town. The filth was evident with garbage and dirt covering the pathways and the residents. Quite the contrast to Bodden

Town where the streets were regularly patrolled and kept relatively clean.

Edward found the green house after wading through the throngs of debauchery and unwanted solicitations. The small house had faded green paint falling off in chips from decay and neglect. Aside from the pale green colour the house was rather plain.

Edward unconsciously eyed the road they were on before knocking on the door to the house. He heard no sound of movement at first, but after knocking a second time he could hear someone bustling about. After much noise and curses an iron peep hole opened up in the door.

The pair of eyes showing had a furrowed brow above them and moved about to scrutinise each of the people there. "What business do you have with me?"

"The Bodden Brothers sent us. I have a letter of introduction here, and you should have received correspondence recently regarding our arrival." Edward presented the letter to the slot.

The man eyed the letter, and then Edward, carefully before snatching it. Edward could hear the sound of the paper being ripped into and then silence as the letter was read. After a moment the door was unlocked and opened for the visitors.

In front of Edward stood an older man, hunched over with a cane in one hand. He did not have grey hair or wrinkles, and appeared to be in good health, save for the cane and a limp from injury, not old age.

"Well, get in here. I don't have all day," Aaron said.

Edward entered first, with his group in a line behind him. The inside of the house was unexpected, but understandable, given Aaron's reclusive habits. The first room was plain with very little furniture and almost every inch covered with books and papers. Shelves filled with books lined the walls and spilled into piles on the floor. Papers from different locations across the globe were strewn about in no discernible pattern, some dating back many years. The house smelled of stale air and old paper.

Aaron walked to a door at the far end of the room as Edward and his friends ogled the many texts surrounding them.

"Come on, then." Aaron beckoned.

Edward focused and walked into the other room to sit down in one of the chairs after Aaron did the same, and his company followed suit. "I trust you know why we are here?"

"Yes, and in another week you shall have your answer. The best I could do on such short notice is find out your man, Daniel Richardson, is a slaver. Richardson's last raid took him to Calabar, in NiTalaa, in the past few months."

Edward's mouth went agape in shock over the name of the village. He shared knowing, and equally troubled, glances with his crew.

"If you are upset with the progress you can show yourself to the door. I only had two days' notice to find you this much..." Cook began, but Anne stopped him.

"No, we are pleased with your results. The location is what is troubling."

Edward picked up where Anne left off. "One of our crewmates has been there for some time. He is coloured."

Cook scratched his chin. "That is troubling. He took many slaves from Calabar. I do not know Daniel's role, but he supplied the ship and men."

"We have more reason to meet with this man than before."

Before they could continue the discussion a knock at the door pulled the group's attention. Cook excused himself with a grumble about not expecting anyone and returned to the other room, closing the door behind him.

"So N-Nassir's village was attacked by slavers?" John questioned.

"That appears to be the case," Anne answered.

"There's a high probability he was taken." Edward stroked his beard. The crew left their carpenter after the death of his child so long ago, long enough that Nassir had to have been there at the same time as Daniel Richardson. *Where are you now, Nassir?*

The noise of a punch came from the front room. William glanced to the door. His brow was low, which brought to mind the perked ears of a hound.

William rose silently, motioning for silence. He went to the door and used another slit like the one on the main entrance to see through. What William saw made his eyes widen and he immediately shut the slit.

"We must leave, now," William whispered.

Edward followed suit by lowering his voice. "Why, what is happening?"

"There is no time to explain. The man who arrived is dangerous and we must leave immediately." William pulled Anne silently from her chair and herded her to the back door.

Edward could not let go of his curiosity, and disbelief over the danger, so he peered through the opening in the door. He could see Cook being held up by the neck by another man dressed in black with slick, jet-black hair, and dark eyes. Edward felt something from those eyes. On the surface they lacked emotion, similar to William most of the time, but Edward could see something in them, deep and endless, like a bottomless well.

A brutal, ruthless corruption filled those eyes. Edward felt that he had seen those same eyes before, but couldn't recall where. Edward was gripped with fear, and he could not turn away.

"I will ask you once more. Tell me where the Blackbeard is and I will spare you pain," the man in black said.

"I told you, he's in Mexico. My sources never lie," Cook replied.

"No, your sources may be free of fraud, but your words are not free of contamination." The man in black pulled out a small needle, like a pin, from his belt. "You will clearly not provide assistance, and only death awaits." He flicked the pin into Cook's neck.

Cook pulled his cane up, pointed it against the man in black's chest, and pulled on a hidden trigger. The man in black pushed the cane to the side, but not swiftly enough. The cane shot a bullet through his shoulder. Blood spurted from the wound, and the man in black dropped Cook to the floor.

Cook tried to flee, but the strength left his legs before he could rise. He crawled on his hands and knees, but in a matter of seconds he fell to the ground. Cook futilely tried to pull himself forward, but then rolled over. Cook's eyes rolled up in his head, he foamed at the mouth, and convulsed in muscle spasms. The seizure gradually lessened until stopping completely. Within moments Cook had died from whatever poison was on the needle.

The man in black watched until the end, after which his eyes moved up to the slit where Edward was still watching.

John pulled Edward away by force. Together, Anne and William, Edward and John, left post haste. John and William agreed to split up and meet back at the ship. John pulled Edward to the right of the home.

The man in black emerged from the back door soon after they started running, and noticed Edward and John turning a corner. Edward glanced back, slowing them down, so John pulled him into a nearby abandoned house.

John took Edward up the decaying stairs to the second floor and then forced Edward to climb a ladder to the attic. John entered the attic, then pulled the ladder up so none could follow and covered the hole with a nearby wooden box.

John slapped Edward across the face. "This is no time to be afraid!" he reprimanded forcefully.

Edward returned from his stupor. "What? I'm not afraid of anything."

"Edward, I've been in enough battles during the war to know when a man is afraid. Whoever that man is, he caused you to feel fear, but fear is not something to be ashamed of."

Edward reflected on what he felt moments ago, and asked himself why he froze. He came to the conclusion that John was correct, and Edward was afraid of the man.

"Something about him screamed danger," Edward admitted.

"Good, good. Use your memory to help condition yourself to the feeling."

Edward closed his eyes and recalled the man in black's eyes, and what he'd said. *He was after me, but who could he be? He was too... dark... to be a marine. An assassin? But who would have hired him?* Even in the shadow of Edward's mind, those eyes held no less power.

John strained his ears to try to hear any noises in the old house. After a few seconds, John and Edward could both hear the sound of slow methodical footsteps marching up the stairs. The man in black had followed them, which neither John nor Edward doubted, and he wanted them to hear those footsteps. They became louder and louder with each step up the stairs.

When the assassin was at the top of the stairs, he searched the different rooms one by one. The sound of the footsteps as well as the not so subtle creaking of the old wood allowed Edward and John to know exactly where he was.

Suddenly, a sword thrust up from below with a thunk a few feet from where Edward and John were sitting. Edward was about to rise and move, but John stopped him.

The sword was removed slowly and Edward once more could hear the movement of the man in black. The sword was thrust into the attic through the floorboards once more, closer to Edward and John, then removed quickly. The footsteps moved into the room directly below them. The sword shot up with more frequency, closer and closer to hitting Edward and John.

The hideous sound of the metal scraping through the old wood sent shivers down Edward's spine. He could not release the image of those eyes from his haunted mind. Edward recalled others recoiling at his own glare. *Are my eyes the same?*

Edward wasn't able to dwell on the question for too long, as the man in black was still approaching. He thrust his sword into the box over the attic entrance and pushed it forward, opening the way.

Edward and John had nowhere left to run, so John rose silently with Edward doing the same. The sound of scraping furniture was heard below as the man in black moved something around for him to step on. He climbed up and jumped to the hole, pushing the box aside as he climbed into the attic.

When the man was halfway up, John rushed over and kicked the wooden box into his face. The box busted with the force and caused the man in black to lose his precarious grip on the opening to the attic. The man fell with a crash.

"Run!" John yelled as he jumped down the hole.

John landed on the lower floor and immediately began running. Edward did the same, landing right next to the man in black. The man grabbed Edward's leg with an iron grip, and he struggled to free himself as the fallen man rose to his feet.

John took a knife from his belt and stabbed the man in black on his forearm above the elbow. The iron grip released. The man himself seemed oblivious to the pain, like his body was deadened to it.

John grabbed Edward's arm and pulled him. "I said run, soldier!" John screamed.

Edward and John ran to the closest window and ploughed through. Glass shattered in their wake, the shards dancing in the light. John and Edward both rolled onto the dirt alleyway between the houses to break the fall and ran to the south, to the ship.

"We will not escape this man by simply running," John asserted.

"What do we do?" Edward asked, glancing behind him. Though he could not see the man in black, he could feel his presence. Edward knew he was still chasing them.

"Stay focused," John commanded.

"Right."

"We'll need a distraction. We need to start a riot," John suggested.

"How do we do that?"

"Start hitting people," John answered as he levelled a large man with a haymaker as he ran.

Edward and John both began punching and kicking the townspeople as they ran. John led Edward to the town square full of people. The townspeople who were hit ran after the two, pushing and forcing more people aside in their wake, causing fights to start in the streets.

In the square, Edward and John indiscriminately hit people standing about. Edward threw one man into a group of other people, and John used some people as shields, causing scraps not even involving him to start.

Before long, the whole square erupted in an all-out brawl of pirates, thugs, and drunken revellers. Edward and John didn't check for the man in black, and continued to run through the streets to the gates of the city.

"John, look!" Edward pointed to the gates.

The merchant guards were closing the gates, and Edward could see Anne and William behind the gates with four horses. Anne was arguing with the gatekeepers, trying to get them to stop closing the gates, but they wouldn't listen. The wooden gates were closed and locked before Edward and John reached the wall.

"This way," John ordered, not stopping.

John went to the side of the wooden wall close to the gate and ran up a set of stairs to a walkway around the perimeter of the city wall.

Guards rushed after them and one man threw a punch at John. John blocked the punch, took a musket from behind the guard's back, and smashed the butt against the guard's face. The guard fell over the side of the walkway to the ground below.

Edward scanned for a way they could jump over the wall safely. "There!" He pointed to a large haystack on the east side. "We can climb the watchtower and jump into the hay."

"Lead the way, Captain," John offered as he fired the musket at a guard.

Edward ran along the walkway. Guards attacked him as he ran and he used his broad shoulder to plough through the men blocking his way. Near the base of the watchtower, one guard gripped him by the shoulders from behind while another attacked with a sword from the front. Edward flipped the guard holding him over his back. The man flew through the air and knocked down the one with the sword.

Edward entered the open watchtower. The inside had four wooden pillars with crossbeams on the ends and a perch at the top for the guards. The walkway was completely open and one had to climb up a ladder to reach the top.

Edward climbed the ladder as John followed behind. Edward switched to the other side of the ladder and stepped onto the crossbeams. He jumped, dropping twenty feet and into the middle of the haystack, softening his fall.

Anne and William had noticed the skirmish and Edward jumping down from the watchtower. They rushed over with the horses and shot at the guards outside the walls of Tortuga with pistols.

John reached the crossbeams and was readying himself to jump when a guard shot at him. He started to jump and was shot through his side. The bullet caused John's jump to turn into a fall.

"John!" Edward yelled as he ran forward. John fell onto Edward, and the two dropped to the ground together. "Are you well, John?"

"S-sorry, Captain. I didn't quite make the jump."

Edward helped John rise. "Will you still be able to ride?"

"I believe so. We don't have time to waste anyway, that man is surely on our tail."

Edward, John, Anne and William all mounted their horses and travelled south. The sounds of fighting slowly diminished as they got closer to the harbour.

"William, you saw the man. Who was he?" Edward asked while they were riding.

"Edward Russell. I believe he is the man who killed William III— your uncle, Anne—and framed me for the murder. If I were to speculate, he was sent by Queen Anne."

"Well, I am the target this time. Anne, I know you were not able to see his face, but do you think what William said is true?"

"I was never involved in my mother's affairs, nor did I wish to be, so I cannot say if she has used an assassin." Anne turned away in disgust. "However, sending an assassin after you is consistent with something she would do. You took her heir away from her and humiliated her, twice. First she sent over a hundred naval ships, and now a covert assassin. She won't stop there, I'm afraid."

"It will take more than one man to stop us," Edward declared, full of bravado, but the feeling the man in black gave him was still affecting him.

Anne smiled at his reassurance, but Edward could tell that she didn't believe him by the look in her eyes.

The four riders reached the harbour in no time, and they rushed to the ship immediately. The crew were conducting menial tasks aboard *Freedom* until they saw Edward and company come in with all urgency. The crew dropped what they were doing to see what the commotion was, but Edward stopped them.

"Prepare to set sail, we must leave now!" he yelled for all to hear.

Edward ran up to the quarterdeck where Herbert was at the helm with Christina at his side. Christina had crutches to help her move around as her leg was still healing. Her wolf Tala was lying at her feet.

"What's wrong, Edward?" Christina asked.

Herbert turned his wheelchair around to face Edward. "Did something happen in town?"

"We met with an assassin. He killed our source of information before he was able to find out where Daniel Richardson is," Edward answered.

Herbert adjusted his glasses. "What do we do now?"

William took over explaining. "We were able to find out where Richardson has been: Calabar, NiTalaa."

Herbert and Christina glanced at each other, eyes wide. "But, that's where…" Christina didn't finish her sentence.

"We know," Edward confirmed. "All the more reason why we need to return there as soon as possible. And, did we mention the assassin? Is the whole crew here, or did some men go ashore?"

"Some did, but all crew members have returned," Herbert reported.

"Good, then get us out of here, helmsman!"

19. CALABAR REVISITED

After a brief stop in Port-de-Paix south of Tortuga, to send a letter to the Bodden Brothers about what happened to their friend Aaron Cook, the crew of the *Freedom* set off for Calabar. The journey would take at least seven weeks, so they stocked up before leaving.

Along the journey, the daily routine of maintaining the ship and training kept everyone busy. Without a fully-fledged carpenter, the *Freedom* needed more time for maintenance, so the long trips served her well.

After a few weeks, Christina was up and about without her crutches and back into training. One day Anne proposed a team fight to promote group dynamics. To demonstrate, she and William showed what they were capable of doing together.

Specific manoeuvres, when performed as one, not only helped cover each other's backs, but also increased their effectiveness. Anne would jump off William's back as he was kneeling down to fire a musket. In the air she would land with a double kick using the downward momentum for additional power. William helped Anne jump higher using his hands to vault her up, and then she would latch onto something and pull him up. They worked beautifully together because of their experience.

"Why can't we train together?" Edward asked Anne after one of the demonstrations. There was a twinge of anger in his voice.

"I wish we could, but the difference in our skill levels is too great. If you wish to train with someone, maybe Christina would be better. Your power and her speed would make a good combination."

"I don't think we should team up, Edward would slow me down." Christina spoke loudly enough for Edward and Anne to hear. Anne could see Christina, and at Anne's questioning expression, Christina winked, to which Anne smiled back.

"Slow you down?" Edward questioned as he turned around.

"Maybe she's right, Edward, you are quite a bit taller, and slow. Christina learns very quickly, so I'm not sure you can keep up," Anne asserted, folding her arms and inspecting Edward up and down.

Edward gritted his teeth. "I can run circles around you, little one."

"Oh yeah, see what happens when you try," Christina challenged.

"We will train together then, and we'll see who is better."

"Yay! Thanks, Captain." Christina smiled with genuine mirth, to Edward's confusion. She thanked Anne and talked with her a bit.

"Why do I feel as if I was tricked?" Edward asked to no one in particular.

Sam was passing by on his way to spar with William. "Cause you wus, mate. Cause you wus." He sauntered off with a laugh.

Anne clapped to grab everyone's attention. "Alright, how about we start a duel then? What about Henry and Pukuh against Edward and Christina?"

Henry and Pukuh walked over at hearing their names. After explaining, the four combatants were more than eager to have a good scrap. They stood on the forecastle deck with the crew watching on the railings or on ratlines.

"Watch out, Ed, I'm going to get payback for before," Henry said. He was in a fighting stance, his massive arms flexed.

"We'll see about that," Edward replied.

"I do not wish to hurt you, girl, so I will ease my blows," Pukuh teased Christina.

"Don't mock me."

The groups fought with everything they had, each working together to defeat the other group. Being the first time working with each other, Edward and Christina were less than graceful, and tempers flared, but they were able to turn things around.

Together Edward and Christina managed to throw Henry overboard and forced Pukuh into the corner of the bow. The crew moved away when the three drew close. Christina whispered something in Edward's ear and he nodded. Edward and Christina backed up a few steps and locked hands. Edward pulled her and swung her towards Pukuh. She kicked Pukuh in the chest and he was pushed to the edge of the deck. Edward put Christina down, ran to Pukuh, lifted his legs, and tossed him over the side. The Mayan fell over into the sea like Henry.

Rope ladders were lowered for Henry and Pukuh while Christina and Edward celebrated. Henry and Pukuh climbed up, and dried off.

"How does being beaten feel?" Christina boasted.

Henry and Pukuh eyed each other and laughed. "We went easy on you two," Henry claimed.

"Oh yea? Round two, right now. We'll show you who the best team is," Edward said.

"We are ready to battle when you are," Pukuh confirmed.

The four fought again, laughing as they bonded. Anne watched from the poop deck, joyful over the smiles on their faces.

"Dangerous, leavin them two together," Sam warned, walking over to Anne.

"What do you mean?" Anne said curtly with arms folded.

"Christina an' the capt'n. She admires him, could turn ta infatuation."

"I see what you are trying to do, but it won't work. Jealousy is not part of my vocabulary. I trust Edward and Christina both."

Sam laughed. "I wusn't trying ta make you jealous, jus' a warning. Love is blind, they say." Sam laughed again and strolled away.

Anne watched Edward, Christina, Henry, and Pukuh all laughing. *I trust Edward.*

The *Freedom* landed on the almost non-existent harbour of Calabar at dusk. The harbour was deserted, save for a few small fishing boats, and the only sounds were the subtle knocking of the boats against the pier and the lapping of the waves.

Edward stepped onto the harbour and scanned the horizon. He was joined by other crew members as the sails were furled and the *Freedom* moored.

"What happened here?" Henry thought out loud.

"Daniel Richardson happened," Edward answered.

Edward and the crew left the harbour and rushed up a small hill to the village of Calabar. What they saw as they topped the rise stopped them in their tracks. Edward's mouth opened wide from the sight of the devastation.

Calabar used to be a thriving African community full of life and promise, but now the village appeared like the remains of a war zone. The ashes of homes made of wood and straw were burnt to the ground. The dwindling populace moved about in a trance, many of them children, women, or the elderly. The grave site was clearly visible from the hill Edward and his crew were on, and larger since last time they visited.

At the sight of Edward and his crew, the few villagers shuffling around shouted something and ran into their homes. "No, wait! We're not here to hurt you!" he yelled, but none listened.

Soon after the villagers ran to their homes, men ran out with spears and muskets. Twenty men ran to Edward and his crew, threatening them back to the ship.

"Return to your ship and leave," one of the men in front warned. He wore a set of tattered and worn trousers made by English hands. He didn't wear a shirt, and his raw and powerful chest muscles were exposed. He was tall and his face looked familiar to Edward.

"Please listen to me. We are not here to harm you." Edward stepped forward.

The man in the lead shot his musket at Edward's feet. "Not another step, unless it is back where you came. We have had enough of the white man taking our people."

Edward motioned for his crew to stay back and not draw their weapons. "We are searching for a friend of ours, Nassir. If you can tell us what has happened to him we will leave with no further discussion."

The leader of the aggressors glanced briefly at his men. "What is your name?"

"Edward Thatch."

The leader lowered his weapon "Nassir has told me of you. You can rest assured, as far as I know he is alive." He turned to his men, speaking in their native tongue, and the men lowered their weapons.

"Thank you. Might I have your name?" Edward asked.

"My name is Dumaka. I am Nassir's brother."

"His brother? Well, you do look similar, but he never mentioned anything about you."

"Well, considering he believed me dead, that is unsurprising. Let us talk by a fire, you must be cold and tired."

"Yes, some rest would be nice."

Dumaka took Edward, Henry, Anne, and William to an open area behind one of the remaining homes. While the fire was started, Christina brought blankets for the crew to help ward off the cold air. She laid one over Anne's back and sat down beside her.

"The ship appeared out of nowhere at dawn about four months ago."

"Four months? That couldn't have been very long after we landed," Anne surmised. She held hands with Edward and sat close to him for more warmth.

"No, only about a month. I did not have much of a chance to reunite with him before he was taken. He was still grieving for his son, but he had fond things to say about you all."

The crew's eyes turned downwards as they thought of their friend and what was happening to him now. "So what happened?" Christina asked. Her eyes held anger hidden deep within them, and she gripped the wooden rose at her neck.

"They took over one hundred villagers as slaves. Nassir and some of the men fought, but were not able stand against their numbers. The fighting enabled us to help the less able villagers to escape into the woods. We are all that remains of our warriors. When I returned, Nassir was gone and his body was nowhere to be found. I assumed he was captured."

"Do you have any idea where they were taking the slaves?" Edward asked.

"One of the villagers who escaped overheard the white men say they were travelling to Boston."

Anne turned to Edward. "That lines up with the location of the American Chestnut tree Alexandre mentioned."

Edward nodded. "Your brother took his possessions with him when he left the crew, and I know his papers of freedom were amongst them. If you have his bag, those papers will help us at least free him."

Dumaka shook his head, his eyes betraying his disappointment. "No, his belongings were in the house over there." Dumaka pointed to the remains of a house burned to the ground in the attack.

Edward nodded. "No matter, we will still head for Boston in the morning. Not having those papers makes things more difficult, but we've been in worse situations. We'll get your brother back."

"I thank you for your concern over my brother, and I have no doubts you will succeed in saving him, but I have another request. I wish for you to save the villagers too."

Edward took a drink of some water as he considered what Dumaka requested. "I hope you realise the difficulty of what you are asking?"

"Yes, but I want you to understand what is happening to our people in America. Nassir, and others who were able to make their way home, have told us the horrors. We have dealt with slavery throughout all of history, but at least here we had some chance of reward for our families. In America, death is preferable to how our people are being treated. My brother helped you to be free, and according to him this is something close to your heart. If you truly are a vessel for freedom, then you cannot stand by as my people die for nothing."

"All I can say is I will try. If the risk is too great for my men..."

"I understand. That you will try is enough for me."

Edward turned to his crewmen gathered around the fire, all the senior officers of the *Freedom*, and Christina. "So we are all in agreement then? We leave for Boston tomorrow, and try to save Nassir and the villagers?"

"Agreed," the crew replied.

Their course was set, and soon the fox-hunt for the elusive Daniel Richardson would end.

20. BONDS IN BOSTON

The trip to Boston would take over two months, so the crew stocked up as much as possible in Calabar before leaving. The people in Calabar were generous in their patronage and provided all they could in the hopes Edward and his crew would be able to bring back their family.

Along the way the crew continued training with Anne and William. The new members *Freedom* had gained from Bodden Town were becoming better at working as a team in battle and out. The crew functioned more as a team, making up for each other's weaknesses and aiding in their strengths.

Jack also participated in the training, having an adeptness in fist fighting and fencing. Anne practiced her eastern fighting art with him to hone his hand-to-hand combat, and, as Alexandre was the best fencer, he helped Jack fence. At first Alexandre lamented Jack's lack of skill, but Jack learned quickly and impressed the Frenchman.

Christina and her pet wolf were nigh on inseparable since their fight in the woods of Mexico. Christina trained Tala some commands in French to assist aboard the ship and in fights as well. The only two who could issue Tala orders were Christina and Edward. If anyone else commanded Tala, she merely gawked at them.

Edward and Christina grew closer as well. They continued their training and created some impressive moves. With Edward's strength he was able to swing Christina around by the hands, allowing them to attack while being surrounded, and at the end Edward vaulted her feet-first at the enemy.

"You two are quite the pair," Anne said as she walked up to the poop deck where Edward was.

Edward scratched his chin through the beard. "You mean Christina?" Anne nodded. "Yes, she and I work well together," Edward pulled Anne in close, gazing deep into her green eyes, "but I think we work better." Edward kissed Anne passionately, and she gladly accepted.

Anne patted Edward on the chest. "I want to talk to you about something."

Edward leaned on the railing of the poop deck, allowing him to overlook the whole of the ship. "I am listening."

"What do you plan to do in Boston?" Anne asked, joining him on the railing.

"I haven't decided. I haven't been to Boston, so I don't know how best to secure Nassir and the villagers, let alone the key."

"Well, doing nothing and letting someone else assess the situation would be a prudent first step."

Edward cocked his brow. "Why would I do that?"

"As I am sure you are aware, England is at war, my mother's war, and the American colonies are at the forefront of the conflict. Boston is an English territory." Anne paused for a moment.

Edward picked up on what Anne was saying, grasping where she was headed. "And so, information on our escape would be popular news. What about the ship itself, wouldn't the *Freedom* be well known as well?"

"There are many ships, and *Freedom* is a common name, I don't believe we have to worry about us being ousted," Anne speculated while she patted the railing.

Edward ran his fingers through Anne's curly red hair. "So I won't be able to leave the ship, but what about you?"

Anne sighed and leaned on Edward's chest. "I resemble my mother, so I too will be confined to the ship."

"We'll have each other to keep company, so I'm not complaining." Edward kissed the back of Anne's head. "But I suppose William will be here too."

Anne turned around and stretched out along the railing, laying her head in Edward's lap. She played with his beard. "I could always send William on some errand so we can be alone." Anne smirked.

Edward laughed. "You're so devious, I love it." He leaned down and kissed her once more. Edward noticed Henry on the quarterdeck, talking with Herbert. "Oh, Henry! We need to discuss something."

Henry strolled up to the poop deck. "Yes?" he inquired.

"I'll need you to act as my proxy in Boston. Apparently, Boston is British territory, which doesn't allow Anne or me to step ashore for fear of being noticed. Isn't it nice to have people in the crew that know about these things?" Edward asked with a smile.

Henry ignored the question. "So you'll need me to find Daniel Richardson for you?"

"Yes, when you find Richardson we'll need to do an assessment of the best course of action to retrieve the key and free Nassir and the villagers. If you present the letter he left, you'll no doubt be let into his home, and while inside you can see what kind of security he has."

"Sounds simple enough. I can pose as someone who wishes to buy the key."

"Something tells me he won't part with the key easily, judging from the trouble he went through, but that's the best option at the moment."

"Might I interject?" a voice asked from behind.

Edward noticed Alexandre listening to the conversation. Alexandre sauntered forward to the three of them. Back hunched, eyes dark, and appearance dishevelled as usual, he presented the air of one too busy for sleep or personal hygiene, but the glint in his eyes bespoke his greater faculties of the mind. "I wish to join this *expédition*."

"Not that I'm saying no, but why?"

Alexandre shrugged his shoulders while shaking his head like the answer was obvious. "You need someone who is capable of seeing things the ordinary cannot. I am the only one *compétent*."

"Are you saying Henry isn't qualified for this?"

"*Non*, I am saying lesser minds will miss the big picture. Anne and William are not fit to leave, so I am forced to step in."

Henry glared at Alexandre. "I can understand you being smarter, but your arrogance is groundless. I'm up to the task."

"*Mon ami*, arrogance has nothing to do with this. I possess a dexterity of mind greater than others, this is fact. If you are still in doubt of this even after my *pouvoirs de déduction* have been tested thus far, then we will play a game: we will see who is able to extrapolate the most useful information from Richardson."

"You're on!" Henry said, extending his hand to shake on the deal, which Alexandre accepted.

"This will be interesting," Edward whispered to Anne.

"Mmm, but I have a funny feeling Alexandre might have been trying to bait Henry for some reason."

Edward stroked his beard. "Seeing how this plays out will be fun."

When the *Freedom* sailed into the port of Boston, the crew expected to see a few ships, but the harbour was filled with fifty or more ships of all shapes and sizes. More than a few of those ships were outfitted for battle and some were even the same size as the *Freedom*.

As the *Freedom* navigated the few small islands in the crescent-shaped port, they passed by many ships docking and leaving Boston. The noise from the travellers rose in the spaces between the land and sea. Colourful sailors and merchants travelled to and fro across the decks of the full-sailed ships.

The noonday sun, the sea air, and the smell of nature from the land could not calm Edward's mind from this sight. He believed a raid could be a fall-back plan if they had issues rescuing the villagers from Richardson's grasp, but the amount of military ships was insurmountable for the *Freedom*. Edward held little hope they would be able to achieve the goal of even saving Nassir.

We must play our cards right if we are to secure the key and Nassir.

Edward and Anne descended below deck before the ship was docked. Edward told the crew to act as if Henry were the captain for the duration of their stay.

Henry and Alexandre, dressed in more elegant clothes than usual, left the ship immediately after docking. Henry paid the harbour master and set out to find Daniel Richardson. Richardson was a famous Bostonian, so he wasn't hard to find.

"Old Richardson lives on the west end of town. Head west and ye can't miss 'is cotton fields," a local businessman suggested.

Henry and Alexandre took a ride in a coach to Richardson's residence. The dirt road was bumpy, but straightforward. "So, Henry, have you pondered on our game? How will you compete with my genius?"

"Worry about yourself," Henry barked, pulling at the decorative silk bow tying his fine brown hair in a ponytail.

"I am not worried," Alexandre said with a hollow smile, slapping Henry's hands away from the bow.

Henry glowered at Alexandre. "You should be. One of our crewmates' lives is at stake."

Alexandre feigned shock and placed his hand over his chest. "*Mon dieu*! You do not think I care?"

"Hard to tell with you, sometimes."

"I very much care. You are all of you so… interesting. Without you for amusement whatever would I do?"

Henry rolled his eyes and folded his arms. "Of course. Wouldn't want the good doctor to die of boredom."

Alexandre grinned. "I also recall you did not approve of a *négre* aboard the ship, so are you trying to act holier than thou, or have you had a change of heart?"

Henry's mouth opened in shock by Alexandre's clairvoyance at knowing exactly how to rattle someone. Henry knew he couldn't lie to Alexandre to save face. "I was raised differently from Edward. Negros aren't my favourite company, but Nassir is part of the family. He's different."

"And the villagers?"

"They aren't my concern. Edward can try to figure out how to save them if he wants, but that already appears impossible."

Alexandre laughed. "Yes, well, *le Capitaine* delights in making the impossible possible."

"You have a point," Henry agreed.

"So, while on the subject of making the impossible possible, how do you plan on convincing our *marque* to part with the key?"

Henry cocked his brow. "You're letting me do the talking?" Alexandre answered with a smile and a nod, and Henry sighed. "I suppose I'll play it straight. Tell him it's needed for our ship and see what he's willing to take for it."

Alexandre appeared bored. "Are you sure it is wise to tell him the truth?"

"I don't see any other way of going about it. He knows the key has some story behind it. Whatever we tell him, there's no way we can downplay its importance. The only thing we can do is remove the key's importance for him."

Henry's last comment seemed to pique Alexandre's interest. "And how does telling him the truth remove the importance of the key?"

Henry couldn't help but grin a bit at evoking more than a passing interest from Alexandre. "Assuming he still has the key, he's no doubt been wondering for years what the key was for. In the letter he left he mentioned something about a hunt, and you said he might be of southern descent. So, he's a hunter. Not that much of a stretch." Alexandre nodded. "So, he's been hunting passively, or actively, for the lock that the key belongs to. After so many years, it's not about the key anymore, it's about the door, about the hunt. If we tell him exactly what the key is for, then the hunt is over, and in the most disappointing way possible. I'm also not the best liar, so we'll be more convincing if he can't tell we're lying."

"Remove the prey, and the hunter is left with no more use for the gun," Alexandre posed.

"Exactly. At least, that's the hope. If we can't get the key or Nassir back from Richardson then we'll have to rely on Edward to get everything."

Alexandre chuckled. "You know, perhaps you are not as dull as I first thought."

"Thank you, I think."

Alexandre and Henry finished their exchange a moment before the coach lurched to a stop in front of a white mansion.

The coachman jumped down and opened the door to help Henry and Alexandre down. Henry paid the man as Alexandre surveyed the property.

To the left and right of the mansion a large field of cotton was primed for harvest. In the field, black slaves by the dozens picked cotton from the small plants in the hot sun. The back-breaking work was made worse by the many guards with whips to punish slackers, or to flex muscle. For every five slaves one guard walked up and down the field.

The mansion itself was two storeys, but, while impressive, rather plain. Each window was either shuttered with black wood panels or covered with lace drapes, making it difficult to see inside.

Some of the slaves were entering and leaving an annex building on the right side of the mansion.

More muscle were stationed at the double doors at the front entrance. When Henry and Alexandre approached, the guards stepped forward. "What business do you have here?" one of them asked, then he spat chewing tobacco onto the ground.

"Is this the residence of Daniel Richardson?" Henry asked.

"Yes, and what brings you to Mr Richardson's residence?"

Henry took out the letter Richardson left. "If you take this to your boss, he will understand."

One of the guards took the letter, and the two glanced at each other and shrugged. "Wait here," the first said, then he entered the building.

Henry scanned the field, taking a rough count of the people there. "There are about twenty guards here," Henry whispered.

"Sixteen, to be exact."

"The fields are low, which would make it hard to sneak in or out without being seen even at night."

"One small group would be best. Leaving with so many *esclaves* is a problem. We also have the problem of taking the villagers through town."

"This doesn't appear good."

"*Non*, it does not."

"Mr Richardson will see you now." The guard who went inside had reappeared without the letter. "I will take you to him."

Henry and Alexandre followed the man into the house. Inside, several guards and more slaves worked. In the centre of the main room, a large set of stairs went up and off to the left and right to the second floor. One of the servants passed through a door to the side of the stairs allowing Alexandre to see into the kitchen where slaves were working at preparing food. In the kitchen, he could see a door leading to the slaves' quarters.

The guard led them up the stairs to the second floor. On the far end, a lavish love seat and chairs were set in front of a fireplace. Along the sides, more closed doors led to various rooms.

The guard opened the first door to the right of the fireplace and beckoned Henry and Alexandre to enter. After the two entered, the guard closed the door.

The room they entered was a large and spacious study with tall bookshelves and ornamental relics, possibly from some ancient tomb. A mediaeval set of plate mail, swords, an Egyptian urn, a stone bird, and several animal heads plastered the walls like trophies. The fireplace from the previous room was mirrored into the study, with a small table holding expensive drinks between two high-backed chairs. At the back was a desk with several chairs in front and one behind. Large windows on the back wall allowed light in and provided a stunning view of the road leading up to the mansion. In the centre of the wall, above the desk and chairs, a key hung in a picture frame.

"Come on in and sit down, gentlemen. We have much to discuss," Daniel Richardson said, standing at the desk. His accent was a southern drawl, not native to Boston.

Henry and Alexandre sat down in the chairs offered. Richardson was still eyeing the letter as he sat down in his seat, a soft metallic click sounding under the desk when he moved his feet.

Richardson was an older man with salt-and-pepper hair slicked back. He had a greying beard on his full face, and the plump aspect of a man used to wealth and having others do the hard work for him. He was wearing a black and red suit with his coat draped over the back of the chair because of the heat.

Henry could smell cigar and wood ash in the air, as well as warm alcohol. The smell of fur and raw poultry also came from the many animal heads adorning the walls.

"Would any of you fine gents care for a drink. Ah have some fine whiskey if ya'll 'er interested." Henry and Alexandre both declined. Richardson peered at the letter once more with a smile. "Ah never thought ah would see this again, boy. Been a few years since ah stumbled across that island. Took some doin' to reach the top, and what do ah get for the trouble? A key." Richardson laughed. "Boy, at first ah was mighty angry, but curiosity has a way of increasin' over time. Ah never was able to find out what the key was fer, nor who left it there. Ah am sure interested if you fellers have any information you can provide."

Henry took the lead. "I believe our story may be rather disappointing to you. I was sold a ship by a magnanimous trickster who left clues as to where to find the keys for specific sections of the ship. The island you found was built specifically for his game, and the key is the next one in the line. Without the key, I have a fraction of a ship."

Richardson laughed heartily. "How positively fascinating, to find intrepid adventurers such as myself. My boy, you remind me of myself in my youth."

Henry glanced at Alexandre awkwardly. "Yes, well, as you can see we need the key so we can continue with our journey. We are willing to pay you for your troubles."

Richardson raised his hand. "I am sorry, my boy, but I simply cannot part with the key. The years have made me attached inexplicably and inexorably to the key. I will, however, purchase your ship from you for a more than generous price and you can be assured she will be in good hands."

Henry's mouth hung open. "I'm sorry, but we are in similar sorts. I cannot part with the ship. We have been at this for years now, and the ship means so much more to the whole crew, not just myself."

Richardson stopped smiling. He didn't seem the type used to being denied something. "Then, no amount of money will change your mind?"

"No. I ask you the same."

"No," Richardson replied with a sigh. "Such a disappointment. Well, gentlemen, if you'll excuse me, I have other business I must attend to."

Alexandre finally took the helm. "There is another *afaire* which you may be more amicable towards. A slave named Nassir may be in your possession, or previously has been, who is actually a free man and our crewmate. We are searching for him to bring him back into our fold."

Richardson laughed. "Your French friend is rather funny. I do have a slave with a savage name of Nassir, but all my slaves are slaves, and as such they cannot be free men. You realise the flaw in your logic?"

"We are not lying," Henry replied, growing more frustrated.

"Produce his papers of freedom and I will have no choice but to comply. No papers, no nigger."

"How much to part with him?"

Richardson smirked, knowing he held all the cards. "I refuse. My slaves are all so precious to me. I cannot spare a single one."

Alexandre stood. "Expect a summons to a court of law soon. We will have our crewmate back one way or another."

"I shall await with anticipation."

Alexandre left the mansion with Henry following closely behind, albeit with a misstep due to confusion. Henry and Alexandre entered the coach and headed back to the ship.

"What was that?" Henry asked.

"That will buy us time to steal the key and formulate a proper plan to save Nassir and the *villageois*."

"How do you expect to prove Nassir's freedom without papers?"

"Depending on certain factors, we may be able to win, but it is a ploy. The rest is up to *le Capitaine* and what he wants to do."

Henry sighed. "I hope you know what you're doing."

"Always," Alexandre replied.

21. BAIT & TRAP

"So he lives on the outskirts of town in the middle of a field, and has over twenty guards?" Edward asked. Henry and Alexandre nodded. "How will we free them?" Edward questioned, frustrated.

"You're giving up?" Anne asked, anger seeping through.

"I don't see any way we can save Nassir and all those villagers. If we cause any trouble, there are a multitude of warships here which can best us. We can't kill the guards without a protracted battle, and before the crew arrives we'll be found out by locals because of the numbers."

"But there must be a way," Christina pleaded. "What if we spread out, small groups of people all heading to the mansion, then we strike at once?"

Edward shook his head, running his hand through his wavy black hair. "No, Boston has a local garrison, not an unorganised militia. We would be outed well before we reached the edge of the city. Barring that, we wouldn't be able to escape for the same reason."

"Then what do you suggest?" Anne asked.

Edward considered all the eyes on him. The senior officers were staring at him, expecting an epiphany of a brilliant plan from Edward like in the past. Edward sighed. "I'm sorry, I don't know what we can do. For now, I will sneak into Richardson's mansion and spirit the key away. Then we can confer with Nassir if he has any ideas on how to escape with his people. Sam, can I count on your help with this?"

Sam nodded. "Aye Capt'n."

"Henry, you mentioned the best way to enter was through the slave quarters, and the key was in a room on the second floor."

Henry nodded. "Yes, the key is inside a picture frame on the wall. He keeps a lot of trophies in the room, and the key is one of his accomplishments."

Alexandre laughed, drawing all eyes to him. "Something to share Alexandre?" Edward asked.

"Oh, nothing of importance. Just, if you steal that key you will be taking a *faux*."

A foe…? Ah, Fake. "The key is a fake?"

"He has a lockbox under his desk with the real key inside."

Henry's jaw dropped once more. "How do you know?"

"He shuffled in his seat and tapped his foot against something metal. The sound was faint, but easy to hear if you were paying attention."

Henry folded his arms. "So what makes you think the key is in the lockbox? You weren't able to see inside."

"You said yourself, the man has *trophées* of his accomplishments. Do you think finding the key was an accomplishment? He was never able to find what lock the key was for. *Non*, the picture frame is not a *trophée*, it is a reminder."

Edward shrugged. "A nice theory, but I don't think the game is won yet. We'll test your theory later. We take both. Alexandre, please draw us a floor plan of the mansion so we can work out a plan to sneak inside. When is the court battle to start?"

"Tomorrow. Richardson is a prominent businessman, so the magistrate is speeding things along for him," Henry responded.

Edward rubbed his face in equal parts frustration and exhaustion. "Well, I guess we also have to deal with preferential treatment. Excellent."

Anne held Edward's hand in support. "But what about the villagers?"

"I don't know, I can only focus on one thing at a time. We need to trick Richardson somehow, but I don't know how. I will think of something in time."

The crew left Edward alone, but he wasn't able to formulate a plan. Alexandre was cryptic as usual, and more interested in seeing what Edward could create rather than suggesting a plan. *Damn Frenchman probably doesn't know any way we can save everyone anyway.*

The next day, Alexandre and Henry both went to the office of the local magistrate who was to see them and Richardson together. Richardson brought Nassir along with him. The office itself was a medium-sized room with small bookshelves and a desk. The four sat in chairs in front of the magistrate's desk.

The portly magistrate wore an expensive coat and a powdered wig atop his head in the English style. "Make your claim, gentlemen," he demanded coldly. The smell of alcohol wafted from his breath.

"This man, Nassir, has been wrongfully taken into slavery. He has already served once before and was freed," Alexandre stated.

"Produce his papers of freedom and let this be done then."

Alexandre glanced at Henry and then Nassir. "We can produce them, but we have not had occasion to discuss their whereabouts with Nassir."

The magistrate sighed. "Then go into the next room and discuss. And be quick about it."

Alexandre, Henry, and Nassir rose and entered the room to the right of the magistrate's office.

"I must say, friends, I did not expect to see you today. Thank you for trying to help me," Nassir said in his thick accent.

"You're our family, there's no way we wouldn't come for you. Edward wishes he could be here, but it's safer for us all if he's not."

"I understand."

"Focus, *messieurs*. Nassir, your brother believes your proof of freedom was burned in the attack on your village. Please tell us this is not so."

"My papers were on my person… until Richardson destroyed them."

"Excellent. Now what?" Henry lamented.

"This is simple, we make a forgery. Do you remember the name of the man who freed you?" Alexandre asked.

"David Cooper was the issuer of the papers."

Alexandre pulled out a piece of paper and pencil. "Do you remember the papers enough to provide his signature?"

Nassir took the paper and pencil in hand. "I stared at those papers every night for five years after I was freed. I can provide the entire wording."

Richardson and the magistrate were laughing and hitting it off. Henry and Alexandre eyed each other with worried expressions.

"We do not have the time, the signature will do. Alexandre will finish the rest," Henry said.

Once Nassir finished the signature, Alexandre pocketed the paper. "What about my people?" Nassir asked.

"We are focusing on trying to free you, and Edward is working on a plan to free the villagers, but you must understand the difficulty," Henry replied.

"I will trust in him then."

Henry and Alexandre both nodded to Nassir and they returned to the other room. "We know where the papers are and will retrieve them for you post haste," Henry told the magistrate.

"Yes, yes. We will reconvene tomorrow." The magistrate and Richardson each poured a glass of brandy and continued talking with each other as if they were the only ones in the room.

Henry and Alexandre glanced at Nassir one last time, as he had to stay with his master. Despair was written on his face, but his eyes held a glint of hope.

"Do you think the forgery will work?" Henry asked in a whisper outside the magistrate's office.

"It is not a question of whether it will or will not, but whether the magistrate will let it work. I fear the man may be *corrompu*. Daniel and the magistrate seem to be *amis*. Perhaps his rise to his current position was not done entirely honestly."

"So, what we do will not help?"

"*Non*, I did not say that. This is merely to serve as a distraction from the real plan. *Le Capitaine* will provide the means for all to escape."

"Assuming he's up to the task."

"You have *doutes*?"

"Let's just say my faith in Edward has been shaky of late."

Alexandre nodded. "Yes, I have noticed. He will come through in the end. He always does."

"What makes you so sure?"

Henry saw something rare: a light deep in Alexandre's normally dull eyes. "I'm not."

In the dead silence of night, two figures stalked through the town of Boston and the forest of chestnut trees on the outskirts. They moved silently, but with purpose. Their destination was a cotton plantation owned by a certain Daniel Richardson.

Edward and Sam ran through the woods and travelled light, carrying no weapons aside from knives and a blow gun with darts provided by Alexandre. The moon was full and shining brightly through the slender leaves above them. The wind was cool and breezy so close to the coast, and brought the smell of fresh chestnuts and grass to their nostrils.

As the two reached the western edge of the forest they slowed down to catch their breath and move with more stealth. Edward and Sam both hid behind the trees as they moved forward, seeing if the coast was clear and then motioning to the other to move forward. When they finally reached the edge they ducked down and hid behind a large tree together.

In front of them they could see the large mansion with adjoining quarters for the slaves along with the large cotton field surrounding the building.

Edward examined the location. "This is the mansion, exactly as described."

Edward could see guards with lanterns walking around the property, though none were close to the forest. The guards appeared more vigilant than they normally would be, which did not bode well in Edward's mind. *Henry and Alexandre must have spooked him.*

"So are we gonna kill these wankers or what?" Sam whispered.

"No, we'll use these darts Alexandre provided. According to him they will knock someone out and leave them with particularly bad aches in the morning."

"Blimey. How does the Frenchman create these things?"

"Alexandre said he had an epiphany when thinking about the gas the surgeon in Winchester used. The gas reminded him of a plant some natives used to help them sleep on one of his treks around the world. He kept some with him and dried the leaves. Somehow he made this from the leaves."

Sam shook his head. "What about when they fall? And what about the other guards?" Sam asked as he motioned to the three on patrol.

"Sneak up and catch them as they fall. I'll attack the two on the left, you attack the one on the right."

Edward and Sam went their separate ways after dividing the darts. Edward moved to the left to a row of the cotton which led behind one of the guards. The guard was standing still and scanning the field with a lantern to aid him. Edward dropped to the ground and crawled into the field of cotton.

Edward crawled between bushes of cotton shrubs, trying to make as little noise as possible. The guard was staring in Sam's direction. Edward crawled forward slowly, inching closer and closer. The guard turned around and walked towards Edward who moved closer to the shrubs and lay motionless.

The smell of the cotton mixed with alcohol as the guard approached. Edward turned his head to watch the approach of the patrolling man. His nose passed over a cotton bulb. Edward's nose itched and he felt an urge to sneeze. The guard was nearly on top of Edward. He took out his blowdart and shot the man with a dart in the neck. Before the guard recognised what was happening, he fell. Edward caught him and let him fall gently to the ground as he let out a sneeze.

The other guards turned to the noise. Edward picked up the lantern and waved. The guards returned to their lookout. Edward allowed himself to breathe again as he wiped his nose.

He moved forward, lantern in hand. The two guards didn't notice anything wrong. Edward moved towards his second target closest to the slaves' quarters. The slightest noise came from the right. Edward and the guard's eyes flashed over, and the man waved back.

Sam must have made his move.

Edward stalked over to finish the trifecta so they could move on. When Edward advanced, the guard waved to him. Edward lowered his lantern so his face was not illuminated.

"See anything, Gary? I don't see nothin' over here. I think the boss is jus' spooked."

Edward shot a dart at the man's neck. The man grunted and his hand moved to the dart. He pulled out the dart and had enough time to focus on the needle before he fell. Edward ran over and caught him so he could let him fall gently to the ground without another sound.

Sam rushed to Edward. Edward had another dart ready just in case. "Sam?"

"It be me Capt'n," Sam whispered back. "Ready to head in?"

"Yeah, let's move."

Before the two could move any closer to the slave quarters, the door opened and another guard emerged with a lantern in hand. Edward and Sam blew out their lanterns and ducked to the ground. The guard peered left and right, and he noticed something was off.

In the darkness, the guard could see the third lantern, but not Edward and Sam. Edward shot a dart, but missed and hit the building. Sam tried his shot, but the guard bent over and the dart flew over his head. The guard picked up the dart Edward shot.

"Damn it, I'm out of darts," Edward said softly.

"I be out too. I used two on the first bloke."

"What do we do?" Edward asked, watching the guard examine the dart.

"I don't know, we wouldn't be havin' this discussion if ye were a better shot."

"Me, a better shot? You're the one who missed twice, I only missed this one."

Thump.

Edward and Sam turned in the direction of the noise and noticed the guard passed out. Upon examination, they noticed that the guard had pricked his finger on the tip of the dart, thus injecting himself with the concoction and knocking himself out.

"What a fool," Edward laughed.

The guards at the front entrance of the mansion heard the noise. "Is everything alright?" one of them questioned.

Edward and Sam both jumped at the voices. "Uhh, Gary's been drinking again," Edward replied.

The guard at the front entrance sighed. "Put him inside, we'll tell the boss in the morning."

"Right," Edward replied.

The guards at the front went back to watching the road. Edward picked up the two unused darts, then he and Sam picked up the man who just fell. They carried the body inside the slave quarters.

The inside was a horrid sight to behold. The annex building next to the mansion was a quarter of the size and no inch of the space was wasted on comfort. Wooden cots lined the walls, with a thin strip down the middle for walking. The cots were stacked on top of each other with barely any space to breathe between them.

Some of the slaves' eyes were on them, but they didn't move for fear they would be punished. The slaves probably didn't know the

The Voyages of Queen Anne's Revenge Collection One

ones before them were not guards.

Edward scanned the annex building, but he could see no guards. "Nassir?" Edward whispered. "Nassir?" he asked a little louder as he moved further into the room.

"Edward?" a voice replied.

A man descended from a cot near the middle of the room. Others paid more attention at the odd display.

"Edward, what are you doing here?" Nassir questioned as he walked over to Edward and Sam.

"We have several reasons, but firstly: I am glad to see you are alright. I cannot imagine how Richardson is treating you."

"I have been through this before, but some of my villagers are children, and they are not coping as well."

"Do you have any ideas for how to reach the shore without raising alarm?"

Nassir shook his head. "I know not of any way without alerting anyone. Trust me, I have been thinking, but I am a simple carpenter, not a trickster."

Edward leaned in close to Nassir and whispered, "Then join us and we can at least save you, then we can think of a way to save your villagers after."

Nassir shook his head. "No, I will not leave without my villagers. I leave with them, or not at all."

Edward placed his hand on Nassir's shoulder. "I had a feeling you would say that. I promise you, I will find a way."

"Capt'n, we'd best be leavin," Sam said.

"Right." Edward glanced over his shoulder. "The other reason we arrived was to retrieve the key for the ship."

"The slaver has a key to the *Freedom*?" Nassir asked.

"Yes, we travelled to the location the clue pointed us to, but the puzzles were solved and we found a note instead of a key. The note was signed Daniel Richardson. Once we procure the key, we will return to the ship and invent a plan to save you." Edward glanced at the near hundred watching him. "All of you."

Nassir hugged Edward. "I believe in your words."

Edward nodded and held Nassir's gaze for a moment before he passed through the door joining the annex building to the mansion. Nassir and the villagers watched as Edward and Sam crept into the mansion. Their hope was leaving, but Nassir knew they would return, and they would all leave as one.

Edward walked through the empty kitchen and pulled out the mock blueprint Alexandre provided. The picture showed a rough detail of where Edward was and where they should go. The kitchen had one exit to the left leading to the dining hall, and another to the right leading to the entrance room. Edward opened the swinging

515

door on the right to peer inside.

Two guards were conversing on the side Edward would walk into, but no others from what he could see. He slowly pulled the swinging door back to a point of rest.

"Take one dart, head through the dining hall, and we'll hit both of the guards at the same time."

Sam nodded and took one of the darts. He went through the door to the dining hall after checking for guards. Edward peered through the swinging door. When he saw Sam at the other door, they both nodded and pulled out their blowguns. They fired the darts at the same time, hitting both of the guards.

The guard Sam shot fell to the ground after a few seconds, but the other was still standing. First, he pulled out the dart, inspected it, and then tried to wake his friend.

Edward's and Sam's shock was written on their faces, and each rushed out to correct the mistake. The guard noticed Sam approaching him, then opened his mouth to yell. Edward ran and clapped a hand over the guard's mouth. The guard struggled and writhed against Edward, but couldn't free himself. Sam punched the man hard in the stomach, then again in the temple, knocking him out.

Edward lowered the guard to the ground. Sam carried a grim expression. "We only have a few minutes before he wakes up," Edward whispered.

"What happened to the dart?" Sam asked.

"I must have picked up the one the other man pricked himself on."

"No use cryin' now. We 'ave to move."

Edward and Sam moved quickly and quietly up the stairs to the second floor. They kept an eye on the corners for any movements in the dark of the upper part of the mansion, but the hallway was quiet and empty.

Edward went to the fireplace and opened the door to the right. He peered through the slit, and saw an empty room. Edward and Sam entered, shut the door, and rushed straight to the desk at the back.

Moonlight from the windows, and the eyes of dead animal heads following their movement, lent an eerie atmosphere to the empty room.

Edward's eyes moved across the trophies, and settled on the key above the desk. He moved a chair behind the desk to stand on top of, and took the key down.

"Isn't that the fake?" Sam asked.

"We don't know yet. We shouldn't make assumptions. Alexandre could easily be wrong about the whole thing." Edward opened the picture frame and pocketed the key. "Take the lockbox," Edward said as he set the picture frame back on the wall.

Sam bent under the table and on the left side, hidden under the legs, was a small iron box with a slot on the front meant for a key. Sam set the iron box on the top of the table.

"Can you pick the lock?"

Sam laughed. "Can you pick a lock, he says? Who do ye think I am mate?" Sam pulled out some tools from his pockets and showed them to Edward.

"Well, get to it. I'd rather not have to take the whole box with us if we don't have to."

Sam went to work on the lock with Edward watching intently over his shoulder. Edward was on edge, and he was sweating from the pressure. The tiny sounds of the clinking metal on metal sounded like gunshots. Sam perspired in concentration, the stress of the situation hitting him as well.

After a tense few minutes, Sam turned the metal pick and the lock clicked. The top of the lock box popped ajar. Edward and Sam both smiled at the sight.

"I'm afraid you won't find what you gentlemen are searching for in that trinket."

At the entrance stood Daniel Richardson, portly with salt-and-pepper hair, just as described by Henry. He held a musket in his hands as steadily as any trained soldier.

Twelve guards filed into the room and pointed muskets and pistols at Edward and Sam.

"The key in the picture frame is a forgery, and there is nothing in the lockbox aside from money and deeds to several foreign estates." Daniel pulled out a slender key on a chain around his neck. "This is the real key. I'm in the habit of trying to open any strange locks I find. Who would believe the owners of the lock would fall into my lap as a gazelle into the lion's maw? One way or another, your ship is mine."

"Over my dead body."

"That can be arranged." Daniel raised the musket once more.

Edward grabbed the lockbox and threw it at the window. Richardson and the guards let loose their guns on Edward and Sam as the lockbox crashed through the pane, shattering the glass. Bullets flew past them as Edward and Sam jumped out the window and fell to the ground below. The two rolled as they hit the ground, and jumped up to run, but were stopped in their tracks.

In front of them were the magistrate's men with weapons ready to fire.

Edward and Sam surrendered. They were shackled and thrown into a carriage to be taken to the local jail.

22. TRICK & SWITCH

Edward and Sam sat on the floor of a small cell, thick wooden walls and iron bars keeping them caged. On the back side of the cell a window with iron bars let air inside. Inside with them were a few local toughs and a drunken old man.

Edward and Sam were both incarcerated until they could have a meeting with the local magistrate about sentencing. Luckily the locals didn't know who Edward was so he was only being tried for attempted theft, but even theft could carry the death sentence depending on the magistrate and the load on the jails.

Overcrowding isn't a problem here, but the magistrate is. If I could get word to the crew...

"So, how's it feel ta be back in prison, Capt'n?" Sam asked with his trademark smirk.

"Terrible," Edward replied. He leaned over to Sam. "We need to find a way out of here."

"Way I sees it, a jail such as this has one weakness: the guard. When they open the door to let someone out, we rush the guard and escape."

"Sounds simple enough. I overheard those two will be let out today, so we can ask them for help." Edward pointed to the two local ruffians.

"Work yer magic, Capt'n," Sam said with a laugh.

Edward sat down beside the two thugs. "We want to escape, what say you help us out?"

The two men laughed. "And why should we help you?"

"Money. If you help us we will reward you with money and take you wherever you wish."

The other man spoke up. "How much money are we talking about?"

"One hundred pounds split between the both of you," Edward replied confidently.

The two men smiled and one offered his hand. "Give each of us one hundred and you have a deal."

Edward sealed the deal with a shake, then told the short version of the plan. They would wait until the two men were let out, then the four of them would jump the guard and run. After sealing the deal, Edward went back over to Sam. The co-conspirators whispered afterwards, laughing and deciding what they would do with the money.

"I suppose that went well?" Sam asked.

"Yes, money is an easy motivator," Edward replied.

After another half hour, the sound of clinking keys could be heard down the hallway between the cells. Two guards, one with the keys and the other with a musket, approached the cell Edward and Sam were in.

"Alright Greg, Jim, time ta go, you worthless sacks of bullshit." The guard set the key in the lock and turned.

Edward, Sam, Greg, and Jim all tensed. The guard swung the door open. "Now!" Edward yelled as he ran to the open gate. The guard's eyes widened and he grabbed the iron bars to close the gate.

Edward balled his fist and was about to punch the first guard when he was sent to the floor suddenly and violently. Greg and Jim attacked Edward and Sam, allowing the guard enough time to close and lock the gate. Once Edward and Sam were subdued, more guards were brought in.

"Why?" Edward asked Greg as the man pinned him down.

"You think we're stupid? You were using us. There ain't no money, and you ain't no captain. Besides, this'll put us in good with the magistrate. No hard feelings?"

Edward and Sam tried to struggle against the men, but neither was able to escape.

The extra guards entered the cell and aimed muskets at Edward and Sam. "Don't you move unless you want to be shot!" the guard with the keys shouted. Greg and Jim moved away from Edward and Sam and then left with the guards through the gate. The gate was locked and the guards left through the hallway.

Sam stood and rubbed his neck where Jim had pinned him. "Well, wonderful."

Edward rose up and moved his arm around to bring the feeling back. "Now what?"

"Don' look at me. I'm not the one with the plans."

Neither am I, apparently.

Edward and Sam sat in silence as the day passed by. Eventually the drunken old man was also let out, this time with five guards pointing muskets at Edward and Sam while they took him out. Edward didn't try anything, and Sam wouldn't if Edward didn't. A guard told them the magistrate would see them tomorrow, and they were given mouldy bread with thin soup to eat.

Later that night, Edward and Sam were trying to sleep on the hard wooden floor when Edward heard a curious noise outside. He rose and peered out the gated window, but he couldn't see anything. He rested his ear to the edge and listened intently.

"Edward," a voice softly sounded in the dark.

Blackbeard's Ship

"Henry?" Edward asked into the darkness.

Henry appeared from the shadows. He was wearing a cloak and kept searching to and fro to make sure no one was around.

"What are you doing here?" Edward asked.

"We bought some time by giving fake *Freedom* papers to the magistrate. He's having them inspected for authenticity as we speak. We were also able to talk with Nassir, he's the one who told us you were captured."

"I'm sorry, Henry. Everything was going smoothly. Richardson is sharp, and I think we underestimated him. I don't know how we're going to get out of this one." Edward's eyes hit the floor, his disappointment in himself evident.

"Don't worry yourself. After seeing you captured, Nassir came up with a plan to save you and his villagers."

"Will his plan work?"

"Trust me, if we play our cards right, this one can't fail."

The next day, the *Freedom* was no longer in the harbour. The ship had left in the early hours of the morning. The crew were in a rush to leave, and headed south to an unknown destination.

Henry and Alexandre, however, remained. They entered the magistrate's office and stepped into pure chaos. People were running around, talking with locals and the authorities about something. Daniel Richardson was there, with Nassir at his side, talking with one of the officials about what happened.

Henry and Alexandre walked up to them. "What is this madness?" Alexandre asked.

One of the officials spoke up to answer. "The magistrate was kidnapped in the night, and, the Devil smiles, so was the mayor and the sheriff and some other officials."

Henry and Alexandre grinned. "Perhaps we can shed some *lumière*," Alexandre said as he handed a piece of paper to Daniel Richardson. Richardson opened and read the paper.

Richardson, if you are reading this, my crew of the Freedom have taken Boston officials as hostages. If you want to see them again, you will meet these demands: Myself, Edward Thatch, and Samuel Bellamy, will be released from prison and surrendered to the crew of the Freedom. Along with us, our crewmate Nassir, his villagers, and the key, you know which one, will be brought to exchange for the lives of these officials. Take all these to Gloucester in four days and the exchange will be made.

After Daniel was finished reading, he pulled the paper away with a flash of rage. "What is the meaning of this?" he asked, shaking the paper at Henry and Alexandre

"Was the paper not self-explanatory? Follow the instructions and your people will return safely," Henry said, then he and Alexandre turned to leave.

"What do you think you are doing, sirs?" one of the officials yelled.

"We are leaving. We will be watching from afar to make sure you follow through with our *demandes*." Alexandre waved goodbye to Nassir as they left. Daniel and the official were not armed and thus powerless to stop Henry and Alexandre. After leaving, they disappeared and were not found again.

Later that evening, a meeting was held with the remaining authorities over how to handle the situation.

"These pirates have our leaders in the palm of their hands. There should be no question we must give in to their demands," one man declared, with some in the meeting agreeing.

"Where is the justice? Doing this will let other criminals know they can make a mockery of our city," another refuted, with an equal amount of people siding with him.

"What of it? All pirates are caught eventually. This Edward Thatch is the infamous Blackbeard we've been hearing about. All we need to do is let our motherland know he is here and the Queen will send naval reinforcements. We can use this situation to our advantage."

Daniel Richardson was also a part of the meeting, being central to the demands. He slammed his fist on a desk. "Is no one taking a mind to my loss in this? They have a snare around my property alone and it is unacceptable any of you think I should transfer my slaves to this pirate!"

"You have an overabundance of plantations in many cities, Richardson. Your duty in this situation is to sacrifice for the greater good," the first man said. "And, might I remind you that several people whom helped you acquire said plantations are amongst those missing?"

The argument continued for over another hour with the participants in the meeting clearly split down the middle. Some were swayed back and forth, but they couldn't reach a consensus on what to do.

The doors to the meeting hall were opened and a newcomer barged in. "I believe I may be of some assistance."

"Who are you? This is a private meeting!" Richardson yelled.

"I am Captain William Wilkinson of Her Majesty's ship, the *Diamond*. I have been tracking the Captain of the *Freedom*, Blackbeard, to here." William stood in full captain's attire, clean-shaven, black of hair, chiselled body and straight posture.

"You are late, Captain. We have captured your man, Blackbeard, but his crew has taken the mayor, along with several other prominent Bostonites, hostage."

"Such a shame. What are their demands?"

"They want their captain and crewmates back, along with the slaves of Daniel Richardson." One of the men motioned to Richardson.

"Then the answer is simple: we will give in to their demands," William confirmed, his hands folded behind his back.

"What?" Richardson yelled. "Those are my slaves we're talking about. You can't order me to surrender my slaves."

One of the Boston officials spoke up. "We've been over this, Richardson. We are willing to compensate you for the slaves."

"And let those pirates just get away with this? That is base cowardice and I will not be a part of it."

William raised his hand before the argument could continue. "I did not say we would be relinquishing them. My plan is thus: We will act the part of cooperating with their demands, then at their desired meeting spot, my crew will attack in the *Diamond*. You will gain your slaves back, and we will capture Blackbeard and his crew to execute."

Richardson was more amicable, but still wary. "But how do you know you will be able to stop him?"

"I know because it is my job to know. Ensure everything is in order when the crew of the *Freedom* arrive for their spoils. If anything is out of place, they will know. I imagine some of their crew are watching to confirm your compliance?" William asked.

"Yes, they are," Richardson answered.

"This is a common tactic of theirs. If the pirates are spooked, then this will be all for naught. As such, I will pose as one of the crewmates aboard the slave ship along with half of my crew. We can buy some time to allow the *Diamond* to sail over by fighting Blackbeard's crew on the slave ship."

Richardson sighed. "Hold a moment now. Who are you truly? You arrive as if from thin air, claiming to be a Captain of a Royal Navy ship, and you are telling us to comply with these pirates demands. How do we know you are not part of the pirate crew as well? Where are your credentials?"

"Hmph," William scoffed. "I assumed, judging from your character, you would be able to measure who you were dealing with on sight. I guess I was wrong. Tomorrow night, join me on the *Diamond*, and I will show you my credentials." Captain William turned to leave, but turned back after a moment. "Please do keep yourself hidden. We do not want these scoundrels finding out I am here."

Richardson gritted his teeth in anger over the gall of this William. *He may be a Captain of the Royal Navy, but he has no right to issue orders in my town.*

Richardson used his skills as a hunter to stalk through the town the next night, making his way to the pier. He had noticed marines in their uniforms manning and cleaning the ship in the afternoon, but something felt fishy.

Richardson sneaked silently through the alleys of the buildings in Boston, doubling back often to ensure he wasn't being followed. The cold night brought the noise of animals, vagrants, and late night drunkards to his ears, but none followed him.

When Richardson reached the pier, he still maintained his vigilance as he passed by the sleeping ships with dropped anchors and solitary guards. When he approached the *Diamond*, the name painted in white on the side, the crew pointed muskets at him.

"Who goes there?" one of them asked.

"I am Daniel Richardson. I was asked to appear by your captain, William Wilkinson."

"At ease, men," William ordered, appearing behind them. The crew lowered their weapons at his behest. "Come aboard, sir. You are welcome, and our credentials await your presence."

Richardson raised his brow, but he didn't ask any questions. He walked up the gangplank to the deck of the ship and followed William to the stern cabin.

"You will have to forgive me for the secrecy, but what you see next must be kept with the utmost confidence. I must have your word."

"And you have my word. On with it, man."

"Please, remain courteous as well."

William opened the door and entered first. Richardson followed closely behind. A woman sat in a high-backed chair behind an oval table. She had red hair falling in curls and beautiful green eyes. She appeared young, but at the same time very mature.

"Your… Your Majesty?" Richardson exclaimed.

Richardson had seen Queen Anne once many years ago in England, before she was Queen, and this woman in front of him looked exactly as he remembered.

William knelt down, and after Richardson recovered from his shock he knelt as well. "Your Majesty, Daniel Richardson is here as I explained."

"You may rise, both of you."

Daniel Richardson rose and his gaze met the Queen's. Her eyes held a force deep within them which hit him deeper than any lion's fangs. Richardson had heard rumours that the Queen could cut with a glance, and now he believed them.

Anne rose from her chair, assisted by a guard at her side, and strode to the front of the table where Richardson stood. She placed her hand in front of Richardson, and he knelt down again to kiss it. "We are sorry for our appearance, but practicality often trumps fashion, especially in battle."

"You look magnificent, my Queen, and, I must say, quite youthful."

Anne laughed daintily, placing her hand over her mouth. "We see the hunter strikes swiftly and charmingly."

Richardson noticed a ring on the Queen's finger, not altogether an abnormality, but the ring itself was what caught his attention. That ring was meant for the heir apparent or presumptive of Britain.

"I must express my deepest apologies for your loss, my Queen. You must be grieving and yet have to deal with such trivialities after such tragedy. It is inspiring to see you in such good health despite the rumours."

There was a slight pause before the Queen spoke again. "Yes, well, we must always set personal matters behind us in times of war. Though difficult, we are recovering. As for those nasty rumours, you should know better than to listen to everything you hear. Now to business. You have doubts about our Captain Commander William, yes?"

Richardson flushed. "I must admit, my doubts feel a bit foolish now, but when posing a venture one must make all certainties when one's livelihood is at stake."

"The necessity is not lost on us. We trust this meeting has proven evident truths about our sincerity in the capture of this villain, Blackbeard?"

"I have no more doubts, but there is one small matter…" Richardson said hesitantly.

"And what might that be? Speak."

"The reward for Blackbeard's capture. As your men are capturing him with my assistance, will I be claiming some of the fortune?"

Anne laughed. "That trifle? Why of course, your collaboration will be met with compensation in full."

"May I keep his ship as well?" Richardson asked.

Anne's demeanour changed. "That is a bit too much. The ship is a frigate as we understand, and could be used for the war effort."

"Then what if I do not take the reward? The ship is important to me, as it relates to the key the pirates want from me."

Anne considered the proposition. "You may keep the ship in exchange for none of the bounty from Blackbeard's head."

"Most excellent. In two days' time I will load a ship with my slaves and your men can be the crew. Together we will capture this villain."

Captain William stepped forward. "Forgive me, your majesty." William bowed and faced Richardson. "As our business is concluded, I wish to remind you, Richardson, to bring the real key with you, as the attack will only begin when this ship catches up to yours. We may need to buy time by letting the pirates test the key on their ship, including the slaves and their crewmates. All must appear in order so we do not scare them away."

Richardson's eyes narrowed suspiciously. "How did you know the key I mentioned worked on Blackbeard's ship?"

William paused for a half-second. "Not a few moments ago you mentioned your desire to take the ship, and how the ship related to the key Blackbeard wants. Assuming the key works on the ship is not a stretch. Do you disagree?" William raised his brow.

"No, you are correct, I did say as much, didn't I? You are most astute, William. I will bring the real key. A true hunter knows that to catch an animal the trap must be well disguised."

Anne went back around to the other side of the table and sat down in the ornate chair. "Now, our business is concluded, and you must excuse us, sir. We must discuss more details with our Captain William."

"Yes, of course. Thank you for this audience, your majesty." Richardson bowed low and then left the room and the ship.

After confirming Richardson had left the ship, William and Anne both let out a breath they seemed to have been holding in the whole time.

Anne looked to William. "Do you think he believed us?"

The next day, Richardson prepared his ship, a large cargo ship without cannons, with supplies and had his own men inspecting the rigging and making it seaworthy. The lowest deck was similar to the slaves' quarters at his mansion: row after row of stacked wooden planks meant to hold as many bodies as possible with no regard for comfort. Many had died during the trip due to those conditions, but it didn't matter to slavers and was a common design choice.

The day after Richardson loaded the ship with his slaves, William and half the crew from the *Diamond* functioned as the crew.

"You have everything prepared?" William asked. This time he was dressed in civilian clothes, akin to what a sailor might wear.

"Yes, the slaves are loaded, I have the key, and the ship was inspected yesterday. She is in fine shape. Is your crew ready?"

"Always," William stated. "Where is Blackbeard?"

"He and the other prisoner are arriving as we speak." Richardson pointed to a coach with barred windows pulling up to the harbour.

The Boston jailers brought Edward and Sam from the coach and aboard the slaver's ship in shackles. Richardson grinned when he saw Edward being brought aboard.

Edward and Sam had been told of the exchange before being brought to the ship, but not that marines were involved. The *Diamond* was in plain view next to the slave ship, and a marine captain, William, was standing next to Richardson. "So my crew is heading into a trap?"

Richardson laughed. "Yes, my boy. And after this is done, your ship will be mine, as I foretold."

Edward struggled, but couldn't do anything in his condition. "I'll make you pay for this, Richardson. Mark my words!"

"Yes, yes. Said the fly to the spider," Richardson replied as Edward was taken below with the slaves.

After the ship was double checked, the sails were unfurled and the ship left the harbour. The *Diamond* followed behind as they left Boston and headed east.

Richardson pointed at the marine ship. "Isn't your ship supposed to be farther behind us for the ambush?"

"The destination is a day away. My people will slow when we are closer," William replied.

The two ships kept moving east, however, and not north to the supposed destination. After a few hours Boston was completely out of sight, and they still hadn't changed course. William gave instructions to one of the crewmen, who ran below deck to carry them out.

Richardson was growing impatient. "Are we not to head north to Gloucester?" he asked.

William was about to answer, but Edward and Sam both appeared from the lower deck. The two were no longer wearing shackles and the crew were welcoming him as a friend. Edward smirked as he approached William and Richardson.

"What is the meaning of this? Why is he not in chains?"

"The same reason why we aren't heading to Gloucester," Edward said with a grin, "and why these men are not actually marines: we tricked you. William here is one of my crew members, as is the woman you spoke with posing as Queen Anne."

Richardson glanced left and right to the many crew members advancing on him. What once were sheep turned out to be wolves. The hunter was now caught in a snare, tightening like a noose. He began sweating with all the eyes on him.

"And what of the mayor and the magistrate?"

"They are currently at an inn in Boston, probably still unconscious thanks to Henry and Alexandre. Once they wake, I'm sure someone will help them. As for you, well, there are a few people who would enjoy seeing you dead, and I don't plan to disappoint."

Edward stepped closer to Richardson. The man kept backing up to the edge of the ship. When he bumped into the railing, he peered over the edge to the water below. Richardson gritted his teeth and reached into his pocket. He pulled out the key to the *Freedom*.

"You forget I still hold the ultimate bait," Richardson hissed as he dangled the key over the side of the ship. "Take me back to Boston or you can say goodbye to the key."

Edward's face turned grim, but he didn't move. "Think about the situation you are in. You cannot win here."

"Oh, I don't think so. You and I, we're birds of a feather. I saw the drive in your eyes that night. You won't let anything stand in your way to retrieving this key, and I won't let anything stand in my way to getting what I want. You would sacrifice everything for this, even your precious crewmate Nassir and his filthy, savage family."

"You're wrong," Edward said.

Richardson laughed with sincere joy. "We're alike, Blackbeard! We both know I'm right. This is the only way to achieve your goals. Turn the ship around, return my slaves, and the key is yours."

Edward couldn't see a way out of the situation without giving Richardson what he wanted. The entire crew watched the deadlock between the two, and no one dared move with the key poised to be lost to Davey Jones' Locker.

"This is all a big game of cat and mouse. Even if we did turn the ship around, you would throw the key into the ocean when we let you free."

Richardson sneered. "That is the game you must play."

William, noticing Richardson's attention focused solely on Edward, saw his chance. He moved in a flash and kicked Richardson in the temple. Richardson fell to the deck with a crack. The key flew up in the air. Edward ran, leaped off of the ship, and thrust out his hand to grab it. The key was inches away, twisting and turning in the air. Edward's fingers touched the tip of the metal but he could not grasp it. The key fell, Edward falling parallel to it, but still he could not reach.

The key fell into the water with a small plop. Edward made a splash as he followed into the drink. The murky water was impossible to see through. Edward scanned the waters, trying to see where the key went, but darkness invaded his vision. Edward swam deeper, searching harder for the dark metal through the murky water.

Edward had lost all hope and started to return to the surface when a splash came a few metres from him as another swimmer jumped into the drink. The crewman swam with ferocity and purpose, deeper and deeper until Edward couldn't even see him.

That's the fastest swimmer I've ever seen. Edward peered at the point where the person had disappeared. After another moment, Edward had to surface for air.

When Edward emerged, several of the crew members were at the side of the ship, including Nassir and some of the villagers, watching the water. When the crew noticed Edward they were relieved.

"Does anyone know who dove into the water?" Edward asked. The crew replied negatively.

Edward swam in the water waiting for the crew member who dove in. The slave ship furled their sails and stopped movement as best as possible, allowing the *Freedom* to sail up beside them. The crew was able to explain the situation to the crew of the *Freedom* in full, and the crewmate hadn't yet surfaced.

Something is wrong.

No sooner had Edward's thought passed than the surface broke and the body of the crewmate float on top. "Bring him aboard the *Freedom*!" Alexandre yelled over the side.

Edward swam over to the crewmate and carried him back to the *Freedom* where a rope ladder awaited him. He climbed to the top post haste, with the crewmate slung over his shoulder.

When Edward rose to the edge of the ship, the crew helped the crewman off Edward's shoulder. The crewman's hand was clenched over something, but his hand opened when he was set onto the deck. The key fell out. The crewmate wasn't moving.

Alexandre leaned over and listened. "He isn't breathing."

23. THE THIRD

Alexandre grabbed the key, then picked up the crewman, to the confusion of others.

"Alexandre, what are you doing?"

"Saving this one's life," he yelled as he carried the crewman to the gun deck. On the gun deck he set the key in the door at the bow end and it opened with a click. Alexandre kicked the door open and rushed inside. Those who followed caught a glimpse of a surgeon's room, with various medical devices and bottled liquids, but once Alexandre was inside, he closed the door and locked it behind him.

Edward knocked on the door. "Alexandre, let us in!"

"*Non*! I am performing surgery. Now leave me be!"

Edward turned to the crew behind him and shrugged. There was no dealing with the Frenchman when he was in one of his moods.

The crew, including Edward, Anne, and Henry, waited in silence in front of the room while listening intently for sounds beyond the door. For an hour, all that could be heard was a random click here or a metallic scraping there.

Edward pulled out a Mayan medicinal herb from his pocket and began chewing on it. The bitter taste hit his tongue and he became lost in thought as he chewed. "Wait a moment," Edward said after a few moments, his brow raised. "How did Alexandre know that this was a medical room?"

Anne, Henry, and the other crewmates peered at each other, as if asking the other people if they knew the answer.

"I noticed him pass a whole day once just sitting with his ear pressed against the door of each locked room," Anne stated. "Perhaps he was able to hear the rattling of the instruments and bottles?"

"Now that you mention it… I saw him with some apparatus up his nose and a tube through the bottom of the door. He was sniffing about with the device. Maybe he… smelled what was inside?" Henry postulated, unsure of himself.

The other crewmates delivered similar strange tales of Alexandre occupying himself by prodding each room to no end. Separately, the stories show how odd the Frenchman is, but together the action painted a picture of a man deducing what each locked room contained inside via process of elimination.

"Alright, so how did Alexandre know the key we received was meant for this door?" Henry asked this time.

"I can tell you that one," Edward replied. "The last two rooms are on this floor at opposite ends. It's a safe bet to think the room at the stern is the captain's cabin, as that is similar to other ships of this rate. The architect of this game would no doubt keep the purpose of each room in mind when thinking about which key we should get next. Benjamin wanted us to survive without cannons for a time, as a test, so they were unlocked second, and after we recover the last key the ship is officially mine. Technically I'm not captain until then, so the captain's cabin should be unlocked with the final key. Alexandre knew that, thus his confidence in knowing the key would unlock this door."

Alexandre emerged from the room, his clothes dyed red in spots. "Excellent deduction, *mon Capitaine*." Everyone stood and stared at Alexandre expectantly. "Victor will live."

Instead of a sigh of relief, the name was met with confusion. "Who's Victor?" Edward asked, curiosity written on his face.

Alexandre rubbed his eyes. "Victor has been with us from the *début*. Since Port Royal."

Edward shrugged, still not recollecting. Alexandre sighed.

Anne's face lit with recognition. "Oh! I remember I had a rather short conversation with Victor once, long ago."

Edward turned to Anne. "Only once?"

"Yes, as I recall he was shy and not very talkative. Perhaps that's why you're unable to recall Victor?"

"I assumed I talked with every crewman aboard at least a few times. Can we see him? I may be able to remember if I see his face." Edward attempted to enter the surgeon's room.

Alexandre blocked the way. "*Non!*" he commanded. "The patient is resting." Alexandre handed a piece of paper to Edward. "Here, play with this. You will need time for this one."

Edward took the paper, the next clue from Benjamin Hornigold. The last clue, leading to the last key for the *Freedom*. Edward was about to open and read it when he stopped himself.

"Wait, you're saying you figured out the clue already?"

"Yes, I read the riddle quickly before performing surgery and discovered the solution during. It was all very fascinating. Now leave," Alexandre ordered, pointing to the ladder.

Edward pocketed the paper and headed up to the main deck. "You won't read the clue?" Anne asked.

"I think we should wait until we finish what we set out to do first. Once we return the villagers to NiTalaa and find out if Nassir will rejoin us, then we can worry about the next key."

"These riddles take some time to solve. Are you sure we

shouldn't start work on it sooner?" Anne asked.

Edward glanced back and forth to make sure no one was listening. "The crew needs a little rest after all the running around we've been doing. This is for the final key, and it will no doubt be the hardest trial we've faced. That means that there's potential some could lose their lives. If we have an excuse to stave that off for the time being, I'll take it."

Anne nodded, but wondered to herself if it was for the crew's sake or his own that he wanted to put off the riddle.

When Edward and Anne returned to the main deck, the crew brought Richardson over to the *Freedom* via a gangplank. "What do you want us to do with 'im?" Sam asked.

"Take him to the brig. We'll deal with him later," Edward replied.

Anne and Edward watched as the crew took Richardson below deck. "I cannot believe I had to act as my mother for Richardson to go along with the plan. I never want to do that again," Anne lamented with folded arms.

"The crux of the plan was convincing Richardson he had a chance to take the *Freedom* for himself," Edward said as he pulled Anne close and rubbed her arm. "Besides, I heard your acting was impeccable. That he was fooled is all that matters."

"Yes, I am happy this worked well." Anne carried a troubled air about her, despite the success of their plan.

"What's wrong?"

"I was thinking about something Richardson mentioned. My mother suffered a loss recently, but he didn't mention what kind. I worry one of my family members might have died."

"We've been travelling much, so news of the world is scarce. There's also a bounty on my head we didn't know about."

"A bounty changes nothing."

"Yes, we're still pirates so there's always people after us." Edward faced Anne and held her by the arms. "Don't worry about what Richardson said. You have us now, remember?"

Anne gazed deep into Edward's dark eyes. "I know, Edward. I'll be fine." Edward pulled Anne close and hugged her. Despite what Anne claimed, Edward could tell she was still holding back her true feelings.

Back in the locked surgeon's cabin, Alexandre was sitting in a chair in the corner of the room. He was meditating as he waited for the patient he'd operated on to regain consciousness.

The reason Alexandre was so adamant that none see his patient, the shy and reserved Victor, was because Victor was not who he appeared to be. The "he" was actually a "she." Victor was the third woman who had hidden her appearance aboard the *Freedom* from Port Royal, and she was the best at hiding her true nature by far. Alexandre had had a hard time discovering the secret as she possessed an uncanny ability to be transparent in a crowd.

'Victor' awoke with a start, sitting up straight on the raised operating table. She wore a thin white tunic stained in blood. She had short-cropped black hair and black eyes with a thin face and small nose. Her lithe body bespoke her agility and natural fitness. Her eyes flitted left and right quickly like a bird with purpose.

Alexandre noticed the change and slowly opened his eyes. "So you have finally awoken. You should rest more, *ma chére*. You are in no shape to be moving."

"What happened?" the patient asked. Her voice carried a hint of a Greek accent.

"After you dove for the key, you fell unconscious. I revived you, then forced you to sleep again so I could perform *chirurgie* on you."

Victor looked daggers at Alexandre, but he was unfazed. "What kind of surgery?"

"A bullet was lodged in your stomach. I noticed weeks ago in our last battle, and you were hiding the pain ever since. If the bullet was left, you could have died. I was planning on knocking you unconscious, but this provided ample opportunity."

Victor examined the remnants of the operation on her stomach. A blood-soaked bandage covered her abdomen.

"I need to change the bandages once more." Alexandre pushed her down to the table gently. Victor grabbed his arm in a vice grip, but after peering into his eyes she let go and lay down. Alexandre grabbed cotton gauze from one of the many cabinets and prepared it. "So, would you have me call you Victor, or will you tell me your true name?"

"Victoria Theriault. You may call me Tori if we are being so intimate."

Alexandre smirked as he removed the old bandages. "You should know by now you cannot lie to me. Victoria is not your *prénom*."

Tori winced as the bandage was taken off. "My given name is not a name I wish to be called. Victoria is the name I chose for myself, and what I will be called."

"Victoria, then." Alexandre dabbed the gauze over the stitching, soaking up the remaining blood first. "Are you not going to ask how I knew you were a woman, or how I knew about the bullet?"

"Why bother? Five times you stopped others from discovering I was a woman. Noticing my pain would be simple."

Alexandre grinned as he wrapped the new gauze around Victoria's stomach. "Six times now. And if you are observant enough to notice, then you must know I will eventually uncover where you are from and why you insist on staying aboard this ship. Tell me now and save us the *difficulté*."

This time, Victoria smiled deviously. "Perhaps you are getting ahead of yourself, surgeon. Only one who doesn't believe they can win would try to force another's hand with sly words."

Alexandre felt an excitement welling inside him like never before. "To finally meet another whose intellect *may* match my own is… nice. I will enjoy playing this game."

Victoria stood, dressed and adopted the mannerisms of a man again. Soon she was indistinguishable from the 'Victor' she claimed to be. "You will lose." Victoria said, a glint in her eyes.

It would take two months to return to Nassir's homeland. During that time Nassir and the other shipmates remodelled the cargo ship and until it was a remnant of its former self. The interior was opened like a proper ship, and could transport real cargo. With the addition of cannons, the villagers could also turn the it into a decent-sized warship.

The crew of the *Freedom* did the best they could to teach the villagers how to sail a ship during that time.

Nassir reunited with the *Freedom*'s crew and heard about all the adventures since he left. He was particularly interested and concerned for Christina. The story of how Christina acquired her 'pet' was particularly disturbing to Nassir, but Christina assuaged him by telling of how Tala was instrumental in saving Anne's life.

The Calabarians also discussed what would be done with Daniel Richardson. Edward expected Richardson would be sentenced to death, but they decided to judge him upon returning to the village. The return to their families would be celebrated with the death of a slaver.

Christina pushed for Richardson to die immediately, but after talking with Nassir she backed down. Her anger towards the slaver festered and grew during the travel, but she stayed her hand for Nassir's sake.

Anne, however, had questions that needed to be answered before his death. Late one night she left the bed she and Edward shared and entered the brig not two feet away. Richardson was sleeping, but Anne prodded his feet with a sword to wake him.

"Oh, the Queen Anne impersonator is here. Come to gloat?" Richardson spat.

"No, you have information I need."

"And what would you want to know from me?" Richardson asked, still lying down with a face of utter indifference.

Anne toyed with the heir apparent ring now on a chain between her breasts. "During our conversation, you mentioned some loss the Queen suffered. A personal tragedy?"

"What of it?"

"What was the loss she had?"

Richardson cocked his brow and considered Anne more closely than before. His eyes moved to the ring Anne was touching, then to her face. Anne's remarkable face, so similar in appearance, and the ring, so perfect a forgery if there could be one.

"Who are...?" Richardson's eyes widened with shock and then he began laughing. "Oh, this is rich. Why, you're the Queen's daughter. But that would mean..." Richardson laughed again.

"What's so funny?" Anne seethed through gritted teeth.

"Ho-ho, I'll never tell, this is too precious, my dear. I know I am heading to my grave, so there is nothing you can do to pry the information from my lips. I must say, though, your family is certainly a piece of work." Richardson laughed all the harder.

Anne, her anger swelling with nowhere to go, left the brig and closed the door hard. The laugh could still be heard through the wooden wall between her and Richardson.

The hot sun was high in the sky as the crew of the *Freedom* landed at the shores of Calabar along with the former slave ship. The *Freedom* once more bore its name on the side, and no longer the name *Diamond*. The two ships were met with unprecedented joy upon landing.

The villagers of Calabar stood at the harbour and cheered as the ships docked. The men helped bring the ships in and tied them to the dock as the crews set gangplanks down.

Wives and husbands, mothers and sons were reunited with joyful tears and embraces.

Nassir and Edward descended together, with Nassir's brother, Dumaka, rushing forward to embrace his kin. After he had a moment with his brother, Dumaka embraced Edward as well.

"Thank you, you saved my brother and my people. I will forever be in your debt."

"I do not deserve your gratitude. Your brother came up with the plan when I was caught by Richardson."

"As I understand, you and your crew were instrumental in putting forth that plan. Without you this could not have happened."

"Saving Nassir and recovering the key for my ship was part of the reason for helping. I was being selfish."

Dumaka sighed. "And through your selfishness you brought joy to all these faces. A good deed is a good deed, regardless of why or how the act was initiated. Be humble elsewhere and accept our gratitude." Dumaka took Edward's hand and raised it in the air. "People of Calabar, this is the man who gave our people freedom again: Edward Thatch!"

The villagers of Calabar cheered for EdwarYd and the crew of the *Freedom*. As Dumaka pulled Edward through the throng, the villagers embraced him, shook his hand and kissed him in thanks for his actions. The same gratitude was showered upon the crew of the *Freedom* as they disembarked and walked to the centre of the village.

The people held a feast in honour of their heroes, and their loved ones' return. After the feast, and after a few hours of song and dance, Richardson was brought from the brig and to the centre of the village. As he was pushed forward, the villagers shouted insults and spat on him, but he did not flinch once.

Richardson was brought in front a fire pit with Edward, Nassir, and Dumaka standing before him. "You are brought before us so we may have justice for the pain you caused our brothers and sisters. For your crimes, we sentence you to death."

"What a crock of shit. You sentence me to death? You niggers don't have rights," Richardson yelled. Edward took out his golden cutlass and handed it to Dumaka. "You were meant to serve our superior race from the beginning of time!" Dumaka tested the heft of the blade, nodding in admiration. "I was affording you greater purpose than your former, miserable lives. You are merely dogs, and dogs are nothing without masters!"

Dumaka fixed the blade at Richardson's neck. "You are no one's master." Dumaka pulled the blade back and cleaved Richardson's head from his body in one stroke. The head and body fell to the ground with a thump, the blood spurting from the stumps left behind.

Dumaka turned his back on the body and lifted his arms in the air, the golden blade in one hand. The people of the village and the crew of the *Freedom* cheered as one. The people of Calabar would never let another take their freedom away.

24. THE ISLAND OF HEAVEN & HELL

"Take care of my brother," Dumaka said.

"I will," Edward assured him as he held out his hand.

Dumaka shook Edward's hand and embraced him before saying a few words to and then embracing his brother.

Nassir walked over to Edward. "Ready?" Edward asked.

"Yes, it is time we leave," Nassir said.

Together, Nassir and Edward boarded the *Freedom*. The crew waved to the villagers as they shoved off and let loose the sails. They continued to wave and holler until the villagers were completely out of sight. Two months' travel had created a strong bond between the crew and the Calabarians, one which would not be broken.

As *Freedom* sailed across the ocean, Edward focused on the paper left in the surgeon's room, the final clue to the location of the last key. That piece of paper meant the journey was almost at an end. Edward sat at of a table at the quarterdeck with Herbert nearby at the helm.

"Are you simply going to stare at the paper, or will you read it?"

Edward returned to reality to see Jack sitting beside him at the small table. Edward chuckled at the comment. "I was thinking on how far we've come because of these little clues. Hard to believe this will soon be over."

Jack pulled out his violin, set his feet on the table, and played a light tune. "This has been quite the adventure. I've been on the sidelines, but I believe it has afforded me perspective."

Edward joined Jack in his relaxation, placing his feet on the table as well. "And what has your perspective allowed you to see?"

Jack closed his eyes as he pondered the question. "I've seen brave men and women die in battle and against deathly traps. I've relived tragedy through the eyes of a father. I witnessed a journey across the world, and a boy accused of being a pirate become a man in a short time." Edward smiled. "But, most importantly, I think, I saw a group of wayward vagabonds and lost souls brought together by that man and made into a family."

Edward was moved by Jack's words and his violin. "You have quite the way with words, Jack. You've almost made a song out of our adventure."

"I considered writing one, and I may after we are done. The journey may be more important than the ending, but there is no song which never ends."

"Then let us move towards that end." Edward opened the paper up to read the clue.

At the point between Heaven and Hell
In the palm of God's left and right hands.
An island of duality sits.
Two crews follow two paths.
At the centre lies the final trial of man.

Edward pondered about the clue for a few moments while Jack read. "The clue seems very simple to me."

Jack handed the paper back after reading. "What do you propose?"

Edward folded his arms. "Well, Heaven and Hell are often depicted as being above and below, and since we are seeking an island this would mean north and south. The point between north and south is the equator."

"Yes, that makes sense. What of the left and right hands? East and west?"

"That would only be logical given the first part. The right hand of God often symbolises a position of honour and distinction. The holy land, Jerusalem, lies to the east, and the New World to the west. I believe the island lies between the New World and the Old."

Jack smiled as he switched the tune to a faster tempo. "You know a lot about the Bible for one who claims to not know anything about God."

"My father taught me a few things when I was younger, but after he disappeared I stopped studying. I have a hard time believing in God."

Jack sighed. "I must admit, with everything that has happened, I find it hard to believe in God as well at times. Then I think on all the blessings He has provided me now, and it is easier to believe."

Edward contemplated Jack's words for a moment, but his mind was not swayed. Edward turned in his seat. "Herbert, you've been listening, yes? Can you tell us what you think?"

Herbert locked the helm and turned his wheelchair. He adjusted his glasses as he wheeled himself over to the table. "You mean about God or about the clue to the key?"

"The key. I think I've had enough theology for one day. No offence, Jack." Edward handed the paper to Herbert.

"None taken," Jack replied while tuning his violin.

Herbert examined the paper. After he read through, he folded the paper and gave it back to Edward. "Your assessment is sound. There is a book in the cabin below called *Atlas Cosmographicae*, would you mind grabbing it for me, Edward?"

"Certainly. I'll be back in but a moment." Edward went below and into the stern cabin, the war room, and after a few moments' search he found the *Atlas* and brought it back up to Herbert.

Herbert read through the dusty old tome, scanning different maps until he found a map of the known world. The map was separated into two half-circles with a line horizontally down the middle. The two circles were separated directly between the New and the Old world.

Edward laughed. "This is perfect. This map shows exactly where the island should be."

"Yes, and we should arrive in about two to three weeks," Herbert estimated.

"But, Captain, what about the last part about needing two crews?" Jack asked, pointing in the general direction of the paper.

"We'll need to return, but there's no harm investigating."

"Fair enough."

Edward gathered the crew and let them know the plan. After the crew realised this was for the last key, they cheered and wanted to feast and break out the strong stuff, but Edward dispelled all hope of merriment.

"You may celebrate and feast after we retrieve the key. Currently, there is nothing to celebrate, but I can assure you once we are done we will have a party to end all parties!" Edward exclaimed.

Much to Edward's dismay, but simultaneous delight, his comment elicited more cheering than before. He was eventually able to calm the crew and focus them on work so they could head to the next island.

When the *Freedom* reached the estimated spot of the equator, Herbert travelled from east to west, moving north and south in a zigzag along the equator to maximise sight for the crew.

Edward peered through a spyglass onto the open sea. The air filled Edward's lungs with the feeling of the sea and invigorated him despite the monotony of their task. Days passed with his and others' eyes behind spectacled vision.

"What I don't understand is how this island was not found before," Edward said to no one in particular.

"Is that really so odd, brother?" Pukuh asked as he joined Edward at the starboard railing on the waist.

"Pukuh, I haven't seen you in ages."

"All this trickery and deception is not my strength. I am a warrior. The only deception I use is when I resemble the tiger stalking my prey."

"Yes, well I'm rather glad we didn't have to resort to a battle to save Nassir. I don't think we would have been as lucky as our previous battles. So you think this island not being found is normal?"

Pukuh leaned against the railing. "Well, yes. Benjamin created this for you, so it is natural you should be the first to find the island."

"What about the last island that Daniel Richardson found?"

"He was meant to find that island, as you are meant to find this one."

Edward stroked his beard. "You say it so elegantly, but perhaps I should ask how, then. How would no one find this island?"

Pukuh shrugged his shoulders. "How would none be able to open the locks on this ship? How does a man have a golden arm? How were any of the islands we travelled to created? How does one travel from the future? These are things men are not able to explain. Over what we have seen, is a lost island so hard to believe?"

"Well, when you put it that way," Edward said, turning around and leaning on the railing with Pukuh.

"My father, after regaling me with amazing stories about his adventures with Benjamin Hornigold, said to me: 'My son, I tell you truthfully, if Benjamin wanted to stop the sun in the sky, he could do so. That man makes the impossible possible.'"

Edward, still sceptical despite all evidence to the contrary, folded his arms. "He must have been some man."

"You two are alike, but perhaps you are a bit more."

"A bit more what?"

"You have done impossible things, and you are being moulded by Benjamin. Soon, I think you can surpass him. If I stay with you, maybe I will see you stop the sun in the sky. Then I will tell my father: this man made the day stand still."

Edward laughed and slapped Pukuh on the back. "You truly do have a vivid imagination, Pukuh."

"Captain!" a man in the crow's nest yelled. "I see land off the port bow."

"Good work, Richard." Edward turned to the stern. "Herbert, did you catch that?"

"Aye, Captain. Changing course now." Herbert spun the helm to port, turning the ship southwest.

As the *Freedom* drew closer to the island, many of the crew crowded around the bow of the ship to watch. Some were on the waist, others hanging off the rigging, and some standing on top of the railing or on the shoulders of others.

The island itself was large and covered in foliage. Palm trees surrounded the island without end, and was too thick to see through. Edward had Herbert do a circle around the whole island, which took several hours, but eventually Edward found what he was searching for on the expansive beachfront.

Blackbeard's Ship

There. A path between the palms. "Land us here, Herbert!" Edward yelled.

Herbert turned the ship to the island and commanded the crew to trim and furl the sails, then drop anchor. The ship slowed until gently gliding to a stop just off the shore.

Edward and nearly the whole crew departed in longboats to the island below. Edward led them through the path. The path so cleanly led through the multitude of palm trees, it had to be man-made.

The canopy of palms swayed with the wind from the ocean, rustling and crinkling as if they were trying to say something to each other or the visitors to their island. The grass too sang its own song for the crew of the *Freedom* as they passed by.

The crew was taken in by the beauty of the island so greatly that when Edward happened upon a set of stone steps he nearly stubbed his toe. His jaw dropped with what he saw.

In front of Edward, two massive stone platforms stood side by side up a set of steps. Beyond the stone platforms was an impossibly tall wooden carving of an angel with a spear standing atop a devil, ready to strike. On the left and right of the carving were two giant stone double doors. The doors were covered by a spiked wooden wall which extended as far as Edward could see, and by his guess around the whole island.

Edward climbed the steps to the top. He noticed a moss-covered stone tablet between the two platforms. He pulled off the slimy and slick moss to reveal a carved tablet depicting people climbing onto the platforms and opening the stone doors.

Edward turned around to the crowd. "Alright, I want half of you to step onto the left platform, and the other half onto the right platform," he yelled.

The crew followed their captain's direction and separated as best they could into halves. Once everyone stepped onto the platforms, nothing happened. The stone doors didn't move an inch.

Edward addressed the crew once more. "Everyone on the left platform, I want you to move to the right platform."

Edward ascended the right platform once more as the crew on the left joined him. As more and more of the crew stepped onto the right platform it slowly descended with the weight until the platform became completely flush with the top of the steps.

Rumbling started underneath their feet. The stone double doors left of the angel and demon opened. When the door was fully open, the rumbling stopped.

The crew stepped off of the right platform to investigate, but as soon as a few left the stone doors closed. Edward called them back, and the door opened again.

"Anne, see what's beyond the door, would you please?" Edward asked.

"Certainly," she replied.

Anne went to the left stone door and peered inside. "There's not much to tell, really. There is a path leading to the left with high walls, and a platform fifty feet ahead. Do you want me to head inside?"

"No. Come back." Anne followed Edward's direction. "Now, to the left platform."

The crew moved to the left platform, and this time the right stone door opened. Anne passed through the right door and examined what lay beyond.

"This side is the same as the other, but mirrored. A path leading to the right and a platform down a ways," Anne yelled.

"Alright, come back. I have an idea of what we need to do." Anne did as requested and returned to the platform as the crew descended the steps and sat down. The only ones left up the small set of steps were Edward, Anne, and Henry.

Edward folded his arms and sat on the edge of the left platform. "We'll need help to proceed through this trial, and not the help Captain Smith provided last time." Edward alluded to the marine captain who chased them halfway around the world before Edward was finally captured and sent to prison. "We need a pirate crew who will cooperate with us on this."

"Do you have one in mind?" Henry asked.

"Well, I think the choice is obvious. We need to find Bartholomew Roberts and the *Fortune*."

"How do you expect to find Mister Roberts?"

"How did you find him to help us escape Portsmouth?" Edward asked the two of them.

Anne leaned against the right platform. "Well, we found Roberts rather by accident, or we had the good *Fortune*, if you would," Anne said with a smirk, "to be found by him. He heard, as the world had, about your capture, and the Bodden Brothers pointed him in our direction."

"Perhaps Roberts left a way to find him with the Boddens, or with the Boddens' information network they may be able to find them anyway."

Henry stepped down from the platform he was on. "So, back to Bodden Town then?"

Edward stood up. "Yes. Back to the ship, men."

Anne stepped ahead, and Edward followed down the steps, but Henry's hand on his shoulder stopped him. "Edward, can we talk for a bit?"

Anne stopped halfway down the steps, waiting for the two of them. "Go on ahead Anne, I'll catch up," Edward said. Anne nodded and headed back to the ship with the crew. Edward sat down, and Henry sat opposite him. "So what did you want to talk about, Henry?"

"I'll make this brief. I want us to make a stop in Badabos."

Edward's brow shot up. "Our hometown? Why?"

"I haven't seen my family in two years. I want to see my mother. I want to see if she's doing well."

"How to say this delicately... No."

"Why not?" Henry asked, anger seeping into his tone.

"Going back is too dangerous, Henry. The people of Badabos know us, and they've seen the ship before. I'm not subjecting the crew to danger because you're homesick."

Henry stood up from the platform. "We can land the ship on the north beach, away from the harbour, only a five-minute walk through the woods to town. None would know we arrived, and I can disguise myself."

"A disguise, really? That's your plan?" Edward scoffed. "You and your father are well known in Badabos, you're bound to be recognised."

Henry motioned towards Edward. "All I need to do is don as big a beard as you and no one will recognise me. Hell, the way you are you would never be spotted either."

Edward was going to object immediately, but shut his mouth for a moment. "You know, that is true. My appearance has changed in these two years. This could work."

"See? Trust me. Everything will be fine. I'll see how my parents are, and then leave. We'll stay a day at most."

Edward folded his arms and stared at Henry. "I don't enjoy our hometown, but I don't want my personal distaste to affect my judgement, so we'll visit for one day."

Henry embraced Edward tightly. "Thank you, Edward."

"Don't make me regret my decision."

"I promise, you won't."

25. THE BLACK DEATH

The *Freedom* landed on the north side of the island of Badabos. Some Badabos natives had joined Edward and Henry before they were labelled pirates, but few were left. John was one of them, but he, along with most, decided to stay on the *Freedom* and opted to send a representative with letters and money.

"John, why don't you join us? If you don a disguise I'm sure no one would recognise you either."

"N-no, Captain, I think I should stay on the ship. The more people we send in the more risk we take. Besides, I don't have any family to see."

Edward frowned. "Well, as long as you're sure."

"I am sure. Please be careful."

"I will."

Edward and Henry travelled into town with a few of the crew. Pukuh insisted on helping gather supplies so he could stretch his legs. He wore civilian clothes, but he somehow managed to carry a concealed spear.

While walking through the forest, Edward and Henry recounted childhood misadventures together in those very woods. The crew smiled at the light-hearted nostalgia amongst the friends.

When they reached town the crew left Edward and Henry, heading off to do their business. "Are you joining me, Edward?" Henry asked. "I'm sure my mother would love to see you as well."

"No, I don't wish to intrude. I will walk around town for a bit then head back to the ship. You can tell your mother I said hello."

Henry nodded and left to see his home for the first time in two years. Edward watched as Henry jogged away between the houses.

Well, now what? Edward scratched his head.

As he glanced about, the town brought back memories for Edward, both joyous and melancholic. The hate he held in his heart was vaporous, like trying to grab smoke. Edward could see the bad memories, but all he caught in his net was nostalgia.

Memories of Henry, Robert, and Edward playing in the streets, going to school, working in the fields. A face long since forgotten filtered into Edward's consciousness as well: Lucy, his former flame. *I wonder if she is still here.*

"So where are we headed, Captain?" a woman's voice asked behind Edward.

Blackbeard's Ship

Edward turned with a start. Behind him stood Christina in a leather vest and a loose tunic underneath. She also wore comfortable trousers and boots.

"What are you doing here?"

Christina placed her hands on her hips. "Am I not allowed on shore?"

"Well, you are, but…"

"As I understood, anyone was allowed ashore as long as they wore a disguise if they were from here. I'm not from here, so there's no risk, correct?" Edward pursed his lips. "I'll take that as a no. Now, I want the full tour. I want to see where the great Blackbeard grew up." Christina grabbed Edward's arm and led him through the streets and into the town.

The two walked along a small market street curving up from the harbour. Christina was more fascinated by the market in Badabos than any island she had been to before. She was laughing and pulling Edward along the whole time, eliciting chuckles from passersby.

When Christina bent down to admire some wares from a local merchant, her wooden rose necklace dangled out in front of her.

"What a pretty necklace," the merchant commented.

Christina glanced at her necklace and smiled. "Thank you." She leaned closer and held the pendant out so the merchant could see better.

"Impressive quality. Would you be willing to part with it?"

"No!" Christina snapped, anger flashing forward in an instant. She pulled the necklace close in a protective stance and eyed the merchant like she would a lecherous vagrant. Others in the market stared at Christina and whispered to each other.

Edward placed his hand on Christina's shoulder, making her jump. She became aware of the eyes on her, and the way she'd acted to the merchant. Christina sincerely apologised to the merchant and explained how the necklace was sentimental. The merchant accepted her apology, and the mournful empathy in his eyes told her he understood what the pendant meant to her.

Edward and Christina traversed the market street for a few more minutes. Christina stared at the ground, melancholy painted on her face, while her fingers unconsciously caressed the rose.

Edward grabbed her hand and pulled her to the northern side of the town. He took her through the different whitewashed and brown houses and stores until they reached the edge of Badabos.

"Where are we going, Edward?" Christina asked.

"To the only spot which matters to me in this stinking town," Edward replied.

Edward took Christina to a small grassy hill which went higher and higher until the whole town was visible at the peak. At the edge there was a straight drop of about two hundred feet to the ocean below. Edward sat at the edge, overlooking the ocean. *Freedom* had arrived in Badabos at about noon, and now the sun was halfway to setting on the horizon. Christina sat down beside Edward, their feet dangling in the air.

"Before we set out on our journey, I, Henry, and our friend Robert Maynard used to come here nearly every day. We used to play games, tell stories, and talk about the ports we would visit when we were older." Edward smiled as he recalled those halcyon days.

"Who is Robert Maynard?" Christina asked.

"Do you remember before we stole the *Freedom* back from Portsmouth, when we bound a marine before departing?" Christina nodded. "That marine was Robert Maynard."

"Oh." Christina laid her hand on Edward's. "That must have been difficult."

Edward gave her a hollow smile before staring at the ocean and the bright sun. The wind breezed gently through his black and her strawberry-blond hair.

"Can I tell you a secret?"

"Of course."

"Betraying Robert wasn't difficult for me at all. I acted without hesitation, and I don't feel ill over what I did. The one thing I feel is confusion over how I don't feel anything."

"Why should you? He would have stabbed you in the back if he had the chance."

Edward whipped his head over and leaned back. He hadn't expected an answer so quickly and succinctly. After Edward took a moment to process what she said, he nodded.

"I guess you're right. Robert was always on the side of the law, which is why he joined the marines. Well, I feel foolish. I'm receiving life lessons from a young pup."

Christina laughed. "I'm not a young pup." She playfully pushed Edward.

Edward grabbed her arm for support. "Don't, that's dangerous." But he grinned.

The two gazed at the ocean, not saying anything. They listened to the people in the town below, their muffled voices filtering to the top of the hill, the breeze travelling across the ocean, and the calls of the birds as they flew over the island.

Christina leaned over on Edward's shoulder. "Thank you, Edward."

"For what?"

"For helping me forget, even if but for a moment." Christina touched the wooden rose hanging around her neck.

Edward wrapped his arm around Christina's shoulder, pulling

her close. Christina wrapped her arms around Edward's waist and held onto him. Warm tears soaked through Edward's shirt, but he did not say a word. Soon, Christina lay on his lap, breathing softly from slumber.

Edward lay back, closed his eyes, and slipped to sleep as well.

Edward opened his eyes and the cliff was gone, replaced by a drab house with a fireplace. A boy was playing with a wooden knight. He wore a smile on his face as he made the knight jump.

Edward remembered the toy Henry lent him so long ago. Edward also knew what happened next.

Edward's uncle-in-law flashed in and grabbed the toy in one hand, an open bottle in the other. His uncle-in-law cast the toy into the fire.

"No!" both the young and old Edward yelled.

"Think ye can bring trash into my house, can ye?" Edward's uncle-in-law yelled. The man picked the boy up by the neck and pressed his body against the fireplace, the flames licking the boy's stomach. Little Edward screamed and thrashed in pain, but the man held him still.

The fireplace disappeared, and the boy Edward lay in front of the door. Edward's aunt stood in front of Edward, protecting him. His aunt and uncle began arguing, but he couldn't hear the words. His uncle back-handed his Aunt, ending the argument, but she refused to move.

Boy Edward rose up. "When my father comes back, he'll kill all of you!" the boy yelled, rushing out the door after.

The house turned to smoke and transformed into the cliff again. Little Edward sat, his head on his knees, bawling. Another boy was consoling him.

"Why did he leave, Rob?" Edward pleaded. "Why did Dad leave me?" He cried between his legs.

"Your dad didn't leave you."

"Then where is he?" Edward yelled, angry.

The young Robert Maynard pulled Edward's arm away from his tear-filled face. "He's waiting for you." Robert pointed to the sea. "He's waiting for you on the sea."

"You think so?" Edward asked, wiping his eyes.

"You always told me he said 'A man knows no greater freedom than the sea.' He wants you to become a man and find freedom, to find him, out there."

"You promise?"

"Promise," Robert replied immediately, his youth-like assuredness in full force.

This was the day Edward decided to go to sea. It didn't matter how, he would make it happen.

The smoke returned, shifting and transforming where Edward was.

"Come back to me," Edward heard whispered in his ear.

Edward was now on the port of Badabos. Beside him was the ship he'd bought, his *Freedom*. Before him was Lucy, the woman he loved, the woman who loved him. The old him. The whaler, Edward.

"Wait for me," Edward replied. The old Edward.

Edward was suddenly staring down at his old self and Lucy as they kissed for the first and last time. Edward was on the port and in the air at the same time. His old self, and yet also his new, simultaneously.

Lucy turned to Edward in the air. Edward peered at Lucy from above, and she aged before his eyes. A scar grew across Lucy's eye, blinding one eye and marring her dainty prettiness. Her eyes changed in the same way as Edward, darkening from the sorrows of life. The eyes carried an edge like a knife, different from Edward's hate-filled eyes; Lucy's filled with what could only be called righteous fury.

Edward could not bear to stare at those eyes any longer and turned away. Edward noticed Lucy's right hand fall away, and was replaced with the claws of an animal. Suddenly, Lucy was no more, and Christina was there instead.

Christina took her right arm, the hand still an animal claw, and removed it from her body. Christina knelt down, offering the arm to Edward on the port, and Edward accepted.

Edward then stared at his counterpart on the port. Edward's beard grew on his face, becoming long, filling with smoke from lit wick. Edward's eyes grew dark as he grew older, until the eyes resembled another's. Foreign and filled with malice, Edward didn't recognise them. Those demonic eyes filled the dream with a darkness Edward couldn't escape. The eyes were dragging him into shadows, whether he liked it or not.

Edward shot awake and a chill crawled up his spine. Within seconds his dream was a forgotten memory, but the feeling he felt at the end remained. "Something's amiss."

Christina rose up, wiping sleep and tears from her eyes. "I'm sorry, Edward."

Edward shook his head. "No, no, not you. Something doesn't

feel right."

Edward scanned the ocean, the harbour, the town itself and back, but he couldn't see what was causing his unease. He rose from the edge of the cliff and Christina joined him. Christina was focused on Edward and his mania. Edward peered at the town again, and like a bloodhound his head moved this way and that. He stood on the tips of his toes as if tracking a scent.

Edward ran back down the hill and into the market street. Many shops were closing despite a few hours of daylight being left. Edward glanced left and right up and down the market until settling on the right, down the market street.

"What do you see?"

"You can't feel that?"

"No," Christina said with confusion evident in her voice.

Edward kept staring down the street trying to see something through the throng of people milling about. His eyes were furrowed and focused like an eagle. Christina also focused her senses in the same direction, imitating Edward. Edward's eyes soon widened with recognition.

Edward quickly grabbed Christina's arm and pulled her into a side street and ran. "What's wrong Edward? What did you see?" Christina asked through laboured breaths.

"Not right now. Keep running." After Edward rushed Christina up and down different streets at random, their legs tired, and they ran out of breath, so he stopped. "I think we'll be safe here, for now."

"Safe from what? What are we running from?" Christina asked while holding onto her knees.

"You recall me mentioning the man in black?" Edward said through ragged breaths.

"The assassin? How could I forget? Your tale of his countenance was riveting. He's here? How did he know to come here?"

"I imagine Captain Smith, our previous pursuant, was forthcoming about our hometown to help this one's investigation. His timing is impeccable."

"I recall you saying he was injured several times when you met with him, but he didn't feel the pain and kept chasing you."

"Well, then you know how dangerous the man in black is. We need to find Henry and leave before he finds us." Edward took a few deep breaths and began walking again, albeit slower.

Christina followed Edward closely. "Why run away? We should fight."

"We are far too outclassed. I'm not sure any of our fighters could match him, even fighting together." Edward weaved through the houses, making his way to Henry's parents.

"But we've been practicing together. We can take him."

Edward stopped and turned around, facing Christina head-on, and gave her a glare so fearsome she was frozen still.

"If we fight him, at the least we will be horribly injured, at the worst we will die. The latter is more likely." Edward turned back around. "We must keep moving."

Christina didn't say another word as they made their way between the houses of the town to where Henry's parents lived. Edward sprinted up to a small whitewashed house of simple design for a poor farming family, and knocked on the door loudly and swiftly. No answer came, so Edward knocked again.

A shuffling noise preceded the door slowly opening. An older woman peeked out behind the door and eyed Edward up and down with confusion and fear. Until she peered into his eyes.

"Edward? Is that you?" the woman asked.

"Yes, it is me, Mrs Morgan. Henry is here, is he not?" Edward asked politely.

"Ed?" Henry's voice sounded behind the door, before it was opened wide. "What are you doing here? What's wrong? Don't we still have a few hours left?"

"We must cut the visit short. The man in black is here."

Henry's eyes widened. He turned to his mother and embraced her. "I am sorry, but I must leave."

"Is something the matter?" she asked.

"No, no, all is well. We are simply being cautious."

"Well, please be careful. I love you."

"I love you too, Mother."

"How touching," an unknown voice said behind them.

Edward, Christina, Henry, and Mrs Morgan turned their heads swiftly. In front of the house was the man in black, the Royal Assassin. His cold eyes filled the group with fear and the image of death flashed before their eyes.

Edward raised his fists, Christina pulled a dagger from her belt, and Henry joined Edward in a defensive stance.

"Hmm, I did not see your ship in the harbour. It must be hidden somewhere. I suppose I can have a little fun for a bit." The man, dressed in a black leather longcoat, flashed a knife from his sleeve and held it lightly in his fingers with the least amount of effort.

He's toying with us. Edward's anger replaced his fear.

The jet-eyed man threw one of his poison needles at Edward. Christina, reacting faster than Edward, pulled him aside. The needle slipped past Edward's forearm. At the same time, the man with the hair slick like crow's feathers ran and slashed with his knife. Christina blocked the strike with her own knife.

Blackbeard's Ship

Normally, the needle missing Edward would be a fortunate occurrence, but someone was standing behind him.

Henry's mother.

The needle hit her in the neck and pierced the skin. She pulled out the needle, peering at it through unfocused eyes before fainting.

Edward turned his gaze to Henry's mother. Henry had bent down and was crying her name. He examined his mother as Alexandre taught those aboard the *Freedom* to do. "She's alive, but I don't know for how long."

The clang and flash of blades brought Edward's attention back to the street. Christina was fiercely attacking the man in black, her anger driving her blade faster and stronger than ever. The assassin deftly blocked and parried the blows with ease.

"You have ten minutes, more likely eight, judging from her size and frailty," the assassin said, still blocking Christina despite looking the other way.

"Edward, my mother needs help." Henry lifted her off the ground.

Edward gritted his teeth and turned back to the assassin. "Take her to the ship, Alexandre will be able to help her. We'll hold him." He pulled out his golden cutlass and began a charge.

Edward slashed down. The assassin jumped back, out of the way. Edward stood beside Christina and lowered his stance. Christina set her foot on Edward's bent knee and flashed another knife into her other hand. The two were ready to battle as one.

The assassin watched as Henry headed north with his mother in his arms, and grinned maliciously. "Interesting."

Edward stared down the man in front of him. A crowd of spectators had gathered behind the man. "So, what is your name, so I may stop thinking of you as 'The Assassin'?"

"My name is Edward Russell, but as we both share a name you may call me by the name I have amongst those who fear me: The Plague."

Edward wasted no more time talking. He ran over, leaping into the air and descending with his blade. Plague stepped to the left. Christina jumped off of Edward's back and into the air with a flip to move behind Plague, then sprang forward to slash at his back. Plague spun, blocked the strike with his dagger, and kicked Christina in the stomach.

She let out a muted cry and doubled over in pain. Edward slashed at Plague. The man in black, surrounded by the air of death, ducked and dodged each oncoming swipe from Edward's golden blade.

After a momentary exchange, Plague jumped away from Edward and Christina once more. "Christina, are you hurt?" Edward asked.

She rose as she clutched her aching stomach. "I'll be fine. I can keep going."

"Eagle and the Bear," Edward said while holding out his golden blade to Christina.

Christina nodded, taking the cutlass and handing Edward her dagger.

Edward threw the dagger at Plague. Plague ducked down. Edward turned and bent down, cupping his hands. Christina ran at Edward, jumped, and landed in his cupped hands. Edward launched her into the air, then ran to the Plague. He grabbed the man in a bear hug while he was distracted by Christina, and turned around. Christina fell with the blade aimed at Plague's back.

"Foolish!" Plague said.

The assassin flexed his muscles. Edward's grip broke. Christina was still falling. Plague stepped forward, pulling Edward with him, and thrust his dagger into the air. Christina was impaled on the short blade. Edward was sliced in the shoulder with his own cutlass. Christina dropped the cutlass as her strength left her. It fell to the ground with a clang.

Plague threw Christina to the ground and she lay in a heap. "Christina!" Edward yelled, holding his shoulder. His eyes were drawn back to Plague. "Damn you!" Edward yelled furiously. "You'll pay for that."

"Doubtful."

Plague flicked his wrist and sent a dagger flying towards Edward's throat. Edward pulled up his hand in a pathetic attempt to guard himself.

From above, a spear swiped the air. The dagger flew away with a metallic ring.

Pukuh landed in front of the kneeling Edward. He didn't have on his usual warrior clothes, but that did not detract from his countenance. His strong back and arms stood stalwart in front of his brother. He had one hand on his hip and the other held his spear at his side.

"Pukuh!" Edward exclaimed.

"Take the little warrior back to the ship, brother. I will take care of this one."

Edward glanced from Christina to Pukuh to Plague. "But…" Edward shook his head and stood up. "Right. We'll wait for your return."

Pukuh and Plague watched as Edward grabbed his cutlass, then picked up Christina. She was bleeding out rapidly. Edward wished Pukuh luck, then headed north to the ship.

"So you share the name of the Mayan God of Death. We are

similar. I'm called Plague."

"I do not know what this 'Plague' is, but it is not your true name, no?" Plague shook his head no. "Then we are not similar. You merely adopted a name of death. I *am* the God of Death."

"Let us hope you live up to the name. I have become rather bored."

Pukuh grinned at Plague's gall, and because he too was bored with those he'd fought aboard the *Freedom*.

Against this man, Pukuh could go wild, and he was excited.

Edward ran through the town, following paths memorised as a child. *Pukuh will win. If anyone can, it's him.*

Edward emerged on the market street where the people of Badabos were walking back to their homes after a long day. They turned to watch the tall man with long black beard carrying a young woman and leaving a trail of blood behind them. Edward kept running through the people and once more into the alley between the houses and businesses.

The blood didn't let up, and kept falling at a steady pace. Christina had fallen unconscious not long after Edward began running, and she was turning pale.

"Hang in there, Christina!" Edward yelled, unsure if his words were reaching her.

Edward picked up the pace as he ran deftly through the trees of the small forest along the path created over the years. Animals turned to watch their passing and cried out at Edward's urgency.

Edward emerged from the trees to a small sandy beach hosting the *Freedom*. The crew aboard were readying to set sail, no doubt apprised of the situation by Henry. When the crew noticed Edward with another body in his arms, they lowered a small dingy into the water for him.

Edward laid Christina down in the small boat, then gave a thumbs-up to raise it. As the crew gently pulled the ropes, Edward climbed up a ladder.

"Someone call for Alexandre!" Edward yelled as he jumped over the railing. "Tell him to bring the needle and thread."

Edward helped the other crewmates on the pulley bring the dinghy and Christina in. After the dinghy was lowered onto the waist, Edward scooped Christina into his arms and laid her down on the deck.

Blood poured onto the ship, soaking into the pine planks. Edward pulled up her shirt and lowered her breeches. The wound was lower and the cut deeper than Edward anticipated

Alexandre rushed to the top deck as Herbert crawled over to his sister's body.

"What happened?" Herbert yelled at Edward.

"Did you not hear the story from Henry?" Edward screamed back. "The Plague is upon us. The man in black. The assassin. He did this when we were trying to fight him. If Pukuh hadn't shown up when he did…"

"How could you let her fight that monster?" Herbert asked, his eyes shooting daggers at Edward.

Before Edward could defend himself, Alexandre pushed between the two of them. "Argue later, fools. I need to work quickly. Hold her down."

Edward and Herbert held down Christina's arms and legs with all their weight, just in case. Alexandre used a needle and thread to pinch closed the wound on Christina's lower abdomen. His thread-work was better than anything Edward had seen, and the wound was closed in a matter of minutes. The wound still bled, but not as badly as before. After Alexandre finished, he washed and cleaned the wound once more with his bottled water and cloth.

Alexandre set another clean cloth over the wound, and made Herbert lay his hands over it lightly. "Press gently. Clean any blood, but do not disturb the thread." Herbert nodded in affirmation, and Alexandre headed back below deck.

"Capt'n! Lookit over there," one of the crewmen exclaimed, pointing to the island of Badabos.

Edward peered in the direction the man was pointing. He was viewing the small cliff he and Christina were on earlier, and he could see two figures moving towards it. *Are they fighting?* "Somebody bring me a spyglass," Edward commanded, and one of the men obliged. Edward gazed through the spyglass and was able to see the scene on the cliff. Pukuh and Plague were still fighting. Edward's heart sank. *Pukuh is losing.* The thought shocked Edward. The assassin was more skilled than Edward's best.

"Is everyone back from the shore?" Edward asked, to which one of the crewmen answered yes. "Set sail! Head to that cliff," Edward commanded as he ran to Christina and knelt down next to Herbert. "Herbert, I need you at the helm. I can take care of Christina."

"Just as how you took care of her before?" Herbert snapped, tears in his eyes.

"Christina will survive, but Pukuh may not! I need you on the helm, no one else can navigate the shoals." Edward stared Herbert in the eyes.

After a moment the ship was pushed off of the beach and the sails were lowered. Herbert nodded and headed back to the quarter-deck. Nassir helped Herbert to the helm. Edward dabbed at Christina's wound. Despite the pain of the needle, Christina hadn't been roused.

Could the blade have been poisoned as well? Edward shook his head. *Alexandre would have noticed. It must be blood loss.*

Anne and William ran up to the main deck and over to Edward and Christina. "Did the assassin do this?" Anne asked.

"Yes, but Christina's wound is stitched, it's up to her will now," Edward said, holding the cloth tight.

Anne knelt down next to Edward, examining Christina's body. "She is strong, she will be fine."

Edward gazed into those green eyes, the ones which filled him with strength when he felt all was lost, and nodded. "Can you take over? There's one more person we need to save."

Anne took the cloth from Edward as she rose to her feet. "Whom?" Anne asked.

"Pukuh," Edward replied, glancing at the two-hundred-foot cliff approaching. "Someone grab a spare sail from the hold, quickly!" he shouted, slashing his hand through the air to emphasise the urgency.

Several of the crew went below deck to follow the order. Herbert was shouting orders to trim and furl several sails to slow the ship in the shoal.

Edward watched the fight between the man known as Plague and Pukuh as it progressed further and further towards the small cliff. The Mayan didn't glance to the side, but Edward could tell he saw the ship.

"Don't slow down!" Edward yelled to Herbert.

Herbert leaned over. "What?" he asked, confused.

"If we slow down, the assassin will jump aboard. We need to speed up so only Pukuh has enough time to jump on."

"How will he know what to do?" Herbert shouted back.

"He'll know."

Herbert shook his head. "Lower the sails. Close-haul to the wind as best you can, men!"

The men who went below returned with a spare sail rolled up and held under their arms. "Up to the poop deck. Pull the sail taut so Pukuh can jump onto it," Edward commanded.

Edward and the crewmen unfurled the sail and pulled it tight in a circle on the poop deck. The crew watched the cliff side as the ship passed under, picking up speed. *This is your chance, Pukuh, jump.* The waist of the ship was passing under the cliff. *Jump, Pukuh, jump!* The stern approached, and the men with the sail were staring straight up. *Now Pukuh!*

Suddenly, a body flew off the edge of the cliff. Nearly two hundred feet the man fell and landed neatly onto the cloth sail, which broke his fall.

Plague! "Crew, attack!" Edward commanded.

Some of the crew drew knives and swords while others ran to grab weapons as quickly as possible. None were prepared for a fight so suddenly.

Edward saw another man jump off the edge of the cliff from the corner of his eye. *Pukuh!*

Pukuh fell towards the ship. He had a dagger in his left hand, and he was holding it outstretched. Pukuh thrust the dagger into the aft sail as he fell into it. The sail broke his fall, and the dagger cutting through the thick canvas slowed him until he was halfway down. Pukuh's grip was lost and he fell to the deck in a heap.

The crew attacked the assassin known as Plague with full intent to kill, but Plague was holding his own. Whether it was shots from pistols and muskets, or slashes from swords and daggers, even simultaneous attacks, he seemed to avoid them even if by the skin of his teeth.

Plague was adept at using each opportunity to his advantage. When he was about to be shot, he pulled a crewman trying to attack him with a sword in close to use as a shield. When he was being attacked by multiple people in close quarters he manoeuvred them around so their own attacks threatened each other.

Edward ran over and knelt down next to the Mayan. "Pukuh, are you well? Can you stand?"

Pukuh was breathing heavily, and one eye was closed in pain. His right arm was limp at his side, and at first Edward thought the arm broken, but the reality was far worse. The Mayan's arm was turning black. Pukuh's hand and half his forearm was overtaken by the devil creeping up it.

Pukuh kept his eyes on Plague. "That man is a demon. One lapse in concentration invites misery."

Edward stared at the man called a demon by the God of Death. The crew was cautious in attacking now that they knew how capable their target was. Plague used the break to search the ship for something, or someone, but his search seemed to be fruitless.

Who is he searching for? I'm sure he heard me say his name. Am I not his target?

Before Edward's question could be answered, Plague was hit with a kick to the chest, sending him back a few steps. William appeared out of nowhere in front of Plague on the cloth sail.

Plague smiled genuinely. "Why, if it isn't William, the Arcing Light himself. I haven't seen you in ages. Not since your disgraceful failure to protect your King. Oh, wait, I mean to say when you betrayed the Crown and killed him. Yes, that was the story… Perhaps I said too much." Plague shrugged.

William's normal facade of calm indifference faded and was replaced with fury. "Edward! Your sword, if you please."

Edward glanced from Plague back to William. Plague wouldn't let his eyes leave William for a second. Edward took out his cutlass and tossed the shining gold sword to William, who caught the blade in the air, not letting his gaze leave the assassin.

"I have been waiting for this day for seven years. No one interfere! This is my fight!" William said.

"Best make it count then, my boy."

The two warriors circled each other, with all eyes on them. William's knees were bent and he held the cutlass close with one arm braced behind the blunt edge. Plague held two knives, one high and one low, while he stalked the small battleground like a lion out for prey.

William moved first, and Plague joined him. The two warriors danced on the *Freedom*'s deck. The two men were evenly matched, and the only sound was the occasional stamp of a foot on the wooden deck or a scraping of metal as they dodged, ducked, and deflected the other's strikes. To those watching, the fight was like a choreographed play.

Edward and Pukuh observed the battle with wide eyes. Edward, at the close angle he was, had difficulty keeping track of the two men. "William will not last. We must remove this man from the *Freedom* or he will destroy us all," Pukuh whispered.

Edward glanced over to Pukuh. The man was holding his right arm, the Black Death still crawling steadily up to his elbow. Edward carefully concentrated on the two fighters in front of him and waited for an opportunity.

William's and Plague's blades flashed as they swung them through the air. William took a wide swing horizontally. Plague ducked down, then jumped up and slashed at William horizontally. William leaned back to avoid the blade then thrust the golden blade forward. Plague jumped back, almost to the edge of the ship.

Edward saw movement in his peripheral vision on the waist of the ship. Christina was still lying there, and beside her stood Tala. Edward knew what he needed to do.

"Tala!" Edward called. "*Épaule!*" he yelled, pointing to Plague.

Tala rushed up the steps and leapt at the assassin. Plague was so focused on William, the wolf caught him completely off guard. Tala bit down on Plague's shoulder, stopping him in his tracks.

"Tala, *courir!*" Edward commanded as he rushed towards Plague. Tala released her prey and ran away. Edward slammed into Plague's chest with his shoulder. The assassin was sent flying backwards. He hit the aft railing and flipped overboard into the water, hitting with a splash and sinking below the surface. Bubbles rose from where he fell in.

"Men, fire at will!" Edward shouted.

The crew ran to the aft railing and fired into the water. The dozen cracks and snaps from the pistols and muskets sounded out, and the bullets popped into the sea where Plague had fallen.

The ship was still moving forward, but the crew continued to fire where they thought Plague landed until they were out of range.

Edward searched the sea, then the aft of the ship in case Plague was hanging onto the back, but he couldn't see him anywhere.

"Captain, look!" A crewman yelled, pointing to the water a couple of hundred feet away.

Plague was treading water, seemingly unharmed. He had swum out of harm's way as soon as he fell into the water. Plague stared at the *Freedom* as she left the island of Badabos far behind.

26. THE BREAK

"William, you must cut off my arm!" Pukuh yelled.

Pukuh was kneeling and holding his right arm extended. The black disease was still silently creeping past his elbow and up his bicep. The progression of the poison Plague had hit him with was rapid, to say the least. Pukuh had trouble keeping his arm steady in the air.

"Someone bring Alexandre!" Edward commanded. Edward knelt down beside Pukuh. "Pukuh, there's no need to go to such lengths. Alexandre will cure you."

"He will not. The poison is spreading too quickly. Do it, William," Pukuh said forcefully; sweat coated his tan face, dripped off his brow, and fell to the wood deck.

William bent his knees and held the cutlass in two hands. Edward stood and approached William. "You cannot seriously be considering this. What are we to do after we cut off his arm, hmm? Let him bleed to death?"

"The man has chosen his path. We will find a way. Step aside," William said.

Edward ignored the order. "If we can find a way to stop Pukuh from bleeding out then we can find a way to stop the poison." Alexandre ran up to the poop deck. "Alexandre! There you are. Can you please talk some sense into these two? You can cure the poison, no?"

Alexandre stared at Pukuh's outstretched arm. Alexandre, his eyes tired and defeated, shook his head. "This poison is beyond me. Dismembering is the only way, and that we have the chance to amputate is a *merveille*."

William and Pukuh both tensed for what was to happen. Edward jumped in between them. "Hold, hold! What will we do afterwards? In case you are not aware, it is rather difficult to start a fire on a blasted ship! How will we heat the oil to stop the bleeding?"

Alexandre folded his arms. "We can produce the same effect with a chemical burn. Continue on, *messieurs*, I shall return presently." Alexandre ran and disappeared to the deck below.

Edward refused to move. "There must be another way."

William inspected Pukuh's arm. The poison had spread halfway up his bicep by now, and was no doubt further along internally. "This is no time to argue. If you will not move I will show you why

I am called the Arcing Light."

William stood straight and closed his eyes while holding the sword at his side. After a moment, William opened his eyes. With speed unparalleled, William ran past Edward in the blink of an eye. When Edward turned around, William was standing behind Pukuh, his back turned and the blade at his side. Pukuh's right arm fell with a thud.

Alexandre ran up to the poop deck with a bottle of clear liquid in hand. He took charge of the situation. "Hold him down!" Alexandre commanded.

Edward, William, and several of the crewmates laid Pukuh down and piled on top of him so he couldn't move. Blood was gushing out of the stump on his shoulder, but Pukuh didn't scream once. His teeth were bared, his eyes were wide, and he breathed heavily like an animal.

Alexandre didn't wait or slow down to warn Pukuh, he pulled the cork stopper out of the bottle and poured the clear liquid over the wound. The perfectly sliced cut boiled and bubbled as the acidic chemical burned Pukuh's flesh. The remainder splashed to the deck and ate through the wood.

Pukuh thrashed and screamed in pain. The sound was like the low rumble of a wolf and then turned to a high-pitched cry of an eagle as Pukuh lost his breath. He continued to howl and writhe in pain against the crewmates holding him down.

"*Mon Dieu!*" Alexandre yelled over the screams. "He should have passed out from the pain by now. Quickly, make him unconscious before he goes mad!"

"Sorry Pukuh." Edward raised his fist and punched Pukuh in the jaw, causing the Mayan's head to strike the floorboards, knocking him out. His eyes closed and his body went limp. The crew fell off of him and let out deeply held breaths. Pukuh's wound was closing like Alexandre had said, but the skin was still boiling from the burns.

"Move him below deck so he may rest," Edward commanded.

The crew lifted the Mayan and carefully carried him down to the waist with Alexandre in tow, hanging onto the blackened arm.

Edward rushed to Christina's still body on the waist of the ship. Anne was at Christina's side, stroking her strawberry-blond hair. "How is she faring?" Edward asked.

"Still pale as a ghost, but her breathing is normal. I think she'll be fine," Anne replied with a smile.

"Let's take her below deck and place her in a bed."

Edward picked up Christina's body with Anne's help and they carefully took her to the crew cabin. On the way, Edward noticed Alexandre and Henry in the surgeon's room next to an obscured body.

Edward and Anne continued down another ladder to the crew's quarters and laid Christina onto one of the beds. Anne filled a bowl with water, then dipped a cloth into it and wiped Christina's forehead.

"I'll be fine here. Henry needs you."

"Thank you, Anne." Edward kissed Anne on the forehead and then ran swiftly back up to the gun deck and into the surgeon's room.

The shelves were lined with bottles in protected cabinets so they wouldn't sway and crash with the movement of the ship. A broad operating table stood in the centre of the room, and at the sides were small cots and chairs. A body lay on the table, covered by a large cloth sheet, and in one of the cots Pukuh was resting.

Edward stopped at the sight of the covered body, then slowly lifted the covering, and saw his fears made true. Henry's mother lay there, dead. A different poison from Plague had reached her heart and killed her before she could be saved. For one last sign of hope, Edward looked to Alexandre, who shook his head and dashed Edward's tiny hope to pieces.

The smell of death already hit the small room and mixed with the scent of unfamiliar chemicals that prickled Edward nose. Edward's eyes also watered, but not from the smell.

Edward wiped his eyes and moved to Henry, who was sitting down in one of the chairs, tears in his eyes. "Henry…"

Henry raised his hand weakly. "Don't, just… don't. I can't take this anymore, Edward."

Edward was taken aback. He didn't know what to say to comfort his friend.

Henry ran his fingers through his straight brown hair. "I can't take the fighting, the killing, and the death any longer. I'm tired, Edward. I want out."

Edward's mouth went agape. "W-what?"

"I want off this ship. I have the money according to the commandments, so I want you to take me to the next port and we'll go our separate ways."

"Y-you must be joking. After all we've been through? After what the assassin did to your mother?"

"The assassin is not the real reason my mother died. He may have poisoned her, but we put her into harm's way."

"What? Us? If we're to blame anyone for this it should be the assassin, not you or I. Listen to what you're saying, Henry."

"I know what I'm saying. The fact of the matter is that we broke the law and these are the consequences. This all stems back to the day you decided to hold the pistol to Captain Smith's head. I'm not saying I'm without blame. I could have left you, but I didn't. I've paid the price of ignoring the truth, but I will not pay any more. I'm done."

"What about all we've been through? What about our friendship?" Edward pleaded.

"I've seen what happens to a friend who disagrees with you. I've made my decision, Edward, and it is final. I won't be your accomplice anymore. I won't be another victim in your never-ending game for freedom."

Upon seeing Henry's unwavering expression, Edward lowered his hands. After the initial shock subsided, anger crept in, and Edward wanted nothing more than to hurt Henry. But Edward saw the covered body of Henry's mother once more, and realised Henry had already been hurt enough.

Edward quickly left the room and closed the door behind him. He was exhausted and it all hit him at once. He shuffled below deck and sat on the edge of his bed. On the opposite end Anne was still sitting next to Christina, and upon noticing Edward she came over and sat next to him.

"So Henry has told you his decision, has he?"

Edward opened his mouth to respond, but the words didn't come. He ended up nodding slightly before he sank to his knees.

After a moment Anne stroked Edward's back. "I won't leave you," she whispered.

Edward shot up. "Promise me," he said grabbing Anne's hand and gripping it like a lifeline.

"I promise you, Edward, I will never leave you."

Edward peered into Anne's steely gaze, the strength of her words reflected in the window of her soul. The oath Anne swore was etched in the deepest parts of her.

Edward fell into Anne's shoulder and she stroked his wavy hair; he took the strength she wanted to impart, until night was upon them.

27. PUSHING HIM INTO DARKNESS

Christina bolted upright, taking a deep breath and waking from the stupor she had been in for so long. She let out a scream of pain as her movement shifted the wound in her stomach. Christina clutched her chest as Anne pushed her back onto the bed.

"Easy, easy, you're still healing. Lay back down, gently now." Anne's voice was soothing but firm.

Tala, sitting at the side of the bed with Anne, had jumped up when Christina awoke and now gazed at her expectantly, panting. Christina petted Tala's luscious fur, calming the wolf down.

Anne lifted Christina's shirt and, sure enough, her stomach was bleeding from the movement. Anne took a dab of water and cleaned the wound before applying a green paste which made Christina wince.

"What's that?" Christina asked.

"This is the plant you recovered from Pukuh's homeland. It will help heal you faster." After Anne applied the paste she covered the wound in cloth to seal it.

Christina's eyes opened wide as she recalled the circumstances of her receiving the wound. "What happened? Was Edward hurt?" Christina asked, nearly bolting up again.

"Edward is unharmed. Pukuh assisted in the fight, affording Edward the necessary time to bring you back here. You lost much blood and were unconscious for several days."

"Days? How did we escape Plague? Did Pukuh kill him?"

"Unfortunately, no. Pukuh was injured with poison and we were forced to amputate his right arm. We only managed to flee because of William and Edward."

"Even Pukuh was no match for him? I never believed it possible." Christina winced and lightly touched the wound on her stomach. "The man's eyes were terrible. It was as if I was struck by a knife... Well, I was," Christina said with a chuckle, "but you know what I mean." Anne nodded. "I don't think I was fighting as well as I could have before I was hit. I imagine that's how people feel when they behold Edward's eyes."

Anne faltered for a moment when she realised what Christina meant. "If Plague has eyes similar to Edward's, he is fearsome indeed. I haven't yet seen the man for myself, but the waves he has caused are clearly visible."

"Can no one stand against him?"

"I fear we may be wholly outclassed." Anne let out a sigh. "We must intensify our training if we are to stand a chance."

"I am with you, sister." Christina raised her hand.

Anne smiled widely and grasped Christina's hand. "I don't have a sister, but I will be glad to call you mine."

"So, sister, what would you say to helping me take a walk? I wish to feel the salt air on my face and see my brother again."

Anne frowned. "Alright, but we must be careful. We don't want the stitches to come undone."

Anne helped Christina up from the bed and then lent Christina her arm. Christina held firm to the offer, with her other hand on Tala's back as she moved on her wobbly legs to the ladder.

After slowly making their way to the gun deck, the two took a break at Anne's insistence. "So what about Tala, has she been cared for?" Christina asked Anne.

"She has not left your side since you were injured, and growled at anyone who approached. Alexandre could not get close, so I have been taking care of you and feeding her. She is very loyal."

Christina scratched Tala's chin. "I wish she was with us when we fought Plague. Things might have turned out different."

Anne nodded. "She actually helped in removing Plague from the ship. She's quite the fighter, as are you... Oh, one detail I neglected to mention: Edward wishes for us to use aliases when in town to help avoid another run-in with the Plague."

"I'll be sure to create one."

"Well, one more flight and we are done."

Christina and Anne resumed their trek up. After some time, the two women reached the top deck and the open air.

Christina took a deep breath in through her nose and let out a joyful sigh as she smiled. She scanned the horizon, taking in the ocean and the crew moving about on the *Freedom*. Her smile soon faded as she noticed the melancholic faces on those passing by.

"Is it because of Pukuh's arm?" Christina asked Anne.

Anne shook her head. "No." Anne opened her mouth, but needed a moment to speak the words. "Henry has chosen to leave the crew," she whispered.

Christina would have reared back in shock had she not been tied to Anne for support. "Why?" Christina's shock blurted out the question, then she added, "No, don't tell me? His mother?" almost directly after.

Anne nodded solemnly.

"Poor Henry. I would not blame him for his decision."

"Nor would any, but Edward seems fit to blame himself," Anne said, her oft-withheld emotions showing for the first time in her eyes and face. "Enough of this bitter melancholy. The crew has yet to notice us here, so let's show them you are well that their spirits may yet be raised."

Anne and Christina roamed the ship and talked with the crew, who, upon noticing her up and about, turned from frowns to smiles immediately. Many gathered around, causing Christina to say a few words to calm a growling Tala, and wanted a recounting of the battle against the Plague. As Christina told her story to those gathered the crew became more animate with each blow and manoeuvre. When the story was over, the men shouted curses to Plague and promised he would be killed for what he did to Christina.

Christina smirked. "You'll need to get in line, boys. The next time I see him I plan on returning his gift to me a thousandfold." As she said the words, she stood a little taller.

The crew laughed jovially while wishing her a swift recovery. After a few more moments of talking, Anne pushed everyone away.

"Back to work, men. Christina needs to see her brother." Anne helped Christina past the men and up to the quarterdeck where Herbert was at the helm.

Herbert was speaking with a crewmate when Christina approached. The crewmate's eyes wandered, which caused Herbert to turn himself around. The sight of Christina up and about nearly brought tears to his eyes.

Christina moved away from Anne and gave her brother a hug. "Don't worry, I'm not going anywhere."

"This is all my fault. I should never have brought you with me to this ship," Herbert whispered, his eyes cast downward as he gripped her hands like a vice. "I never wanted my quest for vengeance to hurt you."

Christina hushed him. "I'm the one to blame because I wasn't strong enough," she whispered. She pulled back, caressed Herbert's cheek, and touched the carved rose on her chest. "You're not the only one on a quest."

Edward stepped down from the poop deck and Christina's gaze was drawn to him.

"Edward!" Christina yelled.

Edward's smile to Christina was accented by cold eyes from a deep depression, but the young girl paid it no heed.

"You have recovered nicely," Edward commented.

"If not for you and Pukuh I would probably not be here."

"We both owe Pukuh a debt. I would have suffered the same fate if he hadn't arrived."

"Henry's mother wasn't so lucky, I hear."

Edward's mouth opened as he was caught off-guard by the comment. "No, she wasn't. If you'll excuse me, Christina."

Christina carried a sad expression on her face as she nodded slightly. Edward descended to the main deck and further into the bowels of the *Freedom.*

Anne approached Christina as she stared at the descending figure of their captain. "He just need a bit more time. The wounds are still fresh."

Christina turned to Anne, concern on her face. "The world seems to be conspiring to thrust Edward into darkness."

Anne's eyes reflected the sadness in Christina's. "The world is full of darkness. Some who live too long in the dark can lose themselves. We can only hope our Edward is strong enough not to let himself be lost."

"Or hope becoming darkness itself is what makes him strong," Christina added.

Anne couldn't be sure, but she noticed a slight grin twitching on the young girl's lips.

The *Freedom* landed at Port Royal a few hours before nightfall. The sun had disappeared behind the heavy dark clouds covering the sky. Garish lightning and screaming thunder loomed in the distance.

The mood aboard the *Freedom* was reflected by the dull and depressing weather. The crew knew why they were there, and none liked it. One of their family was leaving, and they couldn't do anything about it despite varied attempts during the travel from Badabos to Port Royal.

The crew were gathered on the main deck, and after a gangplank was placed over the port side they watched the ladder leading to the lower decks expectantly. Edward stood on the quarterdeck with Anne, Christina, and Herbert. Anne held Edward's hand as they silently watched with the crew.

After a moment of waiting and a clap of thunder, Henry emerged from the gun deck. In his arms he carried a wrapped body, his mother, and over his shoulder he held a sack with his meagre belongings.

When Henry reached the gangplank, he turned around, making eye contact with many in the crew, but not talking to any. His eyes eventually met Edward's. Edward gripped Anne's hand tighter as Henry stared at him coldly.

Henry turned, adjusted the weight on his shoulder, and slowly disembarked. The wind gusted strongly in his direction, urging him forward to Port Royal and further from *Freedom,* from his now former family, from his surrogate brother.

Henry's brother, Edward, also felt the push of that wind. The same sea winds which had guided Edward's father away from him were seeing fit to take his brother from him now. The wind pushed Edward to the sea years ago, and now pushed him to land.

Edward's feet moved of their own volition. He released his grip of Anne and quickly found himself on the gangplank to the harbour of Port Royal. Edward chased after Henry to the main street and out of sight of *Freedom*.

"Henry!" Edward yelled. Passersby stared at the tall bearded figure, short of breath and with desperation in his eyes, and then hurried about their business. Henry stopped, but didn't turn around. "Please don't leave. I need you."

Henry stood stock still, eventually raising his head to the heavens before he glanced over his shoulder. "No you don't," Henry said, and started walking again.

Edward gripped his hand tightly, so tight it shook. He remembered all the times they'd laughed, fought, and cried together, and how those times would never happen again. The feeling hit him like a bullet and, before Edward knew what he was doing, he was pointing a pistol at Henry in a shaking hand. "I won't let you leave, Henry."

Henry sighed and turned around. When he saw the pistol he took a step back. "What are you doing, Edward? Are you out of your bleeding mind?"

The townsfolk who saw Edward pull out the gun either ran away or hid in their houses for fear of what was about to happen. The sky grew darker and the wind shifted, blowing against Edward's face and pulling back his longcoat, but he took no notice.

"I can't lose more of my family!" Edward yelled over the din of the wind.

Henry shook his head. "You don't have a choice in the matter, Edward. You lost me a long time ago." Henry turned and walked away.

"Stop!" Edward shouted.

Henry half-turned. "What are you going to do, shoot me? That won't make me stay."

Edward held the pistol trained on Henry, his hands still shaking, as his friend moved farther away. Edward began lowering the gun when a soldier tackled him from the side.

The gun went off. The bullet hit Henry in the back. Henry took two more steps and fell to his knees. He dropped his bag and his mother's body, then felt at his back. Henry beheld his hand full of blood before falling to the ground.

"Henry!" Edward screamed.

Edward fought the soldier off and ran to Henry, but more soldiers showed up with muskets pointed at him. With clenched teeth and eyes staring at his friend bleeding out on the street, Edward turned and ran. He ran as bullets followed his shadow. He ran as the rain finally set in and the winds urged him back to the sea harder than ever.

The officers chased Edward all the way back to the *Freedom*, now with swords out as the rain made their gunpowder useless. When the crew saw Edward being chased they quickly made the ship sea-ready. When Edward ran up the gangplank and onto the main deck, Anne yelled, "Cut and run!" causing the crew to cut the anchor line and dropping it into the sea. Without the anchor, or the hours needed to raise it, the *Freedom* was able to leave shore immediately.

The *Freedom* sailed back into open water and lost all pursuers in the storm. Amidst the rain, the lighting, and the thunder, none could hear the roars of their captain as he was haunted by his actions.

He truly had lost his brother now.

28. THE HOUNDS OF PORTUGAL

During the weeks of travel to Bodden Town, Edward didn't speak a word of what happened with Henry. Instead, he silently suffered with his shame and sadness. Not even Anne could pry the secret from his lips.

Edward kept his distance, and by the end of the trip his face was cold and like stone. The emotion was drained from his eyes and replaced with detached purpose.

Once arrived in Bodden Town, the gangplank was settled and Edward stalked across with leaden feet. Each foot fell with all his weight, and Edward looked as if he could collapse at a moment's notice.

Edward kept himself up and moving, and headed straight to the Bodden Brothers' home with Anne and John following behind him. When Edward arrived, the gates were opened for him and he was led up to the business room on the second floor he was so used to.

"The brothers with be with you shortly," One of the attendants said before closing the doors to the room behind him.

"Edward, can we talk about what happened? Naturally you would be upset with Henry gone"—at the word gone, Edward winced and closed his eyes—"but this feels different. You can talk to us." Anne reached for Edward's hand, but he pulled away.

Edward stared at the ground, then ran his fingers through his hair. "I fear if I say what happened it will make it become all the more real." Edward searched for an exit, but he had nowhere to escape the interrogation.

Anne glanced at John, concern in her eyes. John pulled Edward close. "It's alright, son, we're here for you."

Edward's eyes flashed open and he pushed John away. "I'm not your son, and you're not my father! Don't you dare pretend to be him."

John looked hurt by Edward's lashing out. Anne pushed forward. "Peace Edward, John meant nothing by it."

"And nothing's all he'll have. I don't need your sympathy, so leave me be. I don't need you two to talk with the Boddens." Edward stared daggers at the both of them.

Anne stared back at Edward with equal fury. "By your leave, Captain." She stalked out of the room.

John glanced at Anne and then back to Edward. "Your father

568

wouldn't approve of how you're acting, Edward." He didn't meet John's disapproving gaze, and John left the room.

Soon after, the Bodden Brothers Neil and Malcolm entered, peering behind them with confusion. "What has happened with the young lass and your accountant?" Neil asked.

Neil and Malcolm were wearing white satin ruffled shirts and loose blue vests with gold trim. The brothers matched, as always.

Edward shook his head and retracted to his current cold and distant demeanour. "Nothing. I need you to find me someone."

"Name them," Malcolm started, "and we shall find them," Neil finished with a flourish.

"Bartholomew Roberts. I believe you helped him find my crew before my escape, and now we are in need of his help again."

The brothers held disappointed expressions on their faces. "Such a shame you had not arrived sooner," Malcolm lamented.

"Roberts was here not two weeks ago," Neil clarified.

"Two weeks ago? Why?"

"He was searching for a man as well," Neil explained. "He was hunting a Walter Kennedy, and lost the trail months ago. He turned to us for help," Malcolm continued. "Our information network is simultaneously the most well-known and secret of the New World." Neil said, which made Malcolm laugh. "Aaron Cook has died, and we have acquired all his contacts with none of the subterfuge."

Edward chuckled; the Boddens having more power meant he had more power. "I recall the name, Walter Kennedy. Roberts said the man stole some of his treasure and left him for dead. Where did you send him?"

"Portugal. Specifically Lisbon."

"Portugal? Why there?"

"The Pirate Priest didn't elaborate, but he claimed Portugal was the last location he would have looked for Kennedy." "Perhaps the treasure you mentioned was in fact stolen from Portugal, and thus the last country Kennedy would think Roberts would head to."

"Your assessment, as always, is sound. I'll need the *Freedom* re-stocked for the trip, and a new anchor, as we cut ours to escape Port Royal."

"We will send word to our suppliers to gather a list." "And then take the cost from your shares, of course."

Edward nodded and said his goodbyes to the brothers, then headed back to the ship. Over the rest of the day and the whole of the next, the ship was resupplied with ammunition and food for the trip to Portugal and then some.

Anne, angry with Edward, ignored the captain until the night of the second day. While Anne and Edward slept on their bed in the crew cabin, the sounds of sleeping neighbours in the swaying hammocks nearby, and the slight lapping of the waves against the side, filled the ship.

"I forgive you," Anne said, her back against Edward's.

Edward turned around slowly. "Forgive me? For my outburst?"

"Yes. I know what you are experiencing is trying, and the wounds were still healing. You will talk with us when you are ready, so I will not press the issue."

Edward kissed Anne on the cheek and returned to his slumber. Edward didn't know when he would be able to talk about what he did. Talking about what he did made it more real, and the reality was what scared Edward most.

Freedom landed on the shores of Lisbon, Portugal, after a month and some weeks of travel. What met the crew was a venerable paradise unlike any they'd had the pleasure of visiting before.

The long stone bow-shaped harbour stretched from the sea and into a large inlet. Along the coast the harbour was broken up by sandy beach. The harbour, inlet, and beach were filled with ships of all sizes and styles and people of several nationalities. A number of warships were docked, as Portugal was involved in Queen Anne's War, siding with the Queen and fighting their neighbour Spain.

The harbour and beach quickly changed to stone houses hundreds of years old. As the *Freedom* approached the harbour, Edward noticed each house had different designs and additions setting them apart, aside from the broad strokes like the common red-tiled roofs. The tiles of stone on the sides of the houses were painted with floral patterns and murals attracting attention with bright colours and unique decorations. The houses and tall buildings were built on rolling hills covering the horizon.

For the first time in a long while, Edward noticed Pukuh coming out from the lower decks. Pukuh was recovering, or as much as one could call recuperating when half the time he was doing push ups with his one arm, and very rarely was let out of Alexandre's sight. Pukuh raised his left hand in front of his eyes, blocking out the harsh rays of the sun. He bid good-day to those wishing him well, and moved to the forecastle deck to gaze at the beautiful scenery.

Edward joined the warrior at the railing. "Breathtaking, don't you think?"

"Yes, this shall be a treasured memory, alongside many I have on this journey," Pukuh replied.

Edward peered at Pukuh's bandaged right shoulder. Alexandre said the wound had long since stopped bleeding, but the bandages were for the sores, which would take longer to heal.

"How's the arm?" Edward asked indelicately.

"Gone, brother, but not forgotten." Pukuh flashed the stump. He took a long breath in as he stared at the railing, and Edward could see tears welling in the warrior's eyes. "I still feel my hand as a demon haunting me, and my fingers yearn to be moved."

"I cannot imagine the pain you feel."

"No, you cannot," Pukuh said with bite. "If not for the princess's dog, that beast would have torn this ship apart."

"Aye, Plague was a tough bastard. You did well, brother." Edward placed his hand on Pukuh's shoulder.

Pukuh shoved the hand away. "Do not pity me! I am weak, and I paid the price." He turned his gaze to the ever-closer town, turning his back to Edward.

Edward's mouth was agape, trying to find the words, but none came. He felt like he was losing another brother.

"Captain!" Herbert yelled, waving for Edward.

"Leave me be," Pukuh said coldly.

Edward stood for a moment, then granted Pukuh's wish and joined Herbert on the quarterdeck. "What is it, Herbert?"

"I see the *Fortune*, she's docked to the northwest," Herbert replied, pointing off the port bow. Providence saw fit to swiftly bring the two together.

"Excellent, bring us around and drop anchor next to her," Edward commanded.

"Aye Captain!" Herbert replied before commanding the crew to furl the sails.

The *Freedom* floated beside the smaller *Fortune* and the anchor was dropped, causing them to draw to a halt just shy of being parallel to one another. The crew of the *Fortune*, upon seeing the *Freedom*, were waving and hollering to their friends.

Edward, Anne, Sam, and John entered a skiff and paddled over to the *Fortune*. A rope ladder was lowered, and the four boarded. When Edward pulled himself over the side of the *Fortune* and stepped onto the waist, he was met with a multitude of grins, albeit with some missing or discoloured teeth.

"The prodigal son has returned," a voice boomed from the stern.

Edward shifted his gaze to see none other than Bartholomew Roberts, the Pirate Priest, in the flesh. At seven feet tall, he stood well above most, even taller than Edward, and his loose white cotton shirt was rolled up to expose his massive hairy arms. He was at all times impressive, intimidating, but, with his smile, welcoming.

"Don't I need money to be prodigal?" Edward asked with raised brow.

Roberts laughed heartily. "Too true, too true. Let us say you are returned and have us a feast, shall we?" Roberts yelled, pulling Edward in close and raising his fist. The crew yelled in agreement to the festivities. "How have you been, young one? Let us head to my chambers so we may speak in private."

"Please, lead the way," Edward said.

Roberts took Edward and company into a cabin at the stern. Inside was a small room with a table, chairs, and a cabinet. Roberts bade the others to take a seat while he took some choice brandy from the cabinet, poured it into glasses and offered some to his guests. After brandy was distributed and Roberts had sat down, he restarted the conversation.

"So, my dear Edward, what brings you all the way to Portugal, and how, pray tell, did you happen upon me?"

"Yes, well, we were searching for you, and the Bodden Brothers helped point us in your direction. We need your help with something. I don't believe I told you the story of our ship and what we've been after this whole time, have I?" Edward asked while sipping his brandy. It had a scent of cherries and the taste was sublime on Edward's palate.

"*You* have not, but I was apprised of the situation by your red-haired beauty before we assisted in your escape," Roberts replied with a nod in Anne's direction. "Otherwise I would not have tested God's will that day and advised you to buy a new ship."

"That makes things easier, but that reminds me: when you met Anne, did you not think I broke the Pirate Commandments?" Edward asked, referring to the code he and Bartholomew Roberts created for how pirates are to act aboard the ship.

"I believe the rule is you had to seduce the woman aboard, yes?" Bartholomew asked rhetorically with a raised brow. "If you can find me any woman you could seduce aboard your ship, I will owe you a gold coin." Bartholomew grin as the others in the room laughed at his jest.

"Fair enough," Edward said with a smile. "Now, to the business of the *Freedom*'s keys. The final trial to reach the last key is upon us, but it's a dual trial." Edward passed the piece of paper with the clue to Roberts. "The trial requires a massive crew of possibly five hundred, or two crews working together. And, since we don't have the former, I was hoping you could help with the latter."

Roberts read over the paper as Edward finished his proposal. "Mmm, this does sound intriguing, but I'm afraid I cannot help you right now. We have problems of our own we must attend to."

Edward glanced to his comrades then back to Roberts. "Well, our business isn't pressing, so if you need assistance then our crew would be more than happy to oblige. You've helped us much in the past, it is only fair we should aid you in your time of need."

Roberts smirked. "A quid pro quo, as it were? You help us and then we help you?" Edward nodded. "The Devil is ever present, but the Lord provides to his faithful." Roberts rose and extended his hand. Edward stood and returned the hand to complete the arrangement.

"Now, tell us what you need."

"We are hunting for Walter Kennedy to pass the Lord's judgement upon him for his betrayal, but we have run into some problems. The Hounds of Portugal are protecting Kennedy, and, furthermore, kidnapped one of my crewmen as hostage."

"Kidnapped? Whom did they spirit away?" Anne asked.

"My first mate, Hank Abbot."

Edward's eyes shot wide open. "How could that happen?"

"Do not mistake these Hounds for some common group of bandits, they are well organised and have been the bane of the populace for some time. The Hounds came in a group upon Hank and a handful of my men in an alley. The Hounds killed everyone but Hank, perhaps to set an example, but they clearly do not know with whom they are dealing."

"And with us here the Hounds don't stand a chance." Edward raised his glass. Roberts shouted a 'Hear, hear!' in agreement before downing the remainder of his brandy. "Do you know who their leader is?"

"Unfortunately there is scant information about them. Rumours state the Hounds are led by a pirate who gathered ruffians and put them to task. Others say the Hounds are a front for a noble, or the Spanish, who are trying to dethrone the King of Portugal. No one knows what the truth is, but whoever their leader is, he is powerful and ruthless."

"Well, as always, we'd best proceed with caution. We'll split into groups and take a few different approaches. Anne, I want you and Roberts to take Alexandre and see if he can glean anything from where Hank was kidnapped." Anne nodded in consent. "Sam, I want you to see if you can be recruited by the Hounds."

"I'm yer man. I'll loosen some purses and try ta make friends in all the wrong places. I'm good wit that sorta thing." Sam laughed with glee.

"John, you and I will see what information we can gather. Maybe we'll have more luck asking around."

"Y-yes, Captain," John replied.

"And don't forget not to use your given names. This is a territory loyal to Britain, so there may be British navy here. Agreed?"

"Aye, Captain!" Edward's company replied at once.

Roberts bellowed a laugh. "So decisive, and no objections from anyone. I always knew you were special, Edward. I can tell great things are yet to come for you. I do have one question before we move forward: Where is your Welsh friend, Henry?"

Edward pursed his lips for a moment, then produced a hollow smile. "We... had a disagreement, and he's... no longer with us."

Roberts had a genuine expression of mourning on his face. "Such a shame. Perhaps someday he will return to the fold."

Edward showed another false smile, and after a moment to compose himself he responded with a simple, "Perhaps." Then with a deep breath he continued. "Let's find these Hounds shall we?"

"Agreed. Whoever their leader is, he must be trembling in his boots now."

In the bowels of a ship, Hank Abbot hung by his arms from the rafters. His body swung with the rocking of the waves. His eyes were swollen and blood dripped slowly from gashes on his cheek. His nose stung from multiple fractures and the horrible stench of rotten wood, vomit, and unwashed bodies. His lips were dry despite his damp surroundings. He had four broken fingers, three broken ribs, and a shattered knee.

Cold water was thrown in Hank's face, causing him to wake from his first moment of sleep in a week. "Wake up, wake up!" a man in front of Hank yelled.

The man was unkempt from head to toe, with long greasy hair, rotted teeth, and beggar's clothes. His eyes were wide and he didn't appear sane. The most striking feature on the man was a medium-sized chest stuck to his right hand. As the man moved around, a clinking sound could be heard in the chest, possibly of gold. Gold forever within his grasp but beyond reach.

The man moved close to Hank's face, staring at him with demented eyes. "This ain't tha time ta be sleepin' Hank, I told ya."

Hank lifted his weary head and spat blood in the man's face.

The man reared back his right arm, the coins clinking in the treasure chest, and punched Hank in the face, breaking his jaw against the solid wood and metal. Afterwards, the man wiped his face off. "That weren't smart, Hank."

Hank gave a weary laugh, and with much difficulty sputtered out, "Worth it."

The two were in a hold in the lower decks of the ship, a hold for prisoners. Hank was in a cage with iron bars surrounding him. Other people were in cages like Hank, but none hanging as he was, and none so bloodied.

Someone from the crew ran down from the higher decks to the

cell with Hank and the other man. "Captain, we received news about the *Fortune*."

The captain of the ship laughed maniacally. "Did they cast off?"

"No, not yet," the crewman replied.

"Well…" The captain paused, gripping Hank's cheeks. "Maybe we need ta teach 'em another lesson." He threw Hank's face away.

"There's more. Another ship showed up, seems to be in league with the *Fortune*'s crew. A fifth-rate frigate, could be trouble if they find us."

The class of ship piqued the captain's interest. "What wus tha name of tha ship?"

"*Freedom*. Isn't that the name of the ship what that famous bloke Blackbeard is on?"

The captain squeezed his fists tight. "I want the captain of dat ship," he seethed through gritted teeth.

"Kenneth?" the crewman asked.

The captain, Kenneth Locke, pulled the crewman in close. "I said, I want tha captain of that ship, and I want 'im now."

"Aye, aye, Captain." The man saluted before running back to the upper decks.

Kenneth turned back to Hank. "Now, where wus we? Ah yea, we wus gonna have some fun before the party starts. I hope ya last 'til then."

29. CACHE-HAND

"What do you see, Alexandre?" Anne asked the Frenchman.

Alexandre, eccentric as always in a silk robe and grey pantaloons, examined the scene of the attack and kidnapping. The bodies of Roberts' deceased crewmen were gone, but blood stained the stone alleyway. The doctor squatted down to peruse the dirt and mud, sometimes dabbing his finger into the wet dirt then smelling or tasting it.

"Assistant, my tools *s'il vous plait*," Alexandre commanded with outstretched arm.

Victor, better known to Alexandre as Victoria, brought Alexandre's bag and dropped it on the ground beside him. Alexandre glanced back to Victoria as she re-joined the others with arms folded.

Alexandre reached into the bag, produced a magnifying glass, and further investigated the scene. He moved around in a squatted position, waddling back and forth as he studied the ground.

"So, anything?" Anne probed, becoming impatient.

Alexandre placed the magnifying glass into his bag and stood up again. "*Non*, nothing. The only thing left is the blood and the *boue*... the dirt, and too much time has passed to glean anything. The soil is local, but I have no way to tell if this area has been contaminated or not."

Anne sighed, and Roberts prayed. Victoria's finger was pointed towards her feet, away from the area Alexandre was focused on. Beside Victoria's feet was something small and white which was barely noticeable.

Alexandre picked up the object in front of Victoria, not commenting on how she had been blocking his view beforehand on purpose. What Alexandre picked up was the petal of a flower. The petal had small purple dots and a yellow hue at what would be the throat of the flower.

"What is that?" Roberts asked.

"This, *mon prêtre de pirate*, is a step in the right direction," Alexandre replied.

Sam drank his glass full of ale to the end without stopping, then slammed the glass on the table loudly. "I win again!"

The man in front of Sam, a large burly brute, finished his ale after another second of drinking. He reluctantly pulled out his coin purse and paid Sam a few coins for their wager.

"Much obliged," Sam said before the man left the table. Sam then nodded to a crewmate who bumped into the man, deftly stealing the purse. "Another round on me!" Sam yelled, to much applause.

Another man approached Sam's table and sat down. "You're good," he commented.

"Not good 'nuff. That last one drowned me. I'll settle for an arm wrestle. What say the winner takes two quid?" Sam offered, placing his arm up to start the match.

"Sorry, I'm not here to lose money. I'm here to offer you an opportunity."

The words piqued Sam's interest, and for the first time he measured the man in front of him. By all appearances he was out of place amongst the rabble in the tavern. He wore a cavalier hat with a feather out the back, and long blond hair flowing past his shoulders. His face was handsome, as if untouched by fists or knives, or even the weathering of the sun. He wore a long-sleeved blue doublet with wide white collar up to his chin. His breeches ended past the knee and he wore long leather boots and white socks in between.

No way this nancy is with the Hounds. "I'm not interested in small time." Sam slapped the barmaid on the behind and winked to her after she delivered his ale.

"Trust me, this is not small time. Now, before I play my hand I want to congratulate you on your boy's cut-pursing. I must admit, I missed quite a few of the exchanges." The man leaned in close and whispered. "Now that that is out of the way, have you heard of the Hounds of Portugal?"

Sam's brow raised. "Who are you?"

The man smiled. "I'll take that as a yes. My name is Philip Culverson, and I am the second in command of the Hounds. We're always seeking promising young men such as yourself, and the rewards are much greater than the pittance you gained here today. Now, I've given you my name, may I have yours?"

"The name's James Bellamy." Sam leaned back and set his feet on the table. "Well, ye answered the 'why me?' and the 'what's in it for me?' Now how about the 'how can I trust ye?' and 'where do I sign up?'" Sam said with his usual hyena's smile.

Philip smirked. "I'm fond of you, James. I'll answer your latter question first: I need to be sure of two things before we take you in. One: You're good on a ship, and two: You're good in a fight."

"I've been sailing since I was a wee mate, and no one's better in a scrap than me," Sam said confidently.

"I'll take the sailing on faith, but the fighting I'll need to see for myself." Philip rose from his chair, picked it up, and smashed it into the back of one of the larger patrons. The other patrons in the dank tavern went silent and watched intently. When the man rose up and turned around he immediately saw Philip and started after him. "Sir, sir, I was not the one who hit you, this man over here did." Philip pointed at Sam.

To Sam's surprise, others in the tavern corroborated the story Philip told. *More Hounds?* Sam tilted his head to the man, rose from his chair, and drank the last of his ale.

The man reared back and swung at Sam. Sam pulled back, letting the man hit air. The man tried to hit him again and Sam smashed his glass into the man's face. The glass broke into a dozen pieces and lodged in the large man's eyes. Sam kicked the man in the chest and he was sent flying back to the bar counter. Sam pulled back his fist, and punched the man's face. The man fell to the ground with a thud, unconscious.

"Another round, if you please!" Sam yelled as he returned to his table.

The crowd in the tavern erupted into cheers and hollering. The barmaid quickly brought him another drink with a kiss on the cheek and a wink.

Philip grinned and bent over to whisper in Sam's ear. "One-Fifteen Rue Passadico, midnight. Come alone and tell them the *Caballero de las Flores* sent you." Before Philip left he dropped a flower into Sam's hand. A white flower with small purple spots and a yellow throat.

⚓ ⚓ ⚓

Edward leaned against the stone building. The rich floral design on the building contrasted heavily with his black leather longcoat and tricorn hat. Edward examined the hat, remembering the circumstances behind his first receiving a captain's outfit.

John had bought the outfit for him the first time they visited Port Royal. Edward was so happy because it felt like the first step in him becoming a real captain. Immediately after Edward received the outfit, however, he found out Henry was about to be hung at the gallows for his mistake.

Anger seeped in when Edward recalled what he did to Henry, and he crumpled the hat. Moments later, John emerged from the building. "Anything?" Edward asked as he reshaped and donned the hat.

"N-no, Captain. Still nothing. Either no one really knows, or they aren't telling us, I c-couldn't tell."

Edward scoffed and started walking down the street with John at his side. "Probably the former, the same as the others. They know nothing about the Hounds save from the rumours we've already heard. None have been captured and the Hounds ransom out high-ranking individuals for coin."

John wrung his hands with his usual trepidation. "P-perhaps the others will have more luck."

"Perhaps. Let's take a break. The day is hot and we've been walking much too much."

John pointed down the road. "There was a pub back a ways. Mayhap we can nourish ourselves as well?"

Edward led the way. "Now that you mention food, I also feel a bit peckish." Edward and John trekked along the cobblestone street, past the colourful houses and into the pub John mentioned.

The pub was a well-to-do establishment with clean stone walls and a well-lit interior adorned with chandeliers. The expertly crafted tables and floors were made of polished hardwood and filled with proper ladies and gentlemen.

When Edward and John entered, sweaty and ragged, the patrons and servers immediately stared at them. Many whispered about the new customers, no doubt appalled by their presence.

Edward paid them no heed and sat down at one of the lavish tables. After a moment a server arrived to take their order.

"Some rum and whatever you're serving today, miss."

"That will be two reals, sir."

"John, do we have any Portuguese currency?" Edward asked.

"N-no Captain," John replied.

"Do you take British currency?"

"Yes, two crowns will do."

Edward reached into his pocket and pulled out and handed three crowns to the server. The gentlemen and ladies were shocked to see such a man give such an exorbitant amount as if it was nothing.

The server smiled, thanked Edward, and went back to fetch the food for them.

"C-Captain, that was worth several bottles of rum and a week's worth of food," John whispered.

"The look on their faces was worth the price," Edward replied as he smirked and waved to the other patrons.

The server brought back their rum first, then in mere moments brought a plate full of steaming vegetables and thick cuts of herb-roasted meat. Edward received more share due to his generosity. Edward and John slowly enjoyed every bit of their exquisite meal.

"John, I wanted to apologise for before," Edward said out of the blue after downing some rum. "What I said was uncalled for. You've always been there for me, and you deserve better."

John was taken aback. "D-don't trouble yourself, Captain. I know how sensitive the subjects were, and I acted inappropriately."

"Nonsense, I know you wanted to help. I couldn't talk about..." Edward paused, the words hard to find. "The truth is... when I tried to bring Henry back I..."

Before Edward was able to continue, a smooth-faced gent in a feathered cap, long blond hair, and a blue doublet sat down loudly at their table.

"Oh, pay me no heed, please continue with your conversation. My business can wait," the man said, absentmindedly smelling a flower in his chest pocket and gazing at everything but the people he rudely interrupted.

Edward gritted his teeth. "You stepped into a private conversation, so you'd best state your business quickly or I'll force you to leave."

The man raised his hands. "I apologise, I meant no offence. I hoped you men were searching for the Hounds of Portugal, but I must be mistaken." The man rose from his seat. "I will leave you to your conversation."

"Hold! Hold, sir," Edward said urgently. "How did you know our business here?"

The man turned back around, took his cap off and bowed. "Philip Culverson, at your service. Knowledge is my game, and my birds told me where I could find you." Philip sat back down in the seat. "I trade information for money, and wherever I stand to profit you can be sure I am there."

"So you know where the Hounds are? How did you acquire such information?" Edward asked, dubious of the stranger in front of them.

"I do know where they can be found, and procured this information by having friends in the right places. Often it is not the questions you ask, but who you know to ask. I know who to ask," Philip said with a smirk.

"How much is your price?"

"This information is a bargain: free."

"Free? Why would you give away this information for free? What profit do you stand to gain?" Edward asked with raised brow.

Philip leaned closer and whispered, "Profit comes in many ways, my friend, and when the one and only Blackbeard is hunting for someone, he can't mean to conduct a pleasant conversation."

Edward frowned at John. They hadn't used their true names all day, yet Philip knew who Edward was. *Perhaps this beard really is a problem.*

"How did you find us out?"

"The name of your ship is famous, and, I mean no offence, but Edward Teach isn't the best *nom de plume* for Edward Thatch, if you ask me."

"Before you take us to the Hounds I have a few more questions. You say our ship is famous. Is my crew in any danger?"

"Do not worry, I've made the necessary arrangements to stall the marines. Your crew is safe, for now. Any other questions before we leave?"

"You said profit comes in many ways. How will you profit from our destruction of the Hounds?"

The smile left Philip's face. "The Hounds took my brother from me. I vowed to make them pay, but, alas, I am only one man. If I can point you in their direction, then my brother will be avenged. Whoever pulls the trigger matters not to me."

Edward peered into Philip's eyes. His story was believable enough, and the man himself appeared to be trustworthy. "Alright, we will avenge your brother after we conclude our business with the Hounds, I assure you. Lead the way and we'll formulate a plan to take them down."

Philip closed his eyes. "Truly I thank you." Philip rose from his seat. "I will show you the way to their hideout."

Edward and John followed Philip out of the pub and into the streets. They ran north through the side streets and alleys. Edward tired and needed to slow down after a few minutes.

"Hold, Philip. I think I ate too much, my head feels light." Edward leaned against a building. John, too, was leaning against a building on the opposite side of the street, until he fell to the ground with a thud. "John!" Edward yelled, stepping closer, but he fell to his knees abruptly. His body was shaking and he was having trouble staying upright. *What's happening to me?*

Philip knelt down in front of Edward. "Did you know the extract of certain flowers cause you to fall asleep when ingested?"

"You did this?" Edward's vision began blurring.

"Yes. Oh, and Blackbeard? Kenneth Locke says hello," Philip said with a laugh.

Edward grabbed Philip's collar, mustered the last of his strength, and punched the man in the face. After delivering the punch Edward fell unconscious.

Philip rose up and spat on Edward's motionless body. He took a handkerchief from his pocket and wiped off his bloody lip. "Let us bring these two back to the ship. Mustn't keep the captain waiting."

As Philip walked away, the Hounds of Portugal took Edward and John in their jaws and away from the safety of their friends.

Blackbeard's Ship

Edward awoke slowly, his head pounding, and the effects of whatever he was drugged with still coursing through his veins. He couldn't lift his head, and his eyes only slightly opened. His feet and hands were bound in chains, and he was hanging from the ceiling of a ship in a barred cell.

Edward moved his eyes around, noticing John hanging beside him in the same dulled state. In the dark ship he could see other barred cells, similar to the one he occupied, with other prisoners. The wooden floor was wet and rotting from too much water exposure. Rats slinked by Edwards' feet on the search for whatever food they could steal.

To Edward's right was the bow of the ship, and to the left, the aft. The aft had a wooden ladder leading upwards. Edward and John were near the middle of the ship on the starboard side.

"John? John, can you hear me?" Edward asked.

John did his best to swing himself around to face Edward. His eyes were open and he appeared unharmed. "I can h-hear you, Captain."

"You're not hurt, are you?"

"No, not that I'm aware. Where are we?"

Edward recalled the words Philip had said to him before he passed out. "We're on Kenneth Locke's ship."

John's eyes bolted open. "Kenneth Locke? B-but you left him on a deserted island."

"Yes, well, he must have escaped somehow. Doing well for himself apparently. He must be out for vengeance."

"Finally awake, ye bastard?" Kenneth Locke said, striding into the hold.

"Look who the rat dragged in." Edward planted his feet as he regained some of his strength. "I thought you were dead."

Kenneth smiled, showing his foul teeth as he entered the cell. "Oh I bet ya would'a enjoyed that real good, ya? I almost did die, a bunch o' times almost, but fortune favours me." Kenneth grabbed Edward by the cheeks. "Don't favour ye much, now does it?" Kenneth threw Edward's face back.

"How did you escape the island?" Edward asked while adjusting his jaw.

"Yer Captain Smith found me, locked me up. When I wus about ta lose me arm," Kenneth lifted his right arm, causing the coins in the chest to rattle, "I escaped. Been huntin' fer ya off and on ever since, and now fortune favoured me once again."

"So now what? You want to kill me? Get on with it. You're boring me."

Kenneth moved so close to Edward his rancid breath invaded Edward's nostrils. "Ye'd fancy that wouldn't ye? I love ta break this to ya: I'm gonna take things real slow with ye. Make ye bleed, make ye hurt, make ye beg for the end before I send ye ta Davy Jones."

Edward grinned. "There's just one problem with your plan Kenneth."

"Oh, whut's that?"

"I'm not very good at begging."

Edward smashed his head into Kenneth's face. Kenneth was sent back to the bars of the cell. Edward jumped from the ground and pushed his feet forward, pressing the chain binding them against Kenneth's neck. Kenneth was being choked against the iron bars of the cell.

Kenneth pulled his right hand back and struck Edward on his side with the heavy chest of gold. The force of the blow was so great Edward couldn't help but loosen his legs, releasing Kenneth. Edward fell back to the ground, his strength gone out of him.

After a moment's breather, Edward spat blood out of his mouth. The blow from the chest hurt more than any other punch he'd received before. "You have quite the right hook, Kenneth."

Kenneth lifted the chest on his right hand with ease, showing it to Edward. "They're callin' me Cache-Hand now. Your face is gonna be best friends with this hand o' mine by the time we reach our destination." Kenneth swung his arm back and uppercut Edward's jaw.

Edward's world went black once more.

30. JOHN THE FEARLESS

Edward shook himself awake. Kenneth was gone, and had been replaced by two men with muskets outside the cell. The ship was now swaying up and down with the waves.

Are we sailing now? "How long was I out for?" Edward asked John.

"An hour. Kenneth released the other p-prisoners, or killed them, perhaps. Either way, we're on our own now."

"I wonder if Hank was with them."

"I couldn't tell, all of the prisoners had rags on their heads."

"Well, if Hank was among them I hope to God he wasn't killed."

"Shut yer holes in there!" one of the guards yelled to Edward.

Edward decided to comply and bide his time. There would be a proper time to fight later, and now, when he was bound in every way imaginable, was not the time.

"Oi," the second guard said to the first, "grab us some eats and chairs, mate. This guard business is a bore, so at least let's be comfortable about it."

"And why do I 'ave to git 'em? Yer new, you do it," the first guard said.

"Precisely why I can't, mate. I don' know where nothin' is."

The first guard glared and pointed at the second. "Alright, but next time yer on yer own."

As soon as the first guard was up the ladder, the second turned around to reveal his face to Edward and John.

"Sam! What are you doing here?" Edward asked in surprise.

"Shhh, ye bleedin' idiot! They'll hear. I did jus' what ye asked and got recruited by the Hounds. I didn't know whut happened to ye until I walked down 'ere not a half hour ago."

"Well, you'll need to play your role a bit longer than expected now that we've left Portugal."

"Aye. Wus sudden too. Luckily I managed ta scrawl out a letter before we left. *Freedom* should know what happened soon."

"D-do you know where we're headed?" John asked.

"Somewhere in Ireland. I found out after we set sail, so the *Freedom* only knows you've been captured and I'm with you."

"T-that is truly unfortunate."

"Did Kenneth not recognise you?"

Sam laughed nervously. "Not yet, at least. He don' seem to re-member me. Got right up close too. Ye seem ta be the focus of his rage, and the year an' some made him forget everyone else."

"Well, at least we can be thankful for that." Edward noticed movement from the ship's ladder. Edward motioned his head that way, causing Sam to turn and see the other guard returning. The three stopped talking.

Over the next week, Edward and John did not see hide nor tail of Kenneth Locke. Various guards came and left during the days and nights, and each time Sam was able to he brought them extra rations to keep up their strength. If he hadn't they would have starved.

The ship docked at an unknown port, and, after Edward and John were blindfolded, they were let out of their cage and led away from the ship. The two were pushed along a sandy beach to a grassy plain, and then to a rocky road for a few hours, until finally being led into a building made of stone.

Edward could hear the crackling of a fire and the sound of wind through small openings high above him. He also heard a snapping noise like a carpet flapping against a wall in the wind. *Are we inside a castle?*

Edward and John were taken down a long winding stone stair-case, then through a hallway and into a room. Their blindfolds were removed. The room they stood in was an old cellar. On the right side of the room two thin beds were provided, but were more fit for holding rocks than men. On the left side of the room a wooden table had been pushed against the wall with two chairs. The back wall was covered by a wooden wine rack which probably used to hold much more wine.

The guards who led Edward and John down to the cellar took the chairs from the table and moved them in front of the door. The two sat watching Edward and John intently, pistols at the ready.

"Where are we?" Edward asked after taking in his surroundings.

"We're at shut yer shit-hole, that's where."

The other guard laughed. "Nice one, Markus," he said, then the two slapped their hands together.

Edward moved to the corner of the room where the beds where, and John followed. "We could easily kill those two and es-cape if they didn't have those guns," Edward whispered.

"We have to w-wait for an opportunity, but it must be tonight. We cannot allow Kenneth to start whatever it is he wants to do."

Edward nodded and lay down on one of the beds. After three hours, a knock came from the cellar door. Edward rose from his bed and tensed.

Sam entered after a few words with the guards. He had a loaf of bread and two cups of wine on a tray. Sam handed Edward the tray.

Sam had his usual hyena smile. "Enjoy the bread, ye bastards."

Edward inspected the bread and noticed a long cut across the middle. Sam winked at Edward, then left the cellar. Edward sat on the bed next to John, his back facing the guards and blocking their view. Edward reached into the bread and pulled out a knife.

He glanced at John; both knew what to do. John moved to the wall of wine and began rummaging through the remaining bottles. Edward hid the knife in his pocket, and walked over to one of the guards.

"I need to take a piss," Edward told one guard.

"There be a bucket over there. Piss in that," the guard said, motioning to the bucket with his pistol while still sitting in his seat.

"Oi, don't touch the wine, old man," the second guard yelled to John, standing up.

"I don't enjoy the wine you provided, so I'm taking another." John's voice was steeled with purpose.

The second guard walked over to John, leaving the first alone with Edward. "That wine's not fer you, old man. Hands off, I said."

John peered over his shoulder and nodded to Edward, which nod Edward returned.

Edward pulled the knife from his pocket and thrust it into the first guard's throat. First came a loud thunk, then blood splashed onto Edward's face and clothes.

The second guard turned when he heard the noise. John pulled a bottle of wine from the rack and smashed it over the guard's head. The guard fell from the blow. John caught the man by the hair and stabbed him in the throat with the broken bottle. He died without being able to make a sound. John lowered the man to the floor silently.

After the two relieved the dead men of their weapons, Edward started to leave, but John stopped him. He motioned to his feet and then removed his boots. Edward followed suit. Barefoot might be difficult after escaping, but they could move stealthily.

Edward went to the door and opened it slowly. No one was waiting outside in the hallway. Edward motioned for John to follow him as he left the room.

Edward and John passed through the short hallway, passing by several wooden doors and up the winding staircase. Edward held the knife in one hand, and the pistol from a dead guard in the other.

When Edward and John neared the top of the staircase they could see two guards at the top standing at the entrance. Sam was one of them. The way the staircase winded Edward was able to stay well out of view from the other guard.

Edward knelt down and tapped the knife against the stone. Sam turned his head to the noise and saw Edward.

"Did you hear something?" another voice said.

"Nah, wus jus' me boot." Sam tapped his foot.

Sam motioned for Edward to back up. Edward and John headed back down the stairs and waited. Sweat beaded on Edward's forehead as the silence and tension turned oppressive.

After a moment Edward could hear Sam say, "Did you hear that?"

"Hear whut?" the other guard said.

Sam didn't reply, and started walking down the stairs.

The sound of footsteps neared Edward and John. Edward backed down the steps slowly. *Whatever you're planning on doing, Sam, do it now please.*

As if hearing Edward's thoughts, a loud cracking noise preceded the footsteps stopping. They started again a moment later. Edward lifted his pistol in the air. Sam turned around the corner.

"Blimey, watch where you point that thing."

"I wasn't going to shoot you, trust me." Sam cocked his brow. "Alright, I almost shot you. I'm sorry, it's been a rough week."

"Well, best stay on yer toes, this is where things git dicey. We have to cross the great hall, up the stairs to one of the corner towers. I snuck some rope up there earlier so as we can climb down." Sam motioned his thumb in the direction of the tower.

"Why not head out the front?"

Sam raised his brow. "The front's too heavily guarded, mate. We'd not make it past one man. Our best chance is ta climb down silent and then make a run through the forest. I 'eard from some boys there be a town not ten miles south of 'ere."

"Lead the way," Edward said.

Sam moved swiftly and silently up the stone stairs, his feet lightly touching each step before moving to the next. The musty air of the castle was oppressive as they walked up, coupled with the smell of blood, sweat, and charred wood from torches on the walls.

When Sam reached the top, he stopped Edward and John, then casually walked through the opening, examining the room before him. After a moment he motioned for Edward and John to join him.

The great hall was an expansive rectangular room with a high ceiling and balcony walkways on the left and right sides. At three points in the middle of the hall were large stone fire pits, permeating the room with heat and an orange-yellow glow. Along the side walls were tapestries depicting battles Edward didn't recognise, and one depicting the crucifixion. All were weathered and worn and contributed to the room's musty smell.

Sam guided John and Edward to the tapestries and pushed them behind the dusty fabrics. As Sam sauntered along in plain sight, John and Edward followed slowly whilst trying not to expose their movement. When John and Edward reached the edge of the first tapestry Edward peeked out from behind and when Sam gave the signal they moved to the next covering.

The castle was quiet. Too quiet. The only noise beyond the crackling of the fire and the billowing and snap of the swaying tapestries was Sam's footsteps. Edward and John did their best to minimise the sound of their feet against the cold floor and muffle their deep breaths.

Where is Kenneth's crew? Or Kenneth, for that matter? Sweat dripped from Edward's brow despite the cold.

Sam whispered, "Stop," and Edward froze with John behind him. The two pressed up against the wall, motionless.

One of Kenneth's crew descended the stairs, an effeminate man with a feathered cap, the same man who had captured Edward and John in Portugal, Philip Culverson.

"James, yes?" Philip asked, brow raised in question.

"You should know, pretty boy, you brought me 'ere," Sam replied, trying to maintain his smooth, cocky, composure.

"Yes, I suppose I did. I haven't had much chance to talk with you since then." Philip leaned against the wall of the castle, in the middle of the tapestry between Edward and John. Philip was centimetres from touching Edward's shoulder with his own. "Tell me: what do you think?" Philip asked, gesturing about.

Sam glanced at where Philip was leaning, then back to Philip's eyes. "This castle be nice an' all, but we be pirates, eh? When do we be pirates? I don' understand why we're torturin' those blokes in the basement if we ain't gettin' us no gold."

Philip gazed into one of the fire pits. "In truth I do not know much either. Kenneth refuses to tell me any details on why he has a problem with the Blackbeard pirates. All I was able to squeeze out of him is that it relates to his hand. Anything involving his hand is a sore subject with my dear captain." Philip lifted himself from his leaning position and started walking away from Sam.

Sam, Edward and John all let out silent sighs at their narrowly avoiding catastrophe. Sam turned around. "So why do you follow him so blindly?"

Philip turned around, walking backwards as he talked. "Despite his eccentricities, he always brings the gold eventually. And, I owe him a life debt."

Sam nodded, and Philip turned back around, heading to the front door of the castle. Sam turned and began walking slowly toward the stairs, listening for the door to open.

"James?" Philip yelled suddenly, making Sam jump.

Sam peered over his shoulder. Philip was standing in front of the spiral stairs leading to the cellar. "Yea?"

"Why is no one guarding the stairs?" Philip asked, pointing to the empty opening.

"Oh, that'd be me, boss. Jus' takin' a walk round the hall ta stretch me legs," Sam replied coolly.

Philip eyed Sam curiously. "Yes… well don't go too far."

After Philip started walking again, Sam did as well. Sam made his way to the foot of the stairs as he watched Philip exit the castle.

"C'mon boys! Let's move," Sam whispered.

Edward and John peered out from behind the tapestry, then ran to Sam. He gestured for them to move up the stairs and to the left side of the second floor. Slow and steady wasn't cutting it, and the three knew that. They bounded up the stairs, Sam trailing behind to not make noise with his heavy boots.

"Head for the stairs at the end of the hall," Sam commanded, pointing to the other end of the balcony walkway.

Halfway past the hallway, the doors of the castle opened and three of Kenneth's crew entered. Sam, Edward, and John all jumped behind one of the tapestries covering the walkway.

"So then the bloke said, 'Oi, she didn't say mittens!'" The three laughed at the punchline Edward, John, and Sam would never know the setup for.

One man stopped and pointed to the cellar stairs. "Ain't people suppose'ta be blockin' the cellar?"

"Yea, two blokes: The greenhorn and Gregory."

"Somethin' don' feel right," the first man surmised, and all three pulled out weapons and descended the stairs.

"Go, go!" Sam whispered urgently.

The three ran up the stairs as fast as they could. Noise was not an issue now, speed was the only advantage that remained. The sound of Sam's boots reverberated off the stone walls loudly as he rushed to the top of the tower.

When the three reached the top, the wooden door to the tower was being opened by one of Kenneth's crew. Edward pulled out the bloody knife. The fat man had a split second to realise his doom. Edward jumped and thrust the knife deep into the man's eye and they both fell to the floor.

John leapt over Edward and cocked his fist, blitzing towards a sitting man on the left side of the circular tower room. The man got to his feet. John delivered an intense blow between the man's eyes. The man fell, unconscious. John knelt down and snapped the man's neck, killing him.

To the right, a third man stood and pulled out a pistol. John flashed demonic eyes at him and the man flinched. Sam kicked the pistol out of his hands, and then delivered another blow to his un-guarded centre. The man fell backwards and out the window of the tower. He plummeted to his death in front of more of Kenneth's crew.

Edward ran to the window, and saw the reaction of the crew-men at the bottom of the tower. They saw Edward and ran to the front of the castle.

"We need to get out of here, quickly," Edward said.

"Jus' need ta find the rope I left 'ere," Sam replied, frantically combing the room. He overturned boxes and barrels and other odds and ends, but couldn't find what he was searching for. "Where is that blasted rope?"

Edward and John both were scouring the room, but their lifeline was nowhere to be found. "It's not here," Edward said, nailing the coffin shut. He could see no alternate escape route, save jumping out the window to their deaths. The three could hear the voices of shouting people from below. "I won't have *all* of us dying here. There's only one thing we can do." Edward tossed the knife to John. "John, you know what to do." Edward closed his eyes and spread his arms.

John adjusted his glasses, flashed forward, and sliced Edward's chest. With John's precision, the wound was superficial at best, but it looked bad to the naked eye. Edward let out a groan.

"What in blazes are ye doin'?" Sam yelled.

"You're the only one who can make it out of this alive, Sam. Punch John to make it more believable."

Sam paused, the pain over what was to come evident on his face. "I can't."

"You must, son," John said, unwavering.

"This is my last command as your captain, Sam. I command you to live." Edward's eyes bored into Sam.

Sam took one last glance from John to Edward, then he reared back and punched John hard in the jaw. Philip and a dozen crew-men burst through the open tower door. John fell backwards, his head hitting the stone wall.

"What happened here?" Philip shouted.

Sam took in a heavy breath and smirked. "Jus' after ye left these jokers busted out and ran fer the tower. I chased 'em and took 'em out."

Philip beheld the scene. Edward lay on the floor, still clutching his stomach and breathing heavily. John spat blood and struggled to rise to his feet, making a show of it.

"Good work, James. I knew you were a good choice for this crew. Shame we lost so many in the process." Philip planted his boot on Edward's stomach, beside the wound. "I guess the Devil lives up to his reputation. You're quite the troublemaker, Blackbeard." Philip pulled the blade out of Edward's stomach. "Take them back to the cellar. I will talk with Kenneth." Philip shoved the bloody knife into Sam's hands, then pulled out a handkerchief and wiped the blood off his palm. "This ends now."

Sam joined Kenneth's crew and took Edward and John back to the cellar. Edward's and John's hands were bound in front of them and they were forced to kneel on the wet stone. Two people stood behind Edward and John with pistols aimed at their heads. Two more aimed muskets from the front, and several more sat in the room, watching them like hawks.

Dad damn these bloody bastards! There be no way out of this now. I'm sorry, Captain. Sam's apology was written in his eyes as he stared at Edward, hoping his words would reach.

After a few moments, Kenneth and Philip entered the cellar together. Kenneth was furious, but no moreso than he had previously been around Edward. His left arm balled into a fist, and no doubt his right hand, inside the chest, was clenched as well.

"Oh, so glad you could join us, Chest-Hand. Thanks for gracing us with your presence. Wait, was it Chest-Hand? No, no, Fortune-Fingers? Money-Mitten? Oh! I remember: Prize-Paw!" Edward jested.

Kenneth shook with rage. He pulled back his right arm and slammed Edward's face with a blow so hard it broke his nose and sent him to the stone.

"Six men! Six men of mine you killed!" Kenneth yelled as he kicked Edward in the ribs. Kenneth kept kicking and kicking until Edward's rib broke with a loud snap, then he stopped to catch his breath. "I demand compensation, and I will collect," Kenneth seethed.

One of Kenneth's men pulled John to one end of the room, and another propped Edward up to watch. Kenneth pulled out a knife and stepped behind John. He set the blade underneath John's neck.

No! Not John! "Kenneth, stop!"

"Oh? What will you do if I don't? Hmm?" Kenneth asked, not removing the blade.

Edward looked daggers at Kenneth. "I will kill you."

Kenneth was not fazed. "You can't kill me when you're dead."

John raised his bound hands. "It's alright Edward, I'm ready to die. The only regret I have is I couldn't keep the promise I made your father. Tell him I'm sorry, will you?" John said, stoic and unflappable even with the blade against his neck. Despite John's strength, he was so old, so tired. Edward had never seen John this way before, and only now realised how much he'd pushed John over these years.

"How can I?" Edward asked, tears streaming into his black beard.

John smirked even in the face of death. "Your father is in the Caribbean, Edward."

Kenneth's blade sliced through flesh, leaving a red streak across John's neck. Blood fell like tiny drops of red rain, joining its clear brethren on the damp stone. John followed the blood, his eyes slowly losing their lustre, and fell to the floor with a thud.

Edward reached out to John, his mouth agape. His mind splintered like shattered glass. He could neither feel, nor speak. As Edward's mind recovered, the shards played the scene of John's death again and again in his mind, coupled with Henry falling to the ground, a bullet in his back. Edward was responsible for both. Edward's heart filled with anger. Anger at himself for Henry, for allowing this to happen to John, and letting his crew down.

Edward peered up at the face of Kenneth Locke. The smug grin on his repulsive face was salt on the wounds.

Edward lunged at Kenneth, jumping over John's body and gripping the man's throat with his bound hands. Edward pressed hard on Kenneth's Adam's apple, choking the life out of him.

"I'll kill you, you fucking bastard!" Edward yelled as he slammed Kenneth's head against the stone. Kenneth's men tried to pull Edward off their captain, but he was too powerful. "Is this what you wanted, huh? You wanted to die? Let me fulfil your wish!" Edward continued slamming Kenneth's head into the stone, blood seeping into the crevices.

Kenneth's men punched and kicked Edward relentlessly. Edward's strength faded from him with each blow and his grip eventually loosened. Kenneth`s crew pulled Edward to the other side of the room and kept beating him until they were satisfied. When they were finished, Edward was numb from the pain. Kenneth recovered and dispensed a few swift kicks as well.

"That all ya got?" Edward sputtered.

"Save your strength, you'll need it to beg for your life," Kenneth said.

Edward used his remaining strength to pull himself up to his feet. He stood tall, towering above everyone else in the room. "I will never beg you for my life, nor will I beg to die. I will live, and I will make sure the last thing you see is my hands around your neck as I choke the life out of you."

Kenneth stepped on John's lifeless body, staring up into Edward's eyes. "Let's see how long your declaration lasts."

31. ESCAPE FROM LISBON BAY

"Where is Edward? He should have returned by now," Anne said to no one in particular. She stood in the stern cabin of the *Fortune*, gazing out a large window to the port of Lisbon, watching the boats and ships and people passing by as night fell.

"Shall I find him for you, your—?" William asked, nearly slipping out what Anne thought was a "your majesty," in front of everyone.

Anne contemplated her answer for a moment. "No, not yet. It's better to stay in one group. If something happens and we must find you too it will waste time."

William nodded in assent. Roberts bellowed a laugh. "He is probably boozing and brawling at this hour."

Anne stared blankly at Roberts as he continued laughing, then turned back to the window. "That's not something Edward would do. He's not a heavy drinker of wine, nor a gluttonous eater, and he is slow to wrath for silly reasons." Her arms were folded, trying to hold in the worry in her heart. *Something is wrong.*

Roberts laid his hand on Anne's shoulder, turning her away from the window. "Edward will be alright. Do not worry, child. As you say he is no fool. He would not run headlong into danger."

Anne turned away from Roberts. "Danger has an uncanny way of finding us, and that is what I am afraid of."

Alexandre and Victor were sitting at the table in the cabin examining the petal they found and talking in hushed tones.

"Are you discussing anything we should be privy to, *chirurgien?*" Anne asked.

Alexandre gazed lazily at Anne with his dark eyes. "Victor and I were merely *débattre* over whether this flower is from Northern or Southern Ireland." Alexandre was content to continue his argument, but Anne pressed for more.

"And what are your assessments?"

"I, correctly, say the flower is from Southern Ireland, as I visited there not a few years prior to moving to Port Royal. Victor has not been there in some time through his own admission, and things have… *évolué* since then."

Anne eyed Victor for an objection so a decision could be

593

made. Victor simply sat staring daggers at Alexandre and then Anne.

Anne took it as Alexandre being correct. "Now we know the flower is from Southern Ireland. That could mean the Hounds' base is there, or it could mean nothing. Until we hear from Edward and John, or Sam, the only fact is the Hounds may have been to Ireland and one of their crewmates fancies flowers, yes?" Anne stared a cold, Queen's stare at Alexandre.

"*Oui.*" Alexandre lost his smug smile and turned away from Anne's glare of disappointment.

"Useless," Anne said with frustration, turning back to the cabin window.

The room was thick with tension. William approached Anne and whispered in her ear. "Perhaps you should sleep, my lady. Waiting is of no use. I will search for him, so you may rest easy."

Anne turned around and patted her hand on William's chest. "Perhaps you are right. Thank you, William."

William bowed slightly, then led Anne to the cabin exit, but halfway there someone knocked on the door. William and Anne both glanced at Bartholomew, as they were guests of his ship and cabin.

"Enter," Bartholomew commanded.

One of *Freedom*'s crewmates entered with a letter. "Uh, Miss Bonney?" the crewmate asked sheepishly, unsure of whom to address. "The harbourmaster had this letter for us. It's addressed to you." The man held the letter in front of him.

Anne took the letter. William peered over Anne's shoulder as she read, and soon Bartholomew joined them.

"It's from Sam," Anne said aloud with excitement. She read the letter quickly and with each line her visage turned a new shade of pale. "Edward and John were kidnapped by the Hounds. Their leader is a man named Kenneth Locke. Sam says they dropped all their previous victims at the west harbour and left Portugal."

"Does the letter mention where they travelled?" Alexandre asked.

"No, Sam was not privy to that information, just that they were headed north," Anne replied.

"Who is this Kenneth Locke?" Roberts asked.

"He was an old crewmate whom we banished and left to die on an abandoned island. Somehow he survived and must be out for revenge. More importantly, Sam wrote that all other people they kidnapped were left at the west harbour. Mister Abbot may be among them."

Roberts glanced at Anne, then to the other members of the *Freedom* in his cabin. "But what of Edward? Time is not to be wasted here, child. The longer you wait the more danger your captain is in. Leave our problems to us, we'll join you later."

"We made an oath. We help you find Mister Abbot, then you help us. We have an obligation to help you in your time of need, and we would help you regardless."

Roberts glanced at the crew again, and they all nodded in consent with Anne's declaration. "You are, all of you, more honourable than any others I have met in my travels. Let us quickly see if Hank is alive, and then we'll save Edward from the clutches of evil!"

Bartholomew left the cabin with the others following behind him. Roberts commanded his crew to take them into the harbour, and the *Fortune* was manoeuvred to the closest opening. Despite the unusual amount of ships and people moving about for this time of night, the crew of the *Fortune* worked like a well-oiled machine. The helmsman swayed *Fortune* in between the myriad of ships and slowly eased the ship into the harbour.

After the gangplanks were set, Bartholomew wasted no time moving ashore to the city of Lisbon, heading straight west. Anne and William followed, but Alexandre and Victor headed back to the *Freedom* to notify the crew of their impending departure.

The three ran quickly through the streets, dodging the occasional passersby on their way west. The hulking figure of Bartholomew attracted attention as he stormed by, a stark contrast to the average William and the slender Anne following behind him.

"Mister Roberts, if we find Abbot, and he is…" Anne couldn't complete the sentence.

"I am prepared," Roberts replied, slowing his pace. "If God's will is to take Hank from me, then who am I to argue?"

Anne felt the resolve in Bartholomew's words; he did not have even a hint of doubt in his heart. *He is a true man of God, through and through.*

"It is not to say He and I will not have some words later if that is the case," Roberts continued with a hearty laugh, causing Anne to smile. "Rest assured, I have faith Hank and Edward are safe. And even those with faith the size of a mustard seed can move mountains!" Roberts said with aplomb before he started running again.

As the three ran, they noticed a crowd gathered in the direction they were headed. At this time of night, it could only mean something of import was happening, and the release of kidnapped nobles would fit. The three made their way to the centre of the disturbance.

A dozen people lay on the ground, wounds covering their thin, malnourished bodies. Surgeons were treating the wounded as best they could, but were focusing on the nobles first and foremost.

"Hank!" Roberts yelled, running to his friend. Anne and William were a step behind.

Hank was lying on the stone ground, a shadow of his former self. His right eye was gouged out, blood staining his ear and hair from the wound, and his left arm and leg were broken, the bone like shattered glass sticking out of the skin. Beneath the surface, his wounds were probably much worse, but he was alive.

"Didn't reckon I'd see ya again, Capt'n. Prayed my damndest." Hank's body convulsed as he coughed up blood.

"We're here now, so save your strength and don't talk."

"No, you need to listen," Hank gripped Roberts' coat. "They sent word to the military. They're gonna attack. Ye gotta run, Capt'n." Hank's last words fizzled out and he fell unconscious.

"Hank? Hank!" Roberts yelled, trying to wake him.

"He's still alive," Anne reassured him. "But he needs help, and if what he said is true we need to return to our ships. Alexandre has the skill to save Hank."

"Yes." Roberts pulled himself together and picked Hank up gently.

Roberts—with Hank in his arms—Anne, and William returned to where the *Fortune* was resting. They couldn't rush for fear of worsening Hank's condition.

When Anne reached the harbour, she could tell something was off. The small boats and ships were docked, and a few large warships in the distance were preparing to set sail.

"We must be off. Those warships will soon be upon us," William said as they boarded.

When Roberts entered the ship with Hank's fragile body in his arms, a crowd of crewmen gathered. "Listen men, our enemies will soon be upon us, so there are two things needing done: Firstly, we need to return to the *Freedom* to warn them, and have their surgeon heal Hank. Secondly, we must escape Lisbon with all haste. Understood?"

The crew responded with a firm "Yes," then set about removing the *Fortune* from the harbour. Once the mooring lines and gangplank were pulled back, Roberts' crew moved the *Fortune* to where the *Freedom* awaited. The *Fortune*'s crew fixed a gangplank across the two ships, and Anne and William crossed.

The crew were busy at work, but stopped when Anne and William came aboard. Alexandre and Victor were there waiting, Herbert and Christina were at the helm directing the crew, and Nassir was preparing the sails with help from the crew.

"Alexandre, Hank is at death's door and he needs your skills." Alexandre nodded and crossed the gangplank with Victor. After they were across, the gangplank was drawn. "All hands, release the sails! Herbert, head for the throat of the bay," Anne commanded.

Herbert nodded and when the sails were unfurled he threw the wheel hard to port, turning the ship parallel to the harbour. As the *Freedom* approached the throat, three ships moved in, blocking the exit.

"Three ships dead ahead!" Herbert yelled.

Anne ran up the steps to the quarterdeck, took the spyglass offered by Christina and examined the ships blocking their path. Two sloops of war on the left and middle, and one sixth-class frigate on the right. All three smaller, but faster, than the *Freedom*.

"We can turn broadside and fire a full volley," Herbert suggested.

"That won't help. Ships are behind us too. By the time we turn full circle we'll be attacked on both sides," William said.

Anne focused on the bay. William was correct: two battleships the same size as the *Freedom* were on a pursuit course. There was no possible way the *Freedom* and *Fortune* would make it out alive in an offensive battle.

"We have one chance," Anne said, closing the spyglass with a snap. "We ram between the sloop and frigate, fire our cannons, and escape. The *Fortune* can escape between the two sloops or follow us."

"What? That's insane!" Christina exclaimed. "Even if we break through they'll attack us on the way. We'll never make it."

Herbert studied the ships ahead of them, then peered over his shoulder at the larger ones behind. "No, Anne's right, this is the only way. The *Fortune* is a sloop, and won't be able to handle a battle head on." Herbert turned the wheel starboard into the wind. "Achieving ramming speed," he said.

Christina didn't appear happy, but she didn't object further. Anne moved to the edge of the quarterdeck to issue orders.

"We need men in the bow deck. Fire those cannons at will! Gunners below deck, ready for broadside volleys. Close-haul the sails. We are pushing through the blockade, men!" Anne yelled.

The crew hesitated only a moment before rushing to work. Alexandre had explained the situation already, but the crew felt odd taking orders from someone other than Edward, Henry, or John.

The enemy ships closed the gap between each other as the *Freedom* picked up speed. The crew on the sloops and frigate fired their cannons. The iron balls hit the ocean, splashing water across the deck. *Freedom* retaliated with the bow cannons, easily hitting the broadside of the frigate. More cannonballs were fired. The iron hit the *Freedom* on the railing and bowsprit, sending splinters of wood flying.

When the ships were close enough, the marines fired muskets and rifles. Anne grabbed a rifle and shot back, with the crew of the *Freedom* following suit.

Night was upon them, and the ships continued to fire upon each other in the moonlight. The large flashes of the cannons and the smaller guns, each with their own puff of smoke, reflected on the water in the pale luminescence.

In the battle, ear-splitting shots from more than six dozen cannons, loud pops from the guns, and never knowing where the next bullet would appear from, made even the hardest of men shake. The crews pressed, either through fear, anger, courage, or blind ignorance, to save theirs and their comrades' lives.

"Brace for impact!" Anne yelled as she gripped the railing.

The *Freedom* smashed into the bow and stern of the other ships. Wood scraped on wood as the sloop and frigate were pushed to the sides.

"Fire port and starboard!" Anne commanded.

The sound of fifty cannons pierced the crew's ears. The cannonballs left their iron prisons and ripped the enemy ships to shreds. The sloop's hull was instantly honeycombed with a dozen different holes, and it began sinking into the bay waters. The frigate survived, for the moment.

The crew of the two enemy ships jumped over to the *Freedom* in droves to escape the sloop, and to attack from the frigate.

A crewmate of the *Freedom* ran up from below deck. "We're takin' on water in the berth," he yelled to Anne.

Anne fired her rifle at one of the marines' legs, then kicked another in the chest, sending the man overboard. She scanned the ship until she found who she was searching for. "Nassir, take men below deck and seal those holes."

Nassir, towering above the marine in front of him, delivered a fierce punch which sent the man violently to the deck of the waist. "Yes ma'am." Nassir immediately went to work, helping free some of his mates from fighting to assist him in the belly of the ship.

Suddenly, the *Freedom* lurched to the port side. Anne peered up and noticed the problem. The sloop sank on its starboard side, and the sails had tangled in the *Freedom*'s main sail. If the sloop sank enough, it could take the *Freedom* with it.

"William, I need you on the sail with me." William nodded and began climbing the ratline to the main top. "Christina, will you be able to protect your brother on your own?"

Christina pulled out a pistol from her belt and fired it on a marine climbing the ladder to the quarterdeck. Out of nowhere, Tala appeared and ripped out another man's jugular before landing beside her companion. "Of course." She grinned, petting the wolf.

Anne nodded and followed William up the ratline to the main top. Some of the marines were crossing over from their mast to the *Freedom*'s main yard.

One man sliced across at William. William ducked down and kicked the man in the legs. The marine fell sideways, cracking his ribs on the spar before tumbling and snapping his neck on the waist below. Another man advanced and attacked. William grabbed the marine's hands and kicked him in the chest. The second man was sent back against a third and they both lost their balance and fell.

Anne gazed solemnly at the dead marines. "So much for trying not to kill them."

William didn't turn around. "After your mother sent the Plague, I realised there is no use saving those trying to kill you. I vowed to protect you, and I will live up to my vow this time, no matter the cost."

William moved forward to the edge of the spar before Anne could reply. He pulled out a knife from his belt and began cutting the rope binding the spars of the two ships together.

Another marine ran across the sloop's mast, about to jump over to the *Freedom*. Anne pulled out a pistol and shot him in the chest. The man clutched his chest and fell backwards.

"I too will not risk the lives of our family on the one I left behind," Anne said. William nodded and returned to cutting the cable.

Anne glanced down from her vantage point. The crew fought tooth and nail against the multitude of men boarding the ship. Christina protected her brother, with Tala's help, from forces boarding the aft. Herbert yelled orders to the crew, despite having been shot in the arm, and occasionally fired a musket as he managed the wheel. Pukuh was there too, trying his best to fight with his left arm.

Cannons were being fired at close range from the frigate, and the sloop was nearly submerged. The *Fortune* was fighting the other sloop ahead of the *Freedom*, and was almost out of the bay. *Freedom* was moving forward, but was severely slowed by the sinking sloop. Behind them the warships were closing in and would soon be within firing distance.

William sliced through the cords several times before throwing them away. "Help me lift the mast, Princess," he said, crouching under the spar.

Anne knelt down and lifted with all her might. William used his shoulder and pushed hard with his legs. The sloop's spar inched up slowly, but not enough to separate the two ships. After a moment's futile struggle William and Anne resigned and caught their breath.

"How are we to move a whole ship?" Anne asked, not expecting an answer.

William was breathing heavily while viewing to the scene below. "We don't need to move the ship, just the mast." William stood staring at the chaos below. "Charles!" He yelled to one of the gunners. The man named Charles ducked down to avoid the rain of bullets and peered up to the sound of his name being called. "Chain shot on the sloop mast!" Charles studied the mast stuck to the *Freedom*, and then to the sloop. He smirked and nodded to William.

William moved back under the sloop's spar, and Anne prepared herself. Charles ran to the bow cabin, dodging bullets and slashes, and returned with a specialty ammo. He held two cannonballs attached by a thick iron chain. Charles loaded the ammo into a cannon, aimed for the sloop mast, and fired.

The cannonballs spun in the air, and the chain hit the mast, rending the hardwood and separating the mast from the ship.

"Can we leave the mast?" Anne asked William.

William assessed the situation. "No, if we leave it and it falls the wrong way as we move forward it could damage *Freedom* or fall on one of the crew. If possible, we need to remove it."

William and Anne pushed and lifted the spar away from the *Freedom*. The sail swayed and pitched in the wind. William dug his back into the heavy wood. Anne lifted the mast like she was tossing a caber, her legs and arms straining with the effort. The two threw the mast to the port side of the sloop and it lurched forward and fell into the water with a giant splash.

Freed from the shackles of the smaller ship, *Freedom* moved quicker towards the mouth of the bay. The frigate was sinking, but the majority of the crew had jumped ship to continue the battle atop the *Freedom*.

Anne noticed several enemies heading to the *Freedom*'s lower decks. "Help rout the enemy on the waist, I'm heading below to ensure we are not sunk." William nodded, then climbed down the ratline. Anne jumped off the spar, grabbed a rope and swung down to the waist.

Pukuh was a few paces in front of Anne, fighting with a spear in his one arm. Pukuh's striking was efficient for not having his right arm, but he had difficulty parrying and blocking blows without the power of two hands.

The man Pukuh was fighting sliced his sword down. Pukuh blocked with his spear. The powerful blow broke the spear in half, leaving the Mayan defenceless. The man lifted the sword high in the air again. Pukuh was on his knees, his teeth gritted.

Before the man could attack, Anne stabbed him in the throat with a long dagger. The man fell to the ground, blood gushing from the wound.

Anne handed Pukuh a dagger. "Use this, Pukuh."

Pukuh accepted the dagger grudgingly. "Thank you, Princess."

Anne ran past those fighting and to the ladder to the lower decks. She jumped down several steps at a time, on the heels of the men heading below. She caught one on the arm, twisted him around, and punched him in the temple. The man fell to the ground unconscious and Anne ran to the next set of steps.

When Anne reached the crew cabin, she could feel a small layer of water on deck, seeping into the bilge. If enough trickled through the cracks, the bilge would fill and the ship would sink.

Anne could see the marines attacking the crew trying to patch holes. As Anne was about to run over and dispatch the attackers, a glint of light caught her eye in the darkness. On the bed Anne and Edward shared lay the golden cutlass Edward used. Anne grabbed the eagle-hilted blade, then rushed to the crew in need of help.

Anne slashed the back of one marine and slit the throat of another. The others were quickly dispatched by the crew. "Patch those holes now!" she commanded. Anne didn't wait to see the order followed through and instead jumped down a hatch located at the centre mast to the bilge.

The lowest part of the ship, below the waterline and the worst spot for a cannonball to hit, was rapidly filling with water. Anne landed feet-first and the water reached her chest even as she stood on the keel.

In the pitch darkness of the bilge, Anne saw five of the *Freedom*'s crew fighting three marines, the latter gaining the upper hand due to having weapons. Nassir and his helpers used timber meant to patch the holes for protection against the swords.

Nassir blocked a slash from one man, the cutlass embedding itself in the wood. The man tried to remove the weapon, but couldn't get enough leverage. Nassir twisted the timber to the side and the man released the cutlass to save his fingers. Nassir smashed the wood into the man's face, breaking his nose. The man fell backwards, clutching his bleeding nose.

Anne stabbed the man through the back as he floated towards her. Hearing his mate die, one of the marines turned and attacked Anne. He slashed at her. The water slowed Anne's reactions and she was barely able to bring the golden cutlass up to block. The man pushed down and his blade dug into Anne's shoulder. She used both hands to push back, only managing to stop the blade from going any deeper.

Nassir attacked from behind and cracked a hammer upside the marine's head, embedding it in his skull. Anger flashed in Nassir's eyes as he swung around, a cutlass in his other hand. The last marine fell, his neck cut half off. Nassir let out a yell, swinging the blade again and again at the dead marine. Great splashes erupted from Nassir's fury as he kept pounding the water.

Anne gripped Nassir's hands from behind. "Now is not the time for you to lose yourself, Nassir."

Nassir took a deep breath and stopped struggling. Anne released him, and he reached into the water to pick up his hammer from the dead marine's head, then went back to work.

The crew helped Nassir, quickly covering the holes with spare planks. Anne helped by holding the planks while the others secured the timber with nails.

"The job is not yet complete, men. This only slowed the flow. We need to clear the bilge of water to bring our full speed back. Then we can cover the beams with tar." Nassir moved to the aft of the ship.

The small space held little, aside from a few spare parts and extra cargo, but one piece of equipment was constant: a chain pump at the aft. Each pump was a chain and a winch, which, when turned, pulled water up and out of the ship.

Anne ran aft, grabbed the winch handle underneath the water along with Nassir and the two began the laborious process of hand-pumping water from the dirty bilge. The other men went to steps at the fore, and opened an entrance to the bilge. They grabbed buckets and helped drain the bilge by running up to dump the water into the ocean.

Over the course of two hours the fighting finished on the top deck, the bilge water was drained, the holes fixed and covered in fresh tar, and the *Freedom* and *Fortune* escaped Lisbon and their pursuers.

Wiping the sweat from their brows, Anne and Nassir took leave of their posts. Anne returned to the top deck. The crew were cleaning the ship of debris, dumping the bodies of marines into the sea, and readying their dead comrades for a funeral pyre.

The disheartened and tired faces said more to Anne than any words could. Lost and leaderless, the crew of the *Freedom* had no energy or morale left. Their captain and quartermaster kidnapped, the first mate gone, a dozen crewmates dead, many more injured, the past weeks and months being hounded by an assassin who took the arm of one of their greatest fighters, all culminated into stress mounting on the shoulders of everyone.

Right now, Edward would deliver a rousing speech, turning the mood and focusing the men. I guess it is my turn.

Anne pulled herself up straight and walked to the quarterdeck. Christina was applying a bandage to her brother's forearm as he sat in his wheelchair. Anne could tell Christina too was in low spirits. Christina afforded Anne a cursory nod before returning to work.

Anne leaned forward on the quarterdeck railing, staring at the crew as they milled about. "Attention, crew!" she yelled. The crew of the *Freedom* stopped all they were doing and moved closer to the quarterdeck to hear Anne. "These past weeks and months have been difficult. We have had our share of battles, and losses, but we must not let this bring us down. We must press onward to save our captain."

Anne's speech seemed less than inspiring to those listening. She pressed on. "Our captain has been taken by an enemy we all know: Kenneth Locke. Unless we find Edward, Locke will more than likely kill him."

"What more do ye want of us? We be workin' ain't we?" another crewmate said, hunched shoulders of defeat hanging on him like a shroud.

"I am asking you to fight," Anne boomed. "I am asking you to fight for your captain, and for this ship's namesake." Anne pat the railing of the *Freedom* before gazing into the eyes of the crew. "This ship is our home, but it is also a symbol. A symbol of what we all strive for, what we would fight for, what we would sacrifice our lives for." Anne pointed to the bodies of the dead crewmates lying in a line beneath her on the waist. "Those men sacrificed their lives for that cause, for you. We all owe Edward our lives and our *Freedom*, and if you are not willing to yell from the bottom of your hearts that you will fight for his *Freedom*, for our family's *Freedom*, then perhaps this is the wrong ship for you." Anne turned her back to the crew and sat on the railing, closing her eyes.

She rubbed her eyes; the stress was wearing on her. She felt defeated. *I failed these people. I am no leader, only a shadow of someone greater.* The image of her mother entered Anne's mind, and bitter tears welled in her eyes.

But Anne's words sank in, and after a long silence, one crewman stood tall and said: "I will fight." Anne turned and focused on the crewman, smiling at his declaration. "I will fight," another repeated, stepping forward. "I will fight," a third chanted. Soon the whole crew repeated the sentiment, their fatigued eyes changing.

"I will fight," Christina joined in proudly, raising her fist in the air.

"I will fight," Herbert resounded with his sister.

The crew all focused on Anne. "For *Freedom*!" she yelled, pumping her fist in the air. The crew yelled the words back to her. "For *Freedom*," she yelled again, louder than before, the strength of the crew boosting her as they shouted the mantra back all the louder. "For *Freedom*," Anne yelled one last time.

"For *Freedom*!" She heard back, even louder than before. Anne observed the crew of the *Fortune* yelling the same declaration to their brothers. They were all waving, hooting and hollering with large smiles on their faces.

The crew of the *Freedom* were back to their old selves, Anne included.

"Where to, Captain?" Herbert asked Anne.

Anne gazed at the fore, the faintest bit of dawn's light on the starboard horizon and wind blowing her long red curls back. "North, to Ireland." She declared.

"Aye, Captain," Herbert said, turning the ship north.

We are coming for you Edward. Do not die on me.

32. DEAD & ALIVE, LOST & FOUND

"I need your help," Pukuh declared solemnly. After Anne's rousing speech, he'd asked to speak with her. He wore a serious expression on his face, like none Anne had seen before.

"Anything you need, Pukuh," she replied.

Pukuh fell to his knees and prostrated himself before Anne. "I want you to train me to fight."

Anne was taken aback at the Mayan's plea. "You are stronger than this. You have trained yourself your whole life, and in time your arm will not be a hindrance to you. Why ask for training now?"

"I wish to fight for *Freedom*, for my brothers and sisters, but I am weak. A weak man thinks he can learn everything on his own." Pukuh raised his head and stared Anne in the eyes. "If I am to fight for Edward, for *Freedom*, for my village, and face Plague again, I must learn how to be the best, from the best."

Anne smiled. "Well said. However, I am not the best. William?" Anne beckoned.

William stepped up to the quarterdeck. "Yes, my lady?" he asked.

"Would you be willing to train Pukuh to fight?"

William peered over to Pukuh, who once more bowed low before William. "Stand," he commanded. Pukuh followed William's orders and even displayed his best attempt at a salute out of respect. "I will train you, but this won't be a master-pupil relationship. We can both learn from each other, so we train as equals, and I will have it no other way. Agreed, Prince?" William extended his left hand to shake on the agreement.

Pukuh lowered his salute and smiled. "Agreed," he replied, shaking William's hand with a firm grip.

The two then left to start training immediately. Pukuh was eager to learn from William, and Anne couldn't be sure, but she thought she could see the inkling of a smile on William's face too.

The recognition of the sun being out finally hit Anne, and she realised she was exhausted. The crews of *Freedom* and *Fortune* had fought through the night without sleeping.

"Herbert, when we can, tell the *Fortune* to drop anchor and we'll allow the crews to rest. It has been a long night."

"Aye, Captain. I will begin now," Herbert said, yawning as he spoke.

Anne descended to the crew cabin, and lay down on the bed she and Edward had shared not a few days before. She could still smell his scent, and when she closed her eyes she could swear he was next to her. Anne drifted off into slumber, Edward forefront in her mind.

"How are you faring, Mister Abbot?" Anne asked, sitting beside Hank in the crew cabin of the *Fortune*.

"Doin' a mite better, Miss Bonney, thanks ta yer surgeon's skills," Hank replied softly.

Hank was still the worse for wear. His body, bruised and battered, was healing, but slowly.

"Stay rested, and when you're better we'll have a drink in your honour. It would be remiss for you to be late for your own party," Anne said with a grin.

"I reckon the Lord himself couldn't keep me from bein' there."

Anne patted Hank on the leg, then advanced to the steps of *Fortune*'s crew cabin where Roberts stood watch. "He claims to be better, but he appears worse. What did Alexandre say?"

"He said to pray and wait. Alexandre has done all he could for Hank, it is up to God now. Two weeks have passed and Hank is able to stay awake long enough to talk, but he can barely keep even the least bit of food down. I fear God may have left us." Roberts gazed at his comrade, struggling to breathe, then his eyes fell.

"Do not say that. The *Freedom* has not given up hope, nor should you." Anne placed her hand over Roberts' and squeezed.

Roberts squeezed Anne's hand back and shook his head. "Aye, I shouldn't give up so easily. Our plight is nothing at the moment, we should be focusing on finding your captain."

"I fear God may have left us there as well," Anne said.

"My dear, Hank is one thing, but Edward is another entirely. He would not die so easily. We will arrive in Ireland soon and before you know it you two will be reunited."

"I hope you're right."

"I know I am. Besides, one should follow their own advice, lest they be a hypocrite." Bartholomew winked, and Anne smiled.

A crew member came down the steps to speak with Roberts. "We can see land, Captain. We'll be arriving in Cloankilty soon."

Roberts nodded to the crewman, then turned back to Anne.

"Let's renew ourselves with some fresh air."

The two went to the top deck of the *Fortune*. The sun was approaching noon, but the cool air made it feel earlier in the day. Anne could see the *Freedom* off the port stern, the crew hard at work under William's direction to keep speed with the smaller *Fortune*. Anne moved to the bow of the *Fortune* and gazed at their destination.

The town was a few hours away and only a small dot on the horizon. As the ships drew nearer, Anne could see the outline of small wooden and stone homes and a small harbour. When *Fortune* was close to landing, Anne was able to see the whole village in front of her. She could tell from her vantage point that the small village had been built with care.

The small wooden harbour led directly to cobblestone streets with various businesses scattered about. One tavern, a blacksmith, bakery, a fishmonger, a butcher, an inn, a church closer to the centre of town, and the rest were homes. A quaint village, but Anne could tell something was off.

"There is no one outside," Roberts commented as he stood beside Anne.

Anne inspected the flags the *Fortune* was running. Plain and white as could be; Roberts ensured the pirate flag they traditionally used for battle was taken off before they were even close to port.

"I wonder why?" Anne contemplated aloud, not expecting a response.

"I guess we'll find out when we land," Roberts replied.

The *Fortune* was brought as close as could be to the small port, then the anchor was dropped into the sea and the sails furled. Anne and Roberts, along with a few of his crew, entered a rowboat to go ashore.

Even as the small rowboat was docking, Anne could see none walking about the town, but she did notice movement in curtains covering the windows. *So there are people.* Anne trekked along the cobblestone street of the town. She went to the closest shop, the butcher, and knocked loudly on the door. No answer. Anne rapped once more. Still nothing.

"Hello? We mean you no harm, we are only here for information," Anne yelled loudly, then tried again in Gaelic.

Roberts joined her. "Nothing?"

"No, the town refuses to answer." Anne turned around, her hands on her hips. She could see another rowboat approaching, this one carrying some of the *Freedom*'s crew. "The curtains move and bend, and I can feel eyes upon me."

"What must we do to coax them out of their homes?" Roberts

asked, glancing about.

Anne strolled down the road. "I think the better question is what has caused the townspeople to act this way." She ambled around a bend onto another long street lined with houses. At the end of the street she could see a fountain spraying water in the middle of a large open area, possibly the town square.

Anne moved towards the town square with Roberts following behind. "Do you know where you are headed?"

"No," Anne replied, not turning around. "Eventually, someone has to leave their home, and we won't depart until they do."

Anne kept walking with Roberts on her tail, unequivocally caught in her pace, as most were when next to the headstrong red-haired woman. Anne slowed down when they reached the small fountain.

She searched the square, and she could see an old man sitting on a bench at the foot of the fountain. He was wrinkled, with long grey hair and a lengthy beard of the same hue, and a cane in his hands. He didn't notice Anne and Roberts, so Anne began walking in his direction, but she was stopped by a voice from behind.

"Anne," Roberts called softly, provoking her to gaze in his direction.

Fourteen men had weapons pointed at Roberts. Bartholomew's hands were in the air. Some of the locals held swords and pikes, while others had more modern pistols and muskets. They approached Anne with caution, and she also raised her hands in the air.

"What do you want with our town?" one of the men yelled in Gaelic.

"We mean you no harm," Anne replied, also in Gaelic.

"What are they saying?" Roberts asked.

"I will handle this, Roberts," Anne replied.

Before Anne could follow through with her promise, things turned from bad to worse. Christina and ten crewmen from the *Freedom* and *Fortune* ran up behind the locals.

"Drop your weapons!" Christina yelled to the crowd.

The locals turned around, moving behind Anne and Roberts, using them as shields and leverage at the same time. What followed was a tense shouting match between Christina, Anne, Roberts, their respective crews, and the locals.

Anne tried her best to yell in English and in Gaelic for everyone to cease talking and lower their weapons, but her voice was a mere drop of noise in the bucket. Roberts also tried to command his men to lower their weapons, but fear drove them to keep the muskets up, if not steady. Christina, in her usual hot-headedness, was determined to shout louder until she was the victor, and the more shouting did not work the closer she was to pulling the trigger on her musket.

"Silence!" a booming voice cut through the din, and all eyes focused on the person it originated from. The old man who was at the bench stepped in between the two crowds and faced the locals with a steely gaze. He talked with one man specifically, the leader of the young men. The young man heatedly argued with the older man until the old man whacked the young one on the head with his cane.

After a flash of contempt, the younger man walked to the edge of the town square, motioning for his crew to follow. The threat was gone as quickly as had come, but the hostility remained. The young men still held their muskets close, disdain evident in their eyes.

The old man passed Anne and entered the street leading to the harbour. "Come now lass, let us talk. The quicker we know what you want the quicker you will leave," he said.

"Thank you, we feel the same," Anne replied with a smile. She turned to Christina, instantly losing the smile. "Take the men back to the harbour and wait there. Don't make more trouble than you already have."

Christina was about to object, but Anne raised her hand, silencing her. She scoffed and stormed off down the street to the harbour, her cherry-blond hair whipping in the wind.

Anne caught up to the old man who was entering a nearby inn, and followed him inside. He sat at a bar stool at the back and ordered something from the barkeep. Anne sat next to him, and Bartholomew joined a moment later.

"So, lass, what do you want with my town?" the old man asked, not wasting time with introductions. He downed his drink in one gulp.

"My companion does not understand Gaelic, can you speak English?" Anne asked. The old man nodded and Anne continued talking in English. "We require information. We are hunting for a group of pirates who took our captain and two crewmates hostage. We have reason to believe they are somewhere here in Ireland."

"There's many pirates these days, too many. That's why the boys you met were hostile. Pirates have been terrorising our coasts for the past year. They've soured our outlook on visitors."

Anne sent Roberts a knowing glance. "These pirates, would you be able to describe their leader?"

"Aye lass, none would forget such a man. His eyes were dark

and devoid of any compassion, teeth rotted, hair matted with grease and face covered in dirt. His most striking feature had to be the chest on his hand, clanging with the sound of treasure and doom approaching. Any who mentioned the chest was killed immediately. Called himself Cache-Hand, he did. That the man you be searching for?"

Anne nodded. "Yes, the same. Do you know where he is hiding himself?"

"I see by your manner you are educated. You already know the answer. I wish I could help you. The best information I can provide is that the ship always approaches from the east whenever they attack, and they've attacked other towns all along the coast. Follow the coast and you may be able to find where they call home."

"Thank you, you have been most helpful." Anne rose from the bar stool.

"One more thing," the old man said, stopping Anne and Roberts before they left. "Gut Cache-Hand and avenge my son, will ya?"

"I planned on it," Anne replied, not missing a beat.

The old man lifted his cup to Anne before downing another large gulp. Anne turned without another word, and left the inn. Christina was waiting at the harbour with arms folded and a sour expression on her face. When Christina noticed Anne, she stalked over to her.

"What did the old man say?" Christina asked.

Anne dismissed the other crewmates crowding around her and Christina, and stared at Christina with cold authority. "Firstly, use your head and be more responsible. Your rashness could have turned this whole town against us. You are not to act without orders again. Am I clear?"

"You and Roberts would have been shot if—"

"Silence!" Anne cut in severely, causing the crew to peer in her direction. "Am I clear?" she repeated.

Christina bit her lip and gave a sideways glance to everyone staring before saying, "Yes, Ma'am."

"Good, now let's leave. We have a clue as to Kenneth's whereabouts." Anne stepped into the small boat, assisted by Roberts.

"Where are we headed?"

Anne moved her red curls behind her ear as she stared at the moving seas and the rolling coast. "We're headed east."

Shortly after, the two ships set sail east of Cloankilty in search of more information on their lost captain and Kenneth Locke. They stopped at each town and port, and every small village in between, asking for information.

Similar to Cloankilty, the townsfolk displayed open hostility because of *Freedom*'s and *Fortune*'s size, and the cannons aboard. Some towns fired upon them before the ships could reach port and forced the crew to turn around and keep heading east.

After weeks of searching and slow sailing, the crews of the *Freedom* and *Fortune* met with a strange sight. They found towns untouched by any pirates. The towns and villages welcomed them, and recounted hearing of attacks on other villages, but were blessed not to be among them.

Anne wondered what made the villages special, and arrived at one conclusion: they were getting close. Kenneth was smart enough not to attack too close to home, but not smart enough to cover his tracks.

Instead of asking about attacks, Anne and the crew started asking the villagers if they had received any warships in port over the last months. They didn't find any more information until landing in Youghal about midday.

The town of Youghal was a quiet, small town of about a thousand residents, with a large port for fishermen and tall ships alike. A port of that size was uncommon in a small town like Youghal, which Anne felt required further inquiry.

Anne, Christina, William, and Roberts all went to the local tavern to see what information could be gathered there first, before trying the local officials.

Inside the tavern, scarcely anyone was present. At midday most would be working in some fashion, and the place only held men who were permanent fixtures. They were the type who had nothing else to do but listen, and had loose lips with the proper motivation.

Anne noticed a few men sitting around the various tables. She motioned for William and Roberts to talk with different people, then she and Christina approached the barkeep.

"Hello sir. I would enjoy some wine to wet my lips, and," Anne plopped a gold piece on the table, not interested in wasting time, "information if the favour suits you."

The tall, thinly bearded man went wide-eyed at the gold and pocketed it quickly before any could see the glint, then turned to a shelf at his back hosting his precious stock. He poured a good wine into two clean glasses and handed one to Anne and the other to Christina.

"English?" the man asked softly. Anne nodded. "Good, the fellows here don't know the tongue, so I suppose your friends are wasting their time."

Anne glanced back to see Roberts joining William, having no success in talking to the locals, but William knew the language.

"What did you want to know? I suppose it's of import if you part with gold."

"Indeed. We are searching for a band of pirates who frequent Southern Ireland. Would you know anything about pirates in the area?" Anne asked, slowly sipping her wine.

At the mention of pirates, the barkeep's eyes widened, then quickly became devoid of expression. "What would a lovely lass such as yourself be interested in pirates for?"

"We have some business with them," Anne replied vaguely.

The barkeep's mouth made a line. "Not heard anything about pirates in these parts. Sorry, maybe they're further east."

"So you have not heard any word about pirates attacking the shores near here at all? What about the harbour, it looks recently expanded to allow tall ships to dock. Care to explain why?" Anne pressed.

The barkeep was sweating. "Nothing wrong with that. Merchantmen frequent here. If that is all, I would appreciate it if you would kindly leave."

Christina slammed a knife into the counter. "He's lying," she said through gritted teeth.

The barkeep backed up at Christina's threat. Anne held Christina's hand at bay. "Now, now, let us not be hasty. May I have your name, sir?" Anne's voice was sweet and inviting, meant to offset Christina's threatening tone.

"Lucas."

"Lucas, we're not here to harm you. We simply wish to find these pirates, and then we will be on our way. Any information you could provide would be of immense help to us. Please."

Lucas peered back and forth between the two women, then leaned in, beckoning them closer. Anne and Christina glanced at each other, then leaned forward, closer to Lucas.

"The pirates own this town. They live in an abandoned castle a ways up the Blackwater River, to the north, but you'll not find them there now. They only return once every six months and left not a week and a half ago. Sorry, that's all the information I can give you. I'll be in trouble if they ever find out. Now, please, leave."

"Thank you," Anne said hollowly, then she turned and left the tavern quickly.

Anne's mind reeled with the knowledge. If the pirates left, there could be only two reasons: Either Edward and John had been killed and they left, or they left with the Hounds. If the latter happened, Anne had no way of finding them. She left the tavern, stepped into the nearest alley, and leaned against the wall of one of the buildings.

"My lady, are you alright?" William asked, pulling her up.

Anne shook herself and separated from William. "I am well, sorry for worrying you. Kenneth's hideout is a castle north of here. We must head there, now." Anne pushed past William.

She stalked ahead as William gazed at her back. William thought if Anne were to stop moving forward for one second she would break. Her hope was all keeping her feet moving. *What will happen if that fragile hope is shattered?*

Roberts and Christina approached William after watching the scene from a distance. "What happened?" Roberts asked.

"Is Anne well?" Christina asked, concern in her eyes.

William's eyes never left Anne's striding figure. "She will be fine for now. Later, however..." William turned to Roberts; the tall brute had a subdued worry in his eyes. "We are heading on foot to the enemy stronghold. They have a castle north of here. Tell your men to prepare for battle, and ready cannons for transport."

"There's no need for the weapons. The barkeep claimed Kenneth and his men left weeks ago," Christina said.

"A small force could have been left behind to guard the castle, or the barkeep could be lying. We would do well to be prepared rather than caught unawares."

"The men have been itching for a fight. I hope the pirates are there. It would be a stain on my honour if the Lord's wrath were to be denied by something so trivial as chance." Roberts punched his fist into his palm, then headed to the harbour.

William then turned to Christina. "Head back to the ship and instruct our men to prepare also. Keep watch over Anne," William said before walking away.

"What are you doing?"

"I will buy supplies for the trek. Cannons will be difficult to carry, we need wagons."

"What? Cannons?"

"Yes, they may be necessary. And if they are not, we will be all the better for it."

Christina grinned and nodded, then returned to the harbour with the others. William purchased supplies, buying several wagons and horses, bullets, and food. He took the supplies to the harbour with some of the locals' help. The residents were astonished at what they saw on the harbour.

Almost three hundred people from the combined crews of *Freedom* and *Fortune* were descending from their ships armed to the teeth. Each man, regardless of stature, was muscular and intimidating. Those itching for a fight wore fiendish grins, and some tossed around daggers and sliced at imaginary foes with their swords. The sight was fearsome, and the villagers who helped William quickly ran away when they realised what was happening.

When the crews noticed the wagons, they worked together to quickly load them with cannons, cannonballs, and spare weapons.

After preparations were complete Anne addressed the crews. "Move out!" she yelled.

The crew slowly made their way through the small town of Youghal as the citizens watched half in wonder and half in horror. When they reached the edge of town they were met with a large crowd of citizens with one standing out in front.

Anne ordered the crew to stop, and she approached the man in front. "Step aside," she commanded, the Gaelic tongue making the words sound all the more cutting.

The man was sweating, but he stood his ground. "I am the mayor of this town and I beg of you, please do not do this. When the pirates return they will kill us."

Anne grabbed the mayor's chest with both hands, shaking him as her eyes bored into his with fury. "Hundreds of your brothers died because of these pirates! Have you not seen the towns ravaged, the eyes of the victims who lost loved ones due to their savagery? The lot of you are without spine, the same as dogs bending to the will of their master." Anne pushed the mayor away. "You deserve whatever fate brings you. Now move, before we do their job for them."

The mayor appeared as if he would object further, but instead stepped aside with his head hung in shame. When he made way, the townspeople followed and allowed the crews room to leave.

The war procession moved out of town, leaving the passive citizens behind as they headed for battle. Soon, all that remained was the marks of footsteps and treads from the wagons.

"She's right, we deserve what's coming to us," one of the citizens said solemnly.

The mayor took a moment's pause, then shook his head. "No!" he yelled as he turned to his people. "We don't deserve a pirate's justice! Nevertheless, we do need to take responsibility. For too long we have stood aside and let those men have their way, but I say no more! We have the advantage here: They think we are too afraid to strike back. So when the pirates come back, we will be ready to ambush them and exact our revenge for what they've done to our brothers and clansmen. Who's with me?" the mayor yelled.

The townsfolk roared in agreement. Anne's scolding had put fire in their bellies once more, and the townsfolk set about making defences for when Kenneth returned, and informing the neighbouring villages to do the same.

Anne and William scouted ahead and found the fortress Kenneth and his men called home.

William scanned for movement along the curtain wall walkways, but found none. "It appears empty."

Anne peered through her rifle sights at the keeps on the corners, taking special note of the arrow slits. "I concur. How long until our men arrive?" she asked, double checking the castle walls.

William glanced at the forest behind him. "Five minutes, give or take."

"We should invade the castle first. The cannons could endanger Edward, John, and Sam's lives." Anne stood up and slung her rifle over her shoulder, but before she could make her way to the castle William stopped her.

William placed his hands on Anne's shoulders and stared deep into her eyes. "My lady, are you truly prepared for what we may see when we enter?"

Anne shoved his hands away. "What a thing to say to one you claim to serve."

William immediately bowed. "Forgive me, My lady. I only meant to help."

Anne sighed. "I am no queen and you are not my subject. Rise," she commanded, and William obeyed. "Tell me truthfully, William, you loved my uncle, yes?"

"Yes, My lady, I did. My hope is to one day make amends for my failing His Majesty."

"So what would you do if you faced his murderer, Plague, again?"

"I would kill him without mercy." William's face was devoid of emotion, but his eyes filled with promise.

"Exactly. I will fill myself with hate until I see Kenneth beneath my heel begging for mercy. Then, I will laugh as his body burns and his bones crack." Anne smiled in a way which made William sweat.

She glanced over William's shoulder to see their small army drawing near. She made a gesture for them to halt their advance. Roberts, Hank Abbot, and Christina all approached William and Anne to see what the plan was.

"William and I will see if the castle is safe, then we'll send you a sign to bring in the troops," Anne said.

"What will this sign be?" Roberts asked.

"We will open the doors," Anne replied before walking to the clearing's edge with William.

Anne and William crouched down behind some bushes and trees. "We'll need to scale the walls so I brought a few grappling hooks." William reached into a small bag behind his back and pulled out two large grappling hooks. "The hardest part will be the castle approach. There is no cover."

Anne took her rifle out. "I will cover you." Anne lay down flat on her stomach and positioned the rifle in front of her between the bushes to allow full view of the castle.

William moved a few paces away for Anne to be able to see through the rifle, then, on the count of three, he ran at top speed to the castle. When he reached the halfway mark the sound of gunfire hailed from the castle. William turned to his side instinctively. The bullet grazed his arm, drawing blood.

Through the rifles sights, Anne noticed a man with a musket. Before Anne could fire a shot, he ducked down beneath the castle wall to reload.

"Stop hiding so I can shoot you," she chanted under her breath, but her prayer was not answered. Anne peered at the castle wall, searching for her mark.

The man who shot William suddenly reappeared halfway across the castle wall. Anne cursed under her breath as she re-aimed a full second behind the attacker. The man took another shot. The bullet hit the ground in front of William and forced dirt into the air. Anne shot. The man ducked. The bullet took a chunk out of the stone behind him.

William removed the grappling hook from behind him and swung it, gathering momentum. He threw the hook at peak speed and it swooped over the top of the wall. William tugged on the grappling hook to secure it, and started climbing.

Anne noticed another man with a musket running across the castle wall. He pulled himself partially over the wall to aim his musket at William. Anne shot him in the shoulder. He dropped his gun and fell off the side of the wall.

William pulled out a pistol from his belt and aimed it above him. The first man popped out from the castle wall and aimed at William. William shot the man in the chest and he slumped down on the castle wall, dead.

William continued his climb unhindered. At the top, he jumped over the edge of the wall and onto the castle walkway.

Anne watched William as he stalked about, reloading his pistol as he walked. After a moment he was out of sight.

Anne tensed at the silence. Sweat dripped from her brow as she stared through the sights of the rifle. Every ambient sound from the forest caused her heart to skip. On the outside her body was calm, but inside the minutes passed like hours as she gazed intently on the castle of their enemy.

The large double doors of the castle opened slowly without warning. Anne called over some of the crew with muskets to stem the possible tide. A figure emerged from the opened door.

"Hold your fire!" Anne yelled.

William was leaving the castle. Anne stood, put her rifle on her back, and then ran to the castle doors where William waited. The crew followed behind her.

"Was there anyone else?" Anne asked.

"None aside from the two we shot. The castle appears to be empty, though I have not had time to search everywhere," William replied.

Anne turned to those who followed her. "Search every inch of this castle. If you find anything, return here," she commanded.

The men dispersed in groups throughout the castle, doing as commanded and searching the castle's every nook and cranny.

"Now, you have a wound which needs to be tended." Anne pushed William to the ground.

She examined his arm, and found his bicep still bleeding. Anne pulled gauze out of her pocket, and wrapped it around William's arm. After she finished, a group of crewmates returned from a room below the castle.

The crewmates had grave expressions on their faces. "You need to see this," one of them said, motioning with his thumb to the stairs leading down.

Anne pushed past and practically ran down the stairs, her hair and cloak swaying with the motion. William and the two crewmates kept in step with Anne all the way down the spiral staircase. At the bottom, they were met with a corridor, doors to other rooms ajar, and light spilling from the room at the end.

Anne stepped forward slowly, taking breaths as she did. She reached for the door, closing her eyes, holding the air in her lungs tightly like a fist clenched. She pushed on the door with one hand. The light from a candle illuminated the room.

Dried blood stained the middle of the floor where pools had previously been. The room stank of gunpowder, vomit, and death. There was no body to account for the blood, just a cot, a table, and an empty wine rack.

Blackbeard's Ship

Most men and women might retch at the scene and the smell, but Anne was not most people. She stared at the blood intently for a time as William searched the room for clues.

"Anne." William held a letter out in front of him.

Anne glanced at the letter, then to William. "Where did you find this?" she asked, opening it.

"Under the bed," William said.

Anne read the letter, and William could tell something was wrong. He motioned for the two crewmen to leave the room and the three slipped out. William closed the door behind them and they went back up the spiral stairs.

"What was that about? What did the letter say?" One crewman asked.

"Nothing good, that much is assured. We shall find out soon enough. For now, gather the crew and tell them to stop searching, we are done here." William instructed.

The crewmen did as instructed and soon the crews of both *Freedom* and *Fortune*, save those watching the cannons and wagons, were in the main hall of Kenneth Locke's castle.

Christina, Tala, and Pukuh approached William, who was guarding the staircase. "Where's Anne? Why are we still here?"

"Anne is below." William motioned behind him. "We found a letter, Anne is reading it now."

"What did this letter say?" Pukuh asked.

"I don't know," William replied.

"Then why are we standing here? Let's find out what it said." Christina tried to walk down the stairs, but William stopped her, causing Tala to growl at him.

William glared at Tala, and the wolf hung her head in submission. "She is not to be disturbed."

"We are wasting time here, brother. Was not our goal to find the captain? Our captain is not here, thus we must be elsewhere."

"I think what Pukuh means is move, William." Christina once again tried to push her way past, more aggressively this time.

William pushed her back. Soon after, an argument erupted amongst the crew who were anxious to leave. William tried his best to calm the crew, but the noise rose louder by the minute, and all communication was breaking down.

Because of the noise, none noticed Anne walking up the steps. When she returned to the main hall, the arguments stopped and all eyes were on her. She gazed at all the hopeful eyes of the people inspired and loved by Edward.

Anne's eyes were red, and she looked tired. "John and..." Anne placed her hand on her mouth, then shook her head and continued. "John and Edward are dead," she stated solemnly, listlessly lifting the letter.

The room quieted. The cold wind from the Irish hills filled the castle, howling hauntingly and sending chills down everyone's backs.

"No!" Christina yelled. "There's no way they could die." She screamed, her eyes closed tightly to shut away the forming tears. Her hand was balled into a fist around the rose hanging from her neck, Ochi's memento.

Anne's mouth made a straight line as she stared at Christina with pity in her eyes. "Read for yourself." Anne shoved the letter into Christina's hands then left, wading through the throngs of crewmen gathered as Christina read the letter out loud.

"This is Sam," Christina started, glancing up to the onlookers. "I hope you find this before that bastard comes back. I tried to help John and the captain escape, but I failed. John and Edward saved my life, and sacrificed their own for me. Kenneth killed them. I'm sorry, I've failed you all, but I'll make it right. I swear I'll kill the ugly sod if it's the last thing I do. If I don't see you again, tell Anne I'm sorry." Christina's hands fell, the letter dropping from her fingers.

The faces of hundreds were filled with melancholy. As the reality of what had happened dawned on those gathered, they realised exactly what the words from Sam meant. Edward, their captain, their brother, was no more. They would not hear him laugh again, they would not be inspired by his words and deeds again, and they would no longer take comfort in his presence. And John, the father some never had, would never express uplifting words to his sons, nor make people laugh with his timid nature, nor watch their backs in battle. And Sam was lost in a den of wolves on a suicide mission, blaming himself for what happened.

Christina shook her head like she was awaking from a dream. Her eyes focused and she ran outside to where Anne stood, the crew following slowly after. "There may still be hope, Anne. There are no bodies here, how do we know they truly died?"

Anne shook her head, pulled the girl closer, and hugged her tightly. They embraced for a moment before Anne spoke. "Sam would not lie to us. He saw John and Edward die," Anne whispered bluntly into Christina's ear.

Christina pushed away from Anne, the tears she tried to hold back rushing down her face. "Then what do we do now? What are we to do without Edward?"

"Simple: We kill Kenneth Locke and make him pay for what he did. I won't let Sam take my revenge from me." Anne's words piqued the interest of the crew, and took them away from their depression as they focused on her. "For too long over this past year we've been on the run. Too long we've been on the receiving end of extortion, slavery, lies, secret assassins..." Anne gazed through the crowd, pointing to Nassir and Pukuh, and Christina, as she spoke. "And death." Anne paused, noticing the crowd hanging on her every word.

"This is the time for revenge." The crew chanted their agreement to her resolve. "Our revenge!" she continued. More of the crew joined in the resonating chant of agreement. "Our comrades' revenge!"

"This is no longer about *Freedom*, as when we first left Portugal. We have our *Freedom*. This is about those whose *Freedom* was stripped from them long before it should have been." Anne paused before gazing at Nassir. "Ochi." Anne turned to Christina. "John," she continued, peering at other crewmates as she listed off names of those who had died on board the *Freedom*. "And our captain, Edward. They had their *Freedom* and lives taken, and, though we cannot restore their lives, we can free their spirits so they may rest in peace. Revenge will be our new charge. Revenge." Anne finished with reverent emphasis on the word.

Christina lifted her hand in the air. "Revenge!" she yelled for all to hear.

"Revenge," Pukuh echoed.

"Revenge," the crews chanted one after the other and then in unison until the whole room was filled with the sound of their voices. The mantra renewed the crew's hope, and bestowed new purpose to drive them forward.

"Our first order of business," Anne stated when it quieted. "Destroy this castle."

The crew yelled their agreement in furious abandon, rushing out of the castle and to the armaments they brought. The cannons were lined up and aimed at the fortress.

"Fire!" Anne yelled, followed soon after by William down their long line of men. Bartholomew and Hank continued the command soon after their counterparts, and the cannons fired in succession.

The sound of each cannon blared like a volcano erupting in sequence. The thunder was ear-splitting and terrified the creatures of the wood, as well as the humans from the town.

The cannonballs smashed into the hewn rock and cut stone, sending pieces flying in all directions. Wave after wave of cannon fire broke into the walls, demolishing the castle bit by bit.

Before long the job was done, and the remnants of the castle were nothing more than a pile of rubble. The first part of their revenge was complete, and the crew returned to Youghal.

The townspeople were waiting. From their faces, Anne could tell they knew what had happened, but some townsfolk decided to see the wreckage for themselves. None talked to the crew as they passed through the streets to the harbour.

Anne held her head high and didn't glance at the mayor or the nearby gawkers. Her focus was on moving forward.

First we will need to resupply, then wait for Kenneth Locke to return. However, one of the townsfolk could send word. Threats of violence should suffice. I may not have Edward's eyes, but I have something close. The mayor was easily dominated, so the others should fall in line.

Anne processed their next steps like a game of chess, keeping a hundred moves ahead of the enemy. So great was her concentration, she did not notice when she arrived back on the ship and accidentally bumped into one of the crewmen on the *Freedom*.

"I'm sorry, I was not watching myself," Anne said absentmindedly and with her head down. She continued walking without waiting for a reply.

"Anne," the crewman called in a familiar voice.

Anne spun her head back in the direction of the voice. *It cannot be!* She gaped with disbelief at the figure in front of her.

"Don't worry. It's really me," he reassured her, as if reading Anne's mind.

Anne burst into tears and leapt into the man's arms. "Edward!" she cried.

Edward wrapped his arms around Anne tightly and ran his fingers through her long red curls in that familiar way. Edward, too, wept as he took in the full presence of the woman he loved more than anything in the world.

"I'm finally home."

33. BENJAMIN'S GAME

The entire town of Youghal was not able to sleep that night due to the raucous partying of the crew of the *Freedom* and *Fortune*. The town's reserve of alcohol was drained during the hours between dusk and dawn, and the butcher made a fortune selling his entire stock off to the hungry pirates. Much singing and laughter and rejoicing was had on and off the harbour. Even some of the townsfolk joined in and made friends with the rebels visiting their home.

On the *Freedom*, Edward was surrounded by a crowd of people from the two crews. Throughout the night, Edward's cup was continuously refilled and food was never far from his reach thanks to attentive friends.

Edward was telling the sad story of his capture to all listening, but to them the tale was of their captain, or friend, surviving against all odds. "For three days Kenneth's crew took turns beating me throughout the day and night. I resisted as best I could, all things considered. People were switched out when I broke their arms, legs, or noses. After that frustrated Kenneth enough, I was poisoned from what I could tell. I don't know what the poison was but my insides burned for a whole day."

"How do you reckon you survived?" Hank Abbot asked, brow raised.

"Well, the only thing I can think of would be either the poison wasn't meant to kill, or because of the special weed from Pukuh's village," Edward surmised, motioning to the one-armed Mayan.

"Did the gods appear with some in their hands for you, brother?" Pukuh jested.

Edward chuckled. "No, over the past months I've been chewing on the leaves. I happen to enjoy the bitter taste, and we had more than enough to go around. Perhaps I gained a defence against poison from eating so much." The company nodded at the explanation. "So after the poison, they decided to up the ante. One night, I was taken to a river a short distance from the castle, Blackwater River. Kenneth and several others shot and stabbed me a dozen times, then Kenneth kicked me into the river and left me for dead. The next thing I remember was the coldness of the water rushing me to the ocean. Somehow, I was seen by a small whaling ship in the early hours of the morning and brought back to Youghal to heal. As you can see, I'm still not quite my old self, but I'm walking again, which I couldn't say a week ago."

Edward's body was bandaged from head to toe beneath his clothes, and where he wasn't bandaged he was bruised in varying colours and stages of healing. Hank had looked as if he'd crawled from hell when he was recovered, and Edward had suffered worse, so one could only imagine how he looked when the whalers saved him.

"Those devils will pay for their injustice on you, I so swear," Bartholomew said with his fist clenched.

The crew joined in with their own curses and promises for revenge against the man who'd killed John and nearly killed their captain.

"No," Edward said. The crew went silent and confused expressions abounded on their faces. "I'm not saying we won't avenge John, God knows I want to, but we can't wait six months. We have a job to do, and that's acquiring the final key to the *Freedom*."

"Edward, we know you've been waiting a long time, and we're so close to the end of the journey we started three years ago, but can't it wait?" Christina asked.

"No, our priority now and always has been finishing Benjamin's game and restoring full functionality to the ship."

"The Hounds need to pay for what they've done, partner, it's not solely your crew who've been wronged, but ours as well," Hank said.

"If you want to break our oath and leave to take out revenge, then you certainly may," Edward replied, slowly standing up from his seat. "But my crew will find another to help us finish this."

Jack Christian, who would normally be entertaining the crews, stood up and tried to calm Edward. "Edward, let's not say something we may regret now, alright?" The wise older man had a calming nature, but Edward was not swayed.

"My orders are final. We will be heading to the Island of Heaven and Hell." Edward turned his gaze to Bartholomew. "If your crew still wishes to maintain an alliance with mine then you may join us." Edward stormed off to the upper deck.

As Edward left, Bartholomew spoke to his crew and calmed them after Edward's harsh words. He was far more understanding and slow to anger than his stature suggested, and he stopped his less patient men from blowing things out of proportion.

Anne told the crewmates not to worry, and left the crew cabin to follow Edward. He had gone to Alexandre's medical cabin. Before Anne opened the door, Jack stopped her.

"May I?" he whispered.

Perhaps Jack is better suited for this. Anne nodded, pulled herself back, and allowed Jack the room. She returned to the lower deck with the crew as Jack entered the cabin.

When Jack opened and closed the door silently behind him, he could see Edward reaching with a shaky hand into the bag of the Mayan crop. Edward chewed on one of the leaves as he sat on the floor in front of the island table in the middle of the room.

Jack joined Edward, took a leaf from his hand and chewed. "Not bad."

The two sat silently as the noises of the party, though muffled, persisted through the walls of the ship from all sides.

"I keep having this dream," Edward chuckled nervously. "I'm standing in a white room, and uh... John's there. Except it's not John, it's my father." Edward fidgeted and tore at the small leaves absent-mindedly as he talked. "My father talks to me, but I can't understand what he's saying. Then suddenly a red streak appears across his neck, and... I'm holding a knife in my hand." Edward laughed again. "I know what the dream means, it's so painfully obvious, and I know I did not kill John, but that doesn't change the fact that I've had the same dream almost every night for the past month." Edward rubbed his eyes and let out a long sigh.

Jack took some of the broken leaves from Edward's hand and chewed on them. "Sometimes when I'm walking through the towns we've been to, I see the image of my wife passing by. I've even stopped a few ladies, but once I take a second glance I see the mirage made plain. Kids too. I see my kids, Maximilian and Jessica, running about here and there, playing with a hoop and stick, alive and well.

"When someone you love is taken from you, it feels as if a piece of yourself is replaced with something... rotten. A sickness of hate which never seems to fade. Sometimes the rot can be healed, one way or the other: over time, talking about what happened, forgiveness and sometimes revenge. The problem is finding out what to do next."

"What do you think I should do?" Edward asked the older man.

"I feel only you can know what's best for you, Edward. If you think we should finish the game then that's the best thing to do. Whether that decision is good or bad, your family will help you through."

Edward turned away from Jack's gaze. After a moment Edward held up his hand in front of him and stared as it shook from the slight bit of strain.

"Whenever I think of facing Kenneth my body tenses and my heart feels as if it's being held tightly, as if a snake coiled itself around and won't release me."

"Fear?" Jack asked.

"Not exactly. I've felt terror before, under the gaze of the man in black I'm sure you've heard about. This is different. I feel powerless to dangers ahead. I feel as if Locke is around the corner, waiting for me to lose concentration, then everyone I love will be dead, or he'll torture me until I no longer have the will to live. Like I'm trying to push down a brick wall, it feels as if I can't stop it from happening." Edward clenched his fist and turned away from Jack. "This is foolish. You lost your wife and kids. My troubles pale in comparison."

Jack squeezed Edward's hand tightly. "Don't ever think that. Your burdens are our burdens, your worry is our worry. It is real and we are here for you. A wise man once told me the worst thing you can do is think you are alone and have no family. You are not alone, and we are your family, remember that."

"Thank you, Jack," Edward said, wiping away tears before they could fall from his eyes.

The two men sat, silent at times, listening to the sounds of the crew outside. And, for the first time in the months since his abduction, Edward relaxed.

When all thoughts of celebration were gone, and the sombre reality finally set in, Edward held a funeral for John. There was no body, so the crew gathered John's belongings and set them in a rowboat.

John was a man of simple means and simple needs. All his belongings amounted to a few gold pieces, two sets of plain clothes and a spare set of leather boots, a journal, and spectacles.

Bartholomew delivered a eulogy as the crews watched the boat float away from the Irish shores. A single arrow was set ablaze and fired into the boat to create a funeral pyre.

Edward stared at the tall fire, the last remnant of a man Edward wished he'd known better. *I promise I will find my father, and I will tell him of your bravery.* Edward breathed deeply the sea air. *Thank you, John. Rest peacefully, you earned it.*

34. TSUNAMI VS. PLAGUE

Thousands of miniscule parts of leaves burned as air was drawn through a pipe. The resulting smoke entered the mouth and lungs of an old man. The old man held the smoke in his lungs for a moment, letting it do its work, before blowing it away to the ether.

"So, ye see, I simply must do somethin'," the older gentlemen said.

Across from the old man, a younger one with slick black hair sat on the deck of a ship. He held his hand to his chin and appeared to be deep in thought.

"Yes, yes, I do see the dilemma. So, let us consider you the ferry captain, and I the passenger. I require passage to a destination, and you require payment to allow passage. What payment would you think suffices to allow me crossing?" The younger man gestured off the bow towards an island that was currently only a dot on the horizon.

"Hmm..." The old man sounded thoughtful as he sucked on his pipe again.

The wind howled across the ocean. The sound of the ocean breeze passed unabated across two gargantuan ships. The crews were deathly silent as they watched the two captains negotiate. The elder was a feared pirate known as William Kidd, the Tsunami, and the younger was a powerful Earl, Edward Russell, but was known in some circles as Plague, a master of poisons.

"Eyes," Kidd offered.

Plague mockingly considered the offer and mulled it over for a moment. "No, I rather enjoy the ability to see."

Kidd took another drag and puff of the weed. "Arms."

Plague was quick in his answer. "I'm rather fond of my arms, so, sorry, but no."

"Legs."

"Again, I have to decline. Though we would have much more in common if this was done," Plague said, gesturing to Kidd's wooden leg, "I find that wood chafes, and I do not wish to have splinters."

"We seem ta be at an impasse, then."

"Well, speaking honestly," Plague held his hand up, "if we are being honest, there is not much of a negotiation occurring here. Generally, when one is haggling a price, there is a back and forth where the price is fluctuating in a downwards direction. If anything, the price has gone up. If I may make a suggestion in your tactics to make the proposition more appealing, perhaps moving from pairs to singles would continue this little transaction we are having."

Kidd sighed. "One eye."

"No."

"One arm."

"Sorry."

"One leg."

"I refuse."

Kidd's face was like stone. He said nothing further, but instead stared down Plague and waited for him to make the next move.

"Wait," Plague said, holding up his finger. "There is another option in our scenario which I neglected to mention. I could threaten to kill the ferry captain unless he allows me free passage," Plague said with a savage grin.

Kidd lowered his pipe and stood up. "Now ye've gone and done it."

The wind howled again moments later, but, unlike before, the din of a battle overshadowed its cry.

35. OF HEAVEN

The *Freedom* and *Fortune* landed on the final island hosting Benjamin's game. The crew of the *Freedom* were familiar with the island, but the *Fortune*'s crew were not used to the strangeness awaiting them.

Edward stepped onto the waist of the ship. "Secure those lines, there could be a storm at our backs and I don't want anything to happen to the ship should the winds change," he commanded. The ship had felt hard waves over the last few hours and Edward didn't want to take any chances.

"Do you think it safer to wait before trekking onto the island?" Anne asked.

Edward mulled the question over for a bit while stroking his long black beard. "There is something strange about these waves. I think they were meant for someone else." Edward kept eyeing the waves crashing against the hull before shaking his head. "I'm talking foolishness, let's ask the expert." Edward turned his head to Herbert, who was preparing to leave the ship as well. "Herbert, what would you say about these waves? Will the ship be in any danger while we are on the island?"

Herbert wheeled himself over to the starboard side and gave the waves he had been watching throughout the voyage a final perfunctory glance, then eyed the horizon. "We don't have to worry, if I'm not mistaken the waves are beginning to subside."

"Perfect." Edward turned back to Anne. "Nothing to worry about."

Anne nodded, but took note of Edward's odd choice of wording earlier. *Meant for someone else? What is your intuition telling you, Edward?*

Edward and Anne gathered gear they felt necessary for the job ahead: Guns, muskets, swords, food, water, rope, lanterns, and various other survival items. The rest of the crew followed suit under William's supervision.

Only a few members of the crew were left to guard the ship, eager volunteers who knew what could await them and opted out in favour of the easy job. Edward warned the men to stay on alert and not to drink any alcohol while on duty. Edward also told Christina to leave Tala on the ship as he knew it would be dangerous. She protested only slightly.

After preparations were made, the crew descended to the sandy beach below, joining the crew of the *Fortune*. Altogether, near to four hundred souls walked on the beach.

Edward walked over to Bartholomew, who, at Anne's instruction, was loaded with supplies like his crew. "How are you feeling, Roberts? Ready for the unknown?"

"I have no need to fear. Your tales of previous trials, while nothing to snub the nose at, were good preparation. My men know we are moving into dangerous territory. Their hearts and minds are prepared."

Edward laughed. "Whatever you think you may expect when we enter the forest, I can assure you, you will be shocked."

Edward led the crews along the path between the swaying palms. Anne ran to catch up to Edward, and William followed closely behind with Roberts. All the senior officers were dispersed amongst the crew. Jack, Pukuh, Christina, Herbert, Alexandre, Victor, and Nassir were peppered throughout the crowd, sharing stories with the crew of the *Fortune* as they trekked through the path.

After a short walk, Edward and Bartholomew emerged upon the small hill in front of the two stone pressure plates. Bartholomew ran up the steps and the sight of the angel fighting the demon and the double doors caused his jaw to drop open.

Roberts turned around to Edward with a big grin on his face, unbecoming of the man's oft intimidating figure. "I see why you wanted to call upon our assistance, my boy! This trial of yours is dipped in Biblical symbolism."

"If anyone can solve deadly puzzles about the Bible, it would be you, Pirate Priest."

Roberts noticed the stone tablet between the pressure plates. "Ah, I understand now. One crew stands on one of these altars and it opens the door for the other to enter."

"Yes, and during our previous visit we found that beyond the doors is a similar slab, which will most likely allow the second crew to enter." Edward observed the two crews crowding around the field near the pressure plates. "So, Roberts, which side do you wish to take your crew through?" Edward asked.

Bartholomew stroked his clean-shaven chin. "Well, I will allow you to be on the right hand of God. Our crew will take the left path."

"Alright, men, onto the right platform," Edward commanded.

The crew of the *Freedom* did as commanded. As more stepped on, the stone slab slowly descended, and before the last few crewmen were able to crowd onto the pressure plate it became flush with the rest of the altar.

A loud grinding could be heard beneath the earth and soon

above ground by the stone doors on the left of the angel. After the sound and movement of the earth settled, Bartholomew and crew entered the open doorway.

Before Bartholomew joined his crew, he talked with Edward. "Well, my boy, if I believed in luck I would take this time to wish you good fortune, but instead I will say this: Let us meet on the other side." Bartholomew stretched out his hand.

Edward smiled and gripped his friend's hand, then pulled him close and embraced him. "Whatever happens, don't die."

Roberts laughed. "Aye, aye, comrade." Roberts then embraced Anne and kissed her cheek before leaving to join his crew.

"When you hear the sound of gunfire, it will mean we are safely inside," Edward yelled when Roberts and crew were halfway through the door.

Roberts waved his hand, and after a few seconds he was beyond sight. Another minute more and the stone doors on the right opened.

Edward left the platform and the crew followed. He entered the door and stood near the entrance, waiting for his crew to enter the path leading to the right. After everyone was inside, Edward took out a pistol and shot at the ground. A few seconds later the ground rumbled once more and the stone doors closed behind the crew of the *Freedom*.

Edward joined his crew and they trekked the path guarded by impossibly high wooden stakes, and past the second stone pressure plate a third of the way down the path. Pukuh waited to talk with Edward.

"So, brother, what do you think awaits us around the corner?" Pukuh asked, pointing with his spear in his left hand to the end of the path which opened up on the left.

"I hate to mimic Roberts, but after all we've seen on our travels I'm not sure I can be surprised from Benjamin's trials anymore."

Pukuh mimicked Edward's response to Bartholomew with a laugh. "If only you knew the stories my father told me of his travels. I used to think they were fanciful tales for young warriors to be inspired by, but never held them to heart as truths. After time with you, I became doubtful. Impossible stories of islands floating in the sky, an invisible city of gold in the middle of a desert, and beasts taller than the tallest ships are sounding not so childish now."

"Maybe we should ask him the truth of the matter once this is over. Speaking of which, do you plan to return home after we are done here?"

"Do you wish me to leave?" Pukuh asked, brow raised in question.

"No, of course not. You never told me how long you planned to journey with us, simply that you wanted to gain experience."

"I still have a ways to go. I believed I was strong, but the man called Plague, he showed me I still have much to learn." Pukuh motioned to his missing right arm. "The princess's do… I mean… William has been helping me turn my weakness into a strength." Pukuh stopped, causing Edward to stop as well. "I am with you until you no longer find a use for me."

"Then I am afraid you will be with me a long time yet, brother." Edward smiled.

Pukuh returned the smile. "I would not have it any other way, brother."

"Edward! You must see this," Anne yelled from the front of the crowd. Half of the crew already passed the bend in the path.

Edward and Pukuh both ran forward through the crowd to see what the commotion was about. When the two turned the corner, their jaws dropped at what they saw.

In front of them was a large field five hundred feet across, lined by more sharpened wooden stakes, and in the middle of the field a massive one-hundred-foot-tall ship stood. The ship was bevelled at the bottom like a normal ship, but from what Edward could see the top was completely flat. On the far right side of the ship a large slanted gangplank allowed entrance to the ship.

"This may be a reference to Noah's ark," Anne surmised.

"Yes, and if we are to follow the rules, we must enter, I suppose," Edward replied. "But let us see if we can bypass that, shall we?" Edward walked over to the side of the ark.

The sides and top were so smooth that from afar it appeared to be carved from a single piece of wood, but upon closer examination the ship was made of planks.

Edward removed a long line of rope from his sac of supplies and tied a grappling hook to one end. The rope wasn't long enough on its own, so Edward took rope from Anne's supplies as well as some other crewmates and tied the ends together until he felt he had enough.

The crew were dispersed about, some examining the outside and inside of the ark and others the wooden stakes, and some talking amongst themselves or watching Edward.

Edward swung the grappling hook around and around, building speed. When the hook reached the apex he threw it into the air at an angle over the top of the ark. Edward tugged on the rope, but the hook slid back down to the ground in front of him. He tried this again and again and again, but received the same result.

"The ark is too smooth." Anne ran her hand along the side of the ship. "We have no choice then, we must enter."

Edward sighed in frustration. "It never gets easier, does it?"

Anne shrugged her shoulders and grinned.

Edward jogged to the entrance at the far end of the ark and entered, followed by Anne, Pukuh, and an excited Christina. On the inside, a wall blocked them from the bulk of the ship, the roof went only halfway up the height of the ark, and a pedestal stood in the middle of the hundred-by-fifty-foot room.

Edward examined the pedestal. On the top of the elbow-high wooden pedestal was a carving in the shape of a book with an inscription.

"Come thou, and all thine house, into the ark. Only when the door to sins of the past is closed may thou be granted entry to salvation," Edward read aloud.

"Edward, look." Christina pointed to the inside walls. Wooden pulleys were set on either side with rope attached to the gangplank. "Those must be to close the doors."

Edward nodded in agreement. He noticed William standing at the bottom of the gangplank. "William," Edward yelled. "Gather the crew in here."

William circled around the field and issued Edward's command to enter the ark. The people slowly lumbered their way into the gigantic structure as they examined the surroundings.

"I want two teams on the pulleys to raise the gangplank," Edward yelled over the din of the talking crew while pointing to said pulleys.

Volunteers went to task and in teams of two began pulling on the wheel spokes, gradually raising the monstrous gangplank. As it closed, the light of the day left, and was replaced with a deep darkness. When the light was completely gone, and the gangplank could be raised no more, a loud clicking and clanking noise could be heard behind the walls.

As alluded to on the carved pedestal, the wall blocking them was lifted by whatever mechanism lay behind the walls of the ark. As the wall rose, light was reintroduced to the crew, and they were able to see the vast interior of the ark in full.

The first fifty feet of the room was open space all the way to the roof. Two massive structural beams supported the left and right sides, with glass panels on the ceiling between the beams to provide light. On the floor between the beams, a carved pedestal similar to the one at the entrance stood. Behind the pedestal were twelve unique statues, six men and six women, and behind those were another twelve statues of animals in a row. Behind the statues, and taking up the rest of the nearly four hundred feet left of the ark, was a wall of wood separated into square cubes about ten by ten feet in size. In the corner of the wall, one of the cubes was open to allow passage, which Edward assumed was the way to exit the ark.

Edward started to walk over to the statues, but was stopped when the sound of gunfire startled him. He turned to see Anne holding a rifle.

"Anne, what are you doing?"

Anne pulled out a spyglass, and peered at the ceiling. "Not even a crack," she murmured. "If we could but break the glass then we may have been able to use a grappling hook, but the glass must be too thick. The bullet lodged into the pane, but did not pierce the glass." Anne handed her spyglass to Edward, and he confirmed what Anne said.

Edward handed the spyglass back. "Well, let's see what we're dealing with." Edward approached the pedestal. Alexandre and Victor were reading the inscription and talking in hushes voices when Edward approached. "May I?" Edward asked.

"By all means, *mon Capitaine*." Alexandre backed away and motioned to the pedestal.

As Edward began reading aloud while Alexandre and Victor moved on and examined the statues. "Of each holy man and woman, six and six they be, you will pair them with the beast according to the heavens. When the Lord gazes upon your pairs and deems them worthy, the path to salvation will be revealed. Six and six men and women shall not sin six times against the Lord for it is the number of the beast. Each sin sends one farther from the Lord, and on the sixth brimstone and fire will rain upon thee and send thee, and thine house, to Gehenna."

"Fire's gonna rain on us?" one of the crewmen asked, worried.

"Whuts this Gehenna? Is that Hell?" another asked.

The crew began talking amongst themselves and the panic could be clearly seen on some faces. They were trapped in the ark. If the ship caught fire there would be no way to survive.

"Calm, please everyone!" Edward yelled. "Nothing bad will happen as long as we solve this puzzle correctly. We've done this before, we'll do it again." Edward's words eased the minds of the crew. "Now, let's figure this out together." Edward examined the human statues.

From left to right, first six male statues, then six female in a line. Each man was adorned in various style of robes and some holy artefacts like rosaries, Bibles, or crosses, except one who was dressed in armour and held a lance. The women appeared to be nuns with plain clothing covering the head, save two with fancier clothing and crowns. At the base of each statue was an inscription.

Edward read the inscription on the first statue. "Monks under my discipline tried to poison me, but God protected me through miracles, and after this I founded twelve monasteries." Edward chuckled at the notion of monks trying to poison one another.

Blackbeard's Ship

"He is Saint Benedict," Alexandre stated matter-of-factly.

Edward noticed the Frenchman standing beside the statue. "So, let me guess, you've already figured out how this is solved and won't tell us?"

"*Hélas*, no. I may be intelligent, but I am not a god. Victor and I were able to deduce five of the statues' names, myself three of the five," Alexandre said loudly so Victor could hear, "and only three of which I can tell you where to set. The rest are unknown to me."

"It is rare for you to say that you don't know something," Edward commented, panic setting in. *If Alexandre can't figure this out, what hope do we have?*

Alexandre chuckled. "Despite what many of you think, I am anything but arrogant. I know what I know, and I know what I do not. There is nothing to worry about, *mon Capitaine*. This puzzle, complicated as it is, is designed for pooling of knowledge. *Venir*, see these statues here?" Alexandre pointed to the animal statues behind those of the humans. "What of these does not belong?" Alexandre asked.

Edward scanned the statues. Each was to scale, starting with a rat, then an ox, then tiger, rabbit, and... "Wait, what is this? It appears to be a large snake, but the next statue is a snake." Edward pointed to the statue to the right of the unfamiliar one.

"That is a dragon. A mythical flying lizard. I am sure you recall the English stories such as Beowulf?"

"Yes, I am familiar with dragons, but where are the wings?"

"This is a Chinese dragon, most often depicted without *ailes*."

Edward cocked his brow. "Then what does this mean? How do we pair the statues together?"

"The Chinese Zodiac. The Chinese relate each year with an animal, repeating every twelve years from rat to pig. The statues each relate to a person, a saint most likely due to the five I—"

Victor audibly coughed to Alexandre.

"The five *we* deduced. Depending on the birth year of the person, the statue relates to an animal from the Zodiac. Once we *determiner* what animal they are, we move the statue to these sections here." Alexandre pointed to a barely noticeable wooden square a small distance from each animal statue. The wooden square was coloured differently from the rest of the wood on the ship, but still smooth, with no noticeable indentation. "Placing the statues will be the easy part, the hard part is deciding where."

Edward nodded. "Thus why having more people is better. More knowledge to figure out who each person is and what year they were born. Each one is too obscure for one person, unless they are extremely well travelled and devout. Amongst a group of almost two hundred, it doesn't seem so farfetched." Edward considered the crew milling about, examining the ship and the statues and talking, and noticed several people, including Christina, Herbert, and Nassir, at the entrance to the strange area which took up the back portion of the ark. "Have Anne and William organise people to work on this, I will examine the rest of this ship."

"*Oui, Capitaine*," Alexandre replied.

Edward joined the group gathered at the back. The sectioned wall taking up the back fifth of the Ark was its own oddity. Edward didn't understand the purpose, but if the pedestal was any indication it would not provide a way out in its current state.

Two crewmen began entering the open section. "No, wait!" Edward yelled, stopping them. "It's too dangerous." He led the crewmen away. "We don't want to take any chances."

Edward took a gander into the entrance. Inside was a hallway leading deeper into the ark with a ten-foot clearance. The hallway itself was about a hundred feet long, then turned off to the right with stairs leading up. On the floor, Edward could see the same discoloured wood separating the hallway into ten-square-foot cubes. Each square was part of a larger cube which made up the final four-hundred-foot part of the ark.

"Well, I'm too curious, so I'm going in," Christina declared, walking to the entrance.

Edward grabbed her arm and pulled her back. "That was an order. If previous trials are any indication then there are probably life-threatening traps awaiting any who enter before the puzzle is complete."

"And what if that's not the case? What if there is something in there which could help in solving the puzzle out here?" Christina argued, waving her arms.

"What are you basing this off of? Your assumption is groundless," Edward argued back.

Christina contested everything Edward said and did not accept his answer. The conversation became rather heated until Herbert interjected.

"Stop, children. Stop!" he bellowed. Christina and Edward both glared at Herbert, but he was unfazed. "I feel it is worth exploring further. Perhaps all we need to do is have the courage to enter and the exit will be right around the corner. Perhaps Benjamin means for us to be afraid, while we waste time here. Is that not something he may do?"

Edward frowned, glancing back and forth between Christina and Herbert. "It sounds plausible," he said. Christina jumped and laughed in glee, grinning at her brother coming to her defence. "But, but," Edward repeated with emphasis, "you must take someone with you in case something dangerous lurks beyond those walls."

Christina instinctively turned to her older brother, and he immediately put his hands in the air. "You cannot be serious," he said with a straight face.

"No, of course not. I don't want to carry you around," Christina replied with loving bite only a sister could manage. "Nassir, would you be a gentleman and join me?" Christina linked her arm in Nassir's.

"Certainly. I will not allow any harm to befall you, Christina." Nassir turned to Edward and Herbert. "Is my protection acceptable to you both?"

Herbert and Edward both nodded in assent. Christina smiled from ear to ear and pulled the larger Nassir by the arm into the unknown. Edward glanced at Herbert and they both watched Christina and Nassir as they walked through the hallway.

"So far, so good," Edward said to Herbert as he leaned on the wooden wall.

As if the Devil was listening, a loud click drew Edward's attention to Christina. She was peering at her feet in the middle of the hallway. Edward's heart seized in his chest. He pushed away from the wall and as he was about to run into the entrance, the wall shifted before his eyes and the entrance moved away from him.

Edward backed away from the wall to see what was happening, partially out of fear and partially out of instinct. The entire back section of the ship began moving of its own accord. The entrance previously in the bottom left corner moved back and disappeared. Each ten-foot cube was moving and changing from its original position, and from the noises the cubes behind the wall were moving as well. After a few seconds the wall stopped, and the ship was so quiet one could hear a pin drop.

All eyes were on the back wall. Edward snapped out of his shock, ran to the wall, and pounded on the wood.

"Christina! Nassir!" he yelled as he beat his fist against the grain. "Can you hear me? Are you hurt?" Edward pressed his ear to the wall, but he could hear nothing.

Herbert glanced at the wall with a confused, panicked expression, and followed suit with Edward. He screamed his sister's name and savagely hit the wall. Edward moved to another spot on the wall and held his hand up for Herbert to stop his shouting and banging. "I hear her," Edward said softly. "I hear you, Christina!" he bellowed. "Are you and Nassir safe?"

"Yes, we aren't harmed," Christina replied. "The sections shifted after I stepped on a switch. I think a maze would be the only way to describe what we're seeing in here. There are so many different paths I don't know where to go next."

"Have you moved since the maze changed?"

"No, we thought it best to stay still."

"Try pressing the switch again," Edward yelled.

Herbert grabbed Edward's arm and pulled him away before he could hear anything else. "Are you insane? We don't know what that will do."

"In case you haven't noticed, it's a little late for objections, Herbert. I was against the idea from the beginning, and now she's lost with no way out. Pressing the switch may reverse what happened."

Herbert made no more objections, but still looked displeased. Edward believed he was lashing out because of his choice to let Christina go.

Edward pressed his ear to the wall to listen again. "...ward? I couldn't hear you. Are you sure you want me to press the switch again?" Christina asked.

"Yes, press the switch," Edward commanded.

"Aye, aye."

Edward backed away from the wall and watched as the ten foot cubes began shifting again. Edward wasn't able to follow the movement exactly, but it did seem to be moving opposite to what it had the first time. A few seconds passed with the crew all watching the spectacle. At the end, the entrance returned to the bottom left.

Christina ran out and searched through the gathered crew to find her brother. She rushed to Herbert and embraced him.

Herbert's hands shook as he pulled his sister close. "I feared the worst had happened."

"I'm sorry for worrying you, Herbert. I'm here. I'm safe."

Herbert pushed his sister back and stared her square in the eyes. "I forbid you from going into that maze again. Edward was right, it's too dangerous."

Even Herbert, the sailing master, could not have foreseen the storm unleashed inside Christina at those words. "You forbid me? I am not a child. Both of you do not realise that." Christina looked daggers at both Herbert and Edward. "I am going back in there, regardless of what you want!"

Herbert matched Christina's fury line for line on his face. "And what if you die, hmm? What then?"

"Then at least I would have had some choice in the matter!" Christina yelled. "I know of the arguments you had with Edward each time I have become injured, and I agree with him." Christina turned to Edward. "But you are equally as guilty as Herbert. Neither of you allow me my freedom despite how you venerate the word so. Ever since your accident, Herbert, you unwittingly shackled me with the chains of a child. I know you were hurt by Calico Jack, but when I am hurt it is not Edward's fault." Christina knelt down next to Herbert and the loving gaze of a sister returned to her eyes. "I am not a child who does not know the dangers of gunpowder. I am a grown woman who understands the risks. I will not shame Ochi by cowering in fear when facing our enemies, nor will I let fear of the unknown stop me."

Herbert's eyes welled up with tears. "I don't know what I will do if I lose you. You are all I have left in this world."

Christina shook her head as she touched her brother's leg. "If that is why you are so afraid, then you have nothing to worry about. How many times must you be told, brother? We are your family." Christina gestured to all the crewmen gathered around.

Herbert turned his gaze from the ark's floorboards and into the faces of those staring at him. Many smiled and nodded when they met his eyes. Herbert's gaze eventually landed on Edward, but then he turned away in shame.

"I am sorry, Edward." Herbert opened his mouth to say more, but the no words came out.

"There is nothing to apologise for." Edward lay his hand on Herbert's shoulder, and grinned. "Until you accept us as your family, we will be here. They say you can choose your friends, but you can't choose your family, isn't that right, men?" The crew responded with a holler and some raised fists. Edward chuckled. "You're stuck with us."

Herbert laughed and wiped a tear away. "I wouldn't have it any other way."

After a moment of silence, Edward grabbed the crew's attention. "Alright, Christina, Nassir, be careful." Christina nodded and jogged back to the maze and entered. Soon after the maze shifted again before their eyes. Edward turned his attention back to the crew. "Where are we on the statues?" he asked no one in particular.

"We set the statues we know of, at Alexandre's direction," Jack told Edward, pointing to the five statues standing next to their respected animal companions. "We are about to move one suggested by myself." Jack smiled as he said that part.

"Which one?" Edward asked as he watched ten crewmates lift the heavy statue of a priest.

Jack grinned sheepishly. "Well, the name was inscribed on the statue already. Saint Francis. There are several saints with the same name, so we don't actually know which one it is."

Edward was shocked. "Isn't this dangerous? We can't afford to make mistakes. The engraving on the pedestal mentioned something about six sins and being engulfed in fire, I think you recall."

Jack ran his fingers through his hair. "Well, yes, we know. We have ideas for some of the other statues, but we must start somewhere. I believe this one to be Saint Francis Xavier, born in fifteen-oh-six, which, according to Anne's math, would be the year of the Tiger."

Edward focused on the crew, a few steps from setting the statue down. "I suppose," he agreed, stroking his beard.

The crew dropped the saint's statue next to the Tiger statue and a clicking sounded. At first Edward feared the worst, then his rational mind went through the steps. *Each statue must have clicked before this.* Edward calmed himself with this, but as he glanced at the crew, he could tell something was off. *There was no noise before!*

Another noise started, bringing Edward's attention to the front of the ark, where they had first entered. The wall which first lifted to allow the crew passage to the interior of the ark was now lowering inch by inch.

"Get away from the front of the ark!" Edward yelled, swiping his hand across the air.

The crewmen near the descending wall snapped out of their stupor of curiosity and ran. When the wall was halfway down, Edward could see two large unlit fire pits suspended in the air in the alcove where the wall used to be. When the wall was close to the bottom, Edward noticed the alcove was slanted and covered in a black, tar-like substance. The black liquid spilled over the falling wall and covered it completely, pooling on the floorboards and oozing out towards the middle of the ark and the crew.

When the wall fell flush with the rest of the ship, a mechanism struck flint to steel and created sparks, igniting the two fire pits. After the fire pits were set ablaze, they began descending slowly. Eventually, the fire would reach the bottom of the alcove and, presumably, ignite the black liquid, and in turn the ark.

Edward took charge of the situation before panic took over the crew. "Move the statue off!" he commanded. The men moved the Saint Francis Xavier statue away quickly. After they moved the statue, all eyes were on Edward, waiting for orders. Their survival hinged on Edward's next words, and Edward knew it. "I want all crewmates to split up among the statues. Senior officers will work at taking information on the possible origin of the person depicted by the statue. If you don't know who the person is, or are unsure, move to another group. I want everyone involved in this, no lollygagging. Seven statues, seven groups. Hop to it, men!"

Each crewmate ran to the nearest statue. Anne, William, Jack, Pukuh, Herbert, Alexandre, and Victor each moved to one of the statues, knowing their role without needing to question. They would guide the discussion as well as possible towards finding the solution of who these priests and nuns were and when they were born.

Edward paced back and forth, watching the crew working together, and the slowly falling fire pits some fifty feet away. When he noticed crewmates glancing at the impending doom, he admonished them to stay focused. Individual crewmates shuffled to other groups when they felt they knew nothing about the statue or had no further input to provide their group.

Edward gradually made his way to Alexandre, who simply observed the group discuss amongst themselves, no doubt analysing every word for something worthwhile.

"So, can you tell me what happened back there?" Edward whispered while Alexandre's group were discussing the exploits of female martyrs who were imprisoned.

"We did a test. We had one in seven chances. We were no farther ahead, so I made the call to use Jack's suggestion. Is that *un problème*?" Alexandre asked, brow raised.

"No, but I wish we were in a better position beforehand, maybe had a few more statues figured out before doing a test. Now we have a timer over our heads. How long do you figure we have left?"

Alexandre considered the fire pits, then his sullen eyes examined the angles and the relationship of the pits to the port and starboard walls. "*Cinquante-six* minutes, give or take."

Edward laughed. "Give or take. I enjoy your humble attitude. Always refreshing." Edward patted Alexandre on the back.

"If you ask me, this timer is, for lack of a better term, a godsend. I find that when under threat of death, humans can work more efficiently. Trust me, I've done tests," Alexandre said with a dark grin. "Also, this has brought those previously unhelpful into the fold as *contributeurs*."

Edward glanced at the teams working together. They had adopted frantic expressions, and argued vehemently that their assessment was correct, but all were involved.

"I believe you may be correct. Let us hope this is enough." Edward peered back to the maze behind him, the loud thumping of the shifting cubes telling him Christina was still alive.

Across the next thirty minutes, Edward and the senior crewmates collaborated on the consensus of their groups. The seven debated amongst themselves on whether their group was correct for their statue.

Four statues had riddles about the people they could be, and three had names on them. They were able to make a list of the possible priests and nuns each statue represented, and figured out which combinations would work, but a problem quickly presented itself.

"We're one statue short," Anne said flatly.

Alexandre concurred. "None of the *combinaisons* work with William's statue."

"So, what does it mean? We don't know who that is?" Edward pointed to the statue in question.

"Apparently so," William concluded.

"It matters not, just position the idols," Pukuh chimed in.

Anne sighed. "Pukuh, there are four possible solutions for this. We have fifteen minutes. We may be able to determine this statue's origin by then. According to the text, if we are wrong it will undoubtedly speed the process of our doom."

"What of it?" Pukuh replied, indignant. "Time for talk is over. We must act, or we *will* die."

Anne glanced to the group, and all agreed with Pukuh's suggestion. "Alright, we'll try it your way."

Anne guided the crew in placing another statue. They believed the statue to be Saint Thomas Aquinas, born in the year of the Dog. As the crew moved the holy man's likeness, the fire pit inched ever closer to the pitch-covered wood, looming like the sword of Damocles. One mistake would that sword down, sealing the fate of the *Freedom*'s crew.

Half the crew's eyes were focused on the statue, and the other half on the pits. The priest's statue was plopped down next to the figure of the dog. Those focusing on the pits and those on the statue swapped focus in the seconds after the statue lowered.

The pits kept lowering as normal, and the relief was visible on Edward's face, and the faces around him. Edward glanced at Anne and Pukuh; they both let out sighs.

Anne commanded the crew to move to the next statue. As the statue was set down next to the figure of the snake, Edward unconsciously held his breath, his eyes intent on the fire pit, and his ears listening for a sound he prayed never arrived.

Click

The noise caused Edward's gaze to shift back to the statue. The crewmates who set the statue down aped in shock. The sound of moving metal grinding and clanging echoed beneath the floorboards. Edward followed the noise with his eyes as it travelled all the way to the front of the ark.

The pits fell. Edward watched in horror as the pits sped to the bottom of the alcove. The noise of the iron chain locking filled the room. The pits stopped, swinging back and forth.

"*Deux* minutes," Alexandre counted blandly, filling the void of silence.

Panic gripped the crew of the *Freedom*. Hope was lost in those few seconds, as was order. Each man tried their own way of escape. Most ran to the sides, hacking and shooting at the wood, but none made a dent. Sweat poured from the faces of those men onto the floor of the Ark through their wasted effort.

Anne and the senior officers did their best to quell the squall of voices and calm the pirates, but theirs was also a futile endeavour. Anne and William attempted to reason with some, but it devolved into arguing. Pukuh took a more direct, forceful approach, but one against a mob did not work. Jack's and Herbert's soft-spoken natures were easily overpowered. Alexandre and Victor stood watching, merely observing the chaos.

Edward glanced back and forth at his crew descending into madness, and he'd had his fill. "Enough!" he roared, slamming his fist into the beam and shaking the ark to its core. In a matter of seconds, all eyes were on the captain. "If we die, we die with dignity." Edward stared his men in the eye, then sat down, facing the fire pits.

As Edward's men watched him sit, their hands, held high in defiance, lowered as well. They still had no hope, but they had regained their pride. The crew did not want to bring shame to their captain's name, nor disappoint the one who had given them *Freedom*. The crew gradually joined Edward in sitting.

Anne regarded the men who, so affected by their captain's simple resolve, changed their outlook completely. She joined Edward at the front of the crew.

Anne leaned over to Edward. "How is your hand?" she asked, peering down at the reddish hue forming on the side of his right palm where he'd hit the support beam.

"My hand is fine," Edward replied, pulling his hand close to his chest. Anne took it and wrapped it around hers.

Edward gazed into Anne's eyes, and she into his. Those green eyes of hers captured him as they always did, and, before Edward knew it, he was far away from the ark, and from the impending doom. Edward became lost in Anne's eyes, and she in his.

"I love you, Anne."

Anne smirked. "I know." Edward pushed her playfully. "I love you too, Edward."

The pit reached its destination. The flames grew and filled the alcove with light. In mere seconds the front of the ark was on fire. After overtaking the black pitch the inferno crawled across the floorboards and set the walls ablaze. Smoke filled the room, covering the glass panels of the ceiling. The wood cracked and let out a howl as moisture turned to steam and escaped. The heat intensified as the fire spread, feeding on the wood and air.

The heat and smoke seemed to rob the moisture from the surroundings, and some of the crew began coughing. Edward's throat was scratchy as well, as if he was swallowing ash.

Edward's ears heard all the sounds of the spreading fire, but one sound was missing now. Edward's head spun around to the back of the ship. The moving maze Christina and Nassir entered had stopped after near continuous movement the past hour. Edward glanced at the left corner, and noticed, despite all odds, the maze entrance back in its original position.

"Edward!" a voice sounded from inside the maze.

Edward stood, his brows furrowed. Christina ran out of the maze, followed by Nassir. She was holding something in the palm of her hand.

It cannot be. Edward's eyes opened wide in astonishment.

Christina ran, pushing through the crowd, towards Edward. She now held the object she had found outstretched above her head.

Edward moved back after recovering from his shock. "Hand it to Anne, quickly!" he yelled over the raging fire.

Christina shifted and jumped in front of Anne, shoving a piece of paper into her hands. Anne examined the paper, and soon her expression changed to awe.

"It is a list of years next to the names of animals," Anne said, as she worked everything out in her head. "Everyone on your feet! Lift those statues!"

The crew jumped to the closest statues not already assigned to animals, picking them up of the ground. Anne yelled out directions to each group, pointing as she did. In less than a minute the statues were set.

Edward couldn't hear another click, but he felt a rumbling below his feet. This time the rumbling moved to the back of the ark, towards the maze.

The maze cubes shifted of their own accord, rapidly moving the insides around to another configuration. Edward watched as the entrance moved from one end to the other, then stopped. The back of the ark stopped moving completely.

"Move!" Edward yelled, pointing to the entrance to the maze, or what could be the ship's exit, and their only hope, now.

Edward ran to the entrance, but didn't enter. He stood at the side, watching as his crew entered. Edward yelled for the men to hurry as he spurred them along with a hand on their backs.

When the crew were gone, Edward took one last glimpse at the ark. The roof collapsed at the front, sending wooden planks crashing down. Flames reached the support beam and started climbing.

Edward entered the maze, running through the tunnel. Anne waited at the back, and when she saw him she started off again to the left. Edward turned the corner and saw stairs heading up for the length of two of the ten-foot squares. After Edward climbed the stairs, he flew down another hallway, and around another left turn at the end. The process was repeated around the perimeter of the maze and up.

A deafening crack resounded throughout the ark, stopping Edward in his tracks. In front of him was another set of stairs, but before he could climb, one of the support beams crashed through the nearby wall. The flaming beam broke the wood to splinters with thunder and screeching. It eventually settled in front of the stairs, blocking the way.

Anne appeared in the right corner at the top, the only spot left open in the wake of the beam. "Edward! Are you unharmed?"

"I'm fine, but soon I won't be," Edward replied, eyeing the hell-fire through the hole made by the beam. The fire had nearly overtaken the whole ark, and the ship was quickly falling apart.

Anne tried to push herself through the small hole to join Edward, but even her slender body could not fit. Edward moved to the left side, but there wasn't any room to squeeze through either.

"Hang on Edward, I'll be right back." Anne called over some of the crew. "Now lift!" she commanded. "Edward, get ready. We'll attempt lifting the beam to let you through."

Edward positioned himself at the top of the stairs in front of the left side of the beam. He grabbed the side and lifted with all his might to help, but the beam didn't seem to move at all. Edward's body was still healing and weaker than normal.

"We need more bodies. Move in as best you can," Edward could hear Anne say.

Edward lay down on a step and planted his feet into the small opening as best he could. He could hear Anne yell "lift!" and he pushed his feet in tandem with his brothers. After a few seconds of no movement, Anne called for rest, then counted down from three.

"Three."

I will not die here.

"Two."

I'm not done yet.

"One."

"I won't let you win, you hear me you bastard?" Edward yelled.

"Lift!" Anne shouted.

Edward bellowed with rage, pushing the beam with all the strength in him. The pillar inched forward. Edward pushed with his back, the movement of the massive beam feeding him with strength. The pillar moved foot by foot, and with the extra room more people joined in lifting it to save their captain.

"Now, Edward!" Anne yelled.

Edward released his feet from the beam and crawled over to safety. When he was on the other side, the crew dropped the pillar and it fell with a thunderous boom as it smashed through more of the ark.

Anne grabbed Edward's hand and pulled him up. "Move!" Edward commanded between ragged breaths. "And thank you." Edward's afterthought compliment drew more than a few chuckles.

Edward, Anne, and the crew ran through the small hallway, then to another left turn, and up a longer flight of stairs. At the top was an opening to the outside.

Edward emerged from the ark to the bright sun and tropical wind. After his eyes adjusted to the new scenery, he could only see half his crew. He noticed the men descending off the side on rope ladders.

Edward guided the remaining crew to move ahead of himself. The crew swiftly descended the ladders while the fire moved closer like a tiger stalking prey. Edward gazed at the front of the ark, the flames changing it into what could have been a funeral pyre.

Anne and Edward rushed down the hundred-foot ladder on the side of the ark. The heat of the flames licked at them as they moved. As soon as the fire was about to overtake their ladder, the two landed on solid ground. They ran forward, putting a safe distance between them and the death trap before collapsing on the grass.

Edward and Anne breathed heavily from exhaustion, and Edward could hear the crew resting from similar effort.

"I didn't think we would make it," he said.

"Our family is lucky. If any other crew had to face this, I don't think they would have survived."

Edward nodded with a grin. "You may be right… but the crew with a *Pirate Priest* for a captain probably would have done well, right?"

Anne laughed. "Yes, that crew might have fared better."

Edward scanned the crowd of two hundred before resting his eyes on Christina. "Christina!" he shouted, beckoning her over.

Christina turned to Edward's voice, and, after ensuring her brother was unharmed, walked over. "Yes?"

"First off, good job, my dear. You saved us." Christina smiled at the praise. "How did you make it back? The maze must have shifted over a hundred times."

"Well, Nassir and I were running most of the time, but we moved methodically. Each time the maze shifted I memorised where we were, and then if we reached a dead end we went back and tried another route. Eventually we found the paper, and retraced our steps." Christina explained.

Edward was dumbfounded at the explanation. "How could you remember?"

Christina laughed. "I trained myself to remember things. It used to be a game I and my brother would play. We used to see who could remember the most numbers in a random sequence." Christina smirked. "I don't enjoy losing."

"Impressive," Anne remarked. "She is a prodigy." Anne whispered to Edward. "Perhaps we should be training her mind too."

Edward simply nodded in agreement with Anne, he was still in awe of Christina's abilities.

Now that they were out of harm's way, Edward stood and observed the area. The crew was in a field similar to the one before they entered the ark, but surrounded by wooden stakes. Edward could find no discernible exit. Some time had passed since the trial was made, as vegetation had grown over the wood, and the grass was long.

On the left side, the side closest to Bartholomew's group, the wooden stakes appeared different, so Edward examined them.

At the wall, Edward noticed a pedestal similar to the ones they had seen many times before here. Edward noticed no writing, only a switch.

This must to open the way to the next area.

Edward pressed the switch. The ground rumbled and he could feel movement beneath his feet spreading to the wall to his left and in front of him. Suddenly the walls dropped down revealing a whole other area, along with a new danger.

To Edward's left, he could see the crew of the *Fortune* fighting an unknown enemy. The sight made him jump, and he immediately drew his golden blade. His crew were shocked and drew their weapons as well.

Edward's gaze was drawn to an altar in the middle of the two fields. Standing on the altar in the middle of Edward's and Bartholomew's crews, was an accursed man with slicked-back hair and black clothing. He was holding a bloodied Bartholomew by the neck, and he glanced nonchalantly over his shoulder and smiled.

It was Plague.

36. FROM HELL

Blood dripped from Plague's hand onto the grey marbled stone of the altar. The blood of the faithful Bartholomew dripped onto the stone and pooled at his feet.

Edward, his cutlass drawn, ran to the altar and jumped atop. The crew of the *Freedom* rushed to the aid of *Fortune*'s crew. The sounds and smells of battle quickly filled Edward's senses.

"Fitting, is it not? Bartholomew, the Pirate Priest, sacrificed in a place such as this."

"Release him, Plague, it's me you want," Edward commanded as he circled the large surface of the altar.

Edward Russell, known by many names, laughed, sending a chill down Edward's spine. "You know nothing, boy." He dropped Bartholomew, and the Pirate Priest fell in a heap on the marble. Plague slowly drew his weapon, a small dagger. Normally innocuous in the wrong hands, the dagger took on the form of deadly claws in Plague's.

Edward leapt forward and slashed. Plague parried the strike, then punched Edward in the nose. Edward fell backwards, but stayed on his feet. Plague thrust his blade at his abdomen, but Edward smashed his elbow into Plague's hand, nearly knocking the dagger from the assassin's grip.

Plague stopped his advance and adopted a more defensive posture. "You've improved, but methinks you stretched yourself too thin."

Edward breathed heavily, staring intently into Plague's eyes. He pulled his sword close to his chest and held it in both hands. *He's right. I'm not yet fully recovered.*

Pukuh and William both jumped atop the altar beside Edward. "Worry not, Edward, we will handle this. We have business with him."

Pukuh flashed his spear forward in his left hand. "This one owes me an arm."

Plague stood up straight. "You act as if I am the only one here, gentlemen." The man with the slick black hair put his fingers between his teeth and whistled loudly. After a second's delay, two people with masks on joined Plague on the altar. "Leave the one in the middle for me, the other two are yours. If you cannot kill them, at least make yourselves useful and keep them busy."

Without a word, the masked people pulled out Katar, stylised Indian daggers. The daggers had horizontal handles to allow the blade to rest just above the knuckle so they could be punched into the victim. The two rushed Pukuh and William, pushing them back and off the altar, away from Edward.

With Pukuh and William gone, Plague resumed his defensive stance, but pulled out another dagger for his other hand.

Edward assessed his opponent. *Knees bent, low to the ground. No way to unbalance him. One dagger near his face, one around his torso. No way past his defence. If I can distract him, I could gain the upper hand.*

Edward peered over Plague's shoulder, widened his eyes a touch, and nodded. Plague glanced over his shoulder, but no one was there. Edward thrust his cutlass towards Plague's face and the man threw his arms up. Edward changed direction mid-way and swiped at Plague's legs. Edward's double-feint worked and he sliced Plague's thigh open.

Plague ignored the injury, but his eyes flashed with anger. Edward could feel the pressure of those eyes, but he would not run this time. He stared straight into the face of fear.

Plague ran forward, his blades dancing in the air. Edward took each thrust, lunge, slash, and cut and returned them in kind. Plague parried Edward's blows, but every so often he slipped and was sliced on the hands, face, and stomach. Edward was nicked in the forehead, hand, bicep, legs. The two men traded jab for jab, neither one cutting deeper than the surface.

Edward jumped backwards to catch his breath. The blood from his forehead seeped into his left eye, blocking his vision. He wiped away the blood and noticed Plague was also short on breath.

"Maybe *you* are stretched too thin, Plague. Did Bartholomew take the fight out of you?"

Plague stifled his heavy breathing and stood up straight. "Hmph. You are nothing before me." Plague postured with bravado.

The Royal Assassin with a penchant for poison pulled a vial from his pocket. Edward tensed and raised his guard. Plague popped the cork from the vial and took a large sniff from its contents before throwing it to the ground and breaking the bottle.

Edward didn't understand what was happening, but he didn't like it. Plague breathed rapidly, but not from fatigue this time, his eyes widened, and his pupils grew large. Plague threw his daggers away and changed to hand to hand combat.

Whatever had been in the vial changed Plague completely, and with the metamorphosis he regained speed and strength before Edward's eyes.

Plague lowered his body and moved inches in front of Edward, and he didn't have time to react. Plague landed an uppercut and Edward's chin flew up. Plague struck him in the stomach. Edward tensed his stomach and took the blow, then slammed the butt of his cutlass into Plague's head.

Plague punched Edward's right hand and he dropped his cutlass, and the assassin took the drop in his guard to kick him in the side of the knee. Edward dropped to the stone uncontrollably, but twisted and struck Plague in the midsection. Plague doubled over, but dropped his elbow on Edward's head.

Edward was pushed down further to the ground, still on his knee. He gritted his bloodied teeth together and balled his fist. Edward jumped upwards, delivering an uppercut square on Plague's jaw. The man's head whipped backwards, and his eyes went foggy as he began losing consciousness.

Plague forced himself back from the brink, his eyes shooting wide open. The assassin clinched Edward's midsection, fell backwards, and slammed Edward's face into the stone altar.

Edward fell to the ground, his head and body aching. He couldn't rise back up; he was *so* tired. Disoriented too. He pulled his body around as he searched for Plague.

Edward could see the two crews fighting against Plague's crew. First, he noticed Alexandre and Victor fighting back to back. Alexandre used a rapier to cut and thrust into his opponents' vital organs with precision only he could pull off. Victor used a small round shield and curved double-edged blade to parry and slice his opponents.

Next, Edward noticed Nassir and Christina fighting together, and Jack and Herbert attacking from long range. Working together, the two groups were dropping enemies left and right.

In those few flickering seconds of movement, Edward's eyes finally found Plague. He too was overlooking the battlefield, searching for something while he caught his breath. Edward followed Plague's gaze to Anne.

Anne was fighting against Plague's men on the side where the ark was still burning fifty feet away. She directed the crew of the *Freedom* during the battle while firing her favourite rifle and engaging in the occasional swordplay.

Plague pulled out a familiar needle from his pocket.

No! Not Anne! Edward moved his body around and tried to push himself upright. *Damn arms! You're stronger than this.* "Anne! Run!" Edward yelled, but Anne was too far away and the noises of the battle too intense for her to hear. *Damn legs, move!*

Plague set the needle into a crossbow bolt, placed the bolt in a crossbow, and aimed it at Anne.

"Anne!" Edward yelled, but to no avail. He pushed his body with all his might, his face turning red and veins showing from the strain.

Plague pulled the trigger, sending the bolt to Anne at incredible speed, and it struck her in the shoulder. Anne stopped what she was doing and pulled the bolt out of her shoulder, confusion on her face. She turned to the altar. Anne saw Plague and Edward, then she stepped forward, but she collapsed on the ground.

"Anne, God, no!" Edward howled, tears filling his eyes, but still Anne did not answer.

"Mission complete," Edward heard Plague say.

Edward forced himself to his feet, anger driving his muscles. He picked up his cutlass from the altar and approached Plague with lethal intent. Plague turned and picked up his daggers again, ready to kill.

Suddenly, Bartholomew jumped up behind Plague. The big man wrapped his massive arms around Plague's arms and pulled them back to expose the assassin's chest. Then Bartholomew wrapped his legs around Plague's, not allowing him any bit of movement.

Plague struggled against the bonds, but at least for the moment Bartholomew's strength was more than Plague could break. "Hurry, Edward. Kill him!"

Edward pulled the blade back and slashed Plague across the chest. Edward's gritted his teeth, and stared into Plague's eyes. For the first time Edward could see fear in the man's eyes.

Plague broke free from Bartholomew and Edward, and fell forwards to the marble, his shaking hand holding himself up. Blood poured from the open wound. Plague turned himself around and lay back on the raised stone.

Edward approached Plague. He leaned over the body of the man who had haunted them the past months. The man who killed Henry's mother, the man who took Pukuh's arm, and had now poisoned Anne.

Plague coughed blood over the marble, and laughed. He continued to laugh and cough blood as Edward stared at him. Plague was dead, and the man himself knew it, yet he kept laughing.

"William!" Edward beckoned.

William rushed over to Edward's side; he was covered in wounds, but thankfully still alive. Edward lifted his golden blade over Plague's head and stared at William. William nodded and placed his hand over the hilt of the blade.

"Go to Hell," Edward said.

Edward and William slammed the golden cutlass down on Plague's neck, severing his head from his body. The man named Edward Russell, the Plague, one of the Immortal Seven, was finally dead.

Though Plague did not live up to one of his names, those who witnessed his death claimed they could still hear him laughing even after Edward delivered the final blow. He laughed all the way to the grave and beyond.

37. THE SHIP'S NAME

Edward ran like a ship with a storm in its sails. "Stay with me, Anne," he said between breaths. Edward carried her to the *Freedom*, the battle still raging on behind him.

Edward had rushed to Anne's body, calling for Alexandre as he did so. The wooden spikes had dropped, revealing a way out in between the two sides of the trial.

"We need *médecine* from the ship," Alexandre had stated.

Edward had nodded, picked Anne up, and started running with Alexandre closely behind.

Edward ran along the walled path to the entrance they were in not hours before. He rushed around the wooden statue and the pressure plates and into the woods.

Anne's breathing was shallow and she was as pale as a cloud on a summer's day. Her eyes were closed in pain, flickering as the light passed over.

Edward cursed under his rapid breath. *How could I be so foolish? All the signs were there. Plague was never meant for me. I should have seen it sooner.*

"Focus, *Capitaine*," Alexandre commanded, noticing Edward slowing.

"Right," he replied, quickening his feet.

Edward emerged from the forest to see three ships. The *Fortune* on the left, the *Freedom* next to it, and on the right a massive second-rate warship.

Edward could smell gunpowder in the air, and bodies recently sent to the next world littered the beach and water surrounding the ships. The *Freedom* had no marks of battle, but the third ship had many holes across the hull from cannon fire.

"Oi! Is anyone alive?" Edward yelled.

Alexandre pulled on Edward's shoulder, trying to pull him back. The Frenchman held a finger to his lips to force a cautionary silence on the captain.

Before Alexandre could pull Edward back into the forest, a man appeared on the fore of the *Freedom*. "Captain! Praise the heavens you be safe," he said.

Alexandre released the captain and the two ran to the ship.

Edward waded through the water and sand, balancing with Anne still in his arms. "What happened, besides the obvious?"

The crewman followed Edward to the side, then dropped the *Freedom*'s jolly boat into the water. "When we saw the warship approachin' those of us leftover from 'ere and the *Fortune* hid in the woods and after theys all left we snuck back and showed the leftovers what-for."

Edward gently laid Anne down in the small boat, but climbed up a rope ladder instead of jumping in. The crewman talking with Edward called others to his aid and pulled the jolly boat back up to the deck.

"Are the boys doing alright?" the crewman asked while pulling hard on the rope. "We saw the enemy head your way, but there were too many for us to stop them."

"All is well, no need to worry yourselves. Bartholomew and I killed their leader, the Plague, and it's only a matter of time before the men finish his crew."

Edward jumped over the railing of the ship as the crew were securing the boat and pulling Anne to the deck. Tala was sniffing Anne and licking her face, trying to wake her. Alexandre was ahead of Edward, running to his medical cabin. Edward took Anne into his arms, and followed the Frenchman to the lower deck.

"What happened to Miss Bonney?" the crewman asked.

"She was poisoned," Edward yelled back before descending the ladder.

Edward took care in transporting Anne down the ladder and the narrow hallway to Alexandre's cabin. She was sweating bullets and mumbling indistinct words Edward couldn't make sense of.

Almost there, Anne. Hold on a bit longer, and Alexandre will save you.

Edward entered the cabin and lay Anne on the table in the middle of the room. At the back of the cabin, Alexandre flew into a frenzy, grabbing a mortar and pestle in one hand and the Mayan plant in the other. He threw the plant in the mortar and crushed the leaves together with the pestle.

"Third shelf, black mushroom. *Vite*!" Alexandre commanded Edward.

Edward jumped to the right side of the room with the various shelves and oddities contained within. He quickly scanned the shelf and found the mushrooms in a glass. Edward removed the glass and handed a mushroom to the surgeon.

"Do you know what poison was used?" Edward asked.

Alexandre dropped the mushroom in the mortar and crushed

the plant and it together with some water. "*Oui*. Our man in *noir* was sloppy. I had never seen the poison used on the Mayan devil, so if he used that again our princess would be gone. This is one I have seen before. I did not have enough time to save Henry's mother, but this time..." Alexandre took out a cloth and wrapped the plant and mushroom paste in the centre of the cloth. "Grab the two bottles in the corner." Edward did as commanded and brought the sealed bottles over quickly. "Now smell each of them, *s'il vous plaît*."

Edward opened the first and took a whiff of the contents. "Smells sweet, but with a hint of rot. Akin to bad wine."

"Close that and try the other."

Edward took the second bottle and repeated the process, trusting Alexandre's process. "Is this vinegar?"

"*Bon*, it is vinegar."

"And the first one?"

"If you wish to kill someone, pour the first liquid on their head." Alexandre smiled devilishly. "We will need it next."

Edward gazed at the bottle with a new appreciation of terror. "Why are they not labelled?"

"Too much work. Now, focus." Alexandre set down a glass and handed Edward the cloth with the plant and mushroom mixture. "Hold this over the glass."

Edward glanced at the liquid Alexandre claimed could kill with a splash, took in a deep breath, and held the cloth over the glass. Edward's eyes were shut tightly and his hands clenched against the glass, his knuckles white in anticipation for the deadly liquid about to be poured near him.

Edward heard some shuffling around him, then nothing. "You may open your eyes," Alexandre said. Edward did as instructed and now saw four wooden clothespins holding the cloth against the glass. "Your dedication to the woman you love is admirable, albeit misplaced. You did not think I would risk pouring the *liquide* over you, did you?"

Edward grinned sheepishly. "No, of course not."

Alexandre gave Edward a knowing glance, then slowly and carefully poured the contents of the first bottle over the cloth. As the liquid passed over the herbs and mushroom it took on a blackish green hue and dripped from the cloth into the glass. Alexandre was meticulous in his preparation, taking his time, which Edward knew was precious in this scenario.

Edward left Alexandre to what he did best and turned to Anne. She was shaking and cold, but her forehead was slick with sweat, like her body was in the throes of a fever.

Edward took Anne's hand and gripped it tightly. "You can make it, Anne. If anyone can beat this, I know you can. If you can hear me, you need to keep fighting a little longer." Edward leaned over and kissed Anne on the forehead before wiping a strand of red hair away.

"*Capitaine*, the vinegar, if you please," Alexandre said over his shoulder.

Edward let go of Anne's hand and grabbed the vinegar bottle, opening it in a single motion. Alexandre held the cloth in his index finger and thumb over the glass.

"When I say now, pour the entire bottle of vinegar over my hands."

Edward cocked his brow. "Why, what are you—"

Alexandre squeezed the cloth together, causing the absorbed liquid to pass through it and over Alexandre's hand. The liquid burned Alexandre's skin as it transferred from the cloth to his hand and down to the glass below. Alexandre shook with the effort to let every drop fall into the glass; his arm convulsed and his eyes widened with pain, but his hands never moved an inch.

Alexandre threw the cloth away and moved his hands to an open area. "Now!" he yelled.

Edward paused for the slightest moment, still in shock from what he'd witnessed. He pulled himself together and dumped the vinegar over Alexandre's hands. The vinegar reacted with the other liquid, providing the surgeon with the needed relief. Edward continued until the whole of the bottle was empty and the room had taken on a smell of sweet vinegar wine, rot, and burning flesh.

"Now, I will need you to make the final *preparation*," Alexandre said, holding his hands in front of him still, showing no sign of pain.

"What do I need to do?"

"Pour a drop into another glass, and fill the rest with water."

"Easy."

Edward took an empty glass and set it on the shelf in front of him. Then, with a shaking hand, he gripped the other glass. Alexandre watch over his shoulder, breathing down his neck.

Edward turned his upper body to face Alexandre. "Do you mind?"

Alexandre backed up a few paces and leaned on the shelf, still watching like a hawk.

Edward took two deep breaths and picked up the glass with the deadly concoction. He gently moved it to the other glass, setting the lip of the first against the edge of the second. Centimetre by slow centimetre Edward tipped the first glass up.

"*Vite*," Alexandre prompted.

Edward closed his eyes in frustration for a moment, then turned to Alexandre. "Stop," he commanded.

Edward turned back to his task, but an idea formed in his head. Edward set the first glass down and pulled a clean cloth from Alexandre's supplies. He took the cloth and dipped the corner into the glass, letting the liquid absorb in. After Edward felt enough liquid was absorbed he positioned the cloth over the second glass, then picked up a clothespin. Edward put the clothespin above the spot on the cloth where the liquid was, then moved the pin down, the pressure pushing the liquid down and out of the cloth. Once a drop fell, Edward removed the cloth and filled the glass with water.

Edward turned to Alexandre, the glass in hand. "Now what?" Edward couldn't be sure, but he believed he saw a small grin on Alexandre's lips.

"Now, you must make her drink."

Edward lifted Anne's head with his left hand while holding the antidote in his right. "Anne, you must drink this. Anne! If you can hear me, I need you to drink this. It will help you."

Edward pushed the glass to Anne's lips. Alexandre dried his burned hands and helped open her mouth. Edward tipped the glass and gradually poured the liquid down Anne's throat.

She coughed, spitting a bit of the liquid out. "Damn," Edward cursed.

"Let her head relax, it will help."

Edward nodded and cradled her head in his elbow. Her mouth naturally opened. Alexandre took the glass from Edward and he took over administering it to Anne.

After a laborious ten minutes, the liquid was gone. Edward gently laid Anne's head back down on the table. She was still sweating and breathing rapidly.

"Now what?" Edward asked.

Alexandre returned his instruments to the shelves. "Now, we wait. The worst is past us. *Se relaxer*, your beloved will live on. Make her comfortable and wait for her to awaken."

Edward nodded, then pulled Alexandre close and embraced him. "Thank you. You saved us all a dozen times over. I know I don't thank you enough for all you've done for our family, and for that I'm sorry." Edward let Alexandre go.

Alexandre smirked. "Careful, *Capitaine*. I may become attached to everyone."

Edward laughed as he picked up Anne from the table. "We both know it's too late for that."

Edward then noticed the audience watching the entire time. He passed by them all, Anne in his arms. The crewmen watched Anne with concern and relief in their eyes. After Edward was outside the room, the crewmen piled into the medical cabin and flooded Alexandre with praise and questions all at once. Edward could see a smile at the corner of Alexandre's lips.

Edward took Anne to the crew cabin and lay her down in their bed in the corner underneath the ladder. He pulled the covers over her, and kissed her on the forehead.

"I won't be long, Anne."

Edward ran back up to the top deck. He jumped over the side of the ship and climbed down the rope ladder to the sandy beach below. He ran to the path, but stopped short of entering. The crew of the *Freedom* and *Fortune* were standing in front of Edward. Bartholomew was leading the pack, waving to Edward.

"My boy! Is Anne well?" he asked immediately. His face was bloody, dirt and cuts covering his body, but Bartholomew appeared no worse for wear.

"Yes, she is fine. Alexandre created an antidote for the poison. I trust your return means the battle went smoothly?"

"Aye, God was with us this day. We only battled half of Plague's crew, given the design of this trial, and when providence sent your crew to our aid the numbers were in our favour."

Edward stroked his beard. "So the other half of Plague's crew is stuck behind the ark with no way out then."

"Right you are. Ah, yes, you should be delighted to have this, I presume?" Bartholomew reached into his pocket and pulled out a key.

Edward smiled. "How did you happen upon this?"

"Writing on the front of the altar indicated a need to sacrifice blood. After you left, Plague's blood pooled on the altar and activated it, opening an alcove with the key inside."

Pukuh and William, injured and helping each other walk, trudged over to Edward and Bartholomew.

"Where is Anne?" William asked, concern evident in his eyes.

"She is in the crew cabin, resting. Alexandre made an antidote for her, so she is safe."

William let out a sigh and nodded to Edward in thanks.

Jack and Hank Abbot were next. The two waved to their captains as they passed. Jack was battle worn, but in good spirits considering. He had overheard Edward's mention of Anne being safe.

Christina, Herbert, and Nassir exited the path after Jack and Hank. Christina ran over to Edward, followed by Herbert and Nassir on her heels.

"Is Anne safe?" Christina asked Edward.

Edward laughed, this being the third time he was asked. "Yes, she is well thanks to Alexandre. If you wish to see her, she is in the crew cabin resting."

Christina kissed Edward on the cheek and then ran off to the *Freedom* ahead of her brother. Herbert and Nassir were fatigued, but uninjured. They both nodded to Edward when he glanced over.

The remainder of the crew passed in waves, some more injured than others, and many asked about Anne despite their own worries. Edward answered their questions with a scolding remark to return to the ship and worry about themselves, followed by assuring them Anne was alright.

Victor arrived last, carrying a body slumped over his shoulder, and something in his hand. This time, Edward ran over.

"Did one of our crewmates die, Victor?" Edward asked.

Victor shied away from Edward's eyes as he replied, "No."

"Then, who...?" Edward examined the body, then noticed a severed head in Victor's hand.

"Alexandre wanted the body," Victor said curtly. "Problem?"

Edward stepped aside. "No, no. Continue on."

Edward couldn't help but stare at the head as Victor walked to the ship. Plague still had a smile on his face, and though his eyes had gone glossy and dull already they were no less potent in inspiring fear. Like the eyes of Medusa, Plague could turn even the most hardened man to stone with his gaze.

"Quite the foe, that one. You know him?" Bartholomew asked.

"Yes, we met him a few times on our journey. He was well known by the name Plague, but his true name was Edward Russell. Anne and William believed him to be a Royal Assassin under direct orders from Queen Anne."

"So he was here to assassinate your Anne?" Bartholomew asked. "I don't understand."

"So I take it Anne never told you?" Edward asked, glancing about.

"Tell me what?"

"She's the princess."

Bartholomew laughed. "Princess of what?"

"Denmark and Norway. Anne is the Queen's daughter."

Bartholomew's jaw dropped and his brow cocked. After several protests, and Edward reciting the fact over and over, Bartholomew eventually accepted the truth.

"But why would the Queen want to kill her own daughter?" he asked, not really expecting an answer.

"I do not know. The Queen could feel betrayed after Anne left her again, or she considers Anne a liability. Any number of reasons, really. The two have a poor history, one Anne isn't keen on sharing, but she'll tell me when she's ready, I'm sure." Edward and Bartholomew stood in silence for a moment, letting the sombre talk overtake the moment.

"Let us remove ourselves from this darkness and see your ship opened," Bartholomew said, patting Edward on the shoulder to get him moving.

Edward smacked the key in the palm of his hand thoughtfully. "Not yet. I started this journey of the keys with Anne, and I want to finish it with her. It would not feel right without her."

"Understood. We will wait for her to awaken. Now go back to her, you don't need to attend my sorry self anymore. I can manage."

"One thing before I leave. Half of Plague's crew is still on the island. Could you organise the crews to bring all three ships out to sea? If we don't have to fight them, all the better."

Edward started walking away towards the *Freedom*, but Bartholomew made him turn around with a question. "What are we to do with so large a ship?"

Edward turned, walking backwards. "We're pirates, aren't we?" he asked, his arms spread open. "We sell it."

Bartholomew smiled widely at the young man's boldness. Edward smiled back to his friend, then turned around to join his crew in returning to the *Freedom*, their home.

On the waist, many were resting from the battle and the brush with death in the ark. Edward examined the injured and ensured the crew was doing well. They were in high spirits now that Plague was dead and Anne was safe, despite being battle weary.

Nassir approached Edward, purpose in his eyes. "Captain, I must show you something. I held to this until now, as now the ship is whole."

Edward was confused by Nassir's cryptic talk. *Will he leave the ship again?* "Lead the way."

Nassir first took Edward to the stern. Right beneath the quarterdeck, there was a small square platform with railings on the sides. The location was in the same spot where Nassir had installed a rope for Herbert to climb down instead of having to traverse the ladder.

"Yes, I've been wondering about this platform. What does it do?"

"I will show you," Nassir said with a grin.

Nassir went to the side of the platform and began pulling on a rope. The platform rose as he pulled, and when he let go it was stationary. Then he pulled another rope and the platform descended again.

"It still requires some testing, and the bow side is not complete, but I thought you would appreciate seeing it."

"Nassir, this is brilliant. This is more than I could have expected. Now Herbert can stay in his wheelchair and travel around the decks. I'm sure Herbert will appreciate that." Edward patted Nassir on the shoulder, and the man smiled.

"That is not all. I have one more surprise."

Next, Nassir took Edward to the bow cabin. The cabin was mainly for storage, and held everything from cannonballs for the top deck to spices which could not fit in the lower cabin. It also had three large twelve-pound cannons for a frontal assault.

Nassir moved to the corner of the room, which held something rather large wrapped in cloth. Edward had no recollection of seeing it before. Nassir unwrapped and revealed the item.

Edward laughed in astonishment. "Nassir, it's beautiful. This is the figurehead you were making, right?"

Nassir nodded and gazed upon his creation with Edward. The wooden figurehead was of a woman with long, flowing curls and piercing eyes wearing a Greek-style robe. The face was akin to Anne, and in the statue's hands were an hourglass and a spear.

"This is not the same statue I was working on before. When you and this ship were taken, I believe the British Navy destroyed the first one I was working on. When I rejoined the crew, I began work on this one. Originally, the likeness was to be of Queen Anne, but later I chose the likeness of our Anne."

"It truly is breathtaking. When next we are at port we will affix it to the bow." Edward stepped closer and stroked the face of the statue. The figurehead was so lifelike in appearance Edward believed the statue would start talking to him.

"Go to her," Nassir said. "This will still be here."

Edward nodded and left the cabin, heading to the lower deck. He passed Alexandre's cabin, which was filled to the brim with injured. Crewmates with lesser injuries were waiting outside. Edward inspected those waiting and peered into the cabin to see Alexandre and Victor hard at work providing care.

Edward continued to the crew cabin and the bed where Anne was sleeping. William was sitting bedside, talking with Christina and Pukuh, with a few other crewmates listening, and Tala at Christina's side.

At the sound of Edward's footsteps, Tala turned her shaggy head his way. Christina noticed Tala and followed her gaze. "There you are, Edward," she said. "We were trying to figure out why Plague was sent after Anne. I say Plague was a warning for us to stay away from England."

"The Queen would never send the Admiral of the Black as a warning. Anne was the main target, but we were all meant to die." William's arms were folded neatly across his chest.

"We don't know that. If we were targets then why not destroy our ships? If they wanted us all to die they could have done it without even stepping foot on shore," Christina countered, combative as usual.

Edward stepped between her and William. "We can debate this later. For now, Anne needs her rest, which means no yelling. We're setting sail presently, and all of you are needed above."

Christina let out a sigh and strode off with Tala and the other crewmates. Edward watched as they left, leaving him, William, and Anne.

"I need you to take over and have us sailing as soon as possible. I'll stay and watch over Anne."

"Some say setting sail without the captain on deck is a bad omen," William claimed as he rose from his chair.

"If you truly believe that, I am Davy Jones."

"Well, as this ship is not the Flying Dutchman, I will see myself above." William passed Edward, but stopped when he reached the ladder. "Captain?"

"Yes, William?"

William stood straight and saluted. "It is an honour to serve on this ship. And, thank you for saving Anne."

Edward was speechless. All he could do was nod to William, causing the man to leave before Edward could wrap his head around what had happened.

Edward sat down at the foot of the bed, and watched Anne as she slept soundly. Her colour was returning and she no longer breathed heavily. She was at peace.

Edward relaxed as the fatigue from the day seeped in. Soon his eyes were closed, and, not long after, he was asleep.

Edward awoke to the sounds of the sea waves lapping the ship. When he opened his eyes he was gazing into the ocean green eyes and ruby red hair on his love, Anne.

"Finally awake?" she asked, chipper as ever.

Edward leaned forward and passionately kissed Anne, embracing her tightly. He held onto her like she was his lifeline in the middle of a storm.

Edward eventually uttered, "I'm sorry."

"Sorry for what, silly?" Anne replied, pulling back to see his eyes, placing a hand on his cheek.

"I almost lost you, and I am to blame."

"Don't ever say that," Anne said forcefully. "It's because of you that I'm still here. You have nothing to be sorry about." Anne smiled and this time she embraced Edward.

After another moment together, Edward pulled away and took something out of his pocket. "Look what Bartholomew found." Edward opened his hand to reveal the final key.

"Have you not opened the final door yet?" Anne asked, her eyes wide.

"No, not y—"

"Well, what are you waiting for?" Anne shuffled herself quickly out of the bed. "The door will not open itself, now will it?" Anne extended her hand to Edward.

Edward smiled and took Anne's hand. Together the two moved up to the gun deck, heading towards the stern and the last locked door on the ship.

"*Capitaine*," Edward heard behind him. Alexandre was standing at the door to his medical cabin, drying his hands. He had noticed the key in Edward's hand. "See me after you are finished. You as well, Princess. It concerns you both."

Edward was suddenly worried. "Is it urgent?"

"*Non, non.* See me when you are done."

"I am sure I have you to thank for still being alive, Alexandre. I'll give you a proper thanks in a moment."

"I look forward to it. God knows I haven't *enjoyed* enough hugs already," the surgeon said with mock disdain.

Anne laughed, then she and Edward continued walking towards the stern, albeit at a slower pace. He and Anne were starting to gather a crowd. Those resting on the gun deck noticed the key, and Anne, and formed a line behind them. Many also expressed their relief in seeing Anne up and about so soon.

Edward, Anne, and a dozen crewmates stood in front of the large and ornate double doors. Edward stared at the key.

"Well go on, then," Anne encouraged with a grin. The crewmates nearby joined in with her.

Edward lifted the key up to eye level, which at his height meant everyone else was staring up at him. "With this, the game is finally over."

After the weight of Edward's words reached his own heart, he turned around and set the key in the lock. After a deep breath, he turned the key, grabbed the knobs to the doors, and opened the final room.

What met Edward's eyes was the most lavishly decorated room of the *Freedom*: The captain's cabin. *His* cabin.

Red carpet with gilded tassels lined the centre of the floor from front to back. Three gold chandeliers hung from the ceiling in a row, following the path of the carpet. On the side walls several tapestries were hung to keep the room warm, and at the back thick, patterned curtains covered windows to the outside.

Like in the bow cabin, three twelve-pound cannons pointed to the outside. They were on wheels and could easily be turned about in the event the ship was invaded and Edward wanted to make a final stand.

On the left side of the room there was a king-size bed with a wooden bedframe which appeared to be carved from a single piece of oak wood. Silk and cotton sheets with gilded embroidery draped the mattress.

On the right stood a desk of intricate design. It held shelves on the bottom left and right sides, with a chair in the middle. The shelves held anything a captain could want: paper, sea charts, navigation tools, writing instruments, and a few books.

A large round table with chairs was set at the back of the room, similar to the one in the war room above, but smaller and more intimate. This one was meant for entertaining and dining rather than meetings, but it did have a grandiose high-backed chair with red upholstery and gold trim, mirroring the war room.

Edward and the crewmates nearby entered and examined the room more thoroughly. Littered about were small knickknacks like swords, guns, books, chests and a dresser full of extravagant clothes, a statue holding a skull, and bottles of various alcohols of rare vintage.

"This was on the table." Anne held out a piece of paper to Edward.

Edward read the paper. "Congratulations. Signed Benjamin Hornigold." Benjamin's seal, a hunting horn, was beside the signature in gold wax. Edward flipped the paper over, but the other side was blank. He laughed loudly and wiped away a tear. "How anticlimactic."

"Indeed," Anne concurred.

"I think this might change your mind, captain," a crewman said, lifting a heavy medium-sized chest to the table. The crewmate opened the chest with a smile, and gold coins fell out the top.

Edward grabbed one of the coins. The other crewmates' jaws were on the floor, and they too grabbed hold of some of the coins, and tested them.

"Real gold!" one confirmed excitedly.

"There must be a thousand gold pieces in here," Edward said, his shocked expression turning to the widest of smiles.

Edward picked up Anne in his arms and began spinning her around. The crew in the cabin were giddy with excitement at the wealth before them. They embraced and danced with glee.

Anne laughed as Edward spun her in the air. He eventually dropped her back down and kissed her. "I think it might be the gold speaking, but I love you, Anne."

Anne laughed and smacked Edward. "I love you too." She kissed him back.

Edward caught sight of the medical cabin through the open doors of the captain's cabin. He glanced at the crewmen grabbing fistfuls of the gold coins, their eyes in a frenzy.

"Hey, leave the gold in the chest. That's for the whole crew, and rightfully half should go to Bartholomew's crew, so no touching." The crew mumbled cries of dismay, but Edward silenced them, then turned his attention to Anne. "We should see what Alexandre wanted."

"Yes," Anne replied.

Edward and Anne returned to the bow where Alexandre and Victor waited in the cabin. Inside on the table lay the body of Plague, his head lying where it normally would be if attached, but a cloth draped over the face.

"What did you need to tell us, Alexandre?"

"There are *deux* things you needed to see. First, this." Alexandre pulled off the cloth covering Plague's chest. The material made a sickening squish as it caught on coagulated blood and was ripped off. "Notice anything odd?"

Edward inspected Plague's chest, and what he saw didn't make sense. A large wound stretched from the dead man's left shoulder all the way down to his right hip. Opposite to that slash, there was another going from the right shoulder to Plague's left hip. The two cuts made an X in the centre of the assassin's chest.

Edward knew the second wound was from him. "Was this from Bartholomew?" Edward asked, pointing to the first wound.

"*Non*, I inquired, Bartholomew shot Plague here." Alexandre pointed to a bullet hole in Plague's stomach. "But this wound was fresh during your battle. I would estimate within five to ten hours old at the time."

"He fought us with this wound? He must have been weak from blood loss even if he was able to stop the bleeding. That's how I was able to win."

"You must give yourself some credit, Edward," Anne said. Edward cocked his brow. Anne pursed her lips. "Yes, you're right. You would not have won otherwise."

"But who wounded him?" Edward asked.

Alexandre shrugged. "We may never know. They could be dead now because of their fight."

Edward nodded. *If Plague was the one who survived with this wound, I would not wish to be the other person.* "And you say you found something else?"

Alexandre turned around, picked up a piece of paper and passed it to Anne. The paper was worn and flexed. The top of the paper read: "The Daily Courant," and the headline in big bold letters read: "Queen Anne's Daughter Dead."

Anne's knees buckled, but she steadied herself on the table in front of her. Tears formed in her eyes. "This is why she wanted me dead. I am a disgrace to her, Edward." Anne handed the paper to Edward.

Edward read the headline and some of the article. The paper stated how Anne Sofia Stewart, daughter to the Queen, was killed by an unknown group a pirates during a trip to Boston. The date of the paper was almost a year ago, a month after Anne assisted Edward's escape from jail.

"This is her way of telling me I'm disowned." Anne wiped her tears away. "It is better this way, yes. I cut my ties long ago, it's only fitting she make it permanent." Anne began pacing the room. "And, I'm still alive. That is my revenge against her. She can tell herself I am dead, but it will never be true."

Edward, Alexandre, and Victor all focused on Anne, not saying anything. "What? Why are you all staring?"

Edward didn't speak, he simply embraced Anne. At first she stood stock still, shaking, then her arms flew up and gripped Edward's jacket like a vice. She stifled sobs as tears fell on Edward's chest.

After a moment, Victor joined Edward in embracing Anne. He waved for Alexandre to join after he seemed content to stand there. Alexandre sighed and placed his hand on Anne's head. Victor pulled on his shoulder and forced him to join in the embrace.

The three let Anne dry her eyes, their gesture saying more than words ever could. "Thank you," she said meekly.

Victor, Alexandre, and Edward released Anne from their embrace. "There is something I need to tell the crew. Something I've been thinking about for a long time, and now I know the perfect way to go about it." Edward turned to Alexandre and Victor. "Could you two gather the crewmates on the waist?" Alexandre and Victor both nodded and left the cabin.

Edward started to walk away, but Anne stopped him. "Wait, Edward. What do you have to announce?" she asked.

Edward leaned against the edge of the cabin door, his hand on the exit. "The ship's name," he said with a smirk, then he rounded the corner.

Anne jumped forward, trying to catch up to Edward, wiping her eyes. "What do you mean? The ship *has* a name!" she yelled out the cabin door.

Edward was at the ladder. "I'll explain what I mean up top," he yelled back, bounding up the steps.

The salty air filled Edward's nostrils. It became a fine day for sailing. The waves from before they landed were gone, the wind was in their favour, and the sun shone all the harder.

The crew waved and called to their captain as he ran to the quarterdeck where Herbert, Christina, and Tala stood. Anne was on his heels and even more people waved and hollered to her, glad to see her awake.

On the quarterdeck, Edward could see the *Fortune* off the starboard side, and Plague's ship sailing with them off the port side, manned by men from both crews.

"Captain," Herbert said, nodding as Edward approached.

"How fares the sea, Herbert?" Edward asked.

"Smooth sailing, Captain. Winds in our favour. Headed to Bodden Town to unload this cargo, I presume?"

"You presume right, sailing master." Edward smiled.

William joined those on the quarterdeck and spoke words with Anne, ensuring she was well. William knelt, examining her closely. After a few words and nods from Anne, William stood straight and the two joined Edward, Herbert, and Christina at the helm.

"William, could you call the crew together? I have an announcement to make."

"Aye, aye, Captain." William turned to the main deck and yelled for attention.

The crew dropped what they were doing and crowded together near the quarterdeck. Jack and Nassir were on the deck, Pukuh was hanging from a bowline, and Alexandre stood beside Victor, with the remainder of the crew walking up from the lower deck.

"Well, men, I want to start off by saying I am proud of all of you for the courage you displayed back on the island, and for all the times I called upon you to be brave with me.

"Over the course of this journey we've solved deadly puzzles in the underground of not one, but two islands, fought against a Marine Captain who chased us halfway across the Caribbean, saw the unimaginable in the Devil's Triangle, fought a plantation owner, and killed an assassin sent by none other than Queen Anne herself.

"That is more than any crew on these seas could say they've done, and you deserve all the praise. Without you, all this would not be possible, so thank you."

The crew pumped their fists and hollered their appreciation back to their captain.

"And thanks to those efforts, we now have a full ship. The final cabin is opened, but before you view the room I have more to say.

"When I received this ship—some of you may not know the story, but I'll keep it brief for those of you who do—I had a night of wild abandon, with too much to drink, and I used my life savings to buy this warship, when all I wanted to be was a whaler. The man who sold me this ship was named Benjamin Hornigold. He created this ship as a game, and that is what set us on this journey for the keys.

"Little did I know at the time, but because of what he did, he still owned this ship. *Freedom* was his ship, and until I retrieved all the keys, this ship would not truly be mine, as it is now.

"As such, this ship needs a new name," Edward said, placing his hands on the quarterdeck railing.

The crew was confused. "But Captain, why?"

"Simple, gentlemen: We have our *Freedom*. This ship is a symbol for all of us. For some, the ship is our home, our escape, our hope. The name was more than just the name of a ship. *Freedom* was what we sought. Freedom from our former lives, freedom from chains, both literal and figurative. But, the ship is ours now, we are free from our former lives, and we are free from the chains.

"We need a new name, and with that name a renewed purpose."

Edward let the crew murmur amongst themselves, allowing the words to sink in and take root. After the crew talked with each other, they agreed with Edward.

"What's the new name?"

Edward folded his arms. "*Queen Anne's Revenge.*"

Anne's and William's jaws dropped. The crew became louder at the sound of the new name. Confusion was the main theme.

Before the crew could ask more questions, Edward raised his hands to silence them. "The reason why I've chosen *Queen Anne's Revenge* is twofold: Firstly, because the name will be a testament to our victory against Queen Anne and her assassin. This ship will be a constant reminder that despite her actions against us, despite throwing everything she sent against us, we are still here, and we are still alive!" Edward yelled, causing many in the crew to cheer. "Whenever people hear of our exploits, it will be a constant mockery against her and all she stands for.

"And the second reason will be our purpose. Queen Anne's Revenge will be the name the world knows, but to us, the true name of this ship is *Revenge.*

"We have our freedom, so we will avenge those who have had their freedom taken away. Our purpose will be to take *Revenge* for those who can't take it for themselves.

"Slaves, the poor, the imprisoned. We will free them from their chains, and take revenge on those who caged them. Who's with me?"

The crew pumped their fists and chanted together in agreement. They were in a frenzy of excitement so loud that those on the other ships could hear it.

"We are pirates! We will steal *Freedom* back for those who need it, and take *Revenge* on those who think they can take it away," Edward yelled. He raised his fist. "Revenge!"

The ship once known as *Freedom*, owned by Benjamin Hornigold, was now and forever known as *Queen Anne's Revenge*, owned by Edward Thatch, the pirate Blackbeard.

EPILOGUE

One Month Later

The noonday sun shone over the *Queen Anne's Revenge*, the wind cooling the ship and all those gathered on it. The ship drifted in the sea off the coast of Bodden Town. The crew of the *Fortune* mixed on the deck with the crew of the *Queen Anne's Revenge*. Everyone gazed at the quarterdeck, and the ceremony being performed.

On the quarterdeck, Christina stood on the starboard side, and William on the port with Jack behind him playing a light medley with his violin. In the centre, in front of the helm, stood Bartholomew, Edward, and Anne.

"Do you, Edward Thatch, take this woman to be your wife?" Bartholomew asked.

Edward was wearing a white three-piece suit with gold and silver embroidery. He had a white undershirt with a vest and longcoat and the pants went to his knees with white socks pulled up. His beard was in braids and his wavy black hair was slicked back.

"I do," he replied.

"Do you, Anne Bonney, take this man to be your husband?"

Anne wore a stunning white dress with a gold necklace. The dress was embroidered similarly to Edward's suit, with gold along the chest and pearls at various spots. It fit Anne's curves beautifully and had a frilly skirt all the way to her feet. Anne's hair was done up, with her curls spilling out at the front and sides.

"I do," she replied.

The two were wearing rings, simple gold bands made from left-over metal from the forging of Edward's cutlass.

"Then by the power vested in me by the Lord above, I now pronounce you husband and wife. You may kiss the bride."

Edward leaned in and kissed Anne. The crews cheered and threw up their hats in celebration of the union. Edward and Anne, both smiling from ear to ear, turned hand in hand, and gazed at their crew. They lifted their hands together, showing the two wedding bands symbolising their eternal bond.

THE END

BOOK ONE OF
THE PIRATE PRIEST

BARTHOLOMEW
ROBERTS' FAITH

1. GOD'S JUSTICE

"Why's it gotta be called *Princess* anyways?" Walter Kennedy asked, his harsh Irish accent in full force.

John Roberts sighed as he relaxed his grip on his mop. "This again? The Lord grant me strength," John recited in his melodic Welsh accent as he dipped the mop into the bucket and returned to work.

The hot sun beat down on the two young men as they toiled away on the slave ship called *Princess*. Other sailors were tending the rigging of the sails, or working with the captain on navigation—which was John's preferred task—or lounging about out of sight.

"All I'm sayin' is we's only makin' three pound a month. Least we could be workin' on a ship with a better name."

John laughed. "So, what would you decree this humble ship's new name to be, Captain Kennedy?" John asked with a mocking bow.

Kennedy stopped working and placed his hand on his chin as he looked away in thought. Roberts also stopped working and watched the wheels in his friend's brain go to work. Sweat dripped off the smaller man's nose, and Roberts felt dampness on his own forehead and hairline.

Since joining the slave ship *Princess*, Kennedy had been equally a source of entertainment and a thorn in John's side. The lithe Irishman's ramblings were so ire-inducing they oft demanded attention in the same way one cannot help but watch a ship as it crashes into a reef and capsizes.

"The *Gallant*," Kennedy stated with pride.

John laughed heartily, his seven-foot-tall frame heaving with each burst of sound. Kennedy was not amused.

"Oi! I should like to see ye come up with something better."

John gradually ceased his laughter and found his voice again. He wiped sweat off his brow and tears out of his eyes. "No, no, the name wasn't the issue, just the appearance you took while pronouncing it. One would think you were some Biblical character come to life. Very theatrical. Would I be able to see the pose again? Perhaps we can have a portrait made when next we land ashore." John gestured as he peered at the sky and said, "Captain Walter Kennedy. I can see it now." John once again went into a fit of laughter, with some of the crew around them joining in.

Kennedy gritted his teeth as he glanced to the onlookers. His brow creased in anger.

Kennedy lunged at Roberts, but the large man sidestepped, mop still in hand, and let out a breath before a chuckle. The Welshman brandished the mop like a sword, with the dirty cloth dripping to the ship's deck in front of him.

"En garde!" Roberts said playfully.

At the prospect of a fight breaking out, the crew became livelier. A group gathered around the two young men to see what was about to happen. The crew hooted and hollered in excitement.

John was holding Kennedy back with his dirty mop. The lithe man stepped in a circle, trying to see an opening but not finding one. John jabbed the mop at Kennedy. Drips of water flew off the end of the mop and hit the smaller sailor in the face. He wiped his face, his expression pure fury, then pushed the mop aside, pulled back his fist, and thrust it at Roberts' face.

"Enough, you two!" The loud shout stopped the fight and the cheers from the crew.

A man pushed through the throng of onlookers and entered the ring the crew had created. The captain of the *Princess* was standing before Roberts and Kennedy, and disappointment was writ large on his face. The man appeared the dainty sort, with his white wig poking out of his tricorn hat, and his perfectly clean appearance, but he gave a look which brooked no resistance.

"I tell you gentlemen: You are trying my patience." The captain grabbed John's mop from him.

Roberts and Kennedy had the good sense to look sheepish in front of the captain. "It won't happen again, Captain Plumb," Roberts assured the man.

"You tell me again and again you two will not fight and you will work harder, and yet here you are again. If you would not seek to antagonise Walter so, John, then perhaps you would not have to lie to me so much. What does the Lord say about liars?"

John was taken aback. "He hates a lying tongue."

"Correct. Take yourself below deck and reflect on your actions," Captain Plumb commanded.

Roberts gazed at the floorboards as he said, "Yes, Captain," and then he walked away.

"And, you!" Captain Plumb shouted with one finger pointed directly at the remaining transgressor. "I expect this deck to be spotless by the time you're done. You hear me, Kennedy?"

The man's mouth opened wide, incredulous at the captain's harsher treatment of him over Roberts. Roberts was looking over his shoulder with a wide grin. Kennedy gritted his yellowish teeth and went back to work with a "Yes, Captain."

Roberts sauntered lazily to the steps and into the lower deck. He entered the crew quarters, which doubled as mess during the day. Far aft was the galley, and towards the bow two thirds of the ship was taken up by the slaves' quarters.

Roberts moved to the galley and secured some dry biscuits when he was sure none could see, and then headed to the slaves' quarters.

Roberts went through a door into a closed section of the ship set apart specifically for the transport of the slaves. The captives were laid out shoulder to shoulder on the deck of the ship, and every two feet up was a wooden bunk for more slaves. They were packed so tightly there was barely any room to breathe.

The smell of sweat, disease and decay filled the room. Roberts had steeled himself against the scent long ago, and the thoughts of where it developed were pushed far from his mind. He didn't want to think about the dead and sick in the cabin. He felt bad enough about his job on board as it was.

Roberts proceeded to the back of the ship and sat down. He handed his biscuits to the nearby slaves, who wordlessly accepted and devoured the gift, but Roberts gave a more generous portion to one in particular.

"Thank you, again, my friend," a slave at eye-level to Roberts said in a thick British accent. The man was thin and frail, of deep complexion, and had long hair on his head and face.

"It is the least I can do, and unfortunately it is also all I can do for you, Talib," Roberts replied.

Roberts' friend quickly consumed the biscuit. "The least you do is the reason I still live now. Please, though, John, you must call me Bartholomew. If your crewmates hear you call me by that name you will be in trouble."

"I care not what mortal men can do to me."

Bartholomew managed a weak laugh. "Yes, that sounds like something you would say. 'Fear not them which kill the body'," Bartholomew recited. "Please, for my sake, call me by the name chosen for me."

Roberts sighed. "You win, I will call you Bartholomew." He told Bartholomew of what brought him to the slave's quarters and the dark-skinned man smiled. Afterwards, John read aloud a few passages from a Bible he kept in his pocket. The worn leather and curled pages bespoke its well-used nature.

After Roberts was done reading, Bartholomew seemed pensive. "John, can I ask you a question about God?"

"Of course. I do not purport myself to be a priest, but I will do my best to answer you."

"What does the Bible say about justice?"

Roberts was taken aback, but began thumbing through his Bible after recovering. "In the book of Isaiah it says, 'For I the Lord love judgment, I hate robbery...'"

"There. He hates robbery. What of my people, who have been robbed?"

Roberts' jaw went agape as he tried to stammer out words. "I don't follow."

Bartholomew stared intensely at Roberts. "My people have been robbed of their lives, of their family, of their homes. Where is the justice for them?"

"Well I..."

"Are all the men aboard godly men as you, John? Is slavery God's work? What does the Bible say about slavery?"

Roberts' face felt hot. "I... I don't know," he lied. *'Inherit them for a possession; they shall be your bondmen forever.'*

"What sin have we done to deserve this?" Bartholomew gestured around him as best as he could in his cramped bunk.

Roberts glanced around to his surroundings. He couldn't push away the thoughts of what was happening now. The slaves were starving, sick, dying, or already dead, and for an unjust reason. The contradiction ate at him, burned him as did Bartholomew's eyes in that moment.

Roberts rose to his feet. "I am sorry, friend, I need to think on a few things." Roberts left the slave's quarters and travelled to the crew's quarters.

Roberts laid himself down in his hammock, the Bible still in his hands and a finger holding a place in the pages. He opened it back to see the same verse he'd read to Bartholomew about justice.

"So I am a liar, a robber, and a sinner, am I?" Roberts placed the open book over his eyes and lay in thought. *Please, God, I am in need of guidance. Tell me what the truth is.*

Roberts lay in silence for a time, before he heard footsteps approaching. He moved the book off his face to see Walter Kennedy next to him. Walter punched him in the gut, but it was more for sport than harm.

"Ah! That's smarts!" Roberts yelled.

"And it's less than ye deserve, John." Walter loosened a scarf on his neck and removed his hat before jumping into a hammock. "One a' these days yer gonna put both of us in dire straits."

"Be thankful it is not today, then," Roberts replied, staring at the ceiling.

Walter glanced over to Roberts while rummaging around in his belongings. "What's got you all mucked up? It's not what the captain said about lying, is it?"

"Not exactly."

"Well, come on then. Spill it or I'll tell all the mates how the captain's got ye salty-eyed and pissin' in yer boots."

Roberts sighed. "I've been thinking about the work we're doing. Are we righteous in our dealings with these foreigners, or are we committing sin?"

Walter scoffed. "You must be joking, right mate?"

Roberts eyed Walter. "No, I'm serious. You are a God-fearing man, are you not?"

"Of course."

"Then what would you say if we were to do this to a man from England? Place him in a two-foot-tall coffin, with poor provisions, next to his sick family, and leave him there while they die next to him?"

"Well, there's the rub. You be thinking of them as us. The Bible says, 'Love thy neighbour as thyself.' These blokes ain't our neighbours. We don't need to treat them with love. The rules don't apply."

Roberts rubbed his chin. "It doesn't feel right."

Walter shook his head. "Alright, then, what does the Bible say about slavery?"

For the second time in his life Roberts was loath to speak aloud the word of God. "It says foreign slaves are property, like cattle."

"There's yer answer. God is with us, so set yer heart at ease." Walter laid his head back in his hammock with finality.

Roberts lay back in his own hammock again, staring at the ceiling once again. *It still doesn't feel right.* The man of God closed his eyes and let the ship rock his hammock until he was sound asleep.

The sound of thunder shook Roberts out of his sleep. His eyes shot open, and he forced his body up to full alertness. He noticed Walter was also awake, nearly mimicking his movements.

Roberts and Walter swiftly jumped out of their hammocks, threw on their boots, and tied the laces tight before running up to the main deck.

Roberts expected to see dark clouds and feel cool rain falling on his face when he reached the waist of the ship, but the sky was clear and the sun still hot. Judging by the sun's position, they couldn't have been asleep for more than an hour at most.

Roberts glanced about for the source of the thunder he'd heard, and soon found the father of the noise. Off the stern, two ships were approaching the *Princess*. At the stern of the *Princess*, he also noticed the captain, the first mate, the quartermaster, and half the crew staring at the coming ships.

Roberts joined his brothers at the stern to get a better view. Walter followed closely behind. He pushed past the smaller sailors to the stern railing, where the captain and senior crewmates were gazing through spyglasses to the ships gaining on them.

The captain put away his spyglass and turned around to face the crew. When he did, a multitude of questions met him. He put his hands up and waved them to calm and silence the crew. Once everyone was silent, he addressed the men.

"Be calm everyone, there is nothing to worry about. I do not want any panic. I will not lie to you, as that will do no good. The ships you see on our tail are pirate ships." Those words spread like wildfire among the men until Captain Plumb raised his hands once more. "The shot they delivered was a warning, and they fly the black flag, not the red, so they should be reasonable men. We will surrender and give them what they want. That is the most sensible action, and the one which will help us keep our lives."

The crew murmured amongst themselves about payment and what will happen if they can't send money back to their families. The captain glanced back and forth between his senior officers.

"Captain," Roberts said, speaking for the crew, "if we give the pirates what they want, will we still be paid our wages?"

The captain scanned all the eyes on him, and then cursed under his breath. "Listen up!" he yelled. "There's only one way we can leave with our lives and our wages. No one mentions the slaves we have aboard. We don't have cannons, and not enough guns to fight against the pirates, so we give them everything else of value and they'll leave. Understood?"

The crew were unconvinced. Roberts once again spoke up. "What do we do with the slaves, sir? If the pirates inspect below deck they will surely see them, and the manifest will show we have slaves aboard."

"John, I'll need you and Walter to move the slaves into the hold. It's the only place we can hide them. Let me worry about the manifest. Go on, now. The rest of you, furl the sails and drop anchor. Slowly, mind."

Roberts nodded and turned around, pulling Walter with him. The two rushed back to the lower deck while the rest of the crew set about their task.

"How does the captain expect us ta get all two hundred into the hold? The pirates'll be on us before we 'ave half of 'em in there."

"I don't know, but we have to. I would rather see these people with us than with those scoundrels."

Roberts and Walter entered the slaves' quarters. "Walter, open the hold hatch. Everyone, please listen. Pirates are approaching. We need you all to move into the hold so you will be safe."

The slaves didn't move, as only a few understood English, save one. Bartholomew moved out of his wooden flatbed and rose to his unsteady feet.

"Bartholomew, please, you must tell your people to hurry. It will be dangerous if they find you here."

"I understand," the man replied before addressing his fellow slaves. He spoke to them in their language and told them what was happening and what they needed to do.

As Bartholomew explained everything, the slaves got up and walked over to where Walter and Roberts were signalling. When Bartholomew finished, Roberts let out a sigh.

"Thank you, my friend. Hopefully we can make it through the day and I will snag us some rum to share."

Bartholomew had a troubled look on his face. "I do not understand. What would these pirates want with us?"

"Slaves are worth money, they could sell you for their gain. The difference is, on this ship you have a fair chance of going to a good home. With the pirates, they will sell you to whomever they wish with no thought but getting the best price wholesale."

"You will forgive me if I do not see much difference at the moment."

Roberts squeezed his friend's shoulder. "Trust me."

"I do," Bartholomew replied.

Roberts' attention was drawn to the hold opening when he heard a loud thumping. He went over to see Walter throwing the slaves down into the hold with no regard for their safety, a knife in his hands.

"What in God's name are you doing?" Roberts yelled, grabbing Walter's wrist in a vice grip.

"What's the problem? Ye said it yerself earlier: they're property, like cattle."

Roberts let go of Walter's wrist, shock evident on his face. He glanced to Bartholomew, his mouth agape as he shook his head, searching for words. "I didn't…" He stared at Walter, furious. "I didn't say that." He clenched his fist.

Walter saw the rage in Roberts' eyes. "We don' have time fer this."

Roberts closed his eyes and released a breath. "I know." He turned to Bartholomew, an apology in his eyes, but the man only nodded, wordlessly telling Roberts he understood. "Help me move everyone into the hold, Bartholomew. As for you," Roberts said, pointing at Walter threateningly, "watch the door."

As Walter walked to the door, Roberts helped lower the slaves into the hold with Bartholomew. They worked swiftly and carefully to help everyone into the small space.

Soon after starting, the movement of the ship halted completely. The crew had been furling the sails when Roberts and Walter went below deck, and the ship's momentum had taken them this far. It wouldn't be long before the pirates caught up and boarded.

Roberts glanced at Walter, who signalled to hurry. He and Bartholomew did their best to rush, but the hold was filled with rope and other supplies. Packing two hundred or so souls into that space was difficult enough to do with a reasonable amount of time.

Halfway through, the sound of a mass of footsteps resounded above. Roberts, Walter, Bartholomew, and the rest of the slaves all eyed the ceiling when they heard the sound. Roberts glanced to Bartholomew, and the two quickened their pace even more.

Sweat dripped off Roberts' face and his arms were getting tired. The tension was racking his nerves, and every sound from above took on the noise of a gunshot.

When the last of the slaves was lowered into the hold, Bartholomew walked over to Roberts. "I suppose it is my turn."

Roberts pulled Bartholomew in for an embrace. "Be safe."

Roberts helped the man into the hold, and he saw a multitude of eyes staring back at him. "Pray for us," Bartholomew said.

"Always," Roberts replied.

"They'll be on us in minutes," Walter cautioned, glancing out the door. Then he took a look around the slaves' bunks. "Oh God, what about the dead ones?"

Roberts swung himself around and noticed what Walter was seeing. Thirteen dead slaves lay in their bunks, rotting. The sight and the thought of what he knew needed to be done sickened Roberts.

"We need to put them in the hold," Walter said finally.

Roberts was glad he didn't have to say it aloud and simply nodded as he steeled himself for the task. He walked over to one of the bodies, and the first one he pulled out of the bunk was a child.

Roberts stopped in his tracks, kneeled, and took a deep breath. The sound of oncoming footsteps above afforded him no time for thoughts of grief. The tall man picked himself back up and walked to the hold opening, where he gently handed the child to his people, and they accepted the dead one in their arms. "I'm so sorry," Roberts whispered.

"Hurry up, mate," Walter said behind him, two bodies slung over his shoulders.

Roberts rose to his feet, facing Kennedy. "Have some respect for the dead." He pulled a dead woman off the shorter man's shoulder and handed her to the slaves.

Together, Roberts and Walter worked to clear the slave section of the dead. They heard a commotion approaching as the footsteps made their way to the deck they were on. When the last of the deceased was in the hold, Roberts closed the hatch.

The door slammed open, and four armed men stepped inside. Though they appeared as normal as any other sailor—woolen caps, heavy coats, and drab pantaloons—they were clearly pirates by their manner. The bloodlust was clear in their eyes, which were quick to size up the nooks and crannies of the room to ensure there were no surprises.

Roberts was still on his knees and he turned and plopped himself overtop the hatch he had just closed. "I swear we wusn't drinkin' again, Captain!" Roberts yelled, his eyes half closed. "Wait a... you ain't tha Captain."

Walter glanced back and forth from Roberts to the pirates, his eyes wide and full of fright. He'd been caught unawares by Roberts' ploy and didn't know how to react. Shock and fear stunned his mind at the worst time.

The first man who'd entered wore a feathered tricorn hat, his brown hair flowing out to his shoulders. He was young, but carried himself with an air of authority. The man approached Roberts and Walter.

"Where is the hold?" The man said with a distinct Welsh accent Roberts picked up on.

Roberts looked around, his eyes still half open. "I dunno mate, when ye find it let me know where it is. The Captain'll be glad to know we didn't lose it."

The pirate did not look amused. "What is this room for?" He pulled out a sword and pointed it at the two. "Be truthful now."

"Storage," Walter suggested.

The pirate peered at his surroundings. "Seems a little sparse for storage."

"We sold it all," Walter replied.

The pirate nodded and walked around for a bit. He took his time, casually examining the room as he circled the bunks. "You know, I've seen a lot of slave ships, and these seem an awful lot like slave bunks to me."

Roberts laughed. "Slaves? Too much work."

The pirate arched his brow. "Oh, is that so?"

"Yea, the real money's in spices, see? Spices, as long as ye pack 'em right, will never spoil." Roberts forced a belch.

The pirate turned the corner of the bunks and walked over to Roberts and Walter again. He knelt to be eye-level with Roberts. "So, where did you put the barrels in this space?" the pirate asked, motioning to the bunks.

"Not barrels, bottles. That way ye can sell 'em fer more."

"Ahh." The pirate nodded. "So, why are you two in here?"

"Havin' a little drink ta celebrate our sales. Shh," Roberts said emphatically, "don't tell the Captain."

"Oh, I wouldn't dare." The pirate examined Roberts up and down. "So, if you were drinking, tell me: where is your drink?"

Roberts remained listless for half a second before flinging his brutish hand forward to try to choke the pirate in front of him. The pirate flashed his sword up and lightly touched the base of Roberts' chin with the tip of the blade.

"Now, now. It was a clever ruse, and might have worked if your Captain's manifest hadn't looked so shoddily done." Roberts lowered his hand. "Now," the pirate began, "get up and move away."

Roberts complied, the sword an ever-present threat on his chin. The other three pirates approached and pointed pistols and muskets at Roberts and Walter while the first one turned his attention to where Roberts had been lying down.

The pirate opened the hold hatch and peered inside. "Well, what do we have here?"

"Leave them alone!" Roberts yelled.

"Sorry, slaver," the pirate snarled, "you won't be getting a payday today." The pirate reached his hand into the hold. "Come, now, people, I'm taking you home."

Roberts cocked his brow. "Home?" he couldn't help but utter.

"That's right, home. We're freeing these people," the pirate proclaimed as he lifted the slaves up to the deck one by one.

Roberts was flabbergasted. He didn't know whether to believe the pirates or not.

Another pirate assisted, and soon all the slaves were back above the hold. "Bring your dead with you; you will be burying them soon."

If these pirates are lying, there would be no point in bringing the dead along. But it still could be part of gaining our trust.

"Everyone to the main deck," the pirate commanded, motioning for the others to follow.

The Negroes followed behind him, with Roberts and Walter being pushed ahead by the pirates. Bartholomew slowed to walk and talk with Roberts.

"This," Bartholomew whispered, "is justice." He passed by to join the other, seemingly former slaves.

The words hit Roberts like a sack of bricks. The words pirates and justice did not exist together in Roberts' mind. They killed, stole, raped, and summarily broke every commandment and committed all seven deadly sins according to what Roberts knew of them. Yet, here they were freeing slaves and dispensing their own brand of justice.

"Move," the pirate behind Roberts ordered as he shoved him with his musket.

Roberts walked with the rest of the group to the main deck. The crew of the *Princess* were sitting in the centre of the waist surrounded by the pirates. The *Princess* itself was flanked on both sides by pirate ships. One was called the *Royal James*, and the other was the *Royal Rover*.

Roberts' eyes met Captain Plumb's, but the captain looked away in shame.

The pirate who'd promised the slaves their freedom appeared to be the captain, as he didn't answer to anyone and was issuing orders to the pirate crew. The pirates had several gangplanks dropped on either side of the *Princess* and guided half the Negroes to board each ship. Once they were across, the pirate captain turned his attention to the crew of the *Princess*.

"So, now the question is: what to do with you all?" he said to no one in particular as he paced about. The sound of his boots rang into the otherwise silent surroundings. "I have a few options, but the first thing I'll do is this: Kill your captain." The pirate pulled out a pistol and fired it at Captain Plumb's head.

The speeding iron ball hit dead on, killing the captain of the *Princess* instantly. The crew cried out as blood splattered on those closest to the deceased.

"Now, the others who wouldn't cooperate," the pirate called, pointing to Roberts and Walter. "You two, come here. Someone give me a pistol." The pirate captain's crew forced Roberts and Walter closer, while another brought him a pistol. "What is this? I want a loaded one, of course." The pirate captain threw it back to his crewmate and the crewmate began loading it. The pirate captain sighed. "Well, I guess I can tell you why I'm killing you while we wait."

Please, God, do not let it end like this.

"You see, your captain told us he was willing to cooperate, but produced a false manifest. As much as we pirates appreciate liars and thieves, we are of course not to be trifled with. So, he was an example to anyone who lies to us. As for you two, you perpetuated the lie, and did a decent job as well, I might add. Too bad you're a slaver; you would have made a good pirate," the captain remarked, staring at Roberts. The crewmate finished loading the pistol and handed it to his captain again.

Just as the captain cocked the gun, someone yelled, "Stop!" The voice belonged to Bartholomew, Roberts' friend. "That is a good man. He was trying to protect us, because he did not know your intentions."

"Hmm." The pirate released the cock on the gun. "Be thankful to your friend, gentlemen. You get to have a choice in your fate."

Thank you, Lord… No, thank you Bartholomew. Roberts' eyes reflected gratitude as he stared at Bartholomew and took deep breaths. Bartholomew nodded to his friend and smiled.

"The rest of you are free to go," the pirate captain announced to the crew of the *Princess*, "as soon as we take what we came for. However, we are short crewmates due to some recent battles. If anyone wishes to join us, they may keep their personal belongings; otherwise we'll be taking anything of value. Do not be mistaken, this life is not easy, but it is not without its rewards. Any takers?"

I can't let Bartholomew leave like this. If these men are still lying, then God knows what will happen to him. Roberts rose to his feet. "I will join you."

The pirate captain turned around to face Roberts. He gave the sailor a once over and then smiled. "Good choice."

2. THE PIRATES & THE PRIEST

The pirates ransacked the *Princess* and took everything of value, even what little spare clothes the crew owned. All they left was enough food so the *Princess* could return to shore and restock. The pirates first piled everything they were taking onto the main deck of the *Princess*.

Roberts found himself on the *Royal Rover* after gathering his belongings. Bartholomew was waiting for him. Roberts thanked the man profusely for his help.

Walter was soon beside Roberts, a pack slung over his shoulder. After some chiding, he gave Bartholomew cursory thanks. No other sailors from the *Princess* decided to join the pirates.

"So, what now?" Walter asked after Bartholomew went to join his people.

"How about you two start putting the supplies onto your new ship?" the pirate captain suggested. "Sorry, I suppose if I'll be ordering you around you should know who I am. My name is Howell Davis, captain of these vessels."

"John Roberts."

"Walter Kennedy."

"Well, if you'll be with us awhile, gents, I suggest you acquire new names."

"Why is that?" Roberts asked.

"And here I thought you were the smart one, Roberts, being from Wales and all." Davis uttered a Welsh curse under his breath before letting out a sigh. "Pirating isn't the most legal of activities. Let's say word comes to your family about your exploits. They could be held accountable for your actions. People search for vengeance at all avenues."

Walter waved off the advice. "My family's all dead, so it don't matter to me." He dropped his pack, returned to the *Princess*, and began carrying the supplies to the *Royal Rover*.

"So, were you born in Wales as well?" Roberts asked.

In response, Davis asked Roberts a question back in Welsh. "I noticed your accent. I was born there, as was my father before me. Whence do you hail?"

"Casnewydd Bach," Roberts replied in his native tongue. "You?"

"Aberdaugleddau. A few days' ride from you, I suppose. Nice to see a fellow Welshman again."

Roberts nodded. The two watched the pirate crew taking the supplies across the gangplanks to the pirate ships. Roberts glanced over his shoulder to see Bartholomew explaining what was happening to his fellows.

"Pleasantries aside," Roberts began, "I joined to ensure these people's safety. If you do not keep to your word..." Roberts left his threat unuttered.

Davis eyed the larger Roberts up and down. "Understood, but I want you to take a good look at my crew and tell me what you see."

Roberts cocked his brow at the odd request, but took notice of the men loading the two ships. At first, he didn't discern anything out of the ordinary—sailors, as any other, in the same clothing as Roberts—but after a moment it hit him.

"So, you see it, yes?" Davis asked.

"You have Negroes, and Spaniards, and is that an Asian on your crew? I've never seen one before." Roberts pointed to one of Davis' men.

Davis laughed. "Yes, I met him on a merchant vessel. He boarded our ship when we were loading the supplies we took and wouldn't leave. He's learning English bit by bit. I tell you, he's a damn stubborn one. There's times I feel he thinks he's captain." Davis shook his head, but wore a smile. He sat down on the port railing of the ship and faced Roberts. "This ship isn't like the ones you're used to. Slave has no meaning on a ship full of criminals.

"I made a deal with some of the men aboard. If we happen across a slave ship then we will free the slaves. In exchange, those men will forgo their shares. Over time, the whole crew was in agreement, so now we use whatever we make to fix the ship and purchase supplies, and then whatever is left over is given to the men. They enjoy the arrangement. Makes them feel good about what we do.

"If I broke my word and didn't free those people, my men would have my head. So, it's in everyone's best interests to take them home."

Roberts nodded, but he still didn't understand how it was possible. Pirates were supposed to be scum, but instead these ones freed slaves and shared earnings.

Davis switched back to English. "Come then, let's move this cargo onto the ship."

Roberts followed Davis and worked with the pirates to unload the *Princess* of its valuables. He was so focussed on the situation aboard the pirate ship, and the state of its crew, that he was oblivious to the awkward feeling of taking his old friends' belongings from them.

Once the two ships were loaded with supplies, the sails were let loose and they headed off with the wind.

Roberts and Walter watched as the *Princess* became smaller and smaller on the horizon. The bad feeling Roberts had about taking his former crewmates' supplies was there in full force now that he was resting.

"Do you think they will tell the authorities about us?" Roberts asked.

"Probably," Walter replied. "We did steal all their things, and Davis killed tha captain."

"Why did you join the pirates, Walter?" Roberts asked.

"Ye jokin', mate?" Roberts shook his head no. "Pirates is where the money is at. Ain't ya heard those stories 'a pirate captains and their wealth? Benjamin Hornigold, William Kidd. All tha pirate captains, some still alive and kicking. Even Davis seems ta be doin' well fer himself, with two ships and a crew like his. This could be my chance ta become a captain meself." Walter wore a wide smile on his face and had a glint in his eyes. Roberts was all too familiar with that glint of future wealth already spent. "What 'bout you? Why did ye join tha pirates, a God-fearing man such as yerself?"

"I wanted to ensure Davis keeps his word and frees the slaves, but now I feel my fears were misplaced. Davis seems to be a man of his word, at least."

Walter laughed. "And now yer a pirate."

Roberts frowned as he saw the *Princess* becoming a dot against the sky and sea, the salt air of the sea whipping at his face. "And now I'm a pirate."

Davis approached Roberts and Walter after the *Princess* was out of sight. "Well, gentlemen," the pirate captain said, getting the two men's attention, "one thing we usually do after liberating a slave ship is have a feast, so why not join us below for some ale and food?"

Walter smiled and walked off to the lower deck. Roberts followed soon after, and Davis walked with him.

"Let's find your saviour and we can eat together," Davis said in Welsh.

Walter, who was ahead of the two, stopped, but Davis waved him along. Walter cast Roberts a sour look, but left down the ladder to the lower decks.

"My saviour?" Roberts asked, confused.

"The former slave who vouched for you."

"Ah." Roberts nodded his head. "Yes, that would be nice. His name is Bartholomew."

Davis' brow cocked. "His real name?"

"Well, no, his real name is Talib. He insisted I call him by his slave name, Bartholomew, so I didn't get in trouble. I suppose now it doesn't matter."

"No, no it doesn't." Davis smiled and the two went down the ladder to the lower decks.

After passing the gun deck, the two went down another ladder to the lowest deck. The smell of ale, meat, and cheese already filled the air, as did the sounds of joviality from many people. The pirates were singing and retelling stories. The Negro pirates were talking with their people, and others were filling their famished bodies.

Davis went to an empty table and sat himself down. Roberts found Bartholomew in the crowd and brought him to the table, and the two sat down with the captain. Another man joined them.

"This is my first mate, Delliger. He's a fresh-faced bastard, but he knows which end of a musket to point at the enemy, so I made him my first mate."

Delliger smiled and went to shake Roberts' hand. "He says that, but we all know I only let him be captain until my time comes. Pleasure."

Roberts smiled and shook Delliger's hand. Bartholomew did the same, and introduced himself to the captain and first mate, thanking them for their help.

"No need to call yourself Bartholomew anymore, mate," Delliger stated. "You're free now."

"With all due respect, on this ship I am not free. Freedom will be when I am with my wife again, so, until then, being called Bartholomew will be part of my penance."

"Fair 'nuff," Delliger replied.

Food was brought over for them to enjoy. Ale, fish, salted meat, and cheese. Bartholomew gorged himself on everything brought to him, so Roberts had to force him to slow down lest he get sick.

"So," Delliger began before drinking from his mug, "how is it you know how to speak English, Bartholomew?"

"I was taught by a former master," Bartholomew replied between bites of food.

"How did you end up acquaintances with Roberts here?" Davis asked.

"I ended up on the *Princess* after my master sold me. After my wife died, I could not work the same." Bartholomew's eyes were cast down, his dark complexion matching his dark tone. "But John must have seen how lost I was, and he told me about the Bible and how my wife is waiting in heaven for me."

Davis eyed Delliger, took a swig of his ale, and then stared at Roberts. "Look, Roberts, what I'm about to tell you is for your own good: a pirate ship is no place for God."

Roberts' eyes shot open. "Explain."

"We're pirates. We've been forsaken by God. The less you care about what God thinks about what we do, the better."

Roberts slammed his fist on the table. "There is always a place for God. Always." The normally dulcet tones of Roberts' accent took on a harsh discord.

Davis glanced around at a few different eyes now watching them. He continued speaking in Welsh. "Roberts, I'm telling you this for your own good. What we do, it'll eat you alive if you think about it the way the Bible wants you to."

Roberts eyed Davis. "Then maybe I didn't make a good choice in joining this ship."

Davis sighed. "Maybe not."

The awkward silence that followed was short-lived, as a crewmate soon ran over to the captain's table. "Captain, there's a ship off the bow."

Davis' eyes lit up. "Is it…?" The crewman nodded with a devious smile. Davis put down his ale and got up from the table. "Men, our luck doubles today. We've found our prey."

The pirate crew hooted and hollered at the news, and after taking a few last-minute bites of food or swigs of ale they rushed back to the main deck.

"What's happening?" Roberts asked.

"We weren't here to attack your ship. We were chasing another, and thought we lost it. Why not join us above? Perhaps this will change your mind about being aboard this kind of ship."

Davis joined his crew and returned to the main deck. Roberts stayed behind with Bartholomew. Most of the former slaves also stayed behind to continue eating.

Walter walked over to Roberts. "Are ye not going ta see what the commotion's 'bout?" Walter asked.

"No, I think it's safer down here."

"Safer?"

"Captain Davis said they've found a particular ship they were chasing. They will probably attack it soon."

"Considerin' we're part of this crew now, we might want to pull our weight."

"You go ahead, I'll catch up."

Walter shook his head. "See ya there, captain's pet."

Roberts took a drink of his ale and began eating again.

"They need you here, John," Bartholomew stated.

"What do you mean?"

"The captain of this vessel thinks there is no place for God here, but he doesn't speak for the entire crew. He may not even believe his own words. I saw in his eyes a need to do good. His crew wanted to free slaves, so he helps to free slaves. He could easily seek fortune alone, or could have killed you despite what I said. 'You shall know them by their fruits.'"

Roberts thought on the events he had witnessed today. He had seen two captains of completely different calibre. One sought to conceal for profit, and the other acted to save people he didn't know. *Davis could have taken the manifest at face value, and left with the spoils. His crew wouldn't have known the difference.*

Roberts rose to his feet. "Tell your people to take shelter. There might be a battle soon." Bartholomew nodded, and Roberts left to join everyone else on the main deck.

When Roberts emerged, he saw people running this way and that to trim and loosen the sails to give the *Royal Rover* some more speed. The smaller *Royal James* was ahead by two ship's lengths, and gaining on the ship in front of them.

The ship being chased wasn't overly special, but, unlike the *Princess*, it had cannons. With its three masts, it appeared to be the same size as a sloop-of-war, but it flew a French flag on its topmast.

Roberts joined Davis at the bow. The captain was peering through a spyglass at the enemy ship, and after a few moments he held his hand in the air and made a fist several times. On the stern of the *Royal James*, Roberts saw a crewmate giving another signal in return, and then that crewmate turned around and issued orders to the crew.

Davis lowered the spyglass and noticed Roberts. "Decided to join us, have you?"

"Consider me an observer."

"Observe away." Davis handed the spyglass to Roberts.

Roberts took the device and gazed through it. He watched the crew of the *Royal James* working tirelessly to move the ship faster. They moved the *Royal James* in line with the French ship to steal the wind from its sails. Roberts also noticed men at the bow, and what he thought were cannons.

Explosions erupted from the bow of the *Royal James*, followed by smoke, and after a few seconds several splashes.

"A warning shot, like before," Davis explained. "If today is a good day, they will also surrender."

Roberts stopped looking through the spyglass for a moment and peered over to Davis. "I would pray for your success, but you said there is no place for God here." Roberts chuckled at his own joke.

Davis chuckled as well. "I don't think God would take pleasure in you praying for us."

"If I cannot pray for sinners, then who am I to pray for?"

"Good point," Davis replied.

"Besides, I think God would appreciate it if there was no bloodshed." Roberts looked through the spyglass again, this time at the French ship. He noticed something about the crew's actions, the way they were moving across the deck. "They're going to turn the ship," he declared, handing the spyglass back to Davis.

"Who?"

"The ship you're chasing. They seem to be trimming the sails quite a bit, but not furling them completely. We're with the wind, so the best bet I would give is that they're preparing to turn and don't want to lose momentum. They're trimming the sails in advance so it's easier to pull them all the way up in a moment."

Davis peered through the spyglass at the enemy ship. "Damn, you're right. It's probably going to try and attack the *Royal James* and break the flank by moving to our port." Davis turned to the crew. "Two points to port!"

The navigator relayed the instructions to the crew, and they set about releasing riggings on the sails and making the ship move to port. As soon as the *Royal Rover* began moving, the French ship made its move as well.

The French ship turned hard to port, just as Roberts had predicted. The wind still blew against its sails, but it wasn't pushed away because the sails were trimmed so much. Instead, the enemy ship was able to turn all the way around while retaining some of its speed. The ship angled itself towards the *Royal James*.

By the time the French ship was turned around, the *Royal Rover* had moved to the port side of its sister ship. The *Royal James* was still moving faster though, and would be upon the enemy too soon.

Captain Davis gave another hand signal, and the crew of the *Royal James* furled some of their sails, slowing it considerably.

"Now it's too late for them to change course," Davis commented. "Even if they dropped their sails, the wind is against them. Thanks Roberts."

The two ships were matched in speed, and headed towards the French ship. They were minutes away from being within firing distance. Roberts could see the French ship better now. It carried twelve cannons on either side, which was more than the *Royal James* but was trumped again by the *Royal Rover*. The name on the side was *Argent*.

"Men, to arms! Ready starboard volley!" Davis yelled. "Have you ever been in a battle before, Roberts?"

"No, I've never worked on a ship with cannons."

"Well, watch out. This is the part where things become interesting." Davis' Welsh enunciated the hard rolling r and Roberts could tell he was excited from the tone.

Roberts watched the ships closely, sweat beading on his forehead. He was terrified, but excited at the same time. He'd heard stories about naval battles, but had never been a part of one.

"Fire!" Davis yelled.

A wall of fire and iron exploded from the starboard of the

Blackbeard's Ship

Royal Rover, and was returned by the *Argent* in kind. A few of the cannonballs hit the water and splashed with a loud plunk. Several hit the sides of the *Royal Rover*, causing the wood to burst from the force. Men were sent flying from the blasts.

The noise of the cannons and splintering wood quickly ceased, but the screams of the injured and orders being yelled continued on. After another moment, the cannons' howl was heard again, followed by chunks of the ship being broken apart and more water being splashed into the air.

"They're waving the white!" one of the crew yelled.

"Cease fire!" Davis ordered in reply. A few cannons fired off again, but after another shout of the captain's order, the thunder stopped.

It was over faster than Roberts had thought it would be. The carnage was still everything he dreamed it as being, but it was swift and forceful, not long and drawn out as he'd expected.

"Oi," Davis called, smacking Roberts' arm. "It's over."

"Right."

Roberts glanced around the ship to see the crew helping those injured to one side so they could be tended to. He was glad to see Walter up and about and unharmed.

"Bring us around!" Davis yelled. When he didn't hear confirmation of his order, he repeated it, but still heard nothing back from the navigator. "Jones?" The captain looked at the wheel, where a few crewmates were gathered.

Davis ran to the other end of the ship where the wheel was. Roberts followed behind. Davis went over beside his crewmates to see a body lying on the ground, blood pooled beneath it.

"Jesus!" Davis cursed. The man took a few breaths, staring at the body of his crewmate. "Alright, move him below deck. Heath, man the wheel and turn us around."

The crew replied with an "Aye, Captain," before following through with their orders.

"That's it?" Roberts asked, unable to keep the shock from his voice.

"Yes, for now," Davis sighed, "that's it. We still have a job to do."

Roberts couldn't help but be ashamed at Davis' cold-hearted attitude, and saw the other crewmates adopting the same stoicism. Their eyes told the truth though: the death of a mate hurt them.

God, please have mercy on this sinner.

The ship was turned around, and was joined by the *Royal James* in the same maneuver as with the *Princess*. They went on both sides of the *Argent* and put down gangplanks for the crew to travel across.

The pirates rounded up the crew from the merchant vessel and put them into a group in the middle of the ship. They kept weapons trained on the enemy crew the whole time.

"Where is your captain?" Davis asked.

The captain of the *Argent* stepped forward. "I am here," he said in a thick French accent.

"I trust you know what we're after?"

The French captain peered to his left and right. "I have an idea."

"Lead the way," Davis commanded.

The Frenchman turned around and started walking towards the stern, and Davis followed behind. Roberts stayed on the sidelines with the other pirates, guarding the crew of the *Argent*. Roberts didn't have a weapon, however; he was committed to observing.

He noticed a sharp movement out of the corner of his eye. A merchant crewmate had pulled out a knife and was rushing at Davis.

"Davis, watch out!" Roberts yelled.

Davis turned around just as the enemy thrust his knife at him. The pirate captain sidestepped and knocked the knife out of the man's hand. One of Davis' crew fired a musket at the enemy, and he fell to the ground dead.

With the commotion ceased, Davis glanced back to the other men of the merchant crew. "Anyone else?" Davis challenged. No one came forward. Davis beckoned Roberts over. "You saved my life, mate. I owe you, and I won't forget that."

Roberts nodded, but he couldn't move his gaze away from the man who had been killed. This was far different from the pirate crewmate who died in front of him. This was a man who he helped kill.

"Come, Roberts, you'll want to see this." Davis motioned another couple of crewmates over, then entered the stern cabin.

Roberts shook his head, prayed silently for the man whom he would never know, then joined Davis and the two crewmates in the stern cabin.

The *Argent*'s captain was kneeling behind a desk, with Davis and the two crewmates watching him like hawks, and with pistols trained on him just in case. The enemy captain opened a compartment in the desk protected by a lock, then pulled out a chest and placed it on top of the desk.

Davis motioned for Roberts to join him. Roberts walked to the other side of the desk. The pirate captain set his pistol on the desk and smiled as he opened the chest.

It was in that moment that John Roberts began to understand the allure of being a pirate.

3. DRINK AND BE MERRY

Roberts was in the crew's quarters of the *Royal Rover*, in the open surgeon's section. The surgeon was tending to the wounded from the previous battle. There hadn't been time to bag Jones' body yet, and so the dead man was lying on a table.

Roberts had had enough of conflict and wanted to be away from prying eyes. He had a decision to make, and didn't want to be disturbed.

"Here," Davis said, handing Roberts four gold pieces before pocketing some for himself.

Davis sent the other crewmates out of the cabin with the *Argent's* captain while he and Roberts stayed behind. The chest full of gold was the treasure the pirates were after, but a quick review of the manifest showed even more plunder to be stolen. Spices, gunpowder, clothes, food, tons of stock to be taken, and soon to be sold.

"What is this?" Roberts asked.

Davis chuckled. "Gold, clearly."

Roberts frowned. "I know that much. What I mean is why are you giving these to me?"

"Consider it an advance share. I'm not sure if the Commanders will allow you part of the booty, considering how new you are and especially since they didn't see you help in the battle. I know without your help the battle would have been more difficult, so I want to make sure you have something to show for it."

"Commanders?" Roberts questioned, a brow cocked.

Davis cursed and rubbed his chin. "That's right, we never told you how this ship worked. There are two factions on board the ship: the Commanders and the Commons. The Commanders are the ones who make the decisions by a vote. The decisions could be as simple as which port we head to next, or who will be captain, should the men have a problem with me or if I have an untimely dinner with Davey Jones," Davis said with a grim chuckle. "The captain has a vote, and if there is a tie the captain breaks the tie.

"The Commons have no say in the vote, but they do vote who

becomes a Commander based on their section on the ship. Depending on how many crewmates are in that section there could be multiple Commanders selected to represent their wishes."

"That is an interesting system," Roberts said, stroking his chin. *Aboard the* Princess *there was no voting on anything. The captain's word was law.*

"We find it works well, as votes aren't hidden. If a Commander didn't vote the way his section wanted him to they could replace him in the next election. The Commanders have to set aside personal feelings to stay in charge, and the Commons always have a chance of becoming a Commander if they play their cards right."

Roberts was still stroking his chin. "Perhaps Walter and I have a chance to climb above our station here."

Davis smiled. "Don't want no more swabbin' the deck do you?"

Roberts laughed and shrugged his large shoulders. "Let's say I've had my fill, and the years have not made the swabbing any more enthralling."

The shorter Davis laughed along with Roberts. "As I was saying, you should keep that gold a secret, as I'm not sure the Commanders will allow you a share. If they do, just decline it this time, as that's probably double what everyone else will get. You'll make yourself look good if you decide to redistribute it to the crew."

Roberts gazed at the gold, this time appreciating just what it was he was holding. On the *Princess*, he'd received three pounds silver or less a month. In his hands now was more than he'd made in a year before, and then some.

Roberts pocketed the money.

The cargo of the *Argent* was unloaded, with no further issues from its crew. Delliger speculated that once the chest and cargo were sold they would have enough to live comfortably for a long while. But he also said that, knowing Davis and the way the crew liked to spend their money, they'd probably be after their next score a week after freeing the slaves.

Roberts went below deck and noticed the injured being tended to, as well as the dead navigator, Jones. He sat down next to the body to think about his options.

There seems to be no end to the conflict I feel today. I would ask God for help, but I already know what the answer would be. 'For the love of money is the root of all evil.'

Roberts held one of the coins in front of him, staring at the gold lustre. *Why should I have to toil for another's gain? God allows men to profit from sin on a daily basis and those same men call pirates who steal their ill-gotten gains the evil which plagues the world. What sense is that?*

Roberts heard footsteps approaching and pocketed the coin.

The person approaching was a crewmate Roberts hadn't been introduced to. He was a short Negro with a timid nature. When he noticed Roberts he stopped in his tracks.

"Ah, sorry misser. I'll come back."

"No, no, I should be leaving anyway. Please." Roberts motioned for the man to approach, and got up out of his seat to leave.

The Negro approached the table holding Jones' body, and he removed his cap. He looked at the body of his crewmate, obviously a friend, with reverence. He turned to see Roberts still there, watching.

"You's the preacher, right?" the man asked.

Roberts laughed. "I suppose so."

"What happens affer we die?"

Roberts hadn't expected that question. He noticed the need in the young man's eyes, so he walked over to the table again and stood next to the man. "Well, the Bible often likens death to sleep, and we will be awoken again to have a final judgement before God. In that sense, your friend here is simply sleeping, but can be awoken only by the Creator. That's not so bad, now is it?"

The man wrung his woolen cap in his hands. "Could ye pray for him, misser?"

"Certainly," Roberts replied.

Roberts prayed for a pirate. He prayed for a man he never knew, and never would know, but who was clearly loved by many, despite his sins.

⚓ ⚓ ⚓

A few days had passed since the battle with the *Argent*, and despite Davis' prediction the Commanders voted to give Roberts a share of the spoils. Roberts followed Davis' advice and declined the gold, asking that his share instead be redistributed to the other crewmates. As the ship seemed to value transparency, the other crewmates knew of his decision, and in short order Roberts was becoming a favoured crewmate.

During meals, many in the crew wanted to sit with him and Bartholomew, often giving him extra meat or ale to drink. They shared stories of their travels with Roberts and seemed to genuinely enjoy his company.

"You know, Bartholomew," Roberts said on the third night of revelry, "perhaps they do need someone like me aboard this ship."

Bartholomew laughed. "Careful, John, don't let the drink go to your head."

The next morning Roberts awoke to a splitting headache, but

after some meat and movement around the ship he felt much better. He spoke with Delliger about what he was to do aboard the ship for the day. As the ship was already repaired as much as it could be, and they had all the rigging men they needed, Roberts was to swab the deck. He was also to be joined by a familiar face, one who seemed to have been avoiding him since boarding the pirate ship: Walter Kennedy.

"This remind you of anything, mate?" Roberts asked with a smile on his face as he swabbed the deck.

"Different ship, same shit. Every time."

Roberts kept swabbing, but glanced over to his companion every so often. As he did, the foul look on the other man's face seemed to grown fouler each time. After a half hour, it seemed to build to a head.

"What do ye keep starin' at me fer, John?"

"No reason," Roberts explained, taking a break under the shade of the sail. "It's just that when we started here, you seemed so happy to be aboard. You even said you wanted to try working your way up to Captain. There's a pretty good chance of that happening here as well. Davis told me about how things work aboard the ship…"

"See, that's me problem. Davis *this*, Davis *that*… Ye two're so chummy already. No one told me 'ow it works on this ship. All I get is a 'mop this,' 'scrub that,' 'hoist those sails, Kennedy.' I'm goin' nowhere fast, and that's all I'll ever have."

"Come now, that's not how it works here. So there are the Commanders and the Commons. The Commons can…"

Walter held up his hand. "I don't want to hear about the stories Davis' told ye. Why don't ye take yer mop elsewhere?"

Roberts didn't say anything else and decided to leave Walter alone. *He'll come around eventually.*

Roberts made his way to the stern as he mopped the deck. The hot sun made him sweat, and the sweat falling on the wood meant he needed to work twice as hard. Eventually he was able to get in a rhythm and didn't have to think about anything other than the task at hand.

The closer Roberts came to the stern, the clearer he heard a noise which invaded his rhythm and made him lose focus. *What is that noise?* He stopped mopping to search for the source of the noise. Eventually he noticed Davis at the wheel, poring over several maps and a compass, and fighting with the wind to ensure they didn't all blow away. The pirate captain was uttering Welsh curses under his breath, which was no doubt the noise Roberts had been hearing.

"What seems to be the trouble, Captain?" Roberts asked.

Davis looked up from his work to see Roberts there. He glanced back and forth to see if anyone else was around, and then answered in Welsh. "I'm in serious trouble here, John."

Roberts spotted the desperation in Davis' eyes and tone. Roberts came closer, and he too spoke in Welsh. "What's wrong?"

"With Jones dead, we're down a navigator. I told the crew a long time ago I was good at navigation. That's the whole reason I'm fucking captain, mate."

"And the problem with this?" Roberts asked, still not understanding his friend's desperation.

"I'm shit at navigation," Davis replied bluntly. "I can't read a map to save my mother's life."

Roberts laughed heartily. "Well, you've got yourself in quite the pickle, then haven't you?"

Davis wasn't amused. "This ain't funny, mate. Hey!" Roberts' laughter slowed to a halt. "If the Commanders find out, they might elect a new captain."

"Worry not. You seem to have the Devil's own luck. I've picked up a few things here and there, being on a ship, so I should know enough to navigate for you."

Davis let out a sigh of relief and moved out of the way to allow Roberts access to his maps and dry compass. Roberts searched through the maps to find one relative to their location, and placed it on top.

"Well, here's the first issue," Roberts said as he picked up the map, and with emphasis while staring at Davis, he turned the map around.

Davis palmed his face in frustration. "You're tellin' me I was lookin' at the maps upside-down this whole time?"

"See here," Roberts said, pointing to the top corner. "This is a compass. See that 'N' at the top? That means north. This is how the map is supposed to face," he gibed.

Davis pushed Roberts. "Shut it, ye git."

Roberts continued to teach Davis how to read a map, how to use a Davis quadrant, and didn't miss the opportunity to jab Davis the captain for not knowing how to use an instrument with his own name in it. He also taught him something about how to read the skies. The information was a lot to take in, and needed to be condensed, but it enabled Davis to manage for the day.

With Roberts' help, the ship was turned around to return them to Anomabu, where the *Princess* had acquired the slaves.

That night, the Commanders held a meeting started by Davis. After a while, Roberts was asked to join the meeting.

They held their meetings on the stern of the main deck. The wind was cold and biting, but Roberts' wool clothes helped against the chill. Roberts joined the twelve Commanders, including Davis.

"Welcome, Roberts," Delliger said, offering a cup of rum to him.

Roberts accepted the drink. "What is it you needed, gentlemen?"

"We'll cut straight to it," Davis declared, with some of the men nodding in agreement. "We've voted you to be our new Navigator, in place of Jones, may he rest in peace."

"Hear, hear!" the Commanders shouted before taking drinks of their rum.

Roberts glanced back and forth between the attendees, his mouth agape.

"That is, of course, if you'll accept?" Delliger asked.

"Why me?"

Delliger continued. "We understand from Davis you have some skill with navigation, and Davis is currently Captain. We always prefer to have several people who can do a job so we're not left wanting."

Roberts ran his fingers through his hair. "What I mean to say is: I've been vocally against being on this ship and the work done here. Why would you choose someone like that?"

"We try to be objective when making our choices, and base it more on skill rather than disposition. Besides, a navigator needs to be assertive. You're a perfect fit... unless, that is... you don't have the skills Davis mentioned?"

Roberts scoffed. "Of course I do, better than you lot."

Delliger smiled, as did the other commanders. "Then it's settled. Let's welcome our new navigator, men!"

The other commanders all hooted and hollered, then drank the rest of their rum in one gulp. The thirteen drank more rum in celebration of Roberts' new position.

Roberts drank in celebration of his first ever promotion on a ship. *And now I'm a pirate.*

"That is definitely wormrot," Roberts noted.

Davis, Roberts, and Delliger were in the bilge of the *Royal James*. Four weeks had passed since the battle and the ship was taking on water. After the crew found the source, Davis wanted confirmation.

"See, here." Roberts picked up a broken piece of wood from the watery bilge. "Look at all those holes," he said, pointing to a multitude of tiny holes in the wood.

Delliger lifted the lantern he was carrying, and he and Davis leaned forward, eyes squinted to see better. Davis nodded with a frown on his face.

"So, what can we do?"

It was Delliger's time to take over. "It depends on the extent of the damage." Delliger examined the wood in the dark bilge. "Looking at the surface, it seems we'll have to replace a lot of wood. Until we examine the keel we won't know if we have to scrap her or not."

"Scrap? Come, now, it can't be that bad, can it? It's just the keel."

Roberts looked at Delliger, both of them hunched over in the bilge, and the two laughed. "How long did you say you've been working on ships for, Davis?" Roberts asked.

"A few years..." Davis claimed, crossing his arms. Roberts and Delliger just stared at him. "Alright, two years."

Roberts and Delliger chuckled. "You'd better be thankful for that pretty face of yours, Davis," Delliger commented, "because that's the only reason you're our captain."

"Aww, shut it! We all know who brings in the gold."

"Well, he's got us there. Come on boys, we're almost to land." Delliger led the other two out of the bilge and they went back to the main deck of the *Royal James*.

Once there, Davis addressed the crew to inform them of the wormrot and that the ship would be more thoroughly inspected. Davis also mentioned that they might need to scrap the ship if the wormrot was widespread.

Roberts relieved the helmsman for the final approach west of Anomabu. With the wind in their favour, they reached their destination within a few hours. Roberts guided the *Royal James* just shy of land, and the *Royal Rover* wasn't far behind, steered by a man Roberts had trained to navigate.

Davis told the slaves, with the help of Bartholomew translating, how they have a friend in the area that will help them relocate to new homes. They couldn't return to a colony without freedom papers, and those were harder to acquire.

Davis and Bartholomew moved to the *Royal Rover* and explained the same thing as Roberts and the crew helped transport the slaves to shore via longboats. Soon, all two hundred were on shore, and Davis' friend was there as well, as he had a home nearby.

Davis gave him a great deal of coin, and they parted ways. Bartholomew approached Davis before he departed back to the *Royal Rover*.

"I wish to join you on your ship," Bartholomew said.

Roberts cocked an eyebrow. "Why would you want that, Bartholomew?"

"Yes, while we could use the extra manpower, I hesitate to bring you aboard," Davis stated, arms crossed.

"I want to join because I have seen something special I have never seen before: people of colour working in harmony with those of none. Also, I have nowhere else to go. The closest thing to family I have is John. I would stay with you to stay with my friend."

Roberts was touched by Bartholomew's words, but still couldn't help but think it was a poor decision. "Bartholomew, this is a pirate ship. There will be battles, and we will be doing things the Lord would frown upon."

"None of these things have stopped you from joining. Previously, you too wanted nothing to do with this ship. What has changed?"

Roberts glanced at Davis, then back at Bartholomew. "I suppose it is for the same reason as you; I've seen something I haven't seen before within these people... Also, the pay is better." Roberts chuckled and Davis joined in laughing.

"Then there should be no objection to my joining."

"What about working on a ship? Have you ever worked on a ship before?" Davis asked.

Bartholomew shook his head. "No, but I know how to cook. I could cook for the crew."

Davis stroked his chin. "That will work. Let's return to the ship, we can restock at Anomabu."

The three returned with the other crewmates on longboats, the former slaves all waving to them as the pirates left.

"Despite my objections, I'm glad you decided to join us, Bartholomew," Roberts reassured the man.

"I couldn't leave you here without being able to repay my debt."

"Your debt?" Roberts asked. Davis' attention was also piqued.

"You saved my life, John, and the crew of the *Royals* gave me my freedom again. I wish to repay that."

"You don't owe us anything, mate," Davis said. "You're one of us now, an equal."

Once they were aboard the ship, and after the announcement of their new cook joining the crew, the men wanted to have another feast. It seemed that the crew drank to intoxication every night, and any excuse to do so again was welcome. They were also genuinely excited to have Bartholomew join them. Many congratulated him and welcomed him to the crew, and also gave him more ale to drink.

"Do you always have celebrations at the drop of a hat?" Bartholomew asked.

"Most of the time," Delliger replied with a chuckle.

"Doesn't it become a problem? What if we're attacked? Not by another crewmate, I mean," Roberts clarified, "but by another ship. With the crew in such a state, we could have a problem."

"Nah, it'll be fine," Davis reassured him. "It's always been like this. It helps the crew relax. This isn't the kind of job where you want to be wound up. Tempers start to flare and things go bad in a different way for us, the Commanders."

"Let us eat and drink; for tomorrow we die," Roberts recited.

"Hear hear!" Davis cheered, lifting his cup.

Roberts, Bartholomew, and Delliger all clinked their glasses together in agreement of the decree. The celebration for their new crewmate continued on into the morning, and the whole crew was incapacitated for several days after.

4. GOD'S JUDGEMENT

The crew were given shore leave at Anomabu, but the Commanders stayed behind to hold a meeting. They wanted to decide on where to sail next after they sold the spoils from the *Argent* and *Princess*. Roberts was recently elected a Commander, and so he joined the discussion.

Captain Davis expressed interest in heading to Príncipe, an island to the southeast which he'd heard was small, but was wealthy due to sugar and cocoa trade. Some of the other Commanders offered a few suggestions, but Davis' seemed the best as the island was not as fortified as others, and made for an easier target. When put to the vote, Davis' plan was chosen.

The *Royal James* was beached and the bilge drained before the crew began ripping off planks from the bottom to replace. They soon found it was futile.

"Look 'ere," the ship's carpenter said, pointing to the bow part of the keel.

Roberts, Davis, and Delliger were all examining the wood closely. A few holes dotted the side of the keel here and there.

"An' over 'ere." The carpenter guided the three to the stern and once again showed them keel there.

"Wormrot," Roberts muttered, dismay in his voice.

"We lucky to 'ave got this far. A few mor' weeks and we'da sunk wit Davey Jones."

"Thanks, Dunham," Davis said.

After the carpenter walked away, Roberts asked, "So, what now?"

"We have to abandon her," Delliger declared. "We can't sail with it like this. We'd have to constantly pump the bilge, and as the weeks pass the possibility of a breach grows."

"This will put a significant dent in our firepower," Davis lamented as he leaned against the ship. "Well, it's not so bad. We were short on men before, so that won't be an issue anymore, at least." Davis chuckled, but there was a definite hint of annoyance in it.

"Do we have enough to buy another?" Roberts asked.

Davis and Delliger glanced at each other, and then laughed together. "You're as green a pirate as they come, John," Davis said eventually.

Blackbeard's Ship

"We stole this ship. It'd be a waste to buy one when one can just be taken. That's the beauty of being a pirate."

Davis and Delliger walked past Roberts. "Buy a ship, he says," Davis commented, and the two started laughing again.

Roberts shoved the two of them, and the three all laughed together.

After informing the crew, they set about removing the cargo and all valuables from the *Royal James* to the *Royal Rover*. The whole affair, including selling what they'd stolen from the *Princess* and *Argent*, took about two weeks.

Their business concluded, the *Royal Rover* headed to the island of Príncipe, a journey which itself would take a further two weeks. During the journey there were many nights full of drunken revelry, and with the crew being at full complement it was even worse than usual. Several fights broke out, but the next morning tempers would subside with the aches the drink had brought on. Aside from those fights, the journey was uneventful.

When the *Royal Rover* reached the harbour of Príncipe they were met with a blockade of two sloops-of-war. Davis had had the foresight to change the flags *Royal Rover* was flying to those of a British man-of-war they'd attacked a few months prior. He also wore the garb of the captain from the same ship. *Royal Rover* was settled just outside the blockade, so as not to provoke the ships.

"Those ships could be a problem," Roberts warned.

"Don't worry, we've done this before," Davis reassured him. "We capture the governor, hold him for ransom, and then abscond with the money. They won't fire on us with their governor on board."

"Then, what happens when we give the governor up? What stops them from attacking us then?" Roberts asked.

"We don't give him up here," Davis said with a laugh. "We take the money, tell the ships to stay in harbour until we're out of sight, then set the governor free in a longboat before we escape."

"Seems you've thought of everything."

"You'll pick these things up eventually. It pays to be prepared."

After a short time, one of the sloops sent a longboat with some men to the *Royal Rover*.

"Hoy!" Davis yelled to the men in the longboat.

"What brings you to Príncipe, gentlemen?" one of the men in the longboat asked. He had a tan complexion and an exotic accent to his speech.

"Straight to the point, I like that," Davis said emphasising his musical Welsh accent. "We're here on a stopover before heading farther east. We need to resupply, perhaps relax for a bit. We've heard stories of Príncipe's beauty and wanted to see it for ourselves."

The man in the longboat examined the people on board the *Royal Rover*, and slowly nodded. "Yes, you may enter," he declared simply. The longboat set off back to its sloop.

Davis ordered the crew to get the ship moving again, and the *Royal Rover* entered the harbour.

"The island is so small. Are you sure you'll be able to ransom enough money for the governor?" Roberts asked.

"See those ships there?" Davis asked, pointing to a few ships docked at the pier. Roberts nodded. "All merchants. This island is one of the biggest exporters of cocoa, and to a lesser extent sugar. Its small size means the wealth from that trade is held in very few hands."

Roberts nodded. *Davis knows what he's doing. If he had been born into a different family he might have been a wealthy business owner.* "So what's the plan?"

"In a few days we'll send word to the governor to have lunch with me on our ship. Once he comes aboard we'll hold him hostage. Then, we wait for the money."

"What about in between?"

Davis smiled. "What else? Take in our surroundings."

After the *Royal Rover* was docked, Roberts invited Bartholomew to a walk around the island. Bartholomew accepted and the two went ashore.

At the entrance to the pier several vendors were selling various foods, and some of the local cocoa and sugar, but not much, as it was generally sold in bulk to merchants.

Roberts bought some cocoa from one of the vendors. Before serving, the cocoa was fried in a large cooking pot. Roberts was told that the beans take long to prepare, so they were already roasted and de-shelled before being fried with a touch of sugar in front of him. The aroma of the toasted cocoa and sugar was heavenly, and permeated the surroundings. After a short time, the vendor removed the beans, crushed them, and served them to Roberts and Bartholomew in a bowl.

"Oh my," Roberts remarked before silently ravaging the beans.

Together, Roberts and Bartholomew devoured the beans in short order. They agreed that it was one of the most delicious things they had ever tasted. Roberts would have purchased more, but the price was high and he wanted to continue his tour.

Roberts' tour was short-lived, however, as the island was even smaller in population than he'd previously thought. There were two inns, a brothel, a bar, a few homes, and off in the distance Roberts spied a small fort which he believed belonged to the governor. A local told him most of the island's inhabitants lived farther inland on plantations.

Roberts and Bartholomew went inland, walking amongst the tropical trees, swaying grass, and chirping birds. The two took in their surroundings with happy hearts and zest for life.

"After being on a ship for a few months, it's nice to be able to stretch and have fresh earth under my feet."

Bartholomew laughed. "I agree."

Roberts realised what he'd said, and to whom. "I suppose you must be even more relieved. You're free, and you have some meat on your bones again."

Bartholomew nodded while patting his stomach. "I do not remember the last time I was able to do something like this without worry. It almost feels too good to be true."

"It is real, as real as can be."

Roberts and Bartholomew continued to walk and talk as they moved farther inland. Eventually they reached an area with tall plant stalks stretching on for hundreds of feet.

"This must be the sugar cane they harvest."

Before they could continue their journey, they heard a commotion nearby. Roberts started walking towards the origin of the noise, but Bartholomew stopped him.

"We should head back."

"What if someone is in trouble?"

Bartholomew let Roberts go, wondering if his friend was being naive or if he knew what was happening and what he was about to do.

Roberts ran over to where the noise originated to see two dark-skinned people, one man and one woman, kneeling before a tanned man. The lighter man, no doubt the master of the plantation, held a whip in his hands, and was yelling at the other two.

After a moment, the man raised his whip. Before he could strike, Roberts grabbed the man's wrist. He turned to see Roberts, the seven-foot giant, in front of him. Roberts released his grip and the man backed up a few paces.

"What is the meaning of this?"

"Do my actions not speak loudly enough? Stop whipping these people."

"And what right do you have to command me to stop? These are my slaves."

"What is their offence?"

The plantation owner scoffed. "I ask again: by whose authority do you speak? I have no obligation to answer, as this is my property and my business. Off with ye before I strike you as well."

"Answer me!" Roberts yelled, the force of which brooked no questioning.

The plantation owner took another half step back, but stopped himself. "These slaves were trying to escape. I am punishing them."

"How much are they worth?"

"Excuse me?"

"You heard me, how much for them?" Roberts said, pointing to the two slaves.

Throughout the exchange, Bartholomew and the two slaves were simply glancing back and forth at the two men. The three did not know what to do, and so they continued passively watching.

"They aren't for sale."

Roberts reached into his pocket, causing the plantation owner to flinch. Roberts held up his other hand as a warning, then pulled out the four gold coins he got from Davis. He showed them to the plantation owner.

"This should suffice."

The plantation owner peered at the gold, then at Roberts. He was visibly confused, and shaken from this sudden altercation.

The wind blew past the group of people, sending notes of the sea and the local vendors' food to them. The air rustled the leaves of the sugar cane and accented the silence surrounding Roberts' offer.

"What is so important that you wish to purchase these slaves?" the plantation owner finally asked.

"What's it to you? I want the slaves, and this is my offer. Do you accept?"

The plantation owner sighed. "My boy, as I said, they aren't for sale. No matter what you can offer me, it will not match my need for them. We are in the middle of a harvest, and I would not be able to find slaves of similar calibre to keep up with the demand. Return in a few months, and we can talk then."

Roberts gritted his teeth and clenched the coins tightly in his fist. The gold hurt his palm as he squeezed.

Bartholomew went over to Roberts' side and whispered in his ear. "I understand your feelings, believe me, I do, but even if you take these two, there are a dozen more you cannot help here, and a dozen more plantations on this island. You will only make it harder on the remaining slaves by taking these two."

Roberts glanced at the slaves still on their knees. Their eyes pleaded with him to keep going, but Bartholomew's hands were pulling him back.

Roberts stared at the plantation owner, his hand holding the whip half-cocked, and noticed something dangling off his neck. The plantation owner was wearing a necklace of the Crucifixion, open for all to see. The idol around his neck a symbol of his faith.

Blackbeard's Ship

Roberts turned around with a huff and walked back to the path, leaving the slaves and the plantation owner alone. Luckily, Roberts and Bartholomew were not able to hear any further commotion behind them.

Roberts headed back to the *Royal Rover* to find Davis. Bartholomew followed closely behind, unsure of what Roberts was about to do. The two found Davis in the mess drinking some ale with some other crewmates.

"Davis, I need to talk with you."

"Sure, mate," Davis said. He noticed the look in Roberts' eyes, and elected to leave the table and talk with Roberts privately. "What is it?"

Roberts paced about now that they had slowed down, unable to keep himself still.

Davis wore a concerned look on his face, and eyed Bartholomew. "John, calm down and tell me what's going on. You're acting as if me mum died."

"I know, I just... I knew what I was about to say before, but I need a second..." Roberts began speaking in Welsh. "Instead of ransoming the governor for money, I think we should ransom him for the slaves on this island."

Davis looked at Roberts as if he had two heads. "Are you mad?"

"No, I am very much in control of my faculties. Well? What do you say?"

"I say you're mad if you think we can."

Roberts continued to pace around the ship, his footsteps loud and pronounced. "Why not? Tell me why it wouldn't work."

Davis shook his head. "Clearly something has happened to cause your ire. I understand, but you need to sit down and breathe. You're not thinking straight."

Roberts sat down and eyed Davis intently. "Well?"

"Well, firstly, it's not up to me. This sort of thing would have to be voted on, as we would be forgoing money. Secondly, this island has many slaves. One governor is not worth so many slaves. The plantation owners would sooner install a new governor than give up so much."

"Does this crew not want to see slaves freed? I thought that was the main objective on board."

Davis laughed. "No, the main objective is staying alive and living like kings while we are." Davis sat down across from Roberts. "It's easy to take slaves when they're being transported, as it's only one ship we have to deal with, and we have the room on our ship to host them. Right now, we're down a ship so there's not enough room. There are two ships in the harbour with almost as many guns as we have on each of them, and that's not even mentioning the merchant ships with cannons on them as well.

"Even if we can get the slaves on board, we wouldn't be able to escape. It's just not possible. I'm sorry."

Roberts looked away in frustration. For a few minutes he just sat silently fuming. "I want it put to a vote."

"Mate, I already told you it won't work."

"I still want the Commanders to vote on it. I have that right."

Davis sighed. "Alright, if this will help you see the folly then we will vote."

Later that night, when all the Commanders were back on the *Royal Rover*, a vote was held on how to treat the ransoming of the governor. Unfortunately for Roberts, the other Commanders were unanimously against his plan.

Roberts was disheartened by the whole affair, and went to sleep without discussing the matter further with anyone. The next morning, Davis came to see him as he was just getting out of his hammock.

"How are you feeling, John?"

Roberts nodded. "Better. I'm sorry about yesterday. I understand what you were saying. It was a foolish plan."

"Do not trouble yourself over it. Would you care to share what provoked your anger so?"

"I noticed yesterday the conditions of the slaves on the island, possibly even the least extent of it, and I felt powerless to help them. My whole life I've been more than privileged compared to Negroes and I've been blind to the plight of slaves, or I looked the other way. I don't want to do so again."

Davis leaned against a hammock. The swaying of the ship moved him back and forth on it. "I understand, but from a pirate who's been living the life for some time to one relatively new, my advice is this: you must choose your battles wisely. We can't change the world.

"Right now, you're too soft. You'll die a quick death if you keep on the way you are. Know when you can help someone and when you have to walk away. Worry about you and your comrades first, the enemy next to you second, and everything else third.

"These men are relying on you to watch their backs and keep them safe. If you're focussed on helping someone else, they'll die. Understand?"

"I understand," Roberts said. He leaned back into his hammock and let out a sigh, then ran his fingers through his hair. "So, how is the ransom plan going?"

"I just had someone send my invitation to the governor for lunch on the ship. With luck, we'll hear from him shortly. In the meantime I have to dress the part of a naval captain."

Roberts examined his friend's current attire. He was wearing little better than rags. From his hat to his boots, every article of clothing bore some sort of tear or damage.

"If you're supposed to be a British captain, then I'm a saint."

"Hey, I said I needed to change. Clothes are expensive. It's another good thing to steal. Nothing beats a wool cap on a cold ship."

"I second that."

Roberts returned to the main deck as Davis went to his quarters to find a change of clothes suitable for the task ahead. He noticed Walter there, swabbing the deck as usual.

"Walter! Have you gone ashore yet?"

"No, I 'aven't," Walter replied curtly.

"Well, might I suggest visiting a local cocoa vendor? They cook them with sugar and while they are a bit dry it is also quite tasty. One of a kind, a must-buy."

"I'll have ta try some then."

"Well, why don't we buy some right now? Soon we won't have a chance to. I'll purchase them for you, if that's what you're worried about."

"I don' need yer charity!" Walter shouted.

Roberts' mood changed instantly. "It isn't charity. I wish to give you something out of kindness. We are friends, are we not?"

Walter laughed. "We wus never friends. I've seen tha way ya always look down on me. At least before we wus on the level. Now, jus' because yer Welsh, you've become a Commander while I'm left in the dust. Jus' leave me in peace. Play with the captain if yer bored."

Roberts was about to object, but realised nothing he said would do any good right now, so he left Walter alone.

He's not wrong. I have thought lesser of his ideas in the past, and I happened to be in the right place at the right time to get where I am today.

Before Roberts could dwell on it further, Davis walked up to the main deck. He wore a new outfit and new hat in the style of a British naval captain. It was even more convincing than the one he'd worn when they entered the harbour. He was dressed in a blue bicorn hat, a blue jerkin with tailcoats over a white shirt, and a cravat around his neck. White breeches and black shoes completed the costume.

Roberts laughed at the sight, especially when Davis began walking with his back unnaturally straight.

"Oh bugger off, it's the best I could do with what I had."

Roberts waved his hand. "No, it's perfect, but that's what's so hilarious. You look like a git."

"Laugh all you want, this is what will win us the day, I'll show you."

"Yessir, Captain, sir."

"Shut it," Davis ordered, but Roberts still couldn't stifle his laughter.

Later that day, while everyone was having supper and drinking too heavily once again, they received word back from the governor via letter. Davis had Roberts read it to him at their table.

"Hello Captain Davies?" Roberts asked, confused by the first line in the letter.

"That's the name I told my messenger to give."

Roberts continued. "May this letter find you and your crew in good health and spirits. Let me first welcome you to our beautiful island of Príncipe. I accept your invitation for a luncheon on your ship, however it will have to be on the morrow. Tonight I would like to have wine at my fort with you. If this is acceptable, please accept a coach I have prepared to bring you and three officers with you. Signed Marco Espada, Governor of Príncipe."

"Well, I suppose I'll be having wine with the governor tonight. Care to join me?"

Roberts thought about it for a moment. "Wine at the governor's fort... That is very tempting. How about a favour instead?" Davis motioned for Roberts to continue. "How about taking Walter Kennedy instead?"

Davis glanced over at Walter Kennedy, sitting and drinking alone, then back at Roberts. "Truly?"

"Please, give him a chance. He's ambitious and I'm sure if you give him a little attention he'll be all the more loyal to you."

"You make it sound as if he's more a dog than a man."

Roberts smiled slyly, a drink in his hands. "Haven't you always wanted a pet?"

Davis frowned. "Not particularly, but I suppose it will be fine having him along this one time. If he proves himself then perhaps I can find him something else to do."

"Thank you, Davis. A chance is all I'm asking for."

"Right. Now, time to put this getup to use. Delliger!" Davis yelled, getting his first mate's attention. "Get Kennedy and another man in some nice clothes, we have an appointment with the governor."

Delliger nodded, and gathered the crewmates together before heading to the crew's quarters to find appropriate clothes. By the time they were changed the sun was down and the coach had arrived to pick them up. Davis told the other crewmates and Commanders to keep watch while they were gone.

After seeing them off, Roberts decided to have a nap in his

hammock. *I do hope Walter makes a good impression. He's on his own now.*

Davis, Delliger, Walter, and another crewmate sat in cushioned seats inside of the four-horse coach as it took them to the governor's fort. If the coach was moving more quickly their ride would have only been a few minutes, but the driver seemed content to leave the horse at a trot.

"Well, at least the ride is comfortable. My clothes feel as though they're meant for a child," Delliger commented, pulling on his collar. "What about you, Walter? How's the fit?"

"Snug," Walter replied. "I find it itches more than the wool," he said, scratching his legs.

"I wonder why that is."

"So, everyone know what's going on tonight, right?" Davis asked.

"I think so. You both confident in your roles?" Delliger looked at Walter and the other crewmate, who both nodded.

"Captain Davies, an' his first mate Delliber. Excellent names," Walter joked with a smile.

"They've always worked in the past," Davis replied.

"Have to learn when to leave well enough alone sometimes. Too many stories in your head and you're liable to jumble them up."

Walter chuckled and saluted. "Yes, sir, Delliber."

The others in the coach laughed along with Walter's jesting.

Suddenly, the coach stopped moving. "That's odd," Davis remarked. He opened the door at the side of the coach. "Driver, why have we stopped?"

Before there was an answer, Davis noticed movement in the trees off the road. He saw people converging on the coach, weapons in hand.

"Die, pirate scum!" someone yelled.

Davis pulled the door to the coach shut and covered his face. A storm of bullets rained on the coach like hail in a storm. The bullets ripped through the wood and fabric, and through the sound of the muskets and men shouting, they could hear horses dying and collapsing to the ground.

After the first wave of bullets, Davis opened his eyes. He felt warmth on his arm, and noticed blood seeping out of a wound on his shoulder, but felt no pain. He glanced around the coach.

"Oh, God, Delliger!"

"Shit, he's dead," Walter said, glancing at Delliger and then at the dead body of the other crewmate next to him. "We're dead!" Walter screamed.

Davis turned to Walter and shook him hard. "It's not over yet, dammit!"

Davis pulled out a pistol and a knife. He opened the door of the coach and fired his pistol at the first man he saw. The man fell to the ground, dead. Davis then threw his knife at another person. The knife made a *thunk* as it hit the man's neck. The enemy clutched his neck and fell to his knees, blood gushing out of the wound.

Davis exited the coach, pulling Walter along. No enemies were on that side of the coach, but he could hear footsteps and shouts on the other side.

Davis started reloading his pistol. "What do you have for weapons?"

Walter appeared dazed. "Uhh, a pistol and a cutlass."

"Alright, go to the front of the coach. We'll fend them off, and then we'll head back to the ship and sail away."

Walter walked listlessly to the front of the coach, and Davis moved to the back. When Davis was just finishing loading his pistol, he noticed Walter running out of the corner of his eye. Walter was running away from the fight and into a field towards the harbour.

"Dad damn you, you coward. You'll rot in hell for this!" Davis yelled.

Davis closed his eyes and took a few deep breaths.

All they that take up the sword will perish by the sword, right John?

Davis opened his eyes and stepped out from the back of the coach to fight against his enemies, as he had done countless times before.

Roberts felt a chill and awoke with a start. A feeling of dread swept over him, and he became restless. The ale he'd drunk earlier had left him a little groggy, but the feeling he now had overpowered it. Roberts jumped off his hammock and walked up to the main deck of the ship to get some fresh air.

Outside, amidst the barrels, cannons, and rigging rope, was Bartholomew. The dark man was staring out at the town in the night. The moon was full in the sky on the horizon, and its pale glow was just starting to replace the sun.

"Beautiful night, isn't it?" Roberts commented as he went to stand beside Bartholomew.

Bartholomew glanced over to him, then back to the moon.

"Yes, it is."

"I forgot to ask you how it's been aboard the ship since you joined."

"Everyone is welcoming and kind, and there are others who've dealt with slavery in the past. They understand where I came from, and offered advice on how to live this type of life."

Roberts nodded and smiled. "That's good. The food has certainly gotten better since you started cooking. I'm appreciative of that fact."

Bartholomew laughed. "Perhaps that has helped in the crew being accepting of me as well."

They observed the quiet town for a few moments until they heard a commotion. The noise of shouting people and loud pops floated to them across the harbour. Bartholomew and Roberts glanced at each other to see if the other was hearing the same thing.

Ten crewmates keeping watch on deck also took notice of the noise, and moved to the starboard side of the ship to catch a better glimpse of what it was.

The noises grew louder until they noticed a man running onto the pier from the town. Because of the darkness, Roberts wasn't able to make out who the man was, but he kept running closer to the *Royal Rover*. When the man was within sight, Roberts realised what his sense of dread had hinted at.

Walter Kennedy ran up the gangplank of the *Royal Rover* and up to the crewmates meeting him on the port side of the ship. Roberts and Bartholomew also rushed over to Walter.

Walter was out of breath and nearly collapsed on the deck. "Trap… Ambushed…" he tried to spit out through deep breaths while doubled over.

"Just breathe, man," Roberts commanded.

Walter took a few big breaths and stood up. "Davis, Delliger, Jerome, they're all dead."

Some of the men gasped. Roberts was visibly taken aback. He couldn't even process the deaths yet. "What happened?" he asked.

"It was a trap, we were ambushed. The governor must have found out we're pirates. I was chased here. We have to cut and run before they signal the ships."

Walter's mention of the ships drew Roberts' attention to the sloops-of-war in the harbour. He looked over the water, and plainly saw the two sloops-of-war circling. Their sails were furled and they appeared to be simply floating there, but the portholes on the gun deck were open, signalling that the cannons were ready to fire.

They wouldn't fire right now, they won't risk hitting the town. They'll wait until we try to leave, and then cut us off.

"You two," Roberts said, pointing to two of the men on watch. "Get below deck and wake everyone up. We need the cannons loaded and these sails down." The two crewmates nodded and dashed down to the lower decks to wake the rest of the crew. "Everyone else: get started on releasing the rigging, and detach us from the pier."

Roberts began to join the men in releasing the rigging, but saw Walter still just standing around. "Walter! Get moving!" he bellowed.

Walter's eyes focussed, he nodded, and then went to the nearest rope ladder and climbed up to a mast.

Roberts helped in preparing the sails for departure while Bartholomew kept watch on the town. Light from lanterns crept ever closer to the harbour, and the din of many voices arrived with it.

After a few minutes, the men Roberts had sent below returned with fifteen others. Roberts went over to them. "Why are there so few?"

"Sir, we managed to wake half the gunners and these men. The rest are tanked."

Roberts examined the men that were able to be awoken, and even they seemed to be only half aware of what was happening. "Damn. We can't fight with only half our guns. I knew drinking on duty would become a problem." Roberts glanced at the harbour and the two sloops, and then took note of the direction the wind was blowing. "Listen up; we have only one chance at this. Tell the gunners to load starboard. Once we're sailing, we can't get caught by both of those sloops, so we have to swoop around and attack the one on the left. Then we can use the wind to head north and out of here."

The men nodded, and one went below to issue Roberts' orders while the others helped their brothers in releasing the sails.

"John, they're here!" Bartholomew yelled.

Roberts turned around to see Bartholomew on the starboard bow, pointing to the town. He followed the man's finger and saw men with muskets lining the pier and taking aim.

"Bartholomew, get down!" Roberts screamed.

The sound of a dozen muskets rang into the night. Bullets flew through the air in a dozen different directions. Bartholomew's hands lifted to cover his ears as he started to kneel, but he was too late.

A bullet struck him through the back. He stepped forward with the force, and then another bullet hit him in the side of his stomach. He fell to the deck.

"Bartholomew! Talib!" Roberts screamed as he ran over to his friend's side. He picked the fallen man up and inspected his wounds. "Talib, Talib, please no. Don't die, Talib."

Bartholomew's eyes opened and he turned his head to face Roberts. "I told you, my name is Bartholomew."

Roberts' legs were warm, and he noticed a pool of blood forming beneath him. "It'll be alright. You're going to live Talib."

"I suppose you can call me Talib now, I think I'll see my wife very soon."

"No, no, no. You're not Talib. Please, stay with me." Roberts grabbed his friend's hand and gripped it hard.

"Or maybe this is God's judgement. Maybe I'll be sent to hell for joining pirates. I guess I'll find out soon."

"No, don't say that, Talib." Roberts heard the pirates around him yelling and more snaps of gunfire from the harbour.

"Thank you for being my friend, John. I wouldn't have been able to go on without you."

"We'll keep going. You're going to live. You are."

Bartholomew's eyes closed slowly. "Goodbye, John."

5. BARTHOLOMEW ROBERTS

Roberts lay in his hammock, staring up at the ceiling of the *Royal Rover*. The waves gently swayed him back and forth as the ship moved in the water.

Roberts' plan had worked. The *Royal Rover* was able to escape by the skin of their teeth by avoiding the pincer and attacking one of the ships as it passed by. They didn't escape unscathed, however; they lost four men, including Bartholomew.

Roberts repeated all the things Bartholomew said to him in his head again and again. *What does the Bible say about slaves? This is justice… There are a dozen more you cannot help… This is God's judgement…*

Ever since Bartholomew died in his arms, Roberts had had a constant ache in the middle of his head. The pain would not cease, and the more he thought on Bartholomew's words, the worse it became.

Roberts pulled his Bible out of his pocket. It had been a while since he looked at it. The worn leather, the bend at the spine, the stale smell all showing signs of heavy use, but it had not been used much in the past weeks.

Is this my punishment?

"Roberts?" a voice rang.

Roberts got up. It was a crewmate of the ship Roberts wasn't familiar with. "Yes?"

"The Commanders wish to see you."

"I'll be there in a moment."

The crewmate nodded and went back up the ladder to the main deck. Roberts lay back in his hammock and once again stared at the familiar planks. After a moment he sighed and got out of the hammock.

Roberts left the crew's quarters and went to the main deck. The sun shone brightly, mocking Roberts with its heavenly light. It was a beautiful day, when Roberts felt it should be nothing but rain.

Roberts walked to the stern, where the Commanders were waiting. Roberts half expected Davis and Delliger to be there, but after a half-second, disappointment and melancholy renewed within him.

Blackbeard's Ship

The third in line, the quartermaster, Hank Abbot, was the one who took charge in Davis' and Delliger's absence. He was a Northern New World colonist who somehow found his way to a ship full of British and African pirates—and the one Asian one, of course.

"Thanks for seeing us, Roberts. We know how close you were to Bartholomew. We would let you mourn, but we cannot wait much longer."

"What is this about?" Roberts asked immediately.

"Well, we put it to a vote, and we reckon you should be our new captain."

Roberts' jaw dropped. "Why? Why me?"

"You know how to navigate, the men respect you, and you saved more lives than some of the men can count here the other day. If not for your decisive action, we'd be sunk."

Roberts rubbed his right temple. "I've been on this ship for at best two months, and you want me to be captain? I can't... I just can't... Find someone else." Roberts turned around and began to leave.

"Wait a darn minute! Why do you refuse?" Hank asked.

"I can't run this ship. It's too much," Roberts mumbled, and continued walking. He left the Commanders in shock, but he didn't care. All he wanted to do was sleep.

The Commanders held another meeting and decided they would need to find another captain. Because the man they felt was the best candidate had refused, they were forced to evaluate others who just fell short.

Each of the Commanders was to bring forward a candidate, and that candidate needed to tell the Commanders what they would want the *Royal Rover* to do next if they were elected. One of said candidates was Walter Kennedy.

This is my chance, Kennedy thought. *I can become a captain, and all I have to do is spin some lies. They already bought that I can navigate, how hard could it be to impress them?*

"So, Walter, what would you want us to do if you were captain?"

"Well, we lost a lot tryin' ta scheme money from the governor, so we need ta capture a ship for some quick cash. An' maybe we can steal the ship too, ta bring us back some firepower. The men need something ta take their minds off tha nasty business we wus just in."

Many of the Commanders nodded at Walter's answer.

"Thank you, Walter. You are dismissed."

Walter left the stern and went below deck to the crew quarters. He had a smile on his face and a spring in his step the whole way there. He went straight to his hammock next to Roberts and lay down in it.

"Better get used ta takin' orders from me, mate. Yer lookin' at yer new captain," Walter proclaimed.

"Oh? I overheard they were considering a few people. What did you tell them our next move should be?" Roberts asked.

"Told 'em we need a new target. That ransom plan was a fool's errand. We need ta capture a ship and leave the whole thing behind us." Roberts didn't reply. Walter sat up in his hammock. "Well?" Walter asked.

"Well what?"

"What do ye think? Ye may need ta vote fer me. Yer a Commander still, ain't ye, mate?"

"It's good."

"Good." Walter nodded, and then he lay back in his hammock.

There was silence for a few minutes as Walter relaxed and let his thoughts of becoming captain of a pirate ship swim freely. He smiled unconsciously as he thought of the prospects the new opportunity would bring him.

The happiness was quickly shattered when he heard Roberts getting out of his hammock.

Walter opened his eyes and sat up. "Where are ya going?"

"I'm going to meet with the other Commanders."

"What? What for?" Walter asked as he too got out of his hammock.

Roberts stopped in his tracks, and then turned to face Walter. "It is better that you do not join me."

"Ta hell with that. Yer goin' ta try an' convince 'em to make ye captain, ain't ye?"

Roberts frowned. "I'm sorry, Walter. I know how much it means to you, but there is something I must do, and I now have the means to accomplish it."

Walter furrowed his brow. "What are ye talkin' 'bout? Ye make it sound as if yer already captain. They 'aven't even made their decision."

Roberts shook his head. "They already offered me the position. I declined it earlier. That's why they're trying to find someone else to fill the role."

Blackbeard's Ship

Walter was confused at first, but confusion soon turned into anger. "This is horseshit! I deserve to be captain."

"I'm not disputing that, Walter, but I need to do this. I won't let Barth... I won't let the men on our crew who died die in vain." Roberts turned away and headed to the ladder.

Walter followed Roberts to the main deck where the Commanders were still conferring at the stern. When the two sailors approached, the Commanders ceased talking.

"John, Walter, is something the matter?" Hank asked.

"He's tryin' ta take back the offer he declined earlier. It's not fair, I tells ye. That position is mine."

"Well, with all due respect, Walter, the captaincy hasn't been decided yet. It isn't your position."

Walter grew more agitated by the minute. *Roberts will ruin everything!*

"Please, John, tell us what you came here to say."

Roberts glanced at Walter, then at Hank. "I am not trying to take back the offer you so graciously gave me earlier. I do want a second chance, however. As a Commander, I did not nominate a candidate for captain, and with your permission I would like to nominate myself. If you allow this, I will tell you what I want our next step to be, and you can judge me on the same merits you judged everyone else."

Hank glanced at his fellow Commanders. "Let's hear what you have to say."

Roberts took a deep breath. "Over the past weeks I've been on this ship, and slightly before that, I've had my faith tested as never before. I've seen men who claim to be with God treat other men like cattle, and I've also seen men who were not religious save those same men and give them freedom.

"I've come to the realisation that those who are with God are not righteous, and I do not want to have anything to do with those men. I also don't want anything to do with a God that says slavery is alright, or who would send men to hell for stealing from evil men.

"For the first time since stepping aboard this ship I truly wish to become a pirate and take something for myself. The Bible says to not take vengeance, as it belongs to God, but I say to hell with it. I want revenge on the people who killed our crewmates.

"Fuck the ransom. I say we return to Príncipe, kill the lot of them, and take everything for ourselves."

Hank smiled. He looked at the other Commanders, and they all nodded to him with the same smiles on their faces.

"I think we are all in agreement. Your plan is certainly the best one we've heard. Congratulations, Roberts, you are our new captain."

The Commanders applauded to their new captain.

"Another matter I feel we should vote on immediately is prohibition of drinking while on duty. We wouldn't have lost those four men if the crew hadn't been drunk."

"I feel I can speak for everyone in saying that we all agree," Hank said. "Now, we should discuss the plan of attack."

Walter stormed off, rage fueling his every step. He couldn't stand to listen to them talking any longer. *You'll pay for this Roberts. Someday you'll regret what you've done today.*

The island of Príncipe was deathly silent in the middle of the night. It had been a week since the *Royal Rover* escaped. Only one sloop was defending the harbour while the other was being repaired.

Roberts and nine men were in a longboat heading to the east of the island, the closest point to the governor's fort. The moon was no longer full, but still provided a decent amount of light to see by. The waves were in their favour, pulling them inland with little need for paddling.

They landed the longboat on a small patch of beach and Roberts helped pull it up and away from the tide. He and the nine men moved silently up a hill towards the small stone fort. Weapons were at the ready, but the thundering pistols had been traded for restrained throwing knives held by skilled hands.

The men went up to the nearest fort wall, adjacent to the entrance. Hank moved to the edge of the wall and motioned for the others to stay where they were. He peered around the corner and then held up two fingers, indicating there were two guards. Hank beckoned another crewmate over, took his knife and scraped it lightly against the fort wall.

Soon after, footsteps from two people approached. Hank and the other crewmate tightened their grips on the knives they held. The footsteps came closer and louder. The crew tensed. The guards walked past the corner of the fort. Hank sprang into action and pulled one of the guards over to his helper. The other crewmate stabbed the guard through the throat. Hank jumped and slammed his knife into the head of the second guard.

Hank and the crewmate pulled the bodies back to the wall of

the fort and turned them over so they blended into the dirt with their dark clothes.

The group waited a moment to see if anyone had heard the noise, and after they were sure it was clear they began moving again.

The crew sneaked along the front wall, and after Hank checked through the door they entered the fort. Past the first door was an earthen ditch twenty feet wide meant to hold cannonballs that breach the first wall, and then another defensive stone wall in front of it. The second wall had an upper walkway around the whole perimeter with a complement of cannons, but it appeared unmanned.

Hank led the crew across a walkway over the ditch and to the next door of the fort. He motioned for the crew to enter the ditch to the sides of the door and hide under the open walkway, then picked up a rock on the stone walkway and joined the crew.

Hank hucked the rock at the doors. After a moment, the doors opened and three guards came out.

"What d'ya think made that noise?" one of the guards asked.

"Ah, it was probably jus' a bird peckin' on the wood."

"Hey, look," the third guard said. "The front gate is open."

The three guards pulled out their weapons and cautiously made their way towards the entrance. Hank motioned for a few of the crew to join him on the walkway. The men stalked the guards as they inched closer and closer to the front gate. The three of them went up behind the guards, and Hank glanced at his companions, each nodding to indicate they were ready.

In one swift motion, the guards' mouths were muzzled and their throats slit.

Roberts couldn't help but admire the coordination with which they acted. *These men have done this before. It was the right choice to allow Hank to lead.*

After the guards were hidden beneath the walkway in the ditch, the pirates moved on to the interior of the fort. As discussed prior to embarking on the longboat, the crew split into pairs and went in different directions to cover the entirety of the fort. Hank and Roberts headed straight to the centre, the most likely spot for the governor's quarters.

Along the way, Hank did the legwork. When they met a guard he killed him without hesitation. He slit throats, threw knives, and strangled his way through the fort as Roberts followed behind him.

When they happened upon a Negro maidservant, Roberts

pulled Hank back and took over. The new pirate captain grabbed the maidservant from behind, his large hands covering her mouth and pinning her arms.

"Please stop, I do not wish to hurt you." The maidservant stopped struggling, but Roberts didn't remove his hand from her mouth. He turned the maidservant around. "Nod if you will not scream, should I remove my hand." The maidservant nodded, and so he cautiously removed his hand.

"Please, sir, I…"

"Shh, shh," Roberts coaxed. "All we want to know is where your master's chambers are. If you show us the way I will give you this." Roberts pulled out a gold piece from his pocket.

The maidservant glanced at the piece, then back to Roberts. "I cannot."

"Yes, you can. Whether you help us or not, soon you will no longer have a master. If you head to the pier, people there will help you escape the island. Stay if you wish, but if you choose to help us this will help you either way."

The maidservant stared intently at the gold. By the look in her eyes it seemed she hoped the lustre of the gold would hold the secret to what she should do. After half a minute, she quietly said, "This way."

The maidservant led the two pirates through the corridors and up the stairs of the stone fort in an almost maze-like pattern. She stopped just shy of walking up a flight of stairs, and turned around to Hank and Roberts.

"His room is in the middle of the hall," she stated, pointing to the hallway through the opening of the stairs.

"Thank you," Roberts whispered. He tried to offer her the gold coin, but she refused.

"I do not want the money. Please just tell me you are true."

"I promise you we will free you and as many other slaves as we can tonight. That is the truth."

The woman almost had tears in her eyes. "Thank God for you, sir. Thank God."

"God has nothing to do with this. Quickly, go," Roberts commanded.

The maidservant went back down the stairs as quickly and quietly as she could. Hank went to the edge of the stairs and peeked around the corner.

"It's as clear as a pasture at sundown," Hank confirmed, walking around the corner and motioning for Roberts to join him.

The two walked along the corridor, still careful not to make any noise and watching their surroundings for other guards. It was quiet, which was a good sign.

"This must be it." Roberts eyed two large double doors. "Ready?" he asked. Hank nodded, so Roberts turned the handle on the door and opened it.

They entered the room and noticed the governor and his wife fast asleep in a canopy bed in the middle of the room. Roberts closed the door behind them. Hank took the right side with the governor's wife, and Roberts took the left with the governor.

The two pirates nodded to each other, and then covered the mouths of their targets. Both of them awoke and sent muffled screams through the pirates' hands.

"Quiet, or your wife dies," Roberts threatened, seething with anger.

The governor looked at his left to his wife, and went silent. His wife was still struggling and screaming. Hank hit her in the back of the head with the butt of a knife, knocking her unconscious. The governor let out a stifled cry.

"I'm going to remove my hand. You scream, and she dies. Understood?" The governor nodded. Roberts removed his hand. "Where are your valuables?"

"There is a loose floorboard under the bed and a chest hidden underneath. Take everything, please just let my wife live."

"Noble words for such a coward," Roberts said.

Hank tied up the governor's wife while Roberts tied up the governor, and then Roberts went underneath the bed to find the treasure the governor mentioned. Just as he'd said, there was a loose floorboard and a chest inside. He took out the small chest and opened it.

Inside the chest were gold pieces, jewelry, and gemstones. Though the chest was small, it nonetheless carried great wealth.

When Roberts got up, he noticed something on the governor's side table. It was a Bible. Roberts scoffed. "Alright, we got what we came for. Only one thing left to do."

"How do you think you'll escape from here? We have a sloop in the harbour. By the time you reach the pier someone will have alerted the militia. Give up now and I'll forget this happened."

"We won't have to worry about the sloop. We've already taken it. And we won't have to worry about the militia, we've already killed them."

The governor was at a loss for words. He stumbled and stammered to say something of value before sputtering out, "Who *are* you?"

"Who am I?" Roberts repeated. The voices of Davis and Bartholomew instantly rang through Roberts' head. *I suggest you acquire new names... This is justice.* "I am those you have killed... I am vengeance... I am justice... I am Bartholomew Roberts." He took up the sword for the first time in his life, and thrust it into the governor's chest.

Roberts watched as the governor fell to the floor and his blood seeped from his body. Roberts had never killed a man before, but he felt no remorse over the death he'd just dealt.

Roberts leaned his elbows against the starboard railing of the *Royal Rover*. He held in his hands his Bible, the Bible he had owned for a considerable amount of time, the Bible he had turned to for advice countless times. He ran his fingers along the broken and worn leather, admiring the beauty of the tattered relic.

Roberts tossed the book into the water and watched it sink into the depths of the sea. He released a sigh when it was out of sight and then he stood up straight.

Hank walked up beside Roberts. "Ready to move on, Bartholomew?"

Roberts smiled. "Yes, I think I am."

THE END

BOOK TWO OF
THE PIRATE PRIEST

BARTHOLOMEW
ROBERTS' JUSTICE

.

1. BARTHOLOMEW THE BEAR

Bartholomew Roberts, the pirate, sat at a table in a bar with some sailors. He was spinning a tale about a recent expedition which saw him and his crew hitting a storm. The tale was as tall as him, given that the goal was to gain their trust.

"I tell you, men, the storm was like none I had seen before. It came and left like a spectre before anyone noticed what was happening. We have two ships and we're lucky they're still with us," Roberts stated before taking a swig of his drink.

The hovel he found himself in was a lively tavern with all manner of immoral men and women finding solace under its roof. The smell of unkempt bodies, spilled ale and wine permeated the surroundings, as did the laughter and talk of general festivity.

"Lucky is not runnin' into no pirates after yer run-in. That's lucky," one of the men commented.

Roberts smiled. "Yea, I'm thankful for that as well." His smile faded. "You've been attacked recently, I take it?" he asked, his melodic Welsh accent undercutting his seriousness.

"Ay, last week on the way here. Took my whole shipment of silks and my savings. Thanks to that I can't even afford another shipment. I need to take on a loan just to keep sailing."

He shook his head. "Tch, tch. Isn't that just the way? What about you gents? Business going smoothly, or are you meeting storms like this gentleman...?" He gestured to the first man with his mug.

"Gerald."

"This man, Gerald, and I?"

"I was shipping ten tonnes of rum," another man at the table explained, "and one tonne of spices. Spices got waterlogged because of some fault in the barrels and the rum burned after one of my men got into it and had an accident. I made sure he had another 'accident' later on." He took a long drink, and he had had one too many already. His nose and cheeks were peach red. "An' now, word spread that my luck is bad and my crew worse, so I got nowhere prospecting."

"Such a shame," Roberts said. *Nothing to steal from you, that is the shame...* He then turned to the third man in the group he'd pulled together from the patrons in the tavern. "What of you, sir? You seem awfully quiet. How are the seas treating you?"

The third man was young, had his hair tied back, and wore a new-looking sailor uniform. He was dressed down, as this wasn't the sort of place one would wear a uniform, but it was clear he was part of some company.

"Things are going well, sorry to say for you gents," he answered in a proper British accent.

Roberts noticed a slight twinge on the corner of the man's lips. He pointed at the man. "Oh! I see that smile. Come now, you old dog, you're holding back on us. You're about to have a payday soon, aren't you?" he speculated with a big grin on his face.

The gentleman couldn't hold back a grin of his own, Roberts' being as contagious as it was. "I shouldn't say."

The charismatic Welshman mocked a frown and then smiled again. "Now you've teased us again. You can't tell half the story and then forgo the rest. The curiosity is liable to eat us alive. Isn't that right, gents?"

The others at the table joined in with Roberts' boisterousness. Together they chided the sailor into telling the whole story, even though he hadn't really said anything to begin with.

"Alright," the man finally conceded. "I do not wish to boast, so I will only say I recently acquired quite a lucrative contract with the East India Company to ship stock west."

With the mention of that name, the other sailors' eyes and ears perked. Roberts whistled. "Sounds profitable indeed. When are you due to ship out?"

"After our ship is cleaned, in near abouts two days."

"And you're sailing the *Decadence*? Three sails, thirty guns?" he asked.

The man nodded. "That would be the one."

"Bartholomew?" someone called.

Roberts turned around to see one of his crewmates timidly approaching, but nonetheless with urgency in his eyes. He waved for his crewmate to join him, but the man shook his head and beckoned his captain over.

"Excuse me for a moment, gentlemen," he said before rising from the table and walking over to his crewman. "What is it? I'm in the middle of finding our next plunder."

The man was wringing his hat in his hands, nervousness creeping through. "It's bad, Captain. None of the men know what to do."

Roberts held his hands up. "Calm. Breathe. From the beginning now."

The crewmate glanced about to make sure no one was listening. "Hank, a few of the commanders, and seven of the crew were taken from a tavern."

"Taken? By whom?"

"The local militia. They're being held in the prison on the other side of town."

Roberts rubbed his chin and muttered a curse under his breath. "Head back to the ship. I'll handle it."

"Sir?" the crewmate questioned, brow cocked.

"I've seen the prison. It's small and only manned by a few people. With the daylight waning, I shouldn't have a problem rescuing the boys. Any more people and we would draw suspicion. Tell the crew I will be back by midnight."

"Yes, Captain," the man stammered before heading out the tavern's swinging door.

Roberts returned to the table, took the last drink of his ale, and placed a note on the table. "Unfortunately, I must be leaving now. Gentlemen, it has been a pleasure."

The captains lifted their glasses to him and said goodbye as he left.

Roberts checked his person quickly to ensure he was prepared for what he was about to do. *Pistol, sword, everything in order. Wait, where is my…* He touched his back pocket, the same pocket that once held a Bible he'd owned for quite a time. That familiar leather book used to be a staple in his back pocket, but was no longer there. *Half a year and still I reach for that book. Davey Jones must be finished reading it by now.*

He put his thoughts back on his crew and moved on towards the prison. Day was starting to leave the port town, and the sun on the horizon shone light on the harbour and at Roberts' back. The golden glow reflected in the wood and stone of the houses as he passed by, and cast his shadow larger than life on the walls and alleys. Seven feet tall as he was, the shadow he cast was great indeed.

He reached the prison at one side of town, and assessed its fortifications. It was a stone building, not really much of a prison, but slightly bigger than all the other buildings in the town. He had heard the prison held close to one hundred prisoners, but at most only twenty guards of the militia were present at a time, and that was during the day.

Directly in front of the prison stood a five-foot raised platform with a wooden hanging beam in the middle. A man already long dead was suspended in the air by a noose. The smell emanating from the body was sickly, not quite at the point of decay, but fouled by excrement. His body was limp and his arms were tied behind his back. Below his neck, his skin was pale; red marks could be seen surrounding the rope tight around his neck, and his tongue involuntarily stuck out of his mouth and had turned purplish. His eyes were still open, bloodshot and staring at Roberts in the eerie way the dead peer at everyone. A placard hung around his shoulders, resting on his stomach, which read "Pirate."

Roberts couldn't help but stare back at the man, wondering what his true crime was, and how he'd ended up being executed. *I will not let my men suffer the same fate.* He had a brief inclination to pray for the dead man, but shook his head and kept walking.

He sauntered around the buildings surrounding the prison. No other buildings were very close to the prison, which allowed him a good line of sight to view it from all angles. Other men and women were still walking about the village, so he was able to blend in while examining his target.

There were two entrances, one at the front with the hanging podium, and another at the back. Each was guarded by two armed men in blue uniforms similar to those worn by the British Royal Navy, but cut off at the elbow.

Though no houses were close by, the prison was in plain view. *I won't be able to enter without drawing unwanted attention. I must find another way.*

When Roberts took another walk round the prison, he noticed a few guards leaving. He observed the men talking and laughing with each other while walking.

They must be finishing their shift. If I can take one of their uniforms I could walk through the front door of the prison...

He tailed the three guards. The people of the town were beginning to disperse as night drew in, and he was able to easily follow them. After a moment, one of the men separated from the group and entered a side street. Roberts followed the lone man.

The guard walked through the side street until he reached a house and turned to enter. He turned his gaze in Roberts' direction. Roberts missed a step. The guard tensed.

There are still people in the streets. I cannot make a move yet. He regained his composure and resumed his stride.

"Keep up the good work, mate," he said as he passed the guard.

The other man nodded as Roberts passed by. He could still feel the guard's gaze on his back. He turned the corner at the end of the street and continued walking to the next side street.

Roberts laid his back against the wall and took a deep breath, wiping sweat off his brow. He pushed himself off the wall and approached the house the guard had entered. At the back of the house there was an exit and an alley to access the side, which he entered.

The side of the house had a few low double-hung louvre windows and the shutters were open. He went up close to one of them, keeping his body close to the wall of the house. Voices travelled out of the open shutters.

"… prisoners give you any trouble today?" s female voice asked.

"Nah, the new ones ain't any trouble," a male voice responded. "The new 'uns are positively jovial."

He must be talking about Hank and the others.

"They're scheduled for execution on the morrow, yet behave better than the local drunks. It's like they're not afraid of the noose. It's unsettling."

"Aww, well I know something to help settle ye," the woman replied.

Sounds of kissing filtered from behind the screen, then the sound of footsteps moving further to the back of the house, and then a door closing. *Here's my chance.*

He moved closer to the front of the house and peered in through one of the shutters. He was looking into the living room of the guard's house, and could see the blue coat resting on a chair next to a table. The chair was too far from the window, so he somehow had to enter the house to get the uniform.

He glanced to the ends of the alley. It was dark, and most everyone was indoors at this hour. The house next to the guard's home was dark, presumably because no one was home, which made things easier for him.

Roberts lifted the window shutter as far as it could go, then climbed up into the opening. He took a moment to check the inside again, and, not seeing any residents in the living room, he continued his entrance. He was not a small man, and so the window was a tight squeeze. He could feel the grating of the shutters digging into his back. The giant took a deep breath and sucked in his gut. He moved his arms up and into the living room, and pushed against the siding of the window as he shimmied his torso through. After a moment of struggle, he was halfway through, and only his legs were dangling outside.

The chair was almost within reach now. *If I can just catch the uniform I won't have to enter all the way.* He extended his arms in front of him. His upper body started to fall forward and his legs flew up in the air. He planted his hand on the floor and then spread his legs out to keep his balance on the window sill.

Roberts reached for the chair, but it was still an inch away. He swatted at it in an attempt to get closer, but it wasn't helping. He kept shuffling forward precariously on the windowsill. The Welshman managed to get one finger on the edge of the chair and clenched his teeth as he pushed down with all his might. The chair moved forward ever so slowly, and with his other hand he was able to grab the coat.

After removing the coat, the chair became a lot lighter, and he didn't have a proper grip on it. It fell through his fingers and made a loud snap as it hit the floor. He cringed and then rushed to pull himself out of the window.

He drew himself up against the wall of the house and flattened against it. He listened intently as he held his breath with the uniform clenched in his hand. After a moment of no door opening, he let out his breath. No one seemed to hear him.

He pulled off his top and attempted to put on the guard's uniform. The uniform was tight across his broad chest, and he was forced to tug on the arm to finally get it to fit. As he tugged, the fabric frayed with a loud rip.

He tensed and stood up straight. He turned as best as he could to inspect himself, and was disheartened. It had ripped on the arms and the bottom of the sides. The uniform normally went halfway down the forearm if it fit, but in Roberts' case it only reached a little over his elbow. His hairy arms were showing, as were the hairs on his chest through the obviously stressed buttons. It was constricting on the arms and chest, and he had a hard time even breathing in the outfit.

It will have to do. Just act the part, and the rest will come together.

He looked up to see a young boy staring at him in the street at the end of the alley. By his snickering the child had been there for some time.

"Run along now, young one, before I teach you some manners," Roberts warned with the back of his palm raised.

The boy laughed and ran off.

Roberts moved deliberately towards the street and back to the prison. He kept his back straight and his gut sucked in as he walked. Along the way, the few people who were still wandering the streets gave him odd looks when he passed. By the time he reached the prison, he was sweating and his arms were beginning to tingle from poor circulation.

He marched up to the doors of the prison, going over what he could say to the men guarding to allow him entrance. *I will tell them I am late for my shift, apologize, and walk through. That will be the simplest.*

When he approached the doors, he half opened his mouth, ready to give his story, but the guards simply moved aside to allow him entrance. Roberts missed a step, peered warily at the men in front of him, and then entered the prison. They seemed to pay him no heed as he passed.

Perhaps this costume doesn't look as tight as I thought.

He found himself in a not-so-great hall. Empty tables and chairs sat in the middle of the room, and racks next to doors on either side of the room held spare weapons. Straight in front of him was another door as well.

He decided to head straight, and went through the door. In the next room was a long hallway with prison cells lining either side. A pair of armed guards were talking with each other in the middle of the hallway.

He glanced back and forth, examining those in the cells as he roamed. The quality of the cells left a lot to be desired. They were small and cramped, with too many people stuffed inside. The smell of faeces and other bodily odours filled the area. The prisoners were loud and some tried to grasp Roberts as he passed by, but he was out of reach.

Each cell was secured with iron bars and thick stone separated the small quarters from each other. There were no windows or openings to allow air to enter, thus the smell lingered with no way of escaping, just as the prisoners did.

As he passed the guards, they nodded to him, once again giving him only a cursory glance and nothing more.

Any in their right mind would think there's something strange; my arms are turning white, I'm sweating seawater and this uniform is splitting at the seams. I suppose I shouldn't look this gift horse in the mouth.

At the end of the hallway a staircase led to the second floor of the prison. He checked the cells at the back before moving on up the stairs.

From his examination, the prison had only two floors, but it felt smaller on the inside. He was sure there were more rooms with prisoners, as he could see doors on either end of the hall. He first entered the room nearest the front of the prison.

Inside the room was a single prison cell, larger than the rest by far, with a small window at the top covered with iron bars and doors on either side like the entrance of the prison. Roberts was taken aback when he saw his crew right in front of him. Some were playing a game of cards on the cell floor while Hank was being questioned by one of the guards.

"I'll ask you again, what ship are you with and what is the name of your captain?"

Hank sighed, and then glanced briefly at the door where he saw his captain. His eyes shot open for a split second before he regained his composure. Hank returned his attention to the guard questioning him.

"I'll tell you again: we belong to no ship and answer to no captain."

"Three times you've denied having a captain, but I know this is not the truth."

A crow perched in the window near the cell and called out,

drawing the attention of the crew and the guard. The crew then glanced to the door and noticed their captain.

Roberts put his finger to his mouth to silence the crew before they cried out. They returned to their game of cards, and acted as if nothing was different. The guard resumed questioning Hank, none the wiser.

Roberts closed the door and silently moved behind the guard. The Welsh giant wrapped his massive arm around the man's neck, and covered his mouth with his palm. The guard struggled and pulled against him, but it was no use. Roberts was far stronger than the smaller man. The pressure against the guard's neck cut off his air; his thrashing slowed as the seconds passed until his arms and legs went limp. Roberts slowly set the man on the floor, then grabbed the keys off his belt.

He took the keys to the cage his crew was set in, and began trying each key on the iron lock.

"Captain, you are a sight for sore eyes," Hank said. "I thought we were gonna be left behind."

Roberts gestured at the card game. "You didn't seem too concerned."

Hank glanced back to the cards, then to his captain again. "Can't let 'em see us sweat, now can we? We have reputations to uphold."

"True enough." With the next key, the iron bars were opened.

The crew exited the cage and thanked their captain profusely. Smiles abounded on all the men's faces, and there was much rejoicing.

"Now, how about we leave this place?" Roberts suggested.

"There's a storage area in that room with spare uniforms we can don." Hank pointed to a door on the side of the room.

"The guards here seem rather inept, so I don't believe we would have issues regardless, but it's better to be safe."

Roberts used the keys once again to open the storage room, and the crew entered.

Inside the room were weapons, piles of clothes, and supplies for repairs. The clothes were not simply uniforms, but also what appeared to be clothes from former and possibly current prisoners.

The crew rummaged through the clothes to find uniforms they could wear. Roberts kept watch at the door. Hank took the clothes from the guard, and then locked the man in the cage before changing into the uniform.

"Sure am glad you came by, Captain."

"Of course I would. I couldn't leave you all here to be hung. What kind of a captain leaves his men behind?"

"You'd be surprised."

"I suppose it has happened to you before?" Roberts asked as he glanced to see his crew still changing.

"Too many times to count, I reckon. The types of men attracted to this life aren't always the most loyal. You're different, though, just like Davis. That's why most of us wanted you as captain: you inspire loyalty in others."

Roberts' face was melancholic for a moment as his thoughts turned to his former captain who'd introduced him to piracy. After a moment he raised his brow with a sly smile. "Most?"

"Aye, most. You can't please everyone. I say don't try, it's the majority that counts anyway."

Roberts smiled. "True enough."

Hank finished changing, and the clothes he had been able to procure were a much better fit than Roberts'. The crew finished around the same time, and returned to the first room.

"So, where to now, Captain?"

"We can escape through the back. Two guards are covering the exit, but it shouldn't be hard to knock them out." The crew nodded. "Follow me."

Roberts opened the door to the prison's second-floor hallway, and after a cursory glance to check for guards, he stepped inside. He guided his crew past the other cells with prisoners still locked in cages.

The prisoners seemed to know something was wrong and became more agitated. They yelled and reached out to the pirates as they passed.

When they reached the stairs, Roberts looked down to the lower level to see the guards trying to silence the prisoners. The commotion on the second floor transitioned below, affording him and his crew an opportunity.

He rushed down the steps and opened the door to the back room of the prison while he watched the two guards. He motioned for his crew to go through the door while the guards were distracted. One by one, the group of fifteen casually went through the door without the prison guards taking notice.

Inside, the back room of the prison was a mirror to the front entrance, complete with weapons on racks off to the sides. Some of the crew grabbed weapons.

Roberts closed the door behind him. "Don't take the weapons," he whispered. "When I was watching the guards, none left the prison with weapons. If we are carrying any when we leave it will arouse suspicion if any locals see us."

The crew followed their captain's advice and returned the weapons. Roberts motioned for Hank to join him at the back exit.

He placed his hand on the door and glanced at Hank. His crewmate nodded. He opened the door, and in front of them were the two guards Roberts had seen when he circled the prison.

Roberts and Hank both grabbed one of the guards, and pulled them inside. Roberts closed the door with his foot while slamming the man he grabbed against the wall. He held his hand against the man's mouth so he couldn't scream. The man muffled something as his eyes shifted back and forth trying to make sense of what was happening. Before he could act, Roberts punched him hard in the stomach and released his grip on the guard. The guard doubled over in pain, and he struggled to breathe. He gripped Roberts' leg, his mouth wide open in a struggle to shout, but instead only saliva escaped and hit the floor of the prison. The man's eyes soon shut as he fell unconscious.

Roberts turned his attention to Hank, who also took care of the guard he grabbed. The two were both breathing hard, moreso from the rush of the fight than the physical exertion.

Hank looked at his captain, and after a few breaths he started laughing. Roberts cocked his brow. "Captain, your uniform has seen better days."

He examined himself, extending his arms and seeing what Hank noticed. The uniform was truly gone now. The seams across the arm all the way up the biceps and underarms were torn, as were the sides of the stomach.

"On the positive side, at least now I can breathe properly," Roberts said with a laugh, which the crew joined in. "Alright everyone, let's walk out of here in groups of two or three and split up. We'll meet back at the ship." The crew nodded and they all left the prison.

Roberts joined Hank and they made their way back to the harbour. It was well into the night so the streets were mostly empty. Any people they did meet did not seem to think them out of the ordinary and paid them no heed. The two made it back to the *Royal Rover* and *Fortune* unscathed and undetected.

After a half hour, all the remaining crewmates who had been imprisoned returned to the ships.

"We've escaped prison for one more day, thanks to you, Roberts." Hank let out a sigh and wiped sweat off his brow.

"We should keep it that way. It would be best to stay on the ship and not venture into town for the time being." Hank nodded. "I suppose I should have asked why you all were arrested in the first place. Do the authorities know we're pirates?"

Hank shook his head. "No, no. It's rather funny, actually. One of the crewmates got into a brawl with someone they shouldn't have, an official of some sort. Before long the whole saloon was in a tussle and the official had us arrested. He kept yelling that we'll be hung for what we did, but I imagine he wasn't very serious. One of the crewmates not captured must have taken it seriously for you to be here." He chuckled.

Roberts didn't laugh. "I believe the official was very serious. The guard I followed to steal this uniform from mentioned that you were to be hung on the morrow."

Hank stopped laughing and gave Roberts a grim, questioning look. He simply nodded to his friend's silent question. "Oh my."

This time Roberts had a hearty laugh. "You almost died, and all you say is 'oh my.' My friend you are either very brave or very much in shock."

"Perhaps a little of both," Hank suggested. After a moment to catch his breath, he found the humour in the situation.

The two joined the rest of the crew below deck, and they celebrated their newly recovered freedom. Stories of Roberts' bravery circulated as quickly as the booze and laughter that night.

The next day, news was surprisingly quiet about the previous night's escape. The pirates heard no whispers about fifteen missing prisoners who escaped the noose, and no officials seemed to be on the lookout for tavern brawlers on the run from justice. However, there was one rumour circulating involving the prison, but not one Roberts, or any really, could have expected.

Roberts and Hank were on the top deck of the *Royal Rover* when they heard the news. A crewman ran up the gangplank, but was out of breath.

"Is something the matter, man? You look as if you've seen an apparition."

"It's about the prison, Captain," the crewmate said between breaths. "I've heard word on something happening there, though I tell you truthfully I'm not quite understanding it."

Roberts and Hank glanced at each other. "Well, let's hear it then."

The crewmate nodded as he took the last few breaths he needed to get back to normal. "No word on escapees, but they say some of the guards were attacked by a bear in a blue suit in the night. The same night we escaped."

Roberts was taken aback. "A bear?"

He nodded. "Yes, Captain. A bear. What do ye figure it means?"

Hank let out a laugh. Roberts and the crewmate looked at him as if he were mad. "It means our captain here is a bit too hairy around the arms, that's what it means."

Roberts shook his head. "You can't possibly…" He raised a brow.

Blackbeard's Ship

Hank was acting giddy, snickering at his own thoughts. "Bartholomew the Bear has quite the nice ring to it." He gripped Roberts' shoulder for support as he burst into fits of laughter.

Roberts' face was stone. "You must swear to me the crew will not hear a word of this." He turned to the crewmate who'd brought them the news, and pointed at him menacingly. "Swear to me."

"I'm quite sorry, Captain," Hank said, regaining his composure, but with the hint of his mood dripping from his tone of voice. "This simply cannot be something the crew misses out on."

Hank went below deck to share the story of Bartholomew the Bear with the crew. Roberts shook his head, but couldn't resist smiling himself at the foolishness of the story.

From that day forward, whenever the story was retold, it was with much more laughter, and greater emphasis placed on Roberts' appearance rather than his courage. The name Bartholomew the Bear stuck with the crew not simply as a jest, but also as a source of encouragement. No matter what happened to his crew, the Bear would be there for them.

2. A SHORT AND MERRY LIFE

Walter Kennedy sat slumped on a stool in a tavern, a nearly empty glass loosely in his hands. "More whiskey," he demanded.

The taverner apologized to another customer he was talking with, then looked over at Walter, but did not move an inch. "Your money ran out. Unless ye got more, ye don' get more."

"Tch."

The taverner waved at Walter and shook his head, then returned to talking with his paying customers.

Walter tipped the glass back until it and his face were nearly vertical. The last few drops of his drink snaked their way across the inside of the glass to his tongue. His nose was engulfed in the mouth of the glass, and the smell of the whiskey filled his nostrils. For a brief moment, through watching of the beads of alcohol and the smell, it was just Walter and the drink, and all other thoughts were drowned away. When the beads were gone, and he put the glass back on the table, the thoughts flooded back.

His fault I have no money. If I was captain, we'd have more money than we'd know how to spend.

The sounds of laughter, talking, music, and clinking glasses pounded in his ears. He'd drunk enough to make himself tired, but not enough to suppress the noise. He heard the door open, letting in fresh air and more noise from outside, but he didn't care to see who wandered in.

Someday he'll get what's comin' to him.

The person who entered walked over to where Walter was sitting and placed a hand on his shoulder. He turned his head around and noticed Bartholomew Roberts in front of him.

Speak of the Devil. He chuckled.

"We must leave, Walter. We're setting sail tomorrow and we need you and the crew sobered up by then."

He shook Roberts' hand off his shoulder and turned back around. "I'll be there."

There was a brief pause before Roberts turned him around again. "I want you back on the ship now, Walter. You've finished your drink. You're a commander now and you must set an example for your Commons."

Walter clenched his jaw and gritted his teeth. "I said I'll be there."

Blackbeard's Ship

Roberts sighed and grabbed him by the arm, pulling him up off the stool. He wasn't strong enough to resist the seven-foot beast in front of him. He saw the patrons staring at the spectacle, sneering at a grown man being treated as a child.

"Get offa' me, ye bastard," he seethed.

Walter planted his feet on the ground and twisted away, causing Roberts' fingers to slip. He lost his footing and fell into one of the patrons, then to the ground.

He climbed back to his feet quickly, seeing that the man he fell on top of spilled his drink all over himself, and was giving him the evil eye. He backed away towards the door of the tavern. The man rose to his feet; his teeth were clenched and his fist was in a ball.

"Get back to the ships, Walter," Roberts commanded. "I'll handle this."

Walter turned and left. *Have fun, Roberts.*

He sauntered back to the ships. By the time he arrived back to the *Fortune* the drink was no longer affecting him, and he felt sober. He boarded the *Fortune* and entered the crew cabin below deck. Along the way he motioned for certain crewmates to join him. He and three others advanced to the back of the crew cabin where two crewmates were lounging and talking.

One of the crewmates' head and face were fully shaved, and he had a tattoo covering half his face. He was cleaning his nails with a large knife when Walter and the men approached.

"Ethan," Walter said to the tattooed man.

Ethan nodded to him. "Welcome back. Have yer fill, did ye?"

"Not hardly. Sit, gents. We 'ave much to discuss." Walter and the three crewmates sat down with the other two on barrels, boxes, and chairs. The Irishman glanced around to make sure there were no prying eyes or perked ears. "Roberts is becoming a problem. Where are we on votes?"

Ethan laughed. "No change since weeks a'fore. Long as Roberts keeps bringing in the money he'll always 'ave people on his side."

"How do we change that then?" Walter asked.

"Not by drinkin' till ye piss yer pants every day, that's fer sure," Ethan jabbed.

"Yer one ta talk, ye bastard."

Ethan shrugged and smiled. "Why don't ye just kill 'im?"

Walter quickly shook his head. "No, no. We can't kill him. I don't want him dead. I simply don't want him to be captain."

"Why ye want him out so bad, then?"

"I thought it was obvious." He looked at his companions, who all gave him looks of confusion. "*I* want to be captain."

Ethan laughed all the harder this time. The other men nervously joined in the laughter. "Wait, yer serious?"

Walter folded his arms. "Yea, of course. I would make a great captain. Better'n Roberts."

"Then tell me, Captain, what makes ye so great? What do ye bring ta tha table that Roberts don't?"

Walter leaned back against the many eyes staring at him, waiting for a response. He could feel sweat beginning to fall across the side of his face. "Well, I can navigate," he lied.

"So can Roberts," Ethan replied, leaning over in his chair, gesturing with his knife.

"I'm better than 'e is. And, ye've seen me in battle, I'm good with a musket."

"I've seen ye hidin' behind the main mast more often than not."

Walter wiped sweat off his brow as he tried to think of what would make him a good captain, a better captain than Roberts.

"Well, anything else, Commander?" Ethan asked long and drawn out.

"I can bring us more booty," he replied at last.

Ethan set his back against the chair and pointed the knife at Walter. "That's a tall order. How do ye think ye'll be able to fulfil it?" Walter didn't know how to respond, and Ethan didn't wait for him to think of something. "The only way for you ta become captain is to gain the support of tha crew. Right now, yer nothin' more than a whinin' babe. Ye talk big, but yer an earsore. Now why don'tcha piss off? I'm tired of listenin' to ye."

Walter gritted his teeth, but didn't say anything. He got up and left the group. *I'll show 'em. I'll find a way; I just need the right opportunity. I'll be captain one way or another.*

⚓ ⚓ ⚓

"Captain, the *Fortune* is signalling us," a crewmate yelled from the crow's nest. He was gazing through a spyglass into the wide open ocean. He moved the spyglass in another direction. "There is a ship North by Northwest."

"That must be the ship," Bartholomew said to no one in particular. "Helmsman, move us one point west."

"How can you be sure that's the ship we're after?" Hank asked.

Roberts smiled. "Just a feeling."

"Another one of your feelings. Of course."

"You don't doubt me?"

Hank shook his head. "Just as a cat never falls on its back, you almost possess a sense for which ship has the best haul. Six months and twenty ships later, your feeling has been there more often than not. I don't know where you get it, if it's luck or some gift from God, but you have it." He turned his attention to one of the sails.

"Ugh, they got the jib rigging all mucked again. We're losing speed." He left to yell at the crewmates working the sails, leaving Roberts alone.

A gift from God? Not likely.

After the jib was freed, and the sails in a more optimal position, the *Royal Rover* started catching up to the *Fortune*. The *Fortune* was well ahead of them, however, and quickly caught up to the enemy ship.

Roberts took out a spyglass to observe the *Fortune*. "What are they doing?"

"What's wrong?" Hank asked after coming back from the sails.

"*Fortune* isn't slowing down for us to catch up. I think they intend to attack."

"Surely you jest?" Roberts handed Hank his spyglass. He peered through the spyglass to the ships in the distance. "Damn," he cursed, then he gave the spyglass back. "Didn't you say you left Walter in charge of *Fortune*?" he asked.

"Yes, and I gave him explicit instructions not to attack until both ships were close. I was hoping to force them to surrender without loss of life."

"Not today, it seems."

"He must have lost control of the ship to the crew. His men are more bloodthirsty than they let on in front of me. I should have left you in charge of *Fortune*." Roberts clenched his fist.

"No use beating yourself up about it. If we can catch up the enemy may still surrender when they realise it's two against one."

Roberts nodded and commanded the men to work harder to improve the speed of the ship. When *Fortune* was close to the other ship—the *Decadence*, he hoped—*Fortune* released the black sail denoting it being a pirate vessel.

"Drop the black!" he yelled to the crewmate in the crow's nest.

The man climbed up a few feet of rigging rope to the very peak of the main mast and unravelled a rope holding in place a small black sail. When the crewmate finished untying the rope the sail revealed itself.

The black sail, newly chosen by Roberts since his taking command of the *Royal Rover*, pictured a crude representation of himself on the left, and the skeleton of death on the right. The two were holding onto an hourglass in the middle of the flag. The flag was mirrored on the main mast of *Fortune* as well.

Fortune was closing in on the firing range of the *Decadence*. Roberts peered through his spyglass at the two ships. He was able to see them clearly, and the *Royal Rover* would catch up within twenty minutes at their speed.

Perhaps Decadence will see our black flag as well and surrender without a fight.

The sound of cannons indicated the battle had begun. Roberts focussed his spyglass on the *Decadence* and he could see billowing smoke from its side.

So much for that.

Fortune and *Decadence* fired back and forth at each other. The larger *Decadence* was firing more cannons, but the *Fortune* was able to hold its own. *Decadence* stayed in one spot while firing, whereas *Fortune* moved away and towards the enemy ship in tune with the cannon fire. *Fortune* was able to hit *Decadence* more often than the opposite.

The sounds of the cannons thundered over the ocean and boomed in Roberts' ears. Because of the *Royal Rover*'s distance there was a slight delay between cannon fire and the sound reaching him.

As they advanced, the smell of smoke overtaking the sea air became ever more apparent. To Roberts that smell was all too familiar, and caused a stir in him he was loath to say he enjoyed. Battle came naturally to one of his size and stature, and as much as he wanted to avoid the activity, when he was in the thick of it he couldn't help but enjoy it on some level.

We're almost within firing range now, yet they haven't stopped. He turned to Hank. "Tell the men to fire a few warning shots at the enemy."

"We're too far away for it to be a credible threat, Captain."

"I understand, but *Decadence* has taken several hits and they know we're getting closer. Perhaps if we remind them of our presence they'll throw down their arms."

"Right," Hank replied.

Hank told the gunners above deck the plan, then went below deck to tell the rest not to open fire when the cannons fired from above. Once everything was ready, he gave the order to fire.

Three shots were fired in succession which landed in the water about a hundred feet from the starboard stern of *Decadence*. Plumes of water shot up from where the cannonballs fell.

Roberts watched the other ship through his spyglass. He could see the crew furiously running around the deck yelling orders, grabbing weapons and preparing for battle on the starboard side. He was able to find the captain, and recognized him as the man he'd met in the tavern. At the angle *Royal Rover* was he wasn't able to see the name of the ship, but now he knew it was the right one.

He noticed the captain and another older man in a heated argument. The captain pointed to the *Fortune* and the *Royal Rover* in between a flinch when a cannonball hit his ship. The other man seemed to be trying to reason with the captain. After a moment, the captain rubbed his face and turned around to his crew. They slowly stopped their frantic activity, and the cannon fire ceased. The man who was arguing with the captain handed him something Roberts couldn't see and then squeezed his shoulder. The captain nodded and then waved a white flag above his head towards the *Fortune* on the port side, and then did the same on the starboard side.

Yes. Now Fortune just needs to cease fire. Roberts turned his attention to the *Fortune*. He wasn't able to see the men aboard very well, but he could see the activity on deck easing, and the cannons eventually stopped firing at *Decadence*.

"Helmsman," Roberts called. "Bring us next to the enemy ship." The helmsman turned the wheel of the ship, pulling them in tighter to be in line with *Decadence*. "Men, prepare to board. Just because the enemy has surrendered doesn't mean we let our guard down."

Over a tense twenty or so minutes, the three ships furled sails and slowed down in tandem. Once their speed was sufficiently reduced, *Fortune* and the *Royal Rover* pulled up next to *Decadence*, tied the two ships together with grappling hooks, and then laid down gangplanks.

The crews of *Royal Rover* and *Fortune* boarded *Decadence* with weapons drawn. Roberts pulled out his sword and approached the gangplank.

"Hold for a moment, Captain," Hank said. Roberts turned and walked over to him. "What will we do about Walter?"

Roberts glanced over across the *Decadence* to the *Fortune*, and noticed Walter wringing his hands. "We can deal with him later. For now, we need to give the impression of unity and strength. Any weakness could be exploited."

Hank nodded and pulled out his own sword. Together, he and Roberts crossed the gangplank to the *Decadence*. The crew was gathered in the centre of the ship and dozens of guns and swords were pointed at them to keep them stationary.

Roberts took a good look at the crew in front of him. The majority of the men were very young, and appeared to be inexperienced. Their hands were not yet calloused enough to be considered seaworthy. He approached one of the young men to examine his hand, and, sure enough, there were jagged, bloody cuts characteristic of rough rigging rope digging into the palm.

No wonder the battle was easy. Two-thirds of the crew are greenhorns. He eyed the gathered men and eventually found the captain. The man he had been having an argument with was sitting next to him, whispering in his ear. The captain was young as well, and the other man looked to be the oldest and most experienced of the bunch. *Perhaps the captain is also new to this.*

He rose to his feet and walked over to the captain. When he approached, the captain recognized him.

"You," the young man said, rapidly standing up.

Some of Roberts' crew stepped forward, weapons drawn. He held his hand up and they stepped back. "Yes, me."

"My father will hear of this when I return home, and you will hang for this."

Roberts chuckled. "Ah, so that's how it is. Your father's influence is what gained you this contract for goods, not any hard effort on your part. It explains the young men in your crew, and this old man being your mentor." He pointed to the man still sitting and the enemy crew around him. "You have to pay more for more experienced sailors, which would have meant less for you in the end." He raised his sword and place it under the chin of the young captain. The captain backed up a few short steps. "Or possibly more in this case," he chuckled. "Tell me, what makes you think you'll be returning to your father?" The captain visibly gulped as he stared at the blade on his chin. Roberts turned to his crew. "Search the ship and take everything of value you can find. This vessel's goods are now ours."

"Have fun while you can," the young captain said, his neck extended to avoid the point of the sword. "You'll be swinging from the gallows soon enough, pirate."

"So much the better," Roberts replied. "I used to be a sailor like the men in your employ, making low wages for hard labour while others gained the profit. Now, I have liberty and power, I take from people who have more than enough to spare, and spend it on the pleasures in life alongside my crew who do the same. If I die from this life, then so be it. My motto shall be to take as much as I can from people like you, and live a short and merry life."

3. EYE OF THE BEHOLDER

Roberts was on the deck of the *Fortune*, standing above two dead bodies amongst the wreckage from the previous fight. Though the inexperience of the *Decadence* crew helped, *Fortune* had not been able to escape unscathed.

He knelt down next to the bodies. "Do we know who brought them aboard?" he asked Hank, who was standing behind him.

"No, but I imagine we'll find out soon enough."

"Though these women had a less than desirable profession, they were still innocents. They shouldn't have been involved in this fight, nor paid this price. First young boys dying from powder accidents, and now this." Roberts shook his head. *I thought I was free of innocents dying under my care.*

The dead women were prostitutes by their dress and had been brought aboard before setting sail.

"Could you run by a vote with the commanders on punishing those who brought these women aboard?"

"What about Walter?"

"No vote is necessary, as, if I recall correctly, decisions relating strictly to battle fall under my jurisdiction as captain. It stands to reason that the punishment for not following orders in battle should be my job as well."

Hank nodded. "I'll run it by the other commanders just in case, but you have my support. We wouldn't have any casualties if Walter followed orders." Roberts smiled and nodded before Hank left to talk with the commanders.

"Oh, Hank, wait a moment," he yelled before Hank was half-way up the ladder. Hank turned around. "We should return to the island to sell our stock."

"Isn't that dangerous given that the *Decadence* is from there?"

"We cut their sails which should slow them enough. We'll have enough time to sell the goods, and if not we can leave on the morrow. Another reason I'd like to go back is so I can return these women to their families. They deserve that much, at least."

Hank wore a solemn smile before he nodded and returned to his task.

Roberts picked up one of the women in his arms and took her

to the surgeon's room at the stern of the *Fortune*. After placing the first woman on a table, he brought the other woman in.

He took a wet cloth and cleaned their wounds as best he could. After the blood was clear he wrapped the wounds on their arms and legs, and stitched the clothes so the wounds weren't visible. After the women were as presentable as he could make them, he put a few drops of scented oil on them to stave off the smell of gunpowder and decay, then wrapped them in a loose cloth.

He left the surgeon's room and returned to the top deck of the *Fortune*. He glanced around at the crew busily taking stock and moving the sails around to give them more speed. His eyes eventually settled on the man he wanted to talk with—Walter Kennedy. He pointed at Walter and beckoned him over.

After a moment of hesitation Walter shuffled over to Roberts. "Yes, Captain?" he said meekly.

"Come with me to the surgeon's room," Roberts commanded, trying to restrain his anger from bursting. "We need to discuss something in private."

He didn't wait for Walter to respond and went down the ladder to the lower deck, expecting him to follow. He entered the surgeon's room and when Walter joined him, he closed the door.

Walter went to the other side of the table. Roberts lifted the cloth off the women and gestured to them.

"What do you see?" he asked.

"Prostitutes," Walter replied.

"Innocents." He stared at Walter, who seemed to physically cower at his gaze.

"Well, whut do ye want me to do 'bout it? They're dead."

"It's not about what I want you to do. It's about what you should have done. They should not have been brought aboard, and if you followed orders and not attacked the ship before we were close this wouldn't have happened. Whoever brought these women aboard will be punished, but ultimately you are responsible."

Walter was silent for a moment before he objected. "Well, I cannot help it if tha men disobey me. If yer lookin' fer someone ta blame, Ethan was the one who brought them aboard and instigated the fight against that ship. He's the one ye ought to be yellin' at."

"I will investigate your claims, and if Ethan was the one who brought these women aboard, then he will be punished accordingly, but I say again you are still responsible for the men attacking

Blackbeard's Ship

Decadence. You say you want to be a captain, yet when given a chance to command you can't keep your men under control." He sighed. "You're only getting half shares of today's haul, and you'll no longer be in command of *Fortune.* You'll be back on *Royal Rover* until you're cleared for command again." Walter opened his mouth to object. "No," Roberts said, holding his hand up. "You had your chance. Now leave me."

Walter's mouth was a line, but his jaw clenched as he gritted his teeth in anger. He left the surgeon's room in a huff.

Later in the day, Hank finished his investigation and found several people who corroborated Walter's story involving the women who died. Ethan was the one who'd brought them aboard from a brothel on the island. The commanders also gave permission for Roberts to mete out punishment to him.

Roberts called him to the surgeon's room where the women still lay. When the two entered, he closed the door behind him. Ethan stood on one side of the table with his arms folded.

"Whut do ye want?"

Roberts pulled back the cloth covering the faces of the women. Ethan's face didn't change, but when he glanced at the women he visibly tensed.

"Do you have anything to say about these women?"

Ethan stopped glancing at the women's faces long enough to stare daggers at Roberts. "Nothin' in particular."

Roberts sighed and pinched the bridge of his nose. "Then you leave me no choice but to leave you at half shares for this haul."

"To hell with this."

"You'll return to full shares after our next raid."

Ethan gripped the table tightly while leaning forward. "Whut for? Some bitch whores died? Whut of it? No one cares if they died."

Roberts' rage burned inside him. "God cares for all his children. These women died through no fault of their own. They have families just like us, and those women at the brothel will mourn for them. The fact you cannot see that explains exactly why you brought them aboard: You didn't care if they died. If this happens again, trust me when I say I will not care if you die."

"Is that a threat?"

"Take it however you want."

"Tch." Ethan let go of the table and stormed out of the room.

Roberts leaned on the table and stared at the faces of the dead women he didn't even know the names of. *Why did I bring up God now of all times?*

As Roberts and Hank strode down the street, passersby stared at them. It was midday and the streets were crowded, but the men and women parted for the pair. Confused whispers met his ears as he passed, but he paid them no heed.

The two each carried in their hands the body of a young woman wrapped in cloth—the two women who'd died aboard the *Fortune*. They were taking them back to the brothel they belonged to.

Upon arriving at the brothel and entering the establishment, they were greeted with even more confused looks. Roberts scanned the crowd of women and men in the run-down house. Men of all stations were patrons and women of all ages were catering to them in the lower floor which functioned as a tavern of sorts. Stairs led to an upper floor with rooms for privacy.

"I need to speak with the madam," he said for all to hear.

An older woman strode down from the upper floor and over to them. Her brow was cocked slightly as she glanced at the bodies they were carrying. "Yes?"

"We need to speak in private, miss."

The madam gazed at the bodies once more. "Yes, of course. Follow me."

The madam turned around and went up the stairs. Roberts and Hank followed. She entered the first room at the top of the stairs and held open the door for the two men. After they were in the room, she closed the door.

"I can imagine what this is about. Show me their faces, please."

Roberts moved to a nearby bed and laid the woman on it. Hank did the same. They removed the cloth off the women's faces and stepped back to allow the madam some room.

She approached the bed with a pained expression on her face. She touched one woman's cheek and examined them.

"Stupid girls," she whispered. "How did they die?"

"They were smuggled aboard my ship. There was a battle and they died when they were hit by wood splinters."

"I told them never to set sail on a ship, but they never listen to me." The madam took a cloth out of her pocket and wiped the hair away from the women's faces.

"Do they have any family?" Hank asked.

"They're sisters, but their parents died long ago. We were their family."

Roberts glanced at Hank, then at the madam. "Then this right-

751

ly belongs to you and the other women." He reached into his pocket and pulled out some gold coins.

"What is this?" the madam asked.

"They shouldn't have been on our ship, and as captain I am to blame. This was for their families, and as you are their family you deserve this. I know this doesn't help with the loss, but I want you and your girls to have it."

The madam pocketed the gold. "Thank you, sir. I will make sure the rest of the girls see this." She opened the door for them to leave. As they left, the madam spoke with one of the girls outside the room. "Jean, fetch Pastor Sean and tell the girls not busy with clients to come up here."

Roberts stopped in his tracks. *A pastor?* "Excuse me? Why are you calling a pastor?"

"Women of our nature can still have faith. Luckily, there is one pastor in this city who practices what he preaches and prays for all sinners."

A pastor praying for harlots? I've never seen such a thing. Roberts turned to Hank. "You go on ahead, make sure the goods are sold and the ship prepped to leave." Hank nodded and exited the brothel. "Would it be alright if I stayed?" Roberts asked.

"Why? If you want some time with the girls you'll need to pay more."

"No, it's not that. I wish to speak with this pastor afterwards."

The madam nodded. Women from the brothel filtered into the room steadily. All were shocked when they saw the women who'd died, and before long many of them were shedding tears. After a time, the pastor entered and was greeted by the women.

"What are all the tears for, dearies? You missed me that much, have ye?" he asked with a smile. He was an older man with a Scottish accent which had softened from age. His frame was average, and his hair was beginning to grey. He had an air of fatherly authority, unlike the regal attitude Roberts was familiar with in other pastors.

"Father Sean," one of the women called through her tears.

The women parted to allow the pastor to see. Pastor Sean glanced at the bed, and then walked over to it. After a moment of silence, he turned around and smiled to the group.

"It appears the sisters are having a right old nap now, aren't they?"

One of the women gave him a confused look. "But, Father, they're dead."

"Not so, my child. They are merely sleeping, but not the same kind of sleep you or I have each night. Though, your sleep might also be a bit different than mine." The women laughed. "There, now that's better. You see, in this kind of sleep only the Lord can awaken them. Don't weep because your sisters are sleeping right now. Be happy that they will soon be with the Lord, at His table."

Roberts recalled a similar conversation he'd had with a man aboard *Royal Rover*. A crewmate had died shortly after he joined, and Roberts told a friend of the deceased the same thing Father Sean did.

"But what about their sins? They died before they could tell you."

Father Sean's smile turned into a frown, but not an angry one. "That is true. Well, what can we do about that?" The pastor smiled. "Can anyone tell me?"

"We can pray for them?"

"Correct, dearie. So let's all join hands and pray for Hannah and Suzan."

Father Sean and the women of the brothel all joined hands and prayed for the women who died. Roberts didn't join in holding hands, but he couldn't help reciting the Lord's Prayer. After finishing the prayer, Father Sean had his own words specifically to ask forgiveness of Hannah's and Suzan's sins.

After the prayer was finished, the pastor continued to console the women and bless them. He was kind and compassionate, just like a fatherly figure.

After the pastor was finished talking with the women of the brothel, Roberts approached him. "Father, could I speak with you?"

The pastor took a step back as he looked him up and down. "Oh my, the Lord certainly blessed ye, son. You would be right at home in Scotland. Come, walk with me and we can talk."

He and the pastor left the brothel and walked in the street together. As they passed the citizens, many greeted the pastor with smiles and called his name. Father Sean returned their smiles and greetings in kind.

"So, what is it that troubles you?"

"Well, before that I wanted to say I've never seen a pastor praying for prostitutes before. Why do you preach to them?"

The pastor laughed. "Why would I preach to those without sin?" Roberts was taken aback by the implication. He never thought of it that way before.

"We are all with sin, and equal in the eyes of God. We all also have an equal chance for repentance and a change of lifestyle. Just as Jesus did, I preach in the hopes that sinners will change."

He and the pastor reached a small building with cross-shaped windows on the front. The building was simple and plain with no steeple as found on many other churches. The church had no door and was open for all to enter as they pleased.

"Come inside and we can talk in private."

He followed the pastor into the church. Inside there were rows of pews and at the front a stand for the pastor to preach from. On the wall at the back was a large window in the shape of a cross to allow light to enter.

The pastor went to the front and sat down in one of the pews. Roberts joined him. "So, what is troubling you, my son?"

He hesitated, trying to find the right words to explain what he wanted to say. "What does the Bible say about slavery?"

The pastor scratched his chin. "In the Old Testament it instructs on how slaves should obey their masters, and how they should be treated. In the New Testament, it reinforces slavery. In the book of Luke, Jesus made a parable out of a slave disobeying and being punished. Does this answer your question? I can't help but feel there is more to this than simple slavery."

Roberts glanced around. "What if a slave is mistreated? I previously worked on a slave ship, and many died because of neglect. And beyond that, men are profiting from these deaths."

The pastor nodded. "Ah, I see. You cared for the slaves, did you?" Roberts nodded. "Well, the Bible does say if a slave dies in the care of the slave owner then they are to be punished. I am loath to admit it, but I feel the way slaves are treated nowadays is far and away from how Moses or Jesus thought they should be treated." The pastor shook his head. "As for profiting from this business, the Bible clearly says the desire of money is the root of all evil. If these men are profiting by way of sin, then God does not approve. That you are not working on a slave ship now is commendable."

"But how can God allow these people to continue to profit? How can God allow evil to continue?"

The pastor laughed as if Roberts was a child. "God gave us life and free will to choose what we wish to do. God is allowing all of us the chance to find him naturally. Think of this Earth as His test. At the end of your life, you will be judged for your actions. It is certainly unfortunate that many suffer at the hands of evil men, but this is not God's doing. Only man is to blame."

Roberts balled his fist. "So what can we do when we see these evil men committing sin? Talking to them—preaching to them—

does nothing. I cannot stand by while they kill the innocent. The women you prayed for today died at the hands of men like that."

"I can understand your frustration, my son, but the path of the righteous is one free from vengeance. Vengeance is for the Lord, not for man."

"What about when God sent the Israelites to war against the Midianites? They were sent by God to kill them because of the sins they committed."

The pastor hesitated. "Yes, that is true. God, through Moses, commanded the Midianites be put to death. That was a war, however, not a premeditated murder."

"So, if I am a soldier then killing is alright?"

The pastor raised his brow. "Are you a soldier now?"

Roberts scratched the back of his neck. "In a sense."

"No man is righteous as all men sin, and no war is good, but if war can prevent further evil then it is just to participate. That was why God commanded the Israelites to wage war against the Midianites. You must think deeply on your enemy and see if they truly are against God and his teachings. Only then will you know if your war is just."

Roberts folded his arms in thought. *As a pirate, do these rules still apply? If we free mistreated slaves and steal ill-gotten gains from the rich, is it actually acting out God's will?* Roberts thought of his departed friend from whom he'd borrowed his name. *Were you right all along, Bartholomew? Is being a pirate like Davis truly acting out justice?*

"Thank you, Father Sean, you've given me a lot to think about." Roberts rose to his feet and the pastor joined him. "I think now I need to buy another Bible."

He turned to leave, but the pastor stopped him. Father Sean reached into his robes and pulled out a small Bible. It was similar to the one he used to own: leather-bound, worn from use but well kept. Father Sean handed him the Bible.

"Take this one."

His mouth went agape. For a moment he couldn't think of the words to say. "I can't, this looks to be something precious to you."

Father Sean nodded. "It has served me well, but I feel you might need it more than I. There are always more Bibles I can use."

"Thank you, Father Sean. For everything."

"You are welcome, my son. I hope you find the answers you are seeking, and may God bless your endeavours."

Roberts smiled. "I hope he does as well."

He left the church and made his way back to the docks. As he walked, he leisurely thumbed through the new Bible in his hands. Its pages were worn, but it was clearly loved and cared for. None of the pages were ripped or torn despite the edges being curled and the ink slightly faded. It gave a faint smell of mint, and he found a mint leaf hidden on one of the pages, possibly functioning as a bookmark.

He stopped in his tracks to inspect the last pages Father Sean had been reading. He was trying to guess what the Father was reading when he found something which spoke to his current state of mind.

'The lions do lack and suffer hunger, but they which seek the Lord, shall want nothing that is good.' Roberts smiled. *Have you been providing for me this whole time?*

"Roberts, there you are."

He looked up to see Hank running over to him with a concerned look on his face. "What's wrong, Hank?"

"I went back to the brothel and you were gone, so I've been searching for you. I got wind you've been outed. We need to leave, now."

"Right." He took one last look at the Bible and put it in his back pocket. It felt snug, but comfortable, natural. "Let's move on to a new adventure," he said with a smile.

Hank smiled and the two ran through the streets back to their ships.

4. GOD PROVIDES

Walter followed Roberts and Hank as they carried the bodies of the dead prostitutes to the brothel. They were unconcerned with what was happening around them, so Walter didn't need to hide. The crowd parted for Roberts, as they often did. His large stature made it difficult for others to walk beside him, and he cast a large shadow.

Bastard thinks God's on his side. Soon he'll be out of the picture and I'll be captain. It won't be long now with Ethan on my side. A few more pushes ought to do, just have to find an opportunity…

When Roberts and Hank entered the brothel, Walter waited on the other side of the street. He watched the brothel entrance to see where they would go next. *They'll probably head to some tavern after this, and then I'll get them.*

After five minutes a prostitute left the brothel and headed further into town. Another five minutes passed and Hank exited the brothel alone and began walking towards the dock. Walter turned his face away in an attempt to avoid being seen.

"Walter," a voice called.

Walter turned and noticed Hank calling. *Damn.* "Hello, Mr. Abbot."

"What are you doing here?"

Walter's face felt hot. "Umm." He glanced at the brothel. "I thought I should pay my respects."

Hank nodded. "Good, good. The captain's in there now. Make sure he's not too long, we don't know how long we have until we need to leave."

"Right, I'll keep that in mind."

Hank left Walter and went down the street back to the dock and the ships.

Now must be my chance. Roberts will probably be in there a while. I need to find an officer of the law.

Walter ran off to the centre of the town, rushing past the men and women in the streets and dodging the horses and merchants carts. He searched the signs on the buildings for the sheriff's office or a constable roaming the streets, something he'd never thought he would be doing.

After ten minutes of searching, he was sweating and breathing heavily. He reached a square and took a moment to stop running and search the crowd. The square was bustling with activity. People were talking and walking, several orators were littered about on small platforms speaking about news and politics, and children were running and playing around.

He eventually saw a man in a uniform walking around and being avoided by the citizens. He couldn't be sure, but he felt this was who he was looking for. He ran over and stopped short a few feet in front of the man.

"Sir, are you a constable? I know someone who needs to be arrested."

The man approached him, his eyes more alert than before. "What crime did you see committed, sir?"

He took a moment to catch his breath again. "There is a pirate, Bartholomew Roberts, at a brothel down the street. The brothel is called Stranger's Delight, I believe."

"I've never heard of this man, Bartholomew Roberts. How do you know him to be a pirate?"

Shit! What can I say that's believable? "I was uhh… on a ship he attacked. He released us, but took all our goods."

The constable rested his hand on his chin. "Hmm." He scratched his chin for a moment as he stared at Walter, scepticism in his eyes.

Great, I get the one smart lawman.

"I'll question him about your claims. Show me the way to the brothel."

He let out the breath he was holding. "Follow me." He turned around and jogged back to the brothel with the constable following behind him.

At the brothel, he and the constable entered and scanned the room. He couldn't see Roberts anywhere. His gaze followed one of the women as they left a room upstairs with an open door. The woman had tears in her eyes as she left the brothel.

He must be up there with the dead whores.

He ran up the stairs and peered into the room. There were about ten women in the room crowded around a bed. They were talking amongst themselves and some were just staring at the bed. He couldn't see Roberts anywhere in the room.

"Oi, girl," Walter whispered to the closest woman. The woman turned around. "Where did that tall man go?"

The woman glanced around as she wiped tears from her eyes. The tears created streaks down her face through the dirt and grime. "I'm not sure. He was here a few moments ago."

"Does anyone know where the tall man who was here went?"

The women in the room turned around, then glanced about the room. After a moment they all shook their heads.

Damn! They must have been too preoccupied with those dead bitches to no-

tice him leaving. He left the room and the constable was waiting for him. "He's gone. No one seems ta know where he went."

The constable's mouth was a line. "Alright, you're coming with me so I can get more information on this Bartholomew Roberts. Something doesn't feel right about your story."

The constable reached out to grab Walter by the arm. He jumped back. The constable's eyes widened, then narrowed as he glanced from his hand to him.

The constable lunged at Walter. He hopped over a railing and down to the first floor. The constable peered over the edge of the railing. Walter fell on the wooden floor of the brothel and was scrambling to his feet.

"Stop! Stop, I say!" the constable yelled as he turned around and rushed to the stairs.

Walter was already on his feet when the constable reached the stairs, and ran towards the exit. The constable was halfway down the stairs. Walter rushed into the streets of the city, glancing this way and that, trying to determine the best way to run.

"Get back here!"

He ran to his right, towards the harbour. The constable was hot on his heels. The Irishman weaved through the crowds of people in his way. He glanced over his shoulder. Luckily, the constable was having as much difficulty getting past the crowd as he was.

He sprinted down side streets, behind buildings, and turned at every corner. He could hear the constable yelling behind him in pursuit.

Sweat poured down his face and he felt winded, but he kept running. His legs burned and his arms were getting tired, but he kept running.

Eventually, the sound of the constable faded until he couldn't hear him any longer. He was a few blocks from the dock when he stopped running.

Walter fell to the ground in a side street and caught his breath. He took out a kerchief and wiped his damp brow and forehead. After a few moments of rest, he approached the edge of the side street and glanced up and down the main street. He couldn't see the constable, nor any others he might have recruited, in the street. He let out a large sigh and headed back to the docks.

When he reached the *Fortune*, Ethan and his friends rose to their feet and met with him. They crowded around him, looks of anticipation in their eyes.

Ethan glanced this way and that. His eye next to the tattoo twitched, and he couldn't keep still. "So, did ye do it?"

Walter looked around and noticed several crewmen talking and doing busywork. "We should talk below deck."

Ethan nodded, and the group went down to the crew cabin. When they were in their usual spot, after removing some other crewmates, Walter explained in a hushed tone what had happened on his mission.

Ethan slammed his fist against the starboard planks. "Bollocks, Walter. Ye screwed us over."

Walter raised his hands. "We can still salvage this. We just need ta go ahead with the other plan."

"It's gonna be hard to convince everyone you deserve ta be captain when ye can't even get a simple job done."

"I can navigate, and unlike Roberts I won't take away yer shares when ye want ta have a little fun onboard the ship. Drinking, prostitutes, tell them they can have it all and more when I'm captain."

Ethan stared at Walter as he bobbed his foot up and down. He had a scowl on his face, which simply wouldn't change. Eventually he let out a "Tch," before looking off to the side. "I suppose that'll do. We just need ta make sure our men are on the *Royal Rover* before this all goes down." He stared at the other men in the group. "You can handle that, right?" The other men nodded. "Alright, let's make you captain then, Walter." He stood up and put out his hand. Walter rose to his feet and shook his hand. Ethan pulled Walter in close and whispered to him, "Don't screw this up, or ye'll be swimming with Davey Jones. Ye hear?"

Walter nodded, but when Ethan and the others weren't looking he let out a large sigh. *What am I getting myself into?*

Roberts, Hank, Walter, and the other commanders sat in the mess hall at a large table discussing recent and future events. The *Royal Rover* and *Fortune* had both escaped before the authorities could find them, and luckily managed to sell some of the cargo in the short time they were docked.

"Alright, we're all in agreement about the division of shares?" Hank asked. The commanders nodded. "On to other business then. Roberts?"

Roberts nodded. "There's been a lot of shuffling around of the crew recently from the *Fortune* to *Royal Rover*. Normally this wouldn't be an issue, as we're all the same crew and it doesn't matter who works on what ship, but it's more than usual. Anyone have any idea what it might be about?" He looked at the commanders, but they all shook their heads. "No one mentioning grievances with crewmates aboard the *Fortune*? No?" He eyed Hank, but his number two shrugged his shoulders. "Walter, I know it's a sore spot, but do you think it could have anything to do with your move back to *Royal*

Rover?"

Walter's face was spotted with sweat. "Possibly. Uhh... Ethan also moved over to *Royal Rover* again, and his troupe could have been a part of that move. From there it could trickle down to other crewmates who're friends with Ethan's friends."

Roberts nodded. "Understandable. Unfortunately, this has left *Fortune* understaffed. When we next reach dock we need to send some crewmates over to *Fortune*." He turned to Hank. "Hank, would you be willing to handle that?" Hank nodded. "Alright, let's put it to a vote."

"Ah!" Walter exclaimed. All eyes turned to him. "I can do that if you want."

Roberts raised his brow. "Why take on extra work? We've been on a ship together for a long time now, and let's face it: you'd rather be in your hammock than not." He smiled, and the other commanders chuckled.

Walter smiled slightly. "Yes, well, I feel the need to prove myself after my mistake on the *Fortune*. If you'll allow me, I'd like to have the opportunity."

Roberts was impressed. "Alright, all those in favour." The commanders replied with "Aye." "Then it's settled. You'll handle dividing the crew at the next harbour." Walter smiled. "Now, speaking of the next harbour, where should we head to next?"

The Commanders discussed options for travel, but none had any solid ideas on where to acquire their next haul.

"Well, there is one option," Hank offered after a bit of deliberation. "We could head West, across the Atlantic."

"To what end?" Roberts asked.

"I've heard the Caribbean is mostly lawless and has many pirate havens. We could head there and see where it takes us."

Roberts rubbed his chin. "Having some stomping grounds would help against situations such as the one we were just in, but how is our food supply? Will we be able to make it?"

"I believe we have enough to travel to Brazil. We can make a stop there, stock up, travel the coast to see if we can find any ships to raid, then head on to greener pastures."

Roberts nodded. "Anyone else have other ideas?"

The other commanders didn't suggest anything, save Walter. "I think we should head north," he offered. "The Irish coast is teeming with small trading villages. We could make one of 'em a base and attack tha merchant ships which arrive. Once we're finished, England and Wales are a hop and a skip away."

"Sounds promising, but dangerous. The British Navy would always be hot on our heels if we stay there. Let's put it to a vote. All those in favour of Walter's plan?" Four commanders and Walter raised their hands. "All those in favour of Hank's plan?" Hank, Roberts, and five other Commanders raised their hands. "Alright, Hank wins the majority vote. We'll be heading to Brazil then."

With the course set, the *Royal Rover* and *Fortune* headed to Brazil. Along the way, when the wind was not in their favour and there was a lull of activity, Walter divided the crew and put men from the *Fortune* over to the *Royal Rover* or vice versa. He seemed overly enthusiastic about the activity, which Roberts found an improvement, given his recent poor attitude.

A week out from landing in Brazil the *Royal Rover* and *Fortune* were hit by a storm and blown off course. Luckily no one was injured through the ordeal, but they landed further south of Brazil than they'd anticipated.

The ships ended up near Ilhéus, so they decided to head there first to repair and sell cargo, and seek out prospects. What they found, however, was disappointing.

The harbour and land of Ilhéus was a venerable paradise. Covered in palms, greenery, and sandy beaches, pristine water and open skies, it was quite different from the eastern shores the crew was used to.

The disappointment was the size and state of the harbour. It was a small harbour with barely any room for large merchant ships. The harbour was littered with small sloops and smaller fishing boats, but nothing worth their time as far as Roberts was concerned.

After docking, Roberts left the *Royal Rover* to talk with the local harbourmaster and see if he could glean any information. He could see a bounty of people staring and pointing at the large ship in port.

Hank joined him and the two walked up the dock to land. They were met by a tanned man who waved to them. Roberts approached and put his hand out to shake. The man took his hand and shook it.

"Do you speak English?"

"Yessir, I am slow, but I speak for you."

Roberts nodded and set his hands on his hips, glancing around at the locals still enamoured by the *Royal Rover*. The smell of fragrant meats and coconut met his nose on the back of a wave of sea air.

"The locals seem surprised to see us."

The harbourmaster chuckled. "Yessir, big ships not come here much."

Roberts glanced at the harbour's bevy of fishing ships. "I can see that." He shielded himself from the hot sun. "We were hit by a storm and had no choice but to land here. Our ship was damaged slightly and we have cargo to sell. We were hoping you would be able to accommodate us."

The local ran his fingers through his hair. "We can fix ship, but cargo…" The man gave a so-so gesture, rocking his palm side to side. "Better to sail north to Baía de Todos os Santos. Big port, many ships."

Roberts nodded with a smile. "Is there any anchorage?" The man seemed confused. "Charge for docking?"

The man nodded. "Ah, five real."

"Do you have any reals, Hank?" he asked.

"I believe so." Hank pulled out a coin purse and rummaged through it, eventually finding five reals he could give to the man.

"Thank you," Roberts said to the local, and then he turned around and returned to the ship.

"You seem to be a in a good mood despite not having any ships to raid."

Roberts laughed and stopped walking. "Well, let's just say I'm confident we'll find something."

"Another one of your hunches?"

"Before we decided where to sail next, I prayed to God for an answer to a question I had recently."

Hank raised his brow. "I haven't heard you talk about God in some time, and from what I recall when you first joined us you used to carry a Bible around with you. You haven't had that since... then."

Roberts nodded. "Yes, we lost too many that night."

"Aye, too many, too much, and some more than others." Hank gripped Roberts' shoulder with a knowing look in his eyes. "I never asked because it seemed like a private matter, but I'm curious: what's changed? Something that pastor said?"

Roberts scratched his chin. "You know, I lost my way because of all the horrible acts I saw committed by so-called men of faith. I thought that if God was with them then I didn't want to be with God." Hank nodded. "The pastor made me see that all men are sinners, but those who profit from evil will never win. I prayed for Him to show me whether what we are doing is just, or if we too are doing evil. I believe if God considers our cause to be just, then He will provide for us."

Hank smiled. "Well, it is certainly odd a pirate can say he is doing God's work, but I hope you find your answer soon." The two walked back to the ship, and when they approached, Hank let out a "Hmm."

Roberts smirked. "What?"

"I was thinking maybe instead of Bartholomew the Bear you should be called the Pirate Priest." He chuckled.

Robert laughed with his friend. "It does kind of roll off the tongue. I like it."

They boarded the ship and told the crew about where they were. It was decided they would repair the ships, perform a boot-topping to clean the barnacles off the ship above the water line, replenish supplies, and then head north to Baía de Todos os Santos.

Roberts ordered the whole crew to work so they could leave as quickly as possible, and in a few days they were ready to leave Ilhéus. They travelled along the coast of Brazil, soaking in the sun and gazing at the tropical locales. The relaxing time after the storm helped improve morale.

When the crew reached Baía de Todos os Santos, Roberts' first thought harkened back to the passage he saw in the Bible he received from Father Sean. *They which seek the Lord, shall want nothing that is good.*

In the harbour of Baía de Todos os Santos were at least a hundred ships of all types and sizes. Large merchant vessels were entering and exiting the claw-shaped bay, but the sight that caught Roberts' and the crew's attention the most were forty-two ships flying the flag or coat of arms of Portugal. The ships ranged from sloops-of-war to small frigates like *Royal Rover*. Most carried cannons, and all of them spread out in the harbour either docked or anchored in the water.

Hank glanced at Roberts. "God provides," he commented.

Roberts chuckled. *God provides.*

5. THE PIRATE PRIEST

Roberts entered the third tavern in his search for someone associated with the Portuguese ships in the harbour. The first two times he had no luck, and he was beginning to run out of steam. Asking everyone who seemed receptive the same questions over and over, and burning through money to purchase drinks for said people, was wearing on his mind and coin purse.

He approached the tavern bar and sat down on a stool. "Ale, please. Dark."

The woman working the bar nodded, and then filled a mug with dark ale from a cask behind her. She handed the mug to him and took his payment. He took the ale and turned around in his seat while he took a swig. After a foamy head, the dark ale went down smooth. It tasted of roasted nuts, a hint of coffee, and dark chocolate like what he ate in Príncipe. It reminded him of his departed friend Bartholomew, and of when they'd tried the roasted cocoa in Príncipe. Roberts would never forget that fond memory for as long as his mind allowed him to.

The tavern he found himself in this time was very open with a second-floor indoor balcony and many tables. In the corner of the room, away from the balcony, was an open space for dancing and a fiddler playing a merry tune for all to hear. It was certainly more upbeat than the other taverns he'd visited, and his mood quickly shifted as he tapped his foot to the rhythm of the fiddle.

"Pretty good, ain't he?" someone asked next to Roberts.

Roberts examined the man who talked to him. He was an older gentleman with dark complexion and a short salt-and-pepper beard. He appeared to be a regular at the tavern by his look. "Yes, quite lively indeed."

"When did you arrive in the bay?"

"Just today. I'm a merchant by the name of Bartholomew Roberts."

"Gabriel." The man moved his ale into his off hand and went to shake Roberts'.

Roberts returned the handshake. He scanned the room, and could see a few men in what he thought could be dressed-down formal attire, but he couldn't be sure.

"Tell me, Gabriel, those men there, do they hail from the fleet of Portuguese ships in the harbour?"

"Yea, they are. The one on the left is a captain of some sort. If he can call himself a captain."

Roberts chuckled. "You seem to not like him."

Gabriel laughed. "Arrogant sod keeps mentioning the ships in their army and how they're transporting supplies."

"Hmm," Roberts replied. He leaned over and nodded his chin at Gabriel. "How would you like to help me and stick it to him?" He gestured to the captain with his ale.

Gabriel leaned in. "I'm listening."

"I have half a tonne of gunpowder I need to sell. The only problem is my supplier gave me shite for powder. Works maybe half the time because the mixture was shoddily done. Too much saltpetre. If you and I can make friends with this captain, get him tanked, and get him to buy my powder, I'll be ahead, and when his crew tries to use it they'll be in for a surprise. What do you say?"

"You want to know how to bring people with money to you?" Gabriel asked.

"What?"

Gabriel produced a pack of playing cards from his pocket. "The prospect of winning more money, and arrogance. When you start to lose, lose loudly," he said with a sly smile.

Roberts couldn't help but smile as well, and the two sat at a table adjacent to the Portuguese men. Not being familiar with card games, especially those played for the purpose of gambling, Roberts didn't need to feign losing. The further into the game they got, the more boisterous the two became, and other people crowded around the table to join the game.

"And I win again, gentlemen!" Gabriel shouted over the other patrons.

"Ugh!" Roberts yelled, throwing down his cards. "I swear you're unbeatable, old man."

"So you don't want to play again?" Gabriel winked at Roberts.

Roberts noticed the wink. "I tell you, I cannot. My pockets have run dry. The Lord is my witness, my wife will have my head."

"Oh come now, I'm sure she'll be happy when you return with double the winnings. Double or nothing."

Roberts shook his head vigorously. "You are too good, and I'm on to your tricks. I'm simply not adept enough at this game to stand a chance." Roberts rose from his chair.

Gabriel held out his hand. "Hold, hold now. How about I let someone substitute for you, to win you back your money? Would that make it fair?"

Roberts smiled, understanding the old man's plan. "Well, I suppose that would be fine, but who will spot for me?" He and Gabriel eyed the other people who were playing with them, but they declined, having seen Gabriel's skills.

Roberts turned around to the Portuguese table. "Oi, you there," He called, pointing to the captain. "I'll split my winnings with you if you can beat this old man at a game of cards."

The captain waved his hand and shook his head. "Find someone else."

He leaned forward. "Come now, I need some help here," he pleaded.

The captain looked annoyed. "I said find someone else, vagrant."

Roberts turned around, defeated. When Gabriel looked at him he shrugged his shoulders. He was out of ideas.

"You heard the man, he's too afraid he'll lose too, so you must find someone else," Gabriel said loudly.

The crowd laughed at his comment.

"What did you say?" Roberts heard the captain say angrily behind him. He smiled at Gabriel, and Gabriel smiled back.

"Oh, that was nothing need concern you, sir."

The captain rose from his chair and approached Roberts' table, with his crew joining him soon after. "It does concern me. You said I was too afraid to lose."

"Well, that isn't something to be ashamed of, sir. Not everyone can be good at these games, it takes a certain skill…"

"I assure you, I have the skills, and I could beat you any day."

The crowd was getting into the argument, and sought to rile the two parties up even further. They were doing most of the work for Roberts and Gabriel. The alcohol might have contributed as well.

"Well, prove it then, young man," Gabriel chided.

Roberts rose and motioned for the captain to sit in his seat. The captain took the offer while staring down Gabriel. "Deal, old man."

Gabriel nodded, and the game began. He lost the first game, but with a few words from him and Roberts, they kept playing. Roberts was behind the captain the whole time, cheering him on and getting him progressively stronger drinks. From his new vantage point he was able to see Gabriel was manipulating the cards somehow. He made sure if the captain won it was by a small margin, which gave him the pleasure of reward but still retained his competitive spirit. Over time Gabriel lost more frequently until he called a stop to the game.

"Well, you seem to have bested me, sir. I had you pegged wrong. I'm all out of money now."

The Portuguese captain, now fully drunk, with his subordinates sleeping on the floor or at their tables, laughed heartily. "Thas right, I win."

Roberts slipped some money from the table into his pocket and then shook Gabriel's hand with the money hidden in his palm. "It was a good game, and I thank you for allowing me the help."

Gabriel shook his hand and took the offered money. "The pleasure was all mine," Gabriel said with a smile before he left.

"Where ya goin'? We're no done yet."

Roberts took some more money off the table and pocketed it, then shoved some in the captain's pocket. He then picked up the captain and put his arm over his shoulder. "Come now, sir. Let's get you a drink on my ship."

The captain looked around. "Ah, what 'bout my men?"

"Don't worry about them, they're taking a nap. They'll join us later."

Roberts carried the Portuguese captain from the tavern all the way to the *Royal Rover*. Several times the captain burst out into song, or tried to brawl with him, but he was able to coax the man back into following him. Eventually he made it back to the ship before midnight.

Roberts, with the help of Hank and a few others, took the captain to the crew's quarters and tied him up. "Thanks, men. I'll take it from here." He knelt down to get almost eye level with the captain. "Captain, you're with those forty-some Portuguese ships, aren't you?"

The captain nodded with far too much movement. "Yea, we're waiting fer two big men-o-war to get us to Lisbon."

Roberts cocked his brow and glanced at Hank. Hank wore the same confused expression on his face. He turned back to the captain. "Why do you need a warship escort?"

"Cause we got the goods. Can't be losin' the king's jewels." The captain instantly sobered up, and his eyes widened. "Oh, I shouldn'ta said that."

Roberts smiled at Hank. "Now, Captain, we're friends, right?"

The captain smiled. "Yea, good old friends now."

"Good, good. As a friend why don't you tell me the name of the ship carrying those jewels?"

The captain's mouth made a line and he shook his head. "I shouldn't."

"What's the harm in telling little old me? I'm a simple merchant," Roberts coaxed. "I want to know so I can know who to trade with." He pulled the money from the bar game. "Tell you what, I'll give you this for helping me find these people to trade with. You help me, I help you, and you help your superiors. We all win."

The captain gazed at the money with lust in his eyes. "I'm helping you?" Roberts nodded. "Ship's named Providence."

Roberts smiled and patted the captain on the shoulder. "Thank you, friend." He rose to his feet. "Hank, gather our twenty best fighters. We're about to go for a swim."

"It's now or never, Walter," Ethan said in a hushed tone. "Hank was left in charge and there are maybe twenty men not with us on the *Rover*. We can take 'em."

Walter was sweating. The thought of what Ethan wanted to do was wracking on him. *This is what I wanted, wasn't it?*

"Boys, leave us and get the men armed." The other men left the corner of the crew cabin. Ethan stood up and stared down at Walter. "I told ye before if ye want ta be captain ye need the support of the crew. The men aren't gonna follow some pussyfooted landlubber jus' because he knows how ta navigate and lets em do what they want. Ye want ta be a leader, ye need ta lead. Show the men yer worth a damn, or else they won't follow you."

Walter looked up at Ethan. *Ethan's right. He has respect from the men because he takes it, not because they give it to him.* He stood up and grabbed a cutlass in his hands. "Let's go," he said confidently.

Ethan and Walter left their usual spot, and Walter could see men lined up in the crew cabin. Each man held weapons in hand and watched him as he walked past them. Some of the men nodded to him and others hooted or slammed their fist on their chest. There was a nervous energy in the crew cabin, and despite all the people and the hooting it was quiet. The pressure he could feel kept his feet moving. He kept thinking on Ethan's words and saying to himself *I must do this*, and *I will be captain*, over and over.

He reached the ladder. He could see the moon's light coming in through the opening to the main deck. He took a deep breath and went up. The men followed behind him and before long over a hundred men were on the main deck of the *Royal Rover*.

Hank was on the main deck with about twenty other crewmates waiting for Roberts to return. When men emerged from the crew cabin with weapons in hand he approached Walter.

"What is the meaning of this?" Hank asked while gingerly placing a hand on a cutlass at his belt.

"I am taking over this ship. Roberts is captain no longer."

Hank raised his brow. "There was no vote on this. You have no authority to take these actions." The twenty men on Hank's side gathered around him.

"The only vote which matters is the vote of the crew, and Walter has ours," Ethan stated. The crew hollered in agreement.

"Tell me this then: Who was the one who gave you revenge for Captain Davis while this coward ran?" Hank seethed, pointing at

Walter. "Who was the one who's found us more booty in the past six months than we've gotten in the past three years combined? Do you think Walter would break into a prison to save you from the noose? Perhaps you should ask your new captain what he plans on doing when he is captain before you continue with this folly."

The crowd of mutineers whispered amongst themselves and Walter could feel the hot breath of doubt on his back.

"I'll tell you one thing I will do," Walter said, stepping from the crowd and turning around to face them. "I won't attack a fleet of forty-two Portuguese ships, putting ye all in danger in the process. Ya think the King of Portugal'll let us alone after we steal his jewels?" The men nodded and the whispers seemed to be more in his favour. "I'll tell ye something else I'll do: I'll let ye drink and bring as many whores aboard as ye wish. Life on a ship as a pirate is hard enough as it is. Ye already put yer life on the line, not bein able to wet yer stick is too much to ask of ye." The crowd was becoming more vocal and turning back to his side. "I want what all of ye want: a nice, easy life where all pleasures are laid out before us. Roberts wants ye ta be good Christian pirates who abstain from the comforts life provides. I'll tell you now, and again if ye stand by me as captain, that will not be how things are run from now on. Who's with me?"

The crowd unanimously cheered for Walter.

"Enough of this," Hank said.

The sound of a cutlass being unsheathed rang out in the midst of the cheers, and all other sounds died out for a fraction of a second. Walter's eyes widened and he turned around to see Hank rushing towards him with his cutlass out.

The sound of steel rang out. Hank's blade was deflected. Walter spun around and saw Ethan beside him. Ethan had protected Walter from Hank.

Hank backed up a few paces, and the twenty men with him drew weapons. The crowd behind Walter and Ethan stepped forward, but Ethan called out for them to stop.

"Hank," Ethan said. "Ye fought next to us over the years, just as all of ye did. We don't want ta fight. Leave the ship and we'll let ye go. We owe ye at least that much."

Hank scanned the eyes of the hundred plus men in front of him ready to fight, then at the men next to him. Walter could tell that the twenty men at Hank's side were scared, but still ready to fight if he chose to.

Hank lowered his weapon. Soon after, all the men on the *Royal Rover* lowered their weapons. "You win."

Hank and the other crewmates on Roberts' side entered a dinghy on the starboard side of the *Royal Rover*. Ethan and a few others lowered the dinghy into the water.

"Roberts will never forgive you for this," Hank yelled when the dinghy was halfway down.

Walter stared into Hank's eyes. "I know," he replied.

Roberts and the twenty men he took with him to raid the Providence were in two longboats paddling back to the *Fortune*. He could see the crew on the deck, waving and calling their attention. There was more activity than he expected in the middle of the night, but he was glad for it, as they needed to leave immediately.

The crew manoeuvred the longboats to the side of the *Fortune* as rope ladders and rigging for the dinghies were thrown down.

Roberts climbed a rope ladder and jumped over the side. "Gentlemen! God has seen our cause as just, and we shall not be wanting for some time." He wore a great smile on his face, and his hands were at his sides. As he looked at the crew he noticed Hank there. "Hank, what are you doing on the *Fortune*? Were you not on the *Royal Rover*?" He scanned the harbour, but could not see the *Royal Rover* anywhere. "Where is our sister ship?" He noticed the dejected demeanour of his crew.

"The *Royal Rover* was taken," Hank stated.

"By whom?" Roberts asked quickly.

Hank looked at Roberts with fury in his eyes. "Walter Kennedy."

Roberts was taken aback. "Why would he do such a thing? Tell me we were found out and he had to escape," he pleaded.

"I cannot, as the truth is far worse. I reckon it was because of his desire to be captain not moving forward. He rallied crewmates to his side with promises of doing away with your commands. Letting them drink while on duty and having their precious whores onboard. They let the crew and me go, and then took the ship north."

Roberts ran his fingers through his hair and turned away from Hank. He ambled to the port railing and leaned against it. He gazed at the water lapping against the side of the *Fortune*.

"Captain, will you be alright?"

After another moment, Roberts turned around with a smile on his face. "I am perfect, Hank. With this I finally have my answer."

Hank looked confused. "I understand what you mean, Captain, but our ship was just stolen from us. We're pirates, yet we were stolen from? Is that not as absurd and aggravating as it sounds?"

Roberts laughed, causing the crew to give him strange looks. "God has provided for us in more ways than one."

Blackbeard's Ship

He went over to one of the newly raised longboats, pulled a heavy chest out, and brought it over to the crew of the *Fortune*. He lifted the opening of the chest, and in the pale moonlight over them the contents of the chest shone bright gold like nothing they had seen before.

Inside the chest was filled to the brim with gold coins. The crew of the *Fortune*, having not seen the contents until just then, began laughing hysterically and cheering. The twenty men who joined him were smiling as they brought the other chests on board. They opened them one by one until twenty-four chests of gold coins and various jewels glittered on the deck of the *Fortune*.

When the hysterics seemed to die down, Roberts explained himself. "Not only has God seen fit to give us this bounty, but with the crewmates who saw fit to betray us gone we have all these riches to ourselves." He raised his hands up to his sides. "We are God's chosen!"

⚓ ⚓ ⚓

Roberts sat in a comfy chair in the captain's cabin. He was reading from his Bible, the well-worn but cared-for Bible he'd received from Father Sean. The ink was slightly faded in spots, the pages curled, but there was life in that book. He could tell so much about the Father from where the book was worn the most, almost as if the Father was right at his side.

A rap at the door grabbed his attention. "Come in," he said.

Hank entered the captain's cabin. "Howdy, Captain. They're ready for you out here."

"Thank you, Hank," he said, standing up.

Hank nodded, and it seemed like he was about to leave, but closed the cabin door instead. He stared at the deck. "Captain, I don't believe I had a chance to say it before…" He paused, and then looked Roberts straight in the eye. "I'm sorry about what happened with Walter. I should have fought him, I should have chased after the ship with *Fortune*. I should have…"

"Hank, stop," Roberts commanded. He walked over to Hank, his friend, his first mate, and placed his hands on Hank's shoulders. "You prioritized the lives of the crew, which was the right thing to do. Davis would have done the same."

Hank smiled, thinking back to his former captain. "'Worry about you and your comrades first' he always used to say." Hank chuckled. "I miss him."

"I do as well." Roberts paused a moment to think of those who had passed on, the lives that had influenced him so much and brought him to where he was today. Davis, Delliger, Bartholomew.

"God's judgement will be brought upon Walter, just as Judas in the past and just as we did the Governor of Príncipe. He will not escape justice." He let Hank go. "Now come, the crew is waiting." Hank nodded.

Roberts and Hank exited the crew cabin, and went to the main deck of the *Fortune*. The whole crew was gathered, waiting for the captain to begin. He stood on the quarterdeck, and the crew sat down on barrels or on the deck.

"Welcome to the first of many Bible studies to come. Let's begin, shall we?" Bartholomew Roberts cleared his throat and opened the Bible he held in his hands. "God created the heaven and the earth. The light and the darkness…"

THE END

OTHER BOOKS
BY THE AUTHOR

The Voyages of Queen Anne's Revenge Series:

BLACKBEARD'S FREEDOM

BLACKBEARD'S REVENGE

BLACKBEARD'S JUSTICE

BLACKBEARD'S FAMILY

The Pirate Priest Series:

BARTHOLOMEW ROBERTS' FAITH

BARTHOLOMEW ROBERTS' JUSTICE

BARTHOLOMEW ROBERTS' MERCY

BARTHOLOMEW ROBERTS' SPIRIT

The Collection Series:

BLACKBEARD'S SHIP (Includes Books 1&2 of The Voyages of Queen Anne's Revenge & The Pirate Priest)

BLACKBEARD'S BLOOD (Includes Books 3&4 of The Voyages of Queen Anne's Revenge & The Pirate Priest)

ABOUT THE AUTHOR

JEREMY IS CURRENTLY LIVING IN NEW BRUNSWICK,
CANADA WITH HIS WIFE HEATHER, AND THEIR
TWO CATS, NAVI AND THOR.

Jeremy's first foray into the writing world was during a writing
competition called NaNoWriMo, where the goal is to write a
certain number of words in the month of November.

After completing the novel he started, and some extensive
rewrites, he felt it was worthy of publishing and self-published
his first novel, Blackbeard's Freedom in September, 2012.

After writing over ten books under two names, his passion for
writing hasn't wavered over the years, and hopes to one day
make it his primary career.

Let everyone know what you thought of his novels by leaving a
review. He loves getting feedback on his books, and loves to
hear from fans of his work.

Want to pirate one of Jeremy's audiobooks? Visit
www.mcleansnovels.com/faith-audiobook-offer for a free copy
of one of his audiobooks.